Praise for the
Chronicles of the Cheysuli:

"With every book, the magic of Jennifer Roberson waxes stronger and stronger. Wrought with an epic mysticism and power, the continuing strands of the Cheysuli saga glimmer with the sheen of excellence as they weave their way into a landmark collection of fantasy literature."
—*Rave Reviews*

"Roberson writes in a beautifully lyrical style, with a perceptive sense of drama that enthralls the reader."
—*Romantic Times*

"Roberson is one of the very best writers working in this kind of fantasy, and the Cheysuli series stands out from the crowd of similar novels."
—*Science Fiction Chronicle*

"Roberson is a master at character building. . . . very good reading indeed."
—*Kliatt*

Jennifer Roberson

LEGACY OF THE WOLF

THE CHRONICLES OF THE CHEYSULI

OMNIBUS TWO

Book Three
Legacy of the Sword

Book Four
Track of the White Wolf

DAW BOOKS, INC.
DONALD A. WOLLHEIM, FOUNDER
375 Hudson Street, New York, NY 10014

ELIZABETH R. WOLLHEIM
SHEILA E. GILBERT
PUBLISHERS
www.dawbooks.com

First paperback printing, June 2001
19 18 17 16 15 14 13 12 11 10

DAW TRADEMARK REGISTERED
U.S. PAT. AND TM. OFF. AND FOREIGN COUNTRIES
—MARCA REGISTRADA
HECHO EN U.S.A.

PRINTED IN THE U.S.A.

For the readers

the Tuble Ocean
Valgaard
Atvia
Andemir
Rondule
Kilore
Homana
Erinn
Mujhara
Lestra
the Idrian Ocean
Solinde
Hondarth
the
Crystal Isle

LEGACY
OF THE SWORD

PART I

One

Hondarth did not resemble a city so much as a flock of sheep pouring down over lilac heather toward the glass-gray ocean beyond. From atop the soft, slope-shouldered hills surrounding the scalloped bay, gray-thatched cottages appeared to huddle together in familial affection.

Once, Hondarth had been no more than a small fishing village; now it was a thriving city whose welfare derived from all manner of foreign trade as well as seasonal catches. Ships docked daily and trade caravans were dispatched to various parts of Homana. And with the ships came an influx of foreign sailors and merchants; Hondarth had become almost cosmopolitan.

The price of growth, Donal thought. *But I wonder, was Mujhara ever this—haphazard?*

He smiled. The thought of the Mujhar's royal city—with the palace of Homana-Mujhar a pendent jewel in a magnificent crown—as ever being *haphazard* was ludicrous. Had not the Cheysuli originally built the city the Homanans claimed for themselves?

Still smiling, Donal guided his chestnut stallion through the foot traffic thronging the winding street. *Few cities know the majesty and uniformity of Mujhara. But I think I prefer Hondarth, if I must know a city at all.*

And he did know cities. He knew Mujhara very well indeed, for all he preferred to live away from it. He had, of late, little choice in his living arrangements.

Donal sighed. *I think Carillon will see to it my wings are clipped, my talons filed . . . or perhaps he will pen me in a kennel, like his hunting dogs.*

And who would complain about a kennel as fine as Homana-Mujhar?

The question was unspoken, yet clearly understood by

Donal. He had heard similar comments from others, many times before. Yet this one came not from any human companion but from the wolf padding at the stallion's side.

Padding, not slinking; not as if the wolf avoided unwanted contact. He did not stalk, did not hunt, did not run from man or horse. He paced the stallion like a well-tamed hound accompanying a beloved master, but the wolf was no dog. Nor was he particularly tame.

He was not a delicate animal, but spare, with no flesh beyond that which supported his natural strength and quickness. The brassy sunlight of a foggy coastal late afternoon tipped his ruddy pelt with the faintest trace of bronze. His eyes were partially lidded, showing half-moons of brown and black.

I would complain about the kennel regardless of its aspect, Donal declared. *So would* you, *Lorn.*

An echo of laughter crossed the link that bound man to animal. *So I would,* the wolf agreed. *But then Homana-Mujhar will be kennel to me as well as to you, once you have taken the throne.*

That is not the point, Donal protested. *The point is, Carillon begins to make more demands on my time. He takes me away from the Keep. Council meetings, policy sessions . . . all those boring petition hearings—*

But the wolf cut him off. *Does he have a choice?*

Donal opened his mouth to answer aloud, prepared to contest the question. But chose to say nothing, aware of the familiar twinge of guilt that always accompanied less than charitable thoughts about the Mujhar of Homana. He shifted in the saddle, resettled the reins, made certain the green woolen cloak hung evenly over his shoulders . . . ritualized motions intended to camouflage the guilt; but they emphasized it instead.

And then, as always, he surrendered the battle to the wolf.

There are times I think he has a choice in everything, *lir,* Donal said with a sigh. *I see him make decisions that are utterly incomprehensible to me. And yet, there are times I almost understand him . . . Almost . . .* Donal smiled a little, wryly. *But most of the time I think I lack the wit and sense to understand* any *of Carillon's motives.*

As good a reason as any for your attendance at council meetings, policy sessions, boring petition hearings. . . .

Donal scowled down at the wolf. Lorn sounded insufferably smug. But arguing with his *lir* accomplished nothing— Lorn, like Carillon, always won the argument.

Just like Taj. Donal looked into the sky for the soaring golden falcon. *As always, I am outnumbered.*

You lack both wit and sense, and need the loan of ours. Taj's tone was different within the threads of the link. The resonances of *lir*-speech were something no Cheysuli could easily explain because even the Old Tongue lacked the explicitness required. Donal, like every other warrior, simply knew the language of the link in all its infinite intangibilities. But only he could converse with Taj and Lorn.

I am put in my place. Donal conceded the battle much as he always did—with practiced humility and customary resignation; the concession was nothing new.

The tiny street gave out into Market Square as did dozens of others; Donal found himself funneled into the square almost against his will, suddenly surrounded by a cacophony of shouts and sing-song invitations from fishmongers and streethawkers. Languages abounded, so tangled the syllables were indecipherable. But then most he could not decipher anyway, being limited to Homanan and the Old Tongue of the Cheysuli.

The smell struck him like a blow. Accustomed to the rich earth odors of the Keep and the more subtle aromas of Mujhara, Donal could not help but frown. Oil. The faintest tang of fruit from clustered stalls. A hint of flowers, musk, and other unknown scents wafting from a perfume-merchant's stall. But mostly fish. Everywhere fish—in everything; he could not separate even the familiar smell of his leathers, gold, and wool from the pervasive odor of fish.

The stallion's gait slowed to a walk, impeded by people, pushcarts, stalls, booths, livestock, and, occasionally, other horses. Most people were on foot; Donal began to wish *he* were, if only so he could melt into the crowd instead of riding head and shoulders above them all.

Lorn? he asked.

Here, the wolf replied glumly, nearly under the stallion's belly. *Could you not have gone another way?*

When I can find a way out of this mess, I will. He grimaced as another rider, passing too close in the throng, jostled his horse. Knees collided painfully. The man, swearing softly beneath his breath as he rubbed one gray-clad knee, glanced up as if to apologize.

But he did not. Instead he stared hard for a long moment, then drew back in his saddle and spat into the street. *"Shapechanger!"* he hissed from between his teeth, "go back to your forest bolt-hole! We want *none* of your kind here in Hondarth!"

Donal, utterly astonished by the reaction, was speechless, so stunned was he by the virulence in words and tone.

"I said, *go back!*" the man repeated. His face was reddened by his anger. A pock-marked face, not young, not old, but filled with violence. "The Mujhar may give you freedom to stalk the streets of Mujhara in whatever beast-form you wear, but here it is different! Get you gone from this city, shapechanger!"

No. It was Lorn, standing close beside the stallion. *What good would slaying him do, save to lend credence to the reasons for his hatred?*

Donal looked down and saw how his right hand rested on the gold hilt of his long-knife. Carefully, so carefully, he unlocked his teeth, took his hand away from his knife and ignored the roiling of his belly.

He managed, somehow, to speak quietly to the Homanan who confronted him. "Shaine's *qu'mahlin* is ended. We Cheysuli are no longer hunted. I have the freedom to come and go as I choose."

"Not *here!*" The man, dressed in good gray wool but wearing no power or rank markings, shook his dark brown head. "*I* say you had better go."

"Who are you to say so?" Donal demanded icily. "Have you usurped the Mujhar's place in Homana to dictate *my* comings and goings?"

"I dictate where I will, when it concerns you shape-changers." The Homanan leaned forward in his saddle. One hand gripped the chestnut's reins to hold Donal's horse in place. "Do you hear me? Leave this place. Hondarth is not for such as you."

Their knees still touched. Through the contact, slight

though it was, Donal sensed the man's tension; sensed what drove the other to such a rash action.

He is afraid. He does not do this out of a sense of justice gone awry, or any personal vendetta—he is simply afraid.

Frightened, men will do anything. It was Taj, circling in seeming idleness above the crowded square. *Lir, be gentle with him.*

After what he has said to me?

Has it damaged you?

Looking into brown, malignant eyes, Donal knew the other would not back down. He could not. Homanan pride was not Cheysuli pride, but it was still a powerful force. Before so many people—before so many Homanans and facing a dreaded Cheysuli—the man would never give in.

But if I back down, I will lose more than just my pride. It will make it that much more difficult for any *warrior who comes into Hondarth.*

And so he did not back down. He leaned closer to the man, which caused the Homanan to flinch back, and spoke barely above a whisper. "You are truly a fool to think you can chase *me* back into the forests. I come and go as I please. If you think to dissuade me, you will have myself and my *lir* to contend with." A brief gesture indicated the hackled wolf and Taj's attentive flight. "What say you to me *now?*"

The Homanan looked down at Lorn, whose ruddy muzzle wrinkled to expose sharp teeth. He looked up at Taj as the falcon slowly, so slowly, circled, descending to the street.

Lastly he looked at the Cheysuli warrior who faced him: a young man of twenty-three, tall even in his saddle; black-haired, dark-skinned, *yellow*-eyed; possessed of a sense of grace, confidence, and strength that was almost feral in its nature. He had the look of intense pride and preparedness that differentiated Cheysuli warriors from other men. The look of a predator.

"I am unarmed," the Homanan said at last.

Donal did not smile. "Next time you choose to offer insult to a Cheysuli, I suggest you do so *armed.* If I was forced to slay you, I would prefer to do it fairly."

The Homanan released the stallion's rein. He clutched at his own so violently the horse's mouth gaped open, baring

massive teeth in silent protest. Back, back . . . iron-shod
hooves scraped against stone and scarred the cobbles. The
man paid no heed to the people he nearly trampled or the
collapse of a flimsy fruit stall as his mount's rump knocked
down the props. He completely ignored the shouts of the
angry merchant.

But before he left the square he spat once more into
the street.

Donal sat rigidly in his saddle and stared at the spittle
marring a single cobble. He was aware of an aching emptiness in his belly. Slowly that emptiness filled with the pain
of shock and outraged pride.

He is not worth slaying. But Lorn's tone within the pattern sounded suspiciously wistful.

Taj, still circling, climbed back into the sky. *You will see
more of that. Did you think to be free of such things?*

"Free?" Donal demanded aloud: "Carillon *ended* Shaine's
qu'mahlin!"

Neither *lir* answered at once.

Donal shivered. He was cold. He felt ill. He wanted to
spit much as the Homanan had spat, wishing only to rid
himself of the sour taste of shock.

"Ended," he repeated. "*Everyone* in Homana knows
Carillon ended the purge."

Lorn's tone was grim. *There are fools in the world, and
madmen; people driven by ignorant prejudice and fear.*

Donal looked out on the square and slowly shook his
head. Around him swarmed Homanans whom he had, till
now, trusted readily enough, having little reason not to. But
now, looking at them as they went about their business, he
wondered how many hated him for his race without really
understanding what he was.

Why? he asked his *lir*. *Why do they spit at* me?

You are the closest target. Taj told him. *Not because of
rank and title.*

Homanan *rank and title,* Donal pointed out. *Can they not
respect that at least? It is their own, after all.*

If you tell them who and what you are, Lorn agreed.
Perhaps. But he saw only a Cheysuli.

Donal laughed a little, but there was nothing humorous
in it. *Ironic, is it not? That man had no idea I was the Prince
of Homana—he saw a shapechanger, and spat. Knowing,*

maybe he would have shut his mouth, out of respect for the title. But others, other Homanans—knowing what Carillon has made me—resent me for that title.

A woman, passing, muttered of beasts and demons and made a ward-sign against the god of the netherworld. The sign was directed at Donal, as if she thought *he* was a servant of Asar-Suti.

"By the gods, the world has gone mad!" Donal stared after the woman as she faded into the crowded square. "Do they think I am *Ihlini?*"

No, Taj said. *They know you are Cheysuli.*

Let us get out of this place at once. But even as Donal said it, he felt and heard the smack of some substance against one shoulder.

And smelled its odor, also.

He turned in the saddle at once, shocked by the blatant attack. But he saw no single specific culprit, only a square choked with people. Some watched him. Others did not.

Donal reached back and jerked his cloak over one shoulder to see what had struck his back, though he thought he knew. He grimaced when he saw the residue of fresh horse droppings. In disgust he shook the cloak free of manure, then let the folds fall back.

We are leaving this square, he told his *lir. Though I would prefer to leave this city entirely.*

Donal turned his horse into the first street he saw and followed its winding course. It narrowed considerably, twisting down toward the sea among whitewashed buildings topped with thatched gray roofs. He smelled salt and fish and oil, and the tang of the sea beyond. Gulls cried raucously, white against the slate-gray sky, singing their lonely song. The clop of his horse's hooves echoed in the narrow canyon of the road.

Do you mean to stop? Taj inquired.

When I find an inn—ah, there is one ahead. See the sign? The Red Horse Inn.

It was a small place, whitewashed like the others, its thatched roof worn in spots. The wooden sign, in the form of a crimson horse, faded, dangled from its bracket on a single strip of leather.

Here? Lorn asked dubiously.

It will do as well as another, provided I may enter. Donal felt the anger and sickness rise again, frustrated that even Carillon—with all that he had accomplished—had not been able to entirely end the *qu'mahlin*. But even as he spoke, Donal realized what the wolf meant; the Red Horse Inn appeared to lack refinement of any sort. Its two horn windows were puttied with grime and smoke, and the thatching stank of fish oil, no doubt from the lanterns inside. Even the whitewashing was grayed with soot and dirt.

You are *the Prince of Homana.* That from Taj, ever vigilant of such things as princely dignity and decorum.

Donal smiled. *And the Prince of Homana is hungry. Perhaps the food will be good.* He swung off his mount and tied it to a ring in the wall provided for that purpose. *Bide here with the horse. Let us not threaten anyone else with your presence.*

You are *going in.* Lorn's brown eyes glinted for just a moment.

Donal slapped the horse on his rump and shot the wolf a scowl. *There is nothing threatening about me.*

Are you not Cheysuli? asked Taj smugly as he settled on the saddle.

The door to the inn was snatched open just as Donal put out his hand to lift the latch. A body was hurled through the opening. Donal, directly in its path, cursed and staggered back, grasping at arms and legs as he struggled to keep himself and the other upright. He hissed a Cheysuli invective under his breath and pushed the body back onto its feet. It resolved itself into a boy, not a man, and Donal saw how the boy stared at him in alarm.

The innkeeper stood in the doorway, legs spread and arms folded across his chest. His bearded jaw thrust out belligerently. "I'll not have such rabble in my good inn!" he growled distinctly. "Take your demon ways elsewhere, brat!"

The boy cowered. Donal put one hand on a narrow shoulder to prevent another stumble. But his attention was more firmly focused on the innkeeper. "Why do you call him a demon?" he asked. "He is only a boy."

The man looked Donal up and down, brown eyes narrowing. Donal waited for the epithets to include himself, half-braced against another clot of manure—or worse—but instead of insults he got a shrewd assessment. He saw how the innkeeper judged him by the gold showing at his ear and the color of his eyes: His *lir*-bands were hidden beneath a heavy cloak, but his race—as always—was apparent enough.

Inwardly Donal laughed derisively. *Homanans! If they are not judging us demons because of the shapechange, they judge us by our gold instead. Do they not know we revere our gold for what it represents, and not the wealth at all?*

The Homanans judge your gold because of what it can buy them. Taj settled his wings tidily. *The freedom of the Cheysuli.*

The innkeeper turned his face and spat against the ground. "Demon," he said briefly.

"The boy, or me?" Donal asked with exaggerated mildness, prepared for either answer. And prepared to make his own.

"Him. Look at his eyes. He's demon-spawn, for truth."

"No!" the boy cried. "I'm *not!*"

"Look at his eyes!" the man roared. "Tell me what you see!"

The boy turned his face away, shielding it behind one arm. His black hair was dirty and tangled, falling into his eyes as if he meant it to hide them. He showed nothing to Donal but a shoulder hunched as if to ward off a blow.

"Do you wish to come in?" the innkeeper demanded irritably.

Donal looked at him in genuine surprise. "You throw *him* out because you believe him to be a demon—because of his eyes—and yet you ask *me* in?"

The man grunted. "Has not the Mujhar declared you free of taint? Your coin is as good as any other's." He paused. "You do have coin?" His eyes strayed again to the earring.

Donal smiled in relief, glad to know at least one man in Hondarth judged him more from avarice than prejudice. "I have coin."

The other nodded. "Then come in. Tell me what you want."

"Beef and wine. Falian white, if you have it." Donal paused. "I will be in in a moment."

"I have it." The man cast a lingering glance at the boy, spat again, then pulled the door shut as he went into his inn.

Donal turned to the boy. "Explain."

The boy was very slender and black-haired, dressed in dark, muddied clothing that showed he had grown while the clothes had not. His hair hung into his face. "My eyes," he said at last. "You heard the man. Because of my eyes." He glanced quickly up at Donal, then away. And then, as if defying the expected reaction, he shoved the tangled hair out of his face and bared his face completely. "See?"

"Ah," Donal said, "I see. And I understand. Merely happenstance, but ignorant people do not understand that. They choose to lay blame even when there is no blame to lay."

The boy stared up at him out of eyes utterly unremarkable—save one was brown and the other a clear, bright blue. "Then—you don't think me a demon and a changeling?"

"No more than am I myself." Donal smiled and spread his hands.

"You don't think I'll be putting a spell on you?"

"Few men have that ability. I doubt you are one of them."

The boy continued to stare. He had the face of a street urchin, all hollowed and pointed and thin. His bony wrists hung out of tattered sleeves and his feet were shod in strips of battered leather. He picked at the front of his threadbare shirt with broken, dirty fingernails.

"Why?" he asked in a voice that was barely a sound. "Why is it you didn't like hearing me called names? I could tell." He glanced quickly at Donal's face. "I could feel the anger in you."

"Perhaps because I have had such prejudice attached to *me*," Donal said grimly. "I like it no better when another suffers the fate."

The boy frowned. "Who would call you names? And why?"

"For no reason at all. Ignorance. Prejudice. Stupidity. But mostly because, like you, I am not—precisely like *them*." Donal did not smile. "Because I am Cheysuli."

The parti-colored eyes widened. The boy stiffened and drew back as if he had been struck, then froze in place. He stared fixedly at Donal and his grimy face turned pale and blotched with fear. *"Shapechanger!"*

Donal felt the slow overturning of his belly. *Even this boy—*

"Beast-eyes!" The boy made the gesture meant to ward off evil and stumbled back a single step.

Donal felt all the anger and shock swell up. Deliberately, with a distinct effort, he pushed it back down again. The boy was a boy, echoing such insults as he had heard, having heard them said of himself.

"Are you hungry?" Donal asked, ignoring the fear and distrust in the boy's odd eyes.

The boy stared. "I have eaten."

"What have you eaten—scraps from the innkeeper's midden?"

"I have *eaten!*"

Anger gave way to regret. *That even a boy such as this will fall prey to such absolute fear—* "Well enough." He said it more sharply than intended. "I thought to feed you, but I would not have you thinking I seek to steal your soul for my use. Perhaps you will find another innkeeper less judgmental than this one."

The boy said nothing. After a long moment of shocked silence, he turned quickly and ran away.

Two

In the morning, Donal found only one man willing to give him passage across the bay to the Crystal Isle, and even that man would not depart until the following day. So, left to his own devices, Donal stabled his horse and wandered down to the sea wall. He perched himself upon it and stared across the lapping waves.

He focused his gaze on the dark bump of land rising out of the Idrian Ocean a mere three leagues across the bay. *Gods, what will Electra be like? What will she say to me?*

He could hardly recall her, though he did remember her legendary beauty, for he had been but a young boy when Carillon had banished his Solindish wife for treason. Adultery too, according to the Homanans; the Cheysuli thought little of that charge, having no strictures against light women when a man already had a wife. In the clans, *cheysulas*, wives, and *meijhas*, mistresses, were given equal honor. In the clans, the birth of children was more important than what the Homanans called proprieties.

Treason. Aye, a man might call it that. Electra of Solinde, princess-born, had tried to have her royal Homanan husband slain so that Tynstar might take his place. Tynstar of the Ihlini, devotee of Asar-Suti, the god of the netherworld.

Donal suppressed a shudder. He knew better than to attribute the sudden chill he felt to the salty breeze coming inland from the ocean. No man, had he any wisdom at all, dismissed the Ihlini as simple sorcerers. Not when Tynstar led them.

He wishes to throw down Carillon's rule and make Homana his own. For a moment he shut his eyes. It was so clear, so very clear as it rose up before his eyes from his memory: the vision of Tynstar's servitors as they had captured his mother. Alix they had drugged, to control her Cheysuli gifts. Torrin, her foster father, they had brutally slain. And her son they had nearly throttled with a necklace of heavy iron.

Donal put a hand against his neck. He recalled it so well, even fifteen years later. *As if it were yesterday, and I still a boy.* But the yesterday had faded, his boyhood long outgrown.

He opened his eyes and looked again upon the place men called the Crystal Isle. Once it had been a Cheysuli place, or so the *shar tahls* always said. But now it was little more than a prison for Carillon's treacherous wife.

The Queen of Homana. Donal grimaced. *Gods, how could he stay wed to her? I know the Homanans do not countenance the setting aside of wives—it is even a part of their laws—but the woman is a witch! Tynstar's meijha.* He scrubbed a hand through his hair and felt the wind against his face. Cool, damp wind, filled with the scent of the sea. *If he gave her a chance, she would seek to slay him again.*

Taj wheeled idly in the air. *Perhaps it was his tahlmorra.*

Homanans have none. Not as we know it. Donal shook his head. *They call it fate, destiny . . . saying they make their own without the help of the gods. No, the Homanans have no tahlmorra. And Carillon, much as I respect him, is Homanan to the bone.*

There is that blood in you as well, returned the bird.

Aye. His mouth twisted. *But I cannot help it, much as I would prefer to forget it altogether.*

It makes you what you are, Taj said. *That, and other things.*

Donal opened his mouth to answer aloud, but Lorn urgently interrupted. Lir, *there is trouble.*

Donal straightened and swung his legs over the wall, rising at once. He looked in the direction Lorn indicated with his nose and saw a group of boys wrestling on the cobbles.

He frowned. "They are playing, Lorn."

More than that. Lorn told him. *They seek to do serious harm.*

Taj drifted closer to the pile of scrambling bodies. *The boy with odd eyes.*

Donal grunted. "I am not one of his favorite people."

You might become so, Lorn pointed out, *if you gave him the aid he needs.*

Donal cast the smug wolf a skeptical glance, but he went off to intervene. For all the boy had not endeared himself the day before, neither could Donal allow him to be beaten.

"Enough!" He stood over the churning mass of arms and legs. "Let him be!"

Slowly the mass untangled itself and he found five Homanan boys glaring up at him from the ground in various attitudes of fear and sullen resentment. The victim, he saw, regarded him in surprise.

"Let him be," Donal repeated quietly. "That he was born with odd eyes signifies nothing. It could as easily have been one of you."

The others got up slowly, pulling torn clothing together and wiping at grimy faces. Two of them drifted off quickly enough, tugging at two other others who hastily followed, but the tallest, a red-haired boy, faced Donal defiantly.

"Who're *you* to say, shapechanger?" His fists clenched and his freckled face reddened. "You're no better'n *him!* My Da says men like you are nothing but demons yourselves. *Shapechanger!"*

Donal reached out and caught the boy's shoulder. He heard the inarticulate cry of fear and ignored it, pulling the boy in. He thought the redhead was perhaps fourteen or fifteen, but undernourished. Like all of them. "What else does your father say?"

The boy stared at him. He hunched a little, for Donal still gripped his left shoulder, but soon became defiant. "Th-that Shaine the M-mujhar had the right of it! That you should all be slain—like *beasts!"*

"Does he, now?" Donal asked reflectively, desiring no further answers. He felt sickened by the virulence of the boy's hate. He only mouthed his father's words, but it was enough to emphasize yet again that not all Homanans were prepared to accept the Cheysuli, no matter what Carillon had done to stop Shaine's purge.

Almost twenty years have passed since Carillon came back from exile to make us welcome again, declaring us free of qu'mahlin, *and* still *the Homanans hate us!*

Lorn came up to press against his leg, as if to offer comfort. It brought Donal back to full awareness immediately, and he realized he still held the redhead's shoulder. Grimly, he regarded the frightened boy.

But not so frightened he forgets his prejudice— Donal took a deep breath and tried to steady his voice. "Do you think I will eat you, boy? Do you think I will turn beast before your eyes and rip the flesh from your throat?"

"M-my Da says—"

"*Enough* of your *jehan,* boy!" Donal shouted. "You face *me* now, not your father. It is you who will receive what punishment I choose to give you for the insult you have offered."

The boy began to cry. "D-don't eat me! *Please* don't eat me!"

In disgust, Donal shook him. "I will not eat you! I am not the beast your father says I am. I am a man, like he is. But even a *man* grows angry when boys lose their manners."

Lir, Lorn said in concern.

Donal silenced him through the link and kept his attention on the boy. "What punishment do you deserve? What I would give my own son for such impertinence. And when you run home to tell your *Da*, tell him also that you sought to harm an innocent boy. See what he says then."

Even as he said it, Donal grimaced to himself. *Most likely he will send his son out to find another helpless soul. Contempt and hatred beget more of the same.* He tightened his grip on the redhead. "Now, perhaps you will think better of such behavior in the future."

Donal spun the boy quickly and held him entrapped in his left arm. Before the redhead could protest, Donal swatted him twice—hard—on his bony rump and sent him stumbling toward the nearest street. "Go home. Go home and learn some manners."

The boy ran down the street and quickly disappeared. Donal turned at once to the victim, meaning to help him up, then thought better of it. *Why give him another chance to revile me for my race?*

But the boy evidently no longer held Donal in such contempt. He scrambled to his feet, tried to put his torn and muddied clothing into some semblance of order, and gazed at Donal with tentative respect. "You didn't have to do that."

"No," Donal agreed. "I chose to."

"Even after—after what I called you?"

"I do not hold grudges." Donal grinned suddenly. "Save, perhaps, against Carillon."

The parti-colored eyes widened in shock. "You hold a grudge against *the Mujhar?*"

"Upon occasion—and usually with very good reason." Donal hid a second smile, amused by the boy's reaction.

"He is the Mujhar! King of Homana and Lord of Solinde!"

"And a man, like myself. Like you will be, one day." He put out a hand and touched the ugly swelling already darkening the skin beneath the boy's blue eye. The brown one was unmarred. "This will be very sore, I fear."

The boy recoiled from the touch. "It—doesn't hurt."

Donal, hearing the boy's fear, took away his hand. "What is your name? I cannot keep calling you 'boy,' or 'brat,' as the innkeeper did."

"Sef," whispered the boy.

"Your age?"

Cheeks reddened. "Thirteen—I think."

Donal gently clasped one thin shoulder, ignoring the boy's sudden flinch. "Then go on your way, Sef, as you will not abide my company. But I suggest you avoid such situations in the future, do you wish to keep your bones whole and your face unblemished."

Sef did not move as Donal removed his hand. He stood very stiff, very still, his parti-colored eyes wide, apprehensive, as he watched Donal turn to walk away.

"Wait!" he called. "Wait—*please*—"

Donal glanced back and waited. The boy walked slowly toward him, shoulders raised defensively, both hands twisting the drawstring of his thin woolen trews.

"What is it?" Donal asked gently.

"What if—what if I said I *did* want your company?"

"Mine?" Donal raised his brows. "I thought you feared it, Sef."

"I—I do. I mean, you shift your *shape*." Briefly he looked at the wolf. "But I'd rather go with you."

"*With* me?" Donal frowned. "I will willingly buy you a meal—even a week's worth, if need be, or give you coin enough so you could go to another town—but I had not thought to take you with me."

"Please—" One hand, briefly raised, fell back to his side.

He shrugged. It was the barest movement of his ragged clothing, intensely vulnerable. "I have no one. My mother is—dead. My father—I never knew."

Donal frowned. "I do not live here."

"It doesn't matter. Hondarth isn't my home. Just—just a place I live, until I find better." The thin face blazed with sudden hope. "Take me with you! I'll work for my wage. I can tend your horse, prepare the food, clean up afterwards! I'll do *anything*."

"Even to feeding my wolf?" Donal did not smile.

Sef blanched. He stared blindly at Lorn a moment, but then he nodded jerkily.

Donal laughed. "No, no—Lorn feeds himself. I merely tease you, Sef."

The boy's face lit up. "Then you *will* take me with you?"

Donal glanced back toward the Crystal Isle. What Carillon had sent him to do offered no place for a boy, but perhaps after. Having a boy to tend his horse and other small chores would undoubtedly be of help.

And there is always room for serving-boys in Homana-Mujhar. He turned back to Sef and nodded. "I will take you. But there are things you must know about the service you undertake."

Sef nodded immediately. "I will do whatever you say."

Donal sighed. "To begin, I will not countenance pointless chatter among other boys you may meet. I understand what pride is, and what youth is, and how both will often lead a boy—a *young man*—into circumstances beyond his control, but this case is very special. I am not one for unnecessary elaborations, and I dislike ceremony, but there will be times for both. You will know them, too. But you must not give in to the temptation to speak of things you should not to other boys."

Sef frowned intently. "*Other* boys? Do you have so many servants?"

Donal smiled. "I have no servants—at least, not as *I* think of them. But there are pages and body-servants where we will go, when I finish my business here, and I must have your promise to keep yourself silent about my affairs."

Sef's dirt-streaked face grew paler. "Is it—because you're Cheysuli?"

"No. And I do not speak of *secret* things, merely things

that are very private. And sometimes quite important." He studied Sef's face and then brought his right hand up into the muted sunlight. "See this? Tell me what it is."

Sef frowned. "A ring."

"Surely you are more observant than *that*."

The frown deepened. "A gold ring. It has a red stone in it, and a black animal in the stone. A—lion." Sef nodded. "A black lion—"

"—rampant, upon a scarlet Mujharan field," Donal finished. "Do you know what that is?"

Sef started to shake his head. And then he stopped. "Once, I saw a soldier. He wore a red tunic, over his ringmail, and on the tunic was a lion. A black lion, rearing up." He pointed. "Like that one."

Donal smiled. "That soldier was Carillon's man, as they all are. So am I. But I am not a soldier. Not as you know soldiers."

"A warrior." Sef dipped his black head down. "I know about the Cheysuli."

"Not enough. But you will learn." Donal smiled and reached down to catch Sef's chin. He tipped up his head. "My name is Donal, Sef, and I am the Prince of Homana."

Sef blanched white. Then he turned red. And finally, before Donal could catch him, he fell downward to smack his bony knees against the salt-crusted cobbles. "*My lord!*" he whispered. "My lord—*the Prince of Homana!*"

Donal suppressed a laugh. It would not do to embarrass the boy simply because he was so in awe of royal rank. "I do not stand on ceremony. Serve me as well as you would serve any man, and I will be well-pleased."

"My lord—"

Donal reached down and caught a handful of thin tunic, then pulled Sef up from the cobbles. "Do not be so—*overwhelmed*. I am flesh and bone, as you are." He grinned. "If you are to serve me, you must learn I am not some petty lordling who seeks elevation in the eyes and service of others. You may come with me as my friend, but not my servant. I left enough of those back at Homana-Mujhar." His voice was gentle. "Do you understand me?"

"Aye," Sef whispered. "Oh . . . my lord . . . *aye!*"

Donal released the ragged tunic. *I will have to buy him better clothing, perhaps in Carillon's colors—well,* that *will*

have to wait. But some manner of fitting clothing will not.
"You shall have to *earn* your passage, Sef." Donal looked
down at the boy solemnly. "Are you willing to work for
that passage?"

"Aye, my lord!"

"Good." Donal squeezed a narrow shoulder. "All I require of you is your company. Come along."

"My lord!"

Donal turned back. "Aye?"

"My lord—" Sef broke off, pulling again at his ill-fitting,
muddied clothing. "My lord—I wish only to say—" He
broke off yet again, obviously embarrassed, vivid color
flooding his cheeks.

Donal smiled at him encouragingly. "Before me, you may
say what you wish. If you speak out of turn, I will say so,
but I will never strike you. Say what you will, Sef."

The boy sucked in a deep breath. "I wished only to thank
you for coming to my aid, and to say that usually I *win*
the fights."

Donal smothered a laugh. "Of course."

"They were five to my one," Sef pointed out earnestly.

"I counted them. You are right." Donal nodded gravely.

Sef studied Donal a moment. Then, anxiously, "You said
I may *say* what I wish. Do you mean I may ask it as well?"

"You may always ask. I may not always answer."

The boy smiled tentatively. "Then—I'd ask you what
you'd do against five men, if *you* were ever attacked."

"I?" Donal laughed. "Well, it would be a different situation. You see, I have two *lir*."

"*They* would fight, too?" Sef stared at Lorn in amazement, then turned his bi-colored gaze to the sky to pick
Taj out from the crying gulls.

"They will always fight, to aid me. That is what *lir* are for."

That, and other things, Lorn reminded him dryly.

"Then five men couldn't stop you?"

Donal understood what Sef inquired, even if the boy did
not. "I do not doubt you fought well, Sef, and that bad
fortune put you on the losing side. You need not make
excuses. As for me, you must recall I am Cheysuli. We are
taught to fight from birth." His smile faded into a grim
line. "There is reason enough for that. Even now, I begin
to think."

"Cheysuli," Sef echoed. He stood very still. "Will you tell me what it's like?"

"As much as I can. But it is never easily done." Donal nodded his head in Taj's direction, then gestured toward the wolf. "*There* is the secret of the Cheysuli, Sef. In Taj and Lorn. Understand what it is to have a *lir*, and you will know what it is to be blessed by the gods."

Sef glanced at him skeptically. "Gods? I don't think there are any."

"Ah, but there are. I am no *shar tahl*, dedicating my life to the prophecy and the service of the gods, but I can tell you what I know. Another time." Donal smiled. "Come along."

This time, Sef fell into step beside him.

Three

In the morning the ship's captain, paid generously before-hand in freshly minted gold coin, cast off readily enough for the Crystal Isle. Donal questioned him and learned all traffic to the island was closely watched by men serving the Mujhar; the man had agreed to transport Donal and Sef only after a close look at the royal signet ring. For once, Donal was glad Carillon made him wear it.

The captain was a garrulous man, perfectly content to while away the brief voyage by telling Donal all about the Queen of Homana's confinement. He confided there were Cheysuli on the island with Electra so she could use none of her witch's ways, and they kept Tynstar from rescuing her. He seemed little impressed with the knowledge that he transported the Prince of Homana himself, being rather more impressed with how he could use the knowledge to his own best advantage in fashioning an entertaining story full of gossip and anecdotes. Donal did not doubt a tale of his visit to the island would soon make the rounds of the taverns, undoubtedly much embellished. He quickly grew tired of the one-sided conversation and withdrew with what politeness he could muster, turning his back on the man to stare across the glassy bay.

Behind them, Hondarth receded. The painted cottages merged into clustered masses of glowing white, luminescent in the mist against a velvety backdrop of heathered hills. Before them, the island grew more distinct as the ship sailed closer, but Donal could see none of the distinguishing features. Just a shape floating on the water, wreathed in clouds of fog.

He became aware of Sef edging in close beside him. The mist shrouded them both and settled into their clothing, so that Sef—wrapped in a deep blue cloak Donal had pur-

chased for him the day before, along with other new clothing—looked more fey than human. His black hair curled
against his thin face—now clean—and his parti-colored eyes
stared out at the island fixedly.

"It should not frighten you," Donal said quietly. "It is
merely an island. A place."

Sef looked at the eerie, silent blanket of sea-spray and
morning fog. Even the crying of the gulls was muted in the
mist. "But it's an enchanted place. I've heard."

"Do you know the old legends, then?"

Sef seemed hesitant. "Some. Not all. I'm—not from
Hondarth."

"Where *are* you from?"

The boy looked away again, staring at the deck. Then,
slowly, he raised his head. "From many places. My mother
earned bread by—by . . ." He broke off uncertainly. His
face colored so that he looked younger than the thirteen
years he claimed. His voice was nearly a whisper. "Because
of—men. We—didn't stay long in any single place." He
shrugged, as if he could dismiss it all. But Donal knew such
things would never entirely fade, even with adulthood.
"She died almost a year ago, and I had no place else to
go. So—I stayed."

Donal heard the underlying note of shame and loneliness
in Sef's tone. "Well, travel befits a man," he said off-
handedly, seeking to soothe the boy without insulting him
with sympathy. In the clans, the Cheysuli rarely resorted to
emphasizing unnecessary emotions. "You are of an age to
learn the world, and Hondarth is as good a place as any
to begin."

Sef did not look at him. He looked instead at the Crystal
Isle as they sailed closer yet. The fog thickened as they
approached, wrapping itself around the ship until it clung
to every line and spar, glistening in the brassy sunlight so
muted by the mist. Droplets beaded the railing and their
cloaks, running down the oiled wool to fall on the deck.
Their faces were cooled by the isle's constant wind, known
to Cheysuli as the Breath of the Gods.

"Will you still keep me with you?" Sef asked very softly.

Donal looked at him sharply, frowning. "I have said I
would. Why do you ask?"

Sef would not meet his eyes. "But—that was before you knew I was a—*bastard*."

Donal made a quick dismissive gesture. "You forget, Sef—I am Cheysuli, not Homanan." Inwardly he shut his ears to the voice that protested the easy denial of his Homanan blood. "In the clans, there is no such thing as bastardy. A child is born and his value is weighed in how he serves his clan and the prophecy, not in the question of his paternity." Donal shook his head. "I care not if your *jehan*—your father—was thief or cobbler or soldier. So long as *you* earn your keep."

"Then the Cheysuli are wiser than most." The bitterness in Sef's young voice made Donal want to put a hand on one narrow shoulder to gentle him, but he did not. The boy was obviously proud as well as uncertain of his new position, and Donal had more cause than most to understand the feeling.

He pointed toward the island. "Tell me what you know, Sef."

Sef looked. "They say there are demons, my lord."

Donal smiled. "Do they? Well, they are wrong. That is a Cheysuli place, and there are no Cheysuli demons. Only gods, and the people they have made."

"What people?"

"Those of us now known as the Cheysuli. Once, we were something different. Something—better." Like the boy, he stared across the glass-gray ocean toward the misted island. Finally it grew clearer, more distinct. It was thickly forested, cloaked in lilac heather. Through the trees glowed a faint expanse of silver-white. "The Firstborn, Sef. Those the gods made first, as their name implies. Later, much later, were the Cheysuli born."

Sef frowned, concentrating, so that his black brows overshadowed his odd eyes. "You're saying once there were *no* people?"

"The *shar tahls*—our priest-historians—teach us that once the land was empty of men. It was a decision of the gods to put men upon the Crystal Isle and give it over to them freely. It is these original men we call the Firstborn. But the Firstborn soon outgrew the Crystal Isle, as men will when there are women, and went to Homana: a more spacious land for their growing numbers. They built a fine realm there, ruling it well, and the gods were pleased. As a mark of their favor, they sent the *lir* to them. And because of the earth magic, the Firstborn were able to bond with the *lir*, to learn what *lir*-shape is—"

"*Shapechangers*," Sef interrupted involuntarily, shivering as he spoke.

Donal sighed. "The name is easily come by, but we do not use it ourselves. *Cheysuli* is the Old Tongue, meaning *children of the gods*. But men—Homanans—being unblessed, all too often resort to the word as an insult." He thought again of the Homanan in the Market Square; the woman who had made the sign of the evil eye; the splatter of manure against his cloak. And all because he could shift his shape from man into animal.

Surely the gods would never give such gifts to us was there any chance we would use them for evil! Why must so many believe we would?

They do not understand. Taj floated lightly, pale gold in the silver mist. *They are unblessed, and blind to the magic.*

Why do the gods not make them see?

Blindness often serves a purpose, Lorn explained. *Sight recovered is often better than original vision.*

Donal looked directly at Sef. "Shapechanger," he said clearly. "Aye, it is true—I shift my shape at will. I become a wolf or falcon. But does it make me *so* different from you? I do not doubt there are things *you* do that I cannot. Should I castigate you for it?"

Sef shivered again. "It isn't the same. It isn't the *same*. *You* become an animal, while I—" he shook his head violently, denying the image, "—while *I* remain a boy. A normal, *human* boy."

"Unblessed," Donal agreed, for a moment callous in his pride.

Sef looked at him then, staring fixedly at Donal's face. His disconcerting gaze traveled from yellow eyes to golden earring, and he swallowed visibly. "The—the Firstborn," he began, "where are they, now?"

"The Firstborn no longer exist. And most of their gifts are lost."

Sef frowned. "Where did they go? What happened?"

The taffrail creaked as Donal shifted his weight. "It is too long a story. One night, I promise, I will tell you it

all—but, for now, *this* will have to content you." He looked
directly at the boy and saw how attentive he was. "I am
told the Firstborn became too inbred, that the gifts began
to fade. And so before they died out they gave what they
could to their children, the Cheysuli, and left them a prophecy." For a moment he was touched by the gravity of what
his race undertook; how important the service was. "It is
the Firstborn we seek to regain by strengthening the blood.
Someday, when the proper mixture is attained, we will have
a Firstborn among us again, and all the magic will be reborn." He smiled. "So the prophecy tells us: *one day a man
of all blood shall unite, in peace, two magical races and four
warring realms.*" Fluidly, he made the gesture of *tahlmorra*—right hand palm-up, fingers spread—to indicate the
shortened form of the Old Tongue phrase meaning, in Homanan, *the fate of a man rests always within the hands of
the gods.*

"You said—they *lost* their gifts—?"

"Most of them. The Firstborn were far more powerful
than the Cheysuli. They had no single *lir*. They conversed
with every *lir*, and took whatever shape they wished. But
now, each warrior is limited to one."

"*You* have two!" Sef looked around for Taj and Lorn.
"Are you a Firstborn, then?"

Donal laughed. "No, no, I am a Cheysuli halfling, or—
perhaps more precisely—a three-quarterling." He grinned.
"But my half-Homanan *jehana* bears the blood of the Firstborn—as well as some of the gifts—and by getting a child
by my Cheysuli *jehan* she triggered that part of herself that
has the Firstborn magic. I have two *lir* because of her, and
I may converse with any, but nothing more than that. I am
limited to those two shapes."

Sef turned to stare at the island. "Then—this is your
birthplace."

"In a manner of speaking." Donal looked at the island
again. "It is the birthplace of all the Cheysuli."

"That is why you go?" Sef's odd eyes were wide as he
looked up at Donal. "To see where your people were
born?"

"No, though undoubtedly every Cheysuli should." Donal
sighed and his mouth hooked down into a resigned grimace.
"No, I go there on business for the Mujhar." He felt the

curl of unhappiness tighten his belly. "What I am about is securing the throne of Homana."

"Securing it—?" Sef frowned. "But—the Mujhar holds it. It's his."

"There are those who seek to throw down Carillon's House to set up another," Donal told him grimly. "Even now, in Solinde . . . we know they plan a war."

Sef stared. "*Why?* Who would do such a thing?"

Donal very nearly did not answer. But Sef was avid in his interest, and he would learn the truth one way or another, once he was in Homana-Mujhar. "You know of the Ihlini, do you not?"

Sef paled and made the gesture warding off evil. "Solin-dish demons!"

"Aye," Donal agreed evenly. "Tynstar and his minions would prefer to make the throne their own and destroy the prophecy. He wishes to have dominion over Homana—and all the other realms, I would wager—in order to serve Asar-Suti." He paused. "Asar-Suti is your demon, Sef, and more—he is the god of the netherworld. *The Seker*, he is called, by those who serve him: *the one who made and dwells in darkness.*" He saw fear tauten Sef's face. "In the name of his demon-god, Tynstar wishes to recapture Solinde from Carillon and make the realm his own, as tribute to Asar-Suti. And, of course, his ambition does not stop there—also he wants Homana. He plots for it now, at this moment—but we know this, so we are not unprepared; we are not a complacent regency in Solinde. And so long as Carillon holds the throne—and his blood after him—the thing will not be done. The Lion Throne is ours."

Sef's hands were tight-wrapped around the rail. "*You'll* hold the throne one day, won't you? You're the Prince of Homana!"

He glanced down at the attentive boy. "Now, do you see why I must teach you how to hold your tongue? Honesty is all well and good, but in Royal Houses, too much honesty may be construed as grounds for beginning a war. You must be careful in what you say as well as to whom you say it."

Sef nodded slowly. "My lord—I have promised to serve you well. I give you my loyalty."

Donal smiled and clasped one thin shoulder briefly. "And that is all I require, for now."

His hand remained a moment longer on Sef's shoulder. The boy needed good food in him to fill out the hollows in his pasty-white face and to put some flesh on his bones, but his attitude was good. For a bastard boy living from hand to mouth it was very good indeed.

Donal chewed briefly at his bottom lip. *Being little more than an urchin, he may not prove equal to the task. He may not mix well with the other boys. But then I cannot judge men by how they conform to others—how boring that life would be—and I will not do it with Sef. I will give him what chance I can.* He smiled, and then he laughed. *Perhaps I have found someone to serve me as well as Rowan serves Carillon.*

The prison-palace on the Crystal Isle stood atop a gentle hill of ash-colored bracken and lilac heather. The forest grew up around the pedestal of the hill, hiding much of the palace, but through the trees gleamed the whitewashed walls, attended by a pervasive silver mist. Stretching from the white sand beaches through the wind-stirred forest was a path of crushed sea shells, rose and lilac, pale blue and gold, creamy ivory.

Donal stood very still upon the beach, looking inland toward the forest. He did not look at the palace—it was not so ancient as the island and Homanan-made at that—but at the things the gods had made instead. Then he closed his eyes and gave himself over to sensation.

The wind curled gently around his body, caressing him with subtle fingers. It seemed to promise him things. He knew without doubting that the isle was full of dreams and magic and, if he sought it, a perfect peace and solitude. Carillon might have banished his treacherous wife to the island, but the place was a sacred place. Donal had thought perhaps the incarceration profaned the Crystal Isle.

But he sensed no unhappiness, no dissatisfaction in the wind. Perhaps the island was used for mundane Homanan concerns, but at heart it was still Cheysuli, still part and parcel of the Firstborn. It merely waited. One day, someone would return it to its proper state.

Donal feared to tread the crushed shells of the pathway

at first, admiring its delicate beauty, but he saw no other way to the palace on its green-and-lilac hill. He took nothing with him save his *lir* and Sef. And, he hoped, his courage.

The isle was full of noise. Soft noise; gentle noise, a peaceful susurration. He and Sef and Lorn trod across crushed shell. They passed through trees that sighed and creaked, whispering in the wind. They heard the silences of the depths, as if even the animals muted themselves to honor the sanctity of the place.

Sef tripped over his own feet and went sprawling, scattering pearly shells so that they spilled out of the boundaries of the pathway, disturbing the curving symmetry. Aghast, he hunched on hands and knees, staring at what he had done.

Donal reached down and caught one arm, pulling him to his feet. He saw embarrassment and shame in the boy's face, but also something more. "There is nothing to fear, Sef," he promised quietly. "There are no demons here."

"I—I *feel* something . . . I *feel* it—" He broke off, standing rigidly before Donal. His eyes were wide and fixed. His head cocked a trifle, as if he listened. As if he *heard*.

"Sef—"

The boy shuddered. The tremor ran through his slender body like an ague, Donal felt it strongly in his own hand as it rested upon Sef's arm. His thin face was chalky gray. He mouthed words Donal could neither hear nor decipher.

"Sef—"

Sef jerked his arm free of Donal's hand. For a moment, a fleeting moment only, his eyes turned inward as if he sought to shut out the world. He raised insignificant fists curled so tightly the bones of his knuckles shone through thinly stretched flesh. Briefly his teeth bared in an almost feral grimace.

"They *know* that I am here—" As suddenly he broke off. The eyes, filled by black pupils, looked upon Donal with recognition once again. "My lord—?"

Donal released a breath. The boy had looked so strange, as if he had been thrown into a private battle within himself. But now he appeared recovered, if a trifle shaken. "I intended to say it was only the wind and your own superstitions," Donal told him. "But—this is the island of the gods, and who am I to say they do not speak to you?"

Especially if he is Cheysuli. Donal felt the cool breeze run fingers through his hair, stripping it from his face. The wind was stronger than before, as if it meant to speak to him of things beyond his ken.

"They know it," Sef said hollowly. And then his mouth folded upon itself, pressing lip against lip, as if he had made up his mind to overcome an enemy. "It *doesn't matter.*"

Donal felt the breath of the gods against the back of his neck. He shivered. Then he helped put Sef's clothing into order once again. "I will not deny I feel something as well, but I doubt there is anger in it. I think we have nothing to fear. I am, if you will pardon my arrogance, a descendent of the Firstborn."

"And I am not," Sef said plainly. Then something flickered in his eyes and his manner altered. He looked intently at Donal a moment, then shrugged narrow shoulders. "I don't know *what* I am."

Donal smoothed the boy's black hair into place, though the wind disarranged it almost at once. "The gods do. That is what counts." He tapped Sef on the back. "Come along. Let us not keep the lady waiting."

The interior of the expansive palace was pillared in white marble veined with silver and rose. Silken tapestries of rainbow colors decked the white walls and fine carpets replaced rushes which, even scented, grew old and rank too quickly. Donal did not know how much of the amenities had been ordered by Electra—or, more likely, by Carillon—but he was impressed. Homana-Mujhar, for all its grandeur, was somewhat austere at times. This place, he thought, would make a better home.

Except it is a prison.

Racks of scented beeswax candles illuminated the vastness of the entry hall. Servants passed by on business of their own, as did occasional guards attired in Carillon's black-and-crimson livery. Donal saw a few Cheysuli warriors in customary leathers and gold, but for the most part his fellow warriors remained unobtrusive.

When the woman came forth to greet Donal, he saw she wore a foreign crest worked into the fabric of her gown: Electra's white swan on a cobalt field. The woman was

slender and dark with eyes nearly the color of the gown;
he wondered if she had chosen it purposely. And he recalled that Carillon had also exiled the Queen's Solindish
women.

He wondered at the decision. *Would it not have been
better to send the women home? Here with Electra, they
could all concoct some monstrous plot to overthrow the
Mujhar.*

How? Taj asked as he lighted on a chairback. *Carillon
has warded them well.*

I do not trust her, lir.

Nor does Carillon, Lorn told him. *There is no escape for
her. There are Cheysuli here.*

The Solindish woman inclined her head as she paused
before Donal. She spoke good Homanan, and was polite,
but he was aware of an undertone of contempt. "You wish
to see the Queen. Of course. This way."

Donal measured his step to the woman's. She paused
before a brass door that had been meticulously hammered
and beveled into thousands of intricate shapes. The woman
tapped lightly, then stepped aside with a smooth, practiced
gesture. "Through here. But the boy must wait without—
there, on the bench. The Queen sees no one unless she so
orders it and I doubt she would wish to see *him.*"

Donal restrained the retort he longed to make, matching
the woman's efficient, officious manner as he inclined his
head just enough to acknowledge her words. Then he
turned to Sef. "Wait for me here."

Sef's thin face was pale and frightened as he slowly sat
down on the narrow stone bench beside the door. He
clasped his hands in his lap, hunching within his cloak, and
waited wordlessly.

"Be not afraid," Donal said gently. "No one will seek to
harm you. You are the prince's man."

Sef swallowed, nodded, but did not smile. He looked at
his hands only, patently prepared to wait with what patience he thought was expected, and wanting none of it.

Knowing he could do nothing more, Donal gave up the
effort and passed through the magnificent door. It thudded
shut behind him.

Taj rode his right shoulder. Lorn paced beside his left

leg. He was warded about with *lir*, and still he felt apprehensive. This was Electra he faced.

Witch. Tynstar's meijha. *More than merely a woman.* But he went on, pacing the length of the cavernous hall.

Electra awaited him. He saw her standing at the end of the hallway on a marble dais. And he nearly stopped in his tracks.

He had heard, as they all had, that Electra's fabled beauty was mostly illusory, that Tynstar had given it to her along with the gift of youth and immortality; so long as she was not slain outright, she—like Tynstar—would never die. He had heard that the beauty would fade, since she was separated from Tynstar. But Donal knew how much power rumors had—as well as how little truth—and now as he saw the woman again for the first time in fifteen years, he could not say if she was human or immortal; ensorceled or genuine.

By the gods . . . separation from Tynstar has not dulled her beauty; has not dispersed the magic!

Her pale gray eyes watched him approach the dais. Longlidded, somnolent eyes; eyes that spoke of bedding. Her hair was still a fine white-blonde, lacking none of its shine or texture. Loose, it flowed over her shoulders like a mantle, held back from her face by a simple fillet of golden, interlocked swans. Her skin lacked none of the delicate bloom of youth, and her allure was every bit as powerful as it had been the day she trapped Carillon in her spell.

Donal looked at her. No longer a boy, he saw Electra as a man sees a woman: appraising, judgmental, and forever wondering what she would be like if she ever shared his bed. He could not look at her without sexual fantasy; it was not that he desired her, simply that Electra seemed to magically inspire it.

I have been blind, he realized. *No more can I say to Carillon I cannot comprehend what made him keep her by him, even when he recognized her intent.* He swallowed heavily. *I have been such a fool. . . .* But he would never admit it to her—or to Carillon.

Electra wore a simple gown of silvered gray velvet, but over it she had draped a wine-purpled mantle of sheer, pearly silk. Unmoving, she watched him. Watching her watching him, Donal made up his mind to best her.

"You come at last." Her voice was low and soft, full of the cadences of Solinde. "I had thought Carillon's little wolfling would keep himself to his forests."

Donal managed to maintain an impassive face as he halted before the dais. A word within the link to Taj sent the falcon fluttering to perch upon upon the back of the nearest chair. Lorn stood at Donal's left knee, ruddy pelt rising on his shoulders.

As if he too senses the power in the woman.

Electra was not a tall woman, though her tremendous self-possession made her seem so. The dais made her taller yet, but even marble could not compete with Donal's Cheysuli height.

It was an odd moment. She stood before him, impossibly beautiful and immortally young. Too young. He came to speak of her daughter, when she appeared hardly old enough to bear one.

He smiled. *I have you, Electra, and you do not even know it.*

She watched him. The clear, gray-pale eyes did not move from his face, as if she judged him solely by his own eyes. Well, he knew what she saw: a clear, eerily perfect yellow; eyes bestial and uncanny, full of a strange inborn wisdom and wildness, and a fanatic dedication to the prophecy of the Firstborn.

We are enemies. We need say nothing to one another; it is there. It was there from the day I was born, as if she knew what I would come to mean to her and the Ihlini lord she serves.

"I have come to fetch home your daughter, lady," he said quietly. "It is time for us to wed."

Electra's head moved only a little on her slender neck. Her voice was quiet and contained. "I do not give my permission for this travesty to go forth. No."

"The choice is not yours—"

"So you may say." Slender, supple hands smoothed the silk of her mantle, drawing his eyes to their subtle seductiveness. "Think you I will allow my daughter to wed a Cheysuli shapechanger? No." She smiled slowly. "I forbid it."

He set his teeth. "Forbid what you will, Electra, it will do you little good. If you seek to rail at me like a jackdaw because of your fate, I suggest you look at the cause of your disposal. It is because of *you* Carillon has made me heir to Homana and your daughter's intended husband. *You*, lady. Because you conspired against him."

Long-nailed fingers twisted the wine-purple fabric of her mantle. Her eyes held a malignant fascination. "Your prophecy says a Cheysuli must hold the Lion Throne of Homana before it can be fulfilled. Undoubtedly all of the shapechangers think that man will be you, since Carillon has let everyone know—no matter how unofficially—that he intends to proclaim you his heir. 'Prince of Homana,' are you not styled, even before the proper time?" Electra smiled. "But that is not the prophecy Tynstar chooses to serve . . . *nor is it mine!* We will put no Cheysuli on the Lion Throne but an Ihlini-born man instead, and see to Carillon's death."

"You have tried," he said with a calmness he did not feel. "You have tried to slay him before, and it has failed. Is Tynstar so inept? Is he a powerless sorcerer? Or has the Seker turned his face from his servant, so that Tynstar lacks a lord?" He waited, but she made no answer. Even in her anger, she was utterly magnificent. He felt the tightening of his loins, and it made him angry with himself as well as with the woman. "Electra, I ask you one thing: have you said this to your daughter? Do you tell *her* what you intend to do? He is, after all, her father."

"Aislinn is not your concern."

"Aislinn will be my *cheysula*."

"Use no shapechanger words to me!" she snapped. "Carillon may have sent me here, but this is *my* hall! *My* palace! *I* rule here!"

"What do you rule?" he demanded. "A few pitiful acres of land, served only by those who serve the Mujhar, except for your loyal women. An impressive realm, Electra." He shook his head. "It is a pity you hold no court. Instead, you have only the memories of what you once had the ordering of." He smiled ironically. "The grandeur of Bellam's palaces in Solinde and the magnificence of Homana-Mujhar. But all of that is gone, Electra—banished by your treachery and deceit. Curse not me or mine when you must first curse yourself."

For the first time he had shaken her composure utterly. He could see it. She trembled with fury, and clutched at the silk of her mantle so that the fabric crumpled and rent. Rich color stood high in her face. "First you must *wed* her, shapechanger, to merge the proper blood. But what is not yet done shall *remain* undone . . . and the prophecy shall fail."

Electra stretched out a hand toward him. He saw the merest crackle and flare of purple flame around one pointing finger, but the color died. The hand was nothing more than a hand. Before a Cheysuli, the arts Tynstar had taught her failed.

"Tynstar's sorcery keeps you young now, Electra," Donal said gently. "But you should remember: you *are* a woman of fifty-five. One day, it will catch up to you." He walked slowly toward the dais, mounted it even as she opened her mouth to revile him, and slowly walked around her. "One day he will be slain, and then what becomes of you? You will age, even as Carillon ages. Your bones will stiffen and your blood will flow sluggishly. One day you will not be able to rise, so feeble will you have become, and you will be bound to chair or bed. And then you shall have only endless empty hours in which to spin your impotent webs." He stopped directly before her. "That is your *tahlmorra*, Electra . . . I wish you well of it."

Electra said nothing. She merely smiled an unsettling smile.

"What of *me?*" asked a voice from a curtained opening. "What do you wish for *me?*"

Four

Donal spun around and saw the young woman gowned in snowy white. A girdle of gold and garnets spilled down the front of her skirts to clash and chime against the hem. Redgold hair flowed loosely over her shoulders, in glorious disarray. Her lustrous white skin and long gray eyes were her mother's; her pride was Carillon's.

"Aislinn!" It was the only word he could muster. For two years he had not seen her, knowing her only through her letters to Carillon. And in those two years she had crossed the threshold between girlhood and womanhood. She was still young—too young, he thought, for marriage—but all her awkward days were over.

He smiled at her, prepared to tell her how much she had changed—and for the better. But his smile slowly began to fade as she moved into the hall.

Aislinn let the tapestry curtain fall from a long-fingered hand. The gems in the girdle flashed in the candlelight. Gold gleamed. A fortune clasped her slender waist and dangled against her skirts. And Donal, knowing that Carillon's taste in gifts to his daughter ran to merlins, puppies and kittens, realized the girdle was undoubtedly a present from Electra.

He looked at Aislinn's face. It was taut and forbidding, set in lines too harsh for a young woman of sixteen years, but if she had heard his final words to Electra he was not at all surprised she should view him with some hostility.

The girdle chimed as Aislinn moved. And Donal wondered uneasily if Electra had somehow purchased her daughter's loyalty.

Carillon should never have sent her . . . not for so long. Not for two years. The gods know he meant well by it, realizing the girl needed to see her jehana *. . . but he should*

*have had her brought back much sooner, regardless of all
those letters begging to remain a little longer. Two years
is too long. The gods know what the witch has done to
Aislinn's loyalties.*

The girl halted before him, glancing briefly at the wolf.
Donal thought she might greet her old friend, but she made
no move to kneel down and scratch Lorn's ears as she had
in earlier days.

Aislinn's pride was manifest. "Well? What say you,
Donal?" Her tone was a reflection of her mother's, cool
and supremely controlled. "What of *me?*"

"By the gods, Aislinn!" he said in surprise. "I have no
quarrel with *you.* It is your *jehana* who lacks manners!"

It was obviously not what she expected him to say. She
lost all of her cool demeanor and stared at him in astonishment. "How *dare* you attack my mother!"

"Donal." Electra's voice sounded dangerously amused,
and he looked at her warily. "Are you certain you *wish* to
wed my daughter?"

He wanted to swear. He did not, but only because he
shut his mouth on the beginning of the word. He glared at
Electra. "Play no games with me, lady. Aislinn and I have
been betrothed for fifteen years. We have been friends as
long as that."

Electra smiled: a cat before a mousehole. "Friends, aye—
at one time. But are you so certain she is the woman you
would wish to keep as your wife the rest of your life?"

No, he said inwardly. *Not Aislinn . . . but what choice do
I have?*

He gritted his teeth and made up his mind not to lose
the battle. Not to Electra. He knew she took no prisoners.
"I imagine you have done what you could to turn Aislinn
against this marriage in the two years you have hosted her."
He glanced at the girl and saw contempt for him in her
eyes. Electra's eyes, so cool and shrewd. Contempt, where
once there had been childlike adoration. "Aye," he agreed
grimly, "I see you have. But I have more faith in Aislinn's integrity."

"Integrity has nothing to do with it," Electra said gently.
"Ask Aislinn what she thinks of bearing unnatural
children."

Shock riveted him. He stared at the woman in horror. *"Unnatural children—"*

"Ask Aislinn what she thinks of babies born with fangs and claws and tails, and the beast-mark on their faces," Electra suggested softly. "Ask Aislinn what she thinks of playing mother—no, *jehana*—" she twisted the Old Tongue cruelly "—to a *thing* not wholly human nor wholly animal— but bestial instead." The perfect mouth smiled. "Ask Aislinn, my lord Prince of Homana, what she thinks about sharing a bed with a man who cannot control his shape— *in* bed or out of it."

He took a single lurching step away from the dais and the woman. "What *filth* have you told her—?"

"Filth?" Electra arched white-blond brows. "Only the truth, shapechanger. Or do you deny the gold on your arms, in your ear . . . the animals your kind call the *lir?*" An expressive gesture encompassed gold and wolf and bird.

He felt ill. He wanted to turn his back on the woman and flee the hall, but he could not do it. He would not do it. He would not allow her to win. "Lies," he said flatly. "And Aislinn knows it. Do you forget?—she has known me since her birth."

"I forget nothing." Electra smiled with all the guilelessness of a child. "But you have the right of it, of course . . . Aislinn knows you well."

Donal stood his ground. "We played together as children, Electra. Scraped knees, tended bee stings, shared one another's bread. Do you think, *lady*, such memories can be destroyed with but a few words from you?"

"I have had her two years, Donal." Electra allowed the violet mantle to slither to her hip, exposing the low-cut neck of her gown and the pale flesh of the tops of her breasts. "Do you recall what I did to Carillon in two *months?*"

He did. And he turned at once to Aislinn. "Two years is more than enough time to fill your head with lies, and she is good at that. But do you forget your *jehan?* It is Carillon with whom you lived for fourteen years before you came to Electra."

A pale hand smoothed the garneted chains hanging from Aislinn's girdle. Her pinched face told him she did indeed recall their childhood friendship and her girlish attraction to him. "I—believe my mother has told me the truth. We are children no longer . . . and why would she lie to *me?*"

"To use you." He had no more time for tact or diplomacy. "By the gods, girl, are you blind? Do you forget why she is here? She will try to bring down Carillon any way she can. Even now she stoops to perverting *you!*"

Fingers tangled in the garneted golden chains. "But—it is not the Mujhar she speaks of, Donal . . . it is *you.* It is *you* she warns me against, knowing your animal urges—"

"Animal urges!" He was aghast. "Have you gone mad? You *know* me, Aislinn—what *urges* do you speak of?"

Her face had caught fire, as if to match the richness of her hair. "We were children, then . . . we are adults, now. You are—a man . . . and she has told me what to expect." She averted her eyes from his, staring fiercely at the floor. "I have only to look at Finn, if I want to see what you will become."

"Finn?" He stared. "What has *Finn* to do with this?"

Aislinn managed to look at him again, though the chiming of her girdle told him how she trembled. "Will you deny that he *stole* your own mother because he wanted her—as an animal wants another? Will you deny that he stole also the Mujhar's sister—who later died because of his neglect?" Aislinn sucked in a shaking breath. "I look at Finn, Donal, your own uncle . . . and I see what you will become."

By the gods, Electra has driven her mad— He felt his hands clench into fists, unclenched them with effort, and tried to speak coherently through his astonishment and anger.

"We will—speak of this another time. In some detail. But for now, I must tell you to have your things packed."

"Have you gone mad?" she demanded. "Do you think I will go with *you?*"

"I think so," he said grimly. "It is the Mujhar's bidding I do, not my own. Aislinn—he bids us end our betrothal. The time has come for us to wed."

For a long moment, she simply stared. He saw how she looked at him, appraising him even as her mother had. What she saw he could not say. But her face was very pale, and there was true apprehension in her eyes.

She turned quickly to face her mother. "He cannot make

me go if I wish to stay with you." The question, even through her declaration, was implicit in her tone.

"You have been with your *jehana* two years, Aislinn—longer than was intended," Donal pointed out. "Carillon allowed you to stay because you wished it. He has been overly generous, I think—but now it is time you returned to him."

Electra smoothed the supple silk of her purple mantle. "He is a shapechanger, Aislinn. He can make man or woman do *anything*, does he wish it." Her cool eyes glinted as she looked at him. "Can you not?"

Grimly, he wished he could slay her where she stood, even before her daughter.

Electra merely smiled.

"I will *not*," Aislinn declared. "I will go nowhere I have no wish to go."

Inwardly, he sighed. "Then you defy your *jehan*, Aislinn. It is Carillon who wants you back in Homana-Mujhar." *Not me,* he thought. *Oh gods, not me.*

"And you do *not?*" she demanded triumphantly, as if she had won the battle and proved her point.

Donal laughed, but the sound lacked all humor. "No," he said bluntly. "Why should I?"

Slowly, so slowly, the color flowed out of her face. Her gray eyes were suddenly blackened pits of comprehension. Color rushed back and lit her face. "*Do you mean—*"

"—do I mean I do not want you?" he interrupted rudely. "Aye, that sums it up. So gainsay your foolishness, Aislinn, and order your belongings packed. Carillon wants you home."

The breath rattled in her throat. "Wait you—*wait* you—" She shut her mouth, tried to recover some of her vanished composure, and frowned at him. "To gain the throne, you must have *me.*"

"Oh, aye," he agreed, "but have I ever said I *wanted* it?"

"But—it is the *throne*—" She gestured. "The throne of all Homana . . . and now Solinde. The *Lion* Throne." Her frown deepened. "And yet you tell me you *do not want* it?"

"I do not," he said distinctly. "Do you understand, now? We were betrothed because Carillon had no sons, only a daughter—and no *cheysula*—no *proper* one—to share his bed and bear him any more children." His eyes went to

Electra, standing stiffly on the dais. "And so, by betrothing his daughter to his cousin's son, Carillon gets an heir for the throne of Homana." He spread his hands. "Me." The hands flopped down. "*That* is why I am here, no matter what your *jehana* tells you."

Aislinn gathered the heavy girdle in both hands, wadding the chain into the soft flesh of her palms. She was pale, so pale; he thought she might cry. But she did not. He saw her reach within herself to regain her composure.

She looked at her mother. She looked at her mother, and waited.

When he could, Donal looked at the woman also. She stood but two paces from him, close enough that he could put out his hands and throttle her. He knew, for the first time, a measure of the futility Carillon had experienced, and knew himself a fool for undervaluing the woman.

Gods . . . even now *she does not give up. She will hound him to his death—* He was brought up short. *Which is what she wants. Even now. Even imprisoned on this island, she will do what she can to slay him . . . even to using her daughter.* He felt ill. *I cannot deal with this—*

Electra regarded him quietly. "Do you see?" she asked. "You may win back a part of her, in time—I do expect it, of course—but there is a portion of Aislinn I will always hold." Her right hand scribed an invisible rune in the air between them, as if she dallied idly. She smiled composedly. "Her *soul*, Cheysuli wolfling. I have made that completely mine . . . and what is mine is also Tynstar's."

Donal watched her hand, so slim and pale, as it closed upon the invisible rune. *By the gods, what has she done to Aislinn?*

He looked at the girl. She stood very still, staring fixedly at her mother, and Donal felt an uprush of chilling apprehension. *There are Cheysuli here—Electra can practice no magic.* And yet he knew, watching the woman, that she retained a measure of her power. How much or how little he could not say, but there was power in her eyes. And Aislinn, Homanan and Solindish, was completely unprotected. Vulnerable to her mother.

Before a Cheysuli, the Ihlini lose much of their power. But not all! There are still tricks they can perform. Electra may only know such tricks as Tynstar taught her, being no

Ihlini herself, but I cannot say she is as helpless as we thought—

Donal looked sharply at Aislinn. He saw how pale she was, how she continued clenching the golden girdle with all its rich cold stones. Her hands were shaking, and yet her voice was quite steady, quite calm.

As if she has made a discovery, and is strengthened because of it.

"Is that why you wanted me?" Aislinn did not move. "For the Ihlini?" She ignored Electra's abortive attempt at speech. "And are you so *certain* your perverted magic has worked on me?"

Donal stared at Aislinn. So did Electra. The silence was unbroken in the hall.

Garnets rattled as Aislinn clutched the girdle. "I have listened to Donal just now. I have listened to you as well, hearing you mouth all the things you have told me these past two years. And—I know you better than ever before: *I know you.*"

"Aislinn—" Electra began.

"Listen to me!" Aislinn's shout reverberated. "I will hear no more lies about my father—*no more lies.* Oh, aye . . . I know what you sought to do—I know why you sought to *do* it! Make the daughter into a weapon against the father." Aislinn's voice shook. "He told me—he *told* me: once he truly loved you. But you gave yourself to Tynstar. You wasted yourself on an Ihlini sorcerer! And now you think to twist me in spirit as Tynstar has twisted my father in body?" Hysterically, she laughed, and the sound filled up the hall. "I *do* know Donal—and he is *not* what you say he is!"

Electra's lips were pale. She stood very still on the marble dais. "He is a *shapechanger.* What I have told you is true."

Aislinn shook her head violently. "What you have told me are *lies!* Did you think I would not know? Did you truly believe I would listen to that vile filth you spewed when I have known him longer than I have *you?*" Again, Aislinn laughed. "You do not live up to your reputation, *mother!* I am amazed at how easily I saw through your plans."

Electra's face was bone-white. Suddenly, even through the magnificence of her beauty, she was old.

But still she summoned a smile. "Then I will tell you the truth in one thing, Aislinn—*heed me well*, I do not lie. What is mine is also Tynstar's, and I have *made you mine*." One hand stabbed upward to cut off Aislinn's angry words. "Wait you, girl, and you will see. Do not seek to denigrate my power when you have hardly known it." This time, it was Electra who laughed. "Run along, then, and pack your things. Perhaps it *is* time I sent you home to the cripple who sired a useless daughter when all he wanted was a son."

"Aislinn, do not." Donal's quiet tone overrode the beginnings of Aislinn's outcry. "Let it be. You know what she is." He touched the girl's arm. He felt her body tremble. "Go. Pack your things. And look forward to seeing your *jehan*, who truly loves you."

White-faced, with tears staining the fairness of her cheeks, Aislinn turned and ran from her mother's hall.

When he could better master himself, Donal turned back to face Electra. "I am grateful to you." He said it very quietly. "You have let the girl see for herself precisely what you are, and I need never say another word. You have made my work easier, Electra. I thank you for it."

"Do you?" The overwhelming beauty was back and all the odd fragility was banished. Electra was once more herself. "Then I am heartened. It will make it so much sweeter when my plans are quite fulfilled."

Donal shook his head. "You have power, lady—that I willingly admit—and no doubt Tynstar has taught you how to use it, but you forget. You forget something very important." He forced a smile. "Aislinn loves her father, Electra . . . and the power of that love you can never destroy."

Electra considered a moment. "Perhaps not," she conceded, "but then must we always speak of Carillon? Why not of you, instead?"

"Does it matter?" he demanded. "You have lost her entirely."

"Have I? No, I think not. She may believe so for now—she is welcome to that innocence—but she will soon see that she cannot deny me. I am no idle practitioner of the little love-spells other women like to think they weave. No, no—I am much more. Tynstar has made me so." Slowly, she gathered up the red-purple mantle and draped it over one velveted shoulder. "Aislinn is all mine. You will see it. So shall she. And in the end, I shall win."

"What can you do?" he demanded derisively. "What spell do you think you can cast? You have seen and heard your daughter, Electra—she is none of yours. How can you think to gainsay us?"

The woman smiled slowly, with all the seductiveness in her soul. "Quite easily, as you will see." Electra laughed once more. "Surely you know the law, Donal: *No marriage is binding if it is not consummated.*"

Five

The ship creaked as she broke swells on her way back toward the mainland. Behind her lay the mist-shrouded island. Already the sun shone more brightly, even as it sank toward the horizon and set the seas ablaze.

"I am sorry for what I said to you in the hall." Aislinn, standing before Donal as he leaned against the taffrail, ignored his dismissive gesture. "I said them because my mother made certain I would, though I did not realize it then. She had told me so much of you, and I almost believed her." The lowering sun set her hair aglow. "I am—shamed by my behavior, which was not fitting for a princess." Her voice trembled. "Oh Donal—I am *so ashamed*—"

"Aislinn—"

"No." She made a chopping gesture with her right hand. Her young face was blotched and swollen with tears, so that most of her burgeoning beauty was replaced with anguish. "I *almost* believed her. Though I have known you for so long. And then, when I heard her confidence—when I heard how she intended to *use* me—I could not bear it! I thought of my father as I looked into your face, and I knew what she meant to do."

Donal turned from the rail to face her directly. "Do you say, then, you did not know before today what it was she sought to do?" He asked it gently, knowing it needed to be asked; knowing also she was extremely vulnerable to the pain engendered by such questions.

The wind played with Aislinn's red-gold hair, though she had braided it into a single plait for traveling. The rope of hair hung down her back to her waist, bright against the dull brown of her traveling cloak. Stray curls pulled free of the braid and crept up to touch her face.

Impatiently, she stripped them back with one hand as

she brushed more tears away. "I—knew something of what she intended. At least—I thought I did." Aislinn shrugged slightly. "Perhaps it is just that now I wish to deny what sway she held over me, so I can find some pride again." She turned away from him. "Toward the end, during my last days, I began to understand better what she wanted. And I knew I wanted no part of it. But I was—afraid. I thought if I told her I wished to go home to my father, she would forbid it. So—I waited. And when I heard you had come, I thought I would ask you to take me back. But—I heard what you said to her, how you reviled her, and I recalled all the things she had told me—about what the Cheysuli can do—and I became afraid again." She lowered her eyes.

She was young. So very young. He was unsurprised Electra had chosen to use her; even less so that Aislinn had so easily been taken in. He could not begin to imagine what it had been like for her in Homana-Mujhar, princess-born and bred by her father the Mujhar, knowing all the while her exiled mother was imprisoned on the Crystal Isle.

"Aislinn." He put out his hands and drew her away from the railing, cradling her shoulders in his palms. "I am sorry for the scene involving your *jehana*. But that is done now, and you must face the things that lie ahead."

Almost at once he felt ludicrous—he was not the girl's father, but her betrothed—and here he was speaking like a wise old man when he was more ordinarily an unwise young one.

Donal smiled wryly. "Listen to us, Aislinn. One would think we hardly know one another."

She moved closer, seeking solace. "I think perhaps we do not." Her eyes beseeched his. "Will you be easy with me? I am sometimes a foolish girl."

"And I am sometimes a foolish boy." Donal set a hand to her head and smoothed back the blowing hair. "We will have to grow up together."

Aislinn laughed a little. "But you are already grown, no matter what you say. While I feel like an infant."

"Hardly that. You should look in the polished silver."

A glint crept into Aislinn's eyes. She arched her brows. "I have."

He tugged her braid. "And vain of what you see, are

you?" He laughed at the beginnings of her protest. "I am no courtier, Aislinn, but I can tell you this much: you are a woman now, and quite a beautiful one."

She touched his bare arm lightly. "My thanks, Donal. I was afraid—I was afraid I would not please you. And I do desire to please you."

It was earnestness he heard in her voice, and honesty, not seductiveness. And yet even in her simplicity, there was a powerful allure about her. She lacked Electra's guile, but none of her mother's power to bind a man.

He disengaged from her as easily as he could and stepped away. He could not afford to be bound.

The same Homanan sailed them back to the mainland, silent now in his astonishment at what he heard and from whom he heard it. Sef sat on a coil of rope nearby, watching Donal and Aislinn with the rapt attention of a hound guarding his master. Taj perched upon a spar high above them. Lorn, deck-bound, paced the length of the ship again and again, as if something troubled him.

Lir? Donal asked.

Something. Something. I cannot say. And Lorn would say no more.

Taj?

The falcon's tone was troubled. *Nor have I an answer.*

Aislinn clutched at the taffrail for support as the ship broke swells. Donal reached out and set an arm behind her back. "Forgive me, Aislinn—what I must ask is harsh, I know . . . but you must realize that others have known what Electra is for years. How can you have escaped it?"

Her young mouth twisted bitterly. "Oh, aye, I heard all the stories. How could I not in Homana-Mujhar? We have all heard the lays from the harpers—how it was the Queen of Homana sought to slay her wedded husband." Aislinn looked away from him, staring instead at the mainland as the ship sailed closer. "I heard them all," she muttered, "but she is my mother, and I wanted to see her. Oh, how I longed to see her!"

"Because she was the stuff of legend?" He could not let it pass.

Aislinn's chin rose defensively. "That, too. She was *Electra of Solinde*, Bellam's daughter, ensorceled by Tynstar himself." Her fair skin was flushed with shame. "And I wondered: did I have any of the Solindish witch in me? I could not *help* but wonder."

"No." Donal shifted against the rail. "Aislinn—you must know I do not blame you. I cannot say I know Electra well—like you, I know her through the legends—but I *do* know that what you said was what she had put into your mind. She is a witch, with powers we cannot fully comprehend."

"And you are Cheysuli." Aislinn's gray gaze, though red-rimmed from her anguish, was very steady. She had more of Electra in her features than Carillon, but he saw a shadow of her father in her pride and confidence. "Can your magic not overcome hers?"

"She can use none on me," he agreed, "because of my Cheysuli blood. But she is free to use what she will on you. You are Homanan—"

"—*and* Solindish." She said it very clearly. "Do you wonder, now, if I am the enemy also? If what she said about me is true, then perhaps I *am* nothing but a tool to be used against my father . . . or even you."

"There is no truth in Electra's mouth." Donal tugged her braid again, and then the hand slipped under the rope of hair to press against the cloak and her back beneath the wool. "We must make a marriage, you and I, for the sake of your *jehan*'s realm. But if you have even the smallest bit of Carillon in you, I need have no fear of Electra's influence."

Aislinn stared fixedly at the shoreline. "You said you did not desire the throne." Her voice trembled just a little. "You said—and clearly—you did not desire *me*."

He was not a man of stone, to hear the pain in her voice and not respond. But he could not lie to her, not even to salve her pride.

"The truth," he said gently. "No. I do not desire you. I think of you as a *rujholla*, not a *cheysula*."

"I am not your sister." Her spine was rigid beneath his hand. "And I do not think of *you* as a brother."

She never had; he knew that. He had known it from the beginning. Before she was old enough to know what betrothal meant, she had decided to marry him.

Aislinn turned and faced him. "We were young together, briefly; you grew up too fast. You already had your *lir*—

you were a warrior, not a boy, and too soon you wearied of playing with little girls. Me. Your sister. Meghan." She shrugged. "You left us all behind. But now—*now*—I am trying to catch up."

He knew what she wanted. Some confirmation there could be love between them. And he knew he could not offer it.

I will hurt her. One day . . . I will have to.

"Aislinn—let it come of its own time if the gods desire it. You are young. There is time."

"I am young," Aislinn agreed, "but I am old enough. The priests will see to that."

Donal touched her braid again. "Aye, so they will. I am sorry, Aislinn. But I will not give you falsehood or false dreams."

She turned abruptly and faced him. "Do you not care for me at *all?*"

He wanted to retreat, but did not. He owed her more, no matter how horrible he felt. And he felt. More deeply than he had believed possible. He was fond of Aislinn, very fond; she had always been a winsome girl, and he had always enjoyed her company. But it was girl to man, not man to woman; he had another woman for that.

"Aislinn," he said at last, "What you know of a man and woman has been twisted by your *jehana.* You would do well to speak to mine, to know the truth of things."

Aislinn set her jaw. It was delicately feminine, but he did not forget what man had helped to form it. "Alix is your mother," Aislinn declared. "She will think only of *you*, and not at all of me."

"She is not blind to my faults," Donal told her wryly. "She knows me very well."

"But would she admit them openly to me?"

He laughed. "Do you think there are so many?"

"Sometimes." She pushed strands of hair out of her face. "They say you are much like Finn. And what I have heard of *him*—"

"From *Electra?*" Donal wanted to spit. "Gods, Aislinn, there is nothing but hatred between them."

"From others. You know what the servants say in Homana-Mujhar."

He overrode her at once. "Most of those stories are false.

They are made-up things, tales to entertain those who enjoy such petty nonsense." He shook his head. "Do you think your *jehan* would keep by him a liege man who had done all the things the tales say Finn did?"

"He is your uncle," Aislinn retorted. "I think you will not admit *he* has faults."

Donal smiled wryly. "Oh, aye, my *su'fali* has faults. Many of them—but not so many as all these people so willingly ascribe to him." He sighed, frowning a little. "But—Carillon says I am more like my *jehan* . . . He said the last part wistfully, revealing more of his feelings than he realized; knowing only he longed to be as much like his father as he could.

Aislinn looked at him sharply. He was aware of the intensity of her appraisal. After a moment she looked away again. "You—never speak of your father. You never did. At least—not often."

"No." Donal turned away to lean against the taffrail, belt buckle scraping against wood. "No. For a long time, I could not. Now, although I can, I find I prefer to keep him private."

"Because that way he is yours, and you do not have to share him." Aislinn stood next to him. Her nearness—and unexpected understanding—was disconcerting. He would have preferred another woman standing at his side, blonde instead of red-haired, but she was not there. Aislinn was. "I never knew Duncan," she said quietly. "I was too young when he died." She cast him a sidelong glance, then looked more directly at him, as if she threw him a challenge. "He did *die*, did he not?"

"He died. As a *lir*less Cheysuli dies." His tone was more clipped than he intended. But it was difficult to speak of his father's fate when he resented his loss so much. He recalled too clearly how Carillon had given him the news, saying Tynstar had slain Duncan's *lir*. Dead *lir*: dead Cheysuli. As simple as that.

Except it was not. He knew—as every Cheysuli knew—that death was the end result of *lir*lessness, but no one knew how it happened. How the life was ended at last.

Your father is dead, Carillon had said. *Tynstar slew his lir.* Very little else had been necessary, though Carillon had said the words anyway. Even at eight years of age, Donal understood precisely what *lir*lessness meant.

"What was he like?" Aislinn asked.

"He was clan-leader of the Cheysuli. A warrior. He served the prophecy." He thought it was enough; at least, for her.

"That says *what* he was. Not *who.*"

Donal pushed the breath through the constriction in his throat. "He was—*more. More* than most. One man may claim he is the best hunter, another may claim the best shot, another the premier tracker. But—my *jehan* was all of those things. Clan-leader at my age, because he was the wisest of those young warriors who survived Shaine's *qu'mahlin*. More dedicated; he knew what faced the Cheysuli and he brought them through it. He brought Carillon to the knowledge of what he was; of what he had to be. Gods . . . he gave up his own freedom in service to the prophecy, knowing he would die. Knowing Tynstar would win their personal battle."

"He *knew!*" Clearly, Aislinn was shocked. "How can a man foresee his own death, and then go *to* it?"

Donal put out his right hand and made the Cheysuli gesture: palm up, fingers spread, encompassing infinity. "*Tahlmorra,*" he said. "My *jehan* had a clearer vision than most, and he did not turn away. He knew what he had to do. He knew what the price would be."

"*Tynstar* slew him." She stared fixedly toward the shoreline. "There are so many legends about that sorcerer."

"Tynstar slew his *lir.*" He shrugged. "One and the same, in the end."

Aislinn looked at him sharply. "Then—he did what a *lir*less Cheysuli does? He simply walked away?"

He was somewhat surprised she knew that much. It was not often spoken of, even in the clans. Cheysuli simply *knew.* But he had not expected Aislinn to know.

"The death-ritual." Donal's hands closed tightly on the rail. "It is customary. But personal for each warrior."

Aislinn shivered. "I could never do it."

"You will never have to."

After a moment, she reached out and touched his arm, as if to comfort him. "So—you came to live at Homana-Mujhar in the wake of your father's death."

"No. I came to spend time there at Carillon's behest, not to *live* there. The Keep is my home."

Aislinn looked at him steadily. "And when we are wed? Do you think *I* could live in such a place?"

He shook his head. "No, of course not. You will live in Homana-Mujhar, as you have always done. But you must know there will be times—perhaps *many* times—when I will go to the Keep. There are—kinfolk there."

Aislinn nodded. "I understand. My father has said I cannot expect you to forget the blood in your veins." She shook her head a little. "I do not understand it—what it is to be Cheysuli—but he has said I must give you your freedom when I can. That you tame a Cheysuli by keeping your hand light." She smiled at the imagery.

Donal did not. Inwardly, he grimaced. And yet he blessed Carillon for preparing the girl for his absences, no matter what images were used.

But she will have to know sometime. I cannot keep her in ignorance forever.

He looked past her at the shoreline. "Aislinn—we are here. You have come home again to Homana."

Her reddish brows slid up. "Is not the island part of Homana, then?"

"The Crystal Isle is—different." He thought to let it go at that, but could not when he saw her frown. "It was a Cheysuli place long before Homana was settled by the Firstborn."

She flicked one hand in a quick, dismissive gesture. "Your history is different from mine."

"Aye," he agreed ironically. *More different than you can imagine.*

"What do we do now?" she asked as the boat thudded home at the dock.

"We see to it your trunks are offloaded, and then we shall find an inn that meets with your royal standards." He took her elbow to steady her. "Tomorrow will be soon enough to start out for Homana-Mujhar."

He had thought, originally, to stay the night on the Crystal Isle, but after his bout with Electra he felt he had to leave, to take Aislinn back to the mainland quickly. The girl had been terrified her mother would use magic on her, to force her to stay against her will. And so Donal had taken her off the island alone with Sef and his *lir*, since Aislinn would have none of her mother's Solindish women with her. And now they faced the journey ahead without a proper escort for the Princess of Homana.

Well, Sef will lend some measure of respectability to the journey. I hope.

Donal watched silently as Aislinn's trunks were offloaded and placed on the dock at Hondarth. Sef, as had already become his habit, stood near him. The boy had been unusually silent since he had followed Donal out of Electra's palace, but then Donal knew he himself had not been the best of company. The confrontation with Electra had left a foul taste in his mouth, particularly since she had nearly accomplished what she had intended.

She almost made me doubt her daughter. She nearly made me wonder how much of Aislinn's soul is still her own. But I thank the gods the girl has her own mind, because it has saved her from her mother's machinations.

He glanced at Sef. The boy was still pale, still secret in his silences, watching as the captain piled up all the chests. The odd parti-colored eyes seem fastened on the distances, as if the island had touched him somehow, and he was still lost within its spell.

Well, perhaps he is. Perhaps he begins to understand what it is to be Cheysuli—what the weight of history is. Does he wish to serve me, he will have to understand it.

The dock was busy with men. Donal turned to one of them, hired him with a nod, and gestured toward the growing pile of chests. "Hire men and horses to take these to Homana-Mujhar, in Mujhara." Briefly he showed the ruby signet ring with its black rampant lion. The man's eyes widened. "Lose none of these things, for the Mujhar's daughter prizes her belongings . . . and the Mujhar prizes his daughter's contentment."

The man bobbed his head in a nervous bow, accepting the plump purse Donal gave him, but his eyes slid to Aislinn as she walked unsteadily down the plank. She was wrapped in the heavy brown traveling cloak. but, with her bright hair, unconscious dignity, and a subtlety of manner that somehow emphasized her rank, her identity was hardly secret.

"See it is done," Donal said clearly. "The Mujhar will reward you well."

The man looked at him again; at the yellow eyes and golden earring. The cloak hid Donal's leathers and the rest of his gold; but there was no need to show it. His race was stamped in his face; a Cheysuli, even one born to his clan instead of a throne, wears royalty like his flesh.

The man bobbed another bow, then quickly went about his business.

Aislinn, having come to stand next to Donal, watched the man closely. "They serve you through fear," she said clearly, as if making a discovery. "Not loyalty. Not even knowing you are the prince." She looked into Donal's face. "They serve because they are afraid *not* to."

"Some," he agreed, preferring not to lie. "It is a thing most Cheysuli face. As for me—it does not matter."

Her coppery brows drew down. "But I saw how it grated with you: his fear. I saw how you wished it was otherwise."

"I do," he admitted. "The man who *desires* to see fear in the faces of his servants is no proper man at all."

"And you are?" She showed white teeth, small and even, in a teasing, winsome smile. "What *proper* man takes on the shapes of *animals?*"

He was relieved to see the humor and animation in her face. So, in keeping with her bantering, he opened his mouth to retort that she should know, better than most, what it meant to be Cheysuli. She had grown up with enough of them around her at her father's palace.

But then he recalled that it was to *him* she had directed her questions, and how reluctant he had been to answer. She had been a child, a girl; he had been older, already blessed with his *lir*, and therefore considered a warrior. Then, he had felt, he had little time for a cousin with questions when there were other more important concerns.

Now he knew he had erred, even as he teased. He would have to spend time with her; he would have to educate her, so she could understand. Particularly if she were to comprehend the sometimes confusing customs of the Cheysuli, which often conflicted with the Homanan ones she knew so well.

Uneasily, he wondered if he could explain them all properly.

"We cannot stay here. We must find an inn, sup, then get a good night's rest so we may start back for Mujhara in the morning." Donal glanced at Sef. "You know Hondarth better than I. Suggest an inn suitable for the Princess of Homana, then go and fetch my horse while I escort the lady."

Sef thought it over. "The White Hart," he said at last. "It is not far—" he pointed "—up that way, and around the corner there . . . it's a fine inn. I can't say I've seen its *best* parts—" he smiled a little "—but I'm sure it'll suit the princess. I'll bring your horse. And should I speak to the hostler about buying another for the princess?"

Donal smiled. Sef had taken his service to heart, seeking to do everything Donal would have a grown man do. "And for yourself? Or do you intend to walk?" He laughed as Sef's face reddened. "Fetch back my horse and you may speak to the hostler. Perhaps he has two good mounts for sale."

Sef nodded, bowing clumsily in Aislinn's direction, and scrambled up the dock-ramp to the quay beyond. He vanished in an instant.

Aislinn frowned. "I have not known you to keep boys before. Especially ones like *that*."

"I took Sef on because he is earnest and willing . . . and because he needs a home." Donal bent to run his fingers through Lorn's thick coat. "He is a good boy. Give him a chance, and I think you will see how helpful he can be." He slanted her an arch glance. "Is it not part of a princess' responsibilities to succor where succor is needed?"

Color flared in her face. "Of course. And—I will do so." She snugged the furred cloak more tightly around her body and turned her back on him, heading for the dock-ramp.

Donal laughed to himself and followed.

Seabirds screeched, swooping over the waterfront. Fisherfolk lined the shore, hauling in their catches. The pervasive smell of fish hung over everything; Aislinn wrinkled her nose with its four golden freckles and set a hand over her mouth. "How much farther?"

Donal reached out and caught her elbow, steadying her at once. "Sef said it was around this corner."

"Have we not *already* gone around that corner?"

"Well, perhaps he meant another. Come, it cannot be so far."

The sun fell below the horizon and set the whitewashed buildings ablaze in the sunset, pink and orange and purple. Lanterns were lighted and set into brackets or onto window ledges, so that the twisting streets were full of light and shadows. Aislinn's hair was suddenly turned dark by the setting sun, haloed by gold-tipped, brilliant curls.

Behind them lay the ocean, gilded glassy bronze by the sunset. White gulls turned black in silhouette; their cries resounded in the canyons of myriad streets. The uneven and broken cobbles grew treacherous underfoot, hidden in light and darkness, until Donal took Aislinn's arm and helped her over the worst parts.

"Maybe he meant *this* corner," Aislinn said, as they rounded yet another.

Lir, Taj said, flying overhead. Then, more urgently, Lir!

Five men came into the street. From out of the shadows they flowed, bristling with weapons. Three behind and two in front. Donal cursed beneath his breath.

Aislinn hesitated, then glanced up at him. He tightened his grasp on her arm, hoping to go on without the need for conflict, but the men moved closer together. All exits were blocked, unless he flew over their heads. But that would leave Aislinn alone.

One man grinned, displaying teeth blackened by a resinous gum he chewed even as he spoke. "Shapechanger," he said, "we been watching you. You with your pretty girl." The grin did not change. He bared his teeth. "Shapechanger, why do you come out of your forest? Why do you foul our streets?"

Donal glanced back quickly, totaling up the odds. With Taj and Lorn, he was hardly threatened, but there was Aislinn to think about.

The man stepped closer, and so did the others. "Shapechanger," he said, "Homanan girls are not for you."

"Nor are they for you." Silently, Donal told Taj to continue circling out of range. Lorn moved away from his leg to widen their circle of safety.

"Donal!" Aislinn cried. "Tell them who you are!"

"No." He knew she would not understand. But men such as these, now bent on a little questionable pleasure, might see the implications rife in holding the Mujhar's daughter. Fortunes could be made.

"Donal—!"

Black-teeth laughed. "Who are you, then? What does she want you to say?"

"Move away, Aislinn," Donal said. "It is me they want, not you."

"Is it?" Black-teeth asked. "What does a man do when faced with a woman who consorts with the enemy?"

"Donal—*stop* them—!"

One of the men scooped up a stone and hurled it at Donal. He heard it whistle in the air and twisted, trying to duck away, but even as that stone missed another one did not. It struck a glancing blow across his cheek, smacking against the bone. And then all of the men were throwing.

He heard Aislinn cry out. But mostly he heard the cruel hatred in their voices as the men taunted him.

"Shapechanger!" they cried. "Demon—!"

Taj, he asked, *where are you?*

About to impale the leader—

Lorn—?

Can you not hear the man screaming?

He could. One of the men reeled away, clutching at his right leg. Lorn released him and leaped for an arm, closing on his wrist. The man screamed again, crying out for help, but the others were too busy.

Black-teeth fell away, clawing at his back. Taj still rode his shoulders with his talons sunk into flesh. Donal, left with three men, drew his knife to face them.

No more rocks did they throw. In their hands were knives. No longer did he face Homanans merely out to trouble a Cheysuli, but men instead intent upon his death.

He was angry. Dangerously angry. He felt the anger well up inside, trying to fill his belly. Not once had he faced a man merely trying to steal his purse; not once had he faced a man simply wishing to fight, as men will sometimes do. Not once had he faced any man attempting to take his life. And now that he did, it frightened him.

But the fright he could overcome, or turn to for strength. It was the anger that troubled him most; the anger that came from knowing they saw him for his race, and marked him for death because of it.

When a man dies, he should die for a reason—not this senseless prejudice—

And with an inward snap of rage and intolerance, he summoned the magic.

Six

He knew what the Homanans saw. What Aislinn saw. A blurring voice. A coalescing nothingness. Where once had stood a man, albeit a Cheysuli man, now there was an absence of anything.

It was enough, Carillon had said once, to make a man vomit. The Mujhar had seen such happen before, when Finn had taken *lir*-shape. Apparently it was true, for one of the men cried out and soiled himself even as Donal changed.

It was so easy. He reached out from within, seeking the familiar power. He sank every sense down into the earth. Almost at once he was engulfed by taste, touch, scent, sound, and all the bright colors of the magic. He was no longer Donal, no longer human, no longer anything identifiable. He was a facet of the earth, small and humble and incredibly unimportant—until one looked at what he had done and would do, and the effect it would have on others. No Cheysuli, fully cognizant of his place within the tapestry of the gods, could possibly deny the need for loyal service. Donal, closer to the tapestry than most, did not even think of it.

The magic came at once to his call, filling him until he thought he might burst. He felt tension and urgency and utter need; a physical compulsion. *Sul'harai*, the Cheysuli called it; having no Homanan word to describe the act of the shapechange, they likened it to the instant of perfect love between man and woman. In that moment when he was neither man nor animal, Donal was more complete than at any other time, for he put himself into the keeping of the earth and took from it another form.

He felt excess flesh and bone melting away, sloughing off his body to flow into the earth. There it would find safekeeping, allowing him to set aside fear for the loss of his human form while he assumed another. It was a manner of trading, he knew; while the earth held his human shape, it gave him another to replace the one he put off. But he could not say which cast was better—or which, in fact, held the essence of the true Donal.

He felt the alteration in sinew and skin. He felt the wholeness that came with being completed. He felt the vivid vitality pouring through altered veins, muscles and flesh. No more was he Donal as the others knew him, having voluntarily put off that mold. In its place was a male wolf, yellow-eyed and silver-coated. And when he heard the screaming he knew the change was done.

Donal bunched his powerful haunches, letting all his strength pour into the latter half of his body. He tensed and the fur of his ruff stood on end until he was hackled to the tail. And then he launched himself at the nearest man's chest, jaws opening to display rows of serrated teeth.

The body crumpled, collapsing beneath his weight. It crashed against the ground, blackened teeth clicking in inarticulate words of pain and horror.

I could take his throat—tear it out—watch the blood spill out to soak into the cobbles. What harm would it do? He sought to slay me. *Why not slay him instead?*

Wolf-shaped, Donal stood over the man, head lowered, teeth bared, almost slavering. A mist of anger and bloodthirst rose before his eyes. Everything he looked at had a fuzzy rim around it, as if it bled over into another form. Black-teeth's gurgling moan of horror was lost as Donal gave in to the wolfish growl rising in his throat. And the other men, their terror-inspired paralysis vanishing, tore away.

Donal could smell Black-teeth's fear. It clogged up his nose until he was immersed in the rankness of the stench. Tongue lolling, he could *taste* the terror. It flowed out of the man like a miasma. And for a moment, a long moment, Donal teetered on the brink. He was angry, *too* angry; he was losing himself fast. In a flicker of lucid disbelief he saw himself clearly: wolf, not man; beast, not animal.

Gods, is this *what they meant when they told me never to resort to* lir-*shape when I was angry?*

He retreated at once, lunging away from the madness.

He realized how close he had come to the fine line between control and animal rage. A warrior in *lir*-shape maintained his own mind and his comprehension of things, but the balance was delicate indeed. Donal had been warned many times that *lir*-shape carried its own degree of risk. Did a warrior grow *so* angry that he lost himself completely within his *lir*-shape, he also lost his mind. He would become a wolf utterly, with all a wolf's savage power. awesome strength, and lack of human values.

And without recourse to human form.

Donal fell back again, within and without, backing away from the sobbing man. He heard his own breath and how it rattled hoarsely in his wolf-throat; how he panted in despair. He heard also the echo of his own anger and his desire to slay the man.

I have come too close, too close—by the gods, I nearly lost myself—

At once, he sought to take back his human form. The response was sluggish, painful; he had gone too close to the edge. What was the essence of wolf in him did not wish to give up its shape.

It hurt. Donal gasped, clawing out toward the earth. He had no wish to stay locked in wolf-shape. Not when he was meant to be a man.

Then, all at once, the shapechange slipped into place. He was on one knee, one hand pressed against the cobbles. Paws turned to hands and feet, fur to hair, canines to human teeth. Man-shape once again, but he was not certain how much of the wolf remained.

Lir!

It echoed within the link. Taj and Lorn, both warning him at once.

He spun around, thrusting himself upward, one hand going up to thwart the blow. He saw Aislinn then, whom he had forgotten—a wild look on her face as she sought to stab Donal with her knife.

"*Aislinn—*"

In the bloodied light of sundown he save the flash of the blade as she brought it up from her side. Not overhand, not slashing downward, as novices usually did. From underneath, jabbing upward, as if she knew precisely what she did.

She does . . . by the gods—she does—

For a moment, for one fatal moment, he hesitated. But she did not. She thrust upward with the knife even as he sought to jerk out of her way, and the blade sliced across the knuckles of one hand. He cursed, jumping back, and then he saw Sef hurl himself at Aislinn.

"No—*no!* I won't let you hurt him!"

Aislinn cried out. Donal saw the flash of the blade as Sef set his teeth into her wrist; the knife was perilously close to the boy's thin face. But Sef ignored it, shutting his teeth into flesh, and Aislinn cried out in pain.

Donal stepped in at once. But Sef's teeth had done their work; the knife fell clattering to the street. Donal prudently kicked it out of reach, then caught Aislinn's arm and one of Sef's shoulders.

"Enough—*enough!* Sef—let be . . . I have her now." Donal caught Aislinn under both arms and set her against the wall, pinning her there with his left hand. The right one he carried to his mouth, sucking at his bleeding knuckles. He tasted the acrid salt of blood and the bitterness of futility.

"Aislinn . . . *Aislinn!*" He held her against the wall as she struggled feebly to get away. "What idiocy is this?"

"Witchcraft," Sef whispered. "Look at her *eyes.*"

Donal looked. To him, they appeared swollen black with fear and senselessness. Her face was the color of death. "Aislinn—this is *madness—*"

But she said nothing at all.

It was Electra. It must have been Electra! Gods, will the woman never give up? Still holding Aislinn, he glanced back at the man on the ground. Black-teeth was alone, deserted by his cohorts. But he remained, gibbering incoherently.

Was all of this planned? Donal wondered suddenly. *This attack, knowing how Hondarth feels about Cheysuli, and then, having failed, an attack from Aislinn herself?*

It made him ill. He felt the slow roiling of his belly and the hollowness of his chest.

He looked at Aislinn again. *Did Electra tell the truth? Has she made Aislinn into a weapon against her father—or even against me?*

Aislinn was still his prisoner. She had fallen into silence, staring blankly at the ground. The hood had slipped from her head to bare the rose-gold hair. It glowed brightly in the sunset.

Donal closed his eyes. He felt unsteady, unbalanced by the attempt. But then no one had ever tried to slay him before, and he did not doubt it was unsettling for any man. *I would not care to repeat it.*

You may have to, in the future. Taj pointed out. *There are enemies in every corner.*

Including my betrothed?

The *lir* chose not to answer, which was answer enough for Donal.

"My lord?" It was Sef. "What do we do now?"

Donal looked again at Aislinn. One of the stones had struck her, bloodying her brow. He lifted his wounded hand to wipe it away, then did not. The hand dropped back to his side. *She gets no tenderness from me, until I know what she plans.* He glanced at Sef. "Did you fetch my horse?"

Sef gestured. "There."

The chestnut stallion stood patiently in the shadows. Donal nodded. "Then find us this inn you suggested."

Sef looked at Black-teeth, still cringing on the cobbles, and at Aislinn, bloodied and vacant. Then at Donal, who still felt distinctly ill. The eyes were huge in his thin, pale face. "What—what will you do to her?"

"I do not know." Donal gestured. "Sef—show us to this inn."

Sef, bent down and picked up the knife. "My lord—?"

"Keep it," Donal told him. "But never give it to the princess, or I may lose more than a little flesh." He sucked again at the cut across his knuckles.

"But why?" Sef whispered. "Why would she try to slay you?"

"I think she has been—*influenced*—by her *jehana.*"

"The *Queen?*" Sef's eyes widened further. "You say the *Queen* set her own daughter on you?"

"Or Tynstar, through his *meijha*, if it is true what Electra told me." Donal gestured. "Sef—walk. I have no wish to tarry here a moment longer."

Sef no longer tarried.

The White Hart Inn was everything Sef said it was. It boasted good food, better wine, warm beds, and spacious rooms. Donal took one for himself and Sef and another for the princess.

Donal led Aislinn up to her room and sat her down on the edge of the bed. Then, gently, he sponged away the dirt and blood on her face with a clean cloth borrowed from the innkeeper, along with a basin of water. Aislinn sat on the bed and let him minister to her, though at first she had flinched from his touch.

When she was clean again, though too pale, he gave the basin to Sef to return. Then he turned to Aislinn. "Do you understand what you have done?"

He was not certain she would answer. She had not spoken since she had attacked him.

But this time she broke her silence. Slowly she looked up to meet his eyes, and he saw how her own were clouded and unfocused. "Done? What have I done?"

"Do you not recall it?"

She seemed bewildered by his questions. "What is it you wish me to recall?"

Donal put out his hand. She flinched back, then allowed him to touch her. Gently he fingered the lump where the stone had struck. There was hardly a mark to show what had happened, though—with her fair skin—he was certain there would be a bruise in the morning.

Yet he did not think the stone had struck hard enough to damage her memories. *Unless they were damaged before . . . by someone with reason to do so.*

Aislinn's eyes, Electra's eyes, regarded him almost blindly. Gently, he traced one brow and then the other with his fingertips. "Aislinn, do you trust me?"

"She said I should not—she warned me I should not, but—I do." She frowned a little. "Is it all right?"

"Aye," he said roughly, "it is all right. I would never harm you. But—I think someone has. I think someone has meddled with your mind." He leaned closer to her. "Aislinn—there is a thing I must do. But I will not do it with you unknowing . . . or unwilling. You say you trust me—let me prove the worthiness of that trust."

Her eyes were almost vacant. "What would you have me do?"

He wet his lips before he spoke. "Allow me to touch your mind."

She put up her hand. Her fingers touched his own. But she did not still their gentle movement across her brow. "You mean to use your magic."

"Aye," he admitted. "I must. I must see what Electra has done."

Her very disorientation seemed to lend credence to his suspicions. Aislinn merely shrugged.

Again, he wet his lips. He slipped his free hand up to cradle her head in his palms. Slowly, with great care and gentleness, he slipped out of his skull and went into hers, tapping the strength of his magic.

Gods, do not let me harm her. If Tynstar has set a trap-link, or Electra— He discontinued the thought at once. The implications were too serious. A trap-link might well have been set in Aislinn's mind, waiting to snare him—or any other Cheysuli entering her mind—and hold him for later disposal.

Unless, of course, the trap was set to slay him.

He dismissed the thought. If such a trap existed, it was already too late.

He felt the slow consummation of his bonding with the earth. He tapped the source of Cheysuli magic, drawing it up through an invisible conduit, until it filled him with power and strength. He sliced through Aislinn's young barriers painlessly and slipped into her mind. And he faced, for the first time in his life, the full knowledge of his power and abilities. He had only to *twist* here, *touch* there, and Aislinn's will would be replaced with his own.

But the thought was anathema to him. He was Cheysuli, not Ihlini.

Aislinn's eyes widened, then drifted closed. He saw how pale she was, how her jaw slackened so that her mouth parted to expose small portions of her upper teeth. She was his completely—

Or is she? Someone else has been here before me—!

He withdrew at once, lunging out of her mind and back into his own, badly frightened by what he had felt. Residue. An echo. A *feeling* of other sentience.

Gods—is it Tynstar? Did Electra speak the truth?

"My lord?" It was Sef, kneeling by the bed. Donal saw how pale the boy's face was; how fixed were his odd-colored eyes. And how fright was in every posture of his body. "*My lord*—did it hurt you?"

For a moment, Donal shut his eyes. He needed time to regain his senses completely. But there was none. He took his hands away from Aislinn's head, and smiled wearily at the boy. "I fare well enough. But I should have warned you—"

"Was that—*magic?*" Sef's eyes were widening. "Did you cast a spell here in *this room?*"

"It was not a spell. We do not cast *spells.* We—borrow power from the earth. That is all." Donal looked at Aislinn. "I had the need to know if sorcery had been worked, and so I used my own."

"Had it?" Sef whispered.

Donal did not hear him. He watched Aislinn, frowning slightly as he saw how she began to rouse. Color was returning to her face.

"My lord? Was it?"

Donal glanced back. "What?—oh, aye. It was. But I could not discover the whole of it, or who had the doing of it. Electra, most likely—or Tynstar, through Electra herself." He suppressed a shudder. "But now, I think it is time we all got some rest. The princess particularly." He glanced back at her. She seemed almost to sag into the bed, though she continued to sit; Donal set a hand onto her shoulder. "Aislinn, I know you were merely the gamepiece. But no matter how small the piece, it can overtake even the highest."

He rose. *How in the names of all the gods am I to tell Carillon what Electra has done to his daughter?*

And then, as he turned to go, he felt a wave of heat wash up to engulf his body. And he fell.

Seven

The Mujhar himself poured two cups of steaming spiced wine. He had dismissed the servant, even Rowan, which was an indication in itself that the conversation was to be expressly private. Warily, Donal accepted the cup and waited.

Carillon turned. "Tell me how Sorcha and Ian fare."

In bed, bathed in sweat and filled with pain, Donal stirred. He groaned, inwardly ashamed of his weakness, yet knowing there was nothing he could do. The sorcery had drawn him in. All he could do was lose himself in memories he would rather forget.

"Ian has a fever," he told Carillon. "A childhood thing, they tell me—but he is better. Sorcha is well." He paused. "My jehana says the child will be born in four weeks. I would like to be with her when the pain comes upon her."

Carillon sipped idly at his wine. But his eyes, half hidden beneath creased eyelids, were bright and shrewd. "Provided you are returned, I have no quarrel with that."

"Returned!" Donal lowered his cooling cup. "Where is it I am to go?"

"To the Crystal Isle."

"The Crystal Isle?" Donal could not see any reason he should go there. It was nothing more than a convenient place for Carillon to keep his exiled wife imprisoned. "Why would you send me there?" He grinned. "Or have I displeased you of late?"

Carillon did not return the smile. "You please me well enough . . . for a prince who has more interest in Cheysuli things than Homanan."

"I am Cheysuli—"

"—and Homanan!" Carillon finished. "Do you forget your mother is my cousin? There is Homanan blood in those veins of yours, and it is time you acknowledged it." Carillon

set down his wine and paced to the firepit. His age- and illness-wracked hands went out to bathe in the heat, and Donal saw the edges of the leather bracers he wore on either wrist. For decoration, most thought, to hide the old Atvian shackle scars. But Donal knew better. Carillon needed them to guard his waning strength.

"I do acknowledge it." Donal damped down his impatience and frustration. *"But I have* lir *and responsibilities to my clan. To my su'fali, who is clan-leader. To my jehana, to my son, and certainly to my meijha."* He paused. *"Would you wish me to turn my back on my heritage and tahlmorra?"*

"Part of that heritage places you first in the line of succession," Carillon said flatly, *still warming himself at the fire.* *"So does your gods-dictated destiny. I would have you remember all the responsibilities you have, for there are those to Homana as well. Not merely the Keep and your clan."*

Donal twisted in the bed. Every portion of his flesh ached until he wanted to cry out with the pain. Fire had settled into the pit of his belly, burning relentlessly, and against his will he began to double up. Fists dug into the flesh of his belly, trying to knead the pain away, but it did not go.

"Do you say I neglect Homana?" he whispered through his pain.

"Aye, I do." Carillon turned to face him squarely. *"You neglect my daughter, who is to be your wife."*

Donal stared at him. The wine cup was forgotten in his hands. The frustration and rising anger melted away into shock. "Aislinn?" he said at last. "But—you sent her away to visit her *jehana.*"

"Aye. And I would have you fetch her back to Homana-Mujhar, so I may have her with me again."

Donal felt a wave of relief sweep through him. If Carillon only wanted her brought back for company, the fetching would not be so bad. "I will go, of course. But—surely you could send Gryffth or Rowan, or someone else. I wish to be with Sorcha when the child is born."

"I will give you leave for that, if you are back with Aislinn in time. I have said it." Carillon's voice was steady. *"But I think it is time you thought also of wedding my daughter."*

Donal tried to smile. "I have thought of it. Many times. But Aislinn is still very young—"

"Not so young. Old enough to be wedded and bedded."
Carillon's tone did not soften. *"And was not Sorcha but
sixteen when she bore your first child?"*

"And it died!" Donal cried it aloud, thrashing against
the bed. Hands were on him, pressing him against the mat-
tress, but he did not know them. "The child died, and Sorcha nearly did! Even with Ian the time was hard. And now
that she will bear *again*—"

"It does not matter." Carillon's voice was implacable. *"It
is past time you got yourself an heir."*

Donal gestured. *"You are only forty. Hardly ancient, no
matter what Tynstar's Ihlini arts have done to you. I doubt
you will die any time soon. Give Aislinn a few more
years—"*

"No." Carillon said it softly. "I cannot. Look again upon
me, Donal, and do not mouth such nonsense. Tynstar's sorcery took away twenty years from me and—for all I feel but
forty in my heart—I cannot hide the truth forever. Not from
you or anyone else." He stretched out his twisted hands.
"You see these. Each day they worsen. So do my knees,
my spine, my shoulders. A crippled man is not the Mujhar
for Homana."

"You would never abdicate!" It was unthinkable in the
face of Carillon's pride.

"Abdication is hardly the point," the Mujhar said. "I
doubt I have so many years left as you would prefer to
believe. I prefer to have the throne secured . . . and so should
you. It is, for all that, a Cheysuli thing."

Donal scowled. *"You play me as Lachlan might play his
Lady. Pluck this string, that one, and the proper tune is
heard. You call my Cheysuli heritage into conversation, and
you know what I will do."*

"Then do it." For a moment, Carillon smiled. "Aislinn is
spoiled, as I have spoiled her, but she is also a warm and
giving girl. I think you will find it no chore to wed my
daughter."

But Donal could not reconcile the loss of Cheysuli freedom with the Homanan title the Mujhar promised.

Aloud, he muttered: "I would rather wait. Not—long. A
six-month. Perhaps a year." Donal twisted. "Surely you can
see your way clear to granting me the time. And Aislinn

will need months of preparation . . . women do, and she is a princess——"

"*Donal,*" Carillon said gently.

"*Aislinn is like a* rujholla *to me.*"

"*But she is not your sister, is she?*"

He felt the sudden desperation well up in his soul. "But I would rather wed with Sorcha!" he shouted aloud. "I will not lie to you—it is Sorcha who should be *cheysula* instead of *meijha*—"

"*That I do not doubt.*" Carillon sounded more compassionate. "*I question nothing of her honor or her worth, Donal, as I think you know. But Homana requires all manner of sacrifices, and this one is yours to make.*"

"So, you would have me play the stud to Aislinn's mare, merely to get a colt." He said it clearly into the room at the White Hart Inn. "Yet even the Cheysuli, who have had more cause than most, cannot sanction their women to be treated as mere broodmares."

"*I have cause,*" Carillon retorted gently. "*I have cause, I have reason, I have more than justification, though kings rarely have need of anything more than whim. Oh, aye, I have all the cause in the world.*" He turned his back on the firepit. "*I have a kingdom to rule as well as I possibly can. I have people to husband. Heirs to beget.*" He smiled, but without humor. "*But then we know I failed at that task, do we not? There is only Aislinn, only a daughter from my loins.*" The smile fell away. "*Do you not wed Aislinn, she will go to a foreign prince. And then we run the risk of losing Homana into the hands of another realm. The Cheysuli, so odd and eerie in their magic, may become little more than game, once again. Hunted, branded demons . . . slain. It happened once, Donal. Can you tell me it will never happen again?*"

Donal could not. He knew it would destroy the prophecy, destroy the *tahlmorra* of his people . . . destroy, perhaps, even Homana herself.

He thrashed, sweating, and doubled up yet again from the pain. With great effort, he gave the Mujhar his answer. "I guarantee nothing, Carillon. I know it as well as you. Perhaps better, since I bear the tainted blood." He did not smile. It was not a joke. In some circles, it was said Shaine's *qu'mahlin* should still take precedence over Carillon's peace.

But those were circles Donal did not patronize, being in no position to know them personally; did he know them, they would slay him.

"I do not do it to you." Carillon's tone was ragged. *Gone was the strength of his rank, replaced with the need of the man. "I do it for Homana."*

Even as he forces me to do it for the Cheysuli. *After a moment, Donal nodded. "I will fetch her back."*

Carillon sighed and rubbed at his eyes. "'I will give you this much—you may have eight weeks of freedom when you have brought Aislinn back. It is—not long, I know. But it is all I can spare." *Twisted fingers slipped up to comb through a silvered forelock. "I would have you fully acclaimed before the year is done."*

Donal, hearing the Homanan portion of his fate sealed, could only nod. Then he glanced up and saw the Mujhar's ravaged face.

Carillon watched him with a hunger and sadness Donal could not comprehend. It sent a chill coursing down his spine. He stared back at the Mujhar, not knowing his own face reflected the very expression that had conjured Carillon's pain. "I have lost you," the Mujhar said quietly. "I am bound as cruelly by my royal heritage as you are by your tahlmorra, *and I have lost you because of it."*

"My lord?" Donal's tone was soft.

Carillon sighed and waved a twisted hand. "It is nothing. Only memories of the man whose face you wear." He smiled faintly. "Your father lives in you, Donal . . . you have all of Duncan's pride and arrogance and convictions. I did not fully understand him and I do not understand you. I only know that by pressing for this marriage, I have lost what little of you I once had."

"You have me still." Donal spread his hands. *"Do you see me?—I am not gone. I stand before you. I will ever be your man."*

"Perhaps." Carillon did not smile. *"It simply must be done."*

"I know it, my lord Mujhar." Donal put out his right hand, gestured defeat. *"Tahlmorra,* Carillon."

"By the gods—" he blurted, lunging upward against the

hands that tried to hold him. Small hands, two sets, one toughened, one soft and delicate. Sef, he knew, and—Aislinn?

His eyes snapped open. He saw the dark wooden walls revolve until the movement dizzied him; he shut his eyes at once. A sour harshness preyed on his throat.

"Lie down again," Aislinn said. "So much thrashing is not good for you—it brings more pain."

He looked at her, and did not protest as she and Sef urged him down again. The bedclothes were soaked beneath him. He shivered. "It was *you*—"

"Not me," she declared. "Oh, aye, it was I who cut your fingers, but I swear I knew nothing of the poison. That, I fear, was my mother."

Weakness washed over him. "Lir," he said raggedly.

Here, upon the roof-beam, said Taj, though Donal could not summon the strength to look.

And I. That from Lorn, sitting by the bed.

Donal's hand moved out to touch the wolf's muzzle. Lorn nuzzled him gently, then pressed his nose into Donal's limp hand.

"Donal," Aislinn whispered. "I am so sorry. I did not *know* . . . I swear it. Oh gods, do not *die*. What would become of me?"

Through slitted eyes he watched her. The single braid was tumbled, as if she had spent no time on it for days. Strands of bright hair straggled into her face and he saw how furrows of concern had dug their way into the smooth flesh of her brow. Her cool, pale eyes were fastened on his face.

Gods . . . those are Electra's eyes . . . He swallowed and knew again the stripped feeling in his throat. "Aislinn, I swear—do you *lie* to me—"

"No!" She leaned forward on the stool, reaching out to clasp his hand. "Oh Donal, no. I do not. Sef has—told me what I did, and what you did after—to find out why I did it. He—he said you found something." Shakily, she touched her temple. "Is there—something in my head?"

"Some*one*," he said wearily. "I do not doubt it is your *jehana's* doing, or perhaps even Tynstar's through the link to Electra."

She paled. "Then—if that is true, it is not that I do these

things willingly. Donal—do you truly think I could mean to slay you?"

"I could not say, Aislinn." Vacancy threatened to steal his senses from him. "I think—I think if they have meddled with your mind . . . you are capable of doing anything."

"Is there no way of *gainsaying* it?" she demanded in horror.

He laughed. It rasped in his throat painfully, and he hardly knew the sound. "Oh, aye—there is always a way. But I think you would not like it . . . and I doubt you would agree."

She stared down at the hand she held, dark against her own, though the illness had lent pallor to his flesh. "I will do what you wish, Donal," she said quietly. "How else am I to prove I am innocent of this connivance?"

"And if you are not?" He had to ask it. "If you are not, and seek this way of advancing Tynstar's bid to throw down Carillon, you would do better to try another method." He shut his hand upon hers almost painfully. "I am not the one to do it—I am still too young, and lack the experience one must have—but there are those who could do it for me." He watched her eyes and saw how she stared back. She was clearly frightened, and there was no hint of satisfaction in her manner, as there might be if she sought the test out of some perverse plan to gain his confidence. "Even unknowing, do you agree to this?"

"Aye," she whispered finally. "I will—do what you wish."

He lifted her hand. "Then I hold you to it. You will be tested. Do you understand?"

She nodded. "But—may I know who will have the doing of it?"

"Aye," he said carelessly, releasing her hand. "I will ask my *su'fali* to do it."

Aislinn's head jerked up. *"Finn?"*

"Who better?" He looked directly at her. "He is clanleader of the Cheysuli. And he has had some experience with Ihlini trap-links before." Donal did not smile.

"But—" She broke off.

"I think," said Donal, "we will know the truth at last."

"I swear it," she whispered. "I did not *know*."

Waves of pain radiated upward from his belly. Donal

felt the cramping of his muscles and knew again the total
helplessness as he curled up against the fire. Even Taj and
Lorn, seeking to lend him strength, could not reach him.
The pain was absolute.

"My lord?" It was Sef, bending over the bed. "My lord—
is there *nothing* I can do?"

"Watch," Donal said huskily. "Watch Aislinn for me."

He heard her indrawn breath of dismay. But he had no
strength to regret his cruelty. He dared not trust her now.

He recovered. Sef brought him hot broths at first to
soothe the emptiness and ache in his belly, then brought
stew when Donal could keep it down and finally, after ten
days, brought meat, bread, cheese, and wine. Donal ate a
little of each food, drank down half a cup of wine, then set
it all aside.

"Enough. I will burst. More will have to wait." He
looked at Aislinn, sitting silently on the stool across the
room, and saw she intended to offer no speech. "Well,
lady—I think we shall be on our way to Mujhara in the
morning."

The light from the lantern was gentle on her face. It set
up brilliant highlights in her hair and painted her face quite
fair, gold instead of silver, though—save for her bright
hair—she had the fairness of her mother. She had changed
from her plain brown gown and cloak to equally plain
moss-green, save for the copper stitching at collar and cuffs.
An overtunic of darker green hid much of her femininity,
though no man would name her boy. Her features were
too delicate.

One day, she may rival her jehana's *beauty, though it be
a different sort. Brighter, warmer, less cold and seductive as
Electra's—well, if I must take her as my* cheysula, *better a
pretty one than a plain.* Then he smiled inwardly, knowing
the irony in his statement. *Already you think of making her
the* cheysula *Carillon wants, when she may be plotting
against your life. Fool.*

No, said Taj. *Practical.*

Realistic. That from Lorn.

Donal sat up slowly, swinging his legs over the side of
the bed. He was still in his clothing, he discovered; Sef,
undoubtedly, had lacked the strength to strip him of the

sweat-soaked leathers, and it was not Aislinn's place to do it. He was rank with his own stench, and ordered Sef to fetch up a half-cask for bathing at once.

Aislinn, still sitting silently on the stool, colored, clenching her hands in her lap. "You will send me out, of course."

"Have you not had your own room?"

"You are *in* it," she said softly. "When you fell, the most we could do was drag you into my bed. Sef would allow no one near you, not even the innkeeper's wife. And so *we* tended you." She shrugged. "We have been together here with you . . . Sef, you see, would not allow me to be alone."

He frowned. "Not at all?"

Her gaze lifted to meet his. "But you said he must watch me," she said simply. "I have begun to think of him as my jailer—or, perhaps, your third *lir*." She did not smile. "He is—obdurate. You chose him well, Donal. I do not doubt he will serve you as well as General Rowan serves my father."

"And so you have been here with me for all this time?" He shook his head. "Perhaps it was best, but I am sorry if it caused you inconvenience. Sef is—unaccustomed to royalty." He sat very straight, then arched his spine to crack all the knots. His midsection was extremely tender, within and without, and his muscles felt like rags. Even the *lir*-bands on his bare arms fit a little loosely—he had lost flesh as well as ten days.

He clasped each band, squeezing it against his arm. Beneath his fingers curved the shapes of wolf and falcon, honoring Taj and Lorn in traditional Cheysuli fashion. When a Cheysuli boy became a man, acknowledged so by the bonding of his *lir*, he put on the traditional armbands and earring to mark warrior status. Donal, gaining his *lir* younger than most, had worn his gold for fifteen years.

"You seem much improved." Aislinn ventured.

"Aye. Weary and sore, but both shall pass soon enough." He rolled his head from side to side, loosing the tautness of his tendons. "You need not be *frightened* of me, Aislinn. I do not take retribution on the woman I must wed."

"Must wed," she echoed, and he saw how tightly set was her jaw. "That is it, is it not?—you *must* wed me. My father has taken the choice from you."

"You knew that." Carefully he rose, steadying himself by pressing his calves against the bedframe. He felt old, at least as old as Carillon— "Gods!" he blurted. "Have you done *that* to me?"

"What?" she demanded crossly. "Do you accuse me yet again?"

"Am I old?" He tried to take a step forward and found it weak, wobbly, lacking all grace or strength. Before him rose the specter of premature aging, and what it had done to Carillon. "*Have you made me like the Mujhar?*"

Aislinn made a rude, banishing gesture. "You can only *hope* to be like my father . . . no man can match him, Donal. Do not try."

He lifted one hand and saw firm, sun-bronzed flesh, taut and still youthful, though the palms were callused and tough. He made a fist, and saw how quickly the muscles responded. *Not old, then . . . just—weakened. But that will pass.*

The hand flopped back down at his side. "Aislinn—"

She rose. The stool scraped against the pegged wood of the uneven floor. "I want to know who she is."

For a moment he could only stare. "Who do you mean?"

"Sorcha." She was pale and very stiff in her movements. And every inch the princess. Donal, who had intended to ask her what had caused her change in manner, suddenly understood it very clearly.

"Ah." He sat down slowly on the edge of the bed. "Sorcha."

"Who is she?"

There was no help for it, he knew; the time had come for truth. Evasion was no longer an option. "Sorcha is my *meijha*," he answered evenly. "In the Homanan tongue it means *light woman*."

Aislinn's gray eyes widened. "Your *whore*—?"

"*No.*" He cut her off at once. "We have no whores in the clans. We have *meijhas*, who hold as much honor as *cheysulas*."

Color stood high in Aislinn's fair face. "You see? There are many Cheysuli customs I do *not* know." An accusation; he did not run from the guilt. "Then it is *so*: because we are betrothed—and because my father would never allow it, having no other male heir—you cannot wed your *mei jha*. You must wed me instead." Aislinn stood rigidly before him: a small, almost fragile young woman, yet suddenly towering in her pride. "Do I have the right of it?"

"Aye." That only; more would be redundant.

"And—Ian?"

"Ian is my son."

Aislinn paled. He realized, belatedly, Aislinn would probably feel a woman with a child posed more of a threat than simply a woman alone. "A *bastard*—"

"My *son*." He pushed himself out of the cot. "Aislinn— I know you only echo what words you have heard before . . . but I will allow neither my *meijha* nor my children to be abused."

"Children!" She gazed at him in shock. "There are *more?*"

There was no easy way. And so he told her as simply as he could. "Sorcha is due to bear another child within the month. It is why I wish to leave this place and hasten back—"

"—to the Keep." She nodded jerkily. "That is why, is it not?—not that you wish to fulfill my father's wishes."

"Aye," he told her gently. "I want to go home to my family."

She stared up at him, clearly stunned as well as hurt. He saw how her mouth trembled, though she fought to keep it steady. "Then—there is no hope for me. I am bound to a loveless marriage . . . and all because of the *throne*—"

"Aye," he said softly. "You have begun to feel its weight—the weight we must share."

"Then I do not *want* it." Aislinn's hands rose to cover her mouth. She looked directly at him. "I will have this betrothal broken." The words were muffled, but he understood them.

For just an instant, he felt a surge of hope well up from deep inside. *Does even* Aislinn *ask it, Carillon will have to break the betrothal. And I will be free.*

But the hope, as quickly, died away, and in its place was futility. "Aislinn," he said helplessly. "I doubt he will agree."

"He will," she said. "He will do as I ask." She drew in a trembling breath and tried for a steady smile. "He agrees to whatever I want."

Donal admired her brave attempt at confidence, even

though it failed. But inwardly, he knew the truth. *He will not agree to this, my determined Homanan princess. Not when realm and prophecy depend so much upon it.*

But he had no heart to tell her.

Eight

"Gods!" Sef breathed. "Is *this* where you live?"

Donal looked at the boy. His mouth hung open inelegantly as he stared about the inner bailey of Homana-Mujhar; though it was far smaller than the outer bailey, the inner one was, nonetheless, impressive. Massive rose-colored walls jutted up from the earth, thick as the span of a man's outstretched arms. The outer wall was thicker yet, hedged with ramparts and towers. The clean, unadorned lines of the walls and baileys lent Homana-Mujhar an austere sort of elegance. But Donal thought the legends told about the palace formed at least half of its fabled reputation.

And we Cheysuli built it. Inwardly, he laughed. Outwardly, he smiled at Sef. "This is where the Mujhar lives, and the princess. I—*visit* here often, but the Keep is my home." Donal gestured eastward. "It lies half a day's ride from here. If you wish, I will take you there sometime."

But Sef appeared not to hear him. He twisted his shaggy head on a thin neck, staring around at the walls and towers and the liveried guardsmen passing along the walkways. In the midday sun the ringmail and silver of their steel glittered brightly.

The iron-shod hooves of the three horses clopped and scraped across slate-gray cobbles. Donal led Sef and Aislinn past the garrison toward the archivolted entrance of the palace. Though he himself preferred a side door in order to avoid an excess of royal reception, for Aislinn he would enter through the front.

And then, as he saw Carillon come out the open door to wait at the top of the marble steps, he knew he had chosen correctly.

Donal turned to speak to Aislinn, then shut his mouth

at once. He saw how she stared at her father; he saw the shock and disbelief reflected in her eyes. Before him the color drained out of her face, even from her lips, and he saw how her gloved hands shook upon the reins.

"Aislinn—?"

"He is—grown so *old*—" she whispered. "When I left, he did not look so—so *used up.*" Aislinn turned a beseeching face to Donal. "What has happened to him?"

Donal frowned. "You have heard the story, Aislinn: how Tynstar used his sorcery to try and slay your *jehan*, and in doing so aged him twenty years. That is what you see."

"He is *worse*—" She spoke barely above a whisper. "*Look* at him, Donal!"

Accordingly, he looked more closely at the Mujhar, and saw precisely what Aislinn meant.

She sees more because she has not seen him in two years, while I—having seen him so often for those two years—do not mark the little changes. But Aislinn has the right of it— Carillon has aged. Tynstar's sorcery holds true.

In truth, the Mujhar was but forty years of age, yet outwardly—because of sorcery leveled against him fifteen years before—he bore the look of a sixty-year-old man. His once-tawny hair had dulled to a steely-gray. His face, though partially hidden by a thick silvering beard, was careworn, weathered to the consistency of aged leather. The blue eyes, deep-set, were crowded around by clustered creases. And though a very tall and exceptionally strong man—*once*—age had begun to sap the vitality from his body. The warrior's posture had softened. Pain had leeched him of any pretense of youth.

That, and Tynstar's retribution. Donal felt a flutter of foreboding. *If he grows so old this quickly, what does it mean for me?*

He saw how stiffly the shoulders were set, how they hunched forward just a little, as if they pained Carillon constantly. Perhaps they did. Perhaps his shoulders had caught up at last to his knees and hands as the disease ate up his joints.

Gods, but I hope I never know the pain he knows, Donal thought fervently. He ignored the twinge of guilt that told him he was selfish to think of himself when Carillon stood before him. *Spare me what Carillon knows. I think I lack the courage it takes to face what he has lost.*

He looked briefly at the hands that hung at Carillon's sides. The reddened fingers were twisted away from his thumbs, almost as if someone had broken all the bones. And the knuckles were ridged with swollen buttons of flesh. How he managed to hold a sword Donal could not say. But he did.

Carillon is what keeps Homana strong . . . Carillon and the Cheysuli. Does he fail any time soon, it is all left to me—and I do not want it!

"Aislinn!" Carillon called. "By the gods, girl, it has been too long!" He put out his twisted hands, and Aislinn—forgetting her royal status and the need for proprieties—jumped down from the saddle before the stable lads could catch the reins.

Donal bent over and caught Aislinn's mare before she could follow the girl up the marble steps. He reined her back, then handed the leather over to the first boy who arrived to take the horse.

Aislinn gathered her skirts and ran up the black-veined steps, laughing as she climbed. Carillon caught her at the top of them, lifting her into the air in a joyous, loving hug. Donal, watching, saw yet again how close was the bond they shared.

It is almost as if she spent no time with Electra. She nearly makes me think she is nothing but a girl not quite become a woman—but I dare not trust her. Not until Finn has tested her.

The Mujhar did not appear an aged, aging man as he hugged his only child. The twisted hands pressed into the fabric of her blue cloak, tangling in the wool. His face, seen over Aislinn's right shoulder, was younger than ever before. But the image faded as he set her upon her feet, and Donal saw again how Carillon had grown older in two years.

"Donal, climb down from that horse and come in!" Carillon called, one arm still circling his daughter's shoulders. "And tell me why it is that the baggage train arrived ahead of you."

"Dismount," Donal said in an aside to Sef. "This is the Mujhar you face, but be not overcome by him. He is not a god, just a man."

Sef's expression was dubious. But he shook free of his stirrups and slithered down from the saddle, scraping his belly against the leather. Another stable lad took his horse; yet a third caught Donal's reins with a low-voiced "Welcome back, my lord."

"My thanks, Corrick." Donal gestured to Sef. "Come with me."

"Now?" Sef demanded. "But—you go with the Mujhar!"

"So do you." Donal gestured him up the stairs, and after a monumental hesitation, Sef climbed.

"You are somewhat late," Carillon said quietly when they reached the top of the steps. "Some manner of delay?"

"Some manner," Donal agreed blandly.

"He was ill," Aislinn declared. "Someone—*poisoned* him."

Carillon made no movement, no sound of dismay. His face tightened a little, but otherwise Donal observed nothing that indicated concern. "Well then, you had best come in. As you do not appear in imminent danger of dropping dead at my very feet, I must assume you are completely recovered."

Donal smiled a little. "Aye, my lord, I am." But he had never been good at lying.

Carillon did not seem to notice. "Well enough. Let us leave off standing out of doors. It may be spring, but it is cold enough to qualify as fall." He turned and escorted his daughter into the palace as Donal, Sef and the *lir* followed.

It is not so cold, Donal thought, concerned. *Not so cold as to trouble a man.* But he said nothing to the Mujhar. He merely followed him into the palace.

"I will have you fed first," Carillon said, "and then *you*, Aislinn, must rest. I doubt not you are weary."

"I have not seen you in two years," she protested, "yet you send me to bed like an errant child."

"You *are* an errant child. Have you not kept yourself from me for longer than I wished?"

Her right arm was at his waist as they paused in the entry hall. He had not thickened or put on weight with advancing age, but he was considerably larger than she. "I must speak with you, father. It is important—"

"Another time." Carillon's tone left no room for argument, even from a beloved daughter. "If you do not wish to look like *me* before your time, you must get the rest you require."

Aislinn, shocked, pulled back from his side. "Do not *say* that! You are *not old!*"

Sadly, Carillon bent and kissed her on the crown of her head. "Ah, but you give yourself away with so valiant a protest. Aislinn, Aislinn, I have seen the silver plate. Give me truth, not falsehood; I value that over flattery."

With tears in her eyes, she nodded. "Aye," she whispered. "Oh gods, I have missed you! It was not the same without you!"

Carillon hugged her again as she leaned against his chest. Over her head, he met Donal's eyes. "Aye, I *do* know the truth. There is much we must speak about."

Mutely, Donal nodded. Then he cleared his throat. "My lord, I would have you meet Sef. It is my hope you will allow him to remain in Homana-Mujhar. Let him be trained as a page, if you wish, or perhaps—when he is old enough—as one of your Mujharan guards. I think there is good blood in him, albeit unknown."

Carillon looked at the boy. Sef was pale but he drew himself up to stand very straight, as if he already bore sword and wore the lion in the name of his Mujhar.

"Do you wish it?" Carillon asked. "I will harbor no boys who do not willingly accept the service."

"M-my lord!" Sef dropped awkwardly to his knees. "My lord—how could a boy wish *not* to serve his king?"

The Mujhar laughed. "Well, you will be serving your prince, not your king—I think you will do better with Donal. But I suggest, first, you put flesh on your bones and better clothing on that flesh. You are too small."

Donal marked how Carillon asked nothing about the boy's background, or how he came to be riding with the Prince of Homana. He did not embarrass the boy, nor did he embarrass Donal with unnecessary questions. He simply accepted Sef.

Sef, still kneeling, nodded. Black hair flipped down into his face, hiding the blue eye. But, for the first time, Donal saw Sef deliberately push the hair back.

As if he has accepted what he is. Well, Carillon inspires all manner of devotion. He smiled. "Enough, Sef—few things are accomplished on stone-bruised knees."

Sef did not move. "My lord," he appealed to Carillon, "is it true you nearly defeated the Ihlini demon?"

"Tynstar?" Slowly, Carillon shook his head. "If that is what the stories say about me, they are wrong. No, Sef—Tynstar nearly defeated *me.*"

"But—" Quickly, Sef glanced at Donal. He was asking permission to speak, and Donal gave it with a nod. "My lord Mujhar—I thought *no one* escaped an Ihlini. At least not *Tynstar.*"

Carillon tousled Sef's wind-ruffled hair. "Even Tynstar is not infallible. More powerful than any I have known, it is true, because of the power he has borrowed from Asar-Suti, but he is still a man. And when faced with a Cheysuli—" He smiled grimly. "Let us say: Tynstar is a formidable foe, but not an impossible one."

"But—" Again Sef hesitated, and again Donal gave him permission to speak. "I heard, once, that Tynstar had slain a Cheysuli clan-leader."

Donal felt the sudden wrenching movement in his belly. *That* he had not anticipated.

Carillon looked at him. Compassion was in his eyes. "Aye," he answered Sef quietly. "Tynstar slew Duncan's *lir,* and so Duncan sought the death-ritual as is Cheysuli tradition."

Slowly, Sef worked it out. And when he had, his eyes turned at once to Donal. His face was a mask of horrified realization. "Then if Taj and Lorn are slain—"

"—so am *I* slain," Donal finished. "Aye. It is—difficult for the unblessed to understand. But it is the price of the *lir*-bond, and we honor it."

Aislinn's eyes widened. "You would not do it if you were *Mujhar!*"

She meant it as a declaration. It sounded more like a question. Donal realized, in that moment, she had assumed once they were wed, the customs of the Cheysuli would not be so binding upon him. And he realized she believed he would turn his back on many of them once he was Mujhar.

"Aye," he told her. "Warrior or Mujhar, I am constrained by the traditions of my people. And I intend to honor them."

"You are Homanan as *well* as Cheysuli—"

"I am Cheysuli *first.*"

He saw shock, realization, and rebellion in her face. And a mute denial of his statement.

Carillon's hands came down on her shoulders. "You are weary," he said in an even tone. "Go to bed, Aislinn."

"No," she said, "first there is a thing we must discuss—"

"Go to bed," he repeated. "There will be time for all these discussions."

She flicked a commanding glance at Donal, as if she meant him to bring up the possibility of breaking the betrothal; he did not. He had no intention of it. Done with waiting, she picked up her skirts and ran.

Carillon turned to Sef. "I am sure you are hungry. I suggest you ask in the kitchens for food." He gestured and one of the silent servants waiting nearby came at once. "Escort the boy to the kitchens and see he is fed until he cannot keep his eyes open. Until the prince or I call for him, he is free to learn his way about the palace."

"Aye, my lord." The young man, tunicked in Carillon's livery, nodded and looked at Sef. He waited.

Sef, still kneeling, looked up at Donal. "My lord?"

Carillon laughed. "I see he knows his master."

Donal gestured Sef up from the floor. "You may go."

Silently, Sef stood up, bowed quickly, and went with the liveried servant.

"I am sorry for what the boy said." Carillon's tone was compassionate. "You need no reminding about your father's fate."

"One warrior's *tahlmorra* is not necessarily easily accepted by his kin," Donal responded evenly. "But I hope the gods grant me a life as effective as his."

"Effective?" Carillon did not smile. "A modest way of describing Duncan's loyalty and dedication. And odd, from his son—"

"It does no good to dwell upon it," Donal interrupted. He felt the clenching of his belly; the sudden cramping of his throat. He had said more of his father to Aislinn than he had said to anyone in a very long time. And it was no easier speaking of him to Carillon, who had known Duncan better than most. "Tynstar defeated my *jehan*, but not before he accomplished what he was meant to."

"Siring *you?*" Carillon's mouth twisted a little. "Aye, he

sired you—and in doing so forged the next link in the prophecy."

The link that excluded a Homanan Mujhar. Donal wondered for the hundredth time whether Carillon himself resented the upstart Cheysuli prince as much as everyone else. So much had been given to him when he deserved none of it.

An accident of birth. No more. And yet Donal knew it was not. The gods had decreed his fate.

Carillon appraised Donal. "For a poisoned man, you seem uncommonly fit. Is what Aislinn said true?"

"True. And I am fully recovered." He was not; Donal knew it. He was weary from the ride, too weary. He needed food and rest. But his pride kept him from saying so to Carillon, who faced more poor health than any man Donal knew.

"Good. Come and show me." Carillon turned abruptly and headed toward a corridor.

"*Show* you?" Donal went after him. "Show you *what?*"

Carillon's stride was crisp and even. His back was rigid. There was no sign of advancing age in him, save for the twisted fingers. "Rowan!" The shout echoed along the corridor. Donal, hastening in the Mujhar's footsteps, frowned into the candle-lit passageway.

Shortly after a second shout, Rowan stepped out of a doorway. His black hair was tousled and damp, and his clothing was a little awry, as if he had only just put them on following a bath. "Aye, my lord?"

"My sword is in my chambers," Carillon said briefly. "Do me the favor of bringing it to the practice chamber."

Rowan's yellow eyes reflected startled speculation. "Aye, my lord. At once."

"Carillon, what do you mean to do?" Donal at last fell into step with the Mujhar.

"I mean to find out what order of skill you claim."

"*Sword* skill?" Donal, hastening his steps yet again, shook his head. "Carillon, you *know*—"

"—know what? That you, as a Cheysuli, claim yourself above the use of a sword? Inviolate to its threat?"

"No, of course not." Donal bit his tongue to repress his exasperation. "I can be wounded as easily as a Homanan—it is only . . . Carillon, will you *slow down*—?"

"Only what?" The Mujhar did not slacken his pace. "Is it *only* that you would simply *prefer* to keep yourself to bow and knife?"

"I am good enough with both!" Donal, pride stung, stopped dead in his tracks. Carillon also paused.

"Aye," he agreed, "you are. But the future Mujhar of Homana must also wield a sword." He stretched out his hand as Rowan came striding down the corridor with a scabbard clenched in his hand. "*This* sword," Carillon said, accepting it from Rowan.

Donal scraped one hand down through his hair and over his face. "Carillon." His voice was nearly throttled in his attempt to remain calm. "Do you forget I am *Cheysuli?*"

"I think that is impossible." Carillon's voice, raspy now, sounded harsh in the shadowed corridor. "You take such pains to remind me whenever the chance arises." Methodically, he held the scabbard in his left hand and placed his right on the heavy golden hilt. At the edge of his hand, set into prongs in the pommel of the hilt, glowed the dead-black stone that had once been brilliant crimson. A blood-red ruby, called the Mujhar's Eye, and perverted by Tynstar's sorcery.

Donal looked at Rowan. He saw nothing in the general's face save a perfect blankness. *Cheysuli blankness. He uses his race to thwart even me.*

At last he looked at Carillon. "You wish me to spar against you."

"Aye. As we have done in the past."

Donal nodded his head in the direction of the sword. "You have not used *that* against me before."

"Then perhaps it is time I did. It is your grandsire's sword."

"He *made* it," Donal retorted. "He never used it himself. The Cheysuli never do."

"Hale was all Cheysuli," Carillon agreed. "But you claim a full quarter of Homanan blood, and *that* much entitles you to learn the proper use of a sword."

Again, Donal glanced at Rowan. And again, he saw the blank expression. *Carillon's man to the core. For all he is Cheysuli, he seems more Homanan than Carillon himself!*

Pointedly, Donal looked at Rowan's left side. At the

sword sheathed there. A Homanan sword, but wielded by a Cheysuli.

Color came into Rowan's dark face. Cheysuli-born, Homanan-bred; adversity had taught him to stay alive, during Shaine's *qu'mahlin,* by ignoring the truth of his origins. And now, though free to embrace the customs of his race, he did not. Cheysuli on the outside, Homanan on the inside; Carillon's right-hand man.

In place of my su'fali, *a proper liege man.*

But Donal did not blame Rowan. Not entirely. Finn's dismissal from Carillon's service had been initiated by someone else entirely, and aided—albeit unintentionally—by Carillon himself.

There was, suddenly, tension in Rowan's face. And Donal was ashamed. *It is not his fault. He was raised by the unblessed. Lacking a lir, he lacks also a heart and soul. But he does the best he can.*

"Come," Carillon challenged, "show me what you know."

Donal looked at the royal sword of Homana, knowing it was Cheysuli. And then he looked at Rowan.

Silently, Rowan pulled his forth. He offered the hilt to Donal.

Nine

The practice chamber had no aesthetics about it. It was a plain chamber of unadorned dark-blue stone, even to the floor, which had been worn into a perfectly smooth indigo-slate sheet from years of swordplay and footwork. Each wall bore only weapons racks: swords, long-knives, spears, halberds, axes, bows, and other accoutrements of war. Wooden benches lined the sides for students who chose to or were ordered to watch. Wall sconces with fat candles in them lit the room with a pearly glow. Donal had been in the chamber many times in fifteen years, but he far preferred the training sessions with Finn and others in the Keep.

Carillon stood in the precise center of the smooth, dark floor. He was still fully dressed, not bothering to shed even his doublet of mulberry velvet. His boots were low-cut, of soft gray leather, lacking the heavy soles of thigh-high riding boots. And in his twisted hands was gripped the gold-hilted sword with its baleful, blackened eye.

Idly, Donal slapped the flat of Rowan's blade against his leather-clad leg. He stripped out of his cloak and dumped it onto the nearest wooden bench. Sighing, he turned to face Carillon. "My lord, this will be a travesty."

"Will it?" Carillon smiled. "Then I am pleased you so willingly admit you lack what skill any soldier should possess." He gestured sharply. "Rowan—the door. It may be the Prince of Homana will not desire anyone to see this—*travesty*."

Briefly Rowan dipped his still-damp head in an acknowledging nod, then pulled the door tightly shut. He crossed his arms and leaned against the wall, watching both men in an attitude of nonchalance, yet intently aware of each.

Donal yet held the sword in one hand negligently. The hilt was unfamiliar, being made for Rowan's hand, but then the hilt of any sword was unfamiliar to him. He had spent hours with an arms-master, being drilled until he thought he would go mad, but he had always been an indifferent student. He knew, did the time come when he would have to fight, it would be with knife or Cheysuli warbow.

Or lir-*shape. This is foolishness.*

"Come forth," Carillon invited, "And tell me how it was you were poisoned."

Donal's short laugh was a bark. "I can tell you that without resorting to *this,* Carillon. And I think the answer is easy enough to come by. It was your *cheysula,* my Lord Mujhar. The Queen of Homana herself."

"Come forth." Carillon's tone brooked no refusal. "*I,* at least, can speak while I spar. Can you?"

He baits me . . . by the gods, he baits *me!* Donal moved forward, clad more comfortably than Carillon in snug Cheysuli leggings and sleeveless jerkin dyed a warm, soft yellow. Though he hated swordplay, he could not help but move into a defensive posture as Carillon settled the rune-kissed blade more comfortably.

Carillon grunted. "Electra, was it? I would have guessed the Ihlini."

"Oh, Tynstar may have encouraged it." Donal shifted Rowan's sword until it rested more comfortably in his hands. "But Electra had the doing of this, I am quite sure. But—not alone. She had help."

"Who? Have I traitor on the island?"

"Traito*ress*, rather . . . though I think it is too harsh a word. I believe she was unknowing." Donal touched his blade gently to Carillon's in brief salute. "It was Aislinn, my lord."

"*Aislinn*—!" The Cheysuli blade lowered slightly before Carillon caught himself. "What is this idiocy?"

Donal shook his head. "No idiocy, my lord—it is the truth. Ask the girl; better yet, ask Sef. He saw what she tried to do."

"Come *at* me!" Carillon rasped. "Tell me this over the sword-song!"

Donal stepped in. He parried Carillon's opening maneuver, parried again, and ducked a vicious two-handed swipe that whistled near his ear. He hissed in startled surprise, then danced aside yet again as the sword swooped back to catch him on its return.

"Say again," Carillon ordered. "Say *again* it was my daughter!"

"It *was.*" Donal skipped aside, blessing his Cheysuli quickness. Sparring this might be, but Carillon did not spar as most men did. He was strong enough to stop a powerful blow even as he loosed it to the full extent of the maneuver, and so he sparred with little held back. *Except he is no longer as strong as he once was . . . gods!—he could take my head with another swipe like that!*

"Do not hang back like a fearful child!" Carillon shouted. "*At* me, Donal! I am the *enemy!*"

The royal blade blurred silver in the air, so that the runes bled into the steel and became invisible. Donal saw only the displacement of air and heard the swoop of slicing steel. He moved in instinctively, answering Carillon's challenge, and tried to turn the blow aside. But his blade was battered aside almost at once, then twisted out of his hands. His wrists and forearms cried out their abuse as he fought to hold on, but the hilt slipped from his hands. The sword fell against the floor.

Carillon took a single step forward. The tip of his blade rested lightly against Donal's abdomen, scraping softly on the gold and topaz of his buckle. "It is your *life,* boy," the Mujhar rasped. "It is not *me* you face, but the enemy. Perhaps a Solindish soldier, or an Atvian spearman. Neither will allow you time to retrieve a fallen weapon."

"Do you expect me to believe such a transparent ploy as that?" Donal snapped. "Or do you say we go to war *tomorrow?*"

The tip pressed more threateningly. "Not tomorrow. Perhaps the day after." Carillon's jaw was set like stone. "I have been receiving regular messages from couriers out of Solinde these past four weeks. Royce, in Lestra, believes there will be a full-scale rebellion before a sixth-month is past."

"Rebellion." Donal felt the clenching of his belly. "You have feared it, I know . . . and you have not let me forget what might happen did Tynstar ever rally the Solindish again. But *why* would they follow him after so many years of peace?"

"Peace?" Carillon laughed. "*You* might call it that, having no knowledge of what war is. But Solinde is far from peaceful. Royce has put down insurgents time and time again, and there is talk Tynstar *does* move, even now, to unite the Solindish rebels."

"If he does—"

"If he does, we will go to war again. Not today, perhaps not even tomorrow—but very soon." Carillon regarded his heir. "Now, as you know so much, tell me about Osric of Atvia."

"*Osric!* The Atvian king?" Donal frowned. "He is at home, is he not, quarreling with Shea of Erinn over an island title?"

"Aye," Carillon agreed. "But what if Osric, deciding to avenge his father's death at Homanan hands—as well as tiring of paying me twice-yearly tribute—quits quarreling with Shea of Erinn and chooses to march on Homana?"

"End the tribute," Donal suggested. "It would give him one less reason to consider such a march."

Carillon's smile held little amusement. "I instigated the tribute in retribution for coming against me the last time. Thorne paid for it with his life, leaving his son to succeed him; therefore the son must also pay for the father's folly. Do I *end* the tribute, Osric will judge me weak. It would be an indication that Homana's aging Mujhar, at last, is losing strength, opening an avenue of attack for Osric. No, no—policy dictates I continue to ask tribute of Atvia. There is no other choice."

Donal had no desire to entangle himself in the intricacies of kingcraft, even verbally. "We were not speaking of the potential for war, my lord, but of your daughter's complicity in Electra's attack on me. Should we not finish *that* topic before we begin another?"

"Gods, but you drive me mad!" Carillon said through gritted teeth. "*Look* at me, Donal! What do you see? An old man growing older, and more quickly than anyone might have thought." Briefly, he shrugged, and a faint wince of pain cut across his face. "It was your father who told me Tynstar gave me nothing I would not experience anyway; that the disease would devour my body eventually *regardless* of what I did . . . and it does. *Oh, aye*—it does. Who is to say I will live to see the new year?"

"*You* are the one speaking idiocy *now!*" Donal was taken aback by Carillon's intensity. "Aye, you grow older, but even now you wield a sword. Even *now* you defeat a Cheysuli!"

"Aye, I do. And no warrior I have ever heard of gives in to an enemy so easily." The tip pressed close yet again. "You speak of Aislinn's complicity? Then you had best speak a little more clearly. *Now.*"

Donal sighed. "I cannot say for certain, Carillon. There is no doubt she was—involved. It was her hand that held the knife." He put up his hand and wiggled his fingers. "Healed now, and easily enough—it was not so much of a cut—but I *got* the cut because Aislinn tried to put a knife in my back. And *would* have, had my *lir* not warned me. And even then, she cut me. It was Sef who held her back."

"Aislinn—did *that?*" Carillon's eyes were on the sun-bronzed knuckles.

"Aye, she did. But I doubt it was her decision—I am sure she was ensorceled."

"How?" Carillon snapped.

"By Electra, my lord—who else?"

The creased lids with their silvered lashes flickered just a little. "Aislinn is her daughter. Do you tell me Electra would stoop to such perversion?"

Donal did not smile. "You know her better than I. Tell *me*, my lord, if Tynstar's *meijha* would."

The breath was expelled suddenly; an explosion of disbelief and horrified acknowledgment. The sword tip wavered against Donal's abdomen. "She would," he whispered. "By the gods, she *would*. And *I* sent Aislinn there—"

"My lord." Donal did not move; not even in the face of Carillon's emotions did he dare give the sword tip a chance. "My lord—what else could you have done? She was of an age where she needed to see her *jehana* . . . even one such as Electra."

"Oh no . . . I could have refused. I *should* have. And now you tell me Aislinn tried to slay you?"

Donal was moved to offer any sort of reassurance, though the transgression was serious enough. He could not bear to see a man who was so strong be overcome by the plotting of his treacherous wife. "My lord—at least she *failed.*"

Carillon was not amused by the purposeful mildness of the statement. "*This* time. But if it is true she was ensorceled, who is to say she will not try again?"

Donal drew in a careful breath. Deliberately he kept his tone light, seemingly offhand. "There is a way. I could determine if the ensorcelment is still in effect."

"How?"

"Let me take her to the Keep. Let my *su'fali* go into her mind."

Carillon's brows drew down. "Why Finn? Why not you? I know you have the power."

"I have tried," Donal said gently. "There is a barrier there, the residue of someone else's presence."

"A trap-link?" Carillon demanded at once. "Do you say Tynstar has touched my daughter through Electra?"

"That—that is better left to Finn to determine."

"Then we shall let him," Carillon rasped, "but only on one condition."

Donal stared. "You speak of *conditions* when this may be your daughter's sanity?"

"When I am forced to. And you force me, Donal." Carillon was unsmiling. "I set you a task. A simple task, for a Cheysuli." Suddenly, the smile was there. "Finn could do it. He *has* done it. That Duncan could have, I do not doubt. And now it is your turn." He laughed. "Are you not their blood and bone?"

Donal regarded him suspiciously. "What would you have me do?"

"Take the sword from me." Carillon laughed again. "Win back your grandsire's sword!"

"From *you?*" Donal shook his head. "Carillon, I could not. More than one realm knows what a renowned fighter you are. The harpers sing lays about you—*I* recall Lachlan's *Song of Homana* even if you do not! I would be a fool to try."

"A fool *not* to." Carillon beckoned with two of his twisted fingers. "Come, Donal . . . take this Cheysuli sword from the hand of a Homanan."

Donal swore beneath his breath. And then, invoking what skills he had learned from Finn and other warriors, he moved in against the blade. He ignored the bite of steel, concentrating instead on the surprise in Carillon's eyes, and lifted a flexed forearm against the flat of the blade in a quick, chopping motion. And then, even as Carillon subtly shifted position to try another attack, Donal hooked a leg around his ankles and jerked him to the ground.

"My lord—!" It was Rowan, moving from his place by the door, until Donal stopped him with an outthrust hand. "Do you want the same?" he asked. "This is between Carillon and me."

"Donal—you do not know—"

"I know well enough!" Donal retorted. "He goaded me into this . . . let him reap what seed he sows."

Slowly, Carillon hitched himself up on one elbow, wincing and swearing. He glared up at Donal. After a moment he stopped cursing and nodded absently. "Perhaps it is not so necessary for you to learn a sword after all. You are dangerous enough with *nothing*."

Donal felt a pang of guilt and concern as he looked down upon the Mujhar. He saw again how twisted were the callused hands. "Carillon, I did not mean—"

"I care naught for what you meant, or *did not* mean!" Carillon's shout was undiminished even by his undignified sprawl upon the stones. "Never apologize for downing your enemy. I might have slain you with that sword; instead, you disarmed me." He smiled. "As I ordered."

Donal bent down. "Here—take my hand—"

"Tend your wound, Cheysuli," Carillon said crossly. "You are bleeding, and I am old enough to know how to find my feet." He found them, pushing himself up from the floor, but he could not entirely hide a sharp grimace of pain.

Donal put a hand to his abdomen and felt the slice in the leather as well as the blood seeping through. The wound did not appear to be deep, but it hurt. Still, he shrugged. "It is nothing. Of no account. Honor enough, in itself." He grinned, relieved to see Carillon standing before him, apparently all of a piece. "It is a scar gotten from Homana's Mujhar, and a token of accomplishment. I am still alive. How many others can claim that after a confrontation with you?"

Carillon eyed him suspiciously. "You have a facile tongue. You must have got it from Alix."

Donal smiled innocently. "My *jehana* taught me only reverence for royalty, my lord Mujhar."

Carillon muttered something beneath his breath and gestured to the Cheysuli sword lying on the ground. "You may at least return my weapon to me. I may have need of more practice—for our *next* meeting."

Donal, laughing, bent and grasped the sword by its blade. He ceremoniously offered it hilt-first to Carillon, making a solemn production out of the gesture. The Mujhar reached out to take it with a muttered oath. His mouth twisted in a grimace of acknowledgment, but before his fingers closed on the hilt, he froze.

"The *ruby!*" The shocked outcry came from Rowan.

Instantly Donal glanced down at the stone set so deeply in the prongs of the pommel. And then he lost his smile.

Like the stare of an unblinking serpent, the Mujhar's Eye glared back at him. But no longer was it the tainted black of Ihlini sorcery. It glowed a rich blood-red.

He felt a frisson of fear and shock. "It was *black*—it has *always* been black—"

"No," Carillon said hoarsely. "Before I plunged it into the purple flames of Tynstar's sorcery, it was red as the blood in my veins. Do you see? *That* is a Cheysuli ruby, Donal, set there by your grandsire's hand. Whole and unblemished, as it was meant to be, until tainted by Ihlini sorcery."

As Carillon closed his hand on the hilt, Donal released the blade at once. And the ruby turned black again.

"*No*—" Donal blurted.

"Aye." Carillon's voice was hoarse, uneven. "By the gods—I understand it." His eyes, rising to meet Donal's, were filled with sudden comprehension. "I know now what Finn meant when he explained it to me."

"Explained *what?*"

Carillon gestured. "How a Cheysuli sword knows the hand of its master. How it will serve well any man who wields it, because it must, but comes to life only in the hands of the warrior it was meant for. Do you not know your own legends?"

Donal stared in horrified fascination at the black stone in the golden hilt with its rampant Homanan lion. "I—have heard. But *never* have I seen the story proven—"

"Then look upon it, Donal. This sword was made for you."

Slowly, Donal shook his head from side to side. "Oh, I think not . . . I think not. I am Cheysuli, and we do not deal with swords."

"A Cheysuli made it . . . as once your race made the finest swords in the world, though none of the warriors would use them." Carillon nodded. "Finn taught me much of the Cheysuli, Donal, and—once, for a very little while— I was Cheysuli myself." He shrugged at Donal's twitch of startled disbelief. "You do not yet understand, but you will. There will come a time—" He shook his head quickly. "Never mind. What we speak of now is how this sword was made for you."

"No." It came a burst of involuntary sound, but he knew no other answer. "Not mine. It is *yours*."

Carillon turned the sword in the candlelight, so the flames ran down the blade and set the runes afire. "Do you see? I know you read Cheysuli Old Tongue. Decipher these runes for me."

Donal looked at them. He saw the figures wrought in the shining steel. He saw them clearly enough to read them, and then he drew back once more. "I will not."

"Donal—"

"I *can*not!" he shouted. "Are you blind? You tell me my grandsire made this sword for me while knowing what would happen, and I *dare* not acknowledge what it means."

"The runes, Donal. I can have them read by another. I would rather *you* read them to me."

He took yet another step back. "Do you not see? If that sword were truly made for me, it means I *must* succeed you. *And I am not certain I can!*"

"Why can you not?" Carillon, stricken, stared at him over the shining sword. "Do you say I have chosen the wrong man?"

Donal clapped both hands over his face. "No, oh no, not the wrong man—the *right* man!" His voice was muffled behind his palms. "But how am I to follow you? After all that *you* have done?" Donal stripped the black hair back from his face. "Gods, Carillon, you are a legend by which all men measure themselves. And you are *living!* Can you imagine how they will measure *me* when you are gone?"

Carillon's aging face lost its color. "It is that, then. You fear you cannot live up to your predecessor."

"Aye." Donal sighed and let his hands drop down to slap against his thighs. "Gods—who could? You are *Carillon.*"

"I do not want that!" Carillon cried. "Gods, Donal, be yourself! Do not think about what others would have you be."

"How not? There is nothing else I *can* do." Donal caught his breath. The sparring session had sapped even more of his strength. The chamber wavered a little. He shoved a forearm against his brow to wipe the sweat away. "Surely you must see it, Carillon. Surely you must hear it. How they worship you even as they curse the heir you chose."

"Curse you—"

"Aye." Donal's throat was dry. His voice scraped through the hoarseness. "There are times I almost hate myself. I play the polished plate and reflect the things they see. Cheysuli. Arrogant. Believing myself better than any Homanan. And yet even as they mutter to one another how I will be *given* the Lion instead of earning it, I wonder if I am worthy of your trust." He looked into the older man's face. "Gods, Carillon—there are times I want nothing more than to turn my back on *you*, so I can keep a piece of myself."

"No," Carillon said hollowly. "Do not think of it. Without you, there is nothing."

Donal raised both hands briefly and let them slap down at his sides. "The *shar tahls* say it is my *tahlmorra* to accept the Lion from you. But—I would sooner accept *nothing* from my *jehan.*"

Carillon flinched visibly. Donal saw it and realized he had hurt the man, though he had not intended to. He would not hurt Carillon for the world, not intentionally. And yet there were times he felt his very presence hurt him, because he knew himself living testimony to Carillon's failure to produce a legitimate son of his own flesh and blood.

"I care nothing for what others may think of you," Carillon said. "They are fools. Homanan I may be, but I am not blind. I spent too many years with Finn to disbelieve in *tahlmorra* and a man's place within the tapestry of the gods." One corner of his mouth twitched in an effort to steady his voice. "There was a time Duncan himself told me how he longed to turn his back on his *tahlmorra* so he could share his life with his son. But his dedication was such that he could not ignore what lay before him, and so he met Tynstar and died. But—you should not judge yourself by others, Donal. Never."

Insecurity suddenly overcame him. "I know I can never be what they would have me be. I am not you."

"Be *Donal*," Carillon said. "By the gods, you will be the first Cheysuli Mujhar in four hundred years!"

"Aye," Donal agreed. "I will have your throne one day. That is more than enough. I will *not* take your sword."

"But it is yours. *Yours*, Donal. You must accept it now." Carillon held it out.

Donal took a single step away. "No. Not yet."

"Do you deny your grandsire's wishes?"

"Aye." Donal stared at the runes. The runes that beckoned him; the runes he had to deny. *And do I deny the power?*

Carillon drew in a raspy breath. "Then—if not now . . . will you accept it at your acclamation?" The Mujhar smiled a little. "Shaine gave me this sword upon *my* acclamation as Prince of Homana. Surely you could accept it then."

"No." Yet another step away. "Carillon—I have no wish to strip you of your power. One day there will be no choice, but for now there *is*. And I have made it."

Carillon's eyes, staring down at the blackened ruby, were bleak in his careworn face. It was the face of a man who sees his own ending, when he has only just gotten past his beginning. It was the face of a man who recognizes his *tahlmorra* and all the futility and insignificance of his presence within the palm of the gods. The face of a man who, when confronted with his chosen successor, knows that successor was already chosen long before.

The Mujhar looked at Rowan. "It is *Donal*," he said clearly. "It is Donal, after all." He laughed, but the sound was the sound of bittersweet discovery. "For all Finn and Duncan told me how important *I* was to the prophecy, it does not come down to me at all." Slowly, he shook his head. "To Donal. I am only the *caretaker* of this realm . . . until another's time has come."

Ten

Donal, mounted on his chestnut, watched sidelong as Carillon mounted his own gray stallion. Tall as he was, he seemed to have trouble reaching up to the stirrup. But he mounted. With less grace than Donal had witnessed before, perhaps, but Carillon got himself into the saddle.

The Mujhar let go a short breath of effort completed and squinted in the morning sunlight, glancing over at Donal. "You look somewhat done in. Did you resort to the wine jug last night?"

Donal, who had resorted to nothing but his own imaginings following the confrontation with Carillon in the practice chamber, shook his head a little. "No. I did not sleep."

Carillon's silvering brows rose. "Did not—or *could* not?"

Donal grunted. "One and the same, last night."

The Mujhar nodded. "Neither did I." He glanced across Donal's mount to the smaller bay horse beyond, its rider nearly out of earshot. "So, you bring your new servant along."

Donal drew rein as his horse fidgeted, stomping one hoof against the cobbles of the bailey. Automatically he looked for Lorn, concerned for his welfare, but the wolf waited at some distance from the horses. Taj perched upon the bailey wall.

"Now is as good a time as any for Sef to see what a Keep is," Donal told Carillon. "But where is Aislinn?"

"Delaying for as long as she can," Carillon said dryly. "She wants no part of this."

"She said she was willing before."

"Aye. Before." Carillon was unsmiling. "*Before* she knew aught of Sorcha and the boy."

Donal felt the clenching of his belly. "Then—she told you how she found out."

"Aye. She was—less than happy about it." Carillon looked directly at his heir. "We have never played games with each other, Donal—we knew one day it would come to this. Even when you and Sorcha grew close—you knew."

Carillon, Donal knew, did not precisely accuse. But he was Aislinn's father and, though he understood Cheysuli customs better than any Homanan, no doubt he felt the relationship between Donal and his Cheysuli *meijha* was an insult to his daughter.

Donal drew in a deep breath that was just the slightest bit unsteady. "I—know. As you say, there have been no games. And I mean no offense even now . . . surely you must see that."

"I see it." Carillon shifted in his saddle, as if his muscles pained him. "Donal—I care deeply for my daughter. I would not have her hurt. But neither do I wish to trespass on Cheysuli customs." He stared down at his twisted hands as he clutched reins and saddlebow. "Aislinn said she wished to break off the betrothal. In the face of her tears and tattered pride, I had to refuse her, of course . . . I had no choice."

"No doubt it is difficult for a *jehan* to deny his child anything he or she wants." Donal made his answer as judicious as he could.

Carillon's smile was slightly sardonic. "Aye. And, soon enough, I doubt not you will learn it for yourself. Ian is of an age to exert his needs and desires."

"I am sorry, Carillon," Donal said wretchedly. "I would spare her as much pain and heartache as I could, were there another way."

"I know that. But—I think there will come a day when you find you must make a choice." He gestured with a nod of his head toward the marble steps. "And here is my tardy daughter." Carillon motioned for one of the stable lads to lead the dun-colored mare forward.

Aislinn's shining hair was plaited tightly, then doubled up and bound with green woolen yarn. The knot of bright hair hung over one brown-cloaked shoulder. Her dark green skirts were kilted up for ease of riding, and her legs were booted to the knees. With the grace of youth she mounted, unaffected in her movements, and gathered in her reins. Like most Homanan women, she disdained a sidesaddle and rode astride.

She glanced sidelong at Donal. He saw how red-rimmed the eloquent eyes were, as if she had cried the night through; her face was a little swollen and her mouth did not hold a steady line. But her pert nose with its four golden freckles was lifted toward the sky. "Do we go? Let us get this travesty over."

Donal, despite the haughty words, sensed her unhappiness clearly. Aislinn was a young girl, badly frightened by what she faced, and resorted to what attitude she could in an effort to control her fear. He understood it. He had done it before himself.

Her horse was close to his own. He leaned out of the saddle slightly and caught the back of her neck, squeezing gently. "You will do well enough."

Her demeanor seemed less arrogant. "Will I?" she whispered. "Gods . . . I am so afraid—"

"Fear has its proper place—or so I am told." He released her and reined his stallion around. "But I think there is little need for it in the Keep."

"But—it is *Finn*—"

"He is the last warrior you should fear. That much I promise you."

Aislinn's hands, gloved in supple amber-dyed leather, tightened on her reins. The dun mare crowded Donal's chestnut. "Then I hold you to your promise."

"If you wish, I will go in with Finn. You have felt my touch before. There is little I can do, lacking the necessary experience, but I can monitor what *he* does." Donal shrugged. "Would it lend you some reassurance?"

Her gray eyes, pale as water, studied him a long moment. Then, reluctantly, she nodded. He saw the twisting of her mouth. "Aye. I want you there as well."

He pushed the mare's mouth away from his knee before her metal bit could bang against him painfully. "Then I will be there."

But her fear remained. He could see it.

"Let us go," Carillon said. "Sooner done, is it done with." He gathered his reins and spurred the gray stallion about. But before he could go, Rowan called for him from the top of the marble steps.

"My lord—my lord—wait you." The general ran down the steps rapidly. "Carillon—a courier has come. From Duke Royce in Lestra." Rowan caught hold of one rein and held back the Mujhar's horse. "I think, my lord, you had best hear what he has to say."

At once, Carillon looked at Aislinn. His indecision was manifest. But even as she reined her horse closer to his, preparing to plead her case, he became more decisive. "Aislinn—you will be safe enough with Donal. You have heard what the general has said."

"You promised to go *with* me!"

"And now I cannot." His tone was gentle, but equally inflexible. "Were this testing not so necessary, I would say it could wait for another time. But it cannot, no more than can this courier." He reached out and caught the crown of her head with one broad hand and cupped his twisted fingers around the dome of her skull. "I am truly sorry, Aislinn . . . but I know you will be safe with Donal."

"You give me no choice," she accused unhappily. "You give me no choice in *anything!*" Wrenching her mare around, she headed for the gates.

Carillon sighed heavily. "Be patient," he told Donal. "She is young . . . and till now her lot as my daughter has been little more than a beautiful game. Now she knows its price."

"I will bring her back before nightfall," Donal promised. "As for what she will face—there is nothing for you to fear. It is Finn who will do the testing."

Briefly, Carillon smiled. "After all these years, it comes again to Finn. And I think it will amuse him." Slowly, he swung down out of the saddle and patted the horse's shoulder. "Safe journey, Donal. And now you had best go after her before she gets so far ahead you lose her entirely."

It was Sef, edging his horse close to Donal's, who remarked about the vastness of the Keep. "There are pavilions *everywhere*."

The oiled pavilions, dyed warm earth and forest tones and painted with myriad *lir*, spread through the forest like a scattering of seed upon the ground. The Cheysuli, when they could, left the trees standing, setting up their pavilions in clustered copses of oak and elm and beech with vines

and bracken still intact. Surrounding the permanent encampment, snaking across the ground, stood the curving
gray-green granite wall.

"It seems so, now," Donal agreed. "When I was a boy,
there were not so many as this. But that was when we
lived across the Bluetooth River, trying to stay free of Ihlini
retribution and Bellam's tyranny." He glanced around the
Keep as they rode through, reining around cookfires and
running children. "This is a true Keep now, with the half-
circle walls and painted pavilions. But for years—too many
years—we lived as refugees and outlaws." He glanced at
Aislinn, locked up in her silence. "It was Carillon who allowed us the freedom to come home."

Sef's parti-colored eyes were fixed on Donal. "It's no
wonder they sing songs and tell stories about him, then.
Look at what he's done."

Donal felt a stab of sympathy for Carillon, even in his
absence. *We have made him into a legend for us to idolize,
and we have stripped him of his freedom. It must be more
difficult for him to live up to the name, and he is the one
who wears it.*

"My father is a great man," Aislinn said flatly. "There
is no one like him in all the kingdoms of the world. *No
one* will ever be able to match him." Her gray-pale eyes
were fastened with great deliberation upon Donal's face.

"Aislinn," he said gently, "I do not compete with your
jehan. And I will not even when his throne has passed to
me." Trying to break the moment, he glanced around the
Keep. "This is smaller now than it was when first we came
here. But some of the clans have gone back across the
Bluetooth to return to the Northern Keep." Involuntarily,
he shivered. "It was cold there—too close to the Wastes. I
prefer this Keep. And now—here is Finn's pavilion."

"Another wolf," Sef said. He pointed at the green pavilion with its gold-painted wolf on the side. "Lorn's father?"

Donal grinned down at the ruddy wolf as Lorn snorted
in surprise. "No. More like grandsire, perhaps, did *lir* age
normally. But as they do not, it makes no difference." He
jumped off his chestnut stallion even as Taj settled on the
ridgepole of the pavilion. "Come down, Sef . . . there is
nothing to harm you here."

"You said that about the Crystal Isle." Sef slid off his brown horse.

"And was there?" Donal looped his reins about a convenient tree branch and turned to help Aislinn down.

"There was," Sef said, "but I didn't let it."

Ignoring the boy's superstitions, Donal ducked under the reins and scratched at the pavilion doorflap. "*Su'fali*," he called. "Are you in?"

"No. I am out, but very nearly in." Finn came around the side of the pavilion with Storr padding at his side. The wolf's muzzle had grayed and grizzled, showing as much of age as a *lir* could, for his lifespan parallelled Finn's. Until his warrior died, Storr was free of normal aging.

Finn's black brows ran up beneath his silver-flecked, raven hair. But for that and a few deep lines etched into the flesh at the corners of his yellow eyes, he hardly looked old enough to have a nephew of twenty-three. The dark flesh of his bare arms was still stretched taut over heavy muscles; his *lir*-bands gleamed in the sunlight. "You have been a stranger to your Keep, Donal. What brings you here now?"

"Aislinn," he said briefly, and sensed her instant tension.

Finn glanced at her. "You are well come to the Keep, lady. Meghan will be pleased to know you are here. She is with Alix just now, but I can send Storr for her."

"No." Aislinn's face was tight with apprehension. "I have not come to see Meghan. I have come because Donal made me promise, and my father insisted I *keep* it."

"As one should, particularly a princess." But Finn had lost his welcoming smile as he glanced again at Donal. "This is not a casual visit."

"No," Donal agreed. "Aislinn, as you know, has been with Electra on the Crystal Isle. She has been—tampered with."

"A trap-link?" Finn's hand shot out and clamped on Aislinn's head before she could move. And by the time she *did* move, crying out and pulling away, Finn was done with his evaluation. "No. Something else. Bring her inside." He turned and pulled the doorflap aside.

Aislinn hung back. She looked at Donal, and he saw the terror in her face. Gently, he set one hand on her shoulder. After a moment, she slipped inside the pavilion.

Sef, like Aislinn, hung back. But for different reasons. "It isn't my *place*," he said. "He'll work magic in there. I'll do better out here."

"Come in," Donal insisted mildly. "What Finn will do is nothing I cannot do myself, and I do not doubt you will be witness to it sooner rather than late. It may as well be now." He settled one browned hand around Sef's arm and ushered him into the pavilion, leaving Lorn to trade greetings with Storr—as well as the grooming ritual—and Taj to converse with the other *lir*.

Finn sat on a spotted silver fur taken from a snow leopard. As clan-leader he was entitled to a large pavilion, and he had accepted that right. Furs of every texture and color cushioned the hard-packed earthen floor, and fine-worked tapestries divided the pavilion into sections. One of those sections, Donal knew, belonged to Meghan, Finn's half-Homanan daughter.

Thinking of Meghan reminded him that Finn had said she was with Alix. And his mother, no doubt, was with his *mei jha*. Quite suddenly, Donal longed to be there as well, wishing to forget all about Aislinn and her troubles.

But he had promised, and he did not break his oaths.

A small firepit glowed in front of Finn. The smoke was drawn up to the top of the pavilion, where it was dispersed through a ventflap. Through the bluish haze, Finn's eyes were almost hypnotic.

Aislinn half-turned as if to flee, but Donal blocked her way. Defeated, she turned reluctantly back. Her fingers crept up to pull nervously at the wool binding her braid.

Finn laughed. "You remind me a little of Alix, when first she joined the clan. All doe-eyed and frightened, yet defiant enough to spit in my face. That *is* what you would prefer to do, Aislinn . . . is it not?"

"Aye!" she answered, summoning up her own measure of defiance. "I want no part of this. It is Donal who says I am—tainted." Her voice wavered just a little. "He said—she has meddled with my mind."

Finn did not smile. He did not appear privately amused, as he so often did. His tone, when he spoke, was quiet and exceedingly gentle. "If she has, small one . . . I will see that we rid you of it." For a moment he studied her silently. "There is no need to fear me, Aislinn. Do you not know me through my daughter? You and Meghan are boon companions."

Aislinn's eyes were huge, almost colorless in the muted light of the pavilion. "But—*I have heard all the stories.*"

"*All* of them?" Finn shook his head. "I think not. You had best ask Carillon for more." Now he smiled, just a little, and looked past her to Donal. "Who is the boy you have brought?"

Donal prodded Sef forward. "Answer him. His *lir* may be a wolf, but it does not mean he will devour you. Any more than *I* will."

Sef moved forward three steps. His hands were wound into the black woolen tunic that bore a small crimson rampant lion over his left breast. "Sef," he said softly, keeping his eyes averted. "I am—Sef."

"And I am Finn." Finn smiled his old ironic smile. "You almost resemble a Cheysuli. Donal has not brought you home, has he? As I brought Alix home?"

Color rushed into Sef's pale face, then washed away almost at once. His eyes, blue and brown, stared fixedly at Finn. "No," he said on a shaking breath. "I am not Cheysuli."

Finn shrugged. "You have the black hair and strong-boned face for it, albeit you are too fair for one of us." For just a moment, a teasing glint lit his eyes. "Perhaps you are merely a halfling gotten unknown on some poor Homanan woman—"

Finn stopped. Donal, looking at him, saw the glint in his eyes fade; heard the teasing banter die. Finn frowned a little, looking at Sef, as if he sought an answer to some unknown question.

Donal laughed aloud. "Perhaps *your* halfling, *su'fali?*"

Finn looked at him sharply. "Mine?"

"You are no priest, *su'fali*, who keeps himself from women." Donal, still grinning, shrugged. "Sef himself says he does not know who his *jehan* was."

"He was *not* Cheysuli!" Sef declared hotly.

Donal looked at him quickly, startled by his vehemence. "Would it matter so much if he *were?*" he asked. "What if he were Finn himself?"

Sef's eyes locked onto Finn's. So intense was his regard

he seemed almost transfixed. "No," he said. That word only, and yet its tone encompassed an abiding certainty.

"No," Finn agreed, and yet Donal saw a faint frown of puzzlement. Then Finn flicked a dismissive hand. "To get to the point: Electra has once more meddled with someone's mind, and this time it is Aislinn's." He looked at the frightened princess. "Sit down, girl, and I will discover what I can."

"Donal tried," she blurted. "He could do nothing."

"I am not Donal, and I have had somewhat of a more—*personal*—experience with such things as Ihlini trap-links." Briefly he looked at Storr, lying on a pelt nearby, as if the words evoked some private memory they shared. "Aislinn, I will not harm you. Do you think Carillon would allow it?"

She stared at the furs beneath her feet. "No."

Donal placed a gentle hand on Aislinn's head. "Sit down. I am here with you, Aislinn."

She shut her eyes a moment. And then she sat down where Finn indicated, cross-legged, across the fire cairn from him.

"Now," he said quietly, "if Donal has done this to you, you know it will not hurt."

"Have *you* had it done?" she challenged with a defiance that only underscored her fear and vulnerability.

An odd look passed over Finn's dark, angular face. The scar twisting across the left side of his face had faded from avid purple to silver-white with the passing of seventeen years, but it still puckered the flesh from eye to jaw, lending him a predatory expression he did not entirely require, having the look of a predator already. "Not—precisely," Finn answered at last. "But something similar was done to me. It was—Tynstar. And your *jehana*. Together, they set a trap for me, and nearly slew me." He studied her face closely, unsmiling. "But I survived, though something else did not."

Aislinn, startled, sucked in a breath. "*What* did not survive?"

"An oath," Finn said flatly. "We broke it, your *jehan* and I, because there was nothing left to do." He reached out and touched her eyelids with two gentle fingers. "You are not your *jehana*, Aislinn, and I doubt she has done much to you that cannot be undone. Be silent, do not fear, and forget the stories you have heard."

Silently, Donal knelt down at Aislinn's side. He watched as Finn put his hands out, reaching through the smoke to touch her face. Finn ran his fingers softly across the delicate flesh of her brow, her nose, her eyelids, keeping himself silent. And then he spread his fingers and trapped her skull in his palms.

His hands held her head carefully, cupping thumbs beneath her jaw and splaying fingers through her hair. For a long moment he only looked at her pale, rigid face with its tight-shut eyes, and then his mouth moved into a grim line. He glanced quickly at Donal. "Do you come?"

"Aye, *su'fali*."

"Then come." The grimness faded into relaxation, and the yellow eyes turned vague and detached. Finn was patently *elsewhere*.

Donal knew what he did. Finn sought the power in the earth magic, tapping the source as he himself had done, drawing it up into his body until he could focus it onto Aislinn. He channeled it into the girl, seeking out the knotted web of Ihlini interference. Could he do it, he would untangle the web and disperse it.

Finn's head dipped down a little in an odd echo of Aislinn's posture. His eyes, fixed and unblinking, turned black as the pupils swelled. His mouth loosened; his chin twitched once; a slight tremor ran through his body.

Donal took a breath and slipped into the link with care. He felt his knowledge of body and surroundings fade away at once, dissipating into nonexistence, until he was but a speck of pulsing awareness in a void of black infinity. It was *nothingness*, complete and complex, and yet it was the essence of everything. Earth power, raw and unchanneled, surged up around him, threatening to smother him.

Carefully, Donal pushed it back. He maintained his awareness of self and the knowledge of what he did, remaining *Donal* in the face of such overwhelming power. And slowly, the power fell back, allowing him room to move. Quickly he sought Finn and found his presence in the void, the bright, rich crimson spark that was the essence of his uncle.

Su'fali, Donal greeted him.

That which was Finn returned the greeting. As they made contact, Donal felt the flare of two Cheysuli souls joined in an odd form of intercourse. Together they would locate and evaluate the residue of sorcery that resonated in Aislinn's mind, and they would free her of it.

There, said Finn within the vastness of their link.

Donal saw it. Caught in the countless strands of Aislinn's subconsciousness was a mass of knotted darkness; a spider's web. It looked tenuous as any thread, and yet he knew it was not. Tynstar's "thread" would be tensile as the strongest wire.

Gently, Finn said. *Gently. Springing the trap must be carefully done, or it will catch unwanted prey.*

Donal crept slowly closer to the trap-link. He prepared to lend Finn what strength he could—

—and felt the sudden painful wrenching of a broken link.

Awareness exploded into a vast shower of burning fragments, hissing out one by one. Donal thought at first it was something within Aislinn, some form of ward-spell, then felt the scrape of a hand upon his shoulder. No longer was he free of his body, but bound by flesh again.

Dimly, he heard Aislinn's garbled outcry. Finn was swearing. Donal caught himself before he fell face-first into the flames, then thrust an arm against the pelts to steady himself. He was disoriented and badly shaken, feeling distinctly ill.

Angrily, he turned. "To touch a Cheysuli in mind-link—"

But he broke it off. He saw how Sef slumped down on the fur pelt just behind, his face corpse-white in the blue-smoked air. The boy shuddered spasmodically and his mouth gaped open as if he could not breathe. Donal thrust himself up in one movement and caught Sef before he tumbled into the fire.

Donal looked back at Aislinn. Finn still held her, and by the look of his eyes he had not stepped out of the link. Aislinn still drifted in the trance and Finn still sought the trap-link. But there was no doubting Donal's broken link had affected them both. The shattering had been too powerful.

Donal closed his eyes a moment. He still felt ill. His ears buzzed. Lights fired in his eyes. But somehow he managed to stand up with Sef in his arms and stagger out of the pavilion.

He set the boy down against a tree. Even as he did so,

Sef began to rouse. Donal, seating himself on the ground, put his head down against his knees and tried to regain his composure.

Lir? It was Lorn, thrusting his nose beneath Donal's elbow. *Lir?*

Even as Sef stirred, Donal raised his head. *Broken link,* he told the wolf. *Sef touched me.*

You should have told him, lir. *You should have warned the boy.*

My fault, Donal said, and blew out a heavy breath.

Color crept back into Sef's face. He blinked, rubbed dazedly at his temple, then tried to sit bolt upright.

Donal pressed him back down. "No. Be still. Do you recall what happened?"

Sef frowned blankly. "I—I was drowning. I was being sucked down. It was like I was buried alive." He stared at Donal. "Was it the magic? Did I feel it?"

Donal sought the best words. "Sef—what you did was done out of ignorance. I understand. And I should have warned you: never touch a Cheysuli when he has gone into another's mind."

Sef's eyes widened. "What could happen?"

Donal rubbed at burning eyes. His ears still buzzed, though the sound had almost faded. "Many things, depending upon the severity of the break, and how deeply the warrior has gone. And a link is a link—in touching me you touched Aislinn and Finn. You might have injured us all in addition to yourself."

Sef sucked in a strangled breath. "Oh my lord, I'm *sorry*—"

Donal caught one thin shoulder. "Do not fret. It is over with. No permanent harm was done, that I can see."

"I was so afraid." Sef looked steadfastly at the ground. I was—afraid."

"Fear is nothing to be ashamed of," Donal told him gently. "It strikes all men, at one time or another, and mimics many things. You were not drowning. You were not being buried alive."

Lorn still pressed against Donal's side. *The boy is more than frightened,* lir. *There is* something . . . *else.*

Is the boy a halfling? Donald asked.

The wolf seemed to shrug. *I cannot say. Perhaps—but I*

leave him to you. Lorn turned and went back to his place on the rug by Finn's tent, sharing it with Storr.

Sef's eyes were fixed on Donal's face. "You are— different," he said gravely. "Never do you make me feel a child. Oh, aye, there are times I deserve chastising, and you deliver it—but never do you treat me as if I were unworthy of courtesy. Others do."

Donal smiled. "Maybe it is because I am used to boys asking questions. I have a son, you see, though he lacks ten of your years."

"A—son?" Sef sat more upright. "But—I thought you were to wed the princess!"

"I am. But I have a Cheysuli *meijha*, and she has given me a son." He glanced back at the pavilion, wishing to go back in so he could join again in the link with Finn.

"I didn't know that." Sef's brows drew down in a frown.

Donal smiled. "Does it matter? You are still my sworn man, are you not?"

"What of your son?"

"He is too young yet. Ian has years before he can serve me as you do." He pulled Sef to his feet. "If the pavilion is too close for you, or you feel too frightened to enter, wait here. I will be out when I can." He released Sef's wrist, but as he did he felt something soft and supple against his fingers. "What is this?" he asked, peeling back Sef's sleeve.

It was a narrow bracelet of feathers bound around Sef's wrist. Brown and gold and black.

Sef jerked his wrist away and covered up the band with his other hand. "A—charm." Color blazed into his face. "Protection against strong magic." His eyes flicked toward the pavilion. "I was—afraid. When—when I was given time of my own to spend as I wished, I went into the city. I— found an old woman who makes charms and love-spells." He shrugged defensively. "I said I was afraid of the Cheysuli, and she gave me this." He exposed the feathered band briefly as the color ran out of his face. "Are you ashamed of me?"

"Only if you paid her all the coin I gave you," Donal said wryly. "Did you?"

Sef's eyes widened. "Oh *no!* Do you think I'm a fool? I only gave her *half* of it."

Donal tried not to laugh and did not entirely succeed.

"Well enough, you drove a good bargain. But Mujharan prices are higher than those in Hondarth, I will wager." He squeezed Sef's shoulder. "There is no need for the charm. Shall I take it from your wrist?"

"*No*—" Sef took a single backward step. "No," he said more quickly. "I know *you* would never hurt me," he muttered, "but what of all the others?"

Donal shook his head and sighed. "There is much for you to learn, I see. Well enough, keep your ward-spell and know yourself safe from Cheysuli 'sorcery.'" He turned to re-enter the pavilion, then glanced back. "You may stay here or wander, as you like. But it will be best that you do not come in again."

Blood came and went in Sef's face. "No, my lord. I won't."

Donal pulled aside the flap and went back inside the tent.

Aislinn, he saw, was slumped over, held limply in Finn's arms. He bent down at once to take her.

"No," Finn said. "She will be well enough. It is only the aftermath." Strain had etched new lines in his dark face. Like Carillon, he had once been touched by Tynstar, and it showed occasionally in his appearance and slowed reflexes. But Finn, unlike Carillon, had not lost so many years. "It was—difficult."

Donal knelt down quickly. "Is she all right? Did you destroy the trap-link?"

Finn frowned. "There was no trap-link, not as I know them. There was something, aye—you saw it as well as I—but not of Tynstar's doing. And I think Electra, even using what arts Tynstar taught her, is not capable of setting one herself. But she did work some form of magic on Aislinn. There was an echo, a residue of—*something*. I could not catch it all . . . it was too elusive. And once the boy broke your portion of the link . . ." Finn shrugged, cupping Aislinn's lolling head as if she were an infant. "I do believe Aislinn was somehow ensorceled to carry out Electra's plans, but I think I have ended that."

"I hope you are certain, *su'fali*," Donal said dryly. "I think I would be disinclined to wed a woman who wishes to see me slain."

Finn grinned. "I do not doubt Aislinn has personal reasons for viewing you with some disfavor—having known

Homanan women before—but I hardly think you need worry about a knife in the back in your nuptial bed." Then the humor slipped away. "Who is that boy?"

"A foundling. He was in Hondarth alone, living in the streets and eating what he could find." Donal shrugged. "He begged to come with me when I had done him a service, and so I let him come. Why? Do you think he may really be your son?"

Finn flicked him a glance from half-lidded eyes. "I will not discount the possibility."

Donal sat back on his heels. "You *do* think he is—"

"I said: I would not discount the possibility." Finn repeated firmly. "That does not mean I claim he *is*."

"No," Donal conceded. He chewed at the inside of his left cheek. "But—why should you think so? Burned dark, he might be one of us—but he lacks the yellow eyes."

"So does Alix. So do many of our halflings." Finn shrugged. "Perhaps he is mine, perhaps he is another's. There is definitely something *familiar* about him, but I think it does not matter."

"Not *matter!*" Donal stared at him in surprise. "How can you be so callous?"

Finn's black brows lifted. "I will force paternity on *no* one, Donal. And he did not seem overfond of the Cheysuli."

"He has not had a chance to know us. Given time—"

"Given time, he may find himself content to be your man." Finn smiled. "Not a liege man, perhaps, but a loyal companion. And I think you are in need of one."

"I have my *lir*. They are more than enough."

"Aye. But you will also have Aislinn." Finn looked down on the sleeping princess in his arms. "Odd, how she resembles both and neither of her parents. It is the coloring, I think—strip the red from her hair and make it blond, and she is nearly Electra come again."

Donal reached out and touched Aislinn's hair, smoothing it against her scalp. She looked younger as she slept, but she was no longer a little girl. "No. Not Electra. Perhaps she has the features, but none of the witch's ways." He sighed and took his hand away.

"Donal." Finn's tone was oddly serious, for a man who only infrequently sought decorum. "I know what you face, now that you must wed her. But you are Duncan's son, and I know you have the strength."

"Do I?" Donal looked again at Aislinn. "I am not my *jehan,* much as I long to be more like him. And I could not *begin* to say if I share his dedication."

"He was born with that no more than any man," Finn said. "He learned it because he had to. So will you." He nodded toward the doorflap. "Go and see your *meijha.* You owe her a little time."

"Aislinn?"

"I will keep her with me."

Donal felt the guilt begin to pain him sorely. "My thanks, *su'fali.* It is every bit as difficult as you warned me, that day so long ago."

The scar writhed as Finn's jaw tightened. "I am not your *jehan,* nor can ever be. But I would give you what aid I can. It is only that eventually you must bear the weight yourself." Again he motioned with his head. "Go and see your *meijha.* I will give you what time I can."

Eleven

Donal stepped outside the pavilion, glad to feel the fresh air again, and found his sister in deep conversation with Sef. In all excitement of having Aislinn tested by Finn, he had forgotten Bronwyn entirely. He had not seen her for longer than he cared to admit. But then, he put her from his mind as often as he could.

No. Not Bronwyn. What Bronwyn could become.

She turned as he stepped out. She resembled their mother mostly, with Alix's amber eyes and lighter complexion, but her hair was Cheysuli black.

Or Ihlini *black. In* that *she could take after Tynstar.*

Donal shut off the thought at once. He could not clearly recall precisely how or when his mother had told him Bronwyn was not Duncan's daughter, but another man's entirely. And neither was he Cheysuli, but Tynstar himself. Tynstar of the Ihlini. No, Donal could not recall the words, but he could all too easily summon up the disbelief and astonishment he had felt.

That, and the fear.

One day, she will learn what powers she claims. She will begin to play with them. . . .

He did not want to think of that day. It had been fifteen years since Alix had escaped from Tynstar's lair bearing the sorcerer's child in her belly. Bronwyn as yet had shown no signs of Ihlini powers, but she had been increasingly moody lately. The *lir* themselves had been unable to predict when she might come to know her powers; all they could discern in her was the Cheysuli blood she claimed from her mother's side, as if Alix's Old Blood were canceling out that of the Ihlini. No one but Alix, Finn, Carillon, Sorcha, and himself knew the girl's true paternal heritage, not even Bronwyn herself. But it was possible her father's legacy might wake in her at any time, and so they watched her more closely each day.

She wore a gown of deepest purple trimmed with wine-red yarn in a linked pattern of animals. Birds and bears and cats promenaded at collar and cuffs. The front of her skirts was hooked over the tops of her leather boots, as if she had been running. As it was Bronwyn, she probably had been. She rarely ever walked.

She is wild. So wild. Someone else might say it was the recklessness of girlhood. But—I cannot help but wonder if there is more to it than that.

"*Rujho.*" Bronwyn smiled at him, exposing even white teeth in a face darker than Sef's but lighter than her brother's. "I came to see you, not knowing you were busy. Sef told me what you sought to do." Her smile faded. "Is Aislinn all right?"

"Aislinn is fine. Whatever was there does not seem to be permanent." He glanced at Sef. "I assume the introductions have been concluded?"

"I told her my name," Sef answered. "Should I have said more?"

"Not unless there *is* more."

Sef looked back at Bronwyn. Donal, having seen young boys impressed with girls before, hid a smile. He had the distinct feeling that Sef, if Bronwyn were interested, would spill more of his life to her than to anyone else, including the Prince of Homana.

"Then I leave you in companionship to one another," he told them. "I have private business now."

"With Sorcha?" Bronwyn asked as he turned to go.

Donal abruptly turned back. Bronwyn as well as anyone in the Keep knew what he shared with Sorcha. She knew also he was betrothed to Aislinn; it was common knowledge in the clans. But Bronwyn was Aislinn's friend, and he did not doubt she felt conflicting loyalties nearly as much as he did, if in a different way.

"Aye, with Sorcha," he said at last. "Bronwyn—you will give Aislinn what comfort you can—?"

Bronwyn lifted her head. She had pulled her hair back in a manner too severe for her young face, braided very tightly and entirely bound with purple yarn. The color was striking on her, but it reminded him of the Ihlini. It reminded him of Tynstar, and the lurid fire he summoned from the air.

"Aislinn loves you," Bronwyn told him. "When we are together—here or at the palace—she tells me how you make her feel." Abruptly she looked away, embarrassed. "Donal—I know what there is between *meijha* and warrior . . . but I do not think Aislinn does. The Homanans do not share."

Donal flicked a glance at Sef. The boy listened, but he did so from behind a tactful mask. That much he had learned of royal customs.

"Aislinn must learn," Donal said finally, knowing he sounded colder than he felt; not knowing how else to sound. "You learned. Meghan learned."

"Meghan and I were born of the clans." Bronwyn's voice was pitched low, as if she recalled Aislinn inside the tent. "There is a difference."

Donal turned to face her directly. "You are nearly Aislinn's age. And you and Meghan know her better than anyone. Tell me what *you* would do in Aislinn's place."

Bronwyn clearly had never considered it. She looked thoughtful, then shrugged and spread her hands. Her expression was deeply troubled. "I have been taught a warrior may have both *meijha* and *cheysula*. It is difficult for me to think of it differently. But—I have heard how Aislinn speaks of you, and how she dreams of the wedding and the marriage—" Bronwyn stopped short as anguish filled her eyes. "Oh *rujho*, be gentle with her. I think she will never understand."

"Oh, gods . . ." he said aloud, and then he turned and left them both.

He went straight to the pavilion he shared with Sorcha without paying much attention to how he got there. He was distantly aware of the normal sounds of the Keep—children laughing, babies crying, a woman singing, a crow calling—and myriad other noises. The Keep had stood so long the ground underfoot was beaten flat, fine as flour. Grass grew only in patches beneath the trees. The wall was a gray-green serpent snaking through the trees, showing a flank of stone. Donal smelled roasting meat.

And then he stood before the slate-gray pavilion he had

adorned with silver paint: running wolf and flying falcon. The breeze caused the oiled fabric to billow as he pulled aside the doorflap, then passed through and set the fire cairn to smoking. Blue-gray, it flowed through the interior like thin, insidious fog.

"Sorcha?" He let the flap settle behind him.

A slim hand caught the edge of the tapestry curtain dividing the sleeping area from the front section of the pavilion. He saw Sorcha's face as she pulled the curtain back, and the hugeness of her belly.

"Gods," he said in surprise, having lost track of the months upon sight of her. "Are you certain you will not *burst?*"

Sorcha laughed, splaying one hand across her swollen belly. "No more than I did the last time."

Donal crossed to her, kissed her tenderly. "Where is Ian?" His hands went to her unbound hair and smoothed it back from her face.

"Meghan has him. I sent him out with her, to give me a little peace. Bronwyn wanted to, but—" She broke off. He knew what she would not say, because she had no wish to hurt him. And he did not blame her for her growing distrust of his sister. None of them could afford to trust too much to an Ihlini, no matter how she was raised.

Except for my jehana.

A brief grimace of pain cut across Sorcha's face. She placed a hand against the small of her back. "A boy, I think. Again. And soon. Very soon."

"*How* soon?" He was alarmed by the pallor of her face. Beneath his questing hand he felt the contraction in her belly. "Sorcha—the baby comes *already!*"

"Oh, aye . . . impatient little warrior, is he not?" Her smile wavered. "Different from Ian. Different from the first unfortunate boy." She grimaced. "I think—I think perhaps I had best lie down after all. Help me—?"

He guided her down onto the pallet of pelts they shared. Sorcha's tawny hair spread against the fur of a ruddy fox; he pulled a doeskin mantle over her and pushed a folded bearskin beneath her back for support. "Should I fetch my *jehana?*"

"Not yet," she answered breathlessly. "Soon. But I want to share you with no one for at least a little while." Her

eyes were green. Half Homanan, Sorcha showed no Cheysuli blood. But she had been born and raised in the clan,
and her customs were all Cheysuli. "Aislinn is here," she
said.

There was bitterness in her tone, and an underlying hostility. Never had he heard either from her before. He would
have questioned her about it, but he saw how her face
stretched taut with effort. Her hand clung to his as he knelt
beside the pallet.

"Aislinn is here," she repeated, and this time he heard
fear.

"Aye. Aislinn is here." He had never lied to her before;
he would not begin now. No more than he would with
Aislinn.

"Does she know about me?"

"She knows."

Sorcha smiled a little. "Proud, defiant warrior, close-
mouthed as can be . . . letting no one see what goes on
inside your head *or* your heart. But I know you, Donal."
The tension in her face eased as the contraction receded.
"I can imagine how difficult it was to find the words."

"Now is not the time to speak of Aislinn." He stroked
her hand with his thumb.

"Tell me what you told her."

"Sorcha—"

"Tell me what you *said*."

He brushed hair out of his face. The urgency in her tone
worried him. "Gods, Sorcha—this is nonsense . . . there are
better times to speak of this—"

"*No* better time." Her fingers were locked on his hand.
"I have borne you two sons and now perhaps another. I
would bear you more willingly; I would do anything you
asked me to." She swallowed visibly. "But I will not give
you up. I will not let you be swallowed up by that witch's
Homanan daughter."

"Sorcha—*you* are half Homanan," he reminded her mildly.

Sweat glistened at her temples. "And I would open my
veins if I thought it would purge me of my Homanan blood.
I would cut off a hand if I thought it would relieve me of
the taint. But it would not—*it would not*—and all I can do
is look at my son and thank the gods he has so little Homanan in him." She sucked in a breath against the pain.

"Gods, Donal—I hate the Homanan in me! I would trade *anything* to claim myself all Cheysuli—"

"But you cannot." He had never heard her speak so vehemently, so bitterly or with a spirit so filled with prejudice. It seemed as if the pains bared her soul. "*Meijha*, do you forget there is Homanan in me as well?"

"Gods!" she cried. "It is not the same with you. *You* are the chosen—*you* are the one we have waited for—you are the one with the proper blood who will take the Lion from Homana and give it back to the Cheysuli—" She shut her mouth on a cry of pain and bit deeply into her lip. Her fingers dug into the flesh of his hand. "Oh Donal, do you see? You will leave us all behind. You will turn your back on your clan. They will make you into a toy for the Homanans—" Sorcha writhed against the pallet. "*Never* forget you are Cheysuli. *Never* forget you are a warrior. *Never* forget who sired you . . . and *do not* allow the witch's daughter to turn you against your heritage with her Homanan ways—"

"*Enough!*" He said it more sharply than he intended. "Sorcha, you are doing yourself harm with this."

"You do *yourself* harm." Her eyes were tightly closed against the pain. "You—do yourself harm . . . by leaving the clan behind. . . ."

"I cannot rule Homana from the Keep," he said flatly. "The Homanans would never accept it."

"Do you see?" she asked in despair. "Already they begin their theft of you."

"I am not *leaving*," he said. "I will come here as often as I may. Sorcha—I am not Mujhar *yet*—"

"But you will wed the Mujhar's daughter, and he will make you *his* son instead of Duncan's—"

"*Never.*" His hand clamped down on hers. "Not that. Never. Do you think I am so weak?"

"Not weak," she gasped. "Divided. Homanan and Cheysuli, because they make you so. But I beg you, Donal, do one thing for me—?"

He gave up, but only because she needed her strength for other things. "Aye."

"Make the Lion *Cheysuli* again . . . and your sons and daughters as well—"

In horror, he watched her knees come up, tenting the

soft doeskin coverlet. The mound of her belly rolled as she cried out. What he had meant to say to her was instantly forgotten; he summoned Taj through the *lir*-link and sent him to bring his mother.

Alix came at once and met her son just inside the door-flap. "You," she said, "must go."

"Go?"

"Go. Anywhere. But go away from *here*." Her hands were on one arm, tugging him toward the entrance. "Do as I say."

He did not move, being too big for her to push this way and that anymore. "Sorcha is in pain. I would rather stay with her."

"Loyalty does you credit, Donal—" Alix stopped tugging, as if she realized the futility in the effort, and merely pointed toward the entrance, "—but this is no place for a man about to become a *jehan*."

"I have been one twice before," he reminded her. "I let you shoo me away then—perhaps I should have refused."

"Donal—just *go*. I have no time for you right now." Alix—still slim in a rose-red gown—turned away from him and pulled aside the curtain. Silver clasps in her dark braids glittered, and then she was gone behind the divider. He heard her speak to Sorcha, but could not decipher the words.

Yet another outcry from Sorcha; Donal walked out of the tent into the light of a brilliant day and petitioned the gods for the safe delivery of woman and child.

And came face to face with Aislinn.

She had shed her cloak, gowned in dark green, and in the sunlight her red-gold hair was burnished bronze. Her face was very pale. "Finn would not tell me where you were," she told him quietly. "He tried to keep me with him. But—Bronwyn told me the truth. I thought I should come and meet my rival."

She was all vulnerability, suddenly fragile in the light; pale lily on a slender stalk with a trembling, delicate bloom. But she was also pride; a little bruised, a trifle shaken, but pride nonetheless. As much as claimed by any Cheysuli.

Donal drew in a deep breath that left him oddly light-headed. "Aislinn—the gods know I have done you dishonor by keeping Sorcha a secret, but now is not the time."

From the pavilion there came the muted cry of a woman in labor, and Aislinn's gray eyes widened. "The *baby*—! You told me the child was due—" She broke off, covering her mouth with one hand, and her eyes filled up with tears. But almost as quickly she blinked them away. "No," she said. "My mother told me tears are not the way to win a man's regard. *Strength*, she said, and *determination* . . . and the magic of every woman born—"

"Aislinn!" He caught her arms and shook her. "By the gods, girl, I am not a prize to be *won*. As for what *Electra* has told you—"

"Then how can I turn your affections to me?" she interrupted. "Can I leash you, like a hound? Can I hood you, like a hawk? Can I bridle you, like a horse?" Her body was rigid under his hands. "Or do I give you over to freedom, and know I have lost you forever?"

He heard Sorcha's warning sounding in his head: —*do not allow the witch's daughter to turn you against your heritage*—

"No," he said aloud. "I am Cheysuli first."

"And Homanan last?" Aislinn asked bitterly. "Is this the heir my Homanan father chose?"

His hands closed more tightly upon her arms. Too tightly; Aislinn cried out, and he loosed her only with great effort. "You push me too far," he warned through gritted teeth. "*Both* of you—pushing and pushing and pushing, pulling me this way and that—dividing my loyalties. What would you have me do?—divide myself in two? Give each of you half of me? What good would that *do* for you? Salve your wounded pride?"

"Give up—" Aislinn stopped dead. The color drained out of her face.

"Give up Sorcha? Is that what you meant to say?" Donal shook his head, knowing only he wanted to go away from it all. "I would sooner give up myself." He laughed a little, albeit with a bitter tone. "For all that, it might be easier."

Aislinn stared at the ground as if she wished it would swallow her up. The sun was blazing off the red-gold of her hair. "I had no right to ask it. I know it. You have told me how it is with—*meijhas* and *cheysulas*. But—I will not lie to you. I want you for myself." Her head came up and she challenged him with a stare. "She has had you longer, but I will have you yet."

Wearily, Donal pushed a strand of hair from Aislinn's face. "You sing the same song. Were it not for me, you might be friends." And then he recalled Sorcha's prejudice, and knew it could never be.

There came another cry from the pavilion, but this one did not belong to Sorcha. As it rose up to a wail of outraged astonishment, Donal knew the travail was done.

So did Aislinn. White-faced, she turned from him and walked regally away.

But he knew she wanted to run.

Alix did not send him away when he entered the pavilion. She did not seem to notice him at all, being too occupied with tending Sorcha and the baby. Softly he approached the partially open divider and stopped short.

Sorcha's eyes were closed; Donal thought she slept. Lines of strain were graven in her face. She looked older and very weary, but there was peace and contentment in the slackness of her mouth.

"A girl, Donal," Alix said calmly. "You have a daughter now."

He could not move. He stood frozen in place, staring down at the bundled baby with her pink, outraged face as she lay snug at Sorcha's side, and knew a vast humility.

"I do not imagine you recall being in a similar position, once," Alix said wryly. "I do not recall it so much myself. But it was Raissa who helped me bear you, as I have aided Sorcha."

"Granddame," he said, and felt guilty that he had nearly forgotten the woman who had died so long before.

Slowly he knelt down beside the pallet and put a tentative finger to the perfect softness of the baby's black-fuzzed head. No Homanan girl, this; she had her father's color.

"Let them sleep. Later, you may hold the girl." Alix rose, shaking out her rose-red skirts. Donal saw the faint shine of silver threads in Alix's dark brown hair and realized his mother, like Finn and Carillon, also aged. But less dramatically. Her skin was still smooth, still stretched taut over classic Cheysuli bones, and when she smiled it lit her amber eyes. "It makes one aware of one's own transience, man or woman, and how seemingly unimportant are such things as dynastic marriages when a son or daughter is born," she said gently. "Does it not?"

He rose also. "You heard Aislinn and me outside the tent."

"Bits and pieces. I was too preoccupied to understand it all." Alix glanced back at Sorcha and the child. "They will do well enough without us. I think we can leave them for a while."

This time when she urged him toward the doorflap, he did not resist. He went with her willingly.

He walked with her to the perimeter of the Keep, along the moss-grown wall. Unmortared, it afforded all manner of vegetation the opportunity to plant roots into cracks and crannies, digging between the stones. Ivy, deep red and deeper green, mantled the wall against the sunlight. Twining flowers climbed up the runners and formed delicate ornamentation; jewels within the folds of the velvet gown. He smelled wet moss and old stone; the perfume of the place he knew as home. Not Homana-Mujhar. Not the rosered walls and marbled halls, hung about with brilliant banners. No, not for him.

Even though it would be.

"Aislinn has loved you for some time, since she was old enough to understand what can be between a man and a woman," Alix said gently. "Surely you knew she did."

"I thought she might outgrow it."

"Why should she? Do you not wish for love in this marriage?" At his frown, his mother laughed. "Oh, I know— the Cheysuli do not speak of love, seeking to keep such things impossibly private. But you will have to learn to deal with it, Donal, as your *jehan* and *su'fali* did." When he said nothing, having no answer for her, Alix caught his right hand and stopped him beside the wall. She turned the hand over until the palm was face-up and the strong brown fingers lay open. "With this hand you will hold Homana," she said evenly. "You are the hope of the Cheysuli, Donal, and a link in the prophecy. Deny this marriage and you deny your heritage."

He expelled a brief, heavy breath in an expression of irony. "Sorcha said *differently*. Sorcha said the marriage would force me to turn my back on my heritage."

Alix squeezed his hand and then let it go. "Sorcha is—bitter."

"She never was before." He shook his head in bewilderment. "Is it because the child was coming?"

"Partly." Alix touched him and urged him into motion once again. "I do not doubt she was frightened as well as in pain—the birth was exceedingly easy, but she could not have predicted that. As for bitterness. . . ." Alix stopped to pull a flower from the earth; delicate, fragile blossom of palest violet. "For all these years she has known you would one day marry Aislinn, not her, but it was easy to set that knowledge aside. Now she cannot. Now she must face it, and she does not want to do it."

"She hates Aislinn. That, I think, I can readily understand; I do know what jealousy is. But—*jehana*, she hates the Homanans as well." Again he shook his head. "How do I deal with *that*, when I am meant to be Mujhar?"

Alix cupped the blossom in her hands. "A violet flower among the white is easily plucked, Donal. Easily crushed and broken. There is no protection from the others when your coloring is different." She lifted her head and looked at him instead of the flower. "I do not speak of blond hair and green eyes. I speak of blood, and the knowledge of what one is. Prejudiced, aye, because she is more Cheysuli than Homanan—and yet no one will give her that."

"In the clans, people do not care. *You* are half Homanan; have you felt different from any other?"

"Aye," she said softly. "I spent seventeen years with the Homanans and twenty-four among the Cheysuli. But still I feel mostly Homanan; I do not doubt Sorcha does as well."

"But she was *born* to the clan—"

"It does not matter." She lifted the fragile blossom. "This flower is violet. It bloomed this color. It will never be able to claim itself another color, no matter how hard it tries." She smiled and let the blossom fall to the ground, where it settled into the trembling carpet of snow-white blooms. "Once it might have been purple. But never will it be white."

Donal stopped walking. He turned to face his mother. "Then—if I am that violet flower, I will never fit in with the white Homanans."

"No," she said. "But why wish to fit in when one must rule?"

He turned her to face the way they had come. "Let us go back. I want to see my son as well as my newborn daughter."

"*Jehan?*"

The soft voice intruded into his thoughts. Donal turned, shielding the newborn body in his arms, and saw his son standing in the doorflap with Meghan at his side. Ian's black hair was curly as was common in Cheysuli childhood, and his yellow eyes were bright as he gazed at his father. But his expression was decidedly reticent.

Donal put out a hand. "Come, Ian . . . come see your new *rujholla.*"

The boy moved quickly across the floor pelts, dropping down to kneel at Donal's side. His curiosity was manifest, but he did not touch the baby until Donal pulled back the linen wrappings and showed him the crumpled face.

He glanced at Sorcha as she drifted slowly back into sleep. "Your turn, *meijha*—I named the last one."

Sorcha smiled drowsily. "Isolde, then. I like the sound. Ian and Isolde."

Donal smiled at his rapt three-year-old son. "She is Isolde, Ian. And she will require your protection. See how small she is?"

Meghan, who had brought Ian soon after Donal had returned to his pavilion, moved forward and craned her neck to peer over Donal's shoulder. "Black hair," she said, "and brown eyes, which will lighten soon enough. A Cheysuli, then, with little Homanan about her."

Sorcha's smile widened, and Donal saw triumph in her eyes even as she closed them.

He glanced up at Finn's daughter. There was no bitterness in *Meghan*'s tone, only discovery and matter-of-factness; it seemed neither to trouble nor please Meghan that she was the image of her Homanan mother: tawny-haired, blue-eyed, fair-skinned; Carillon's dead sister to the bone. And she claimed all of Tourmaline's elegance and grace, even at fifteen years. Yet she lived among the clans with a *jehan* who was clan-leader, and she felt no lack that she bore Homanan blood in her veins. No lack at all. If anything, she was more Cheysuli than most because Finn saw to it she was.

No Homanan marriage for Meghan. Finn will wed her to a warrior. Donal smiled ruefully. *But then I am sure she will have more than enough to choose from.*

He glanced up at Alix regretfully. "Will you take Isolde? Much as I would prefer to stay, I promised Carillon I would have Aislinn back by nightfall. And—there are things to be settled between us." When Alix had taken the baby, Donal bent forward and kissed the drowsing Sorcha softly on the mouth. "Sleep you well, *meijha.* You have earned a sound rest."

He rose, scooping Ian up into his arms. "And a hug for you, small warrior. You will be busy from now on." He glanced at Meghan. "My thanks for seeing to him. Soon enough you will have your own children to tend."

She laughed, blue eyes dancing in her lovely face. "Not *so* soon, I hope. I wish for a little freedom, first."

"Do we go?" Ian asked as Donal carried him from the pavilion.

"No, small one, only I am going. You must stay here." He saw Lorn get up from his place in the sun by the door-flap and shake his heavy coat, yawning widely.

A cub and a bitch, Lorn observed. *How symmetrical.*

Donal snorted. *A boy and a girl, lir. There is nothing wolflike about either of them.*

Unless the boy bonds with one of my kind.

Do you say he will? Donal hoped suddenly for greater illumination into the bonding process, wondering suddenly if all the *lir* knew which of them was meant for each Cheysuli born.

Lorn paused and lifted one hind leg to scratch, doglike, at his belly. *No. Such things are left to the gods.*

Taj's shadow passed overhead. *Perhaps he will gain a falcon.*

Or a hawk. Donal nodded. *I would like him to have a hawk. How better to honor his grandsire?*

As you do yours? Lorn asked.

Donal, heading toward Finn's green pavilion, glanced sharply at the wolf. *How do I honor Hale?*

The sword. Taj said. *One day, it will be yours, as it was ever intended.*

Donal did not respond. Instead, as he approached with Meghan, he watched how Sef and Bronwyn sat together in front of Finn's pavilion, speaking animatedly. His sister's purple-wrapped braid hung over one shoulder, coiling against her skirts. Unlike Meghan or Aislinn, Bronwyn lacked conscious knowledge of her femininity. She moved and acted more boy than girl, though Donal knew she would outgrow it.

Now, as she laughed and chattered with Sef, he saw how she would lack the pure beauty Meghan and Aislinn already began to claim, but her light would be undiminished. She was his mother come again.

And who else? his conscience asked. *Is her* jehan *in her as well?*

He stopped by them both, still holding his son, and looked down upon them as they glanced up in laggard surprise. He saw how Sef had peeled back his right sleeve to show off the feathered band; how Bronwyn had drawn pictures in the dust with a broken stick. Runes, not pictures, he noted on closer inspection. But none were Cheysuli.

Bronwyn sprang to her feet and obscured the runes at once, hands thrust behind her back as if she meant to hide the stick. Purple skirts were filmed with dust, tangled on her boot-tops, but she ignored her dishevelment. "I heard the baby has come!"

Troubled, Donal nodded. "The baby has come. A girl. Sorcha has named her Isolde."

"May I see her?" Her face was alight with expectation.

"No." He almost cursed his shortness. "Not now. She is sleeping. So is Sorcha. They need time alone." He saw how her bright face fell. "Later, *rujholla.*" And she *was* his sister, for all she was Tynstar's daughter; he hated to disappoint her. She had had no say in what man sired her.

But he dared not give her the chance to prove herself Ihlini.

Slowly the color spilled out of her face. "What is wrong? Is it something I have done? You are so short—"

"No." Again, he said it more sharply than he intended. Against his will, he looked once more at the runes she had drawn in the dust and then tried to obscure. Odd, alien runes, with the look of sorcery.

"*Rujho—?*"

"Nothing," he said. "You have done nothing wrong. Bronwyn—what are those?" He would ignore the runes no longer.

She looked down in surprise at the drawings in the dust, then shot a glance at Sef. It was mostly veiled beneath lids and lashes, but he saw the silent signal.

As if she means to protect him . . . "Bronwyn!" The tone was a command, and he knew she would not ignore it.

"A secret game," she answered promptly. "We took an oath not to tell." Deliberately, she erased the rest of the runes with the toe of one booted foot.

He looked into her face and saw nothing of guile, only the expression she normally wore. And that mask he could not lift. "Bronwyn—" But he broke it off when Finn came out of the tent. With him was Aislinn; Donal's brows slid up in surprise. He had not thought she would seek him on purpose.

Before Finn could protest, Donal set Ian into his arms. "We must go, or the sun will set before we reach Mujhara." He grinned as Ian locked an arm around Finn's neck and snuggled closer. Without thinking about it, Finn settled the boy more comfortably; he had had practice enough with Meghan.

Donal bent and kissed Ian briefly on the forehead. "Care for your new *rujholla*. I will come back to you when I may." He turned and helped a silently staring Aislinn mount her horse. Then he retrieved the reins of his own mount and swung up into the saddle. Even as he settled, Lorn was at the horse's side and Taj was in the air.

Finn reached out and caught one rein. "How does Carillon fare?"

Donal saw the true concern in his uncle's face. For all they hardly saw one another now their paths had parted, Donal knew there remained a link that would always bind Finn and Carillon. Prince and liege man had spent five years in exile together; two more when the prince had become Mujhar. It was treachery that had parted them, and a broken oath that held.

Donal glanced briefly at Aislinn. But he saw no use in lying; she herself had marked her father's deterioration. "He ages," he said quietly. "Each day—more so than most men, I think. It is the disease . . ." He paused. "Is there nothing to be done?"

The sun shone off the heavy gold bands clasping Finn's bare arms as he rubbed idly at the chestnut's muzzle. He said nothing for a moment, but when he looked up into the sunlight Donal saw how he too had aged.

Gods, they shared so much . . . and now they share so little.

"Tynstar did not give Carillon anything he would not have suffered anyway, one day," Finn said tonelessly. "He merely brought it on prematurely. We cannot undo what the gods see fit to bestow upon a man."

"He is the *Mujhar!*" Donal lashed out. "Can the gods not see how much Homana needs him?"

Finn sighed. "No doubt there are reasons for it, Donal. The gods do nothing without them." Abruptly he slapped the stallion's shoulder. "Go back, then. See Aislinn safely to her *jehan*. Do not tarry here longer if Carillon is waiting."

He serves him still . . . he would not admit it, but he does. In his heart, if nowhere else. He shifted in the saddle. "Aye, *su'fali*. Have you a message for him?"

Finn lifted a hand to block out the blinding sunlight. "Aye," he said. "Tell him I will come to Homana-Mujhar."

"*You* will?" Donal stared. "You have not been there in seventeen years!"

Finn smiled. "I think it unlikely I would miss my *harani*'s wedding. I will come to Homana-Mujhar."

Donal laughed, and then he reached down to clasp his uncle's arm as it hugged Ian closely. "My thanks, *su'fali* . . . it has been too long. I think even the servants miss you."

"No. They miss the *stories* they told about me . . . no doubt they want fresh fodder." Finn slapped the stallion on his broad chestnut rump. "Go. Do not let the Mujhar fret about his daughter."

"No," Donal agreed. *But I will fret about mine, and with no one the wiser for it.* He motioned for Sef to mount his horse. "Tarry no longer, Sef. I do not wish to lose the sun before we reach Mujhara."

The boy caught his reins from the tree and climbed up into his saddle. He looked intently down at Bronwyn. "Perhaps I will see you again."

She still clasped her arms behind her back. Her amber eyes were slitted against the sunlight; they almost looked yellow. "Aye. Come back. Or I will come to Homana-Mujhar."

Sef eyed Donal. "If my lord allows me to."

"You will come to Homana-Mujhar, Bronwyn," Aislinn put in. "You and Meghan. When I am Queen, I will have to have women by me—I would have both of you."

Finn frowned at once. "Meghan does not belong at court. Her place is in the Keep."

"Jehan," the girl protested softly. "If Aislinn needs me there, of course I will go."

His tone was implacable. "This Keep is your home, Meghan. Homana-Mujhar would stifle you."

"Could I not learn it for myself?" She put a slim hand on his bare arm, and Donal saw how already she claimed a woman's gentle guile. "The Keep will always be my home, just as it is yours. But did you not spend years out of it?"

"Aye," Finn said harshly. "And you have heard what such folly brought me." His eyes were in Aislinn, but his tone indicated it was not the girl he saw. "The witch may no longer be there . . . but her memory survives."

Twelve

Donal's personal chambers were, perhaps, a bit ostentatious for a Cheysuli warrior better accustomed to the Keep—and preferring it—but he could not deny that the luxuries conferred a comfort he occasionally appreciated. Thick woven carpets of rich muted tones softened the hard stone floor; woolen tapestries of every hue hid the blank rock walls. A single fat white beeswax candle set in each of four shadowed casement ledges turned the stained glass into jewel-toned panoramas of Homanan history.

The chamber was warm as well; Donal's body-servant had lighted a fire that tinged the air with the smell of oak and ash. Donal did not doubt Torvald had also set warming pans beneath the bedclothes of his draped tester bed, but he had no intention of seeking his rest so soon. The sun had barely gone down. Aislinn had been delivered. It was early yet, and a task was left to do.

On the table near the bed rested a flagon of rich red Ellasian wine and four silver goblets. Donal filled two goblets, then motioned to Sef.

The boy, hanging back by the half-open door, stared. "*Me*, my lord?"

"There is no one else in the room." Donal smiled. "I poured the wine for you. Will you join me in a toast?"

Slowly, Sef moved forward. He accepted the goblet from Donal's hand and peered into the wine-filled depths. Light from candles and fire set the goblet's contents aflame and bathed Sef's pale face with a rosy glow. The hammered silver cast sparks of light into his eerie eyes. "My lord," he said, "a toast?"

Donal raised his goblet. "To my daughter. To Isolde of the Cheysuli."

Sef's breath fogged the silver of the goblet as he peered

nervously at Donal. "But—shouldn't this be shared with someone other than *me?*"

Donal shrugged. "Perhaps, were I the sort to care about such things. But, I can hardly ask the Mujhar to bless the birth of my bastard daughter." Donal did not smile. "*You* are here with me, and I would have you share my toast."

Sef stared at him over the rim of his silver goblet. Then, grinning suddenly, he drank deeply.

Watching the boy, Donal was glad of his companionship. He felt flat, empty, as if he yearned for a fulfillment he could not quite comprehend. He only knew he felt cheated of time with his *meijha*, his son, and his daughter, and all in the name of Homana.

Sorcha has the right of it. Fearing me for a shapechanger, the Homanans will do what they can to strip my Cheysuli habits from me and put Homanan in their place.

Instinctively he looked for Taj and Lorn, knowing no Homanan in all the world could strip him of *those* habits. Because if he were, there would be no Prince of Homana. There would be no Donal at all.

Lorn lay curled upon the tester bed, half hidden behind gauzy draperies. Like Donal, the wolf did not ignore luxury when it was offered. Taj had settled upon his perch in a corner of the chamber, setting beak to wing to smooth the shining feathers.

"My lord?" It was Sef, upper lip painted with wine until a tongue reached up to carry the smear away. "You said once I could ask you any question."

"Aye." Donal sat down on the nearest stool. "Why? Have you one?"

Sef's face was very solemn in the muted wash of candlelight. "Aye, my lord. I wondered why you do not like your sister."

Donal nearly dropped his goblet. "Sef! What makes you ask such a thing?"

"You said I could."

Donal, still shocked, stared at the boy whose set jaw indicated a burgeoning stubbornness. "But—*that* question," Donal said, when he could make sense out of his words again. "What would make you ask it? Of *course* I like my *rujholla.*"

Sef averted his eyes and stared down into his goblet, as

if his brief courage had failed him. "My lord—when we were at the Keep today . . . I—" He shrugged with discomfiture, "I just—thought perhaps you didn't like her. I mean—you seemed troubled by something." The eyes flicked up to meet Donal's again. "Was it because of what Bronwyn drew in the dust?"

Donal tossed down the remaining wine in his goblet and set it down on the rug with a thump. The boy's words troubled him deeply, but not because Sef had noticed his reaction at the Keep. Because he had reacted at all.

"A game," he said. "She said it was a game between the two of you."

"She told me it was—*magic*." Sef hunched thin shoulders. "I—I didn't want to draw the signs, but she said if I was to prove I was grown—" Color came and went in the fair face. "She said I was to draw the same signs *she* drew, because we could make the magic stronger. But—I was *afraid*." Sef's fingers clutched the goblet more tightly. "I remembered what you said about Cheysuli meaning no one any harm, but—I was afraid. She said I had to. And then she—laughed." Abruptly he drank more wine. It slopped against his face and washed over the rim of the goblet, trickling down the front of his livery. This time he did not lick the spillage from his upper lip. "My lord—Bronwyn frightens me. . . ."

And me. But Donal did not say so.

He bent and caught up his goblet, then rose and went to the table to fill the cup again. He did not look at the boy, did not consider the contradiction between the boy's words and his earlier actions, being too lost within his thoughts, and when he heard the voice at first he thought it was Sef's.

And then he realized it was Rowan, standing in the open doorway. "The Mujhar desires your presence in the Great Hall at once."

Rowan's smooth Cheysuli face, as always, expressed controlled calm neutrality. But Donal heard a faint note of tension in his tone.

He frowned. "I have just now gotten back from the Keep. Is it truly so important?" He made a gesture that included the remaining goblets. "Can you not join us in a drink to toast my daughter's birth?"

The candles sent a wash of light and shadows across

Rowan's dark face. He wore a plain doublet of dark blue velvet, freighted with silver at the collar; it glinted in the candlelight. "Electra," he said, "is free."

Sef gasped, shocked, then drew back awkwardly into the shadows, as if he knew it was not his place to interrupt prince and general. He clutched the goblet but did not drink.

A blurted denial died on Donal's tongue. He had only to look at Rowan's face to know the truth. "How?" he asked instead.

"We do not, as yet, have all the information we need. A messenger came—" Rowan shrugged. "The news was simply that the Queen had disappeared."

"From the *Crystal Isle?*" Donal shook his head. "There were Cheysuli with her!"

"They are dead," Rowan said. "Simply—dead. It appears they were poisoned. As for the Homanan guards . . . once the Cheysuli were dead, Electra was free to use her magic."

Unsteadily, Donal set his goblet down on the table. "Cheysuli—murdered?"

He could not conceive of how it had been accomplished. Cheysuli warriors with attentive *lir* did not succumb to poison, not when they guarded a known witch. Not when they guarded the woman Tynstar called his own.

"Poison," he said intently, recalling his bout with the same. "Could she have grown it, or had it grown?"

"All food was brought in from Hondarth. *All* food," Rowan said. "The Cheysuli inspected it."

"Tynstar," Donal said instantly.

The faintest flicker of consternation creased Rowan's brow. "Every precaution was taken." His voice, once untroubled, now was underscored with frustration. "She was guarded by Cheysuli for that very purpose. *No* Ihlini could have gotten past the warriors."

Donal, frowning, chewed at his bottom lip. "I would not put it beyond Electra's abilities to concoct the poison herself, with Tynstar's help. They are linked. How else could Electra have entered Aislinn's mind?"

Rowan shook his head. The firelight picked out the faintest flecks of silver in his thick black hair. "All in all, it is less important to know how it was accomplished than to discover where she is. Where *she* is Tynstar will also be . . . and he is the one we must slay."

"Then—it is war." Donal felt the breath leave his chest. "By the gods—*it is*—"

"Did you think it would never come?" Rowan said grimly. "Did you believe the Mujhar spoke of the possibility out of boredom, having nothing else to do?"

Donal heard the faint undertone of scorn. Aye, he was due that from Rowan. Too often the general had watched Carillon's heir seek escape from princely duties. Too often that heir had turned his back on Homana-Mujhar to spend his time at the Keep.

The gods know Rowan has sacrificed enough for his lord. He would expect me to do the same.

But for the moment, he put off the guilt and lost himself in consideration. "You wish to know where Tynstar is?" He frowned, staring blindly toward the hearth. "He is in Solinde. He will rouse the nobles in the name of Bellam, their fallen king, *and* in the name of Electra. He needs her. To the people, she is the rightful Queen of Solinde. And he will promise sorcerous aid from the god of the netherworld . . . the Solindish, having turned to such things before, will turn to it again."

The dark flesh drawn so taut over Rowan's prominent cheekbones softened just a little. He did not smile, but a weight seemed to lift from his velvet-clad shoulders. "You have more awareness than I expected—I thought Carillon would have to explain it all to you."

Donal shook his head intently. "I have learned more over the years than you may know, for all I was a poor student. But I see it more clearly now." He thought again of Electra, free; Electra, aiding Tynstar. *Oh gods, how do we stop the carnage that will come of this alliance?* He blew out a breath and looked at Rowan. "We will have to go to Solinde."

There was a glint of appreciation in Rowan's eyes. "We move an army into Solinde. Our borders are patrolled, but we will need to send aid, and soon. We cannot afford to let Tynstar breach our borders."

"When?"

"That is for Carillon to say. But I think you will know soon enough, if you go to see him as he wishes."

"Of course." Donal looked for the boy. "Sef—the time is your own. I will send for you if I need you."

"Aye, my lord—*my lord*—!" The boy hastened forward as Donal turned to go. "My lord—if you go to war . . . will you take me with you?"

Donal looked down on the anxious boy. "War, I have heard, is not particularly pleasant. Perhaps you would do better staying here."

"I'd rather go with you." Sef's tone was defiantly adamant, but his thin face was hollowed with fear.

I am his only security, Donal realized in surprise. *He would rather go with me into danger than stay behind in safety.*

He set one hand on Sef's thin shoulder. "I will not leave you, Sef. Your service is with me."

The Great Hall lay deep in shadow. The candle racks were crowded with pale, fat tapers, but all had been snuffed out. Donal smelled the faint odor of beeswax and smoking wicks; that, and the scent of dying coals. The firepit—a trench stretching the length of the massive hall—was heaped with ash and glowing coals. The center of the hall was illuminated only by the pit, and a single torch in a bracket near the throne.

For a moment, night-blinded by distorting shadows, Donal believed the place deserted. He stared down the length of the hall, frowning into the darkness, but then—as his eyes became accustomed to the glow from the firepit coals—he saw Carillon at last.

He sat sunken into the ancient wooden throne carved in the shape of a lion. It crouched on curling paws with claws extended, gilded with golden paint. The headpiece was a snarling face, rearing up over Carillon's head. The lion seemed almost to spring out of the darkness as if it sought prey.

The torch cast flickering light across the wood, glinting on the gold. Illumination painted Carillon's bearded face and crept down to silver the knife at his belt. A Cheysuli longknife with a wolf-shaped hilt, made and once owned by Finn.

Donal halted before the dais. He felt oppressed by the huge hall. The arching hammer-beamed timbers loomed over his head; the far wall, full of weapons, crests, and leaded casements, menaced him as it never had before. He took a deep breath and tried to steady the banging of his heart.

"Rowan—told me." His voice echoed in the vastness of the blackened hall.

Carillon did not stir. "Did he? Did he tell you what it means?"

After a moment, Donal nodded. "It means war has come at last."

Slowly Carillon leaned forward. The torch behind the throne spilled light down his back, setting the crimson velvet of his doublet aglow like a dim beacon amid the shadows of the dais. "War was *expected*. I am not taken unaware by the news. But—the manner of it is somewhat *un*expected." He put his age-wracked hands to his weary face. His fingers massaged the flesh of his brow and pushed back a lock of hair from his eyes. "Electra, with Tynstar—after all these years . . . we face potential disaster."

Donal stepped forward. "We face *war*, my lord. Forget those who are involved, and think only upon the strategies necessary."

The hands dropped from the face. Carillon actually smiled. "Do you seek to teach *me* what war is about?" But before Donal could answer, he waved a twisted hand. "No, no, say nothing. The mood, for the moment, has passed. It is only that I recalled what she did to me so many years ago—how she nearly castrated me, without even touching a blade. Ah, no—her weapon was merely herself. Gods—*but what a woman she was.*" Stiffly, he pushed himself up from the throne. "I do not expect you to understand. But what you *must* comprehend is that paired, they are doubly dangerous. Tynstar will use her to gather all the Solindishmen he will need—the warhost will be massive. It will be an exceedingly difficult conflict." He moved to the torch and took it down from its bracket. "Donal—do you do as I bid you?"

Donal watched him step off the dais and walk purposefully toward the far end of the hall. "Usually," he answered cautiously.

"Then do so now." Carillon's voice echoed. "Come with me to the Womb of the Earth."

A grue ran down Donal's spine. The hairs stood up on the back of his neck. "I have—heard of it," he said. "In the histories of my race."

Carillon took the light with him, leaving Donal in the shadowed darkness of the throne. "Now you will see it, Donal. Now you will go where I have gone."

"You!" Donal turned to stare after the Mujhar. "You have been to the Womb of the Earth?"

"A Homanan." Carillon's tone was scored with caustic irony. "Aye, I have. I thought Finn might have told you."

"There are secret things in every man's life." Donal belatedly followed in Carillon's wake. "My *su'fali* does not tell me everything . . . nor, apparently, do you." He stopped short as Carillon halted at the edge of the firepit.

"Here," the Mujhar said. "The entrance is—here."

Donal frowned. His gesture encompassed the tiles of the floor. *"Here?"*

"Blind," Carillon muttered in disgust. "A Cheysuli warrior—and blind." He thrust the torch into Donal's hands and stepped over the rim of the firepit. Before Donal could blurt out his surprise, the Mujhar kicked aside unlighted wood and pushed away the residue of former fires.

Donal coughed as a layer of ask rose into the air. Carillon bent down and grasped an ash-filmed iron ring set into the bottom of the trench. Donal heard the grate of metal on stone, and then Carillon went down on one knee. His breath was ragged in his throat.

"Carillon—?" Donal moved forward at once, bending to touch one hunched shoulder. "My lord—?"

Carillon shook his head and waved a hand. "No—no—I am well enough. But—I think it will require a younger, straighter back." Slowly he rose, one hand pressing against his spine. "Give me the torch. The task is yours to do."

Donal handed him the torch and stepped into the firepit. Frowning, he bent and grasped the ring with both hands, half-expecting to flinch from the warmth of the metal. But it was cool to the touch, though gritty with ash and charcoal.

He spread and braced his legs, gathering his strength. Then, grunting with the effort, he peeled back the iron plate that formed a lid and let it fall clanging against the stone. He stared down into blackness.

Stale air engulfed his face. Instantly he lunged backward, seeking a safer distance. "Gods," he said, "down *there?*"

"Why not?" Carillon asked. "The last man down there was me."

Donal scowled. He knew what Carillon did. The Mujhar had only to appeal to his pride, and his invitation became a thing Donal *had* to do.

"I have the light," Carillon sounded suspiciously amused. "I will lead the way."

"Should I summon my *lir?*" Donal said with subtle condescension, though he still felt genuine consternation.

"No. There are plenty of them where we go." Carillon stepped past Donal and slowly made his way down the narrow stairs.

Donal was left alone in the darkness of the hall. After a moment, he followed the guttering torch.

It is a hole in the earth, Donal thought. *A deep, utterly black hole, seeking to swallow me up.* Down he went, following the Mujhar. *Carillon has gone mad. The news of Electra's escape has driven him over the edge.* But even as he thought it, he knew it was not true. Electra's escape would simply make Carillon more careful in his planning.

He could hardly see, for the torch Carillon carried smoked badly in the darkness, casting shadows into indistinct planes and hollows so that walls merged with ceiling and the steps, shallow and tapering, faded into opacity. He put one hand against the nearest wall, to steady himself.

The surface was cool, growing more damp with every step. He smelled the moldy odor of dampness, the spice of ancient stone. It filled his senses with the perfume of agedness, and his belly with trepidation.

"There are a hundred and two of them." Carillon's voice echoed oddly in the narrow staircase. "I counted them, once."

"A hundred and two?"

"Steps." Carillon's brief laugh was distorted. "What did you think I meant? Demons?"

Donal did not laugh. His bare arms and face were filmed with clammy moisture. His hair hung limply against his shoulders and fell into his eyes. "How much farther?"

"We are here." The echo sounded closer. Torchlight flared up to fill the passageway and Donal saw that they stood in a space the size of a privacy closet. The Mujhar waited. Against the blackness, painted by torchlight, his hair formed a silver nimbus. "Do you see?" Carillon pointed.

Donal looked. He saw almost immediately what the Mujhar indicated: a line of runes carved into the damp stone walls. Time and seepage had shallowed the figures until they were little more than faint greenish tracings, but Donal recognized the shapes.

He looked at Carillon. "Cheysuli built this palace. It does not surprise me that in the very foundations would be the Old Tongue runes."

"Firstborn runes." Carillon did not smile. "It was your father who brought me here, Donal. With no explanation, he brought me here to show me the Womb of the Earth, so I would know what it was to be Cheysuli."

Quick resentment flared in Donal's chest. "You are Homanan. No man save a warrior can know what it is to be Cheysuli."

"For four days, I did. It was—necessary." Carillon put out a hand to the wall, seeking the proper stone. He found it, pressed, and a portion of the wall turned on edge.

A gust of stale air rushed out of the vault, but it was tinged with the tang of life. Shut up the place may have been, but it was not a deathtrap. A man could go in with impunity.

Carillon thrust the torch through the opening and the flames lit up the darkness. Donal, still hanging back at the bottom of the steps, saw the merest trace of creamy color within the vault, and the sheen of polished marble.

The torchlight was cruel to Carillon's face. Donal saw every crease, every line, every etching emphasized by the flames. But the eyes were endlessly patient.

He stepped past the Mujhar and entered the cream-colored vault. Torchlight danced and hissed, sending the shadows scuttling up walls and ceiling into cracks and crevices. The walls seemed almost to move as he entered, and he saw how the gold-veined marble took life from the roaring flames.

Lir. Lir upon *lir*, leaping out of the stone. He saw bear and hawk and owl and boar, fox and wildcat and wolf. He saw all the *lir* and more, lining every inch of the marble walls and ceiling. No surface was untouched, uncarved.

"Cheysuli i'halla shansu," Carillon said very quietly. *"Ja'hai, cheysu, Mujhar."*

Donal spun and faced the man. The words had been fluent and unaccented: *May there be Cheysuli peace upon you*, and *accept this man, this Mujhar*. He almost thought it was a Cheysuli who spoke the Old Tongue. But it was Carillon, Homanan to the bone, who faced him in the vault.

He drew in a careful breath. "Are you not a *little* premature?"

"Because I ask the gods to accept you?" Carillon smiled. "No. Acceptance may be requested at any time; only occasionally is it given when one asks it." For a moment, he said nothing. When he spoke again, his voice was eloquently gentle, as if he spoke to a simple child. "Donal—you *will* be Mujhar. But it is up to you to make your peace with it if the gods are to accept you."

Resentment flared; he thought of Sorcha, begging him not to leave his heritage behind. And here was Homanan Carillon admonishing him the same. "My *tahlmorra* is quite clear, my lord Mujhar," he said with a deadly pointedness. "I accepted it long ago, since neither you nor the gods— nor my *jehan*—ever gave me a choice."

Carillon did not indicate that the answer—or tone— troubled him in the least. He seemed supremely indifferent to Donal's feelings, as if what his heir thought was of no importance to him when weighed against the balance of the present and the future.

"Look around you, Donal," he said gently. "No man who is to be Mujhar can avoid facing his heritage. Duncan proved that to me when he brought me here. For all I am not Cheysuli, he made me see it was *your* race which made Homana strong. I accepted it and, for a brief time, I accepted the gift the gods saw fit to give me. For me, it was held within those depths." He nodded in the direction behind Donal's head. "For you, it may be something else."

Slowly Donal glanced around the vault. Gold and ivory gleamed. Momentarily he thought he saw a falcon's wingtip move; then he saw the patch of blackness in the floor. It was a hole. A perfectly round hole, extending into the depths.

"Oubliette," he breathed. Swiftly he looked at Carillon as the implications came very clear. "You do not *mean*—"

Carillon's voice was perfectly steady. "For me, it was required. For you—I cannot say. It is a thing between you and the gods."

Donal moved closer to the oubliette. The torchlight was swallowed up, and he could see nothing past the perfectly rounded rim. Nothing at all.

And yet he saw everything.

He closed his eyes. The iron collar of comprehension was locked around his throat. "When will the marriage be made?"

"Within the month." Carillon sounded neither surprised nor pleased, as if he had expected the comprehension. "It gives us time to gather guests so it can all be done quite properly. I cannot have Tynstar believing he has frightened me into this move merely to secure the throne."

"Of course." Donal was aware of an odd lack of emotion in himself. Shock? He thought not. Perhaps it was merely that there was no more room for vacillation. "And the march into Solinde?"

"Within two months after the wedding." Carillon did not smile. "It gives you time to beget an heir."

The flames roared in the marble vault with its ivory menagerie. "Do you take the torch with you?"

"Of course. It is a part of the thing."

Donal nodded. Curiously, he felt no fear, no desperation, no resentment of Carillon's calm pronouncement of his fate. He merely felt that all of it had to be done, in order to temper the links in the chain they forged.

He smiled at Carillon. "*Ja'hai-na*, my lord Mujhar. *Cheysuli i'halla shansu.*"

Thirteen

He heard the scrape of stone on stone; the sibilant grate of limestone wall against marble floor. The torch was gone, leaving only the crackle of vanishing flames in his ears and the blossom of fading fire in his eyes. When the noise and the light were gone, he was left alone in darkness.

Donal shivered. The vault was cool, but he thought the quiver through his body came from more than merely that. He was not precisely afraid, but neither was he perfectly at ease. Given the choice again, he might walk out of the vault instead of allowing the Mujhar to leave him.

He sucked in a belly-deep breath, held it a moment, then released it. He shut his eyes, seeking to measure the darkness of the vault against the darkness all men claimed, and found it brighter behind his lids. He opened them again.

"Shansu," he said, to see if the word would echo. It did, but oddly, falling away into the oubliette that gaped in the floor of the vault.

He put out his hand toward the wall that formed a door. He found it silk-smooth from the skill of the master craftsman who had brought the *lir* to life. Like the walls, the door was made of marble except for the corridor side, which was dark, pitted limestone. Through the darkness, he knew this side was a perfect creamy ivory, veined with purest gold. In another palace, it would be a monument for all to admire; in Homana-Mujhar, it was a place of subtle secrets.

"Ja'hai," he said. Slowly, he moved away from the wall. The edge of the pit felt near. Carefully, he poised himself on the rim, and knelt to make his obeisance to the gods. *"Tahlmorra lujhala mei wiccan, cheysu."*

He tucked his boots beneath him, settling his knees against the marble. His palms he pressed flat against the

floor; his fingers curled over the circular rim of the oubliette. He bowed his head and opened himself to what the
gods would send him.

Silence. Darkness. A perfect cessation of movement.

He sat. He felt the beating of his heart. He felt the rush
of blood through his veins. He heard the quiet whisper of
his breathing. He let himself go.

Slowly.

One piece at a time.

He freed himself from the bindings of his body, and let
his spirit expand. He felt his awareness slipping away.

He let it slip—

—and then it came rushing back.

Light blazed up in the vault. He stared blindly at the
marble wall so full of shining *lir*, and saw the shadow cast
upon it.

Slender. Hooded. Cloaked.

Moving toward me—

—and the torch raised to strike him down.

Donal thrust himself upward, spinning in place at the
edge of the oubliette. He saw only the outline of the
shrouded figure; no face, merely two delicate, slender
hands. And the torch.

The flames burned his eyes, now used to darkness, and
he knew the fire would blind him.

In silence, he thrust up his bare left arm. He felt the heat
of the flames as they scorched his flesh; he smelled the
stench of the charnelhouse. Pain blossomed. He heard himself cry out.

Again the torch thrust for his face; again he thrust it
away. He felt the burned flesh of his arm crack, and the
sticky wetness of blood.

The attack had done its work. Off-balance, teetering on
the brink, Donal reached out to catch the assassin's arm
and caught the flames instead. He fell backward into
darkness.

With a muted scream, he stretched out his arms and tried
to catch the rim.

*Fingers scraped. Bone bruised. Clawing grip slipped and
released.*

His head, thrown back on an arching neck, knocked
against the edge of the marble pit.

Tumbling.

Blind, he felt his body twisting helplessly. He had no coordination. A hand scrabbled briefly against a wall; an elbow banged; bootleather scrapped itself raw. But mostly he tumbled, touching nothing but air.

Blind. Deaf. Tasting the hot acid spurt of bile into his throat.

And then he opened his mouth and shouted a denial of his fate.

His arm dragged briefly against the silk-smooth, rounded wall. Muscles protested, stretching; he heard the chiming scrape of metal against the marble.

His *lir*-band.

Gods—I am a Cheysuli warrior! Why fall *when I can* fly—?

He thrust out both arms. Human arms, lacking feathers or falcon bones. Frenziedly he reached for *lir*-shape, but nothing answered his call.

Slow . . . it is so slow . . . I will never *strike the ground.*

And if he did not strike the ground, perhaps he would not die.

He felt the air against his body. There was no wind, except air rushing past as he fell. The part of him that was falcon, the part that understood the patterns of flight realized he would have to slow himself significantly if he was to alter a downward fall into the uprush of life-saving flight.

He twitched. Sweat broke out on his body. He reached for the shapechange again.

Upside down. The jerk of trapped air against outstretched wings.

Carefully he tipped one wing, swung over, and tried to angle a climb. But he had miscalculated. The sudden change in size and distribution of his weight sent him slicing through the air, directly at the wall. His fall was curbed, but now his momentum smashed him toward the marble.

The falcon's wings strained toward even flight. Willpower lifted him upward, veering away from the wall. And yet the oubliette, in its purity of form, nearly defeated him. The left wingtip caught the silk of the marble and the vibration ran up into his body. His direction changed. He slipped sideways unto the opposite side.

Left wing snapping with dull finality.

Somehow, he flogged the air. Pain screamed through his

hollow bones and reverberated in his skull. Still, somehow, he flew. Perhaps he had not fallen as far as he had feared. He flew, desperately shedding pinfeathers, and reached the edge of the pit.

Falling.

He felt the floor rise up to strike him, battering brittle bones, and then he lost the shapechange. In human-form, Donal flopped across the stone.

Sound filled up the vault. He heard it clearly: a husky, raspy, throaty sobbing, as if it came from a man with no breath left to cry aloud.

He was wet with sweat. His leathers were soaked, rank with the smell of his fear. He lay belly-down on the floor of the vault and pressed his face into the stone, compressing flesh against the bone.

No light.

The torch was gone. He lay in total darkness. But for the moment he did not care; all he wanted was to know he was alive.

His left arm, he knew, was broken. An injury in *lir*-shape translated to the same in human form. How badly the bone was broken he could not say; the dull snap of his falcon's wing indicated it was not a simple fracture. It was possible the bone had shattered. Bound, it might heal, but it was difficult to bind up flesh already badly burned.

"*Lir*," he said aloud. It hissed in the darkness of the vault.

He gathered what strength he could and sent the appeal through the link. Lir . . . *by the gods, how I need you!*

When he could, Donal pulled his sound arm back toward his body, doubling the elbow beneath his ribs. He tensed, levered himself up, then curled up onto his knees to sit upon his legs. The left arm he cradled briefly against his belly, rocking gently on his heels as if he were a child, but left off both cradling and rocking almost immediately. It hurt too much to move or touch the arm.

"My thanks," he said aloud, and heard the hoarseness of his voice. "If this was the test of acceptance . . . I would not care to repeat it."

He tried to regulate his breathing. He tried to hoard his waning strength. *Lir*-shape was gone, he knew; he was in too much pain to hold either form. But it would do little good if he could. With the wall shut, even a wolf or falcon would know captivity.

He felt the sweat of pain drip off his face. He shut his eyes and waited.

"Donal."

A band of dull pain cinched his brow like a fillet of heavy iron. His lip bled from where he had bitten it. He tasted the salt-copper tang. Sweat ran down his face; no more the dampness of fear.

He dared not open his mouth, even to ease his lip, or he would disgrace himself.

"Donal." It was Carillon's voice, from where he stood at his bedside. "Donal—Finn is here."

His eyes snapped open. Through a haze of fever and pain he saw Finn come into the room. "*Su'fali,*" he whispered hoarsely, "tell them no, tell them *no*—" He shifted against the bedclothes, trying to outdistance the pain. "*Su'fali,* tell them no. They want to take my arm."

Carillon looked at Finn compassionately, but tension was in his tone. "The bones are badly broken. And the burns—they could poison him in three days."

"You cannot take his arm." Finn moved toward the bed with Storr padding at his side. "You know better, Carillon."

"What do I know? That foolishness about a maimed warrior not being a useful man?" Carillon thrust out his twisted hands. "See you these? *I* am crippled, Finn—but I rule Homana still!"

Finn bent over his nephew. "A maimed warrior cannot fight. He cannot hunt. He cannot tend his pavilion. He cannot protect his woman or his children. He cannot protect himself." He felt Donal's burning brow. "You know all this, Carillon—I was the one who told you. A maimed warrior cannot serve his clan, nor can he serve the prophecy. He is useless to his people."

Carillon stood at the bedside. He was trembling. Donal saw it in his hands, in his face; in the rigidity of his spine. The grayish pallor of shock was slowly replaced with the flush of rising anger. "You threaten that very prophecy by sentencing him to death."

"I sentence Donal to nothing. I will heal him. Is that not why you sent for me?"

"And if the healing does not work?" Carillon challenged.
"Occasionally it does not."

"Occasionally, when the gods see fit to deny it." Finn
did not spare a glance for the lord he had once so loyally
served. "Donal—what happened?"

His arm pained. "Carillon took me to the Womb of the
Earth," he said breathlessly. "He left me there. I—gave
myself up to the gods. But someone came. Someone—came
at me with the torch. I—fell." He shut his eyes a moment.
"When I could, I took *lir*-shape, but I could not control
the fall. I—could not—fly properly. And so—I hit the wall."

Finn nodded. He glanced around for a stool, found one,
hooked it over with a booted foot. In the light from a dozen
candles, the gold of his *lir*-bands gleamed. "Nothing more,"
he said quietly, sitting down upon the stool. "Nothing more
until I am done, and the arm is whole again." Briefly he
smiled. "*Shansu*, Donal . . . I will take the pain away."

"*Ru'shalla-tu,*" Donal said weakly. *May it be so.*

He closed his eyes. He felt the encouragement of both
his *lir* and the presence of Storr as well. Finn did not touch
him—he merely sat on the stool and looked at Donal—but
after a moment his eyes went opaque and detached. The
yellow was swallowed by black.

Donal drifted. He was bodiless, bound by nothing but
the pain. It flared and died, pulsing in time with his heart;
he wondered if they were linked. But then, slowly, he felt
the pain diminish, and the beating stopped altogether.

Am I dead? he wondered briefly, and found he did not
care.

Floating—

—painlessness swallowed him.

Donal slept for three days following the healing, and on
the fourth he got out of bed. In dressing he discovered
there was no pain in his healed arm, no stiffness in the
bone. Only new flesh, too pink against the sunbronzing of
older skin.

Shall we come with you? Lorn inquired as Donal tugged
on his boots.

No. I only go to see Carillon.

Taj, fluffed to twice his size as he hunched on his perch,
emitted a single permissive sound. Lorn yawned, stretched,

then rose to seek out a warmer place in Donal's bed. Wolflike, he turned three times in place before settling down. *Lir*like, he thanked Donal for his leftover warmth.

Donal went at once to Carillon's private solar to speak of what had happened, and found Finn and Alix there as well. He had vague memories of them standing at his bedside, discussing the state of his health; he recalled also that he had tried, once, to tell them to go away, so he could get some sleep. He had slept, but he did not know if they had heeded his suggestion.

Alix sat on a three-legged stool before the fireplace, indigo skirts spread around her feet as she nursed a goblet of hot wine; Donal could see the faintest breath of steam rising from the surface. Finn sat in a deep-silled casement, silhouetted against the sunlight and framed by chiseled stone. At his feet lay Storr, eyes shut. Carillon filled a tooled leather chair with his legs stretched out before him. From the tight-drawn look of the flesh around the Mujhar's eyes, Donal knew he was in pain.

"*One* good thing has come of this. . . ." Donal shut the heavy door. "It brought my *su'fali* back to Homana-Mujhar."

Finn swung a booted foot. His smile was very faint. "I said I would come to your wedding. This is not so very premature."

"Should you be up?" inquired his mother. "Finn told us you might sleep for days."

"I have." He waved her back down as she started to rise. "And aye, I should be up—or I will take root in that bed." He scratched idly at the new flesh above and below the heavy golden *lir*-band on his arm. "Well, at least this way you two aging warriors may speak of old times without a hundred sycophants listening to every word."

Carillon shifted in the chair, clutching an armrest with one hand. "Old times can wait. For now, we need to learn precisely what has happened." He moved into a more upright position, straightening the hunched shoulders. "Gods . . . when I remember the howling Lorn set up . . . and Taj would not stop flying around the hall. . . ." He shook his head. "I left you alone in the Womb because that is the way it must be done. *Lir*less. Absolutely alone. I gave orders for *no one* to enter the hall. How could anyone have known?"

"The Womb is not entirely secret," Finn pointed out. "All Cheysuli know of it—though not precisely where; we are taught about it as children. It is one of the first lessons the *shar tahls* give us." He frowned. "Still—I doubt any Homanans would know of it, save yourself. Who else is in this palace?"

"Oh Finn, you cannot expect us to believe someone from Carillon's *household* did this!" Alix shook her head. "They are too loyal to Carillon."

"Loyal to Carillon and *Homana*," Finn said evenly. "Rank aside, there is a fundamental difference between Carillon and Donal."

Alix looked back at him levelly. The sunlight lay full on her face, leaching shadows from planes and angles to give her youth again. Donal could almost see the seventeen-year-old girl Finn had stolen from Carillon, then lost to his older brother.

But the moment was fleeting; Donal, looking from his mother to his uncle, saw only a warrior and a woman, kin to one another through their father. Hale was in their faces.

And had it not been for that jehan *and Carillon's foolish cousin, none of us would be here.*

"Foreigners, then." Carillon scratched at his beard. "Well, there is Gryffth. The Ellasian Lachlan sent me—was it fifteen years ago?" He frowned, plainly shocked to find so much time had passed. "But he is the only foreigner in the palace at the moment. And Gryffth I trust with *my* life, as well as Donal's. He helped Duncan and me win Alix free of Tynstar." Carillon shook his head. "No, not Gryffth."

"No," Finn agreed. One boot heel tapped against the wall.

Donal perched himself upon the edge of a sturdy table and helped himself to wine. "I could not begin to hazard a guess. I know there are Homanans who would sooner see me something *other* than Carillon's heir—and back in the Keep, no doubt—" he shrugged a little, mouth twisted wryly "—but I doubt any of them would wish to have me *slain*—" Abruptly, he set the wine cup down. "No—perhaps I am wrong. My reception in Hondarth was not precisely—warm."

"What are you saying?" Carillon sat upright in his chair. "What have you been keeping from me?"

Donal saw how attentively Finn and Alix waited for his answer. And so he told them all, briefly, of the confrontation with the Homanan and the manure that had been thrown. "I felt it was not significant enough to tell you," he said finally to Carillon. "It was—unpleasant—but nothing to fret the Mujhar." He turned the cup in circles on the wooden tabletop, idly watching how the silver rolled against the satiny hardwood finish. "But—I *do* begin to see that not all of Homana is reconciled to the ending of the *qu'mahlin.*"

"Nor ever will be," Finn agreed.

Alix, mute but obviously disturbed, picked worriedly at the nap of her indigo skirts.

"I am not surprised," Finn went on calmly. "I think there are many Homanans who care little enough that we *exist*— there is nothing they can do about that, short of starting another *qu'mahlin*—but I also think they would actively resist a Cheysuli as Mujhar. And you are next in line."

Donal frowned. "But would they try to have me *slain?*"

Alix's mouth was grim as she looked at Finn. "Would they?"

He shrugged. "It is possible. Shaine's *qu'mahlin* was a powerful thing. It bred hatred and fear upon hatred and fear, and fed off of violence and ignorance." He glanced at the Mujhar. "I remember what it was like when Carillon and I came back from Caledon. The purge was over, but there were many Homanans who desired to see me dead." For the first time a trace of bleakness entered his tone. "We would be wise not to discount the possibility that the *qu'mahlin* still exists for those who wish it to."

"Even *now?*" Donal demanded. "You and Carillon came back nearly twenty years ago. Time has passed. Things change. People get older and less inclined to violence." He shrugged. "Perhaps there are some bigots left, but surely not enough to do Homana harm."

Finn eyed him. "I am fifty. *Old*, to your way of thinking, *harani*. And would you consider *me* a nonviolent man?"

Fifty. Donal had not counted up the years lately. To him, Finn was ageless. And certainly never incapable of violence. "No," he said distinctly, and Finn smiled his ironic smile.

Carillon rubbed wearily at his brow. "Gods—will it *never* end? What will happen when I am dead?"

"When you are dead it will be Donal's problem." Finn stretched out one foot and touched the toe of the boot to Storr's left ear. "There is another problem for us to settle before that one comes upon us."

"Such as: who tried to murder my son," Alix said flatly. "Oh, aye, let us turn our attention to *that*."

Donal shook his head. "I saw nothing clearly. Only light, fire—a shape. Someone hooded and cloaked."

"Think back," Finn advised. "Call up the memory. Think what you saw before you fell."

"Fire," Donal repeated, recalling that too clearly. "Flames from the torch. It was thrust at me—I threw up my arm to block it." He suited action to words. "I was thrown off balance—I stepped back . . . and fell." He shuddered, recalling the sensation of weightlessness. "I did not even hear the wall open."

"Think again," Finn said patiently. "You saw a hooded, cloaked figure. Tall? Short? Heavy? Slender?" The toe caressed Storr's ear, flipping it up and down. "Think of everything you saw—even the bits and pieces. If there is an assassin in this place, he will likely try again."

Donal was conscious of their waiting faces, reflecting expectations. He frowned in concentration, summoning up the memory in vivid recollection. "Much shorter than I—even you, *su'fali*. Slender. The cloak was not a large one. And I remember hands." He sat up so rigidly he nearly overturned the table. "Hands! The hands upon the torch!" He stared blindly at Finn, seeing only the hands upon the torch. "Slim, pale, delicate hands, clutching a torch that seemed too heavy, too awkward for a man—" He stopped short. Stunned, he turned to Carillon. "My lord—it was a *woman*—"

Color drained out of Carillon's face and left it a bearded deathmask. "By the gods—*say it was not Electra*—"

Finn shook his head. "Electra is not here. Believe it—I would know it. The trap-link has bound us forever."

Donal still stared at Carillon. "But—what if it were *Aislinn*—"

"Oh, Donal, *no!*" Alix cried as Carillon thrust himself out of his chair.

"Have you gone mad?" the Mujhar asked hoarsely. "Do

you think *Aislinn* could seek to push you into the Womb of the Earth?"

"No more than *Bronwyn* could," Alix said.

Donal's hand, reaching for the goblet, knocked it over abruptly. He heard the dull chime of silver rim against dark hardwood; the sibilant splatter of wine against carpeted floor. But he did nothing to pick up the overturned goblet. Instead, he looked at his mother in something akin to shock.

"How can we say that?" he asked. "How can we say for *certain* Bronwyn would never do it?"

Alix thrust herself up from her stool. "Have you gone *mad?*" Unconsciously, she echoed Carillon. "She is your *sister*—"

"And Tynstar's daughter, do not forget." That from Finn, still seated in the casement. "Alix—*before* you seek Carillon's knife to throw at me—make yourself think clearly a moment." He swung his foot again idly. "She is Tynstar's daughter. Ihlini as well as Cheysuli, no matter what you have done to hide it from her and everybody else. Who can say what Bronwyn is capable of if the Ihlini in her seeks to dominate?"

"No," Alix said tautly. "Not Bronwyn, how could she? She is at the Keep."

"Not *Aislinn*," Carillon said. "Look to another culprit."

"Aislinn tried to slay me in Hondarth," Donal reminded him deliberately, and saw the shock in his mother's face. "Aye—I did not tell you. It was Electra's ensorcelment. But who is to say she has not tried it yet again?"

Carillon thrust a hand in Finn's direction. "You said he *tested* her!"

"I tested her." Finn slid out of the casement and stood before his Mujhar. "I swear—I tested her. There was an echo—a resonance—I thought I had rid her of it."

Donal grimly picked up the fallen goblet and set it straight again. "And if you did not?"

"If I did not, and she *is* Tynstar's weapon, there is yet another test," Finn said simply. "Let her try again."

Donal opened his mouth to protest vehemently, but his intention was overridden by a thin voice raised on the other side of the door. "My lord! My lord! A message for you from the Keep!"

"Sef," Donal said, and went to tug open the heavy door.

Sef nearly fell into the room. His hair was blown back from his face and he breathed as if he had run all the way up three flights of spiraling stairs. "My lord—a message from the Keep. From your *meijha*." He paused, caught his breath. "She says your sister is missing. Bronwyn is not at the Keep."

Donal heard the swift, indrawn breath from Alix standing behind him. "What else does Sorcha say?" he asked the boy.

"She says you had better come home to look for Bronwyn. She has been gone since yesterday."

Oh—gods . . . was all Donal could manage in the face of his mother's fear.

But it was Finn who had the answer. "*Lir*-shape," was all he said. "It will be faster than going by horse."

"Wolf-shape, then," from Alix. "You have no recourse to wings."

Lir, Donal called, and led the way out of the solar.

And behind them, as they left the old man with the boy, Carillon cursed his infirmities.

Five wolves and a falcon fled through sunlight into the shadows of the sunset. Silver Storr and ruddy Finn; ruddy Lorn and grayish Donal ran shoulder to shoulder with Alix, the pale silver wolf-bitch with black-tipped tail. And above them all flew a fleet golden falcon.

In *lir*-shape, Donal was aware of an edge to his apprehension. He was frightened for what they might find once they found her; he was worried that they would not find her at all. And if they did not, and she had come at last into a share of her father's powers, only the gods could say what Bronwyn might do to them all.

But the edge began to creep out from under his fear and express a new emotion. Anger. Frustration. Impatience and helplessness. And they drove him to the edge of infinity.

What if I stayed *in wolf-shape?* he wondered. *What happens if a warrior chooses to give up his human form for the other shape he claims?*

Inwardly, he flinched away from the questions. All Cheysuli, male and female alike, were taught that *lir*-shape was only a temporary guise, borrowed from the earth. *In borrowing, the borrower must return that form which is bor-*

rowed. Donal had always believed the statement redundant; borrowing something meant it *had* to be returned, or it was stealing. Even as a child, he had understood the concepts very well.

But now, so lost within the essence of the shape, he wondered how it could be considered stealing when what he wore was an integral part of his *self.*

A lirless Cheysuli is not a man, but a shadow. He dwells in darkness of mind and body. He is driven mad by the loss, and gives himself over to death.

There was a ritual, of course, because there had to be. Otherwise, the giving over of a life to the gods would be considered suicide, and that was taboo.

Vines and creepers slashed Donal's face. A thorn tore at his muzzle, drawing beads of blood. Curving nails dug deeply into the damp, cool soil, gouging furrows and leaving tracks. But the tracks were spoor of the wolf, not the trail of a man.

He heard himself panting. But how could he be weary? In this shape he had almost endless endurance, because he knew how to pace himself.

Odors filled his nose. Moist earth, old wood, rotting bark, nearby stream . . . but mostly he smelled fear. On himself and on the others.

Can a warrior maintain lir-shape as long as he desires it?

As a child, he had asked his father. Duncan had told him a warrior probably could retain *lir*-shape for as long as he desired; perhaps *longer* than he desired.

The last had frightened him. Intuitively, he had understood. A man left too long in *lir*-shape might never turn back into a man.

But would that be so bad?

No. But what if he were ever to change his mind again, and found himself locked inside the body of a wolf or falcon forever?

No, he decided. *No.*

Weary. So weary. His left foreleg ached. And then he recalled how it had been burned, broken, in human form; the healing could not give back that which had been lost. The magic was not absolute. He had not given the injured limb enough time to recover.

Through the *lir*-link, he passed the message to Lorn. He

must stop. Stop. It was dark now, but the moon, full, had risen, and they were nearly there. They could walk the rest of the way.

Donal stopped running. He panted, head hanging; he tucked his tail between his legs. Slowly, so slowly, the shapechange altered his body. He faced them as a man again.

Man-shaped, he leaned against the nearest tree. "—Sorry," he said. "Too tired—can we rest?"

Alix put a hand upon his arm. A hand, not a paw. "We should have ridden at least half the way."

Donal shook his head. "No. We needed to get home as quickly as possible."

Finn's smile was very faint. "Sorcha should not worry; you will always be Cheysuli."

"Because I call the Keep home?" Donal laughed breathlessly. "Aye—I could not become a Mujharan if the prophecy commanded it."

Alix glanced around. "We are almost there. Oh gods, let the girl simply be *lost* . . ."

"Unlikely." But Finn's tone was gentle. "She is *your* daughter, Alix . . . with all your stubbornness. Perhaps—"

"Perhaps *what*, Finn?" Alix scraped fallen hair away from her face. "Perhaps she decided to visit another Keep? No. She was helping Sorcha with the baby."

Finn's hand clasped her shoulder gently. "*Meijha*, do not fret so—"

Donal nearly smiled at Finn's use of the inaccurate term. Alix had never been Finn's *meijha*, but that had not stopped him from wishing she would someday change her mind.

"Do you not fret about Meghan from time to time?" Alix asked in irritation. "You are a *jehan,* Finn, as much as I am a *jehana.* Tell me you do not know what that entails."

Looking at them, Donal saw two worried people. More worried than they intended him to know. For only a moment, he saw the possibilities through their eyes: *Bronwyn, Ihlini, attempting to use her burgeoning powers . . . or instinctively seeking her father.*

"But she thinks *Duncan* is her *jehan.*" He said it aloud, distinctly; Alix and Finn looked at him in surprise.

"Aye, of course, but—"

Finn's hand across Alix's mouth cut her sentence off. He made a quieting gesture with his other hand and they instantly obeyed.

In silence, they waited. And in silence, they heard the other approach.

Because in the forest, at night, absolute silence betokens a *presence* coming.

Bronwyn—? Donal wondered briefly. *She knows how to move as quietly as any*—

But it was not Bronwyn. It was not a woman. It was a man. A man who had once been Cheysuli.

He was a shadow within shadows, a wraith among the trees. There was no sound, only silence; the silence born of the passing of a spirit on its way to the afterworld. Insubstantial, Donal thought; yet it had substance. It was not a wraith, but a man. Not a shadow: a man who was once a warrior.

A warrior without a *lir*.

Out of the shadows a man stepped into the luminescence of the moon, and they saw his face clearly: old/young; human/inhuman; of sorrow and bittersweet joy. And his face, in the moonlight, was Donal's, but carved of older, harder wood.

"Forgive me," he said; two words, but filled with an agony of need.

Donal felt his senses waver. For an instant, the ground seemed to move beneath his feet. He put out a hand to steady himself, and when his fingers touched the trunk of the nearest tree he found himself turning to press against it. Clinging to it. *Clinging*. as if he could not stand up.

And he knew, as he clung, he could not. He could only press his face against the bark and let it bite into his flesh.

Jehan? Jehan? But he could not ask it aloud. He no longer had a voice. No tongue. No teeth. No mouth. He had lost the means to speak.

He shut his eyes. Tightly. So tightly he saw crimson and yellow and white. When he opened them again he blinked against the shock of sight once more, and realized the impossible remained.

It is *my jehan*— And yet he knew it could not be.

It was Alix who moved first. Donal expected her to run

to Duncan. To grab him, kiss him, hold him. To cry out his name and her love. But she did none of those things.

Instead, she turned her back.

Her face, Donal saw, was ravaged. "If I look—*if I look*—he will be gone . . . gone . . . *again*. If I look—he will be *gone.*

Gone . . . Donal echoed. *But how can he be* here?

The bark of the tree bit into his face. But he welcomed the pain; it kept him from losing possession of his senses.

Slowly Finn reached out and closed a hand around one of Alix's arms. Donal saw how the fingers pressed against the fabric of her gown—pressing, *pressing*—until Donal thought she would cry out because of the pain.

But Alix did not.

It was Finn.

"No," Duncan said. "Oh no . . ."

"You." Finn's voice was ragged. *"You* stoop to apostasy—"

"No—" Alix, wrenching free of Finn's hand, spun around to face Duncan again. "How can you call a miracle *apostasy—*?"

"He can," Duncan said. "He must. Because it is the truth."

"Because you are *alive?*" Alix shook her head. Donal saw how she trembled. "I begged you not to go. Why waste a life? But you denied me. You said you had to go because your *lir* was slain." She tried to steady her voice. "How can you come back now? Why did you stay *away*—if the death-ritual could be left unheeded?"

Finn stopped her from going to the man. "Wait."

"Wait?" She tried to wrench free again. *"Wait?* Have you gone mad? That is *Duncan—"*

"Is it?"

Duncan moved a single step closer to all of them. And his face was free of shadow, open to them all.

It was in the eyes. Donal saw it even as Finn and Alix did. Emptiness, aye. Sorrow: an abundance of it. Such pain as a man, left sane, could never know.

But there was no sanity left in Duncan.

Oh gods . . . oh gods—! Donal shut his eyes. He felt the trembling start up in his limbs; the roiling in his belly. *He is back—he is back—and yet he is not my* jehan—

Finn jerked Alix back beside him. "*Rujho*," he said, "stop."

Duncan stopped. His head twisted quickly, faintly, oddly to one side, jerking his chin toward his shoulder. Twice; no more. A nervous tic, Donal thought dazedly. He knew other men who had them. But—this was something more.

"I need you," Duncan said. "*I need you all.*"

"Why?" Finn asked flatly. "Why does a dead warrior need help from any man?"

"*Finn*—" That from Alix, in horror, but he cut her off again.

"A *lir*less man is a dead man, of no value to his clan. He is half a man, and empty, lacking spirit, lacking soul." Finn's chant sounded almost bitter. "Is that not what we believe?"

We believe—we believe— Donal bared his teeth. *But how do we believe? My jehan has come back to us—*

Duncan twitched again. Briefly, so briefly; Donal almost did not see it. But he found himself, in fascinated horror, anticipating yet another.

"I need your help." Duncan's hair was silver in the moonlight. "I need your help. I need to find the magic to make me whole again."

"Whole? You are *lir*less. How can you be whole?"

"Finn!" Duncan cried. "Would you have me *beg* for this?"

Do not beg, do not beg—not you—*not Duncan of the Cheysuli—that man* does not beg—

Without waiting for an answer, Duncan dropped to his knees. His head, tilted up, exposed the look of mute appeal. He was a supplicant to his brother. To his wife. And to his son. "Can you not *see* why I come to be here?"

Now, they could. Clearly. It showed in the eyes; in altered pupils, altered shape. It showed in the set of his shoulders, almost hunched upon themselves. It showed in the mottled skin of his arms, bare and naked of *lir*-gold. It showed in the bones of his hands: fragile, brittle bones, rising up beneath the flesh to fuse themselves together and turn the fingers into talons.

Not a man. But neither a hawk. Some place between the two.

"Cai was *dead!*" Finn cried. "How is this possible?"

"I am abomination," Duncan said. "Can you make me whole again?"

"But—you are *lir*less." In Finn, the cracks began to show. "*Rujho*, you are *lir*less . . ."

"You can make me whole again."

Alix, trembling, went down on her knees before the kneeling man. She put out her arms and drew him in until his face was against her breasts. "*Shansu*," she said, "*peace. We can make you whole again.*"

"He is *lir*less!" It burst out of Donal's mouth in something near incoherence.

Alix did not hear. "I promise. I promise. We will make you whole again."

"Tynstar took the body. Tynstar took the body," Duncan said against her breasts. "I could not give my *lir* proper passage to the gods."

"Oh gods," Finn said. "Oh—*gods*. . . ."

"I could not die," Duncan said. "There was no ritual. Tynstar had the body, and there was no ritual."

"*Shansu*," Alix said. "We will make you whole again."

"Not without Cai's body," Finn said. "Oh *rujho*, surely you must see!"

Duncan's head twitched against Alix arms. The taloned fingers came up in a twisted gesture of supplication.

Donal at last wrenched himself from the tree and faced them all. "The earth magic!" he cried. "There are three of us, and the *lir*. More than enough, is there not? We can summon up the healing and make him whole again!"

Alix stroked Duncan's silver hair. "Do you see? Your son is much like you. He will be a wise Mujhar."

"Donal—" Finn began, and then he shut his eyes.

"Make me *whole* again," Duncan begged.

Lir. For the first time, Lorn spoke. *Lir, what he requests is dangerous.*

But it can be done?

There is much power in the earth, Taj said from a nearby tree. *With three of you to summon it, augmented by three lir, you can call upon powerful sources. But there is danger in it.*

And worth it, Donal said. *This man is my jehan!*

Slowly, Finn knelt down. He bowed his head in acquiescence.

Dangerous, Lorn said.

Shakily, Donal went to the kneeling triad. There were so many things he wanted to say to his father, whom he had not seen in fifteen years. So many, *many* things; he thought none of them would get said.

"Join hands," Finn said. "The link must be physical as well as emotional and mental. What we do now will stretch the boundaries of the power; if those boundaries break, all will be unleashed. The magic will be wild."

Donal, kneeling between father and uncle, looked at Finn sharply. "Wild—?"

"Before there were men and women in the world, there was magic in abundance. And all of it was wild. It made the world what it is. But it must be held in check if *we* are to live in the world."

"Then—*this* could destroy the world. . . ."

"Duncan would never risk that," Alix said suddenly. She looked at the silver-haired man. "*Would* you? That much risk?"

His malformed hands trembled in hers; in Donal's. "I am abomination. Make me whole again."

"*Duncan* would not risk it," Finn said quietly. "But this man is not Duncan."

White-faced in the moonlight, Alix looked at Finn. "Then—what we do is *wrong*."

"Is it?" Finn looked at Donal. "Is it wrong to do this, *harani?*"

Deliberately, Donal looked into the eyes of the raptor who had once been his father. "It is not wrong if we can control the magic. Stretching the boundaries is not evil, if we learn from what we do. A risk not taken means nothing of consequence is ever learned." Donal drew in an unsteady breath. "I say it must be done."

"Down," Finn whispered. "Down . . . and down . . . and down. . . ."

Drifting.
—drifting—
—*down*—

He sank through layers of earth, of rock, of *rock*, drifting, drifting down, until he was a speck of sentience in the midst of omniscient infinity, aware only of his insignificance in the ordering of things.

Alone?

No. There were other specks, all black and glassy gray, as if they had burned themselves out. As if the infinity had become, all at once, finite, and the sentience emptied out.

Down.

—down—

—*down*—

Jehan, he asked, *are you here?*

Down.

He felt the void reach out for him. Reaching, it caught him. Catching, it tugged him in; tugging, tugging, until he was a fish on a line; a cat in a trap; a man at the end of a sword—

—with the hilt in another man's hands.

Pain.

The sword pierced flesh, muscle; scraped across rib bone. And entered the cage around his heart.

—*pain*—

He cried out. The speck, in the midst of the void, cried out to the other specks that he was in pain, *in pain*, and he knew it should not be so.

The line was cut; the trap was sprung; the sword was shattered. And Donal, hurled back through infinity to know finiteness once more, heard the words screamed from his mother's mouth: "*Ihlini trap-link*—"

And then he knew the truth.

Not my jehan *after all?*

Pain.

He lay on his face. His mouth was filled with dirt and leaves. He spat. The sound reverberated in his skull.

Lir. Lorn, whose muzzle was planted solidly in Donal's neck, shoving. Donal felt the tip of a tooth against the flesh of his neck. Lorn's nose was cold.

Lir. Taj, who stirred dirt and debris into Donal's face with the force of his flapping wings. The falcon was on the ground, but his wings continued to flap.

He felt a hand on his arm. "Donal. *Donal!*"

Finn's voice. Hoarse. Donal allowed the hand to drag him up from the ground. He flopped over onto his back.

Through slitted lids and merging lashes he saw Finn's face. In the moonlight the scar was a black ditch dug into the flesh; the other side of his face was dirty. Scraped. As if he had been hurled bodily against the ground. His leathers were littered with dirt and leaves.

"*Gods*—" Donal shoved himself up from the dirt. He wavered on his knees, pressing one hand against the ground. And then he saw his mother. "*Jehana*—?" Stiffly, he crawled across the clearing. "*Jehana?*"

Finn sat down suddenly in the dirt as if he could no longer stand. One hand threaded rigid fingers through his silver-speckled hair; he stripped it back from his eyes. He bared the face of his grief to his nephew, who still could not believe. Storr sat down next to Finn, leaning a little against him, as if he knew without his support Finn would surely fall.

"He was *sent*," Finn said. "That was not my *rujho*. Not your *jehan*. Not my *rujholla's cheysul*. That was Ihlini *retribution*." He lifted his head and looked at Donal. "He was *saved*, and he was *sent*. We are alive because of Alix."

Donal could only stare at his mother's body.

Finn's voice droned on. "We are alive because when she saw how the trap-link would swallow us all, she threw us out of it. There was power enough in the trap to slay four *hundred* Cheysuli, *four hundred* . . . not just *four* . . . but— she threw us out of the link . . . and let it swallow her."

Donal's vision wavered. He blinked. He could not say if it were tears or the aftermath. He thought it might be both.

Alix was clearly dead. She lay sprawled on her back, arms and legs awry, spilling awkwardly from her clothing in the obscenity of death. Blood still crawled sluggishly from nose, ears, mouth. Her amber eyes were closed.

Transfixed, Donal looked slowly from mother to father. Like Alix, Duncan was sprawled in the dirt. The silent shadows lay across him, hiding malformed hands, hunching shoulders, the predatory eyes.

But not the fact that Duncan was not—*quite*—dead.

Donal twitched in shock as life spilled back into his body. Awkwardly he scrambled across to his father. He saw the blood in Duncan's nostrils. He felt it in his own.

"*Jehan?*" His voice was a ragged whisper as he hunched beside the form. "*Jehan*—have we made you whole again?"

"A toy," Duncan said thickly, and there was—briefly—sanity in his eyes; his human, Cheysuli eyes. "Tynstar—made me—*a toy*—"

"*Jehan?*—"

"For fifteen years—a *toy*—"

Almost frenziedly, Donal dragged Duncan's head and shoulders into his lap. Tentative hands stroked his father's silvered hair. "*Jehan*," he begged, "do not *go*—I have only just *found* you again—"

And in his arms, his father died.

Fourteen

Donal sat in his mother's pavilion. Around him were her belongings, waiting for her return: wooden chests filled with clothing and trinkets; the tapestry she had painstakingly worked for his father so many years before; cook pots and utensils; the jewelry his father had given her; many other things. And all of them spoke of Alix.

She had, over the years, made Duncan's things hers, though she had given many to her son. The pavilion no longer was the clan-leader's pavilion; that was Finn's. But once, this pavilion had known the laughter the three of them had shared; the tears; the evenings of stories and future plans. Once it had known fullness. Now it knew emptiness.

He had spent the long night with Sorcha, trying to ease his grief in her words and her womanhood. She had soothed him as only she could, and yet he had found himself longing for another woman entirely. The one Sorcha could not be.

They had spoken of his father; of what Duncan had once been, and who, but not what Tynstar had made him. For Donal, the memory of the night before was too vivid. Too real. He needed time to understand it and put it in its place. If he could ever find a place for what he had experienced.

In the morning he had left Sorcha, his children, his *lir*. He came alone to his mother's pavilion and sat upon the ragged bear pelt she had kept long past its usefulness, saying Duncan had given it to her and she would never be rid of it. He had sat on it as a child, and now he sat on it again; a man grown, but knowing himself helpless as the child he had once been.

A slim hand slid inside the doorflap and pulled it aside. Donal heard the sibilant scrape of fabric against fabric. He

watched in silence, waiting, as Bronwyn slipped into the
pavilion. Her black hair was mussed, pulled loose from its
single braid. Some hung into her face, veiling much of it
from Donal. She was smiling a little, as if she knew a secret.
Her amber eyes were alight with inner knowledge. But she
was different. Very different. Aside from the fact she wore
the leathers of a warrior in place of traditional skirts, he
thought she looked more alive than he had ever seen her.

She saw him and stopped short. "Donal!"

He waited.

The flap, half-closed, was caught on Bronwyn's shoulder.
But she did not slide it free or step away. She stood in the
shadows of the entrance and stared at her silent brother.

"Are you healed?" she asked. "Your arm?"

"Healed," Donal said. "Bronwyn. Where have you
been?"

She looked away from him, staring at the pelted floor.
Color came and went in her face. And then she seemed to
make up her mind to face him down. She lifted her head
again. "I wanted to see if I could do it. And I *can*. I have
the Old Blood, too."

He stared at her blankly. He was full of his mother's
death and the ruination of his father; he could not comprehend anything Bronwyn said. "Old Blood?" He thought
only of Tynstar's blood.

"Aye," she said firmly. "*Jehana* said perhaps someday I
might be able to learn as *she* had learned. And so I made
up my mind to do it."

"Do what?" His response was sluggish. The aftereffects
of Alix's throwing him out of the trap-link had not entirely
dissipated. He still felt weak. Disoriented.

"Take *lir*-shape," Bronwyn answered "I went away to try."

Awareness returned at once. "*Lir*-shape! *You?*"

Color surged into Bronwyn's face. "Aye! Do you think
I am not worthy because I am a woman?"

Donal thrust himself to his feet. "Do not mouth such
foolishness when our *jehana* is dead!"

He had not meant it to come out so badly; so cruelly.
But all he could think of was his mother dying to save them
all while Bronwyn played her games.

But perhaps they were not games. Not if she could shapechange. And he could not discount the possibility; Alix had

claimed the gift. If her daughter did as well, perhaps the Old Blood might yet counteract the Ihlini in her.

"*Dead.*" Bronwyn gaped at him. "Our *jehana*—?"

"Last night." He saw the twitch of shock in her face; the beginnings of comprehension. "It was an Ihlini trap-link."

Bronwyn flinched visibly. "Ihlini! But—*how?*"

He could not tell her how. That meant he must also tell her of his father; he could not do it. It was too private. Too personal. The pain was his alone.

"*Donal*—"

"Tynstar laid a trap. He wanted Finn and me as well . . . all he got was our *jehana*."

"*Tynstar*—" Bronwyn's amber eyes were full of tears. "*Tynstar* slew our *jehana*—?"

"She has been given passage to the gods." With Duncan, but Donal did not say it.

Disjointedly, Bronwyn fell down upon her knees. She stared blankly at the unlighted fire cairn. Donal, still looking for some indication of guilt, some telltale sign she dissembled, saw only grief and bewilderment. "Why would he want our *jehana*? What would he want with her? Why would he slay our *jehana*—?"

He knew she would not hear him. And so he did not try. He simply went to his sister, knelt down, and pulled her against his chest so she would not have to grieve alone.

"*Rujho*," Bronwyn begged, "why would he slay our *jehana?*"

"Retribution," he answered unevenly. "The *Ihlini* require no reason."

"Dead," she whispered. "Dead? But—I wanted to tell her about it. I wanted to say what I did. I wanted her to know how her blood is in me, too. The *Old* Blood . . . as much as in her son." Bronwyn pressed her face against his shoulder. "I wanted to have importance . . . I wanted to be someone who *counted* . . . I wanted to be *different* . . ."

Oh Bronwyn, he mourned, *you are more different than you can know.*

Her tangled hair was soft beneath his chin. He smoothed the knots against her scalp as if she were a child, and in his heart he knew she was, regardless of her age. As much as he himself was, in his bitter grief.

"I wanted her to know," Bronwyn sobbed, "and now she never will."

"*Shansu*," he said, "*shansu.* Be certain that she knows."

After a moment, Bronwyn drew away from him. "Donal—what happens to *me*, now? What becomes of me?"

One last time he pushed a lock of hair out of her face. "You may stay here, if it suits. The Keep is your home. Finn and Meghan are here; so is Sorcha and the children, and all your clan-mates. But—if you prefer—you may come to Homana-Mujhar. Aislinn could use the company. There is a wedding she must prepare for—in less time than I care to acknowledge." He felt the twist of reluctance in his belly. Fifteen days. But he knew better than to ask Carillon for a delay, even in light of the circumstances. Homana was at stake.

"Wedding," Bronwyn echoed. "I do not feel much like a wedding. Even a royal one. Not without my *jehana*—" But she shut her mouth on anything more, as if she could not dare to say what she felt.

Slowly he stood, pulling her up as well. "I am sorry, but I must go back—"

"*Now?*" She stared at him. "After what has happened?"

Donal sighed, wanting refuge from the bewildered pain in her voice. He did not blame her; he wanted to stay as well. "Much as I would prefer to remain, Carillon would have my head. There are responsibilities—" But he did not explain them to her. In her grief, she would never understand. "*Rujholla* . . . do not forget our *su'fali*. You may find comfort in comforting him."

After a moment, Bronwyn nodded. "Tell Aislinn I will come. But—not just yet. I think I could not bear it."

He bent and kissed her forehead, hoping to offer solace. But what he found was doubt. *Oh gods . . . what if I am wrong? What if the Old Blood in her is tainted by the other?*

And yet he knew he might be doing his sister a grave injustice. He had no proof it had been Bronwyn in the Womb. None at all. The possibility seemed remote, now that he knew where Bronwyn had been.

And Aislinn? Where was she?

He said nothing more to Bronwyn. He left her to grieve in private, according to Cheysuli tradition.

*   *   *

The guests had gathered. The vows had been said. The acclamation was made. In the space of an hour Donal went from unnamed Prince of Homana to the actual thing itself; there was an instantaneous change. He could feel it in the air. A tension. A vibrating urgency. No more was it a *some-day* thing; Homana would have a Cheysuli Mujhar.

When the feasting was done and the hall was prepared for celebratory dancing, Donal discovered he was now the prey of many courtiers. In his years as informal heir, the men who inhabited Carillon's court had mostly tried to ignore him. No doubt they had thought—or, more likely, *hoped*—the Mujhar might elevate a bastard son to legitimacy and send Donal back to the Keep. But the Mujhar had not; Donal was not certain there *were* any bastard sons, though there had been rumors of one or two. And so now the circle was halfway complete; the shapechanger was Prince of Homana.

They oppressed him, the noblemen of Homana. They stifled him with their insincere sudden change of regard, expressing condolences for his mother's death as an opening gambit. He stood his ground for as long as he could, using the Homanan courtesy traditions Alix had taught him as well as what diplomacy he had learned in his years within the palace walls. But courtesy and diplomacy ran out; he retreated. And at last, tiring of his evasiveness, they left him alone.

They do not know me, though all have known me for years. They realize they must deal with me one day, and would rather gain sway with me now, so they may lay the groundwork to make me a puppet-prince, and a Mujhar—when it comes to that—in their pockets.

He knew also that the freedom he had just won would never last; soon enough they would learn his moods and his habits, and would play him like a harp.

Donal stood well back from the dancing and laughing and drinking. He leaned against the tapestried wall and watched in silence, considering his newly won rank. And against his will he touched the golden circlet on his brow.

Carillon had put it there during the ceremony. It represented his princely status; it represented the future of Homana. A simple circlet of plain, unworked gold, lacking significant weight. But it was enough to bind him eternally to his *tahlmorra*.

Donal smiled. *But if they expected me to be a Homanan prince, no doubt my leathers shocked them. Good.*

As a concession to Homana, he wore the royal colors. His jerkin was crimson suede, his leggings were black; black boots were stitched in scarlet. A belt of filigreed gold set with rubies the size of his thumbnail clasped his waist. But for that and his *lir*-gold and newly gained circlet, he was a conservative Cheysuli. Other warriors were not so subdued.

He leaned against the wall. But this time he watched Aislinn as she left her women to dance. He watched as she swayed to and fro with a glittering young Homanan nobleman, touching fingertips and dancing flirtatiously.

She moved with a grace almost foreign to her. Aislinn had, growing up, been a coltish girl, even when attempting regal dignity. Since her sojourn on the Crystal Isle with Electra, she had learned a new and supple grace that was almost sheer seductiveness. There was nothing coltish about her now.

The bright, rich hair swung at her hips as she moved. Unbound, as was proper for a maiden, it flowed loosely over her shoulders, cloaking the pale blue gown. At ears and throat and waist glowed sapphires set in silver.

Electra's wedding jewels from Carillon long ago. It is no wonder he nearly made Aislinn take them off. But even a Mujhar cannot take back what is given freely, and so she has a legacy from her jehana.

He looked more closely at her as she danced with the nobleman. In the weeks since Finn had healed his burned and broken arm, Aislinn had been busy with wedding preparations. They had hardly seen one another. Seeing her now, he thought the preparations were well-made; she was lovely. She was almost a woman, with girlhood nearly banished completely.

What is mine is also Tynstar's.

He heard the words clearly, as if spoken into his ears. He snapped upright, free of the wall, and sought Electra in the throng.

But all he saw was Aislinn spinning slowly in the dance.

He stared. Her hair, a rich red-gold, seemed to fade before his eyes. He saw how it blurred, running into a duller color, until the red was replaced with silver-gray. And then the silver turned to white.

But not the white of age. The pure white-blond of youth; Electra's ensorceled youth.

Aislinn's eyes caught his. She stared at him as she stepped lightly through the pattern. He did not know what she thought; he was aware only of her eyes. Electra's eyes, pale as water and full of subtle promises. But the dreams she promised were nightmares.

The heavy girdle spun out from her twisting skirts. He saw how the silver tangled; heard how it chimed, the dull clink of interlocked links. A rattle of stones as the sapphires clattered. And then the laughter was in his head.

What is undone shall remain *undone . . . what is mine is also Tynstar's.*

Donal flinched as a winecup was pressed into his hand. "Drink deep," Finn advised. "It will be a long night before you can bed your bride."

He looked up again at Aislinn, shaken to the core. Gods—is *Electra somewhere* here?

"I must kiss you for luck!" It was Bronwyn, coming up to clasp his arms. "Bend down, Donal—you are too tall for me!"

He saw how the blue-enameled torque and earrings glittered against her skin. She had none of the dark coloring of the Cheysuli, showing the Homanan in her instead.

Or the Ihlini? He bent slowly, still lost in what he had heard inside his head. "You are certain this will work?"

"Everyone says it will. It must be done. you know." She kissed him soundly on one cheek, then laughed up at him. "Every woman who wants a *cheysul* must kiss the most recent bridegroom."

"*Every* woman—?" He recoiled in exaggerated horror.

"Every single one." She twisted her head to seek someone in the crowd. "There—Meghan will undoubtedly be next."

"Meghan! Meghan is too young to think of marriage— and so, for that matter, are you."

Bronwyn laughed. "I am only a year younger than Aislinn. Perhaps by the time *I* am sixteen, I will have found a *cheysul*." Her amber eyes glinted. "After all, I am dancing with *men*, not boys. I have danced with Gryffth, and Rowan *himself* has already asked me twice."

"Rowan is being polite." Donal unthreaded his arm from hers. "Then go dance, *rujholla*. Do not keep your partners waiting."

Laughing, she whirled in a swirl of sky-blue skirts and hastened back to the throng of young women.

"She is nearly grown," Finn said quietly. "She has the right of it—by next year she may be wed."

A twinge of unease unsettled Donal's belly. "It may be best we do not let her wed. We—do not know what powers she might claim in the coming years."

Finn looked at him squarely. "If you stifle her, Donal— if you seek to keep her leashed, no matter how light the chain—you will surely twist her spirit. Right now, there is nothing of Tynstar in her."

"And when there is?"

"*If* there is . . . we will deal with it then."

"As we must deal with her ability to assume *lir*-shape?"

Finn looked sharply at Donal. "*Bronwyn?* Are you certain?"

"She says so. Did she not tell *you?*"

"No." Finn frowned into his wine. "She—has kept very apart since Alix's death. Oh—she spends time with Meghan, but not much with me. I have tried. . . ." He stopped speaking. His dark face was stark, as if he deeply regretted his inability to deal with Alix's daughter. "She spends more time with Storr than with me, but if she has learned how to take *lir*-shape, that is why."

"Storr said nothing to you?"

"Storr said nothing to me when *Alix* learned to shape-change." Finn's tone was wry, but Donal saw the trace of remembered pain in his uncle's eyes. "The *lir* protect those with the Old Blood. More so, I sometimes think, than they protect those without."

Donal frowned. "Then could they protect her against herself?"

"If she began to show signs of Ihlini powers?" Finn shrugged a little. "Who can say? All we know is the *lir* are constrained against attacking the Ihlini, no matter what the odds. "

"Gods," Donal said, "what my poor *rujholla* faces—"

"We do not know," Finn said deliberately. "She may be free of the evil, even *with* the blood."

Donal swirled wine within the confines of the goblet. "Aye, but—" He broke it off. A stranger approached, and he had no wish to share Bronwyn's parentage with anyone but Finn.

"May I join you?" the stranger asked.

Finn turned to face him, then fell back a step. For a moment there was blatant shock in his eyes. "Carillon did not tell me *you* were coming."

"I was not certain I could." The man—tall, very blond, with a silver circlet banding his head—smiled at Donal. "I think your nephew does not recall who I am. But why should he?—it was nearly sixteen years ago when last he saw me, and he was only a boy."

Donal released a breath of laughter. "I remember you, Lachlan! How could I *not*? It was your *Song of Homana* so many of us sang the summer when you had gone." He shook his head. "No more the humble harper, are you, with all your fine clothes and jewels." An eloquent flip of his hand indicated the blue velvets and flashing diamonds. "No more hiding your identity, but the High Prince of Ellas in all your power and grace."

"Eloquent, is he not?" Finn observed lightly. "I think he gets it from me."

Lachlan's smile was warm and nostalgic. "Does he get anything from *you*, Finn, it would surely be your gift for inspiring—trust." The jibe was gentle. but the sting was clearly present. And then it faded. "I have just come from Carillon. Donal—I am sorry for Alix's death. I admired and respected her greatly. But—as for *Carillon.* . . ." Briefly, he glanced over his shoulder. Near one of the trestle tables Carillon stood head and shoulders above the men who clustered around him; Homanans, mostly, but a few Solindish guests. "In his letters, Carillon said Tynstar had stolen away his youth, but I did not realize he meant as much as *that*." Lachlan's voice was even, but Donal heard the undertone of concern. "Is there nothing to be done?"

Finn shrugged. "He ages. All men age. Tynstar has merely given it to him sooner."

Lachlan regarded Finn's expressionless face closely. "And have you tried to reverse it with your magic?"

"It cannot be done," Finn said flatly. "Ihlini powers and Cheysuli gifts are in direct opposition. We cannot undo what an Ihlini has done when it is of such magnitude as *that*." Briefly, he looked at the Mujhar. His eyes belied his tone. "I think he has accepted it."

"Perhaps I, with Lodhi's aid—"

"No." Finn's voice was flat and inflexible. "It is a part of his *tahlmorra*."

"Lodhi," Lachlan muttered, "you and your *destiny*—!"

Donal cleared his throat. "Lachlan—where is your harp? Have you left your Lady behind?"

The Ellasian's blond hair shone in the candlelit room. Unlike Carillon or Finn, he seemed not to have aged at all, save for a fine tracery of lines at the corners of his blue eyes and faint brackets at his mouth. Blond, he was a stranger; Donal recalled him from a time when he had dyed the fair hair dark.

"No. She is in my chambers. Why?—do you want a lesson?" Lachlan smiled. "When you asked me once before, as a boy, I said you had the hands of a warrior instead of a harper." He glanced at his own supple hands. "And, as for tonight—surely there will be *other* things for you to master."

Finn's tone was subtly mocking. "And what have *you* mastered since last we saw one another?"

"I?" Lachlan's handsome face smoothed into a hospitable blankness, while diplomacy ruled his tongue. "I have mastered happiness, Finn . . . and you?" The tone altered a little. "How is it with *you*—now that Tourmaline is dead?"

Donal saw the taut muscles of Finn's jaw relax just a little. It was shock, he knew; Finn, with most things, was imperturbable. But then no one mentioned his dead *cheysula* to his face.

Finn's face remained expressionless, but only the habitual solemnity of a Cheysuli gave him the control. Donal saw through it quite easily.

But then the control was released. Donal saw his uncle's eyes naked for the first time in his life, and the intensity of the pain stunned him.

Finn looked directly at Lachlan. "Had I to do it over again, I would give her up to you."

The High Prince of Elias was clearly shocked. "Lodhi—*why?* Torry wanted *you.* She went with you willingly."

The tone of Finn's voice was hollowed. "*You* could have kept her alive."

Color drained out of Lachlan's face. His hand, holding a goblet of gold filled with rich red wine, shook enough to make the metal glitter. "But—it was you she wanted. All along. Carillon made it quite clear."

"And you she should have taken." Finn glanced at Donal. "It is—hard to admit it when one has made a mistake. I was too selfish, too proud. Duncan had won Alix—I would not allow Torry *also* to go to another man when I wanted her for myself. I was—wrong. But the price was exacted from her."

"I am sorry," Lachlan said finally. "I had no right to bring it up. This is not the time for recriminations—I banished those long ago." Briefly, he smiled. "And I am wed now myself—a lovely woman. She loves me well, and I am content with her."

Finn smiled ironically. "Where would you find such a fool as *that?*"

Lachlan grinned back, unoffended. "In Caledon, of course, since our realms have made a peace at last. We have two sons."

Finn's mouth hooked down sourly. "Aye, your House runs to boys. How many brothers have you?"

"Five. And five sisters." Lachlan laughed at Donal's startled glance. "Speaking of that: would you care to meet another of Rhodri's sons?"

"Who?" Finn asked suspiciously. "Is this one a harper, too?"

"No. Not even a priest of Lodhi, though he does, when he must, admit to calling upon the All-Wise. Usually when he is in dire need of assistance." Lachlan turned and gestured. A young man approached: blue-eyed, dark-haired, well-dressed in quiet brown with little jewelry. He moved with Lachlan's fluid grace. He was not as tall and did not claim the same purity of features, as if they had blurred in him somehow, but he was handsome enough and his mouth was expressively mobile.

He looked at his brother quizzically; there was a glint in his sleepy eyes. "Aye, my lord High Prince?"

Lachlan sighed. "This is Evan, my youngest brother.

Twenty years divide us, but we are closer than the rest. All the others are dutiful sons; Evan and I are the rebels." He smiled at his brother. "He decided to come to Homana because he had heard all the lays I sang of Carillon's exploits. He said he must meet these Cheysuli warriors, to see if the stories were true."

Evan executed a graceful bow before a startled Donal. "I must admit I expected something other than *civilized* behavior from you, my lord. I thought Cheysuli were spawned with tails and fangs."

For a moment, Donal thought he meant it. Then he heard the ironic humor in Evan's tone. He smiled. "Beware your back—when the moon is whole we seek the souls of such men as you."

Evan grinned and took the goblet from his brother's hand, swallowing most of the wine before Lachlan could protest. He handed it back with a challenging smile. Then he nodded at Donal. "She is a lovely bride, my lord."

"My name is Donal, and aye—she is."

Evan appraised him briefly. "I would drink to your future gladly—had I some wine."

Donal lifted his own winecup. "Then we shall go and find some. My cup is drunk quite dry."

"And I have none at all," Evan pointed out.

They went directly to the nearest trestle table holding all manner of liquor. Donal judiciously stayed with the vintage he had already tasted; Evan, methodically precise, tried four cups before he found the wine he preferred. Then he offered several elaborate toasts in honor of the Prince of Homana and his bride, all spoken in the husky unintelligible language of Homana's eastern neighbor. Having scorched his throat with the words, Evan returned to Homanan and his wine.

The Ellasian prince was full of good spirits, sweet wine, and dry wit. He was patently unimpressed by Donal's rank or warrior status; he was too obsessed with having a good time. Donal, accustomed to wary dealings with Homanans disturbed by his shapechanging or turned obsequious because of his rank, found it a novel experience. He relaxed with Evan as he only rarely relaxed with others. They were, he decided, *kinspirits*, drawn together by mutual liking, respect, and circumstances.

Evan watched the dancers. Donal watched Evan. "Will you inherit the Ellasian throne?"

Evan burst into laughter, nearly spraying wine all over himself. "I? *Never!* There are four brothers between Lachlan and myself, and *he* has two sons. And his wife has conceived again; likely *it* will be a boy, and I will be farther away from the throne even yet." He grinned. "Only if war, famine or plague slew all of *them*, leaving only me, would I inherit Ellas." He shrugged, sounding insufferably contented with his lot. "I am insignificant within my House. I find I prefer it that way."

"Why?" Donal was fascinated.

"As Lachlan said—I am somewhat a rebel son. Being insignificant leaves me the freedom to be whom I wish and to do what I wish. Within the bounds of reason. Of course, there are times my father forgets the order of my birth— was it fourth? No? Fifth?—but all in all I like it better this way." His sleepy blue eyes were shrewd behind dark lashes. "Lachlan is the heir—you have only to look at him to see what the title means. He far preferred being a priest of Lodhi the All-Father and a simple wandering harper, but he was firstborn, and therefore High Prince of Ellas. Those years he spent with Carillon were his freedom. Now he must be a proper son to our father."

Donal looked at Lachlan still in conversation with Finn. "And does he resent it?"

Evan laughed and quaffed more wine. "Lachlan resents nothing. He has not the darkness in him for that. None of us do." He grinned and arched an eyebrow. "That is Ellas for you, Donal: a land of laughter and happy people." His eyes followed the pattern of the dance. "Your wife enjoys herself with countless Homanan nobles. Is it not time *you* partnered her?"

"It is customary for the bride to dance with all the men before she dances with her husband." He shrugged. "Or so I have been told. Dancing is a Homanan custom. I learned because I had to."

Evan watched as Aislinn slipped through the pattern. "But she should not have so much freedom just after you have wed. She will think to seek it much too often."

Donal regarded him in amusement. "What do *you* know of women, Evan? You are younger than I."

"Twenty," he said, unoffended. "I know more than you think. Now *there* is a lady I would care to know better than I do at the moment."

Donal looked. He shook his head at once. "Never Meghan."

"Why not?" Evan demanded archly. "Do you think I could not win her?"

"To win *her* you would have to win her father . . . and that you could never do."

Evan tossed back a gulp of wine. "In Ellas, I have frequent experiences with fathers. When they know who I am, the thing is always settled."

"Finn, I fear, would be less impressed by your rank than with your intentions toward his daughter."

Evan's head turned sharply. "Finn? The Cheysuli?"

"My *su'fali*—" Donal smiled. "*Uncle*, in Homanan."

"Then—she is Carillon's niece—" Evan frowned. "Perhaps I looked too high. Still, she is a pretty thing . . . no, I think not. Why antagonize Cheysuli or Mujhar?" He tapped his silver cup against his teeth. "What of *her?*"

Again, Donal looked. And again, he shook his head. "No."

Evan's brows shot up beneath his dark brown hair. "No? Why say you no? Is *she* close to the Mujhar?"

"Closer to *me*, Ellasian. Bronwyn is my sister."

Evan swore in disgust. "Are there *no* women here who are not kin to royalty?"

"Very few." Donal grinned and pushed his cup into Evan's hands. "I think I will do as you suggest and dance with Aislinn . . . before you look to *her.*"

Fifteen

Before Donal could reach Aislinn, Carillon intercepted him. "Donal—come with me. There are men you should meet."

Politics, of course. "I mean to dance with Aislinn." He thought perhaps an appeal to Carillon's parental prejudice would delay the need for such discussions.

Carillon smiled, seeing through the tactic at once. "Aislinn can wait a few moments. These are men you will need to know." The Mujhar's hand was on Donal's arm as he turned him away from the dance floor. "I know, this is your wedding celebration—but you will soon learn that such occasions offer opportunities other times do not."

Reluctantly, Donal went with him to the knot of noblemen. Two of them he knew, having seen them year in and year out in Homana-Mujhar while they danced attendance on Carillon. Three others were strangers to him, but their accents were Solindish.

Carillon conducted the introductions smoothly with light-headed authority. The nuances told Donal the Mujhar meant to emphasize that this Cheysuli was now the Prince of Homana; did the Solindish seek to discount him, they discounted the man who would one day rule their realm.

But it was the Homanans Donal watched more closely. He expected hostility from the Solindish; it came as no shock when he perceived it, however veiled. But the two Homanans, watching him silently, seemed tense, expectant.

Gods—it is worse than I thought it might be. Surely Carillon can see it. These men and others like them will never accept me as Mujhar.

Carillon's hand was on Donal's shoulder. "Of course we all realize the alliance between our two realms precludes any more war—" his smile was eloquently bland "—so I doubt Donal will ever see it. No doubt he will value the ongoing peace as highly as I do." Carillon inclined his head at the Solindish nobles. "It will be a mark of Donal's tenure as Mujhar that his reign will know only peace, and will no longer need petty squabbling." The hand tightened. "It would please me well to know I am succeeded by a man who can hold the peace so truly."

"Peace is indeed something all of us desire," murmured one vermillion-clad Solindishman.

"Of course, I do not doubt the people of Solinde will be somewhat alarmed by the ascension of a Cheysuli in place of their own Solindish House—" Carillon's smile, once more, held the faintest touch of irony "—but perhaps by the time it comes to that, they will be reconciled to Donal."

There was a quick exchange of glances among the Solindishmen *and* the Homanans, Donal noted.

"Perhaps it is time I sent for Duke Royce to come home from Lestra," Carillon mused. "He has been regent of Solinde for more than fifteen years—he is no longer young. I think Solinde might benefit from another, younger man." He did not smile as he looked at the Solindishmen. "How better to accustom a realm to its future Mujhar than to send that man there now?"

Gods—is he serious? But Donal dared not show his surprise at Carillon's intentions.

One of the Homanans stared. "You send him there *now?*"

It was not, Donal knew, the reaction Carillon wanted. At least, not from the Homanans.

The Mujhar shrugged. "First he and my daughter shall spend some time together as befits those newly married. At Joyenne, I think, before they go to Lestra." Carillon's hand tightened yet again on Donal's shoulder, as if he meant to pull him closer in a brief hug of parental approval.

And then the woman screamed.

Donal spun even as Carillon did. He saw a mass of colors, staring eyes and open mouths, all clustered within the hall, all running into another in a collage of shock and stillness. And then he saw the man with the sword in his hand.

His thoughts were disjointed. *—coming at Carillon . . . a sword—at a wedding—? But—no man may bear a sword*

*into the Mujhar's presence . . . and all the guards are in
the corridor—*

His own hand flashed down to clasp his long-knife and
came up filled with steel and gold. Next to him, Carillon
too had armed himself. But the enemy's sword, even as it
sliced through the air in a blaze of shining steel, fell free
of the assailant's hand. And the man himself, so close to
the Mujhar, dropped a moment later to join his weapon on
the floor.

A knife, hilt-deep, stood up from the dead man's back
in the very center of his spine. Donal knew the blade at
once: a royal Homanan knife, with rampant lion and ruby
eye. And he knew what man had thrown it.

Carillon stood over the body. But he did not look at
it. Instead, he looked at the warrior who had thrown the
royal knife.

Finn's bare arms were folded across his chest. "It does
appear, my lord, you lack a proper liege man."

"Aye," Carillon agreed. His tone, though light, sounded
hoarse in the silent hall. "Since I lost the one I had for so
many years, I have been unable to find another."

The question was implicit in his tone. Donal, staring at
Finn, felt a strange wild hope build up in his breast.

*Gods—did Finn return to Carillon . . . things would be
as they were before—* Except he knew they would not. Time
had altered them both.

Finn smiled faintly, darkly. "Aye," he agreed. "It is difficult to find a man well-suited to the post. I have always
understood a liege man to be—irreplaceable."

"Unless replaced with the original warrior." Carillon's
face was perfectly blank.

Donal looked not at Finn but at Rowan. The most loyal
and dedicated of all Carillon's generals wore, as Donal did,
the colors of the realm. But Rowan's garb, rather than
Cheysuli leathers, was the silks and velvets of Homana.

Yet it was not the clothing Donal looked at, but the face.
The sunbronzed Cheysuli face which had abruptly lost its
color, gone ash-gray in shock. Rowan's hand was on the
hilt of his long-knife, as if he had intended to draw it in
Carillon's defense. And yet—he did not look at Carillon.
He looked instead at Finn.

He waits, Donal realized abruptly. *He waits for Finn's*

*answer. Though he is no proper liege man, he is everything
else to Carillon. He has served him so well for all these
years. I do not doubt he felt he could take Finn's place in
some small measure—perhaps more—and now he realizes
Finn might return to Carillon's side.* Donal blew out a
breath. *I would not wish to live like that, ever on the edge.
Ever wondering.*

But at last the wondering could stop.

Finn looked down at the dead man. The golden hilt glittered in the torchlight. "No," he said finally, with the faintest note of regret underscoring his tone. "I think those
times are done. I have a clan to lead. Warriors to train."
He looked up and met Carillon's eyes. For a long moment
they seemed to share an unspoken communication. Briefly,
Finn looked at the twisted hands and the hunching of Carillon's shoulders. "There *is* something I can offer you. If you
will let me do it.

"Aye," Carillon agreed, "when I have cleared my hall of
vermin." He replaced his own knife—a wolf's-head Cheysuli long-knife—then bent and pulled the bloodied knife
from the assailant's back. He gave the royal blade over to
Finn, then motioned to the guards who had come in at
the woman's scream. Quickly and efficiently two of them
gathered up the body, the sword, and took both from the
hall. The other six waited for Carillon's command.

He did not look at the Solindish noblemen who clustered
near the center of the crowd. "Take them—" a wave of his
hand indicted all six "—and escort them to their quarters.
They will return home in the morning."

"But—my lord Mujhar—!" The gray-haired lord in vermillion velvet spread his jeweled hands wide. "My lord—
we had nothing to do with this—!"

"On the day of my daughter's wedding, I have been attacked in my own hall," Carillon said inflexibly. "Let there
be no more diplomacy between us, Voile—our two realms
will soon be at war. This assassination attempt might have
won it for Solinde before the thing was begun, had it succeeded. But it failed, and you are uncovered—like a grub
beneath a rock—your plan has gone awry." He signaled his
guards to surround the Solindish nobles.

Donal watched the guards take the Solindishmen away.
In a flurry of low-voiced commands Carillon ordered the

music and dancing begun again; the celebration would continue. Then he and Finn took their leave from the hall, and Donal slowly put his knife back into its sheath.

He turned, meaning to find a servant with wine, and nearly stumbled over Bronwyn who stood directly in his path. He caught her arms and steadied her, marking how pale she was.

Her hand went out to touch him. "Donal—how do you fare?"

"Well," he told her. "Bronwyn—the thing is over now."

Fingers locked on the blue enameled torque around her neck. "The sword came so *close*—"

"I am well," he repeated. "Come, you had best go back to our *jehana*."

But Bronwyn stood in place. "Why does Carillon think it was *him* the assassin wanted?"

Donal frowned. "It *was*, Bronwyn. Who else would such a man want?"

"You," she said distinctly. "Oh Donal . . . I saw how the man looked at you. Not at the Mujhar." Her amber eyes began to fill with tears. "It was *you* he wanted, *rujho*. I swear—I saw it in his face."

"Bronwyn—" He glanced past her toward the door through which Finn and Carillon had gone. "Bronwyn— are you quite certain?"

"Aye." Earrings flashed as she nodded her head. "I danced with him, *rujho*. He asked me questions about you. I thought nothing of it—most people do not know you. But then he left me. He left the hall. And when he came back, he had a sword."

Donal frowned. "Were you not made suspicious by all the Solindishman's questions?"

She stared up into his face. "But—Donal . . . he was a Homanan."

He felt his blood turn to ice in his veins. The flesh rose up on his bones. "Bronwyn—are you *certain*?"

"Aye," she said. "Oh Donal, I am *afraid*—"

No more than I am, rujholla. But he did not say it aloud. Instead, he looked for his new wife. "Where is Aislinn?"

Bronwyn gestured. "There—do you see her? Over in the corner."

He saw her. He saw how she stood away from the crowd,

as if she could not bear to be a part of it. Sapphires and silver glittered. In both hands she held a hammered goblet and raised it to her mouth. He saw her grimace of distaste once she had swallowed. But he could not say if it was the wine that caused it, or the failure of the assassin.

Aislinn . . . I think there are things between us to be settled.

Donal looked down at Bronwyn. "Stay here, with the others. I think it is time I took my *cheysula* from the crowd."

"But—what of the bedding ceremony?"

He smiled grimly. "I think, tonight, it would be better Aislinn did without it." But he did not say he intended more for Aislinn than a simple nuptial bedding.

He left his sister behind and smoothly worked his way through the crowd. The thought of dancing had fled his mind completely, though it was expected of the High Prince and his princess. Somehow, the assassination attempt had ruined his taste for celebration.

As he reached her, Donal put out his hand and took the goblet out of hers. Aislinn stared at him in surprise. "Do you want it? Or do you *need* it?" Suspicion made him cruel.

"What?"

He looked into her face. He saw pale pink underlying the pallor of her cheeks; the hectic glitter in her gray eyes. Sensuous eyes; he knew, for all she was still young, she had learned something of a woman's seductive ways from her incredibly seductive mother.

He reached out and caught one slender wrist. "You tremble, Aislinn. For me or for your *jehan?*"

"I thought he would slay my father—"

"He did not want Carillon. The assassin was after *me*."

"*You!* Why would he want *you?*"

Her surprise was sincere. He could not doubt it. It was less than flattering, perhaps—in an odd sort of way—that she would think him so insignificant a target, but he was relieved. He did not think the emotion was feigned.

"There are some men who might desire me dead," he told her evenly, still appraising her reactions. "Undoubtedly some women, as well; Electra, perhaps?" He saw how her color faded. "Carillon ages. He will not hold the Lion forever. How better to wrest the throne from the proper line than by slaying the man who will inherit from the Mujhar?"

"Oh *gods*," she said. "Will it always be like this?"

That was not precisely the reaction he had expected, not if she were a part of the plot against him. "I hope not," he answered fervently. "If *this* is what the rank entails—"

"You do not think you are up to it?" Her tone was very cool. In her silver and sapphires, she was more like her mother each moment.

"Well," he said, "I think Carillon will rule for years yet. By the time he is ready to relinquish the Lion, I *ought* to be up to the task." He smiled at her blandly. "You are hiding in the corner, Aislinn. Are you avoiding me?"

Color rushed into her face. Her wrist went stiff in his hand.

"Are you?" he asked in surprise.

"A—little. I have been told what to expect of the bedding ceremony."

She sounded faintly disgusted as well as uncomfortable. He smiled. "Aye. They will do all they can to discomfit bride and groom. A Homanan custom, I am told; in the clans, a woman moves into a warrior's pavilion, and that is that."

"That is *all*?" Her gray eyes were huge. "At this moment, I would prefer this were a Cheysuli ceremony."

"Then we shall make it one." He closed her hand within his own. "Come with me. We will escape the predators."

Arrangements had been made for them to share royal apartments on the floor above their separate personal chambers. No one attended them; even the corridor was deserted. Privacy was absolute. But Donal took care to lock the door anyway.

Aislinn stood at one of the narrow, glassless casements. He wondered what she saw, staring so fixedly out of the opening. Her back was to him, and he clearly saw the rigidness of tension in her spine.

She turned. The heavy girdle clashed. He heard the rattle of the sapphires in the thickness of her skirts.

The room was made of shadows. The draperied bed was a cavern full of promises. He could almost hear the whispered endearments, the sighs of lovers pleased.

Aislinn faced him in silence. The wash of light from a single candle touched her hair with gold. At her throat shone the silver torque with its weight of brilliant sapphire. "I am—a little afraid."

He leaned against the door so that the carved wood pressed into his spine. He watched her, saying nothing. He could not, for the moment. He was taken too much by surprise. Somehow he had not expected the strong desire he was suddenly feeling.

For Aislinn? When there is Sorcha, who is everything to me?

Everything, perhaps. But for the moment there was also Aislinn.

Slowly, Aislinn moved away from the blackened casement. She went to a table. There was a flagon of wine and two gleaming goblets; a gift from the Atvian king. The bowls of the goblets were glass. The stems were wrought silver, flowing up around the bottom of each bowl in the shape of raven's wings. In the decanter, the wine was red as blood.

Aislinn filled the goblets, then offered one to Donal. "Will you share the nuptial cup?"

He pressed himself off the door. He approached. He saw how her long nails curved around the wine-filled crystal. When he reached her, he put out his hands and closed them over hers.

"*Shansu*," he said. "Do you think I would hurt you, Aislinn?"

"You would never hurt me," she answered clearly. "I have seen the look in your eyes." Unexpectedly, she smiled.

Donal, still clasping her hands and the goblet, lifted it toward her mouth. "I hope the vintage is good."

The rim was at her lips. Luminance flowed across her face. "The cask was a gift from my mother."

Abruptly, he jerked the goblet away. Wine splashed across them both, staining the pale blue silk of Aislinn's gown in a vivid blood-red gout. He felt the splatter on his arms, against his face. The wine was tepid, warm as blood; he nearly gagged on the heavy scent.

The goblet fell. It struck the carpet and shattered.

"Do you risk yourself as well?" he demanded.

"Risk? What risk? It was a *gift*—"

"To you? Or meant for me?"

Color flowed out of her face. Wine droplets glittered against the smooth flesh of one perfect cheek, then rolled down to splash against the gown. "Do you forget, *husband,* that *I* was to drink as well?"

"No more than *I* forget you spent two years with that witch on the Crystal Isle." he answered. "How am I to know she did not dose you with the poison bit by bit each day, until you grew immune?"

"You *fool!*" she snapped. "Do you think I would wish for your death?"

"I accuse you of nothing." He could not, yet; there was no proof of complicity.

"Finn *tested* me!" she cried. "You yourself were there. Am I not free of the taint of sorcery?"

"You have been tested." That much he could give her.

"But you still distrust me." The vivid hair curtained her face on either side. "Do you not? Do you think the assassin was also my doing? Do you really believe I desire to slay you when all I *desire* is *you?*"

He took three steps, reached out, caught her wrist. He looked at the slim, delicate hand. He could see it again before his eyes: the creamy, gold-veined vault with all its marble *lir,* and the hands that held the torch meant to thrust him to his death.

"Aislinn," he said, "you frighten me. I know not what you will do."

"You are a fool." She said it without heat. "A fool, to be afraid, when I would never slay you. I would slay anyone who *tried.* I love you, Donal."

He believed her. In that moment, he was certain she told the truth. And Finn *had* tested her.

Silently, he unfastened torque and girdle. He left both in a spill of silver and sapphire across the dark wood of the table. And then he took her to the bed.

Slowly he untied the lacings of her gown, baring her smooth, pale, delicate back. As he touched her, her flesh responded.

Naked, she lay against the bedclothes. She watched him with the eyes of a woman desiring a man. And so he divested himself of his clothing and slipped into bed beside her. *Perhaps it will not be so ill-matched a union after all . . .*

But as he put a hand upon her breast, Aislinn screamed.

All he could think to do was clamp a hand over her mouth. But she lunged away from him before he could, scrambling to the farthest corner of the bed.

"*Aislinn*—" He got out of the bed at once, afraid he might frighten her further.

"Wolf." She said it with cold precision. "Your blood is the blood of a wolf—your hands the claws of a wolf—your face the *face* of a *wolf—do you think I will lie with you*—?"

He stared at her in horror and his flesh crawled.

Aislinn twitched. He saw an alteration in her eyes. Briefly, a cessation of hostility, replaced with bewilderment. But as he opened his mouth to say her name, she twitched again and the words spilled out of her mouth.

"Beast, not man . . . not a *human* man . . . she has told me—she has told me . . . she has said it would be like—"

"Aislinn, *no*—"

"She said you will take me as a wolf because you can take me no other way." A shudder wracked her body. "Donal? Donal? What is wrong? Donal?" One trembling hand covered her mouth. "What is *wrong?*"

"Aislinn—" slowly he moved one step closer to the bed "—she has filled your head with lies—"

Aislinn's eyes were black. "Wolf—*wolf*—no man . . . no man . . . demon *instead*—to take me as a *wolf*—"

"Aislinn, I *promise* you—"

"Donal—" She twitched. "Do you think I will breed with *you?*"

He felt the trembling begin in himself. Facing her, he could not help it. She crouched, beastlike, against the tester of the bed, knees thrust up beneath her chin and one hand twisted into her brilliant hair. But her other hand came up sharply and made the gesture against Cheysuli evil.

"*Beassssst,*" she hissed "*I will bear you no demon children!*"

Before such fear and hatred, he was totally unmanned. All thoughts of bedding her, no matter how tender, fell utterly out of his mind. Staring at her, all he could see was Electra. Electra on the dais of the palace on the Crystal Isle, facing him defiantly:

"*No marriage is binding if it is not consummated.*"

"Aislinn," he said, "oh Aislinn, do you see what she has done?"

Tears were running down her face. "Donal—? What is wrong? *What has she done to me—?*"

"She has *twisted* you—" But he stopped. Aislinn was beyond comprehension.

Sickened, Donal put on his leathers again. And then he turned back to her. "Aislinn—"

"I will not lie with a wolf!"

Clumsily, Donal unlocked the door and went out. In the darkened corridor he stood, sickened and bereft, wanting only to lick the pain of injured pride. He thought at once of Sorcha, longing for the comfort of her arms. But he could not go to the Keep. Not on his wedding night.

A sound. He looked up sharply and saw movement in the shadows. He heard the sibilance of silk against the stone. His hand went at once to his knife. He half-drew it, then saw the shadows take on the form of a man and woman embracing. The sound became a feminine giggle.

After a moment, the couple moved closer yet, into the spill of torchlight. The man glanced up as he heard the slide and click of knife going back in its sheath. "What— is it Donal? Have we disturbed the bride and groom?" Closer yet, and the man's identity was revealed.

"Evan." Donal found he could say nothing more.

The Ellasian came onward, one arm slung around the woman. Donal did not know her, save to know she was Homanan. Evan apparently had given up his attraction to women who were kin to royalty and had found a willing girl of noble birth. "Do you tarry out *here* while your bride awaits? Or has she sent you away while she divests herself of her clothing?" Evan kissed the girl quickly, then grinned archly at Donal. And then the grin faded.

Evan kissed the girl again, more soundly, then patted her silken skirts. "Go back," he said, with only a hint of regret in his tone. "I have business with the prince."

Her protest died. She slewed her dark eyes in Donal's direction, then gathered up her skirts and hastened back along the corridor.

Evan faced Donal squarely. "There is no need to speak. I have only to look at your face." His sleepy blue eyes held nothing of humor in them. "I know a remedy, my lord, if you will accompany me."

Donal stirred at last. "There is no remedy for this."

"Ah, but there is. I promise you, there is." Evan smiled. "Will you show me the taverns of Mujhara?"

"*All* of them, Ellasian?"

Evan merely shrugged. "As many as you can . . . and before the break of dawn."

Slowly, Donal smiled. "Let us set this city afire."

Sixteen

The Cheysuli were not brawlers ordinarily. They were warriors, bred in adversity and trained to slay quickly and effortlessly in order to protect kin, clan, and king. To fight for the sheer enjoyment of such things seemed utter foolishness. Yet Donal, who had imbibed so much harsh wine he no longer saw anything without a blurred halo surrounding it, found himself embroiled in the midst of a tavern brawl.

He did not precisely recall how it began. Merely that somehow he had discerned an insult to his person and his race, and that redress was necessary. He dimly recalled the offending man had gone down easily enough—and then everyone else in the common room joined in the affray.

He felt himself waver on his feet. Then a shoulder came against his spine and braced him. Without looking he knew, it was Evan, giving him what aid he could.

And I need it—

The tavern was a shambles. Groaning bodies sprawled under tables and fallen benches, counting bruises and fingering cuts. Other bodies, still limply strewn in corners of the room, did not move at all. Donal was dimly aware he and Evan had accounted for all the wreckage; the knowledge made him groggily happy. He was upholding the honor of his race.

The Ellasian fights like a Cheysuli . . . pity he must go home with Lachlan, now the marriage is made—

A great weight landed on him from behind. He folded beneath it, experiencing mild surprise as his face scraped against the wine-stained boards of the plankwood floor. He struggled briefly, felt an arm wrenched behind his back and grunted with unexpected pain. Then he was jerked to his feet and held quite still by a powerful arm thrust around his throat.

Evan, he saw, was in a similar position. The foreign prince was bruised and bloodied, his face battered, but he was smiling. He did not appear unduly perturbed by the sudden cessation of the fight or that he was so easily contained.

"I will pay the damages," he announced. "There is no need to hold us for the watch."

A short, squat man wearing the rough woolen tunic and breeches of a dalesman pushed his way through the wreckage and stopped before Donal. He was thickset, a common sort, with small brown eyes and a small, pursed mouth. The mouth formed his words oddly, twisted by his thick dalesman's dialect.

He stared up into Donal's battered face. "Shapechangers be not welcome here." He spat on Donal's boot.

Donal swallowed. "I was," he said, "before the Homanans began to lose."

Small brown piglet eyes, malignant and unblinking. "Shaine the Mujhar put purge on your sort, shapechanger. Years ago, 'twas . . . and those of us'n here still be holdin' with't."

Donal was dizzy and disoriented, but the mists were clearing from his head. He stared at the pig-eyed man in dazed amazement. "Shaine is dead. *Carillon* is the Mujhar."

"Demon-spawn," the short man said clearly. "Your kind'll be burnin' in the name of good an' clean Homanan gods, unspoiled by the foulness of shapechanger demons."

Donal heard stunned disbelief in Evan's voice. "You would slay a man because of *his race?*"

"Demons," the man repeated, and spat again against the floor. Mucous fouled Donal's boot. "I be Harbin, leader of these men. We all of us'n here be servin' the memory of the *rightful* Mujhar of Homana."

"Shaine is *dead!*" Donal repeated. "Carillon is in his place."

"Carillon be a weaklin' king, bespelled by Cheysuli magic. We don't be followin' him."

Donal became aware of the tension in the tavern. This was not some simple disagreement or mere displeasure over the outcome of the fight. Carefully he took a breath, feeling the arm press more tightly against his throat cutting off the indrawn breath. "Carillon has declared the *qu'mah-*

lin ended. Do you slay me, you slay a man sworn to the Mujhar."

Harbin stared up at him. Thick arms were crossed against his wool-clad chest; his heavy boots were planted firmly against the plankwood floor. "Carillon be bespelled. He holds Homana because of that. Because of his masters, the shapechangers. E'en now he plots to be givin' the throne back into the hands—the *paws!*—of demon-spawn. Us'n be helpless to reach Carillon himsel', but can reach the Cheysuli." His eyes shone in the candlelight. "One at a time, us'n be slayin' them. Us'n begin with you."

"No!" Evan cried. "You know not whom you threaten!"

Harbin ignored him, staring fixedly at Donal. Then his lips stretched wide over strong yellowed teeth as his eyes took in the *lir*-bands, belt, and circlet; the earring shining in black hair. "You be, for all, a *wealthy* demon." He jerked his head. "Strip him of his gold!"

Donal struggled briefly, was contained, and had to stand stiffly as hands grabbed for belt and knife and circlet. But when they sought to pull the *lir*-gold from his arms and ears, it was Evan who shouted to them.

"*Look* at him! He is the Prince of Homana!"

Harbin's head snapped around on his neck. "What folly you be speakin' at me, stranger?"

"He is Carillon's heir—" Evan grimaced as an arm nearly shut off his voice. "He is your prince, you fool—he is *Donal of Homana*—"

Harbin looked back at Donal sharply. He motioned the others away, save for the men that held him captive.

"Is it true?" a voice asked in belated discovery.

"Hold yon tongue!" Harbin snapped. He moved closer to Donal. His broad, stubbled face wore a scowl of consideration. "Is't true? Be claimin' yersel our prince, you be? Carillon's own heir? You wear enow *gold* for it!" He laughed suddenly, harshly. "Donal o' Homana, is't? Us'n caught us a prize *worth* the burnin'!"

"If he *is* the prince—" one man began.

"Hush'ee!" Harbin shouted. "He be a shapechanger. See that beast-gold on his arms and in his ear? The mark of *demons* on him." Harbin's breath came quickly and noisily. "Must be burned for it. Must be sacrificed."

"We can't burn him *here*—" another protested weakly.

The dalesman's piglet eyes narrowed as he picked at his yellowed teeth. "No. But he can still be cut here, and the body taken away for proper offerin'." He nodded. "Aye, aye—no one be takin' notice of a drunken man carried out of a tavern in the middle of the night." He spun around suddenly and faced Evan. "You be fearin' for your *own* life, stranger? Nay. We be not *evil* men. We be burnin' only demons."

Evan's mobile face was darkening with bruises. His mouth twisted as he sought to speak clearly. "He is your *prince*—"

"There bein' the greater offerin'." Harbin turned back, indicating a long wooden table still upright in the center of the common room. "Lay him there, and pin him down. On his back, barin' his throat to the gods. We be makin' this sacrifice as our old'uns did."

Donal felt fingers dig into his arms, broken and grimy nails scoring bare, vulnerable flesh. He bared his teeth at the closest man and saw him fall back in terror. But the others bore him to the table.

Fingers hooked into the heavy bands on either arm. He felt the nails cut as they twisted into his flesh. The *lir*-gold was forcibly dragged from his arms until he was naked without either band. But when a man set hand to the earring, Donal tried to jerk away.

"Lay him down!" Harbin shouted. "Pin him to the wood!"

They threw him down and stretched him flat on his back. His shoulders smashed against the table as they pinned him with countless hands, forcing his head back so that it hung off the end of the tabletop.

His senses reeled. He heard Evan shouting. Frenziedly he lashed out with a booted foot, smashing at any flesh and bone he could reach, but they caught and held him, jerking his legs apart until he was spread-eagled and utterly helpless. Hands grasped at his hair and yanked down his head, baring his throat to the blackened roof beams.

Donal cried out hoarsely, unconsciously reverting to the Old Tongue of his race. He writhed on the table, straining to break free, but he was held too firmly.

Lir! he screamed. *Why did I leave you behind?* Blood

welled into his mouth as he bit the inside of his cheek. *By the gods . . . I have slain myself—*

Harbin drew a shearing knife from his belt and approached, eyes fixed on the bared column of Donal's throat. Viewing the dalesman upside down, Donal saw only a face twisted by madness and the rising of the blade.

Gods . . . I should have stayed with Aislinn—

He opened his mouth to cry out a denial—

—*a wailing howl curled around the corners of the common room and echoed within the timbers of the roof.*

Then another came, closer still, and no man dared move.

The horn window smashed as the ruddy wolf leaped through and drove straight at Harbin, taking him in the throat. The knife fell as Harbin fell and the gurgling cry breaking out of his throat was the last sound he ever made.

A second man screamed as a striking bird of prey streaked in through the broken window and stooped, slicing with upraised talons at wide-open, staring eyes.

Rigid hands released rigid flesh. Donal, freed, came up from the table in a writhing twist. He stood atop the wood, balanced above them all, breath hissing between his tight-locked teeth. He felt a terrific upsurge of rage and the tremendous backlash of fear. He loosed himself, summoning up the magic, and blurred before them all.

Men ran screaming from the tavern, stumbling over others as they fought to escape the nightmare. Some did not make it, for Evan had caught up a fallen sword and cut off several fleeing men, driving them into a corner where he held them.

Lorn, blood-spattered and ablaze with fury, released his third kill. He turned, seeking other prey. Taj, having raked the eyes from one man and sliced open the face of another, screamed from the rafters.

"Hold!" Evan shouted. "Donal—it is *done!*"

Donal, locked in wolf-shape, heard the shout as a blur of sound, meaningless to him. He was caught up in the sheer lust for blood, snarling in ferocious joy as he stalked a man already bloodied from the encounter. Nails scratched against stained wood. Tail bristled. Hackles raised. Ears went flat against the sleek, savage, silver head.

"Donal," Evan gasped breathlessly. "There is no more need to fight. Look around you!"

The wolf moved away from the man who huddled pitifully against an overturned bench, crying and shaking. For a moment the wolf stared fixedly at the Ellasian, yellow man-eyes eerie and half-mad. But then he seemed to understand. The animal shape slid out of focus, blurring to leave a void in the air. Then Donal stood in its place. Blood ran from his mouth and painted his naked arms, but he was whole, and wholly human.

Four men had escaped. Evan held three against the wall. Five lay dead and two more badly wounded. Donal, standing in the middle of the tavern, shuddered once, and was still.

"Were I a vindictive man—" he said hoarsely, "—were I a man such as Harbin, I would order my *lir* to slay you all."

Evan stared at him. "Donal—don't. Do not besmirch your race and name."

Donal pushed a forearm across his sweat-damp brow, shoving sticky hair aside. He left behind a smear of blood. "Should I not? Should I let them go?" For a moment, he shut his burning eyes. "Gods—what has happened here?" He opened his eyes again and looked around the tavern blankly. "What madness infects Homana?"

"Donal," Evan said.

He shook his head. "No. I will not slay them. I will not besmirch my race and name." Again, he pushed dampened hair from his battered face. "But I will let them see what it is to be Cheysuli." He moved toward the three men Evan held in the corner. "Step away from them, Ellasian. This does not concern you."

Evan, dropping the sword in a gesture of distaste, did as he was ordered. He moved to the broken window and watched as Donal paced slowly closer to the men. He held them with only his eyes, pinning them to the wall.

"We claim three gifts," he told them clearly. "One is the gift of *lir*-shape, which you call the shapechange. A second is that of healing, which you refuse to believe, believing instead we are demon-spawn and evil. And the third, the final gift, is truly terrible." Donal drew in an unsteady breath. "It gives us the power to force a man's will, to replace it with our own. It is the gift of *compulsion*." His voice was a whiplash of sound. *"Look at me."*

They looked. They could do nothing else.

Donal held them all. "Take your wounded and care for them. Tell your women and children what you have done this night, and what you meant to do, and what both things have earned you. And know that you will never again lay hands upon a Cheysuli with ill intent." He stared at their blank, slack faces; their empty eyes. He had taken will and initiative from them, putting his own in the places left empty by his magic. The surge of anger within him was so powerful he wanted only to break them all, destroying their minds with a single, savage thought, but he did not. "Go from here," he said thickly, and turned away to lean against the table that had nearly been his beir.

The men gathered up their dead, their wounded, one by one, and carried them from the tavern. When they were done, leaving Donal alone with Evan and the *lir*, he set a hand to his aching head. "Now—you have seen what it is to be Cheysuli."

Evan, slowly sitting down on a righted stool, nodded. "I have seen it."

"And do Lachlan's lays exaggerate?"

"No." Evan smiled faintly. "I think even Lachlan cannot capture what it is to see a man shift his shape into that of an animal. But I think also the magic exacts a price from the men who know it fully."

Donal bent down. He gathered up the fallen *lir*-bands. In his hands, the gold seemed to recapture its luster. "It— exacts a price," Donal agreed. Carefully he slid both bands over his hands and up his forearms, until they rested in place above his elbows. "I walked too close to the edge of madness." Again he bent. He scooped up his belt, his knife, the golden circlet of his rank. And then, too weary to rise again, he sat down and leaned against the table.

Lorn came to him at once, pressing his muzzle against Donal's chest. Donal hung one bruised arm around the wolf's neck and hugged him briefly, putting his bloodied face against Lorn's ruddy head. Taj fluttered down from the rafter and settled on the table, pipping at Donal quietly.

"What do they say?" Evan asked.

"They wish me well," Donal told him. "They wish I might have kept myself from the encounter. They wish I had not seen fit to go out with an Ellasian princeling when I might have remained at Homana-Mujhar instead, and safe from such violence." He smiled. "They wish me nothing I do not already wish for myself." .

"*I* could not have said the evening would end like this!" Evan was clearly affronted. "In Ellas, we do not have madmen out to sacrifice others for their blood."

Donal draped the filigreed belt across one forearm as he propped the elbow across his knee. The rubies glowed dully in the torch-lit room. Like blood. Like all the blood on his arms. Absently, he smeared it across his flesh and dulled the gold as well.

"In Homana," he said, "we have two races vying for a single throne. A Cheysuli throne, once—we gave it up to the Homanans four hundred years ago. For peace. Because they feared our magic. And now, because of Shaine, they fear us again, and seek to usurp us."

"You *will* be the king of Homana."

Donal looked at the Ellasian. "One day. One day, when Carillon is dead . . . and if I am still alive."

"There will always be fools in the world, and madmen." Evan indicated Harbin's body. "You will have to cull them, Donal. Before they cull you."

Donal rubbed the heel of his hand across his gritty eyes. "Evan," he said. "Gods—I am weary unto death. What I have done this night is not lightly undertaken. I will pay the price for such sorcery." He stared blearily at the Ellasian. "Will you see to it I am brought safely home?"

"Of course," Evan agreed, surprised. "But why do you ask?"

Donal managed a final, sickly smile. Then he toppled sideways to the floor.

On the first day, he built a shelter out of saplings. He wove them together with vines. He took stones from the ground and made a fire cairn in the center of the shelter. He lighted a fire and put herbs into the flames, until smoke rose up to fill the tiny shelter.

He stripped out of his leathers and folded them into a pile outside the shelter. He took off armbands and earrings, setting them on top of the piled clothing. Naked, lirless, alone, he entered and sat down, cross-legged, and allowed the smoke to cloak his body.

It grew warm within the shelter. Too warm. What flesh had first shrunk from the twilight chill now exuded sweat

*that formed in droplets and ran down sun-bronzed flesh to
the earth. Breathing grew labored, and husky.*

*He did not close his eyes. Smoke entered them. Burned;
burning, his eyes began to water. Tears coursed down his
face to drip against his chest, where it joined the sheen of
sweat that bathed his flesh.*

*He sat. He waited. When the herbs and wood burned away
and the rocks of the cairn grew cool, still he waited. He did
not eat. He did not sleep. He did not move at all.*

*On the second day, he stalked and slew a silver wolf. He
drained the blood from the body, and then he smeared it
onto his flesh from head to toe. It dried. Itched. Flaked. But
he ignored it.*

He ate raw the wolf's warm heart.

The taste was vile.

But he disregarded it.

*On the third day, he bathed in a glass-black pool. He
scraped blood and grime and smoke-stench from his flesh
with heavy sand. Blood speckled up where he scraped too
hard; his blood; that which was now cleansed as the flesh
was cleansed, as the spirit was cleansed; that which made
him Cheysuli.*

He had sweated out the impurities from within.

*He had slain his other self; devoured that which had
nearly devoured him; renewed the self he had slain in the
bloody christening ritual.*

He was cleansed.

I'toshaa-ni.

"Five days," Rowan said. "You might have told the
Mujhar."

Donal, holding Ian in his arms as he stood before his
pavilion, met Rowan's eyes levelly. "There was a thing I
had to do."

A muscle ticked in Rowan's jaw. "You might have told
the Mujhar," he repeated implacably. "The Ellasian prince
came back telling a tale of near-murder and violence . . .
and yet *you* see fit to leave the city without a word to
anyone."

"I saw fit." As Ian squirmed, Donal set him down. The

boy steadied himself against his father's leather-clad leg,
then ran off to chase a new-fledged hawk as it tried to ride
the wind.

Rowan held the reins of two horses. One of them was
Donal's chestnut stallion. "You have no choice," he said.

"There is ever a choice, for me." Donal did not smile.
"I did not flee, general. I did not run from Carillon's wrath.
I came home to my Keep because there was a thing I had
to do. A form of expiation." His face still bore traces of
the tavern beating, though most of the soreness had passed.
"*I'toshaa-ni*, Rowan . . . or do your Homanan ways preclude you from comprehension?"

Dull color darkened Rowan's taut brown skin. For the
briefest of moments Donal saw the general's tight-shut
white teeth when his lips peered back as if he would speak.
But he did not. He merely pressed his lips together again
tensely and held out the reins to the chestnut horse.

"I might prefer *lir*-shape," Donal said quietly.

"Do you challenge me?" Rowan's voice gained emotion.
There was anger in it, raw, rising anger. "Do you challenge
me?" He cut off the beginnings of Donal's answer with a
sharp gesture. A Cheysuli gesture, quite rude, demanding
the silence of another. "Aye, I know what you do, *my lord*.
You look down from your Cheysuli pride and arrogance
and count me an ignorant man. Unblessed, am I?—a man
without a *lir?* Do you think I do not know? Do you think
I do not *feel* your opinion of me?" Rowan stared at Donal
with a predator's challenge; with the unwavering stare of a
dominant wolf facing a younger cub wishing to fight for the
rule of the pack. "*Lir*less I may be, Donal, but—*by the
gods!*—I am Carillon's man! What I do, I do for Homana.
You would be better to think of me as someone who means
you well, rather than your keeper."

Resentment rose up in Donal's belly. But also guilt, and
a tinge of honest regret. Mutely, he took the reins from
Rowan's hands. "I was in need of cleansing," he said in
low voice. "Rowan—I needed *i'toshaa-ni*."

"No doubt you will need it twice or thrice before this
war is done." Rowan swung up on his horse, pulling his
crimson cloak into place across the glossy rump of his tall
white stallion. He looked down upon Donal, and his face

was very grim. "Carillon has no more time for the follies of youth in his heir. And neither, I think, do I."

"You!" Donal mounted and spun his horse to face Rowan squarely. "You are not of my clan—my kin—you are not even a proper warrior. Aye, I look down on you from Cheysuli arrogance—how can I not? You are a *lir*less man, and yet you live. You live, while the *lir* you might have had is dead all these long, long years."

"Would you rather have *me* dead?" Rowan's hand caught the reins of Donal's horse. "By the gods. boy, you may be Duncan's son, but you have none of his sensitivity. I hear more of *Finn* in you—too quick to judge another man by what feelings are in yourself." Still he held the fretting stallion. Dust rose into the air. "Do you think I feel nothing? Do you consider me little more than Carillon's puppet, titled out of courtesy?" Rowan's lips drew back. "*Ku'reshtin!*—you should know better. I *earned* what rank I hold, which is more than you can claim. *No*—" Again, the sharp gesture cut Donal off. "I was born, as you were, to the clan. But Shaine's *qu'mahlin* raged, and my life was endangered the moment I drew breath. My kin, in running, were slain, and I was left to the Ellasians who found me. Am I less a man for that? Am I less a man because I claim no *lir?*" His eyes held Donal's without flinching. "Less a *warrior*, aye, as you would count a warrior—but not less a *man* than you. I am what I have made myself. And I am content with that." For a moment, his hand tightened on the reins of Donal's horse. "Homanan puppet, some men call me. But what will they call you? *You* claim the Homanan blood . . . while I am *all* Cheysuli."

Donal glared. "I claim nothing but the favor of the gods."

Rowan laughed. The sound rang out raucously, and he threw the leather rein back at Donal. "Do you, now? Are you better, then, than others?" But he stopped laughing. The ironic humor left his voice. Donal saw the tautness in Rowan's mouth and heard the too-smooth note of elaborate condescension in his tone. "And does your divinity preclude you from lying with your wife?"

Donal felt his breath flow out of his chest. He stared back and saw minute disgust in Rowan's eyes.

Disgust . . . with me . . . "What has Aislinn said?"

Rowan shrugged with studied negligence and gathered in his reins. "You will have to ask *that* of Carillon."

"Then let us do it." Donal set heels to his horse. "By the gods, *let us do it*—"

Seventeen

Carillon sat in his favorite private solar, soft-booted feet propped up on a three-legged footstool and torso slumped back into the depths of a padded velvet chair. In his hands he cradled a goblet of pale yellow wine; he nursed it, sipping almost absently. A fresh flagon sat on the table beside the chair.

Donal, facing him, felt impatience rise. He had sought out the Mujhar and confronted him, demanding to know what Aislinn had said of their failed wedding night. Carillon had said nothing, merely waving him into silence as if he must think things over. And so Donal waited.

Taj perched atop the high back of a second chair; Lorn, sleepy-eyed, slumped loosely against the stones in front of the fireplace. Neither offered comment: Donal thought they, like he, waited.

Carillon stared fixedly into the half-gone goblet of pale sweet wine, as if he dreamed. Donal thought he looked lost somehow, elsewhere entirely; there was a slackness about his spirit, a lessening of the intensity Donal had always known in him. But after a moment he stirred. "I am told you left Aislinn to seek entertainments with Lachlan's brother; that you embroiled yourself in a brawl that quickly became more than a misunderstanding. Evan says you are fortunate to be alive."

"Aye." Donal controlled his voice with effort. "I am—fortunate. But I left Aislinn because she would not have me lie with her. There were—impediments."

"Impediments?" Carillon straightened in his chair. One hand gripped the goblet, the other clenched on the knobbed end of the wooden chair arm. "If you speak of a young bride's natural modesty, you should know that a caring husband can overcome *impediments* such as that." He did not smile. "You and Sorcha were quite young when first you lay together. And yet you managed it. Why could you not manage this?"

Donal felt the coil of distaste and embarrassment tighten within his belly. "She would not have it," he said quietly. "She swore she would not have it. There were—words of insult. Words meant to hurt, to unman me—and they did." Donal looked straight at the Mujhar. "What I heard were Electra's thoughts, Electra's words in Aislinn's mouth, and I refuse to lie with *her*."

Carillon sat forward in the chair, hunching both hands clutching the goblet. "Electra," he said hoarsely. "*By the gods*, I wish that woman were dead!"

Donal moved forward. "But she is not," he said evenly. "She is alive, and well, and no doubt abetting Tynstar as he seeks to attack Homana." He paused before the Mujhar, a man grown old before his time, and aging too quickly even now. "But—she is also here, my lord . . . within your daughter's mind. And while she dwells there, there will be no heirs to the Lion Throne."

For just a moment, the twisted hands on the goblet shook. Wine spilled, splashing against the soft leather of Carillon's boots. "And so they shall win this realm because there are no children of my daughter and her husband," he said. "War becomes—incidental. Unnecessary, somehow. Because they can destroy us another way." Carillon drank. He tossed back the wine as if it were water, then poured a second goblet. But this time he only stared into it, his face lined with bitterness and regret.

And then he looked at Donal. "Can you not shut her away? Shut her out of Aislinn's mind?"

Donal shrugged. "She is the parasite and Aislinn is the host. A rapacious parasite . . . and a fragile, erratic host."

Carillon sighed and shut his eyes. For a long moment he kept himself in silence. Then, "Name me a monster, if you will, but I must bid you to use force. Use the power I know you have."

Donal stared at him in shock. "You would have me force your daughter?"

"Not *rape*." Carillon shook his head. "No, never that. Use the third gift. *Compel* her to lie with you. I know you will not harm her." He pushed himself out of the chair.

"Poor Aislinn—it is not her choosing, what Electra has done to her. She has become a valuable gamepiece, a gamepiece which Electra can use to raze the House of Homana. She *infests* Aislinn now, so that against her will Aislinn heeds what Electra intends, even to attempting murder." He ran twisted fingers through the heavily silvered hair. "But one way of making certain Electra does not succeed is to overcome her with magic stronger than what she has learned from Tynstar."

"It is *force*," Donal said. "Kin to rape, or worse—you ask me to take her will from her and replace it with my own."

Carillon set the goblet down on the table and moved slowly to one of the sun-drenched casements. He stared out, but Donal thought he saw nothing. "It is not force if it be replaced with willingness."

Donal crossed to the table and picked up Carillon's goblet, meaning to wash the foul taste from his mouth with a swallow of sweetened wine. But the Mujhar, turning back, saw it. "No!" he said sharply, crossing to catch the goblet from Donal's hand. "No—I am sorry . . . it is my favorite, and the cask is nearly empty. Until more is delivered, I am limited to a single goblet each night . . . and I am a selfish man." Carillon smiled. "I think you might do better to keep yourself from wine this night and think of what awaits you in your bed."

Donal shook his head. "I have no taste for this."

"I do not ask you to *have taste*," Carillon said raggedly. "I ask only that you perform a service any man should be ready and willing to perform."

"Ready and willing!" Donal threw at him. "This is your *daughter*, Carillon . . . not some silly chambermaid!"

"Do you think I do not know?" Carillon shouted back. His voice shook a little, and Donal saw the anguish in the depths of the fading blue eyes. "Ah gods, would that I had never married the woman, so this would not be necessary. *Would that I had wed someone else—*" He broke off. Tears shone in his eyes. "They warned me. Finn, mostly. And Duncan. Even Alix and my sister. *Do not wed Electra*, they said, *she is Tynstar's meijha and will only seek to slay you.* Oh, aye, they had the right of it . . . and now I pay the price."

Donal drew in a deep breath, knowing somehow he had

to offer comfort to the man. "You took her for the alliance between Homana and Solinde. You have spent these past fifteen years teaching me the rudiments of kingcraft—I think I understand at least a little of it. You wed her because you had to."

"Had to?" Carillon's twisted smile was bittersweet. "Oh, aye—I had to. For the alliance . . . but something else as well." He stared into the goblet. "Aye . . . there was sorcery and witchcraft, but much more to the woman than that. She was—unlike any other I had ever known. Even now. And—I think I even loved her . . . for a little while." Slowly, he lifted the recaptured goblet and drank down what remained of the pale, sweet wine. "Do what you must," he said at last. "but be gentle with her, Donal."

Looking at him, Donal felt a chill of apprehension run down the length of his spine. *Gods . . . grant me health, grant me the kindness of never putting such choices before me.*

He waited until it was very late and most of the servants were abed. Then, telling his *lir* to remain in his chamber, he went down the corridor to Aislinn's suite of apartments, and pushed open the heavy door.

He had half expected it to be locked. But perhaps Aislinn, knowing her actions had driven him into the city streets and then to Sorcha in the Keep, thought he would not return to her. And so his way was unimpeded as he entered the darkened chamber.

One candle burned in the far corner. Donal had never understood the Homanan penchant for leaving candles lit when sleep was sought; if there were demons sent to catch a man, a candle would not stop them. And if it were meant to ward off mortal enemies, the light destroyed night vision and left the victim more vulnerable than ever.

But he did not blow it out. He wanted Aislinn to know him when she saw him.

Noiselessly he walked to her draperied bed. He could see nothing through the sheen of silk and gauze. But he could hear her breathing.

Gods . . . does Carillon know what he asks? But he knew the Mujhar did.

Quickly Donal shed boots and leathers. Naked, he stripped aside the draperies, prepared to slip into the bed—

—and found Aislinn waiting for him, kneeling amid the folds of the coverlet.

In the shadows of the curtained bed, her eyes were blackened hollows. Dim candlelight threaded its way through the draperies and burnished bronze her red-gold hair. She wore a thin silken nightshift; nothing else, except her pride.

"You knew," he said.

"I knew. No one told me, but—I knew." She drew in an uneven breath. "All my life I have been brought up to know my task in this world is to bear children for my lord. All my life I have known my firstborn son would become Mujhar in his father's place, as *you* will when mine is dead. Well . . . there will be no son if I do not lie with you."

She was frightened even as she smiled a wry little smile, stating the obvious; that much he could tell. But frightened of *herself*, not of him. "It is not *you*, Aislinn," he told her. "It is what that witch has done to you."

She swallowed visibly. "I know it. But—knowing it does not undo what she has done."

Gently, he asked, "You know what *I* must do?"

Aislinn briefly shut her eyes. "*Gods*, Donal—I would trade almost anything to make this bedding pleasurable for us both! Do you think I *wish* to spew such vileness from my mouth?" Her fingers were locked into the neckline of her nightshift, twisting at the fabric. "For as long as I can remember, you were the man I wanted. Even as children, I knew I could go to you for anything. And now—*now*, when I can have you—I drive you instead to *her*."

Her. Aislinn knew very well what competition Sorcha offered. And yet he did not, for the moment, see jealousy in her face. Only dashed hopes and forlorn self-hatred, because Aislinn blamed herself.

He nearly put out his hands to reach for her, to touch her hair, to stroke her shoulders, but he stopped himself. "Aislinn," he said gently, "if there were another way I would seek it. I have no taste for this."

She nodded. And then her eyes beseeched him. "Do you think—it is possible whatever my mother did to me has faded? Perhaps—perhaps it was meant only for the wedding night."

"Perhaps." He knew better—she grasped at straws—but said nothing of it. "Aislinn—come and sit beside me." He himself sat down on the edge of the bed, knowing the posture was unthreatening. And after a moment, she did as he had bidden.

She laughed an odd little laugh. "I feel like a fool. Like an untried girl, nervous before her lord."

"Are you not?"

She sighed. "I am. Donal—" She stopped short, glancing sideways at his nudity, her eyes dark with passion and fear. Tentatively, she put up a hand and touched the *lir*-gold on his arm. "Do you never take it off?"

"Rarely. It is a part of me." He let her touch the gold, knowing the motion took more than a little courage.

Her fingers explored the armband. "I see Taj and Lorn in the patterns," Aislinn said. "The craftsmanship is superb—I have seen many fine gifts offered to my father, but none, I think, so fine as Cheysuli *lir*-gold. The knife he wears—"

"Finn's, once. They exchanged knives when they swore the oath of liege man and Mujhar."

"And broke it." Aislinn shook her head a little. "What I know of Finn and what I am *told* are two different things. All those stories . . . and yet, he is different from what is said. It seems odd, to know a man, and yet realize others know him differently from the years before I was born."

Donal thought of his father. He had been told countless stories of Alix, Finn, Carillon, and others about Duncan. So many of those stories dated from before his birth, even before his mother and father had married, Cheysuli-fashion. For many years he had treasured the tales, storing them away in the sacred trunk of memory, cherishing all the contents. And now Tynstar had smashed that trunk, destroying the memories.

"I remember when you were born." He did, though not well. But perhaps it was time they began to fashion their own memories for the future. "There was rejoicing throughout Homana, that the Queen had been delivered of a healthy child." He did not say how that rejoicing had been tempered with disappointment; Homana had needed a son.

Her fingers had left the gold to touch his arm. Now she withdrew them. "The *Queen*." Aislinn's mouth twisted. "When men speak of the Queen, they link her name with Tynstar. Not with Carillon, who wed her and *made* her

Queen of Homana. *No*. With that vile, wretched Ihlini!"
Bitterness balled her hands into fists. "I wish—I wish he
were dead! I wish someone would slay him!"

"Someone will, someday." No longer did she seem intimidated by his nudity. "Aislinn—"

She did not let him finish, turning instead to face him
squarely. Hesitantly, she reached out both hands to touch
his shoulders, closing fingers on the muscles. "I want it. I
want *you*—I have *always* wanted you."

Donal did what he had desired since he first pulled back
the draperies. He set his hands into her hair and threaded
persuasive fingers, tugging her closer to him. For him, at
that moment, Sorcha receded; his present was only Aislinn.

"Gods . . ." She breathed it against his mouth. "No one
said I would feel like *this*—"

"Who could?" he asked. "Electra? You see what she
has done."

"My mother is a fool—" Aislinn was in his arms, twisting
shoulders free of her garment to press her bare flesh against
his. "My mother—"

He felt her body abruptly go rigid beneath his hands.
"Aislinn—?" But even as he said her name, he knew what
was happening.

"No!" she cried. "No, *no*—" The shudder wracked her
body. Donal saw her head arch back, back, until her throat
was bared to him and her hair spilled down against the
tangled sheets. The sound she made was one of terror
mixed with madness.

"No more!" he hissed. "By all the gods of the Firstborn,
I will *not* let Electra win—!"

A physical link was not necessary, but he sought it anyway. Aislinn, utterly limp in his arms, he lay on her back
against the bed. He knelt over her, sinking hands through
her hair to cup each delicate temple. He felt the pulse-beat
beneath the flesh, against the palm of his hands.

"Not this time," he said grimly. "Not *this* time, Solindish
witch—"

But what Electra had done was not easily broken. Donal
met resistance as he sought a way through the barriers to
Aislinn's subconscious. Something battered back at him,
trying to throw him away. Instantly he threw up his own

shields and advanced, gritting his teeth against the intensity of Electra's spell.

"Aislinn . . . *fight* her . . . fight *Electra*—not me!"

But Aislinn was too lost within the ensorcelment. She fought him mentally and physically, sweating and crying in her efforts.

He would lose. And by losing, lose Aislinn entirely. He could not see any way to win without risking Aislinn's welfare.

The witch set her trap very well indeed . . . if she does not catch me in it, she may well catch her daughter—

And then he realized there *was* a way to win. It was not fair. He risked Aislinn even as Electra risked her, but if he did not try, she was lost without a fight of any sort. Donal thought she was worth more than that. And so he sought the essence of the shapechange.

He would not change before the girl—did not *dare* to, when that was Electra's key—but he could use a measure of the concentration *lir*-shape required. It was honed sharp as any blade, but offering danger to Aislinn as well as himself. It was a matter of balance again. In such circumstances as these, he could tip over the edge so easily.

Donal summoned up the strength. And without warning the helpless girl, he tore through her mental barriers and forced his will upon hers.

He had told Carillon it was tantamount to rape. Donal knew only that as he forced his will upon the girl, he forced more than mental persuasion.

And yet, even as he fought to win Aislinn back from her mother and the Ihlini, Donal became dimly aware of a part of himself that *understood* the need for compulsion. A part of him knew physical release as well as mental was required, since he sought consummation as a result of forcing her will, and not just persuasion. With a man, there was no question it was merely a mental rape. The compulsion was never sexual. But with a woman, with *Aislinn*, whom he desired anyway, the compulsion was linked with intensifying need.

Perversion? He thought not. But—would he think it *was* while lost in the power of such overwhelming desire?

Man, not wolf . . . man, not falcon . . . And yet he knew, as he slid closer to the edge, it would not be difficult to shift into either form. It was possible he might mimic the being his father had been, neither one nor the other; a *thing* caught between.

He felt a wild rage building up inside of him. Not at Aislinn. But at Electra. At Tynstar. For using an innocent, vulnerable girl as bait to trap a Cheysuli. For setting up the obscene circumstances that required such violence.

For turning him into an animal, even in human form.

Will they never stop? Will they never give up their abuse of human beings?

Distantly, he heard Aislinn crying out. So near the edge, *too* near the edge; he silenced her with the only gag he had left: his mouth.

Aislinn, I swear . . . I never wanted it this way. . . . And until the night of their wedding, Donal had not believed he wanted it at all.

Now he knew he had wanted it longer than he cared to acknowledge. He recalled clearly the young woman who had met him on the Crystal Isle: haughty, defiant princess; later, vulnerable, frightened girl. An assassin as well, but it was yet another facet of her being. She was neither the complaisant, spiritless woman so many Homanans were, nor the cold, powerful sorceress Electra had made of herself. Aislinn was merely—Aislinn. And in their mutual battle against her mother, each sought release whatever way they could find it.

Sul'harai. He did not know the Homanan word for the concept. He only knew that with Sorcha, the experience was familiar. The simultaneous sharing of the magic in their union. Not one-sided. That was easy enough for a woman; easier for a man. Simultaneous. And now, he found he wanted it as much with Aislinn.

"I *will* win, Electra—" And with the strength of the *lir*-bond, Donal smashed all of Aislinn's barriers and left nothing in his wake, emptying her resistance like a seedbag spilling grain.

And as she lay empty before him physically and emotionally, he replaced the abhorrence Electra had put there with a terrible need for him.

Not rape . . . not rape, if she wants me as I want her—

But he realized, as she roused to his hands and his mouth, the compromise was a curse as well as a blessing.

Because if the time came Aislinn ever turned to him out of *genuine* affection, he would never know it.

At dawn, Donal stood at the edge of the oubliette. One torch roared against the silences of the vault. Light rushed across the creamy, gold-veined marble, and the *lir* leaped out at him.

He teetered. Closed his eyes. *Oh gods, what have I done—what have I done to the girl—?*

The torch roared. Everything else was silence.

Except for his screaming conscience.

Remorse? That, and worse. Yet he welcomed the guilt, the anger, the horror; the sickness that turned his belly. It meant he was a man after all, not a beast; not a *thing* who took and was pleased by the taking, not caring *how* it was taken or who was hurt. When she awakened Aislinn would recall only a part of what had happened, because the compulsion worked that way, but *he* would know it all. He would remember everything.

See what I have become?

He stared down into the void. It was not death he sought; not suicide. Not a form of expiation, to pay for the loss of his soul. He had no wish to die regardless of the reason. Suicide was taboo; he was too much a warrior to consider denying himself the afterworld. But he wanted a way of assuaging some of the *pain*.

"My lord—?"

Donal spun at the brink of the void. He was reminded suddenly of the other time he had visited the Womb, and how someone had tried to push him in. Memory flared; he threw up an arm against the assassin.

"*My lord!*" Sef's voice, and shocked. Memory faded; Donal saw the boy standing just inside the open door. His odd eyes were stretched wide in fear. "You do not mean to *jump*—"

"No." The weight of the Womb was at his back, begging him to give himself to the *Jehana*. "No, Sef—I do not mean to jump." Donal felt sweat sting his armpits; he smelled the fear on himself. No, he had not meant to jump, and yet he had come close to it regardless. "What are you doing here?"

He said it more sharply than he intended. Sef's face

blanched white.. "I—couldn't sleep. Bevin had a girl with him, and—" He broke off, plainly embarrassed. Sharing a room with Bevin meant sharing a room with many women as well. "I—went out to walk. I—went to the Great Hall, to see the Lion sleeping." Color washed back into his face. "There was a stairway in the firepit, and so I came down to see where it went." He looked sidelong at the walls with their leaping *lir*. "What *is* this place, my lord?"

"The Womb of the Earth." Donal saw no sense in secrecy, not when the boy had seen it himself. "Cheysuli made it long, long ago. Legends say a man who will be Mujhar must go back into the Womb to be reborn a king."

"Have *you*?"

"Gone in? —no. For me, I think there is no need." He did not pursue it further. For Carillon, the rebirth had been required; for a man born to the clans with the gifts of the Old Blood, there were other initiations.

Sef stared around the vault. "So many animals . . . they look so alive."

"They are not. At least not now." Donal frowned a little. Who was to say the *lir* had never been alive? Perhaps they only waited for the Firstborn to come again before they broke free of the stone.

Donal shivered. And Sef, staring at the oubliette again, mimicked him unconsciously. "My lord—this place frightens me."

"Then let us leave it together. There is nothing more for me here." Donal took the torch from the bracket. "Come, Sef. I think it is time you learned some geography."

"My lord?" Sef stared.

"Maps. If you cannot sleep, look at maps. It is better than counting trees."

He led Sef out of the vault and back up the one hundred and two steps to the Great Hall with its sleeping Lion. Donal shut the hinged plate and kicked ash and logs back over the iron to hide it. Then he took Sef to one of Carillon's council chambers. Donal set the torch into an empty bracket, selected the appropriate map and spread it out on the table, then lighted the fat white candle. He touched a blue-shaded portion of the map. "There. That is Solinde."

"*All* of that?" Sef stood next to the stool upon which

Donal sat. The boy stared avidly at the map, hands clasped behind his back, afraid to touch the valuable hide.

"All of this, aye." Donal's finger swept around the blue borders of the realm. "Lestra is here, you see . . . the city, at the moment, is loyal; but much of the aristocracy is not—these men want to sever the alliance between Homana and Solinde, to claim the land their own."

"But—don't they also want Homana?"

Donal glanced at the boy as he hung over the map. "*Tynstar* wants Homana. The Mujhar believes the Solindish aristocracy would be content enough to ignore Homana, given Solinde again—but under Tynstar's dominion, they give tacit approval to the war. The armies will ride against us while Tynstar, as ever, watches from a distance."

"Then—Solinde isn't really your enemy," Sef said. "It's the sorcerer, isn't it?"

Donal sighed, smiling wryly. "You ask things I am not fit to answer. These are questions with historical implications—being clan-born and bred, I know more of the Cheysuli than the Homanans. But I can tell you this much: for years upon years, Solinde—under Bellam—fought to take Homana. Bellam, being an acquisitive man, wanted Homana for himself. But I do not doubt Tynstar blew a fire from the embers with exceedingly careful breaths." Idly, Donal rested his chin in the palm of one hand. "Bellam is dead now and Carillon holds both realms—but I doubt the Ihlini will ever give up entirely. They will ever be our bane."

Sef frowned, screwing his pale face into an expression of concentration. "Then—if you slew the demon, Tynstar—we would be free of this war?"

"Perhaps not entirely, but I do not doubt Tynstar's death would have great effect on Solinde. In time, did he die, the traditional enemies might make a lasting peace."

Sef straightened from his hunched position over the table. "Then—why not send someone to slay him?"

"Tynstar?" A wry smile that twisted Donal's mouth. "Could *that* be done, it would have been long ago."

"But—he's a *man*, isn't he? A sorcerer, aye—but a man. Can't he die like others?"

Donal regarded the boy's intensity. "Tynstar is a man, of course, and no doubt he can die. But he has escaped death for three hundred years—it will never be easily done."

Sef blanched. *"Three hundred years—?"*

"He has the gift of immortal life from Asar-Suti himself."

"Gods—" Sef whispered. "How will we ever win?"

"With my help, it will hardly prove so difficult." Evan of Ellas, striding through the open door, grinned at them both. "I am coming with you."

Donal stared at him in shock. "I thought you had gone home to Ellas! After that tavern brawl—"

"That brawl?" Evan asked nonchalantly. "I have seen worse in a brothel. No, I have not gone home to Ellas. Not yet. I prefer to stay here a bit."

"To come to war." Donal shook his head. "A foolish way to pass the time, Evan. Ellas has no stake in this. If she lost a prince—"

"She has seven others, if you count Lachlan's sons." Sleepy eyes alight, Even shrugged negligently. "I have neither wife nor sons—that I know of—with which to concern myself. I will come with you."

Sef spoke up before Donal could. "But what would the Crown Prince say?"

"Lachlan?" Evan's brows rose, though he looked a bit surprised at Sef's presumption. But it was Donal he answered, not the boy. "Lachlan knows he cannot gainsay me when I put my mind to a thing." He grinned. "You need my help, Donal. You may as well admit it."

"It isn't Ellas's war," Sef said.

Donal glanced sharply at the boy. Sef stood stiffly by the table, facing Evan squarely. His chin was thrust upward, as if he prepared to do battle. "Sef. This is better left to the Prince of Ellas and me. You may go."

Sef stared fiercely at Evan a moment, then abruptly turned to Donal. "Aye, my lord. But—" He broke off and shrugged. "I just—I just want to come with you."

"And you think I will not take you if the Prince of Ellas comes?" Donal shook his head. "Sef, I have already said you may go to war with me—though I do not understand why you would *want* to, any more than I understand *him.*" His glance included Evan. "You may come. *Now*—you may go."

Sef went. Donal shook his head and Evan, staring after

the boy, merely sighed a little and shrugged. "He worships you, Donal. I think he would give his life for you."

"So long as he does not have to." Donal looked at Evan and began to smile. With the Ellasian prince he felt a weight lifting from his soul. Before Evan, he was free to be the man he so seldom had been able to be. "I think we will show Solinde how two princes can force a realm to its knees."

Evan raised one dark eyebrow. "If we can destroy a single tavern, we should surely have no difficulty with an entire kingdom."

Eighteen

When the Homanan army marched at last across the western borders into Solinde, it met with little resistance. Carillon took care to distinguish between Solindish crofters and citizens who had no stake in the battle beyond trying to survive while their realm was battered by war, and those who supported Tynstar. Much of the realm still served Carillon's interests, albeit reluctantly. Still, the tension was apparent from the moment they crossed the border.

The Cheysuli moved within the ranks independently, under the command of their clan-leaders who dealt directly with Carillon. Donal, who had grown up in the aftermath of Shaine's *qu'mahlin*, had known only a grudging peace between the two races. The incident in the tavern—compounded by recollections of his reception in Hondarth and the reaction to his wedding—served to remind him that the restoration of his race was hardly completed.

He found that most of the soldiers accepted the Cheysuli readily enough—the races had fought together to help win Carillon his throne—but there was uneasiness within the ranks. It was Carillon who kept the peace. And Rowan, whose Homanan ways and Cheysuli appearance made him a man of both and neither races.

Evan proved an easy companion for Donal. Together they argued and debated and discussed all manner of strategy in all varieties of emotions, but always recognizing the bond of true friendship. A bond Donal had never experienced before, being caught between his Homanan rank and Cheysuli warrior status, and he found it was one he valued greatly. It was not the same as the link with his *lir*, but it was very satisfying nonetheless.

Now, seated across the table from Carillon in the Mujhar's crimson field pavilion, Donal realized his present companion was somewhere else in spirit if not in body. Carillon, done with eating, sat back on his three-legged campstool. One hand cupped the footed silver goblet filled with his favorite wine.

It was mid-summer and temperate. An evening breeze rippled the brilliant fabric of the pavilion. Light from the setting sun crept through the weave of the fabric and splashed color into the interior, so that the blond wood of table and chairs was dyed a rich ocher-bronze. The silver shone golden in the light.

Donal smelled roasting boar, spitted in the center of the camp. He smelled the bouquet of Carillon's wine and a faint tinge of bitterness he ascribed to the coals in the brazier. He smelled the aroma of war, though they had barely met a soul in battle. He smelled death and futility, and the strivings of men who would spend their lives in defense of a throne they would never see, a throne that one day would be his.

Carillon slowly turned his goblet in circles on the wood. "Where is Evan tonight? I invited both of you."

Donal smiled. "You recall those Solindish crofters' daughters who felt compelled to follow us? Evan found several more than willing to share their favors with him. He sends his regrets."

Carillon laughed. "I am glad one of us can lose his cares in a woman's flesh tonight." Abruptly, he sat upright on his stool. "Gods—I have forgotten! A message for you from Aislinn came earlier today—I put it aside and forgot it. There—in the small chest by my cot."

Donal pushed back from the table and rose, going at once to the teak casket near the bed. Inside it he found a parchment scroll sealed with wax, stamped with the royal Homanan crest.

He broke the seal. He was afraid as well as curious; in the two months since the army had marched into Solinde, there had been no letters from Aislinn. There had been nothing but silence between them.

Donal read the message, then stared blankly at the lettering. "She has—conceived."

Carillon rose slowly to his feet. "She is certain?"

"There has been confirmation." Donal sucked in, a deep

breath. "Well, my lord . . . forced or not, it seems to have succeeded."

"Thank the gods," Carillon said fervently, "the throne is secured at last."

Donal shook his head. "Only if the child is a boy."

"You have already sired one—is it so foolish to think there may be another?" But Carillon turned away to pour more wine in his goblet, not bothering to wait for a response, though Donal offered none.

He watched Carillon drink. Of late the Mujhar drank more and more, no doubt to ease his pain. Even in the dry warmth of a Solindish summer, his swollen joints ached.

I could not bear it, Donal knew. *I swear—I could not bear it . . . and he leads us all to battle.*

He looked again at the message, penned in a wavering hand. From Aislinn herself, he did not doubt; a scribe would do it more carefully.

Gods, what is she thinking . . . what does she think of me? "She says she is well," he told Carillon. "But—first births are often hard. With Sorcha—" He broke off abruptly, knowing it was not the time to speak of his *meijha*. But then he turned sharply to Carillon. Of late there had been a bond between them of mutual affection and circumstances. Donal recalled how Carillon had taught him to read a map and explained the battles he had fought with Finn at his side. But now, with the specter of Sorcha suddenly between them, he felt the faint tension rise up to mock them both. "You hate me for that, do you not?" Donal asked. "For keeping Sorcha when Aislinn is my *cheysula.*"

Carillon moved to one of the supple leather chairs and sat down slowly, lowering himself carefully into the seat. "I have learned, over the years, to respect many Cheysuli customs. I admit I do not understand most of them, but I have learned what integrity there is in your race. Though, given a choice, I would prefer you set aside your *meijha*— for my daughter's sake—I will not ask it of you."

"You did not answer my question."

Carillon smiled. "No, I did not. Well enough." He shifted in the chair and drank more wine; the pale, sweet wine with its acidic bouquet, that Carillon allowed no one else to touch. "I do not hate you, Donal. I kept myself to Elec-

tra when we were together because I desired no other—
she would inspire fidelity in any man, regardless of his
tastes . . . but it does not mean I cannot comprehend your
ability to wed one woman and keep another as well." He
gazed into the brazier coals. "For all that, I am the *last* to
speak of such things as a man desiring only one woman
when there is another one he cares for. The gods know I
wanted your mother badly enough, even when both of us
were wed to other people." There was pain in his voice as
he said it, immense pain; he had taken the news of Alix's
death very badly.

Donal's hand closed spasmodically on the parchment,
crumpling it into ruin. "My *jehana*—?"

Carillon turned. In his eyes was an arrested expression.
"Did she never tell you?"

"My *jehana?*" It was all Donal could manage.

Carillon sighed heavily and rubbed his eyes. "An old
story, Donal. . . . I thought surely you must know it by
now." Twisted fingers scraped silver hair back from his
pain-wracked face. "Gods—I cannot believe she is gone.
Not *Alix*. After all she has been to me . . . after all she
has done. . . ."

And my jehan? Donal wanted to ask. *You say nothing
of my jehan. Is it that even in death you compete?*

Aloud, Donal said, "What old story, my lord?"

Carillon shook his head after a moment. "I never
stopped caring for her, Donal, even after she wed your
father. Even after she had borne you." He swirled wine in
his goblet. "I wed Electra. And when that marriage was
finished, I turned again to your mother."

Possessiveness overruled Donal's empathy. "Even while
she was Duncan's *cheysula*—?"

"No." Carillon looked at him. "Your father was already
*lir*less. Dead—or so we believed." Carillon's brow furrowed
a little, as if reflecting a measure of his grief. "The day I
took you and your mother back to the Keep, I asked her
to marry me. I would have made her Queen."

My jehana, *the Queen of Homana*— But the wonderment
did not last. "She wanted no one but my *jehan*." He said
it a trifle cruelly, but he felt threatened by Carillon's admission. For so many years he had known how deeply his
parents had loved one another, and how deeply Alix

grieved for Duncan. Now, to think of her wed to Carillon—

"No," Donal said. "She was Cheysuli." He thought it was enough.

Carillon lifted his head and looked directly at Donal. There was no hesitation in his tone, no tact. Just raw, clean emotion. "It would have made you my son . . . as much as if you were my own."

Donal stared at the aging face; at the lines and creases and brackets put there by Tynstar's sorcery. He saw sorrow and regret and anguish in that face, and an almost inhuman strength of will coupled with unexpected vulnerability.

Donal drew in a breath. "I never knew, my lord."

Carillon smiled a little. "She would not have me. She would not put another man in Duncan's place. And so we did not wed—" He broke off a moment. When he resumed, it was with careful intonations so as not to display the magnitude of his grief. But Donal heard it regardless. "Together, they died. And you are still Duncan's son."

"My lord!" The urgent voice came from outside the pavilion.

"Rowan—" Carillon straightened in his chair. "Come in at once!"

Rowan pulled aside the flap and came through part way, so that the crimson fabric hung over one shoulder like a cloak. "Carillon—you had best come. There is something you should see."

The Mujhar pushed himself up from his chair awkwardly and moved at once to pick up his sword and sheathe it. The black ruby glittered in the candlelight; Donal, seeing it again, felt guilty that he had not yet accepted it from Carillon. But somehow he *could* not.

"Come." Carillon went with Rowan out of the pavilion. Donal, waiting for his *lir*, threw down the crumpled parchment and followed a moment later.

Outside, Donal frowned. Something was—different. Something was—not right. There was a tension in the air, a sensation that set the hairs to rising on the back of his neck. A prickle ran down his spine.

Sorcery. That from Taj, flying above in the darkness.

Ihlini, Lorn agreed as he paced next to Donal's left leg.

The light was wrong. Instead of normal deepening twilight, it was nearly black as pitch. Torchlight illuminated the encampment, but the flames seemed almost muted, swallowed by the darkness. Something muffled sight, sound, smell, as if the camp had been swept beneath a carpet.

Rowan took them westward to a line of gentle hills that rolled out to ring the camp. He gestured briefly to the moon hanging so low against the starless sky: its face was filled with darkness. A thick, viscid darkness. The color was deepest purple.

Carillon stopped at the crest of a grassy hill where another man waited with his wolf. In the light from the dying moon, the slender stalks of grass glowed a luminous lavender.

"Ihlini," Finn said.

Donal frowned. Wreaths of cloying mist rose up from the flatlands below the hills: bog steaming in a storm. There was the faintest of hisses, almost lost in the heavy darkness. "Some form of spell?"

"More like a warning—or a greeting." Carillon's hand was on his sword. "Who can say what Tynstar means by anything he does?"

Rowan, next to them, frowned. "How can he summon sorcery before so many Cheysuli?"

Carillon's eyes did not stop moving as he studied the lay of the land and the mist that rose to obscure it. "Here, there are four times as many Homanans. Tynstar strikes at *them*."

Finn's expression was stark in the purpled moonlight. "Even face to face with a Cheysuli, the Ihlini still have recourse to simple tricks and illusions. With so many Homanans present, he need not concern himself with us. He need only play upon the superstitions of the Homanans, as he has done in the past."

Lir, Donal said. *I wish you could do something.*

Nothing, Lorn answered. *You know the law. We cannot fight Ihlini.*

And yet Ihlini fight us.

I did not say the law was fair. Lorn's tone was ironic. *I only know we of the* lir *honor what the gods have given us.*

If I *die, you and Taj are dead.*

It is all a part of the price.

Too high, Donal retorted. *You should tell the gods.*

Why not do it yourself?

Ground fog rolled. Within the violet wreaths flashed tiny sparks of deepest purple, as if fireflies danced in the mist.

"The men are understandably—*concerned*," Rowan said pointedly.

"They are afraid." Finn had no time for wordplay. "As Tynstar means them to be."

Donal glanced around. Behind the rim in the shallow bowl gathered all of the Homanan army. He heard whispers and mutters and curses as the river of fog flowed over the hill and downward. The muffled silence of the night was palpable.

Donal shivered. Lir—*call me a coward. I do not like this at all.*

Taj still hung in the air. *Then all of us are cowards.*

Carillon gestured sharply to Rowan. "Go and speak to the captains. I will not have my men fleeing Ihlini *illusions*."

"Aye, my lord, at once." Rowan departed with alacrity, wading through rolling fog.

"Donal? Donal?" It was Evan's voice, as the Ellasian climbed the hill. "Is this what you meant when you told me about Ihlini magic?"

Donal waited until Evan had reached the top of the hill. "Somewhat," he answered tersely. "Evan—it is not a joking matter."

The Ellasian prince frowned as he looked out across the blackened land. "No," he said after a moment. "It is not. *Lodhi!*—but what a coil!"

Donal looked at his uncle worriedly. "You think he intends no harm, then—if he uses only illusion?"

Finn shook his head. "It is not Tynstar's way to join in battle without first seeking to fill men's minds with fear." His mouth hooked down. "What better than to win before blood is shed?"

"That would never stop him," Carillon answered. "He will spill all the blood he must."

"*Look!*" Evan cried.

The mist parted, sliced neatly as if cloven with an ax. In the wound stood a fountain of purple flame with a heart so brilliant it burned a pristine white. The illumination pouring from the fountain filled the world up with light, bathing each face with a starkness from which there was no hiding. Men squinted, holding up their arms to shield their eyes. Picketed horses screamed and tried to bolt. Cries of fear rose from the clustered mass of men.

Carillon spun around to face them all, thrusting up a belaying hand. "No! It is only Ihlini *illusion.* Do not fear what is not real!"

But Donal watched the burning fountain. It cracked open and spilled out a sinuous gout of flame that crept across the grass. Blackness spread out around it; what it touched it consumed, and anything else nearby.

"Lodhi!" Evan whispered dazedly.

A serpent, Donal thought. *Tynstar's serpent, sent to do his slaying for him—*

"Carillon," Finn warned.

The Mujhar turned. Ten feet from them all, on the crest of the hill, the writhing serpent halted. It coiled, rose upward, stretched itself toward the sky. It thickened, as if it had been fed. It swelled, as if heavy with child.

And then the swollen belly split open, and the serpent gave birth to a man.

He was wrapped in a purple cloak so dark it was nearly black. A silver brooch glinted at one shoulder; silver earrings flashed in his lobes; a ring was on one hand. But it was the eyes, not the jewelry, that Donal saw more than anything else; the eyes, black and beguiling, set in the smooth flesh of eternal youth. The smile, framed by black and silver beard, was singularly sweet.

For the first time Donal faced the man who done so much to destroy his life, and he found he was afraid.

Gods—I am not fit to hold the throne—I can barely look *at the man—*

"I bid you farewell, Carillon." The voice was warmly affectionate, lacking the hostility Donal had expected. "We have been good enemies, you and I, but I am done with you at last. The time for your death has come."

Donal looked quickly at Carillon. He could not conceive of what *he* might say, did Tynstar speak to him. But Carillon was more accustomed to facing the man.

The Mujhar laughed aloud. "Tynstar, you *fool*—what makes you think you will succeed *this* time? Have you not failed repeatedly before? Even the last time we met, nearly sixteen years ago, you could not end my life. Oh, aye, you *shortened* it—but I am still alive to thwart you."

Donal was more than a little amazed by Carillon's composure *and* the audacity of his answer. But then, the Mujhar had had years in which to refine his courage.

Tynstar's smile was genuinely amused. "It is true you have guarded yourself well. The Cheysuli ever serve their Mujhar." He looked at Finn. Then at Donal. "But now there is one of their *own* who waits to take the throne—and you are no longer needed."

Carillon shook his head. "You will not put me in fear of the warriors who serve me so well. I am not Shaine, Ihlini. I do not succumb to such transparent tricks as these."

The flame around Tynstar rippled, as if the serpent writhed. "Shaine succumbed to his own fears and inner madness. You will succumb to something else." Light glinted off his silver ornaments. "Carillon, you have played out your part in the prophecy. You are toothless now, like an old lion—useless and merely a bore. There is another who serves the prophecy now, even as it serves him." One hand rose to point directly at them. "Do you see him? You have only to look at the warrior who wards your left side, so solemn and silent beside you." The sorcerer smiled. "A man at last, Donal . . . no more the boy I sought to make my own so many years ago."

Unconsciously, Donal put one hand to the flesh of his throat. He could feel the kiss of the iron collar, the weight of his vulnerability. Then he forced his hand away. "You are a fool indeed if you think I will turn against Carillon."

Tynstar smiled. "No. I am quite aware of the folly in trying that. You are not so pliant as I could wish. No, you will not turn against Carillon . . . but you will not have to. He will be dead within a year."

"And the throne?" Carillon rasped.

"Mine," Tynstar said simply. "As it was ever meant to be."

"*Mine,*" Donal retorted. "The Lion will never accept an Ihlini. The gods intend it for *us.*"

Tynstar, cloaked in purple shroud and brilliant flame, merely shook his haloed head. "Your *shar tahl* has failed your clan, Donal. You know nothing of the histories."

"*Ku'reshtin!*" Donal swore.

"*Resh'ta-ni,*" Tynstar returned equably, clearly fluent in the language.

Donal stared. But he told himself anyone could learn

the Old Tongue—including an Ihlini—if there were reason enough to do it.

Casually, Tynstar made the gesture of *tahlmorra*. "I shall have to instruct you, I see, to reduce your alarming ignorance."

Finn laughed. "An amusing idea, Ihlini. *You* instructing *us*?"

"I know the truth of the histories," Tynstar said. "And I will willingly share them with you."

"I will not listen," Donal told him flatly. "Do you think I would heed *your* words?"

"Take them to the Keep with you and question your *shar tahl*," Tynstar challenged. "See then who lies. See then who speaks the truth." He put up a silencing hand. "Have you never wondered why the Firstborn left Homana to the Cheysuli? Have you never wondered precisely *how* an entire race died out?"

"You are an unlikely tutor," Carillon told him. "I think you had better go—or do what you came to do, so we may end this travesty."

"I come, I go—I do as I wish." Tynstar did not smile. "Heed me well, all of you—I give you insight into a truth you have never encountered." Again, the hand was raised. He looked directly at Donal. "Cheysuli warrior, you are— with a little Homanan blood. Because the shapechangers serve the prophecy of the Firstborn, who gave it to them before the race died out. Do you know why?"

"A legacy," Donal answered. "We are the children of the Firstborn—"

"—who were the children of the gods." The flame burned more brightly around Tynstar, as if it answered some secret bidding. "But are you so proud, so insular, so *arrogant*, as to believe they sired no others?"

A blurt of sound escaped Donal. He felt Lorn go rigid beside him.

"What are you trying to *say*—" But Finn was interrupted.

"They sired a second race," the sorcerer said. "They sired the Ihlini . . . who bred with the Cheysuli."

"*No!*" burst simultaneously from Finn and Donal.

A rasp. Metal sliding. It hissed, almost like the serpent cloaking Tynstar. Carillon drew forth his Cheysuli sword.

Tynstar laughed. "That cannot slay me, Carillon. Have

you not tried with it before? Have you not seen the black-ened stone?"

"Aye," Carillon agreed evenly, "and would you care to see it again?" Before the image in the flames could answer, Carillon turned and thrust the sword into Donal's reluctant hands. "Show him. *Show him the blackened stone!*"

Donal held the edged blade in one hand, clasping it be-neath the hilt. He could feel the runes against his palm. Slowly he raised the sword, thrusting outward with a stiff-ened arm as if to ward off evil. Against the flame the sword was a silhouette, lacking all colors save the blackness of the night. As if Tynstar had leached it of life.

But then the ruby turned brilliant crimson and set the hill afire.

The fog evaporated at once. The ruby blazed, and as its magic burned away the Ihlini mist Donal felt the thrum-ming of power in his hand. He thought at first he might drop the sword, so startled was he by the growing strength, but he found he could not. From him the sword took life; from the sword he took strength. A perfect exchange of power.

Tynstar's smooth face exhibited mild surprise, but very little concern. "So—Hale's sword at last finds its master. I feared it might happen one day. I thought perhaps I might gainsay him in time when I slew him in the forest, but obviously not."

"*You* slew him!" Finn took a single step forward. "It was *Shaine's men* who slew my *jehan*—"

"Was it?" Tynstar smiled. "Do not be such a fool. I sought Hale because I knew his was the seed that could destroy the Ihlini race. Think you I could let him live?" A dismissive wave of a graceful, negligent hand. "Lindir I intended to slay as well, before she could bear the child—but she escaped me and fled to Homana-Mujhar. So I slew Hale after I slew his *lir*—I meant to take the sword. But he had given it to Shaine." For a moment his beautiful, bearded face altered into something less sanguine, much more malevolent. "I should have known it would be Alix's child for whom it was meant. I felt it in her, before she lay with Duncan. I should have slain her too, as I took Dun-can's hawk. It would have gainsaid the prophecy and saved me the trouble of meeting you here."

Donal lowered the sword. The ruby had dimmed a little, as if knowing much of its job was done; only Tynstar remained, surrounded by his cocoon of living flame. The fog and the serpent were gone. "You slew her anyway. And my *jehan*. When you sent him to trap us."

"That was not my idea," Tynstar said. "It was my—*apprentice's* suggestion." He smiled. "Was it not a good one? Nearly successful, as well."

Donal drew in an unsteady breath, recalling how his mother and father had died. "I do not believe your *lesson*."

Tynstar's shrug was slight. "I know your prophecy very well, Donal. I helped *make* it, merely by being born three centuries ago. I understand what a *tahlmorra* is much better than you or any other Cheysuli, for I have known the gods much longer than any of you."

"Dare you speak of *gods* when you worship that filth of the netherworld?" Carillon demanded.

"I worship nothing," Tynstar retorted. "I *serve*, even as you pretend to serve. The Seker does not require the nonsense of obeisance and ritualistic loyalty. He *knows* what lies in a man's true soul." He touched the brooch at his left shoulder. "Aye, I am an integral part of the same prophecy that orders Donal's life—but I serve it not. I seek only to break its power, before the Ihlini are destroyed." For a moment, there was a touch of humanity in his eyes. "Can you not see? I do this for the *salvation of my race*."

No one answered. Donal stood with Finn, Evan, and Carillon as the *lir* locked themselves in silence, and looked at the Ihlini. The sword was heavy in his hand.

"Salvation." After a moment, Donal shook his head. "I do not believe you. Were the Ihlini truly children of the Firstborn, we would not be mortal enemies."

"Ask the *lir* why they will never attack an Ihlini," Tynstar suggested.

Donal could not answer. Neither did Taj or Lorn.

Tynstar smiled. "You are idealistic, Donal—or perhaps merely young. Comprehension will come with age. You see, we Ihlini desired more gifts than those the Firstborn gave us. More—power. We turned to the only source that would heed us when the Firstborn would not—"

"—Asar-Suti," Carillon finished.

"The god of the netherworld, who made and dwells in darkness." That from Finn.

"Aye," Tynstar agreed. "A generous lord, in fact. He did not stint what powers he gave those who wished to serve him." His eyes were on the sword still clasped limply in Donal's hand. "But the Firstborn sought to destroy us when they learned of our oath to serve the Seker. Knowing they would die before this destruction could be accomplished, they fashioned a prophecy instead, and left the destruction to the Cheysuli—"

"No," Donal said.

Tynstar did not allow the interruption to interfere. "They instilled within you all a perfect and blind obedience that even now binds your soul. They gave each warrior a fate and called it a *tahlmorra,* to make certain the task would be fulfilled. They turned you into *soldiers for the gods,* as dedicated to preserving and fulfilling the prophecy as we are to its downfall. Because that fulfillment, once achieved, means the annihilation of my race." Tynstar's voice was harsh. "An Ihlini *qu'mahlin,* Donal—instituted by the Cheysuli."

Donal shook his head. "The prophecy says *nothing* of annihilation. It speaks of a Mujhar of all blood uniting four warring realms and two magic races. Is *that* so horrible a fate?"

Tynstar's teeth showed briefly. "It means the mingling of Cheysuli blood and Ihlini, Donal. It means the swallowing of our races and a merging of the power. No more independence. No more—apartness. The Ihlini and Cheysuli will die out, drowned in each other's blood."

Gods . . . tell me he is wrong . . . Donal felt as if he had been walking in darkness all of his life. Blind. Deaf. Mute. Yet now he could see and hear and speak. Tynstar had given him sight and hearing: Tynstar had loosed his tongue.

But he did not speak. He lifted the sword and hurled it at the image as if the blade were a spear.

The ruby blazed a trail of incarnadine fire as it arced downward toward the column of flame that housed Tynstar's image. The sword fell, slicing through the fire like a scythe; a ringed hand flashed up and slapped the blade aside. The sword fell, point first, and stuck into the ground.

There it stood, sheathed in flame, like a headpiece to a grave.

"No—" Finn caught Donal's arm as he started forward blindly.

"Wait you—" Carillon whispered.

The ruby flickered. Tynstar, smiling, reached down to touch the stone with a single finger. Again, it flickered. Then it turned to black.

Tynstar laughed. "Shall I make it *mine?* I have only to shut my hand around the hilt. I will take it into my hands and caress the shining blade—until the runes are wiped away. And then Hale's sword will be nothing but a sword, intended for any man, even a common soldier." He reached down, threatening languidly; one finger touched it, another; the palm slid down to rest against the grip.

"No!" Donal cried.

And then, as Tynstar sought to shut his hand upon the hilt, the ruby blazed up again.

The Ihlini cried out. He snatched back his hand instantly; Donal heard his breath hissing in startled comprehension.

But the hand stretched out again. It lifted. Paused. Considered. The silver ring winked in the sorcerous flames.

Tynstar scribed a rune in the air and split the darkness apart.

Nineteen

"My lord . . . *my lord—*"

Hands caught at his shoulders, urging him to rise. Donal, mouth tasting of dirt and flame, realized it was Sef.

"My lord—*please* . . . are you hurt?"

He thought perhaps he was. His head was filled with a darkness rimmed by colored light. Sef's voice was distant, fogged, distorted by the humming in Donal's ears. Even the hands on his clothing did not seem real.

"My lord!" Sef cried in desperation. "Please—get *up—*"

Slowly, Donal rolled onto his side, then pressed himself upward. He sat on one hip, braced against a stiffened arm. Squinting against the brilliance in his head, he tried to see Sef's face.

Abruptly, he recalled what had caused his present condition. He jerked around, drawing his legs beneath him as if preparing to leap. Splayed fingers pressed against the ground; the other hand half drew the long-knife at his belt.

But there was no enemy. Where Tynstar had been was only a charred patch of smoking ground, and the sword.

The sword. Still it stood upright, though tilted, sheathed in the earth from which it drew power. The moon, clean and unobscured once more, flooded the hilltop with silvered light. The rune-kissed blade shone with an eerie luminance. The ruby, cradled in its golden prongs, was a crimson beacon in the night.

"My lord?" Sef whispered.

Donal came out of his crouch. He rose slowly, aware of a faint tingling numbness in his bones. But he did not approach the sword. He looked instead for the others.

Lorn stood but two or three paces away, legs spraddled as he shook his coat free of dirt and debris. Taj still spiraled in the air. Evan was sitting upright, spitting out dirt and muttering of Lodhi and sorcerers. Finn stood even as Donal rose. He went at once to Carillon and put down a hand to him just as Rowan arrived.

"Carillon—!" In his urgency, Rowan nearly shouldered Finn out of the way. "My lord?"

Finn did not give ground. His very silence transmitted itself to Rowan, who—bending down to aid Carillon—glanced up at him in irritated impatience.

Watching them both as Carillon sat up and brushed his clothing, Donal was struck by their eerie resemblance. In the moonlight the differences in their faces were set aside. All Cheysuli resembled one another, but some more than others.

They are alike in more than appearance, Donal thought. *Both of them serve the Mujhar. Finn may have given up his rank as liege man to Carillon, but the loyalty is still there.*

He saw the momentary flash of possessiveness in Rowan's eyes. No, he had not taken Finn's place when the oath had been broken; no man could. But he had made a new place at Carillon's side, and Donal knew he was indispensable. Facing Finn, it would be difficult for Rowan to give way.

"Get me up from here!" Carillon said testily, and caught Rowan's outstretched hand. Donal saw how Finn remained very still a moment, and then moved a single step away.

Relinquishing the service yet again . . . Donal saw the pain graven deeply in Carillon's face; the taut starkness of his expression and the incredibly tight set of his jaw. Like Donal's; like everyone else's, his face was smeared with traces of ash. Moisture glittered on Carillon's brow, and Donal realized it was the sweat of unbearable pain.

And yet he bears it . . . Donal moved to him at once. "My lord—Carillon . . . how do you fare?"

Briefly, Rowan's teeth were bared in a feral, possessive snarl. "How does he fare? *Look* at him, Donal! How do *you* fare after what Tynstar did?"

"Enough." The word issued hoarsely from Carillon. He stood nearly erect as they surrounded him, allowing the pain no opportunity to swallow him whole. One hand rested on Rowan's shoulder as if in placation; Donal saw how the sinews stood up against the flesh of Carillon's hand and knew he clutched the shoulder for support. "Tynstar is—gone. Let us go as well: down from this hill to our pavilions. Tomorrow, I do not doubt, we will be tested by the Solindish.''

"He sought to slay us," Donal said. "Who is to say he will not do it again?"

Carillon's eyes were couched in brackets of strain. "That was not an attempt to slay us. That was his manner of leave-taking. No doubt he *might* have tried to slay us, but the sword prevented that." A fleeting grimace crossed his face as he glanced back at the shining sword. "Hale's blade begins to serve its master."

Donal shivered once. "No. That sword is *yours*."

Sef, standing between Donal and Evan, wrenched his head around to stare. "*That's* the magic sword?"

Donal looked at him sharply. "What are you saying, Sef?"

The boy shrugged self-consciously. "I—I've heard it's got magic in it. There's a story around Homana-Mujhar that it'll be *your* sword, and when it is—"

"Enough!" Donal cut him off with the sharp Cheysuli gesture. "There are better things to do with your time than listen to stories. Go on, Sef—go back to camp. Is there nothing for you to do?"

Color moved through the boy's face. For a moment his vitality dimmed, then came rushing back. He flicked a glance at the Mujhar with his odd, uncanny eyes, then looked directly at Donal. "But they say the sword was made for *you*."

Donal's bones tingled. His head ached. He glared at Sef through eyes that burned from smoke and flame. He pointed at the sword. "Then go and fetch it, Sef, and see what nonsense you mouth."

Sef shrank back. "No! *I* can't touch it!"

"Do not be foolish, Sef." Donal, still somewhat disoriented, felt his patience slipping. "What is to keep you from touching the sword?"

"It—it might stop me." He shrugged. "Somehow. It *might*. You don't know it *wouldn't*." Furtively he looked at the sword. "It's a magic sword, my lord. It isn't meant for a boy like *me*."

"Donal." Carillon's voice, with the snap of command in it. "Fetch the sword yourself. I have no more time to waste on Tynstar and his tricks."

The Mujhar turned away. With Rowan's aid he made his

way down from the crest of the scorched hill and walked through his gathered army, speaking quietly to frightened men. Finn and Evan were silhouetted against the horizon, lighted only by the moonlight. Lorn waited as well, and Taj, still drifting in the heavens.

Donal turned from Sef to fetch the sword. The blade was half-buried in charred earth. He reached down, clasped the hilt and tugged.

At once he felt again the thrumming of life in bones and muscles; the promise of power and strength. *Gods . . . is* this *what has kept Carillon strong all these years as his body decayed? A sword—?*

He pulled it free of the earth. The blade was perfectly clean, unblemished by ash or dirt. The runes seemed to writhe upon the steel.

In the silvered darkness, Sef's pale face was almost translucent. "Hale's sword," he said, "is not meant for such as me."

"This sword," Donal said deliberately, "is meant for any man who can wield it."

"Oh?" Finn's voice held a familiar undertone of irony. "Is that why it warded us against Tynstar?"

Evan shook his head. "In Ellas, magic is limited to such things as simple tricks and potions, or to the harpers of Lodhi. You have seen Lachlan's power. But I have never seen *anything* like this."

Donal looked down at the sword. In his hand, the grip was warm. The ruby blazed bright red. "Nor have I." He could deny the sword no longer. And so he turned and left the hill.

The pavilion held two cots, two stools, one chair, a tiny three-legged table. Tripod braziers stood in two of the corners. The fabric was pale saffron. The candlelight, thrown against the sides, painted the interior burnt gold, pale cream and ivory. It reminded Donal of the Womb with all its marble *lir*.

He sat in the chair. Beside him slumped Lorn, sleepy-eyed in the glow of fat white candles. Taj perched precariously on Donal's chairback; he could feel the meticulous balance of the falcon. In front of him stood the table, and set on the knife-scarred wood was the sword. No more did the ruby blaze, but neither was it black. It was the rich blood-red of a Cheysuli ruby, no more, no less—yet full of significance.

"In the clans, it is held a Cheysuli-made sword has a life of its own when matched with the proper master. I have heard of others made for foreign kings and princes because of all the legends . . . but this one—*this* one Hale made for Shaine. I know the story. It was Shaine who gave it to Carillon when he became Prince of Homana . . . it has been his weapon for years and years. It is a part of the tales they tell about him. And now he thrusts it upon me, says it is mine—"

Evan, sprawled inelegantly across the cot, shrugged. He held a cup of wine in his hand. "Perhaps it is. Does it matter so much?"

"Aye. Cheysuli do not use swords."

Evan snorted. "Then what is the use of *making* them?"

"We do not, now. When the *qu'mahlin* was declared, no longer did we make weapons with which to arm the Homanans." Faintly, he frowned. "If—*if* it is true Hale made that sword for me—why? I am Cheysuli."

"And Homanan, are you not?"

Donal shifted in his chair, disturbing the falcon. Taj reprimanded him gently. "Aye," he said grimly. "But none of me wants that sword."

"And if Carillon leaves it to you?"

"I will not use it," Donal declared. "Never will I fight with it. There is my knife, my bow—even *lir*-shape. Why would I want a sword?"

Evan smiled. "Just because you don't *want* it, does not mean it wasn't *meant* for you."

Donal's smile was wryly crooked. "You sound almost like a warrior discussing his *tahlmorra.*"

Evan drank for a moment, then shifted his posture to sit more upright. "Well, every man has a fate. Some men make theirs. I may not be Cheysuli, but I am a son of Lodhi— for all I may not seem so."

"The All-Father," Donal said wryly. "Is it true you Ell-asians believe he sired *all* of you?"

"Well, He did not precisely lie with my lady mother, if *that* is what you mean." Evan grinned and drank again.

"But aye, in a way, He did. You see, Lodhi lay with a single mortal woman, and from that union sprang Ellas."

Donal, losing interest, looked again at the sword. He rubbed absently at his chin. "This sword is Carillon's—" Abruptly, he rose. He snatched up the sword and went out of the pavilion, ignoring Sef's startled question as the boy rose up from his mat outside the doorflap. Donal ignored everyone as he strode through the encampment; he was intent upon his mission.

Carillon's crimson tent stood apart from the others. Tall wooden stave torches had been thrust into the earth around the pavilion to bathe it with light. Shadows flickered against the crimson fabric; Donal saw there were no guards.

No guards—?

And then he heard the Mujhar's startled cry of pain.

Donal ran. He felt the grip settle more comfortably into his palm. His fingers found ridges meant to cradle his bones; the remaining space beckoned his other hand. The metal was warm, alive; he could feel the power rising. It bled into his body and spread to fill the very marrow of his bones. He almost *wanted* to fight.

His free hand ripped aside the crimson doorflap. Automatically it dropped the fabric and went unerringly to the hilt, closing around the gold. He felt the blade rising, rising, incredibly light in his hands and yet substantially weighted as well. The balance was perfect. The sword was a part of his body, an extension of his hands, his arms, his mind—

—"*No!*" he shouted as he saw the man bending over Carillon's body in the cot.

Candlelight flashed off the blade. The reflection struck full across the man's face as he turned; Donal saw a haze of gold and black and bronze. And eyes. Yellow eyes, staring back at Donal.

The blow faltered. His arms sagged. Donal let the weight drop down, releasing his left hand so that the sword dangled limply from his right. "By the gods, *su'fali* . . . I might have had your head—"

"And regretted it later, no doubt." Finn straightened. His hands were empty. But he stood at Carillon's bedside, and the Mujhar was clearly unconscious.

"What are you doing?" Donal demanded in alarm. "What is wrong with Carillon?" He moved closer to the cot, fingers clenching the sword hilt. "Gods—he is not *dead*—"

"No." Finn glanced down at the Mujhar's slack face. "No, not yet."

"Yet?" Donal stopped beside the cot, but he did not look at Carillon. He stared instead at Finn. "You do not mean—"

"—I mean he has little time," Finn said flatly. "Are you blind, Donal, to say you do not know it?"

"But—but he is so strong—" Donal gestured with his empty left hand. He *rules*—"

"—stolen time," Finn said, and his voice had roughened a little. "Tynstar took it from him—I have stolen it back. A little. Not enough. But as with all things, it carries a price." He looked down at Carillon. "Donal—are you prepared to be Mujhar?"

"No!" It burst out of him instantly. "No, *su'fali*—no."

"Have you learned nothing from Carillon?"

At last, Donal looked down at the man who ruled Homana. He saw how the flames overlay the face and emphasized the slackness of the flesh, the banishment of the strength inherent in Carillon's bones. The beard had silvered, thinning, so that the line of the jaw was visible. The hair, fallen back from his face, no longer hid the fragility of his temples; Donal saw clearly the hollows of age, the upstanding threading of veins, the prominent bones of the nose.

But it was not the face that shocked Donal. It was the leather that had been wrapped around Carillon's naked torso. Stiff leather, laced together; it held his spine perfectly straight, almost too straight. Straps ran over both broad shoulders. The leather bracers, which Donal had always believed were mere cuffs providing some measure of support, were reinforced with metal.

"Years ago, when the disease began to twist his spine and shoulders, he had that made." Finn's tone was expressionless. "It allows him to resemble a man instead of a blighted tree. It allows him to hold the sword you have just returned."

He is dying. I see it, now— "Gods!" Donal whispered. "Oh, *su'fali*—say it is not true."

"I will not lie to you."

Donal felt pain knot up his belly, rising to fill chest and throat. "Is there *nothing* you can do?"

"I have done it." The tone was minutely unsteady, yet tight, controlled. "I gave him *tetsu* root."

Donal blanched. *"How much?"*

Finn's smile lacked humor. "Enough to do some good. And it has. He has been—better—since the wedding."

Donal felt a chill. *"Su'fali—tetsu* root is deadly."

"So is growing old." Finn looked down at Carillon's unconscious body. "It was his choice, Donal. I did not force him. I did not hide it in his wine. I simply told him about *tetsu* and what it could do for him. He said he would take the risk."

"Risk? There is no risk! *Tetsu* always kills." Donal gestured emptily again. "Have you known a man to set it aside once he has begun drinking it regularly? *I* have not. Every warrior who desires it has taken it once, then twice, and soon enough there is no stopping it, not until the root slays. By the gods, *su'fali*, you have given him over to death!"

"I have lessened some of his pain," Finn declared. "For him, I could do no less."

Donal stared at the Mujhar. All the grief welled up and made him feel helpless. Carillon was dying more quickly than was natural. Tynstar had seen to that. But Finn, in a final obscene service performed by a loyal liege man, had made it more immediate.

"How long?" he whispered.

"A month. Two. Perhaps a little longer." Finn looked down at his friend. "What Tynstar did tonight destroyed many of Carillon's defenses. His will has been such that he would not give in to disease or drug. But now—time is running out."

Donal tried to swallow down the swelling in his throat. "Does—does he know it?"

"He knows it."

Donal looked down. He would not cry before his uncle, who would have no tolerance for such things. Instead, he stared hard at the sword. In his hands the ruby glowed, catching the candlelight; the rampant lion seemed to move upon the hilt.

"Do not tell him I know," he said, barely above a whisper. "Do not tell him I came." Mutely, he held out the blade to Finn. "Say I sent a servant with the sword."

Finn relieved him of the weapon. *"Ja'hai,"* he said. *"Ja'hai, cheysu, Mujhar."*

"Not yet," Donal said. "Oh, no . . . not yet. Not while Carillon breathes."

"He will breathe a little longer," Finn said, "but one day he will stop. And you will hold the throne."

"Su'fali—do not."

"Do not what? Speak the truth?" Finn did not smile. "You will have to accept it, Donal. It is for this you were born."

Donal looked at Carillon. And then he turned away.

Twenty

Donal gasped at the impact of bodies meeting. The Solindish soldier weighed more heavily on him than he had expected. He reached in, thrusting a forearm against the man's sword hilt, and drove the blade off course. The tip of the sword hovered, then drifted back near his ribs; he leaned away, pivoting from the hips, and took a firmer grasp on the long-knife in his right hand.

He thrust. The tip struck leather-and-ringmail, catching in steel circles linked together. The blade scraped; a screech of subtle protest. Donal wrenched it away and thrust yet again. Upward this time, beneath the Solindishman's arm. He sought the vulnerable, unmailed flesh of the armpit.

The gap—there!

The blade slid in. He felt it catch on leather, slowing, then digging deeper into flesh, where there was less resistance. The entire length of the blade sank in; he twisted.

The Solindish soldier cried out. His sword wavered in his hand, then fell free altogether. Blood pumped out of the man, flooding his side and painting his ringmail red. Donal felt the warm wetness flow down to wash across his hand, his arm, dripping from his elbow.

As the man sagged, the knife went with him. The hilt slipped out of Donal's blood-smeared hand. He followed it down, bending to regain the weapon; as he caught the hilt once more, he heard Evan's warning cry.

"Donal! *'ware sword!*"

He dropped to one knee, ducking instantly. The whistle of a blade near one ear told him how close he had come to losing his head. A wrench freed the knife at last; he twisted, spinning on the knee, and came up offensively, slipping beneath the swinging sword. One hand caught the soldier's wrist, the other thrust again with Cheysuli long-knife.

Again, blade met ringmail. Cursing inwardly, Donal tried to draw back and thrust again. But this man brought up a knee in an attempt to catch him in the groin.

He twisted and caught the blow on the thigh. He grunted as the impact nearly knocked him down; grimly, he stood his ground and leveled a vicious knife swipe at the Solindish soldier. The swordsman's reach was greater, but the maneuver nonetheless took him by surprise. He jumped back instinctively and left Donal free of the sword.

Donal backed away. First one step, then another. And then, as the soldier prepared to follow, he flipped the knife in his hand and threw it with a snap of his wrist that sent the blade slicing through the tough leather collar at the man's throat and through it, into the flesh beneath.

He turned. Evan, he saw, had engaged yet another soldier. The field was filled with men: Homanans. Cheysuli, Solindish. Those of the clans he knew by their *lir*-gold and yellow eyes; the Homanans and Solindish, save for blazons on their tunics, he could not tell apart. In the midst of battle, one grimy, blood-stained face looked very much like another.

From the corner of his eye he saw a flash of muted gold, feathers blurred in flight. Taj, stooping, scythed through the air. Donal watched him choose his target: the swordsman who confronted Evan. The Solindishman, intent upon his Ellasian prey, never saw the bird. Taj closed talons on leather gauntlets, slicing through to rend flesh and muscle.

"Hah!" Evan cried as the man staggered back, sword falling from wounded hands. "My thanks, Donal!"

"Not my doing," Donal returned. But the conversation went no further. A dying Solindishman, falling at Donal's feet, struck a final blow. Knife blade flashed in the sunlight of midafternoon; tip bit through the leather of Donal's left boot and into flesh, cutting to the bone. Donal, staggering back, wrenched himself free of the knife. But not before he realized he had lost most of his mobility.

He hopped back again, favoring the wounded leg. Curses filled up his mind and mouth; teeth gritted, he hobbled away from the dying man.

Lir, It was Lorn, shoring up his side. *Lir, seek help.*

Not yet, he answered, testing the leg. *I can still stand well enough.*

He sheathed his bloodied knife. Quickly he unstrapped his compact Cheysuli warbow, pulled an arrow from the quiver and nocked it, seeking out a target. But even as he raised the bow, preparing to let fly, he smelled the stink of sorcery.

Tynstar—? he wondered vaguely.

But there had been no sign of the Ihlini since the battle had begun.

Fog. Fingers of it, violet, drifting along the ground. And then, almost instantly, the fog thickened. Stretched. Swallowed up the field.

He could see nothing. His eyes were filled with haze. The smell of it, sickly sweet and cloying, coated his tongue, and he bent to spit it out. Damp, malodorous arms seemed to twine around his neck, putting fingers into his ears. He was cold, wet, nauseatingly sickened by the smell.

"Donal! *Lodhi*—there are *demons*—"

Evan's voice, raised in honest horror. Donal turned, staggering on one leg, and tried to locate his friend. But the vapor was like clay, sealing up his eyes. They burned. They teared. He cursed.

Lir? Lir—?

Here, Lorn's voice sounded distant, swallowed up by the fog. *Lir—this is the Ihlini's doing.*

Donal put away his arrow and the bow. Neither could help him now. *Taj?* he asked.

Above, the falcon answered. *Lir—it is everywhere—I can see no sky—*

"Evan!" Donal shouted. "Tell me where you are!"

There was no answer. In the depths of the heavy fog Donal could hear other voices, all muffled, all indecipherable. But the tones were clear enough. Fear. Horror. Blind, unreasoning terror.

"Evan!"

"Demons!" Evan shouted. And then the Ellasian screamed.

Lir, go to Evan, Donal ordered, hobbling through the choking mist.

I cannot even find you, Lorn retorted. But then the wolf

loomed up through the fog, a solid ruddy shape in the pervasive violet shroud. Lir, *you are limping.*

Aye, Donal agreed. He felt safer with the warmth of the wolf against one knee. *Gods—where is Evan—?*

Here, sent Taj. *To your right by seven steps.*

Seven steps. Donal hobbled. It took him more than seven steps. But at last he saw the body, belly down, sprawled against the ground.

"Evan!" Fear shot through him. He dropped to both knees, ignoring the pain in his leg, and put one hand on Evan's shoulder.

The Ellasian prince came up from the ground in a twisting, convulsive lunge. His blue eyes were wide in a pale face, his mouth agape in fear. But a knife in his hand, and he nearly thrust with it.

Donal fell back, sprawling on his rump against the earth. "Evan—*wait* you—"

Breath rasped in Evan's throat. He stopped hunched, legs spread, nearly swaying on his feet. "Donal?" He peered uncertainly. "Lodhi—is it *you?*"

"I," Donal agreed. It felt better to sit than to stand. "What demons do you mean?"

The knife shook a little. "There was one. There was. It came at me out of the fog . . . *Lodhi!*—but what a vile, horrid *stinking* thing it was! It had no mouth—no eyes . . . it was a slimy, foul, wretched *tentacled* thing—" Evan shuddered. "It wrapped itself around my head and nearly smothered me—" He turned his head and spat upon the ground. "*Lodhi*—I can still *taste* the horrid thing!"

"But now it is gone?" Donal had seen nothing. He thought it likely the demons were illusion called up by the Ihlini for those of the enemy who were not Cheysuli.

Evan sucked in a steadying breath. "Gone. I thought—when you touched me—I thought it had come again. But now even the fog is clearing." Evan looked down at Donal. "You are hurt."

Donal glanced down at the torn, bloodied leather of his boot. "A slice. Nothing more."

Evan knelt, putting away his knife, and peeled aside the leather. In the flesh of Donal's shin, not far above the ankle, was a deep, clean-edged cut. "To the bone, and beyond. You are fortunate the bone is whole." He reached

out and caught Donal's elbow. "Come up. I will see you
to a chirurgeon's tent."

Donal glanced around as he fought to regain his balance.
"The battle seems to be ended. I see both sides with-
drawing."

"But no victory, I will wager." Evan steadied Donal's
progress. "How much longer will this Solindish folly
continue?"

"In two months, we have got nowhere," Donal said.
"Neither side has won. Who is to say how much longer this
will go on?"

"Aye," Evan agreed grimly as Lorn trailed Donal. "*We*
have the Cheysuli, but the Solindish have Tynstar and his
minions. The advantages are cancelled."

Donal sighed, wincing as movement jarred his aching leg.
"We *will* win, Evan . . . the gods are on our side."

The Ellasian snorted. "Aye. And no doubt the Solindish
claim the same thing—just that *their* gods are different."

Donal gritted his teeth. "Let us cease discussing war."

"Aye!" Evan agreed. "Why speak of war when there are
women in the world?"

Regardless of his pain, Donal had to smile.

Carillon came in as the army chirurgeon tied the last
silken knot of the stitches in Donal's leg. Donal himself
was too intent on locking his teeth against the pain to pay
much attention to the Mujhar, but he was aware of Carillon's entry.

"Not serious, then?" the Mujhar asked.

The chirurgeon shook his head. "Hardly, my lord. It will
hamper him a little, but should heal well enough."

"Good." Carillon's bulk blocked most of the sunlight
from the open doorflap. "Rumors said you had nearly lost
the leg."

"No—though it feels like it *now*." Donal scowled at the
chirurgeon as he bound the calf with tight linen bandages.

"Do you think you will need a crutch?" inquired Evan
in mock solicitude.

Knots tied off, Donal brushed the chirurgeon aside with
a muttered word of thanks. Then he glanced up at Carillon.
"My lord—"

His words trailed off. He was faced again with the advancing age of the Mujhar; with the knowledge of what Finn had done to him. And Carillon's willingness.

"Aye?" Carillon waited.

"No," Donal muttered, looking away. "Nothing."

"Courier!" called a voice. "Courier for the Mujhar!"

Carillon turned back toward the entrance. "Here!"

A moment later a young man in royal livery bowed before the Mujhar. "My lord—messages for you and the Prince of Homana."

Carillon accepted them. Like Donal and Evan, he was obviously weary, clothing torn and bloodied. Hands soiled by the dirt of sweat and boiled leather closed around the scrolls, and Donal saw again the leather bracers at his wrists.

"Yours." Carillon passed one over.

Donal, frowning, broke the crimson seal. He read the two brief lines and the signature, and felt the cot shift beneath his weight.

He became aware, suddenly, that Carillon was demanding to know what was wrong. His face must show what he felt. When he could, Donal looked up and met the anticipatory eyes. "Aislinn, my lord. She has miscarried of a son."

For a long moment Carillon stood unmoving in the sunlight as it slanted inside the tent. But then he reached out and caught the parchment from Donal's hand, nearly tearing it in half. He read it, and then he shut his eyes.

Slowly, so slowly, one hand crumpled the message. The parchment crackled in the silence. Donal saw how the fingers spasmed, shutting, and how the callused, grimy hands took on the aspect of a corpse's.

The Mujhar expelled a breath that hissed upon the air. His eyes, when he opened them again, were filled with a quiet desperation. "I am sorry," he said at last. "The loss of an unborn son . . ." He did not finish the sentence.

Donal felt the kindling of distant grief into something very real. *A son unborn . . .* It had happened once before, when Sorcha had miscarried his first child. Ian and Isolde had come into the world safely, and he had grown complacent. He had thought Aislinn would bear him a healthy child; he had not considered a loss. He had not thought of what it meant to lose an heir.

"My lord—" Donal stopped and cleared his throat. "My lord—Aislinn says she is recovered. She says she does well enough."

"Aye. For which I thank the gods." Carillon looked at the scroll given to him. "Perhaps this is from Aislinn as well—perhaps there was something more she wished to say—" He broke the seal, read the message, then stared blindly at them all.

"My lord—?" Donal nearly rose.

Carillon turned away from them. He stepped into the opening and shouted for Rowan. He said nothing at all until the general came, and then his words lacked all ceremony. "Osric," he said clearly. "Osric of Atvia invades through the port of Hondarth."

"*Osric—!*" Donal blurted.

Rowan hardly glanced at him. "He means, then, to march on Mujhara while we dally here with Tynstar."

"Aye." Carillon sighed in utter weariness. "To protect one we risk the other."

"There is no other way," Rowan said flatly. "You must, my lord."

The Mujhar nodded. "He has been stopped a week out of Hondarth, on his way to Mujhara just this side of the fenlands. The domestic troops hold him for now, but for how long?"

Rowan's tunic was stained and torn. The rampant lion hung in tatters. "We are a month's march out of Mujhara. Osric is only a week away from the city. My lord—we must go *now.*"

"And lose Solinde entirely." Carillon grimly crumpled the message. "That may be Tynstar's plan. Can you not see him, Rowan? He suggests to Osric the time is now—the Atvian sails to Hondarth while we wrestle here with Tynstar. Faced with no army to gainsay him, Osric takes Hondarth and marches toward Mujhara. Once he overcomes what few domestic troops there are, he has trapped us between Tynstar and himself: a grub between two stones." He turned to Donal. "Do you understand what we must do?"

Donal felt a hollowness in his belly. "We must stop them both, somehow—Tynstar as well as Osric."

Evan frowned. "My lord—if you were to shift your warhost from Solinde to Homana, would you lose this realm entirely?"

"With Tynstar here?—of course." Carillon looked at Donal. "Tell me what we should do."

Donal stared down at the earthen floor of the infirmary tent. "We fight on two fronts, my lord. We split the army in half."

"Our only chance, and a desperate one." Carillon turned back to Rowan. "Speak to the other officers and the clan-leaders as well. We will leave half the army here—I want the Cheysuli here to fight the Ihlini—while the rest of us go to Osric. Rowan, you will come with me to Mujhara." He cast Donal a level glance. "And you. But you will remain in Mujhara only a week or two, and then return here to command the army."

"Carillon—*no*—" That from Rowan, even as Donal thought to echo the identical words. "He is unschooled in warfare *and* the leading of men. Leave *me* here instead."

"You I take with me." The tone was inflexible.

"Rowan has the right of it." Donal pushed himself up from the cot and rose, suppressing a grimace of pain. "What do I know of leading men into battle?"

"These are veterans." Carillon's voice was harsh. "These men do not require you to hold their hands. They will teach you what there is to know—it is time you learned how to conduct yourself as a soldier must in order to survive—and to keep others alive as well."

"Then why send me to Mujhara?" Donal demanded. "Why not leave me here?"

"Because Aislinn is in Mujhara." Carillon's face was completely expressionless. "It is difficult to conceive a child when man and wife are so many leagues apart."

"*By the gods*—" Donal said raggedly. "She has only just recovered! There is no *decency* to this—"

"There is no time for such things as *decency* in war," Carillon said baldly. "I have an heir; you do not. It is necessary for you to make one." He turned back to Rowan again. "Make certain my half of the army is prepared to leave in the morning."

"Ay, my lord Mujhar." Rowan stepped aside as Carillon brushed past him.

"He is gone mad," Donal said hoarsely. "By the gods—
I think he has—"

Rowan raised his brows. "What madness is there in trying to hold Homana—and in serving the prophecy?"

"Like *this*—?"

"If this is what it takes." Rowan did not smile. "Be ready
to ride in the morning."

The borderlands of Solinde did not have the varied
beauty of Homana. The land was flat, and low, scrubby
trees barely broke the straight line of the horizon; to Donal
it looked as though it stretched forever.

A barren, dismal place . . . fitting for the Ihlini.

He and Carillon rode out ahead of the army bound for
Homana. Not far. Just barely out of eyesight. Rowan had
protested the lack of escort regardless, but Carillon had
overruled him.

The Mujhar rode in silence. Donal, watching him with
subtle, sidelong glances, saw how the morning sun glinted
off the silver of his hair. He wore few ornaments to mark
his rank: his ring and a collar brooch of gold and emerald.
His clothing was exceedingly simple: ringmail over a boiled
leather hauberk. Black breeches. Thighboots. Bracers
banded with slender ribs of steel.

*Gods, what a man he is—what a warrior still . . . would
that I could have known him before Tynstar stole his
youth—*

And what will they say of you? Taj asked, wheeling idly
in the air.

Of me? Inwardly, Donal grimaced. *That I could never be
Carillon's equal.*

Is that truly what you desire? Lorn asked from beside the
stallion. *Did he not make his own way in the world just as
you yourself will?*

Aye. Donal sighed. *What they say, I will know in time.
And perhaps they will have the right of it after all.*

On the crest of a rise, Carillon halted his horse. Still
he sat in silence, staring eastward toward Homana. Donal,
waiting beside him, heard the buzz of a bee in the air.

"I thank you for coming with me to this place," Carillon
said at last. "You might have refused."

"Refused *you*—?"

Carillon rubbed his beard thoughtfully. "Aye. You may refuse me, Donal. I have not stripped you of your freedom *entirely*—it only seems that way."

The chestnut stallion stomped to discourage a bothersome fly. Dust rose. Donal smelled the pungent tang of freshly crushed plains grass. Absently, he tapped his mount with a heel and reprimanded him gently, urging him into stillness. "It is—difficult to refuse you."

"Because that is what I wanted." Still Carillon stared eastward. "But I am done telling you what you must be, what you must say, how you must behave. I am done locking the shackles around your wrists." At last, he looked at Donal. "I have brought you here so I may ask your forgiveness."

Donal started, frowning. "Forgiveness—? From me?"

"Aye," Carillon said gently. "Duncan left me a chunk of naked metal and I did my best to shape it into a sword— even to tempering it to my liking, knowing what weight and balance I desired. But I am no arms-master, and I may have unwittingly set blemishes in the steel." His mouth hooked down in a brief ironic twist. "Now I seek to blood the blade after keeping it sheathed for nearly sixteen years."

"My lord—"

"I am sorry, Donal. I could offer you countless reasons and excuses for what I have become—and what I have done to you—but I am finished with that. I am finished with—much." His brows twisted briefly; Donal heard the undertone of despair in the steady voice. "I am sorry. I am sorry. For you . . . for Aislinn . . . for the child that must come of this." He looked at his ruined hands as they clasped the saddlebow. "Last night I said there was no time for decency in war. Perhaps I meant it then, but it is not true. War may be obscene, but it is also necessary. So is decency, if you are to retain a measure of humanity." His faded blue eyes met and held Donal's. "My wars are nearly over. It is you who will fight them for me, and eventually for yourself. I pray you do it with the decency I denied . . . and the humanity you will need."

"*Ru'shalla-tu,*" Donal said thickly. *I pray the gods it may be so.*

Slowly Carillon smiled. "*Ja'hai*, Donal. *Cheysuli i'halla shansu.*"

After a moment, Donal put out his arm. Their hands met and locked in the firm Cheysuli clasp. "Accepted," he said. "May there be Cheysuli peace upon *you*."

Carillon at last broke the clasp. "We had best go back to the army. Rowan will be worried."

"As well he should be," agreed a sinuous voice. "Have I caught you two alone?"

Donal spun his horse even as Carillon mimicked him. Before them, unmounted, stood Tynstar. And with him was Electra.

She laughed. "We have taken them by surprise."

Tynstar smiled. "I think we have made them mute."

"No," Carillon said. "Hardly that. But I *am* surprised you come to us here. The army is not so far."

"What I mean to do will not take much time," Tynstar said benignly, "and whenever has an army been able to gainsay *me*?"

Electra's cool gray eyes watched Donal. He felt the power of her gaze. "You wanted Carillon, and now we have the wolfling as well. Will you give him to me, my love?"

Donal felt a frisson slip down his spine. Apprehension filled his belly. Lir—

What is there to do? Lorn asked wretchedly.

Taj circled in agitation. *It is law,* lir, *our law, given by the gods. We do not attack the Ihlini.*

Because we are bloodkin? For the first time, Donal wondered if Tynstar's falsehood might hold some truth after all. *Is that why you keep the law?*

Neither bird nor wolf answered.

Tynstar smiled sweetly. "If you want him, Electra, I will give him to you when I am done with Carillon."

Donal straightened in his saddle. "If you think I will sit idly by while you attack Carillon, you are a fool indeed."

"Not a fool," Tynstar answered. "Merely—patient." He raised a hand noncommittally. "For now, I do not desire your meddling."

The Ihlini flicked a single finger. A blow knocked Donal off his horse and into nothingness. He floated, bodiless and mindless, knowing only fear and helplessness and a strange, wild grief. Then he landed against the ground and all such fleeting sensations were knocked utterly from his head, along with the breath from his lungs.

He struggled up on one elbow, trying to catch his banished breath, and saw the tableau take life before him. Taj flew in circles, shrieking in desperation; Lorn tipped back his head and howled in despair.

Donal's leg throbbed. He sank his teeth into his lip, tried to rise, and found himself fastened to the ground. He could not move at all.

"You sent Osric to Hondarth," Carillon challenged.

"I take Homana how I can," the sorcerer agreed. "Would you not do the same? You have learned what it is to be ruthless in order to get what you desire."

Carillon glanced back at Donal. Indecision and concern showed briefly in his eyes. But the indecision faded; Donal saw him smile—

—and set spurs to the flanks of his stallion.

Carillon rode at Tynstar. The Ihlini, unmounted, was prey to a galloping horse. He was prey to the sword the Mujhar drew.

But he merely lifted a languid hand and split the air with flame.

Concussion knocked Carillon from the saddle. Donal saw the Mujhar crash against the ground, sword dropping free of his hand.

Another gesture brought a bolt of lightning lancing out of the sky. It blasted the ground around Carillon's sprawling body, splattering him with dirt.

"Slowly," Electra said. "Let him know he dies."

"Old man," Tynstar said, "shall I release you from your pain?"

Slowly, Carillon pushed himself to his knees. Donal saw how his body trembled, how the chest heaved in complete exhaustion. Dust filmed his face; part of his beard was burned away.

He slumped. Slumping, his hands went to the ground. Fingers splayed. Elbows stiffened. He braced himself with every ounce of his waning strength.

Gods— Donal begged, *do not let it end like this!*

Failing, Carillon's body curled forward, slumping—

—but did not fall. Instead, he jerked the knife from his belt and hurled it through the air.

"*No!—*" Electra screamed.

The knife went home high in Tynstar's chest.

Carillon laughed. "Whose death today, Ihlini? Mine—or is it *yours?*"

Tynstar's right hand clawed at the hilt. A hissing exhalation poured from between his lips. "Seker—" he said, "Seker—I call upon the Seker—"

"What?" Carillon asked, still kneeling on the ground. "Do your powers begin to fade? Do you call upon your god?"

"Seker—" Tynstar hissed. "I call upon the Seker—"

"Before a Cheysuli warrior?" Carillon climbed unsteadily to his feet. "I think the petition will fail."

Tynstar thrust his right hand upward into the air. The fingers shook. "Asar-Suti!" he shouted. *"I summon you to me!"*

Carillon did not wait. He hurled himself forward and came down near the forgotten sword. He rolled rapidly and thrust his failing body upward, leveling the blade in a vicious, scything sweep.

Electra screamed. Tynstar's upthrust hand dropped limply back at his side. He stood a moment longer, then buckled at the knees.

But his head struck the ground before his body did.

The scream went on and on. It sliced through Donal's head like a blade, and then it stopped. Abruptly.

Electra simply stared.

Donal slowly got up. He looked at the severed neck. The blow had been quite clean, no wasted effort.

Blood, thick and viscid, oozed slowly from the trunk. But the color was not red, but deepest black.

Carillon turned to Donal. "How do you fare?"

"He did not harm me, but—*Carillon, look to Electra—*"

The Mujhar spun around. But Electra made no move to attack. Instead, she walked unsteadily toward the decapitated body and knelt beside it.

White-blond hair spilled down her breasts and trailed into the blood. Slowly, the blackness benighted the shining strands. It stained the pale lilac of her gown.

"Electra." Carillon walked slowly toward his wife. "Electra—he is dead."

She leaned forward. She moaned. She put her hands on

the bloodied shoulders of the body. She slid them down across the torso in a morbid caress.

She jerked the knife from the chest—

—and came up, spinning, aiming for Carillon's belly—

—in time to spit herself on the hilt of Carillon's waiting sword.

"Such beauty . . ." he whispered in a ragged, helpless voice.

The knife dropped from her hand. Knees buckled. She fell, and Carillon caught her.

Carefully, he pulled the blade from her body. He set the sword upon the ground. Then he shut the lids of her gray-pale eyes and straightened her silken skirts. Her hands, still stained with Tynstar's blood, he folded beneath her breasts. The glorious hair, half-black, half-blond, he smoothed away from her flawless face.

Carillon knelt. Donal saw the bloodstain spreading beneath Electra's folded hands. Black. Black and thick and viscid.

With Tynstar dead—with Electra dead . . . is Aislinn free at last?

The Mujhar rose. He took up the sword again. He turned to face his heir. "You must go back. Return to the encampment. I must go on to vanquish Osric—I will send your regrets to my daughter."

Donal stared. "But—I thought you wished me to go to her."

"I was wrong." He looked down at the body of his wife. "Once, she must have been a woman. A woman . . . not a witch." Slowly he sheathed his sword. He clasped Donal's shoulder, squeezing firmly, as if he were young again. "Go, my lord. Win back Solinde for me."

Donal turned away. He mounted his chestnut stallion and eased his throbbing leg into the stirrup. Taj perched on the saddlebow; Lorn stood by his side. He turned westward, toward the camp that lay so many miles behind them.

But when he looked back he saw Carillon standing over the bodies of his wife and the Ihlini.

As if he mourns them both—

Twenty-One

Sef's odd eyes were stretched wide in shock. "The demon is *dead?*"

Donal sat on the edge of his cot and worried at his boot, trying to strip it off without causing more pain to the injured leg. Sef stood stock still in front of his master, not helping.

"Aye." Donal caught heel and toe and pulled, gritting his teeth. "At last, we are free of Tynstar's plotting . . . it may be this war will end sooner than we hoped." His foot moved in the boot. He tugged harder, grunting with effort. "Sef—help me with this. Stop gaping at me like a fish."

Sef's usually efficient hands caught the boot clumsily and pulled it off. "But *you* did not slay him—?"

"No. The Mujhar did." Donal, frowning, felt at his bandaged leg. "But it was Electra who slew herself. Had she not tried to slay Carillon, she would not now be dead." He wiggled his toes experimentally. "So we are rid of them both."

"And now?" Sef asked. "What happens to all the other Ihlini—the ones who still fight here?"

"The race is still powerful," Donal told him. "All of them claim some measure of the dark arts. But without Tynstar to lead them, I think perhaps we will have less trouble with them all. Carillon cut the head from the serpent—it may be all the little snakelets will wriggle about in confusion, with no knowledge of how to strike." He stretched out carefully and lay back on his cot. *"Ru'shalla-tu."*

Sef, moving to the table to pour a cup of wine, twisted his head to stare over his shoulder. "What do you say?"

"May it be so. Old Tongue saying." Donal scrubbed the heel of his hand across his forehead. "Gods, but when I

recall the sight of Tynstar's head falling from his body—"
For a moment, he shut his eyes and summoned the vision
again. "And all the blackened blood—"

Sef spun around, nearly spilling the wine. "Blackened
blood! Tynstar's blood was *black?*"

"Black and thick and heavy." Donal levered himself up
on one arm and accepted the cup of wine. "Electra's too—"
He grimaced. "It is enough to give one nightmares."
Abruptly, he looked at Sef with his pale face and staring
eyes. "Gods, I am sorry. I should not have spoken so
plainly."

Sef shrugged. "No. No, better I know the truth . . ." He
shrugged again, as if to ward off the gooseflesh of fright.
"But—what will happen now? Here—to us?"

Donal sipped. "We continue to battle. The Mujhar and his
portion of the army will try to stop Osric before he reaches
Mujhara—here, we must put a stop to the Solindish-Ihlini
uprising."

"Then—we will stay here until this war is done—and
then return to Homana?"

Donal nodded as he swallowed down the wine. "Aye.
Carillon has left me a task. I am to lead these men while
he confronts the Atvian."

"Then—Osric doesn't know the demon has been slain."
Sef frowned. "Does he?"

"No. Perhaps it will aid Carillon's campaign—he will go
against Osric knowing the sorcerer is dead, while Osric an-
ticipates Tynstar's help." Donal smiled. "A surprise for the
Atvian—one that should help our cause."

Sef's voice was tentative. "Then—*these* are politics?"

Donal laughed. "More like strategies. But often enough
they appear to be one and the same."

It was gloomy inside the tent. Night had fallen; candles
illuminated the saffron interior of the pavilion and turned
it pale ocher and dull gold. Evan had absented himself to
spend time with one of his women; most of the encampment celebrated Tynstar's downfall. Donal had passed on the
news calmly enough, then retired to rest his throbbing leg.

"I will rest, Sef. If you wish to go out and celebrate with
the other boys, please yourself."

"My thanks." Sef had grown a little since joining Donal's
service, but he was still thin, still almost delicate. The

sleeves of his tunic and shirt were too short now; bony wrists protruded.

Inwardly, Donal smiled. *More clothing, yet again.* "You may go, Sef. I will not need you again until the morning."

The boy grinned crookedly. "I will drink the cider, my lord—I will drink a toast to the victory over Tynstar!"

"Go." Donal waved a hand, and the boy ran out of the tent.

He sipped his wine. He stared into the shadows and thought of how he had come to be the victim of circumstance. Nearly twenty-four years before a child had been born to a warrior and his woman. Their freedom, like the child's, did not exist. The gods had seen fit to give them all another fate.

Taj perched upon the chairback. He pipped softly, preening his feathers into perfection, hardly aware of Donal's presence. On the floor, next to the cot, lay Lorn, curled upon rough matting, nose covered by the tip of his ruddy tail. He twitched, and Donal knew he dreamed.

He sighed. He stretched out to set the cup of wine upon the table, and then he lay back, head pillowed on arms thrust beneath his neck. He shut his eyes, and slept.

He dreamed. He saw a palace and a dais and a woman upon the dais. She was beautiful. She was deadly. She had the power to twist his soul.

Beside her stood a man. Cloaked in black with a silver sword hanging at one hip. In his outstretched hand glowed a violet rune. It danced. Subtly. Seductively. Promising many things.

From behind them came a girl. Half-woman, half-child, trapped between youth and adulthood. Like her mother, she was lovely, but her beauty was unfulfilled. Like her father, she was strong, but without a will the strength was blunted.

"Donal," someone said, "Donal, you must come."

He frowned. None of the mouths had moved. The rune still danced in the sorcerer's hand.

"Donal—*rouse* yourself—"

A hand on his shoulder, and he was suddenly awake. *Awake*—the dream was banished. He blinked dazedly at Evan and saw how the sleepy eyes were filled with grave concern.

He bent at once and picked up his boot, pulled it on with effort. Evan waited, solemn-faced and silent. There was no frivolity in his face; no hint of celebration.

Donal rose, suppressing a grimace of pain. "Is it better told or shown?"

"Shown," Evan said. "Words would not describe it."

Lir, Donal summoned, and they went with him out of the tent.

Evan led him through the encampment to a hollow in the hills ringing the huddled tents. Not far. But away from the bonfires and clustered soldiers who still celebrated Carillon's victory over Tynstar.

The night was cool. The light had changed; it was nearing dawn. He had slept longer than he intended.

He saw three men standing at the edges of the hollow. Two Homanan sentries. The other a Cheysuli.

Finn turned as Donal came up with Evan. His face, like the others, was solemn, etched with tension. But there was something more in the eyes. Something that spoke of a hope destroyed.

He put out a hand and halted Donal. "There is grief in it for you."

Both sentries held flaming torches. Light hissed and flared, shedding faulty illumination. In the hollow, Donal saw shapes huddled on the ground, sprawled awkwardly in the macabre dance of death. Outflung arms, legs; limp, questioning hands. Faces, stricken with amazement and terror. Open eyes, staring into the heavens.

Boys, all of them.

One of the sentries stirred. "My lord—the others would not have them at the fires. They said it was for men to do, without the company of boys. And so they came here to celebrate on their own."

Donal counted the bodies. Fourteen that he could differentiate from others. Fourteen boys who had run messages between the captains and tended their noble lords.

As Sef had.

His head snapped around as he stared at Finn. "Is he here?"

Mutely, Finn gestured to one of the sprawled bodies. It was mostly hidden by another.

Donal went to the body and knelt. The flickering torchlight showed him shadowed, ghostly faces; slack, childish mouths. He gently moved the body off Sef's legs, then beckoned one of the sentries over.

The torch was unmerciful. Sef's head was twisted slightly, so that his face was turned away. But his neck was bared, and the cut in his throat showed plainly. From ear to ear it stretched. The ground was sodden with his blood.

Red blood, Donal thought. *None of the blackened Ihlini ichor*— "Fourteen boys," he said aloud. "Surely *one* of them must have heard the Solindish coming."

"This was Ihlini-done," Finn told him grimly.

Donal snapped his head around. "Are you certain? This smells of raiders to me."

"It is meant to. But see you this?" Finn held something out.

Donal, frowning, took it from his uncle's hand. It was a stone, a round, dull gray stone with a vein of black running through it.

"An Ihlini ward-stone," Finn explained. "Apart from the other four, it is worthless. But it tells us who was here."

"Dropped?" Donal rolled the stone in his hand. "Used to make them helpless—silencing their cries . . ." He looked again at Sef. Near one bent knee lay a flaccid wineskin. Donal smelled the tang. Wine, not cider; boys had tried to mimic men.

Carefully, Donal closed the staring odd-colored eyes. He recalled Carillon performing the same service for Electra. And then such grief welled up as to nearly unman him before the others. "Gods—" he choked "—why did it have to be *boys*—?"

"Because they knew what it would do." Briefly, Finn touched Donal's rigid shoulder. "I know what he was to you. I am sorry for what has happened."

"To *me*—?" Donal stared up at his uncle. "What of you? What if he *was* your son—or kin or some other kind? What *then*, su'fali?"

The scar jumped once. "It changes nothing," Finn said evenly. "The boy is dead."

"Dead," Donal echoed. Gently, he touched Sef's right wrist. He felt the feathered band. He recalled how it was meant to be a charm against sorcery.

Cheysuli sorcery.

Deftly, Donal untied the knot in the leather lace on the underside of the cool, limp wrist. He took the band and tucked it into his belt-purse.

Not strong enough, he told the murdered boy. *Was I not charm enough against the sorcery you feared?*

But then, looking again at the fourteen bodies, he knew he had not been.

Donal rose stiffly. He could not look at Finn. "We need a burial detail."

The other sentry inclined his head. "My lord—I will see to it." With the torch smoking in his wake, the Homanan went away.

PART II

One

Donal stared gloomily out at the drowning world from the open flaps of his saffron pavilion. It was late evening, just past supper. It was cold. Summer was gone; fall had settled in. In Solinde, it rained during the fall. He was bored, restless, and weary, and heartily wishing Carillon had left someone else to lead the army.

He had led it, now, for two months. Occasional word came from Carillon that Osric of Atvia still pressed them on the plains between Hondarth and Mujhara. Worse, it seemed unlikely there would be any immediate resolution. Osric, Carillon claimed, was a master strategist. The two armies were utterly deadlocked.

Donal sighed and turned away from the rainy darkness to watch Evan rattle a small wooden casket. It held ivory dice and slender sticks of rune-carved wood. The Homanans called it the fortune-game. There were two levels of play: a straightforward dicing game for unimaginative gamblers, and the more elaborate rune-stick portion involving portents and prophecies.

I weary of prophecies. Let Evan play at being Seer—I have enough to concern myself with.

The Ellasian prince had unmatched skill with both dice and rune-sticks. Dice and sticks fell his way repeatedly, but Donal knew he did not cheat. The game itself was not Evan's, but won from a Homanan soldier in an unconnected wager.

Evan rattled the casket. "Come, my lord of Homana— let us see what your fortune says."

Donal smiled wryly. "Have you wearied of taking my coin? *Now* you wish to steal my fortune also?"

Evan raised dark brows in feigned indignation, one hand touching his heart. "*I*, my lord? Do you mistrust me, then?

But here—I will show you. . . . *I* shall throw and read you what I see."

Donal watched idly as Evan chanted over the rune-sticks and dice as he rattled them in their casket. Boredom settled more deeply in his bones.

Solinde, of late, had been peaceful. The Ihlini, perhaps stunned by Tynstar's death, were quiet. The Solindish did not attack. The most recent encampment had stood safely for three weeks. It was possible the rebellion was over; also possible the Solindish meant to trap the Homanans into leaving prematurely. And so the warhost waited.

Evan spilled out the dice and rune-sticks across the wooden table. Ivory rattled; rune-sticks rolled, then settled. Evan frowned in concentration. "Ah!" he cried in discovery. "Fortune looks kindly on you, my lord. See here the rune signifying the *Wanderer?* And the die here for modification? It means within days you shall find yourself traveling on a journey filled with adventure and discovery—see you here? *Jester* and *Charlatan.*" Evan's grin was sly. "A *Woman* as well, Donal—see you this rune here?"

"I see the folly of idleness," Donal retorted. Before Evan could speak, he scooped up dice and rune-sticks without dropping them into the casket, and threw them across the table. "There. Read them for me now."

Evan stared at the pattern. After a moment he lifted his head and met Donal's eyes squarely. "You mock the game, my friend. Not wise. Now what you see is a genuine destiny."

Donal snorted. "I was promised a *destiny* long ago, Ellasian—all Cheysuli are. Read me my fortune."

Evan looked back at the tumbled dice and rune-sticks. He touched none of them, but he pointed to the indicators. "There. A Minor rune, representing *Youth*. But, coupled with a Major one, *so*—" he pointed to another rune on the same stick "—that is the *Magician*, Donal, and a very powerful rune."

Donal, still smiling, nodded. "Say on, Seer."

Evan's habitual sleepy expression was gone. "Here—this is the *Prisoner*. This die signifies time spent—months. And this rune is another Major—it is the *Executioner*." He met Donal's eyes again. "Conjoined with what I threw just before you did, the fortune is a powerful one."

"Aye?" Donal waited.

Evan sighed. "*Wanderer*: you will embark upon a journey. *Charlatan* and *Jester*: you will meet those who are more than what they seem. *Woman* is obvious—perhaps she is also the *Magician*. And at the end of the journey there is imprisonment and potential death—there is an *Executioner*." Evan gestured. "There, my friend, is your fortune."

"A full one," Donal said lightly. "You do not underplay the moment, Evan."

"I underplay *nothing*—" Evan began, but his words were drowned out in a shout from outside the pavilion. Donal heard his own name called.

He turned to the doorflap at once. Framed in the opening was a cloaked and hooded man, nearly indistinguishable from the rain and darkness. "My lord." The voice was raised to reach above the downpour. One hand came up to move the hood and the shadows shifted.

"Rowan! Come in." Donal stepped aside at once and gestured the general in. "Word from Carillon?"

Rowan moved past him into the pavilion. Rain ran down the muddied cloak and splattered against the hard-packed floor; he threw it back from his shoulders. He wore leather-and-ringmail, and his rumpled crimson tunic was stained with blood and grime. The brazier cast harsh shadows across his face and limned his weariness.

"My lord," he said without ceremony. "Carillon is dead."

Donal stared at him. For a moment he felt nothing; as if the words were syllables of nonsense. But then they came together into a sentence he understood. Shock reared up in his soul. "Carillon . . ." he whispered.

Rowan reached into his belt-pouch. From it he took an object and placed it on the table. In the candlelight, the bloodstains shone dark red.

A ring. A gold ring, set with a black stone, and into the stone was carved the rampant lion of Homana.

Rowan bent his head. Silver shone in his hair. And then, with a gracelessness that emphasized his grief and utter weariness, he knelt upon the floor. "My lord," he said. "You are Mujhar of Homana."

Donal looked down at him. Rowan knelt stiffly and his head was bowed. The wet cloak molded itself to his body

and tangled on his spurs. He was wet, wet and weary, and
stark pain was in his voice.

For a moment Donal shut his eyes. Beneath his lids he
saw Carillon as he had seen him last. Standing over the
bodies of Tynstar and Electra, knowing he too would be
dead before the year was out.

He knew. He knew—I knew . . . and still I am unprepared.

He looked blankly at Rowan again. No. It was not right.
The posture was incorrect. He was not the man for whom
the homage was intended. "Get up from there," he said
unsteadily. "You do not kneel to *me*."

Rowan raised his head. "I kneel to the Mujhar."

Again, the words were unconnected. He heard them, but
he could not acknowledge them. Slowly he shook his head.
"*Carillon* is your Mujhar."

The older man's face did not change expression. It was
a mask, a blank, weary mask, hiding what he felt. "You
are in his place, my lord. And I must offer my fealty."

"Get up from there!" Donal shouted. "You do this purposely!" His voice cracked. He stopped speaking. He felt
the trembling in his body. And then, only then, did he see
the tears in Rowan's eyes.

He nearly turned away. He could not face the man's
grief, or it would swallow up his own. Instead he stared
blankly at the ring.

Now it is meant for me. He looked down at his right
hand. On his forefinger the ruby signet ring meant for the
Prince of Homana. No longer was it his. He must replace
it with the other. *Gods . . . I am not worthy.*

"Donal." It was Evan, speaking softly. "Donal—will you
keep him on his knees the length of the night?"

Abruptly, Donal looked back at the general. He saw how
the sun-bronzed skin had lost much of its color. It was
stretched taut over the strong, prominent bones, shadowed
in the light. Rowan looked almost old.

He has lost so much . . . Donal bent. He caught Rowan's
left arm and raised him up. "Do you think I would not
accept you?" His voice was steadier now. "Did you think
I would *dismiss* you?"

"I am Carillon's man," Rowan said clearly. "I can never
be anyone else's."

Donal did not answer at once. He lacked a voice; the

words. Somehow, he had always known it. Rowan was Carillon's man, as he himself had claimed. For more years than Donal had been alive, Rowan had served his lord. He had dedicated his life to Carillon utterly. And now the task was finished.

He will never serve me. To him, I am a makeshift man, not fit to assume the Lion. I can never take Carillon's place.

He looked at the older man. "Surely you will aid me. My task will not be easy."

"Nor was his." The tears were gone from Rowan's eyes. His face was a mask again.

Gods—he will never *acknowledge me.* Donal looked at the ring again. He felt empty and full all at once. Empty in spirit because Carillon was gone; full of the grief it brought. "Rowan," he said softly, "I will need your help."

The other Cheysuli drew in a deep, uneven breath. "Years ago, Carillon gave me an estate as a reward for my services. I have had it administered for me through all the years I remained at Homana-Mujhar . . . but I intended, when this time arrived, to leave royal service."

"Leave." Donal felt the apprehension spill into his belly. "Do you think I can do this alone?"

"I doubt you can do it at all." The tone was uninflected. It made the words more cruel.

"Oh, *gods,*" Donal said. "Do you hate me so much?"

"I do not hate you at all." Neither tone nor expression changed. "You are not—Carillon. That is all. It is not fair, I know . . . but then nothing is fair. Is it?" Rowan's eyes were filled with bittersweet empathy. "You are resented by the Homanans because Carillon made you his heir. Oh, aye—they begin to accept the prophecy, but they would prefer to accept it *later.* With you, that time is now." Rowan sighed and closed his eyes briefly. "There are foreign realms who view the succession with alarm and distaste: *they must deal with a man who shifts his shape.* And, of course, there are the Cheysuli, who view you as something like unto an avatar of all the ancient gods. How can I hate a man as swallowed up as *you?*"

Swallowed up— Aye, he was, or would be. The Lion would regurgitate a different man.

Fear lodged in his throat. "Rowan—*I will* need *your help.*"

After a moment, Rowan nodded. "And I will see that you have it."

Donal turned to the table and poured a cup of wine. He offered it to Rowan. "Here. You are in need of food and rest. But for now . . . will you tell me how it was? Supposedly it is a painless ending."

Rowan, accepting the wine, looked at him sharply. "Painless? His *death?*"

Donal gestured emptily. "I am told the root is—gentle. That at the last a man simply slips away in his sleep. I had hoped it would be so for Carillon."

Rowan stared, the wine forgotten. "Root? What do you say?" Then his mouth dropped open. "Are you speaking of *tetsu?*"

"Aye," Donal answered. Then, in shock, "Did you not know? I thought he told you everything."

Color drained from Rowan's face. "Gods—was *that* it? I knew he was in pain—the disease was eating his bones. But not once—*never* did I think he would resort to such as *tetsu.*" His mask had slipped. There was bewilderment in his face. "But where would he get it? It is a Cheysuli thing, and kept hidden from Homanans." He looked at Donal questioningly. "How would he know of *tetsu.* and who would give it to him?"

Donal felt his jaw clench. "It was Finn who gave it to him."

Shock flared in Rowan's eyes. *"Finn!"* He caught his breath. "Aye—*it would be!* Leave it to Finn to give poison to Carillon!"

"For the pain," Donal protested. "He said Carillon desired it."

"And so he stole more time!" Rowan said bitterly. "Did he tell him what it would do? Did Finn say to him he would lose what little time was left?" His hands shook in his anger.

Donal's fingers curled against his palms until the nails bit in. "I am certain Finn told him everything. He is not a murderer, Rowan."

"He has been that, and worse." Rowan's tone was harsh, the words clipped. "Most of the stories of him are true."

An answering spark of anger flared in Donal's chest. "Finn was loyal to the Mujhar! What he did was because

Carillon desired it! Do you dare intimate to me that Finn *wanted* him to die?"

Rowan shut his eyes. "No . . . no . . . I—do not. No. Forgive me, I am not myself. But—*tetsu* root? *Why?*"

"He was in pain," Donal answered. "Did *you* not tell me that often enough?"

The older visage was haggard in the candlelight. Rowan passed a hand across his face and rubbed at his circled eyes. "Gods—he meant to rule until the end . . . he meant not to give himself over into imbecility from the pain . . . aye, I see it. A man such as Carillon would take *tetsu* and give up quantity for quality. It was his way." Suddenly a breath of ironic laughter issued hollowly from his mouth. "And then, for all that, it was Osric who took his life."

Breath spilled out of Donal's body. "Osric! *Osric?*"

Rowan nodded. "Three weeks ago we rode into battle against Osric. And it was done with. We had won the day. We had only to gather our dead and wounded." He drew in a heavy breath. "I saw him. Carillon was mounted, standing on a hilltop. Just—looking. Looking across the battlefield as we went out to gather our dead. I saw him sitting there, watching . . . I wondered why he was so still. Now, I think it might have been the root. It—affects a man's perceptions." His brows twisted together in a spasm of grief. "I—saw him fall."

"Fall—"

Jerkily, Rowan nodded. "He fell." The words spilled out. "He went down by the hooves of his horse. For a moment I could not understand—Carillon would never fall!—and then I saw the arrow in his chest." He stopped talking. "I was—too far . . . *too far*—I could not reach him in time. But—I saw the Atvian archer—I saw him ride up to my lord. Even as I ran across the hill, I saw him kneel down by my Mujhar. I shouted—*gods, how I shouted!*—but the archer did not listen. And by the time I reached my lord, the Atvian was gone."

Silence. Donal heard the sibilance of the rain. It ran off the pavilion and splattered against the ground. "More?" he asked raggedly.

Tears ran unchecked down Rowan's Cheysuli face. "He knew it was done," he said. "He said I must not trouble myself to send for a chirurgeon. He said—he said he wished

Finn were with him, or Duncan, so they could take away the pain." For an instant, his voice shook. "He told me it was Osric himself—the Atvian archer was Osric . . . that he named himself to Carillon as he knelt down beside him. And then—then he said I was to carry the sword to you, because now you would accept it."

"The sword . . ." Donal echoed. "Gods—now it *is* mine." Rowan's face was gray. "My lord—Osric has the sword." *"Osric!"*

"I could not tell Carillon," Rowan whispered wretchedly. "That is what the Atvian took."

Donal recalled the sparring match he had had with Carillon so many months before. How they had discovered that, in his hand, the blade knew its true master. Not Carillon's sword at all, for all it served him. Meant for another man.

Donal looked down on Rowan. "Then I will have to get it back."

Rowan's voice shook. "I served him for twenty-five years." He spoke with a dry factuality, as if that would somehow hide his grief. "I was twelve. Did you know that? Twelve. He was only eighteen himself, but he was so far above me I could hardly see him for the brightness of his spirit. And he saw to it I was saved . . . he saw to it I was rescued, while he remained in iron." His smile was bittersweet. "I swore then I would do what I could to serve him. Even while he and Finn kept themselves in exile, I did what I could to serve him. I kept his memory alive." The smile faded away. "And when he came home, he took me into his service—my *tahlmorra*, if you will—" He smiled no longer. "And now it comes to *this.*" He nearly crushed the silver cup. "That service is ended by Osric's arrow."

And that arrow makes me king— Donal turned away from Rowan. He could not bear to look at his face.

On the table he saw the ring, still stained with Carillon's blood. *His* ring, now. Slowly, with a dreadful fascination, he drew off the one on his forefinger and set it down beside the other. His son's, if Aislinn ever bore one.

And I pray the gods she will . . . I am in need of an heir, am I to be Mujhar. His inward smile was ragged with irony.

Donal took up the heavy black ring with its incised rampant lion. Carefully he pushed it onto his naked forefinger and felt his flesh form itself to the metal.

He turned to Evan. "See to it the general has food and rest. Then find Finn and have him wait for me here. I will come to him when I can."

"But how long should he wait?"

"Until I have come back." Without picking up his woolen cloak he went out into the rain.

He ran. He thought it might ease the pain. But it only deepened it. He felt it fill up his belly until he wanted to vomit onto the ground. But he was empty. He was empty of all save grief and fear.

He ran—

—and when he stopped, it was because he knew he had to. Because his lungs burned and his belly ached and his soul had shrunk up within his chest. There was nothing left but breathlessness and sorrow, and a wild, wild rage.

He stood upon an escarpment. Below him lay the valley and the encampment. The sky was brackish with clouds; neither moon nor stars shone against the darkness.

He clenched his right fist and felt the heavy ring bite into his finger. "You take them all," he said aloud. "My *jehan*, my *jehana*—the boy . . . now Carillon as well. You take them *all* from me—and you thrust this upon me too soon!"

Do you think yourself unworthy? Taj, spiralling in the misty drizzle.

I am *unworthy.*

You are a Cheysuli warrior. You are worthy of anything. Lorn's tone was inflexible. It sounded like Carillon's.

Donal shook his head. "I am afraid," he said clearly. "Do you understand that? *Afraid.* Because I cannot begin to rule as he has ruled. I cannot be Carillon. I cannot take his place!"

Lorn's eyes glinted. *You are not meant to take his place. You are meant to make a new one.*

Taj circled closer. *In death, as in life, he served the prophecy.*

"He was Homanan, not Cheysuli! Why did *he* have to take the risk?"

A life without risk is empty, Lorn retorted. *A life not risked for something as high as the prophecy of the Firstborn is not a life at all.*

"And mine?" Donal demanded. "What is mine to be?"

Lorn pressed against his leg. *Why not have the Ellasian dice you your destiny?*

Donal's laugh was bitter.

Taj circled more closely. *Who is to say he will be wrong?*

Donal stared across the soaked plains. He saw the guttering sparks of reluctant fire cairns built beneath fabric rainbreaks. His army—*his* army—spread across the land like a silent tide.

And it was time he returned to it.

When he ripped aside the doorflap on his pavilion he found it empty save for Finn. For a moment he thought perhaps his uncle did not know, but then he saw past the subtle control.

The scarred face was perfectly blank. But the fury and grief in his posture was such that it struck Donal like a blow.

Donal drew in a slow, even breath. "I go to Homana in the morning."

Finn, half-hidden in the shadows, did not move at all. "You have an army here."

The flat impersonality of the tone shocked Donal. Their eyes met across the pavilion. Then Donal made a dismissive gesture with his hand. "Solinde, for the moment, is quiet. I will go to Homana."

"Why?" Finn demanded.

Rain ran from Donal's soaked leathers and spilled across the floor. "You were his liege man for nearly ten years. You commanded Cheysuli and Homanan alike in the wars that won Homana back from Bellam's tyranny. I need you to command this army while I fetch home my sword."

Finn smiled tightly. "The Homanans will never suffer a Cheysuli in command."

"They have suffered *me* these past months!"

"At Carillon's behest."

"What of Rowan?"

"At Carillon's behest!"

Donal brought his right hand up into the light so that the ring was clearly visible. "*At their Mujhar's behest*, surely they will accept you as temporary commander."

Finn moved forward until he stood no more than two paces away from Donal. His breath hissed through his teeth as he spoke. "*I* will go to Homana and slay the Atvian serpent. *I* will take his life. Not you. *I* am owed this death!"

"Are you?" Donal held his eyes. "You said once I must choose my own path. I have done it. You will remain here and command the army, *as once you did for Carillon,* and I will go to Homana."

Finn bared his teeth. "*I* am owed that death!"

"I," Donal said. "I am his heir. I will do it. Osric will die by my hand, and I will bring home the sword again."

Finn spat out something in the Old Tongue that set the hairs to rising on the nape of Donal's neck. He felt color drain out of his face. "Insult?" he asked, and heard the waver in his voice. He fought to steady it. "I am your bloodkin, *su'fali!* I have spent my life honoring you for wisdom, strength, and power, and now you offer *insult*—"

"Aye!" Finn snapped. "And will again, do you mean to deny me this."

"*I am your Mujhar!*" Donal's voice was hoarse with the effort of swallowing the shout. "Do *you* fail me in this, think you the *Homanans* will accept me?"

Finn's hand spasmed as he closed it on his knife. "I want only the life of a *single Atvian lordling*—"

"*Shansu, su'fali,*" Donal said gently. "Do you think I do not grieve at least half as much as you?"

The scar writhed on Finn's dark face. For a moment there was such grief and anguish in his eyes Donal feared he might go mad. But Finn contained his emotions.

When he could, he drew in a slow breath and released it carefully. "Duncan would say I am a fool . . . too impetuous for my own good—he told me so often enough—and perhaps it is the truth." Finn's voice was hoarse. "Perhaps I am. Perhaps I must recall all the good advice he gave me and let his son offer it as well." The sigh was ragged around the edges. "I suppose—so long as Osric is slain—it matters little who has the doing of it."

Donal reached out his arms and waited, and at last Finn accepted the brief clasp that sealed their bond again. "Osric will be slain," Donal told him clearly. "That I promise you."

Two

He thought it a little like the Womb of the Earth. The
walls were intaglioed with marble carvings, but the stone
was pale pink and the shapes were not *lir* but men instead:
the sarcophogi of kings.

Effigies and marble coffins filled the shadowed vault.
Donal stood in the half-open doorway and looked in on
the silent dead. It was a Homanan thing to carve likenesses
of the dead into polished stone. A Homanan thing to hide
them away in privacy. A Homanan thing to store them all
together in the bowels of Homana-Mujhar, which was a
Cheysuli place. To Donal, the practice was abhorrent.

Aislinn was within. She was alone, unaware of his presence. Grieving by herself. Of all the candleracks only one
was lighted, throwing the intaglios and effigies into stark
relief. The illumination emphasized the sepulchral silence
of the mausoleum. But Aislinn did not seem to care. She
held a single candle over a plain, undressed marble coffin.

Donal moved through the doorway. His step sounded
loud in the vault; Aislinn spun around with a gasp and
dropped the candle onto the coffin. It rolled, snuffed out,
spilled hot wax across the stone. A curl of smoke drifted
upward and filled Donal's nose with the odor of scented
beeswax.

"Donal!" Aislinn gasped, one hand clutching at her robe.

He moved into the vault, a fat candle clenched in his
hand. The flame flared and guttered as he moved, striking
odd shadows across the pinched face before him. He saw
the glint of tears and the lines of bitter grief.

"They have put him here?" he asked. "Why here? Why
not above the ground, in freedom?"

Her eyes were black in the muted light. "This—this is
where all the kings are placed."

"Shaine too?"

"Sh-shaine?" She stared at him in amazement, as if she could not believe he would speak of such inconsequential things in the face of her father's death. "No. When Bellam took the palace, Shaine was already dead. He was not entombed with honor. Bellam disposed of the body; no one knows where those bones lie."

"Good," he said quietly. "Shaine was not deserving of any honor."

"Donal—!"

He looked at her levelly. "Shaine was a madman and a fool. Carillon deserves better company."

She turned from him then, lurching back to face the marble coffin. Her hands went flat against the undressed lid. Fingers splayed out. She bent her head, and Donal saw how her shoulders trembled. "I saw him," she whispered. "I *saw* him. They told me I had to see him while they prepared him for entombment—so that no one could claim the Mujhar yet lived, and use that for some purpose."

He heard the note of horror mixed with anguish. "But he does," Donal told her. "The Mujhar *does* yet live."

She spun, pressing her back against the coffin. "*What*—"

He overrode her unfinished question. "I am Carillon's heir, Aislinn . . . *I* am Mujhar of Homana."

Color drained from her face, but her voice was surprisingly steady. "You do not waste time."

"I have none." The light from his candle played on the red of her heavy braid, turning it to gold. "Do I falter now, the war may well be lost. There is no time for a leisurely expression of royal grief. Not even for Carillon."

"Then why do you come *here?*" She was wrapped in a robe of cerulean velvet. It slid off one shoulder and displayed the linen of her nightshift; he had thought to spend his time in the vault alone, since his arrival was quite late, but Aislinn did not look as if she had slept at all.

"I came to see how you fared," he told her, "and to bid my good-bye to Carillon."

Tears glittered in her eyes. "I fare well enough—for a woman who has lost both unborn son and father."

He wanted to go to her, to take her into his arms and offer the comfort she needed. But he was afraid. Cheysuli honored the dead with deep respect and solemnity, and the keening of women was abhorrent. He dared not sacrifice his own tenuous control to acknowledging Aislinn's need.

"I am alone," she said. "I have no one in all the world."

He held himself very still. He felt the pain blossom in his chest, then slowly rise to fill up his throat. He found he could hardly breathe.

Slowly, he set his candle down on the coffin. Then he touched her fingertips. When he felt their trembling he knew he was undone.

Aislinn moved into his arms. She clung but she did not break down. She cried but it was silently, with a sort of dignity he had not expected. Somehow, it made the moment more poignant.

"How long do you stay?" she asked at last, when the tears had dried on her cheeks.

"I do not stay," he answered. "I must go on to the Keep."

Aislinn stiffened. "You go to *her?*"

"Aye, there is Sorcha," he admitted, "but also there are my children."

She stepped back from him, leaving his arms empty again. "Then—you will not spend the night with me?" He saw how she twisted the fabric of her robe. "You—forgo a husband's responsibilities?"

"Aislinn," he said gently, "you recall how it was last time. Are you prepared for that again?"

"I think—I think there will be no need." Color flared in her face. "I think you will find me a willing wife instead of a lunatic girl."

He looked at her. It was true there was greater awareness in her eyes. Save for a natural embarrassment and proper modesty, she appeared to lack the fear she had shown before.

Perhaps—now that Tynstar and Electra are dead—she is free of the link entirely.

After a moment, he shook his head. "Aislinn—I am sorry. But tonight there is no time. I must go on to the Keep, and then I will join the army. There is a death I must mete out."

"Osric's?"

He nodded.

"I thought it might be that. Well then, I will not keep

you. It is not my place to reprove you for avenging my
father's death." She turned, reaching for his candle. "Will
you sup with me? You look weary. After that, I will not
gainsay you."

Somberly, she led him from the vault.

He ate. He drank. He told her what he could of the
battles in Solinde. She listened attentively, and he found
she had gained a new maturity in the months since he had
left her. The shape of her face seemed different. Excess
flesh had faded so that he saw the line of her bones clearly,
as he had seen them in Electra. No more the young woman
who only hinted at adulthood; conceiving the child and then
losing it had done much to banish her girlhood.

They were alone. His *lir* were in his apartments in another wing. They dined in her chambers; the servants she
had dismissed, saying they would tend to themselves in
privacy.

Now, as she set her goblet down, she regarded him more
closely. "You look so weary, Donal."

He leaned against one elbow. "I came directly from Solinde. It is taxing to hold *lir*-shape so long without proper
rest, but I felt the circumstances warranted the sacrifice."
He sipped from his cup of wine. "That is partly why I am
out of sorts. If I was cruel to you in the vault, I am sorry
for it."

"You are unhappy." She poured more wine for him. "I
see it clearly. The heirship has been a long one, and now
that it has ended and the throne is truly yours, you find
you do not like it."

"I never wanted it," he said wearily. "I told you that,
once. But—Carillon needed an heir, and I have a drop or
two of royal blood."

"More than a drop," she retorted. "For all you flaunt
your Cheysuli blood, there is Homanan in you as well. And,
as for heirs—we should make some of our own." Her long-
lidded eyes flicked a slanting glance at him. "Do you not
agree?"

He smiled. "I agree. And when I am done with this war,
I shall do my best to sire some."

"Will the war take so long?" Reddish brows knitted together over her lambent gaze.

Donal scratched an eyelid thoughtfully. "Osric has entrenched himself in the plains just north of the fenlands. Mujhara is not precisely *threatened* . . . but it might be if we do not continue to hold him. While our strength is split, there is little we can do. Carillon meant to stop him permanently—now it is up to me."

She reached across the table and caught his hand before he could withdraw. "Donal—stay with me this night. Delay a day or two."

Her flesh was warm against his. "I have said why I cannot. And you agreed you would not gainsay me."

"I lied." Her single braid had loosened so that her bright hair tumbled around her face. Deftly she undid the lacing until the hair fell free of its confinement. The robe slid off her shoulders; through the thin fabric of her nightshift he could see the lines of her breasts.

"Aislinn," he said, "enough."

"No." She rose, pressing her hands against the table. She shook back her hair and smiled. "I am free, Donal. No more Ihlini magic. I can be what you wish me to be."

He was not indifferent to her. But in his weariness, in his single-mindedness, he thought he could refuse her. "Aislinn, please be *patient.* We will have our time."

Slowly, she rounded the table and stood behind his back. Her hands settled on his neck. "That time is *now.*"

"Aislinn—"

"Do you think I play a game?" She bent forward and pressed herself against his rigid back. Her hair hung down to fall across his shoulders. "This is not a game. This is my *retribution.*" Abruptly she caught two handfuls of his hair. *"Do you know what it was like?"* she demanded. "Can you *conceive* of what it was like? Can you *consider* what it is to know such utter helplessness as what you gave to me?"

He caught her hands and rose, stepping free of the stool beside the table. "Aislinn—this is nonsense—"

"Is it?" Her wrists were trapped in his hands. "*I* say it is retribution."

He shook his head, baffled. "Aislinn—are you mad—?"

"You will stay the night with me." He saw the intensity in her clear gray eyes. "I want you to know what it is like. *I want you to feel the helplessness,* as I did, knowing I could *do nothing!*"

He wavered. A shudder coursed through his body. His tongue felt thick in his mouth. "Aislinn—what have you done?"

"Sought power where I can get it." Her long eyes were wide and watchful. "You have drunk much wine, my lord. You are weary. You require rest. But when a husband is stubborn, a wife must make shift where she can."

"By the gods—*you are your* jehana's *daughter*—"

"I am what I must be." Her image wavered before him. She retreated. He followed, trying to catch a hand so he could hold her still.

She said nothing as he fell against the bed. He struggled to push himself upright, clinging to the carved tester and heavy tapestries. His clawing hand pulled down the silken folds.

"You *will* know what it is like," she said in a hard, brittle voice. "I want you to *feel* what it is like. I want—"

But he did not hear what else she wanted.

He dreamed of Sorcha. And sought release in her supple body.

Donal sat bolt upright in the bed, shocked into full wakefulness so quickly his heart lurched within his chest and his head pounded. He thought he might be ill.

He stared at the woman blindly. He swallowed twice, tasting a flat foulness on his tongue. "Aislinn, *what have you done?*"

She turned from her belly to her back. Languorously, she stretched, then pulled silken sheets up demurely to cover her nakedness. "I took your will away."

He rubbed at his face with one hand, trying to vanquish the tingling numbness. His body told him he had lain with a woman last night; his mind recalled nothing of it. "I did not intend to spend the night—I was going to the Keep, and then on to the army."

"I know." Aislinn's smile reminded him of Electra's. "What was it like, my lord, to know yourself so helpless?"

He swore violently and got out of the bed, but clutched one of the testers for support. "Witch. No better than your *jehana*—"

"We will not speak of her." Aislinn hitched herself upright in bed and wrapped herself more tightly in the sheets. "I did not *bewitch* you, Donal . . . I merely drugged your wine."

Dizzy, he sat back down on the edge of the bed. "But— why did you not simply *slay* me? The gods know you have tried before. Unless you have a different plan, now that Electra and Tynstar are dead."

"Plan?" Aislinn frowned. "What do you say? Why would I try to slay you? What do you mean—I have done it before?"

He glared at her sourly. "In Hondarth, Aislinn. Do you not recall? That is a fine example."

Color rushed into her face and one hand flew to cover her mouth. "But *that* was my mother's doing!"

"And last night was yours." He rubbed at his head again, suppressing a groan of pain.

She shifted closer to him, kneeling at his side. "I did not mean for you to feel ill. But you drank more wine than usual—you swallowed more of the drug than I intended." Her hand, reaching out to his shoulder, fell away. "By the gods, Donal!—what do you expect me to do? Last time you took my will from me with your magic and forced me to lie with you. I only wanted you to know what it was like! Can you blame me? And—and—it is true we need an heir. We cannot put off such need."

"We can." *—And now we will.*

"We *cannot!* Do you think I am blind to the require- ments of a queen?" Her eyes were blazing at him. "You seek your light woman, my lord—what *else* am I to do when I am in need of a son?"

"Aislinn—"

"I want a baby," she said with a desperate dignity, "to replace the one I lost."

He opened his mouth to answer harshly, then shut it again. He had never thought what it was to be a woman, waiting only to bear sons to inherit a throne. And in Ais- linn's case it was imperative she bear them soon; sooner, now Carillon was dead.

He slumped on the bed and stared at her; at her pale eyes and paler face. She had much of her mother's beauty and all of her father's pride.

Slowly, he rose from the bed and dressed. He said noth-

ing until he was done, and then he walked to the door.
"Perhaps a woman must do a thing she dislikes for a reason
that demands it—but I cannot *forgive* you for it. No more
than you have forgiven me."

"I do not want *forgiveness!*" She rose up on her knees
before him. "If you cannot bring yourself to get sons on
me I will do what I have to do." Her voice shook with
tears. "Go back to your light woman, Donal—go back to
your shapechanger whore!"

It was all he could do not to cross the room and take
her throat into his hands. But he did not. "You have delayed me long enough," he told her curtly. "Now I must
ride directly to the army, without stopping at the Keep."
He looked at her angry face and felt his own anger inten-
sify. "You had best hope for a son from this travesty . . .
you will get no more children from me."

Her anger fell away. "But—Homana must have an *heir!*"

"I have a son already."

Aislinn scrambled out of the bed. She stood before him,
perfectly nude, but her fury was unimpaired. "You would
not claim *her* child Prince of Homana!"

"If there is no other, what else could I do?"

Pale fists clenched. "The Homanan Council would *never*
accept a bastard by your Cheysuli whore," she said flatly.
"Never."

Donal smiled grimly. "I am Mujhar. In the end, they will
do as I tell them."

Aislinn glared back at him. But the quality of her anger
had undergone a change. Her tears were dry. He saw a new
awareness in her eyes. A cool guardedness in her appraisal.

She smiled Electra's smile.

Donal took a horse from Homana-Mujhar, knowing if he
went straight to the army in *lir*-shape he would be too
weary to go directly into battle. He sent Taj on to the Keep
to pass word to Sorcha that he would not be home after
all. He did not relish the confrontation when at last they
did meet. She would claim the Homanans turned him from
his Cheysuli heritage, and in a way, he thought perhaps she
was right.

As the fleet bird disappeared Donal felt a twinge of regret. Without Taj he felt half naked. A part of himself was

missing, and would be, for a while. He had told Taj to fly ahead to the army when he had finished his business at the Keep. Still, he was more fortunate than other warriors. He would lack the ability to assume falcon-shape while separated by such distance, but his link to Lorn remained intact.

Donal slowed the horse as the forest grew more dense. The track narrowed to little more than a footpath, but hoofprints marked the ground. Branches slapped at his head. Fighting the vines grew tedious.

Lorn, trotting ahead, glanced over one shoulder. *Catch me if you can.* With a flick of his tail he was gone.

The wolf was at home in the forests of Homana; the horse was not. But Donal gave it a try.

He bent low in the saddle, hugging with his legs while his heels urged the stallion faster. He rode high on the chestnut withers, shifting his weight unobtrusively. Hands gave the bit to the horse. Flying mane whipped against his face and he tasted the acrid salt of horsehair.

Lir—lir—lir—

Lorn's agonized scream scythed through Donal's mind as the path before the horse fell away into a pit. He felt weightless and a sudden blaze of fear.

Donal threw himself free of saddle and stirrups.

He caught a twisted, buried root in one hand. Gnarled and whiplike, the root dropped him three more feet before jerking him to a halt. He felt shoulder muscles tear.

He swung in perfect silence, eyes shut tightly against the pain as he reached out with his other hand. As he grasped the root he pulled himself upward, taking the weight from his injured shoulder. Sweat ran down his face as he tried to detach himself from the link with Lorn, for the wolf's pain compounded his own. Taj was too far; there was no hope of flying out.

He swung himself gently against the earthen wall of the pit, clinging with both hands. Slowly he forced himself upward, hand-over-hand, boot toes digging into the crumbling sides. Inch by inch he rose, dragging himself upward to the rim. For a moment he hung suspended, gathering his strength, then lurched upward and clawed at the tangled roots that fringed the pit.

He grunted with effort; tasted the salt-copper tang of blood against his teeth; smelled the sweat of his effort and the stench of his growing fear. The link with Lorn vibrated with the intensity of the wolf's pain. But he dragged himself over the edge of the pit and fell down against the ground.

He coughed. His breath whistled in his throat. His belly heaved as it tried to draw in breath. *Lorn!* he shouted silently, and received no answer through the link. Only pain. Pain and emptiness.

Donal struggled to his knees, nursing his aching shoulder. Dazedly he pushed himself to his feet and staggered toward the trees, trying to follow the thin threat of contact with his *lir*.

—*bind a* lir *and a Cheysuli is bound . . . harm a* lir *and a Cheysuli is harmed . . . trap a* lir *and a Cheysuli is trapped*—

The litany clamored inside his skull. His *jehan* had explained it once in terms a boy could understand; a boy who had received his *lir* too soon, sooner than anyone else. He had never forgotten the lesson.

He fell against a tree, jarring his sore chest and aching shoulder. He stumbled on, responding to the desperate compulsion in his body.

Lir—lir—lir—

He tripped. He fell to hands and knees.

A figure stepped out of the trees and stood before him. Donal, half-blinded by pain, saw the boots first, then slowly looked up.

He saw a slender figure in dark, unremarkable clothing. Pale, delicate hands. And in those hands was clasped the sword with the rampant lion on its hilt.

Donal's head rose. He saw the smooth, youthful face; the parti-colored eyes.

Sef smiled. "My lord Mujhar, this is well-met. Though you seem discomfited at the moment."

"You—you are *dead*—"

"Am I? No. That was another boy. But I am glad the illusion held. I lost one of my ward-stones, you see."

Donal gasped. "*You* are Ihlini—?"

"My name is Strahan," he said, "not Sef. I am the son of Tynstar and Electra."

Donal sat back on his heels. "Electra *lost* that child! In Hondarth—on the way to the Crystal Isle—my *jehan* said she *lost* the child—"

Sef—Strahan—smiled. "So she wanted him to think. But—when you are Electra of Solinde and you have loyal women by you—there are many secrets you may keep . . . many illusions you may hold."

"Not before a Cheysuli."

"Look at me, Mujhar. Tell me if I lie."

Donal looked. No more did the boy give him humility and innocence. He gave him truth. He smiled the pure, beguiling smile of his father, with all the lambent beauty of his mother.

Donal grasped at his knife with his left hand, knowing his right arm too numb, too weak and sore to accomplish the task. But the boy set the tip of the sword against his throat, and Donal did not move.

"I hold your wolf, warrior, and therefore I hold you. Do you wish him to live, do nothing to gainsay me."

Donal spat blood from his bitten lip. "It was *you* in the Womb of the Earth. It was you all those times."

"Of course. *I* gave the poison to my mother so she could escape imprisonment. *I* hired the Homanan to attack you in the hall, knowing he would fail. I wanted you afraid. I wanted you uncertain. I wanted you in a place special to the Cheysuli, so I could slay you there."

"Not Aislinn," Donal said. "And—not *Bronwyn*, either."

Strahan smiled. "Not Aislinn. Not Bronwyn—*this* time." The smile widened. "What is it like to know your wife and sister are bloodkin to the enemy? They are, do not forget. Aislinn through her mother, Bronwyn through her father. What is it like, *Cheysuli*, to know you are kin to Ihlini?"

He echoes Tynstar's words . . . Donal swallowed heavily and looked at the rune-worked sword. In Sef's— Strahan's—hands, the weapon was huge. The ruby was half the size of his fist. "How did you come by Carillon's sword?"

"Carillon's? Or yours?" Strahan laughed. "Osric brought it to me. I had joined him by then—in the aftermath of my 'death'—and I asked for it. As proof that the murderer of my mother and father was dead." Fierce anger and a powerful hatred burned deeply in the unmatched eyes. "He *should* have left Carillon to me. He *should* have let me slay him. I would have given him a much more fitting death." His teeth showed briefly in a smile echoing that of his father. "Do you wonder why I touch the sword now? Do you wonder how I *can?* Because of you, *my lord*—you have been so remiss in your responsibilities. Oh, aye, this sword knows you—a little. But you have not had the ritual performed. You have not held it long enough in your possession for it to know an enemy's hand each time one is laid upon it. It knew me on the hilltop—knew me for what I was—but it has been too long now since you touched it. And without the ritual, the power is reduced."

No one has spoken of a ritual to me— But Donal shook his head. "*I* should have known you. Through my *lir* . . . an Ihlini is ever known."

"No," Strahan said gently. "Not while I wore the feathered band."

Donal's left hand went at once to his belt-pouch. But he did not try to open it.

The boy laughed. "Look upon it, Donal. See what has helped me so well."

Unwillingly, Donal unfastened the pouch and took out the feathered bracelet. He looked at it mutely. Such a simple thing. A slender band of braided feather: black and gold and brown.

He met Strahan's eyes. "How could *this* gainsay my *lir?*"

"They are from your father's hawk."

Breath rushed out of Donal's body. He stared blindly at the feathers in his hand, and recalled his father's body in his arms. *How could I not have known—?*

"A token, but powerful," the boy explained cheerfully. "My father took the hawk's body. And then he took Duncan. With them both, dead *lir* and live warrior, my father fashioned a powerful spell. It hid my identity. It allowed me to come to you. It even made Finn wonder if I were *kin!*" Strahan laughed. "And it made it an easy thing to infiltrate the palace."

I kept this to recall Sef's murder . . . but it is a tool of my own. He looked up at the boy again. "What do you intend to do with me?"

"Make you a *toy*," Strahan said. "The way I made one of your father."

Three

Inside his head, the memories were at war.

He recalled his father from his childhood, when Duncan had been clan-leader and responsible for people other than his son. But he had still made time for that son, teaching him what he could.

He remembered Duncan in his madness, with empty eyes and taloned hands.

He recalled the first time his father had taken him hunting, to teach him what he must know about tracking animals and slaying them to help feed the clan.

He remembered Duncan begging for their help, begging to be made whole again; a man.

He recalled how his mother had taken care to keep his father alive in his memories when Duncan was gone because all too often memories faded into nothingness.

He remembered how Alix had saved them all by sacrificing herself.

But mostly he remembered how his father had died in his arms, knowing himself a toy in the hands of Tynstar's son.

And Donal knew *he* was, also.

No! he cried. *I—am—*

"—not!"

He jerked awake. He heard his breathing rasping in the confines of the cabin. The echo of his shout. The clank of heavy iron as it rattled at wrists and ankles, bolting him to the bunk aboard the ship.

Oh gods . . . He remembered it *all*, now. How Strahan had captured him and thrown him into irons, abusing Lorn to keep Donal a subdued, well-mannered prisoner.

"Tell me something." The boy's voice; Donal opened his eyes. "Tell me something, Donal . . . why was it so easy?" Strahan stood in the cabin just inside the door. He wore dark blue tunic and trews of the finest wool, belted with leather and silver.

Donal swallowed. He had no intention of answering Strahan, but his throat was very dry.

"All my life my father taught me the Cheysuli were not men to be taken without expending great effort . . . yet you fell easily into my hands and make no effort to break free." Black brows knitted over hooded eyes. "Is this an example of the power of the *lir*-bond? I have heard how consuming it is—how a warrior gives up his life when the life of a *lir* is taken . . . but Lorn is not yet *dead*. Merely—*confined*."

Strahan did not elaborate on the confinement, but Donal knew very well what the wolf had undergone. He could feel it in himself as he lay chained to the bunk. Weakness. Hunger. Disorientation. Great thirst. Fever. And while Lorn suffered, so did he. So *would* he, until the wolf was free and well.

The boy moved closer to the bunk. "I expected more from you. In all our months together, you led me to believe you were a warrior. But I see no warrior. Just a *man*—a *human* man, caught within my trap." Yet another step closer. *"Where is the falcon, Donal?"*

Donal heard the change in tone. Strahan was a boy, but a boy with recourse to all the arcane arts of the netherworld. It made him old though young. It made him seem a man when he was not.

He is not a fool . . . and I dare not treat him as one. "Taj is dead." His voice was mostly a croak.

Strahan laughed. "Do you expect me to believe *that?* I *know* what that death entails, Donal. I know about the madness."

"Taj is dead."

"Do not undervalue me!" Color stood high in Strahan's face. "I will paint you a picture, *my lord*. Let us say the falcon is dead. Because you have the wolf, you need not concern yourself with the death-ritual; you are released from the responsibility. But I hold Lorn. Lorn is—ill. The wolf is not himself. And while neither are *you* yourself, precisely, I would hardly claim you mad." Strahan shook his head. "With Taj dead and Lorn so close, you would not be sane."

"What lies has Tynstar told you?"

"None at all," the boy said gently. "It is no secret to me. A *lir*less Cheysuli, left alive, loses what mind he has left. But because your race is so proud, so strong, so *arrogant*, you cannot bear to see any warrior lose his mind along with his *lir*. And so you created a ceremony. Glorified suicide." Strahan smiled. "Oh, aye, I know about the taboo. A Cheysuli would never stoop to suicide. But what else does a warrior do when his *lir* is dead? He gives himself over to whatever force will slay him."

"No—"

"*Aye.* I know it, Donal. Do you forget I held your father?"

Donal lunged up against his chains. "Get out of my sight!"

"No."

"He was not—a *toy* . . . he was a man . . . a *man*—you did not defeat the warrior! Therefore you did not defeat the man! You did not defeat my *jehan*—"

"Oh, but I think I did." Strahan stared at Donal. The faintest underscore of comprehension edged his tone. "And, in doing it—I think I defeated *you*—"

"He was a *man* . . . not a beast, not a bird, not a *thing*—" Donal sucked in a breath. "He was Duncan of the Cheysuli, from the line of the Old Mujhars . . . in the days when the Lion of Homana still belonged to *us*—"

Strahan looked down upon him. "Us," he echoed. "Aye. My father has taught me, too. How the Lion belonged to us all."

"*No!*" Donal shut his teeth into his lip. *No more—give this boy no more words to twist around*— "The Lion was ever ours. *Cheysuli*—never Ihlini. Tynstar spun a tale—"

"Tynstar spun *nothing*," Strahan retorted. "My father told the truth."

"The old gods take you," Donal said weakly. "There are nothing but lies in your head."

"And nothing but truth on my tongue." Strahan stood next to the bunk. "Even *if* my father lied, do you think he would ever claim kinship to you? Would he admit to a taint so willingly if there were no need for it?"

"*Taint.*" Donal nearly spat. "Cheysuli blood would be his saving grace."

Strahan's lips peeled back from his teeth in a smile full of spite. "Then consider us nearly *saved*, my lord. Consider us full of grace."

"Ku'reshtin," Donal swore weakly, but the boy had left the cabin.

He did not know where Lorn was. He had wakened on board a ship in heavy iron, half senseless from the blast of power Strahan had leveled against him. He knew Lorn still lived for the link was intact. His Old Blood gave him the ability to converse with his *lir* regardless of the presence of Ihlini, but he could not break through the wolf's pain. He was, more or less, alone.

Yet again he entered the link in search of Taj, knowing it likely the falcon was still too distant to hear his pattern; knowing also it was worth trying. With Taj free, he had a chance. The falcon could rouse the others and warn them of Strahan's purpose.

But there was no answer from Taj. All Donal could do was detach himself from the link and hope Lorn would recover in time.

He hung in his chains and sweated into the thin blanket on his bunk.

Donal was brought on deck under close guard. He squinted against the sunlight and nearly fell. Confinement in irons had stiffened his muscles and slowed his reflexes. He caught himself against the taffrail and wrenched himself upright, then realized where Strahan had brought him.

By the gods—does he think he can hold the Crystal Isle? This is a Cheysuli *place!*

The mist still clouded the island, closing down over the ship. It settled into his furred leathers. He looked past the dock to the beaches and saw the fine white sand; the forests that lay beyond.

Strahan stood nearby. He was wrapped in a crimson, fur-lined cloak as fine as any Donal had known in Homana-Mujhar. "When last we were here you brought me as a servant, thinking to elevate a homeless orphan from the degradation of the streets." He laughed. "All my talk of demons—all my talk of fear! Enough to lull you to my purpose." He gestured.

"I have made the island mine. I have Atvians and Ihlini to serve me. Fitting, is it not, after you so eloquently told me how the Firstborn came from here?" His odd eyes were fixed on Donal's face. "How does it feel, warrior, to know I have made this an Ihlini place?"

Donal, clinging grimly to the rail with manacled hands, did not choose to answer. What he saw and what he knew conflicted in his mind, for before him stood a slender, delicate boy who had yet to reach proper manhood, and yet claimed all the burgeoning power of the Ihlini.

Tynstar spent more than three centuries learning his arts. Strahan is a boy—those centuries stretch ahead. What will he be in a hundred, two hundred years from now?

The Atvian guards took him from the deck and led him off the ship. Donal stood silently on the dock, watching how Strahan ordered the unloading. He tried to get some glimmer, some indication from the gods that they watched what Strahan did, but there was nothing. The wind was empty of omniscience.

Strahan turned to him and laughed. "Where are your old gods *now*, shapechanger? How could this have happened?" Silver glinted in his ears. No more was he the urchin but a well-dressed young man instead, clothed in fine woolens and glittering ornamentation.

It was useless to remonstrate, to offer Strahan worthless threats and promises. If Lorn recovered, there was a chance Donal could escape. If Taj at last heard his seeking pattern, the falcon could carry warning to Finn and the others as well. But there was no certainty of either.

"Your wolf, Donal."

He swung around, taking an involuntary step forward. He saw a crate, a wooden crate, rolled end over end down the plank, from the ship to the dock below. He heard a muted yelp.

Pain blazed through his mind. *What has Strahan done? Lorn—what has he done to you?*

Guards held him back. He was helpless to aid the wolf. All he could do was mouth incoherent appeals, but he voiced none of them to Strahan.

The boy gestured. "Release him. I want him to understand what it is to confront a dying *lir*."

Donal jerked free of the loosening hands and stumbled

across to the chest. He fell to his knees, seeking to work stiff fingers through the single narrow opening admitting air to the wolf. He touched a crusted nose.

Lorn! You must not fail!

The wolf's pattern was very weak. *No water—no food—little air—*

You cannot die . . . Lorn, I beg you—

You have another, Lorn answered weakly. *You will not be lirless. You will not face the death-ritual.*

Donal tried to thrust his fingers more deeply but the wood compressed his flesh. *Lorn I will not let you die—*

It is better so. I grow weaker. Were I an unblessed wolf of the pack, the others would slay me to protect themselves. The crusted nose pressed briefly against his bruised fingers. *Lir—there is also another reason.*

There is no *reason worthy of giving in!* Donal said angrily. *Have you gone mad? I need you!*

As I weaken, so do you, Lorn told him. *Do not deny it—I can feel it in the link. Do you lose strength because of me, the Ihlini will have his victory.*

Donal could not deny it. In the days since Strahan had taken them both he had known a steady lessening of his strength; a gnawing weakness in his spirit. While Lorn was so ill from his injuries and captivity, Donal was affected as well.

Lir—I will not *allow you to die.*

"Come," Strahan said. "It is time you saw your quarters."

Hands on his arms dragged Donal from the chest. Donal lashed out in fury with manacled hands and booted feet, seeking to slay what he could reach, but the guards were well-prepared. He struck out again; then froze as he heard a low wail of pain from Lorn.

Lir—?

He turned. He saw the sword in Strahan's hands. The tip of the blade protruded into the crate through the narrow opening. "Do as I say," Strahan ordered. "Accompany my servants."

"And if he dies?" Donal challenged. "How will you make me obey you then?"

"If he dies, so does your will." Strahan smiled. "You will live a while longer because there is still the falcon, but when I am done with you the madness will be a *blessing.*"

One of the Atvians thrust an arm into the air. "My lord— *look!*"

A fleet falcon swept through the air toward the ship. It circled neatly over them all and dipped toward the dock, screaming its agitation.

Taj! Donal cried within the link. *Go! Seek Finn and the Cheysuli. Tell them it is Tynstar's brat who holds me—the boy we thought was Sef—*

"By the Seker, it is the falcon!" Strahan shouted. "I will slay *both* of them."

"Taj," Donal shouted. "Go!"

Strahan took two steps to Donal and set the tip of the sword against his spine. "I know you. I know your heritage. Alix's son, are you not?—and she with all the Old Blood. Seek you the shapechange? Do not. Or I will slay you here."

"Slay me, and you lose your tame Mujhar." Donal bared his teeth, feigning a smile.

"I plan to replace you one day," Strahan pointed out. "It can be sooner rather than later." He raised one hand. In the other, the sword wavered, tilted downward, too heavy for him to hold up. The tip bit into the wood of the dock.

Fingers stiffened, snapped apart. From the tips came a blinding stream of brilliant light. Deepest purple, tinged with sparks. An echo of the power Donal had seen in Tynstar.

He aims for Taj— Donal turned on the Ihlini, striking out with shackles and chains. He struck through the flame streaming from Strahan's fingers and felt it spark and burn against his skin, raising crimson weals. Then the fire abruptly died, for the boy lay gasping and blue-faced beneath Donal's weight and throttling fingers.

Hands were on him, jerking him from the boy. Donal teetered at the dock's edge as they thrust him roughly away. He saw that Taj still flew unmolested toward the mainland and released a sigh of relief.

Strahan got unsteadily to his feet. The sword lay on the dock, but he ignored it. "Punishment," he promised hoarsely. "You will be sorry for that."

He thrust both arms into the air as if he invoked a deity. Donal, recalling how Tynstar had tried to summon Asar-Suti, thought Strahan intended the same. He saw the air darken around the pale hands; smoke rolled out of the mist. It wreathed the hands in flame.

Strahan laughed. "Would you care to meet my *lir?*"

Donal's flesh rose up on his bones. "The Ihlini *have* no *lir*—"

"No? Well, perhaps she is not a *lir* precisely—but she is made of the same blood and bone." Crimson sparks shot out of the smoke as it spun around his hands. "She comes from the netherworld, from the Gate of Asar-Suti. And such a lovely, lovely demon—" the flame and smoke exploded "—shall I fly her for you, Donal?"

Black smoke and flame took substance. Donal saw talons, wings, a wickedly curving beak. And a pair of golden eyes that watched him with a malicious intensity.

"Sakti—" Strahan hissed, "—*take* the falcon for me!"

Donal spun. *"Fly!"* he shouted at Taj.

The falcon dipped and dove, streaking from the hawk, but Sakti was relentless. She gained, caught up, struck out with raking talons.

"Taj . . . *fly!*"

Taj flew, but the demon-hawk flew faster. Sakti rose, stooped, struck down with curving talons. One pierced the falcon's breast.

"Taj!" Donal screamed.

The falcon fell out of the sky.

Taj—
—Taj—
Taj?

He drifted. He dreamed. He cried. He knew himself half mad.

Lir—
—lir—
Lir?

He slept. He wakened. He cried.

He could not help himself.

—"Wanderer," Evan said, *"you will embark upon a journey."*

The dice and rune-sticks fell, rattling on the wood—

—"Jester and Charlatan: those who are not what they seem—

—Youth—

—Imprisonment—

—Executioner—

—*Why not have the Ellasian dice you your destiny?*
—*Who is to say he will be wrong?*—
—*wrong*—
Wrong.

He slept.
Dreamed.
Drifted.

—*Your* shar tahl *has failed your clan. You know nothing of the histories*—
—*They sired also a second race*—
—*They sired the Ihlini*—
—*who bred with the Cheysuli*—
"No!"
—*who bred with the Cheysuli*—

He wakened shouting *No.* But there was no one there to hear.

For a long time he forgot who he was or why Strahan held him. And then he remembered.
He remembered *why.*

He was alone. He was locked within a room that held a comfortable bed, a bench, a table, and high narrow casements that let in the mist and muted sun. The iron remained on his wrists, but he had the freedom of the chamber.
Freedom.
It almost made him laugh.

Lorn he could not reach. There was a barrier in the link. But not the utter emptiness that would signify Lorn's death. The wolf lived, but Donal could not touch him.

He tried to follow the days by scratching runes into the bedpost with the buckle of his belt, but he knew he had lost track. The light was somehow wrong. The fog occluded the sun. He could not judge the season or the time.
But it was cold. One brazier was not enough.

* * *

He ate.

He drank.

He was left entirely alone.

The door crashed open. Donal spun around.

Strahan stood within the chamber—

—and so did Finn and Evan.

The boy laughed. "It pleases me to reunite you, now that I have you all."

Donal's breath rattled in his throat as he stared at Finn. "He—took—*you?*"

"Evan and I came to rescue you." The tone was wry, reproving.

The Ellasian grinned. "You might at least give us your gratitude."

"Why?" Dorsal demanded. "How could you come *alone*—?"

"It seemed the best idea." Finn and Evan seemed well enough. Unharmed, and certainly less than horrified by the presence of Tynstar's son.

Donal glared at Evan. "What will High King Rhodri say when he learns his youngest son has fallen prisoner to Strahan?"

"Probably that I am a fool, and no loss," Evan said lightly. "Perhaps I am, and it is not . . . but I thought to aid a friend."

Donal thrust out his hands, displaying the heavy shackles. *"How?"* he demanded. "By wearing Ihlini iron?"

The scar twisted on Finn's cheek as he laughed. "I see a lengthy confinement has not improved your temper."

Donal stared at him. He felt his mouth dry up. "How long?" he asked. "How long have I been here?"

No one answered at once. And then Strahan laughed. "Have you lost count? Did you not see the season change? It worked—it *worked*—I made you forget *everything*, even the time of year!"

Donal recalled how he had made marks in the bedpost to keep track of time. One day, he had stopped. And then the time was lost, and *he* was lost, and now he could not recall how long he had been a prisoner of Strahan.

Gods . . . is this how the madness begins?

"It *worked!*" Strahan exulted. "Do you not recall all the times you begged me for your name? How you begged me for a polished plate so you could see yourself? You believed yourself a hawk—a *hawk*, not a falcon. Mimicking your father?"

"Six months," Donal whispered in horror.

"Winter has come and gone," Finn said gently. "Donal— let it go."

He looked at his hands. Hands only. The fingers were fingers, not talons. But he recalled it, a little; he recalled how he had feared the shapechange as he slept. As Strahan teased him with his power. *By the gods . . . I think we have all gone mad—*

He stared at Finn and Evan. "You are fools." His tone was inflectionless. "Fools, both of you . . . you have given Homana over to Tynstar's son."

"I think not," Finn answered. "You see, the boy is just a boy—still learning about his power. He may be Tynstar's son, but can he lead his race? He is young. *Young*—and youth has a way of tripping over hardships before the highest goal is won." He turned to Strahan. "Did you think we *fell* into your hands when we made certain you would take us?"

Color shot into Strahan's face. "What do you say to me?" he demanded. *"What do you say to me?"*

"That it is time for us to go."

"You *cannot!* I hold you! You are my prisoners!"

Finn's hand was in his belt-pouch. "It is time for us to go."

The boy stretched out his hand. At his fingertips danced a rune of brilliant purple. "I am Tynstar's son. *I am the Ihlini!*"

"And you have lost one of your ward-stones." Finn held it up so all could see it: a small round rock, dull gray, with a single streak of black. "Boy," Finn said, "do you know enough to be frightened?"

Clearly, Strahan did. He backed away, clutching at the crimson robe he wore over dark gray winter leathers. His thin face turned white, then splotchy red; the rune snuffed out in his hand.

Finn smiled. "I do not suppose you have the other four somewhere upon your person—?"

Strahan turned and ran.

"Apparently he does not." Finn returned the stone to his belt-pouch. "I think it is time to go, before he fetches the rest of the stones."

Donal stared at his uncle. "Why? What would happen if he did?"

"Together, the ward-stones augment his power. Apart, they can be used against the sorcerer who made them." Finn gestured toward the door. "Do you tarry, I will think you wish to *stay*."

"I need Lorn."

"We will find him." Finn preceded him through the door. They ran down a corridor. "What of the other Ihlini?" Evan asked.

"They die like other men." Finn led them down a staircase and through an airy chamber. "You have a knife, Ellasian — surely you can use it."

They went down. Down and down, into the bowels of the palace.

"Su'fali!" Donal cried. "I can touch him . . . *there*—Lorn is here!" He gestured at a narrow wooden door half hidden by an arras.

Finn tore it aside and jerked open the unlocked door. "Storr," he said in satisfaction. The wolf held a guard at bay.

"Lorn—?" Donal asked.

"Through there, I would hazard." Finn indicated a second door. "And now, Ihlini—safe journey to your god—"

Donal's chains clashed as he shouldered open the door. He stumbled inside, ducking his head, and nearly fell over his *lir*.

"Lorn!" He dropped to his knees beside the wolf.

Lorn lay on his side in soiled straw. The visible eye was rolled back in his head. The tongue, protruding from between his jaws, was dry and crusted. But he breathed. Barely, but he breathed.

Donal touched the lusterless, matted fur. Lir—*I will not allow you to die—I order you to live—*

He felt the faintest flicker of amusement from the tattered edges of the link. *But it is the* lir *who have the ordering of the Cheysuli.*

Fingers spasmed, then dug more deeply into the pelt. He felt the ladder of Lorn's protruding ribs. *Will you live?*

You still have need of me.

Donal wavered in relief, then bent and set his face against Lorn's shoulder. *I could not bear it if you died.* Then he smiled up at his uncle. "I think he will be all right."

Finn knelt and gathered the wolf into his arms. "I will take him. You are not much stronger than he." He rose and jerked his head at Evan. "See he comes, Ellasian. We have gone to too much trouble to lose him so easily now."

Evan grinned and grasped Donal's arm. "Come, my lord— we must steal ourselves a boat."

Four

They won free of the palace proper without coming to harm—Evan slew three Atvian guards—but the high white walls of the bailey proved a greater foe than man. Locked and attended gates denied them an exit as easy as their entrance.

They ducked down into the darkness of full night, hiding themselves in shadows and vegetation. Finn tended Lorn while Evan watched for guards. Donal knelt against the wall and pushed a trembling forearm through sweat-dampened hair, aware the six months of captivity had leached him of grace and quickness. He rested his head against one doubled knee, trying to catch his breath, and felt the hard cold iron of Strahan's shackles on his arms.

Gods—is this what it was for Carillon when he wore Atvian iron? Inwardly, he shuddered. *It is a perfect humiliation.*

"Donal—?" It was Evan, hunching down beside him. One hand touched Donal's leather-clad shoulder.

Donal lifted his head. "I am well enough, Evan . . . see to yourself."

Evan, laughing softly, withdrew the hand. "Without me, my proud Mujhar, you might still be Strahan's prisoner. Do I get no thanks from you?"

Donal smiled into the darkness. "Would a prince accept *payment* for the aid he rendered a fellow prince?"

"Mujhar," Evan corrected. "Aye, he might . . . could he win it in a fortune-game." Slanting shadow across the Ellasian's face hid his eyes and nose, but not his mobile mouth. He grinned. "But there may be a better reward than that. There was a young woman I admired at your wedding celebration. Could you give her good word of me, it might be payment enough."

"Which one?" Donal asked dryly. "I cannot recall them all."

"You said her name was Meghan."

Chains clashed as Donal glanced at Evan sharply. "And do you forget?—I also told you who sired her." He indicated Finn crouching not far from them with Lorn still cradled in his arms. "Say to *him* you wish to know his daughter better."

"Were you to give *him* good word of me—"

"I think he knows you better than most." But the levity quickly faded. Donal moved over to kneel beside his wolf. *Lorn?*

I have not died yet, lir.

Donal smiled. Then he glanced up at Finn's face. "He requires proper healing."

"And will have it . . . but not just here."

Donal peered through the bushes at the wall. Absently he chewed at a broken thumbnail. "We can hardly scale the walls with an injured wolf—"

"Scale them? Why not fly over them?"

Donal looked back at him sharply. "Taj is—lost. I have no recourse to falcon-shape."

"Do you not?" Finn's mouth hooked down as he shook his head. "Can you not even trust your own senses, Donal? Or your own *sense*. Were Taj truly lost, how could Evan and I have found you?"

"But—I thought you somehow knew Strahan had come here—"

"How?" Finn's voice was underscored with contempt. "Am I omniscient? Did Evan throw the rune-sticks? And how were we to know the boy was Tynstar's get?" Grimly he shook his head. "Imprisonment has not improved your sense anymore than your temper."

Donal hunched forward, trying to keep the chains from clinking. "I *saw* it, su'fali! Strahan summoned a demon-bird from Asar-Suti, and she slew Taj. I saw him fall!"

"The hawk injured him, aye, and he fell. But he was not slain." Finn indicated the wall with his head. "Do you think that is Strahan's hawk? Or is it more likely a falcon?"

Donal's head snapped around. Now that Finn pointed him out, the bird was visible. But only as a shape in the shadows. There was no light to give the bird name or color.

Hope and longing leaped up to fill Donal's chest. *"Taj?"*

I am here, the falcon said. *Why do you tarry*, lir? *Do you come, or do you stay?*

"Leijhana tu'sai," he muttered aloud in a prayer of thanksgiving to the gods. Then, within the link again: *Finn says I must fly over the walls.*

You have done such things before.

Donal laughed to himself wryly. *I am somewhat weary, lir—this has not been an easy imprisonment.*

Then why not leave it behind?

Donal shook his head in resignation. *How many guardsmen, Taj? Ihlini or Atvians?* If they were Ihlini, he had no recourse to *lir*-shape. And Taj could not help him attack them.

Six Atvians.

"Six," Donal said glumly. "And I am only one—"

"Are you?" Finn asked. "I thought you were Cheysuli."

Donal scowled at him; then turned to Evan. "There is something you must do for me. When a warrior assumes *lir*-shape, that which he touches also changes. I would prefer *not* to take the shackles with me; I need you to hold them, and as I change from man to falcon you must pull them free of my wings. Can you do that?"

Evan shrugged. "It does not sound particularly difficult."

Donal smiled a little. "And if the change encompassed *you?*"

The Ellasian's blue eyes widened a trifle. *"Could* it?"

"Who can say?" Donal, grinning inwardly, held out his shackled arms. "Catch hold, Evan, and we shall find out."

The Ellasian, after only a momentary hesitation, reached out and closed his hands around the heavy chains at wrists and ankles. Donal, doubled up in a sitting position, drew in a deep breath and shut his eyes. The shapechange required extreme concentration, and of late the concept had become an alien one.

He felt the peace come rushing in to fill him up with a marvelous sense of well-being. All the pain and anguish of the past six months melted away into nothingness. He was at peace within himself, and from the center of that calm he reached out to tap the powers that gave him the gift of the shapechange.

Donal froze. Even as he tapped the power and felt it run up from the earth to encompass flesh and bones, he thought of the *thing* his father had been. And he could not face himself.

"Donal!" Finn's voice sounding oddly frightened. "Donal—*go one way or the other*—"

So, he *was* a halfway thing. Even Finn saw the difference. Instinctively he reached out to his falcon. *Taj?*

Trust me. Trust yourself. What Strahan did was Ihlini-wrought, and not of good, clean earth magic. Do you think the gods would allow the magic to fail when it is you who asks it?

No. And he reached out again, let the power enfold him utterly, and took flight as the shackles and chains crashed against the ground.

Two falcons drove out of the darkness at the guardsmen, striking with deadly talons and hooked, sharp beaks. They were not large birds, not as dangerous as eagle or hawk in full attack, but in darkness—and unexpected—even a small creature can prove powerfully effective.

Men screamed and fell to their knees, arms flailing at the birds. When three of them groveled in the dirt, clutching bleeding faces, three others drew swords and slashed viciously at the attacking falcons. One sought safety in a tree. The other flew to the ground and became a man.

A blade dipped as the hand that held it clenched in spasmodic fear; the tip bit into dirt. Donal stepped close and broke the man's neck with a single blow, then caught up the sword and turned to face the other two.

He smiled. Leijhana tu'sai, *Carillon . . . the skill will not go unused after all*—

He spun, whirling, as one man sought his unprotected back. He swung, felt blade bite through leathers and wool, then more deeply, splintering ribs and sundering flesh. But his hands were ungloved in the nighttime chill, and the gush of warm blood slicked the grip of the blade. It slipped in his hands, and as the man crumpled to the ground he took the sword with him.

The last guard came at him as he turned, lacking knife, sword, or bow. Donal's arms rose slowly as he lifted them away from his body, hands spreading in the air. He saw the faintest flicker of the sword in the torchlight near the wall; he leaped back, nearly tripped over the dead man's body, then lunged backward yet again.

Lir— he began.

I am coming, Taj replied. *You require my help after all.*

The falcon swept down out of the tree and dug his talons into the guardsman's hands upon the hilt. He bit out a startled oath and dropped the sword. Taj veered away, but as he did the guardsman drew his long-knife.

Donal watched the knife blade. But the guardsman was no fool; he swung with his other arm and smashed it into Donal's face. Ringmail bit in and scored his cheek; Donal swore viciously and jerked his head away. The knife sought his abdomen even as he held the ringmailed wrist.

The Atvian slammed him against the gate. The left arm slid up to crush Donal's vulnerable throat.

Thank the gods he is not Ihlini— Donal took *lir*-shape instantly and left the guardsman staggering against the gate. He darted up, then flew down again and took back his human form.

The Atvian plunged forward with his knife. Donal slid easily aside. He caught the man's slashing arm as it drove past him and snapped it against his upraised thigh.

He caught the knife as it fell from spasming fingers. He allowed the man to fall—

—he spun—

—threw—

—the knife was buried in the back of the Atvian's unprotected neck.

Three more— Donal turned, prepared, but the Atvians provided no threat to him. All three still groveled in the dirt, hands thrust up before their bleeding faces. One man had lost both eyes; the other two bled badly from mouth and nose.

All cried piteously for help from their gods and Strahan. And the man who faced them.

Donal turned away. Grimly he unbarred the gate and thrust open one of the leaves, whistling for Finn and Evan. They came, accompanied by Storr, and Lorn clasped in Finn's strong arms.

"Six," Finn remarked as he passed by Donal into the darkness. "A warrior after all."

"I slew only three," Donal retorted.

"Ah," said Evan, nodding as he slipped by. "That does somewhat diminish your accomplishment."

Donal departed the gate and followed them to the dock. "Which boat?" he asked.

"The closest!" Evan answered.

They ran—

—and Strahan's black hawk exploded out of darkness.

Donal was hurled to his knees as the tremendous weight drove into back and shoulders. Talons closed. Leather tore open; so did flesh and muscle.

He arched, straining upward in an effort to catch the hawk in his hands. Pain vibrated through his body until he thought he would scream with it. But his fingers could not touch the bird.

Evan thrust with his knife. But Sakti drove upward, avoiding the blade with a snap of her powerful wings. She shrieked, wheeled, stooped. Talons slashed past Evan's desperate defense and drove again into Donal's back. She hurled him onto his face.

Donal was half-blind with pain. He tasted blood in his mouth from having bitten his tongue. His face pressed into sand and seashell; he dug handfuls of fine-grained sand. *"Su'fali!"* he cried. Sand and shell crept into his mouth as Satki's weight ground his face into the beach. "By the gods, *su'fali—gainsay this demon-bird—"*

"No warbow!" Finn raged. *"Had I my bow—!"*

"Do something!" Evan shouted, diving at the hawk. "Lodhi!—how can we stop this thing—?"

Finn set Lorn down upon the beach. Hastily he sought stones. Those few he found he caught up in his hands, and searched for the hawk. She spiraled over their heads, drifting in apparent idleness; her cries were malevolence given tongue.

One by one, Finn hurled the stones at the hawk. His aim was good, but Sakti was too swift. Strahan's borrowed demon began to play with them all.

Donal pressed himself upward, biting his lip to keep back his cry of pain. His back and shoulders were afire, but he thrust himself to his knees. "She—seeks to delay us—for Strahan—" he said breathlessly. "We must ignore her—go on—get away from here—"

"How?" Evan demanded. "That *thing* is more than hawk!"

"Demon—" Donal gasped. "Strahan summoned her from the god of the netherworld—"

Sakti wheeled. Stooped. But her target was Evan now.

His breath exploded from his chest as the hawk drove into his ribs, talons closed, knocking him to the ground. But this time Finn was prepared. He waited as she rose, preparing to stoop again, and as her wings snapped closed he drew his knife and hurled it into the air.

The blade glinted in the moonlight. It sliced upward toward the hawk. Sakti, screeching, turned aside. But one foot shot out and talons grasped, closing on the hilt. Wings snapped shut. She stooped. Now she drove at Finn.

He dropped to the ground, rolling as the hawk came at him. One lone talon slashed across his shoulder, tearing fur-lined leather. But she released the knife, and as she hurled herself upward to stoop again, Finn thrust himself to his feet and caught the hilt as it fell.

Sakti soared, wings extended against the stars. Finn waited. And when she snapped her wings shut he hurled the knife again.

Taj darted out of the darkness directly at the hawk. Sakti's size dwarfed the falcon, but Taj did not give in. He flew straight at her and turned her from her course into the path of the oncoming knife.

The blade struck home in Sakti's chest. She screamed; screaming, she fell. But her talons were still extended.

Donal, head tipped back to stare upward into the sky, cried out as the talons sank into the side of his neck. Sakti's weight threw him over onto his back; the talons dug deeper still.

He clawed at his neck, seeking escape. Sakti quivered and was still, but even death did not loosen the clutching talons. It was Evan who at last pried them free and clamped a hand over the wound in Donal's neck.

"*Lodhi!*—how he bleeds!"

"—to death, do we not stanch it." Finn pressed Evan's hand more tightly against the wound. "You must keep it shut—I will take Lorn . . . Ellasian, get him *up* from there! We must take him into the forest."

Donal was half-senseless. He felt Evan urging him to his feet, but his limbs would not obey him. He thought it would be easier and far less painful did he simply remain lying on the beach with the cool sand under his twitching body.

"Up—get you *up*—" Evan panted. "*Lodhi*, Donal—do you wish to bleed to death?"

Evan's hand was clamped to Donal's neck. The pressure hurt. Donal's own hand rose up to peel the Ellasian's fingers away, but Evan withstood his feeble attempt.

"Finn—can you not compel him? Can you not use a little of your magic?"

"Not here; not I. Too many Ihlini present. *Donal* might have the ability—" his voice broke off a moment "—*carry* him, if you have to!"

Evan dragged him from the ground. Donal stumbled, staggered, nearly fell again. His neck was bound up in pain. "Gods—" he said hoarsely, "—*gods*—"

"Bring him," Finn said harshly; and carried Lorn from the beach into the forest.

—pain—

He stumbled. Evan held him up. He staggered. Evan kept him from falling. He nearly vomited. Evan merely held on more tightly and gave him what words he could of encouragement. But most of them were in Ellasian.

—pain—

His left shoulder was wet with warm blood. It soaked through his leathers and dampened the fur lining, until he could feel it running down his arm in rivulets. It dripped from his fingers to the forest floor, splattering onto his boots.

—so much pain . . . pain and blood—

He staggered. But Evan held him up and mumbled Ellasian encouragement.

"Here!" The call came from Finn, hidden by trees and shadow. "Hurry, Ellasian—"

Evan hurried. Donal could not. But at last they broke from the trees into a clearing, and saw the tumbled ruin.

Finn came out of the crooked doorway, lacking Lorn, and helped Evan carry Donal. "Bring him inside. It is cold, damp—offering little enough shelter—but perhaps Strahan will forget this place exists."

"What *is* it?" Evan asked.

Donal, half-dragged, peered through slitted eyes. He saw

huddled green-gray stones taller than Carillon, set in a haphazard circle. Slotted darkness lay between them; they had lost their uniformity, the perfection of their edges. They gaped apart, like a man missing most of his teeth.

"This place was once used as a place of worship by the Firstborn," Finn said grimly, half-carrying his nephew. "There are a few remaining in corners of Homana. . . . I do not doubt this is the first, the oldest. Perhaps it will be our protection against the boy. Here—let us settle him here, against the wall."

Donal moaned as they put him down on the cold, damp ground. The stone was hard and cruel against his torn back.

"Lay a fire," Finn told Evan.

"With what, my *will?*" Evan demanded. "I have no flint."

Finn dug into his belt-pouch. "Here. Use your knife and your wits. This calls for cautery."

Evan caught the flint as Finn tossed it. "Can you not use your healing powers?"

"I am one man. I have not the strength to seal so deep a wound. And you are not your *rujholli* with his magic harp."

Evan turned and went out. He brought back chips of wood and broken branches and piled them carefully. Sparks flew from the flint as he used his knife upon it, but none caught in the kindling.

"Princeling." The twisted title, from Finn, was an insult. "Too gently raised in Rhodri's hall."

Evan said nothing, but Donal could see the grim line of his mouth. Finn, kneeling next to his nephew with one hand shutting off the blood, watched impatiently as Evan worked the flint.

"*Su'fali—*" Donal's voice was little more than a broken whisper. "Is this how you treated Carillon?"

Finn stared down at him. His yellow eyes were black in the dimness of the chapel. Starlight shone in through the broken beamwork, but not enough to illuminate the place. "When he was deserving of it," he said at last. Donal saw the crooked smile. "That was most of the time."

The kindling caught at last and began to smolder. Carefully Evan coaxed it into a flame, fed it more wood, then set the knife blade in the fire.

"Patience, Donal," Finn said softly. "*Shansu, shansu*—I will not let the boy prevail."

Blood still coursed from beneath Finn's pressing hand.

Donal felt weakness and lethargy seep into his flesh and spirit. Could he sleep, the pain would go away—

"Donal!" Finn said sharply. "Do you forget your *lir*? He needs your aid. When the wound is closed, we will heal him. But I need you for that—do not give in now!"

Donal reached instinctively for Lorn, but his own pain and Lorn's weakness threw up a barrier in the link. He could sense the wolf's presence—or was it Storr's?—but nothing more. Taj as well was denied to him.

Evan sighed and rubbed an arm across his eyes. The knife blade glowed crimson at the tip; heat slowly spread up the steel. When it had reached the hilt, Evan took off his fur-lined velvet doublet and folded it into a wrap to protect his hand as he held the knife. He took it out of the fire and carried it back to Finn.

Donal, transfixed by the glowing blade that danced against the darkness, opened his mouth to tell them no.

Finn nodded. "I will take my hand away. You must sear it quickly; I may not be able to hold him."

"Aye," Evan said roughly. "I am sorry, Donal—"

Finn released the wound. Blood welled up afresh, spilling down Donal's chest. But Finn caught his shoulders and pressed his back against the wall. "*Now*—"

Blood hissed as the blade came down. Fluids popped; flesh was seared together. Donal's body spasmed and arched like a man in the clutches of death. Finn held him, spoke to him, but Donal heard nothing. He was eaten alive with pain.

"Enough," Finn said. He shut his fingers in the leather of Donal's winter shirt. "Rouse yourself! Lorn has need of you."

Donal's hand clawed at the cauterized wound, then spasmed away as the pain renewed itself. "Gods—have you *slain* me?"

"Rouse yourself," Finn repeated. "Do you deny your *lir*?"

Sense crept back. With Finn's aid, Donal got up onto his knees. At Lorn's side he shut his eyes and waited for weakness to pass, then set his hands against the dry, staring coat. "Help me, *su'fali*. . . . I have not the strength to do it alone."

"Nor I." Finn's tone was uncommonly gentle. "Let yourself go, Donal. Give yourself over to the earth."

Donal's head bowed down. The puckered seam in his neck blazed up as if newly cauterized. Donal shut his eyes.

Give myself over . . . give myself over to the earth. But—what am I to do if the earth does not wish to give me up when the healing has been completed?

But he could not wait for an answer he knew would not come. Instead, he sank his awareness into the warmth of the earth and sought Finn's presence in the darkness. He found it. They linked at once, then sought the healing magic.

A spring, bubbling up from underground. It flowed. It encapsulated their spirits, examined them, understood their need, and went onward to the wolf. It flowed, bathing him in its strength, until the wounds were healed and the bright burning of his spirit was renewed. And then it flowed away.

"Done," Donal mumbled. "See how he sleeps?"

"Done," Finn agreed. "*Shansu*, Donal . . . it is your turn now."

Donal opened his mouth to answer. Nothing issued from his mouth, not even a final sigh. He felt himself slump sideways and struggled to halt his fall, knowing the landing would hurt his wounds, but his body did not obey.

He felt Finn catch him, and then he sank down into a sleep as deep as any he had known.

Five

Donal roused to pain. It burned in neck and shoulders, down his back. He felt as if someone had flayed him alive and left the bones to molder in the ruins.

He lay perfectly still, still wrapped around the warmth of Lorn's furred body. He felt the regular lifting of Lorn's side; heard the subtle thumping of his heart. He lay relieved, with weary exultation: he was free of Strahan, and the wolf would recover fully.

Slowly, he pushed himself into a sitting position. He grunted against his will; torn flesh and muscles protested. An exploratory hand told him someone had bandaged the talon wounds in his back and shoulders. Finn, most likely—and with Evan's velvet doublet. He felt terribly weak, battered.

He scowled, trying to clear his vision. He saw gray-green stones surrounding them in a tumbled circle. Some stones stood upright, sentinels in the dawn; others tilted against neighbors; a few lay on the ground. Broken beamwork littered the center of the chapel; a ruined altar stood farthest from the fire Evan had built.

Finn squatted by the makeshift cairn. "Well?"

Donal turned his head carefully. The flesh pulled; he touched a puckered seam half a man's hand in length in the hollow where neck and shoulder met. "You have butchered me, *su'fali*."

"We did not touch your face," Finn retorted. "When the marks of battle have faded, no doubt Sorcha will find you just as pretty as before."

Donal scowled.

Finn stood, stretching elaborately. Mist drifted in the chapel and dew beaded on the stones. "I will fetch us something to eat. I go no farther until my belly is full again."

"Make it plump game," Donal advised. "If Evan is as hungry as *I* am, we shall need a sizable breakfast."

Finn loosened the Homanan knife in its sheath. Donal, looking at the heavy hilt with its rampant royal lion, thought again how bitter it must be for Finn to know Carillon was dead.

For so many years his task was to keep him alive . . . yet in the end, he aided his death.

Finn glanced over at Evan, still curled up on a pile of leaves. "The Ellasian sleeps like the dead," he said scathingly, and then he went out of the chapel with Storr trotting at his side.

"I am neither asleep nor dead." Evan rolled over and sat up. "I was merely trying to get warm."

"Then move to the fire." Donal did so himself, albeit slowly, and put more wood on the flames.

Evan got up, twisted to unkink his neck and spine, then moved to the fire and squatted down. "What is Finn about?"

"Hunting breakfast." Donal saw how Evan's beard had come in, forming dark stubble along his jaw. He scratched at it, grimacing, and Donal blessed the gods for seeing to it the Cheysuli could not grow beards. *Too much trouble to take it off each morning.* He was amused by the transformation in his Ellasian friend. Evan's normally immaculate appearance had undergone a decided change. He was dirty, grimy; his clothing was soiled and torn.

Evan put his hands out over the flames. His fingers were scraped. Nails were broken. There was not much remaining of the prince who had come to Donal's wedding. "I am sorry for the pain," Evan said, looking at the bright red weal in Donal's neck. "Finn said it was the only way."

"It was." Donal did not finger the puckered seam. "But I do not see why you did not simply sever the rest of my neck."

Evan's mobile mouth hooked down wryly. "I considered it seriously—but I thought Homana might wish to see her new Mujhar. She has not; you know. . . . Strahan took you too soon. There are rumors you are dead."

"And if I am?" Donal looked at him squarely. "You are the son of a king and know of such things. In Ellas, what would happen if the High King were slain?"

Evan shrugged. "Lachlan would become High King. There would be no great stirring among the subjects—do you forget Rhodri has so many sons? And Lachlan himself has two—by now, perhaps three. There would be an unremarkable passing of the throne from one man to another."

Donal stared into the fire. "Not here. No, not here. Without me, Homana is Homanan again." He bit at a torn flap of skin on one thumb. "Perhaps that is what all of this is about."

Evan frowned and added more wood. "What do you say? This is Strahan's doing."

"Strahan's, aye—but who else's? There could even be Homanans. Not all are reconciled to Carillon's heir." He stood up for the first time, collected his senses, and glanced around. "Gods—this place—it makes a man feel humble."

He moved around the chapel slowly, looking more closely at tumbled stone and broken beamwork, fallen altar and vine-choked foundation pedestals. It was sunrise, but only the faintest tinge of orange shone through the mist. It filled up the place with bronze and gold.

Donal picked his way through the debris to the altar. It leaned haphazardly sideways, propped up by another stone. Its pedestal was shattered. But on the face of the altar were runes, velveted with lichen, corroded by dampness and time.

He bent, picking at the runes with a broken nail. Pensively, he frowned. And then, when he could piece together a portion of the inscription, he let out an involuntary blurt of sound.

Evan left the fire. "What is it?"

"It is no wonder we were not disturbed last night by Strahan or his minions. This is a holy place."

"Finn said it is a chapel."

"*Was.* Look at the inscriptions—see how they border the altar?" Another gesture indicated the other stones. "Each one is inscribed, I will wager, though time has hidden the runes. See you here? *These* runes—see how they are cut so deeply into the stone?" He tapped with the broken nail. "This place offers the guardianship of the gods to any who would seek it of Cheysuli or Firstborn blood. Sanctuary, Evan. Even the Ihlini cannot touch us here."

Taj's scream cut through the mist like a scythe.

Donal spun around and felt the scabbing of his wounds tear apart. "Evan—*come!*"

He ran. He felt the fire in his neck and back and shoulders, but he did not pay attention. He ran.

Thorns snagged at his flesh and leathers as he leaped over fallen trees and skipped across tumbled boulders with the borrowed energy of fear. He heard Evan coming behind him, cursing the briers, but Donal had no time for oaths. Only prayers.

He broke from dense undergrowth into a tiny clearing. He stopped. He stopped so quickly Evan ran into him from behind. But he said nothing to Evan's irritated question. He could not. He could not speak at all.

Finn lay on his back in the clearing. His limbs were sprawled in an obscene parody of his normal fluid grace. He stared upward into the misted sky and blood ran from his mouth.

The sword stood up from his ribs like a royal standard. The hilt was gold, lion-shaped; the pommel stone was baleful black.

Su'fali— Slowly, jerkily, Donal moved across the clearing until he stood at Finn's side. He knelt, knowing shock and pain and a tremendous, blossoming grief. *"Su'fali!"* he shouted.

Finn's left hand lay loosely clasped around the blade. Fingers were stained with his blood. Already his furred leather shirt was sodden.

As if it had been twisted in his body . . . Donal felt the wild grief break free. He swore softly in the Old Tongue, repeatedly, with all the pain and rage he felt.

Finn's mouth moved in a tiny smile. "You have, at least, learned enough of the Old Tongue for *that*."

"Su'fali . . . su'fali . . . what can I do?"

"Do not grieve, kinsman. It is a warrior's death."

"Who?" Donal heard his voice quaver. "Who has done this to you?"

"The boy. Retribution, he said, for the loss of *jehan* and *jehana*." Finn's face twisted briefly with immense pain; the scar writhed upon his cheek. "He—wanted the sword back when he was done with me. He tried to take it back. But— I am Hale's son and perhaps the sword knew me—the magic came, the sword-magic— Strahan was denied even as he put his hands upon the hilt—" Muscles in his jaw stood up. "He wanted you as well, *harani*—he wanted to slay you with the sword Hale made for you—to prove the legend false—"

"Say no more," Donal begged. "Waste none of what strength is left—"

"He said you had denied the sword time and time again, diluting the magic—but *he* was willing to claim it—" A trickle of blood overspilled Finn's lips. "You must claim it, *harani*. The sword is yours." He swallowed heavily. "It begins . . . it begins again . . . with yet another generation—"

"Say nothing," Donal ordered desperately. "Be silent, *su'fali*—I will seek the magic—"

"There is nothing you can do," Finn said clearly but as from a great distance, "Release my spirit when I am dead. You know the custom, Donal. The rite for a warrior slain in battle."

"Aye." The word rasped in Donal's swelling throat.

Finn's fingers traced the shining blade and left a smear of blood. "Strahan sought to hurt you by slaying me, but he has given you back the sword that will, in the end, defeat him. Justice from the gods."

Justice? No, I think not—not when it slays my su'fali—

"Say you will take it . . ." Finn's voice was just barely above a whisper. "Say you will take it and slay Osric of Atvia with it—to avenge Carillon's death—"

"What of *yours*—?" Donal cried.

"My death does not matter. It was ever my *tahlmorra* to die in the service of the Mujhar. And—I have served them both—" Briefly he shut his eyes as pain spasmed across his face. "Donal—"

"Aye?"

Finn struggled to tap the last of his reserves.

"You never . . . never understood Carillon . . . his reasons for doing things the way he did them. Oh, I know—you are young, and youth lacks compassion and comprehension . . . but—he did what needed doing in the best way he knew how." Again pain twisted his face. "I—did not always agree—but I cannot dispute results. He took

Homana out of the flames of war and oppression and made her whole again. He restored our race to freedom—"

"*Su'fali*—" Donal begged "—speak not of Carillon *now*—"

"Should I not? But you are so much alike, Donal—when I speak of him I speak of you." Faintly, Finn smiled. "There are differences, of course . . . but you claim the same pride and strength and determination. I pray the gods you use them as well as he did."

Donal swallowed painfully. "I swear—I will see to Osric's death."

Finn caught Donal's hand in his own. The firm grip was weak now, like a baby's tentative grasp. "I do not—do not go into death without having done a portion of my service . . . the boy—the boy lacks an ear—"

"*Su'fali*—"

The bloody hand closed more tightly on Donal's flesh. "I bequeath Homana to you, kinsman. . . . Answer your *tahlmorra*."

Donal could not speak.

Finn's eyes were nearly shut. "I would ask—one more thing—"

Donal closed his own.

"*Claim the sword*," Finn whispered. "Make it yours from this moment forth."

"*Su'fali*—"

"Do as I command." The voice was little more than a sound. "I am clan-leader of the Cheysuli. . . . You may be Mujhar, but you are still a warrior of the clan."

Donal heaved himself to his feet. He stood over the dying man. "*Su'fali* . . . I am honored."

"*Ja'hai, cheysu, Mujhar*," Finn whispered. "*Cheysuli i'halla shansu.*"

"Accepted." The Homanan word hurt his throat. "*Shansu, su'fali.* Peace."

Donal put out both hands and touched the hilt. The ruby blazed brilliant red. He shut his hands in a stiff-fingered, unsteady grasp.

And pulled.

"*Ja'hai-na,*" Finn whispered as blood ran out of his body. "Oh, Alix . . . you would be so proud of your son—"

Donal stood over the dead warrior with Hale's sword grasped tightly in one hand. He felt the silent keening begin to well up in his soul. He dared not let it become audible; such things were not done. Such things dishonored the code of his clan. But as his face twisted with the pain he could not help but wish he were a small child again, unknowing, and free to cry out his fear and anguish.

When he could, he looked from the warrior's face and stared blindly at Evan. Tears ran down his face. "I am King," he said hoarsely. "Mujhar of Homana and Solinde. And I would trade it all *could I have him back again!*"

Evan's face was still and white as he slowly pointed.

Donal turned. He dropped the sword instantly when he saw Storr. Storr, who stood silently by a huge spreading oak.

Donal fell to his knees and gathered Finn's beloved *lir* into his arms. *Wolf, O wolf . . . he is gone . . . everyone is taken from me—*

You are not left alone, Storr said gently but with a frightening hollowness. *You have your lir—the Ellasian—Rowan—the women who care for you so.*

Donal pressed his face against the silver pelt. *But I lose them, one by one . . . I lose them all . . . my jehan and jehana—Carillon—Finn—now you—*

And one day you will lose more.

Donal drew back. Storr was wiser than anyone he knew. *You are in pain,* he said in alarm as he saw how heavily the wolf panted.

It does not matter. It is time for me to go.

You will die if I do not heal you!

You cannot heal a shattered lir-bond. The wolf pressed his muzzle against Donal's arm. *I am too old. My time is used up. And—I have no wish to survive, now my lir is gone.*

Storr—wait—do not leave me alone—

The magic has ended, kin of my lir . . . it is time for me to go.

Donal shut his eyes. *I will miss you badly, old wolf.*

No more than I shall miss you. Storr's tone was bittersweet. *I had much of the raising of you.*

Donal smiled. He passed a gentle hand through Storr's pelt once more, caressed the grizzled muzzle, and knew he could not gainsay him. *I will tend him, Storr. I will tend your lir as he is due.*

He is deserving of honor— The wolf's sigh was heavy, ragged; the sound of a life used up. *He is deserving of much.*

"Safe journey, old wolf," Donal whispered aloud.

And in his arms there was nothing but dust.

Six

Donal and Evan stole a boat on a night with no moon and sailed to Hondarth, where they shed their heavy boots and slipped overboard near the docks, swimming the rest of the way so as not to give warning to the Atvian fleet. Lorn swam strongly, apparently fully recovered, though still a little thin; Taj flew ahead and waited, perching on the seawall.

They splashed out of the harbor under cover of a dark night sky, wrung water from their clothing and headed up toward a seaside tavern. Donal clenched the sword in his left hand, for he had no belt or scabbard. The blade gleamed in the infrequent wash of torchlight; the ruby, black in Strahan's grasp, glowed blood-red in his.

"I am trusting my life to you," Evan whispered as they crept into the shadow of an alley by the tavern.

Donal raised his brows and slanted a curious glance. "To me? What of yourself? I thought you ever claimed yourself a valiant fighter."

"Oh, aye, I am, I am . . . but certainly not as accomplished as *you*. After all, you have wolf and falcon by you and the ability to shapechange—what have I?" He grinned. "And you carry that sorcerous sword."

Donal looked down at the sword. He thought perhaps it was ensorceled somehow; he recalled how it had warded them against Tynstar; how it had felt like a living thing in his hands when he had nearly beheaded his uncle.

Briefly, he shut his eyes. *Su'fali, oh su'fali*—

A sound. His eyes snapped open. He saw two men passing in the darkness, on their way to the tavern. Donal looked down at his bare feet and wiggled icy toes. "I could use a pair of boots. My feet grow weary of this abuse."

Evan grinned. "Shall we relieve those two sailors of theirs, then?"

"Aye. But quietly . . . *quietly*."

Evan ran lightly through the darkness from the alley with Donal at his side. A moment later they dumped two unconscious bodies into the shadows, stripped them of their scuffed, fish-oiled boots and tugged the footwear on.

Donal winced. "Too small."

"Mine will do well enough—and no, I will not trade with you." Evan pushed a forearm across his grimy face. "What do we do now, Mujhar?"

Donal chewed a ragged fingernail. "I have already turned thief with the acquisition of these boots . . . I think I shall have to worsen my lot and steal a horse as well."

"No," Evan said. "These horses broke loose of their tethers. We only seek out their owners."

"Ah." Donal smiled. "And where might we *look* for these owners?"

"The army might do," Evan said thoughtfully. "Rowan is there—doubtless he could use two more horses."

"And two more men—?" Donal went softly after the two horses tied to the tavern's front wall. He released one animal and handed the reins to Evan, then took a mount for himself.

Hooves clopped against the cobbles. Donal bared his teeth and cursed, wishing he could somehow muffle the iron shoes. But at last he and Evan reached another deep pocket of darkness in the rabbit-warren of seaside buildings. They mounted and headed north.

"I should have made *you* steal them," Donal said. "It is you who requires a mount. I can always *fly*."

"The proof of a real king lies in his humanity."

Donal scoffed. "What nonsense do you mouth?"

"A man who will rule others must learn to treat them as he himself would wish to be treated."

Donal laughed. "Such wisdom from a renegade prince!"

"Well, my father said those things. Rhodri grows pompous at times." Evan plucked his torn linen shirt, still wet and grime-stained, from his skin. "I fear I no longer resemble a prince, my lord Mujhar . . . nor do you much resemble a king."

Donal unsheathed the old sword attached to his saddle.

It was hardly worthy of the name; likely the sailor had carried it for appearances in port. He leaned out of the saddle and dropped it into a running gutter, hearing the splash and clank of poorly tempered steel.

Carefully, he slid the Cheysuli sword into the sheath and slid it home. The old leather scabbard was too short; the blade extended a handspan from the lip. But it would do. "I am not yet a king," he said absently, settling the blade.

"You are Mujhar. The difference lies only in the name."

"First I must slay Osric." Donal wished for a cloak against the cold; winter had passed into the edge of spring, but nights were still quite cool. "Only then will I be worthy of assuming the Lion Throne in Carillon's place."

"Well," said Evan, "I think it is worth the doing. And I think you will succeed."

Donal smiled grimly and rode on, one hand resting on the glowing Mujhar's Eye. Beside him ran the ruddy wolf; above him flew the falcon.

They crept around the outskirts of the Atvian host and found the Homanan army settled upon a wide plain. It was patently obvious the plain had been the site of repeated battles. The ground had been churned into a fine, pale feathering of dirt. No grass grew. There was no vegetation, but the miasma of too much death.

Donal slipped through the Homanan lines like a wraith, with Evan close behind. He spoke quietly to the guards who challenged him. When they saw clearly who it was, all men fell to their knees and swore allegiance. It was a forcible reminder of Carillon's death. Donal—accepting the fealty offered wholeheartedly—nonetheless felt the weight of the burden usurping any pride he might have felt by the reception.

Rowan's vermillion field pavilion was separate from the others, perched atop a swell of a hill overlooking the spreading plain. The moon was nonexistent; Donal could see the tiny fires of Osric's host on the other side of the field.

He dismounted, forgetting the sword at his saddle, and handed the reins to a young boy, who bowed his head shyly. Black-haired, he reminded Donal of Sef.

Until he remembered who—and what—Sef was.

Lorn flopped down outside the doorflap. Taj perched upon the ridgepole. Donal took a deep breath and pulled the flap aside.

Rowan glanced up from the map he studied. Black brows drew down; no doubt he was irritated by the unannounced intruder. But his mouth dropped open as he saw Donal clearly in the candlelight. The map rolled itself back into itself. "Donal! We had begun to fear you were dead."

"No."

Rowan shook his head. "We received word from Finn a month ago, before he and Evan went in to get you free. But—we had begun to think the attempt had failed." Rowan's gaze sharpened as he saw the weal burned into Donal's neck. "By the gods!—What is *that?*"

"A token from the boy." Donal moved into the pavilion as Evan came up behind him. "How fares the army?"

Rowan gestured them to stools and hooked one over for himself. "Well enough. We do not advance, but neither does Osric. He is a master strategist. He lacks our numbers, but he knows how to make his few work in his favor. It is a long, drawn-out affair, my lord. And now—he hangs back. As if waiting for something."

"He waits for me," Donal said.

Evan, who had remained standing in the entrance, moved forward. He set the unscabbarded sword down on the table with a thud and folded his arms. "He waits for *that.*"

Rowan started, staring at the blade. "Carillon's sword! You have got it back!"

"I said I would," Donal said grimly. "Osric gave it to Strahan."

"And you took it back from the boy—"

Donal looked away. "No." His voice shook a little. Slowly he reached out and touched the rune-kissed blade. "No . . . I did not *take* it. Strahan—left it unintentionally."

Rowan drew in a breath. "Have you slain him, then?"

"No." Donal could hardly look at him. "He left it because it was not his, but mine. He left it because Finn saw to it he left it. My *su'fali*—" Donal broke off sharply. When he could, he met Rowan's waiting eyes. "He—is slain, Rowan . . . by the sword made by his own *jehan.*"

"*Finn*—" Rowan's breath ran ragged. "Not *Finn* . . ." he begged. "No. Oh . . . no—*no*—"

Donal could find no words to answer Rowan, so he gave him only silence.

After a long moment, Rowan slid awkwardly off his stool and knelt in the dirt of the pavilion floor. "Forgive me, my lord," he whispered. "I did not give you proper honor when you came in."

Donal stared at the general's bent head. They had ever been at odds, it seemed. Rowan served Carillon, not his heir, and that exacting a service had made him intolerant of Donal's small rebellions. But Carillon was dead. And now Finn. It left him with no one at all.

Save me. Donal bent and clasped Rowan's shoulder. "I have said I will not have you kneeling to me."

"It is done."

"Not this night. Rowan—I need your help."

Rowan stood up. "And I have said you will have it."

Donal tried to ignore the pain in his back. Finn had not had time to heal the talon wounds. "I am Mujhar," he said. "Cheysuli . . . but I do not suit."

Rowan, turning to pour three cups of wine, frowned. "Why do you say that?"

"The prophecy speaks of a man of *all blood* who unites four warring realms. Blood of *two* races flows in my veins—not four."

"Four realms," Rowan said thoughtfully, pouring the cups full. "Solinde and Homana, of course—we are ever at war with Solinde, it seems. And Atvia might be the third. But—which realm is the fourth?"

"Ellas?" Donal turned to Evan.

The Ellasian sat down on his stool near the doorflap. "I think not. Ellas has never fought overmuch. *Never* with Homana or the other realms you name. No . . . when we fight, we fight the Steppes . . . and occasionally Falia and Caledon." He shrugged. "It is why we wed their princesses so often—to settle alliances. For a while."

"It leaves Erinn." Rowan handed out the wine. "Erinn of the Idrian Isles. Not much larger than Atvia—but we have never fought with Erinn."

Donal frowned. "Shaine's first *cheysula* was Erinnish. The one who bore Lindir, my Homanan granddame."

"But we have not treated with Erinn since then." Rowan indicated the map he had been studying. "There has been no reason to. Erinn and Atvia fight one another like two male dogs over a single bone with each turn of the season—some question of a title and imagined insults—but *Homana* has never been involved."

Evan shrugged and stretched out his legs, displaying his stolen boots. "Perhaps that is the key. Perhaps Erinn fights Atvia, and Atvia fights Homana, while Homana battles Solinde." He held up a fist. One by one he flicked up a finger as he named the names. "Homana—Solinde—Atvia—Erinn. Four realms."

"But—I lack the bloodlines." Donal shook his head. "I am not the man in the prophecy."

Rowan's brows lifted a little. "Perhaps your son will be."

Donal grimaced. "I think it *extremely* unlikely Ian would ever be accepted as my heir. He is a bastard, and the Homanan Council—"

"I do not speak of Ian," Rowan said steadily. "Aislinn has conceived."

Donal let out a rush of sound. "*Aislinn—*"

Rowan nodded. "The child is due in two months. We pray this one will be full-term."

Gods . . . she has won . . . that night she drugged me— Donal shut his eyes. *Does she serve Strahan, that child will be a travesty!*

"Donal, there is more." Rowan's voice was expressionless. "It concerns your *meijha* and your children."

Donal's eyes snapped open. "What do you say?"

Rowan took a breath. "Aislinn—summoned Sorcha to Homana-Mujhar. What they discussed I cannot say . . . but not long after it was announced the queen would bear a child, Sorcha took the children and left the Keep."

"*Left—*" Donal was on his feet. "Aislinn has *sent them away—*?"

"They are well, Donal." Rowan said it sharply. "They are well. Aislinn meant them no harm. But Sorcha has taken the children and gone up across the Bluetooth, into the Northern Wastes."

"To the other Keep—?" Donal slammed down his cup so hard wine slopped over to spill across the table. "I cannot believe she did it . . . not *Aislinn*—but" His resolve hardened as he recalled how she had tricked *him*. "I swear—if she does this out of spite or to serve Strahan, I will do to her what Carillon did to her *jehana*. Send her *away* from me—"

"Donal." Rowan cut him off in mid-spate. "She was not harmed, and neither were the children."

"Sorcha would never do it," Donal said flatly. "She would never leave me. She would not take the children away."

Rowan shrugged, plainly uncomfortable. "Who can say what happened between Aislinn and Sorcha? They probably argued over you. Sorcha would never give you up. But neither would Aislinn." He shook his head. "Never Aislinn. She is too much like her father."

"And she is pregnant," Evan said casually. "My mother bore twelve of us. I recall how she was with several of my sisters. Breeding women occasionally have—odd notions."

"I do not care if Aislinn has *odd notions!* I will not allow her to do this to my *meijha* or my children." He set one forefinger into the spilled wine and tapped the map. "I will slay Osric—I will *win* this war—and then I will fetch them home."

"How?" Rowan asked. "We have been fighting Osric for more than half a year. Half our army remains in Solinde; Osric supplies his men from Hondarth. Do you propose to end this war tomorrow?"

Donal heard the underlying hint of contempt in Rowan's tone. He did not blame him; no doubt it was hard for Rowan to serve another, younger master, who had less knowledge of war than *he* did. It was a bittersweet service. *Like an old dog separated from an older, beloved master.* Donal sighed. "Not tomorrow. I propose to do it tonight."

Rowan laughed. But there was nothing of humor in his tone. *"How?"* he repeated.

"I will go to him as a Cheysuli . . . and fight him as a king." Donal's eyes were on the sword.

Evan snorted. "How shall you get through the lines?"

"Not through them, Evan—*over* them . . . as a falcon."

Evan said nothing more. His silence was heavy; he frowned, but swallowed his wine and sat unmoving on his stool.

"When?" Rowan asked.

At least he does not try to gainsay me— "Later, when

darkness is hard upon us. When I have made this sword truly mine."

Rowan drew in a careful breath. "Do what you must do. I will not argue with the gods. But Donal—you have no heir."

Donal caressed the shallow runes in the gleaming steel, dragging broken nails across the incised edges. "I can name none now living. But—should aught befall me and Aislinn bears a son, *he* shall be Mujhar."

"*Executioner*," Evan said suddenly. "The rune might have meant the boy for slaying Finn. Or you, for slaying Osric of Atvia."

"It does not matter," Donal said calmly. "I will see to his death regardless."

With his *lir,* he stood on the field of battle. Behind him stretched the endless leagues of Homana and the endless Homanan army. *His* army. And before him, clear to the dark horizon, lay the massive Atvian warhost.

The moon was a nacreous curving sliver in the blackness of the night. But he could see by the light of the ruby.

Donal had feared, at first, the stoneglow would give him away. But what illuminated the area around him was apparently invisible to Atvians and Homanans alike, for no man came to investigate.

Or else each army believes it something inconsequential.

Donal smiled. The ruby—and the sword—was hardly inconsequential. He had come to believe it at last.

The sword was naked in his hands. Unsheathed, the steel was silver in the moonlight. A bright, white silver, wrought with eloquent runes. Oh, aye, he could read them. He could read what was written there. What Hale had put there for him.

Ja'hai, bu'lasa. Homana tahlmorra ru'maii.

Donal nearly laughed. How he had run away. How he had turned his back. How he had repeatedly refused to accept a gift meant for him alone.

"*Ja'hai, bu'lasa. Homana tahlmorra ru'maii.*" Donal spoke the words aloud. First in the Old Tongue, and then in the language of Homana: "*Accept, grandson. In the name of Homana's tahlmorra.*"

He released a tremendous breath. And then slowly he

bent and knelt upon the ground. The tip of the blade he set into the powdered dirt, and then pressed downward against the crossguards. When he let go, the sword stood up of itself.

"*Lir*," he said aloud. "I lack the proper words. I do not know the ritual."

A ritual is what you make it, Lorn said.

Taj flew down and lighted upon the crossguard. *Say what words you will, and they will be enough.*

Donal wet his lips. Tension knotted his belly. When this thing was done, he would have to confront Osric of Atvia. For all he was willing to take on the task, he was not sure he could do it.

He drew in a breath and held it. Slowly he closed both hands around the blade just below the hilt. Below Taj's talons. And then, summoning all his courage, he jerked his hands downward, downward, until they touched the ground, and he felt the pain fill up his palms.

"*Ja'hai-na!*" he cried. "*Ja'hai-na, Homana tahlmorra ru'maii!* I accept in the name of Homana's *tahlmorra!*"

He sat back on his heels. His fingers sprang open rigidly; he saw the blood pour forth. It spilled through his fingers and down his wrists to splatter the ground.

His arms shook. Pain ran the length of his forearms to his elbows, then up into his shoulders. Shock filled his belly with sickness. "*Ja'hai-na*," he breathed. "Accepted."

Still the blood flowed out of his hands to spill against the soil. He saw how the drops soaked in almost immediately, as if the battlefield had not had its fill of the blood of men. And yet he could smell it. He could smell the stench of war; the stink of rotting bodies. All had been burned or buried, but still he could smell the stench.

"More?" he asked. "Is that what you want, Homana?"

But the earth did not answer him.

Donal looked at the sword. The runes ran red with his blood. But the ruby seemed dull by comparison.

Slowly he reached out his hands. He closed both of them upon the pommel and shut away the ruby from the light of the virgin moon. And then he shut his eyes and emptied himself of the knowledge of who he was.

He needed to know *what* he was.

—*he was a boy again, so small, and listening to his father.*

*Listening to the man who was clan-leader of the Cheysuli,
wiser than everyone save the* shar tahl, *who kept all the
histories.*

*"You are a Cheysuli warrior, a child of the Firstborn, and
beloved of the gods. You are one among many; a man who
is more than a man; a warrior who serves more than war,
but the gods and the prophecy. In you lies the seed of that
prophecy, dormant now, but waiting for the day when you
will awaken at last and comprehend the* tahlmorra *of a kingdom. Not of a boy, of a man, of a clan. Of a kingdom, and
you will be its king. You will be what no one has been for
nearly four hundred years: a Cheysuli Mujhar of Homana.
The man in the prophecy."*

Donal opened his eyes. Took his hands away from the
sword. The blood-bathed ruby glowed more brilliantly than
ever. And when he looked at his palms, he saw the wounds
had healed.

Osric of Atvia, when Donal finally found him, was ensconced in a huge black field pavilion ringed with smoking
torches. He was alone. He sat at his table and pondered his
maps, plotting new strategy. Four braziers and two tall candleracks illuminated the interior of the tent. Light flashed
off ruddy hair banded by a plain gold circlet; it glinted as
he absently smoothed the map with a thick-fingered hand.
His broad shoulders threw odd shadows on the fabric behind him: black on black. He scratched idly at his heavy,
sun-gilded beard.

He was not old. Perhaps thirty, a year or two more. He
was a hardened fighter in his prime; Donal knew he faced
harsh odds. But he would not turn from them.

Donal stepped into the glowing light and smiled, carrying
the sword. Osric, glancing up at the faintest whisper of
sound, froze. His blue eyes widened minutely, then narrowed; he did not otherwise indicate alarm or fear. He
appeared more irritated than anything.

"Hist?" he asked curtly in his Atvian tongue. But then
he saw the sword. He pushed himself to his feet. "You are
Donal." Now he spoke Homanan, accented heavily.

"I am the Mujhar."

"How did you come by that sword?"

Donal watched him. "You took it from Carillon. I got it back from the boy."

"Strahan gave it to you?"

"After a fashion."

Osric was very tall, massive as a tree. Donal recalled Carillon's description of Keough, Osric's grandsire, and thought this man must resemble him. He knew himself outweighed badly, outreached as well, and undoubtedly outmatched when it came to deadly swordplay.

"Strahan held you captive, I was told."

"I was freed. I brought the sword out with me." He paused. "It is *mine,* Osric. My grandsire made it for me."

Osric's blue eyes glittered. He was so vital Donal could sense the strength moving in the man. "I have heard that sword holds magic. Shapechanger sorcery." The blue eyes dipped to the sword, then lifted to Donal's face. "Hale was your grandsire, then?"

"Aye. You see, do you not, I am not an upstart warrior who wishes to grasp at a throne? I have a lawful right to it, Osric. I have blood in me that harks back to the Mujhars of old, and the Cheysuli Mujhars before them."

"*I* have the right of conquest," Osric said. Then, "How did you come through my lines?"

"I flew."

"Flew?"

Donal smiled. "I am a falcon when need be—or a wolf whenever I choose." He pulled aside the doorflap. Lorn came into the pavilion silently. "You have chosen a bad enemy," Donal told the Atvian lord. "We Cheysuli do not sit idly by while you try to usurp our homeland."

Osric still stared at Lorn. "My grandsire died because of a wolf," he said slowly. "In Homana, it was—inside Homana-Mujhar. It was whim—a *wolf's* whim. It did not slay with tooth or claw—it slew by using fear."

Donal laughed aloud. "That wolf, *ku'reshtin,* was my mother."

Osric's teeth showed briefly. "No matter. I know the truth of you. Hold that sword if you wish—I know the truth. The Cheysuli have no sword-skill. I do not mind slaying Homana's shapechanger Mujhar, but I would prefer a better match."

Donal shrugged. "It was Carillon who taught me. Judge my skill by the reputation of my master's."

Osric's eyes narrowed. "Carillon is dead. *I* was the one who slew him—as once he prophesied." He smiled suddenly as Donal started. "Did you not know? Aye—Carillon prophesied our meeting. He told it to my brother, Alaric, when I sent him here some sixteen years ago." He laughed. "Carillon said—if I recall it right—that if we ever met on the field of battle, one of us would die." He studied Donal closely. "Carillon's reputation? Overpraised, I think. As for yours? Let us make one now." He turned. He caught up his own broadsword from his cot, swung back and advanced on Donal.

The hilt settled comfortably in Donal's hands. He felt the warmth of the metal. The odd, vibrant *life* sprang up again.

Osric was a master swordsman. Donal discovered that very quickly. The Atvian's bulk gave him both superior reach and strength, but slowed down his reactions. Donal was quicker than Osric.

He ducked under two whistling slashes that clove the air near his head. He felt their wind in his hair. Still he ducked away, not yet engaging the man. *I am no swordsman, for all I boasted to him—there is too much I have left to learn—*

Osric needed no lessons. He shattered the edge of the table with one huge swipe of his broadsword and laughed aloud as Donal stumbled back hastily. Teeth gleamed in his sun-gilded beard as he lifted the blade, teasing Donal with its tip. "You are mine, fool. Homana falls as *you* fall."

Donal skipped back as Osric's blade flashed by his ribs. He stumbled over a brazier, overturning it; rolled to his feet as he blocked a blow with his blade. Coals burned his legs and feet, charring the leather of his boots, but he ignored that as Osric came on.

"Homana has stood firm against you for over half a year without me," Donal pointed out, moving constantly: "What makes you believe the realm will fall do *I* fall?"

"It is the way of battles involving kings." Osric struck again; Donal ducked. "Soldiers require leadership, royalty preferred. But slay the king and the army is slain, though most men walk away." Osric shifted his stance. The sword was a splinter in his tremendous hands. "Atvia is but a

small place. I grow weary of an island. A realm the size of
Homana will suit me well enough."

Donal moved back. "After Homana—Solinde? Your
present ally?"

Teeth gleamed in Osric's beard. "Too soon to say,
Cheysuli."

The sword seemed to hum in Donal's hands. He felt it
protest his poor skill, as if it were disappointed by his lack.
Donal set his teeth and set up a fence of steel, trying to
maintain his ground as Osric sought to batter him down.

He stepped back, back again. The table pressed against
his spine. Donal threw himself onto the table in a bid to
roll away and gain his feet, but Osric's sword was in the
way. It settled at his throat.

"True," Osric said. "The Cheysuli have no sword-skill."

The ruby blazed up and created a nimbus around them
both. Osric, crying out, fell back, eyes popping in their
sockets. His own sword shook in his hands, but he was too
much a warrior to give over to fear so easily.

Donal pressed up from the table. Osric brought his sword
down. Blades clashed. The immense strength of the Atvian
drove Donal down again. His torn back pressed against
the wood.

The nimbus continued to hum. It splashed blood-red light
across Osric's face until his blue eyes turned Ihlini purple.

Donal felt the numbness beginning in his hands, felt the
sword cleave to his grasp as if it was part and parcel of
his body. Runes glowed white the length of the blade—
he swung—

—Osric's sword broke in a rain of shining steel.

He stood there with nothing in his hands but a useless
hilt. His mouth hung open: a tombstoned cavern in red-
gilt hair.

Donal, still flat on his back on the table, felt the sword
lift him up; felt the power surge through his arms from
shoulder to fingertips. He was lifted; he thrust. The blade
slid home in Osric's belly.

That for Carillon. That for my su'fali.

Seven

Donal took back his human form in front of Rowan's pavilion. As he pulled open the doorflap he met Evan in the entrance. "Osric?" Evan demanded.

"Atvia lacks a lord." He could still feel a residual warmth and vitality in the sword. The ruby was red against his hand.

"Good." Evan had shaved; put on fresh clothing worthy of his rank. The stolen boots had been replaced with finer footwear. "You are unharmed?"

"As you see me." But Donal thought Evan did not see him clearly. There was a drawn tautness at the corners of his eyes and mouth, as if he spoke automatically with little thought for what he said. "Evan—what is it?"

Evan stepped aside and gestured limply for Donal to enter. His hand scraped against the fabric as he let the flap down again. "A messenger came early this morning, just at dawn, while you were still in Osric's encampment."

The pavilion was empty. The bedclothes on Rowan's cot were rumpled. One cup of wine, half-filled, stood on the table next to a pile of maps. A fly buzzed around the rim.

Donal sat down on a stool, hunching a little; he lay the blade across his thighs and fingered the hilt with its rampant lion. "This message was for me?"

"No. For me." Evan frowned a little. He looked almost bewildered. "My brother is—High King."

Donal looked at him sharply. "Rhodri—?"

"Dead of a sudden fever." Evan combed a hand through his dark brown hair. "It took him too quickly—the leeches could do nothing."

Donal stood up again. He understood the puzzled grief in Evan's eyes better than before, now that he lacked Finn.

He reached out and clasped Evan's arm briefly. "I am sorry. Do you ride for Ellas immediately?"

After a moment Evan shook his head. "I would have. At once, of course—I should go home and pay my respects. But—Lachlan has said no. He gives me leave to remain here." He shrugged a little. "He says—he says all of Ellas knows how I honored my father, and that now I must honor the wishes of her new High King." His eyes were full of grief and lethargy; his anchor had been taken from him. "He says I must stay with you."

Donal stared at his friend. His own emotions were detached, as if Finn's death had drained him of the capacity for grief, but he understood what Evan felt. *He has only just discovered how much his* jehan *meant to him, for all he has spoken casually of their relationship.* Donal sat down again. "Why would Lachlan wish you to stay here? I am more than glad of your company, but perhaps you would do better to go home."

Evan's mouth hooked down on one side. "He heard of Carillon's death. Out of sorrow and a wish to keep Homana whole, he is sending five thousand men." Evan smiled. "The Royal Ellasian Guard . . . which was, I know, dispatched once before to Homana, when Carillon needed aid. Out of respect for Carillon's memory, Lachlan wishes to make certain Homana does not fall. But—I think there is more, though he did not say it. I think he fears for Ellas as well. Does Osric take Homana, there is a good chance he will turn his eyes to Ellas one of these years. Why not gainsay that now by sending aid to Homana? He could not do so before—my father preferred to stay out of Homana's troubles—but now he is High King. He may do what he wishes."

Donal sighed, staring pensively at the sword. "Whatever Lachlan's reasons—his gesture is more than welcome."

Evan nodded. "Rhodri was a worthy king. Ellas loved him. But Ellas also loves Lachlan, the scapegrace, priest and prince who wandered as a harper for three years, riding with an exiled Homanan lord as he sought to win back his realm. He will be a valuable ally, Donal."

Thinking deeply, Donal scratched at his forehead beneath the thick black hair that hung nearly into his eyes. "Five thousand men may be more than enough to swing this battle to a conclusion. Unless, of course, Osric's death is enough. It may be that Lachlan's gift is not necessary. But regardless, I must leave Rowan in charge of the Homanan troops, while you lead the Ellasians." He frowned. "It would give me time to go up across the Bluetooth."

"Still you will go?"

"I will. And I will bring Sorcha and the children home— home to Homana-Mujhar."

Evan sucked in a whistling breath. "Not wise, Donal. Aislinn is already jealous—installing your light woman and bastards beneath the same roof may not be for the best."

"I do not care." Donal looked up from the sword. "I am not totally blind to Aislinn's reasons for what she has done. But there are other factors I must consider. She is Electra's daughter. It means I can never view her without suspicion—has she not given me enough reason for that?— because it may be that she has a measure of her *jehana*'s power. For all I know, the Solindish blood in her holds stronger than the Homanan."

"She bears a child, Donal. Possibly a son, and heir to Homana."

Donal laughed. "I have no intention of *slaying* her, Evan! Nor do I wish to beat her. I intend only to put Sorcha and the children where I knew they will be safe."

Evan shook his head. "Do not put her so close to Aislinn. Donal—this is merely jealousy. Once Aislinn has borne her own, she will not resent Sorcha's children so much."

Donal shook his head. "For a man who has neither children nor *cheysula*, you know much about both."

"I have five sisters," Evan retorted, "and—at last count—fourteen nieces and nephews. Perhaps more, by now—my sisters breed like coneys. I speak from experience, Donal."

Donal sighed. "Well, nonetheless, I will go to the Northern Keep and tend to my *meijha* and children. *Then* I will see to Aislinn."

Rowan gave him a new sheath and belt for the sword, since Carillon's was missing, presumably somewhere in the Atvian encampment unless Strahan still had it. But the new one suited Donal's taste. It was plain dark leather oiled to a smooth sheen, worked with Cheysuli runes from top to bottom.

Donal slid the blade home until the hilt clicked against the lip. He looked at Rowan. "Your workmanship?"

Rowan's angular face was solemn. "Aye. My blood showing in me at last. I have the Cheysuli skill."

Donal looked at him in surprise. "Then you are finally admitting openly to your heritage."

Splotches of color formed in Rowan's face, flushing the sunbronzing darker still so that the yellow of his eyes was emphasized. "I have not had to deny it for many years," he said with a quiet dignity. "Not since I acknowledged the truth to Carillon."

He will judge everything in his life by Carillon. Donal sighed and tried to summon what little he knew of tact. "I know you have never had a *lir,* but you *are* Cheysuli. You might have sought a clan instead of the Homanans when you were old enough to know the truth."

Rowan shook his head. "I did not seek the Homanans, Donal. I was *raised* Homanan. Oh, aye . . . I knew what I was *inside,* but how could I fight Homanan habits that grew to be second nature? A child becomes what he is made . . . and I was made Homanan."

Donal frowned down at the rune-worked blade. "We are so different. The races. So—apart. We are different men. And I think you cannot be both."

"You can." Rowan smiled a little. "One day, you may see it. One day you may *have* to. You yourself are less Cheysuli than *I* am, if we are to speak of blood—and yet you are the one who claims the races are different." He shook his head. "You do realize, of course, that even though Homana has a Cheysuli Mujhar once more—that the Cheysuli race will not last forever. We will be swallowed up by the truth of the prophecy."

Donal looked at him sharply. The words, oddly, echoed what Tynstar has said; what Strahan had emphasized. And Donal did not like it. Somehow, it *threatened* him. "We have lost nothing in thousands of years. We still claim the *lir* and all that bond entails. The earth magic that heals, the power to compel—"

"Aye." Rowan interrupted calmly. "But have you never thought that when the goal of the prophecy is attained and the Firstborn live again, there will be little room left for the Cheysuli?"

"There will *always* be Cheysuli in Homana." Donal's tone obliterated room for speculation. "Homanan-raised you may have been, but not Homanan-*born*. Did you not set the runes into the leather of this scabbard?"

"Some things a man never forgets." Rowan looked at the devices he had tooled. "I remember—when I was very small—how my *jehan* used to write out the runes with a chunk of coal on a bleached deerskin. It fascinated me. I would sit for hours before the pavilion and watch his hand draw the runes—making magic. And the birthlines, when the *shar tahl* showed me mine." He smiled reminiscently. "I remembered all the runes. So I pieced together the prophecy and the runes, and put it all into the leather."

Donal watched the changes in Rowan's face. In that instant he felt closer to the man than ever before. In that instant, Rowan was Cheysuli, and Donal could understand him. "What else do you remember?"

The smile fell away. "I remember the day the Mujhar's men came across my family. How they slew them all, even my small *rujholla*. I remember it all very well, though for years I denied it."

"Because your new kin never said you were Cheysuli."

"They never knew." Rowan shrugged. "They were Ellasian, come to Homana for a new life. They found a small boy wandering dazedly in the forest, unable to speak out of fear for what he had seen, and they took him as their own. They were—good people."

"But they were not Cheysuli."

"Half of *you* is not," Rowan retorted. "When I look at you, Donal, I see and hear a Cheysuli warrior, because that is what you desire to show to people. You have all the Cheysuli characteristics—including that prickly pride—and you certainly bear the stamp. But you also are Homanan, because of Alix. You should let it temper that pride. Do not become *so* Cheysuli you cannot understand the people you will rule."

Donal's fingers closed on the leather scabbard. "I—I would prefer to have nothing but Cheysuli blood in my veins."

"But you do not. There is Homanan as well. Else you

would not be part of the prophecy." Rowan sighed. and shook his head. "You are what they have made you, your mother and your father. Duncan was all Cheysuli, and Alix—out of a wish to keep alive the husband she had lost—did what she could to make you Duncan come again. It is—not necessarily bad. I could think of worse warriors for you to emulate—including Finn." Rowan flicked one hand in a silencing gesture as Donal moved to protest. "Finn was what the prophecy made him. He was what Carillon needed for many years. But—people change. They grow older, they mature. Carillon no longer needed him. And neither, now, do you."

Donal shook his head in violent disagreement. "I need him badly, my *su'fali*. There is so much left for me to learn."

"You will learn it. But first you must learn to acknowledge the Homanan in you as well as the Cheysuli."

Donal lifted the hilt. "Do I not wear this now? What Cheysuli has ever borne a sword—except, perhaps, for you?"

"It is a beginning," Rowan agreed.

"It is *more* than a beginning," Donal muttered. "It is an alteration of tradition."

"Perhaps it is necessary." Rowan smiled. "You are the first Cheysuli Mujhar to hold the Lion Throne in four hundred years, Donal. *That* is alteration."

Pensively, Donal nodded. Then he sighed and looked up at Rowan. "There is a thing I would have you do."

The general shrugged. "What I can, I will."

"Win this war. Win this gods-cursed war, so I can begin my reign in peace."

Donal rode northward through Homana, bypassing Mujhara entirely, until he reached the Bluetooth River. On the southern bank he pulled in his horse, staring at the river. It had been sixteen years since he had last seen the Bluetooth, when Tynstar's Ihlini servitors had taken him toward the Molon Pass for entry into Solinde. He had been Valgaard-bound, prisoners, he and Alix, but he had escaped because of Taj and Lorn's aid in accelerating his ability to take *lir*-shape. Alix had not. He had left his mother behind, crossing the huge river on his escape to Homana-Mujhar. Then it had been much colder, for winter had only recently left the land. Now it was spring and the waters were quick, unclogged by ice and slush. He stared at the wooden ferry on the far side and wondered if he should wait for it, or cross Cheysuli-fashion.

Taj, perching in a nearby tree, fixed him with a bright dark eye. *Do you recall it,* lir?

I recall.

You sought the air then. Shall you do it again?

Donal turned to stare over his shoulder, searching for Lorn. A moment later the ruddy wolf broke free of the dense vegetation fringing the riverbank.

No—I will ride. I will have Sorcha and the children with me.

Lorn shook dust from his coat. *Then I must swim this river, unless you bribe the ferry-master to let me pass with you.*

The ferry-master, when he banked his wooden vessel, accepted Donal's gold eagerly. He slanted an apprehensive glance at the wolf, eyed Donal closely, then gestured them both aboard. Donal led the horse onto the thick wooden timbers and waited for Lorn to join him.

The man cast off and began the lengthy process of pulling the ferry back across the wide river. But it did not keep him from watching Donal, or from talking.

He hawked, spat over the side into the water, and jerked his head. "Na' meanin' to offend ye, but 'tis curious I am. Be ye a halfling, then?"

"Halfling?" Donal was startled by the rough northern dialect. The language seemed hardly Homanan.

"Halfling. Aye. Lookit yersel'. Yon color is Cheysuli, but ne'er I seen one dressit like ye. Leathers, they wear, and gold. Be ye only half, then?"

In shock, Donal realized the Homanan clothing Rowan had lent him after his escape from Strahan robbed him of identity. He had put off the torn and soiled leathers, replacing them with black soldiers' breeches; linen shirt and rich brown velvet doublet, which hid the gold on his arms. His hair, left uncut for too long, hid his earring.

He eyed the ferry-master speculatively. "Were I to say I was all Cheysuli, what would you do?"

The man laughed, hawked again, spat over the ferry again. "Indeed, nothin'. On'y curious, master. But ye don't be lookin' like'ee others. Ne'er hae I seen one wear a *sword*."

Donal's hand dropped to the heavy hilt. Possessively, he shut his fingers upon it. "A new custom."

"Yon breed be fierce, master. I seen many of 'em here, crossin' south, bound for the Mujhar's city." Interest flared up in the man's brown eyes. "Hae ye been to Mujhara, master?"

Donal smiled. "Aye."

"Big as they do say?"

"Bigger."

"Hae ye seen yon palace, what called Homana-Mujhar?" His dialect—and several missing teeth—ran the syllables together until they were nearly indistinguishable.

"Aye, I have."

"Ye'll say 'tis grander than I can 'magine, doubtless."

Donal patted his horse's muzzle. "Aye, it is."

"And be he the man they do say he is?"

"Who—the Mujhar?" Donal shrugged. "Tell me what they say."

The ferry-master pulled hard upon the ropes. His mouse-brown hair was long, clubbed back with a strip of leather. He wore rough woolen clothing and heavy boots. Brawny muscles played across his back and shoulders as he pulled against the current. "They do say Carillon chose hi'self a right'un. A man even the 'lini give a wide road to."

Donal smiled wryly. "I thought the Ihlini feared no one."

The man eyed him. "I dinna say they *feared* 'im. The 'lini, most likely, fear nae man. But up here I carry passengers from all lands and all races, and I do say I hauled a few 'lini sorcerers 'cross this beast." He shrugged. "Man doesna say nae to gude gold."

Donal stared across the swift-running river to the far side. He shivered slightly as the chill wind blasted from the frozen mountains of the Molon Pass, several leagues away from the river, but close enough to wall them in on one side. "I would have thought," he said lightly, "that Ihlini sorcerers had no need of a *ferry* to cross this river."

The ferry-master laughed. "Aye, so ye *would* think—but they dinna fly. Nae more than ye do, master."

Donal smiled. "But I do."

"Fly?" The man shook his head. "Ye be jestin' wi' me, then."

"No." *Nae*, he said silently, liking the dialect.

The man eyed him closely. "Then why be ye takin' my ferry?"

Donal laughed. "I do not *always* fly. Besides, I will have company on the way back." He studied the man a moment. "Do you fear me, ferry-master?"

"I hae heard of yon sorcery. Na' feared to say I 'spect it."

"Respect and fear are two different things." Donal leaned idly against the rail. "You have a Cheysuli Mujhar. Do you fear him?"

"I do fear what it might be meanin'." The ferry-master's head rose and he met Donal's eyes squarely. "The legends do say the shapechangers once held Homana, and gi' her oop to men of my race. Now ye hae it back. 'Tis no wonder honest Homanans wonder what it all be meanin'."

"There is no danger in it for any Homanan," Donal told him. "The Mujhar means to keep peace in this realm."

"That I'll be havin' to see fer mysel', then."

"So you shall." Donal gestured. "We are nearly there."

The man whipped a quick look at the bank, hauled on the brake ropes and brought the ferry in smoothly. Donal led the horse onto the bank and mounted. As he waited for Lorn he saw the ferry-master watching him in a mixture of curiosity and suspicion. Donal raised his hand in a brief wave, then put his horse to the northernmost track.

The Keep was set in the toothy foothills of the mountains. Like most Keeps, it was ramparted by high stone walls that wound their way up slopes and down again to encircle all the pavilions. It was a harsh blue-gray stone, almost indigo, that greeted his eyes, not the warm grayish-green he was more accustomed to. In the Northern Wastes, many things were different.

He rode up to the entrance and paused. Three warriors guarded it; even now, nearly twenty years after Carillon ended the *qu'mahlin*, the clans knew better than to trust any stranger who rode in. Even one who appeared Cheysuli.

One of the warriors came forward from the wall. His yellow eyes appraised Donal shrewdly, marking the characteristic Cheysuli features; marking also the Homanan clothing. There was calm politeness in his tone as he offered casual greeting, but Donal saw the slight trace of contempt in the eyes.

Gods—he does not see a warrior . . . he sees a city-bred Cheysuli— It nearly made him cringe.

"I am Kaer," the warrior said. "Have you business in our Keep?"

Not quite the ritual greeting of warrior to warrior—well, I can expect no better. Not hiding all my gold, even with the lir. Donal looked down upon Kaer. "My business is with my kin, who shelter here. Sorcha, my *meijha*, and our children, Ian and Isolde. I am Donal, son of Duncan."

Kaer's expression altered at once. Quickly he made the subtle hand gesture denoting acknowledgment of his rudeness; rarely did a warrior admit to such before another warrior, since Cheysuli were rarely rude, and so an apology was never spoken. The gesture was enough.

"My lord Mujhar." He reached out to catch the stallion's reins. "I will escort you to the clan-leader at once."

It was proper for a visiting warrior to meet first with the keep's clan-leader. Donal badly wanted to see Sorcha and the children, but he forced himself into patience as he dismounted, gave up the reins of his horse to Kaer and went with him across the Keep toward a rust-colored pavilion. On the side a yellow mountain cat was painted.

Kaer paused, called for entrance, was granted it and pulled aside the flap. He spoke quietly to someone inside. A moment later he turned and gestured Donal within, then disappeared with the horse. Donal saw Taj light upon the ridgepole. Lorn flopped down beside the doorflap to exchange greetings with the sleek tawny mountain cat who sprawled upon a rug.

Donal went in. A Cheysuli sat cross-legged before the small pavilion fire, but he rose fluidly as his guest slipped through the doorflap. He smiled. "Be welcome among us. Do you hunger, you will be fed. Be you weary, safe rest is yours."

Donal felt the brief flicker of nostalgia rise up, tempered with a touch of sorrow. So many times, as a boy, he had heard his father say those traditional words to a stranger being welcomed into the Keep. And then Finn. Now they were said to him.

"*Cheysuli i'halla shansu*," he returned. "I am Donal, son of Duncan and Alix. My *meijha*, Sorcha, is here."

The yellow eyes flickered, then assessed him shrewdly,

though the warrior's face remained bland. With a flash of insight Donal realized he would be judged more harshly by his own race than by any Homanan. The Cheysuli had waited for four centuries for one of their own to regain the Lion.

Now one has, but they do not know me as well as they would like to.

The clan-leader nodded. "I am Tarn." He reached out to clasp Donal's arm in a gesture of welcome, then indicated the thick brown bear pelt spread by the fire. Donal sat down accordingly and accepted the cup of honey brew from Tarn's own hands. "I have heard of the war you wage against Osric of Atvia." Tarn poured his own cup full and drank.

Donal nodded, sipping at his portion. It was warm, rich, and satisfying; he had drunk too much wine of late, and found he missed the traditional liquor of his race. "We have left warriors from my clan in Solinde, but I think the rebellion dies. Osric is slain now, and we will soon boast an additional five thousand soldiers from Ellas. The war should be over soon." He did not ask why Tarn had not sent warriors of his own; it was not the proper time.

Tarn nodded. "We are isolated here. But we hear many things. Such as Tynstar's death—and the rising power of his son."

Donal slowly released a silent breath. "Strahan is yet a boy, but powerful. He has learned well from his *jehan*. I do not doubt Valgaard will soon be inhabited again—if it is not already."

"We have heard nothing of that." Tarn set down his cup. "You have come to see your kin."

Donal was relieved the casual talk was ended. "Aye. And to thank you for taking them in. But now I shall have them come home with me."

"I—think not. Not all of them." Tarn's voice was steady. "Donal—it is unhappy news I bear. Shocking news, as well. I wish there were another way—" He broke off, then said it plainly. "Sorcha has taken her life."

Donal dropped the cup. It overturned against his knees, spilling hot liquor across the fabric of his breeches to soak into his skin. But he felt nothing. Nothing but total shock.

"Sorcha?" he whispered. "*Sorcha—?*"

Tarn nodded. "I sent a messenger to Homana-Mujhar, not knowing where you were."

Donal stared blindly at the man. "I was—I was—" He stopped speaking. He could not form another word. All he could do was stare at the blurred face before his burning eyes.

"*Shansu*," Tarn said compassionately. "It grieves me to give my Mujhar such news."

"Suicide . . ." he whispered. "Oh—gods—*no* . . . she has forfeited the afterworld—"

"Aye." Tarn would not meet Donal's eyes so as not to acknowledge a grief that should be private.

"But—*why?* Why would Sorcha *do* such a thing?"

Still Tarn avoided his eyes. "The women came and spoke to me and told me what Sorcha said before she did the unspeakable. It was—grief and anger and loss, the loss of the warrior with whom she had shared her life."

"She had not *lost* me—"

"It was anger, much anger; she told them the Queen had sent her here. Banished your *meijha*, to keep her from your sight." Tarn's voice was carefully modulated; he would not be judge or arbiter, merely a spokesman for what had happened. "She told them she had lost you to the Homanans and to Homana's queen; that you had turned your back on all your Cheysuli heritage."

"Aislinn sent them here . . ."

"That is what we were told. Sorcha and your children were banished here, never to go south of the Bluetooth."

"But—*suicide*—" He could not conceive of the woman doing the unspeakable.

"Sorcha was—half-mad with grief and anger. I spoke to her when she came. Donal—she could not face life without you. Sharing you was bad enough, she said; she could not bear losing you altogether. Not to the *Homanans*. And so she emptied her veins of blood."

Donal stared blindly at the damp liquor stain on his breeches. *She said she wished to, once. To be rid of the Homanan taint . . . Oh gods—Aislinn is no better than her jehana—* He shut his eyes. *What am I to do?*

"I am sorry." Tarn said it gently, more gently than Donal expected; Sorcha was not deserving of compassion to a clanleader's way of thinking. She had done what was never to be done. "What will you do, my lord?"

Donal heard the rank without surprise. Another time, he might have remarked upon it; Cheysuli rarely gave rank to another man, and never to warriors other than the *shar tahls* and clan-leaders.

But things are different, now. He looked levelly at Tarn. "I would like to see my children."

"At once. Wait here—I will send them." Tarn rose and stepped outside, speaking quietly to someone. When the flap was pulled aside again, Donal saw his son.

Ian came in silently and conducted himself with grave correctness, waiting for encouragement before he moved closer yet. He was four now, and Cheysuli pride was already apparent in every line of his slender body, from the lifted chin to the squared shoulders. He wore winter jerkin and leggings.

I wonder . . . will he find his lir *as young as I did—?*

Then a woman came in with Isolde and he banished everything else from his mind. He took the girl from the woman's arms. When the woman went away again, he sat alone with his children.

He snugged Isolde into his lap, settling her against his chest. She was just over a year now; he realized, with a sense of shock, he had lost too much time. Since Isolde's birth he had wed, gone to war, been held imprisoned for six months—too much, too much time. He cradled her silky-haired head in one hand and felt the uprush of grief and anger.

Oh gods . . . oh gods . . . why do you do this to children? Why do you take so many people? From me . . . and now from my children as well. Why do you do this to us?

He held Isolde there against his chest, eyes closed, softly caressing her wispy raven curls. He felt a child himself, badly in need of comforting . . . but his *jehana* and *meijha* were dead. Even Finn, who might have mocked his grief—while understanding it better than most—could do nothing to help him now.

Donal drew in a ragged breath. He looked over Isolde's head to the face of his son and saw a matching conflict there. Ian was frightened, confused, lost. Badly in need of something he could easily comprehend.

No different from myself . . . "She loved you." Donal knew perfectly well he broke Cheysuli custom by even discussing the emotion, but he did not care. Things were different now; he wore a sword at his side. "She loved you—and so do I."

Tears welled up into the wide yellow eyes. Trembling, biting his lower lip, Ian came forward and knelt at his father's side. His right hand hesitantly twined itself into the wide sword belt at Donal's waist; the other hastily wiped the fallen tears away.

"*Jehan*," he began in a small, soft voice, "where do we go now?"

Donal slid an arm around Ian's slim shoulders. Isolde, cuddled against him contentedly as a kitten, scratched at the nap of his velvet doublet. "We go to the place that will be your home."

Ian brightened. "The other Keep?"

Donal stared into the beseeching eyes of his son and realized with a sickening wrench that a Cheysuli keep would never again be home to any of his children. His line, and theirs, would come to know only the walled palaces of kings.

Already, it begins. He squeezed the boy's shoulders. "Ian, you will go to the Keep and see your clan-mates as often as you wish. But you I will have by me."

Ian's fingers tightened on the sword belt. "Will she come back?" he whispered. "*Jehana?*"

"No," Donal told him. "*Jehana* will never come back."

Silently, his son's face crumpled, and he began to cry.

Eight

In the bright, cool light of mid-morning three weeks later, Donal rode through the gates of Homana-Mujhar. Isolde he held in one arm, guiding the stallion with the other; Ian sat perched behind him on the broad, smooth rump, clutching his father's sword belt.

Donal was weary unto death. He had refused Tarn's offer of an escort with a woman to care for the children; in some strange, possessive way he felt it better *he* should tend to the children his *meijha* had borne him. And so he had ridden alone with his children and his *lir* and knew somehow it was best.

He halted the stallion by the marble steps leading to the archivolted entrance. Lads came flying from the stables, all vying for the horse. They challenged one another for the loudest greeting, but fell silent soon enough when Donal did not answer.

He swung one leg across the stallion's neck, turning in the saddle so he would not dislodge his son. Isolde was pressed against his chest. He steadied himself against the saddle, then offered an arm to Ian. The boy slid off as well, clutching his father's hand.

For a moment, Donal shut his eyes. He drew again on what little strength he had left. Then he ordered the horse put away and turned to climb the steps.

"Jehan—" It was Ian, moving closer to Donal's side. "This is Homana-Mujhar?"

"Aye." The tone was flat, lifeless; he was too weary to summon another. "Come up, Ian—there will be time later for you to gape."

He hardly saw the servants who bowed or curtseyed. He saw only endless corridors and marble pillars. And then he saw his sister.

She ran. Both hands clutched at her skirts, pulling them nearly up to her knees as she hastened down the corridor. "Donal—is it *true?*" She stopped short in front of him, breathless. "He said Sorcha was *dead* . . . he said he came from across the Bluetooth—"

Black hair tangled on her shoulders. Donal thought she looked genuinely shocked. Well, she would be; she and Sorcha had been close. But looking at her, he remembered Strahan. He remembered how closely their blood was linked.

Even as Aislinn's is linked. He placed his hand on Ian's head. Then he summoned one of the women servants forward. "Take the children. See they are fed and given rest. They are weary. It has been a brutal journey."

To his *lir* he said, *Go to my chambers and wait.*

"*Donal*—" Bronwyn began, but he waved her into silence as the woman curtseyed and took Isolde from his arms.

"Go with her, Ian. See how your *rujholla* goes with her?" Without the weight in his arms, he felt empty. Isolde began to cry. "Ian, do as I have said. And see to your *rujholla*." he gave Ian a gentle push in the direction of the woman, then turned to face his sister. "Where is Aislinn?"

Bronwyn reached out and caught the velvet of his doublet. "Donal—is it true?"

"Where is Aislinn?"

She stared up at him in perplexed disbelief. "Can you not answer my question? The warrior came down from the north bearing horrible news about how Sorcha had taken her life—can you not even tell me?"

"She is dead." It hissed between his teeth. "*Tell me where Aislinn is!*" He set her aside deliberately and started down the corridor.

"Donal—*wait*—" Bronwyn hastened after him. The wind whipped from her passing cast shadows against the walls. "Donal—she is *resting*—"

"Is she in her chambers?"

Bronwyn caught his arm and tried to hold him back. "Aye, of course—she wearies quickly now the birth is only a month away—*rujho*—wait . . . you are hardly back, and I heard how Strahan kept you prisoner. Donal—*wait*—"

Again, he forcibly set her aside.

"Donal," Bronwyn called, "what are you going to *do*—?"

He did not know. He thought Aislinn might give him the answer.

He said nothing as he entered her chambers. He made no sound. He shut the door. Aislinn looked up and saw him, and terror was in her eyes.

"Donal! *Donal*—" She pushed herself more upright in the bed, scrabbling in satin pillows. "Donal—*wait you*—"

Still he said nothing. He crossed the room to the bed and stood there, staring down upon her. She looked so young, so *defenseless*—

—and so perfectly willing to drive Sorcha to her death.

"D—Donal—!"

"Should I trouble myself to listen to your lies?"

She shook. Her lips were colorless. "I knew—*I knew*— when the messenger came, I knew what you would think—"

"You *sent* her there. You banished her from her home." He saw how her taut belly pushed against the linens of her nightshift. "Did you think it would mean nothing to her to lose her *home* as well as me?"

"Donal—I did not *send* her! She went of her own accord."

"Do you say you did not meet with her?"

"We met. We *met*—I called her to the palace. But I never sent her away. I merely *warned* her—"

"Warned her about *what?*"

"That I would never give you up." Tears ran freely down Aislinn's face. "Oh gods, all I did was say I would fight her for you. I *never* sent her away. Donal—I *swear*—"

He bent over her and pressed her shoulders against the pillows. "—swear nothing! Let me see for myself instead."

Her mouth shaped his name in a cry of terror, but by then he was in her mind.

He felt the shock of the contact reverberate through her body. Her head pressed back against the satin, but her eyes were not closed. They stared at the timbers of the roof beams; blind, senseless eyes, filled with emptiness.

Faintly, very faintly, he heard the protests from his distant *lir*, who knew very well what he did. And he deliberately ignored them.

—barriers—

Weak. Hardly enough to justify the name. There was no defense as there had been before; no effort to gainsay his entrance. He pushed against her barriers and felt them go down, collapsing, like a castle made of sand.

—fear—

That he could deal with easily. For the first time in his life he did not try to soothe her. He did not try to banish the fear from her mind. Instead, he intensified it, letting her see what he could do.

Aislinn moaned.

—a stirring in her mind—

Donal smiled grimly.

—retreat—

Pursuit.

He allowed his awareness to seek out her own, impinging itself upon her will, until she turned and ran from him. In his arms, limp and twitching, she was helpless; in her mind, chased by his will, she was even more so.

Aislinn moaned. She spasmed once, and was still.

Beware the trap-link, even now— He warded himself quickly with what skill he had, drawing in upon himself. He focused, focused, until he could slash through the web of deceit—

—and then he found there was none.

For a moment, he retreated. Then he touched her awareness again, probing it tentatively. He recalled how he had made contact with *something* before, something that had caused him to withdraw as quickly as he could. But this time, there was nothing. No shadow of a link. No trace of any meddling. Aislinn was simply *Aislinn*.

—and nothing but innocence—

He touched her emotions then. Fear was uppermost. But he caught also the last fading traces of love and trust, as though she knew, even as he forced her, he would never hurt her.

But I have!

Donal withdrew at once. He fell out of her mind and into his own, aware he had stolen will and wits from her. It was worse, far worse than what Finn had done in his testing. This time it had been much more.

"Aislinn!" His hands still clasped her shoulders. She hung limply in his arms. But her eyes were open. And blank. "Aislinn—*come back*—" He shook her. *Oh gods— what have I done to her*—?

He heard, dimly, voices outside the door. Bronwyn, calling to ask him what was wrong. But he could not take time to answer.

He pulled Aislinn against his chest, pressing her against it as if she were a child. "Aislinn—*Aislinn*—oh gods, do you hear me? Aislinn—*I was wrong*—"

Her belly moved. He felt it. It spasmed against his own. In horror, he realized he had brought on her labor too soon.

Carefully, so carefully, he lay her down against the bed. Still her eyes stared blankly at the roof beams. Donal felt bile rise up to fill his mouth, and turned to flee the room.

Bronwyn stood in the open doorway, one hand pressed against her mouth. Behind her stood several others; faces he knew but could not name.

He stopped. He stared at them. And then, as, Aislinn cried out in pain, he pushed through them all and ran.

—and ran, until he burst through the hammered silver doors and nearly fell into the Great Hall.

It was empty. Sunlight slanted through the stained glass casements and cast their shapes upon the floor, all tales of Homanan lore. That, and Cheysuli history. But Donal hardly saw them.

Instead, he saw the Lion. It crouched upon the dais as if it stalked him, hunching in long grass. But there was no grass, only the cold heart of rose-red stone and the ivory, gold-veined marble dais. The Lion was brown and gilt and gold; its shape was static, trapped in aging wood. But Donal could almost see it beckon.

Slowly, he walked the length of the hall. He was surrounded by ornaments of the past, relics other men kept to remind themselves of what they once had been. Tapestries worked by their women to show their feats of strength and glory. Weapons hung up upon the stone, stained dark with forgotten blood. Banners, some faded to dreary monotones; keepsakes of ancient wars. But even without them, even without the banners, weapons, and tapestries, and the glowing, brilliant casements, there was yet another monument to the men who had lived before.

And its name is Homana-Mujhar.

Donal stopped before the dais. In the dim, pink light of mid-morning in the hall, he looked upon the Lion. And felt old. Old and wrong.

He sat down. But not upon the throne. Instead, he turned his back on the silent Lion and settled upon the dais. He stared into the firepit, empty of coals or logs.

He thought of going to his chambers, but he could not face his *lir*. Even in their silence, Taj and Lorn would make him confront the truth. And so he faced the guilt alone.

His eyes burned. His throat was raw. His chest was heavy with the weight of what he had done. He waited for someone to come.

—to tell me she is dead—

But he was not expecting Evan.

He heard the footsteps. He did not look up. He stared blindly at the fabric of his breeches stretched over his doubled knees. He sat with elbows in his lap; hands dangled between his thighs, hair falling into his face.

Evan walked the length of the hall until he reached the dais. After a moment's hesitation, he joined him on the smooth, cool marble. "Is there anything I can do?"

"No." He hardly knew his own voice. "I think *I* have done enough."

Evan sighed. For the briefest moment their shared silence was almost companionable, lacking the tension of knowledge. "I arrived a week ago. There was no need for me to stay—the war with Atvia is over." He shifted his seat upon the stone. "When you slew Osric, you took the heart from them. Two days after you left, the Atvians sent an envoy to our camp, offering their surrender."

"That is something." Donal ran a hand through his hair and stripped it from his face. "Evan—"

"Alaric, I think, will also offer fealty," Evan went on, "but—he is home in Atvia, fighting Shea of Erinn over a silly, pompous title: Lord of the Idrian Isles." His tone was underscored with contempt. "Still, I think he will come. I think he will ask alliance." Again, he shifted on the dais. "Rowan has gone on to Solinde. The rebellion there is nearly finished; he should be home in a month or two, with words of victory. I do not know why those fools still fight. . . . They lack Tynstar now. Their cause is no better than it was before. They should give up."

"They want freedom from Homana," Donal said dully. "I might be moved to give it to them—except Carillon was the one who won the realm, and I cannot let go of what he has held. Not if I wish to keep the Homanans satisfied." He sighed. "If I could know Solinde would never again invade Homana—" He shook his head. "But I cannot. Not yet. Perhaps—someday."

"Perhaps. After more wars."

Donal thought of the battles he had seen. He thought of how he had slain Osric in retribution for Carillon's death, and because Finn had asked it. He had been proud to know that he had accomplished the task his uncle had set him; now, seated on cool, hard marble with the Lion crouching behind him, he could think only of the young woman, Carillon's daughter, whom he had effectively slain.

He shut his eyes. "You know what I have done."

"I know what you have done."

"And will you curse me for it? I know the others will. The Homanans—" He broke off. "Gods—they have every night. I nearly slew the Queen. And if I am exceedingly fortunate, this will not begin a war."

"Aye," Evan agreed. Then, gently, "How could you think it of her, Donal? Aislinn is not the enemy."

"Not the enemy, no; the victim. Sorcha's victim, as much as Sorcha was victim herself." He buried his head in his hands, pressing his forehead. "Oh, gods—how can I believe it? Sorcha—gone . . . and making Aislinn look so guilty!"

"She must have been very unhappy. To love you so much and yet hate you so much—"

"Hate *me?*" Donal's head snapped up. "It was *Aislinn* she hated, and the Homanans."

"And you. For leaving her, even briefly." Evan shook his head. "I never knew her. I cannot explain much about her, except to say that there are women—and men—whose affection becomes obsession."

"She said I would turn away from the clans. Turn away from our customs. Seek instead the Homanan way of living."

"And you did." Evan put up a silencing hand. "No, *I* know you did not—but it probably appeared so to her. You were gone for months on end. You wed Aislinn, then went away to war. Returned long enough to get a child on your

Homanan wife, then got captured by the Ihlini. Sorcha met with Aislinn, as Rowan said, and undoubtedly the discussion was—*heated*. Aislinn has a powerful pride. No doubt Sorcha thought she had lost you for good, and to the *Homanans*. And so she went away, intending to take her own life, but intending also to make it look as if Aislinn had driven her to it.''

''And succeeded.'' He dug fingers into his hair. ''Evan—'' He broke it off. Meghan had come into the hall.

''Donal?'' Her call echoed in the timbers. ''Donal?''

She comes with news of Aislinn— Donal shut his eyes. ''Aye?'' he said. ''Meghan—I am here.''

She picked up her skirts and hastened toward the dais. ''Donal—you have a son!''

He stared at her as she arrived before them both, a little breathless; gods knew how long she had been looking for him. ''A son?''

Tawny hair tumbled over her shoulders. ''A healthy son, Donal. She has given you an heir.''

He felt the guilt rise up to stab him in the belly. ''Aislinn?'' he asked hoarsely.

Meghan raked a hand through her shining hair. ''She is—very weak. Donal . . . you had best go to her.''

He felt cold, cold and empty, sucked dry of all but the knowledge of his guilt. Slowly he pushed himself to his feet. ''Aye . . . I will go.''

When at last he looked upon his wife, he saw a child in the bed; a child whose glorious hair spread across the pillows in rich red disarray. Her fair skin was whiter still with the waxy look of the ill. Gold-tipped lashes lay against the dark circles beneath her eyes. The bedclothes were pulled up under her chin, but one arm lay across the coverlet, blue-veined against the fairness of her flesh.

Oh gods, what have I done to her? How could you let me do it? But he knew, even as he asked it, the question was unfair. He had only himself to blame.

Donal sat down on the edge of her bed. He was alone with her, having dismissed her women, and now all he wanted was to see her looking at him from her great gray, shining eyes.

Electra's eyes— Abruptly he shook his head. *No, her own. I am done laying Electra's machinations at the feet of her innocent daughter.*

He smoothed the strands of fine hair back from her brow. He traced the winged line of her eyebrows and the cool silk of her eyelids. "Aislinn," he said. "She was all I ever wanted. A Cheysuli warrior may take as many women as he chooses, providing the women are willing, but for me— for me it was always Sorcha. Ever since we were young." He looked down on her pale, still face. "You yourself are so young—you cannot know what it is to love someone from childhood—" He broke it off. *By all the gods!—I wrong her again, as I have wronged her all along. I pride myself on knowing I have loved Sorcha all these years—and all the while I was no younger than Aislinn is now when I knew what Sorcha meant to me. She bore me a child when she was not so much younger than Aislinn is now. Gods— I have been such a selfish brute—*

He clasped her hand in his. Then, slowly, he slid off the bed and knelt beside it, setting his forehead against the silk of the counterpane.

He sent the call winging deep into the earth, praying the magic would answer him though he had already used it wrongly. He could not afford another mistake. Not with her life at stake.

Donal drifted. He felt the wispy, tensile strength of the magic in the earth. He abased himself before it, admitting freely his guilt. He did not hide what he had done. He opened himself up to the omniscience of the earth and let it see what manner of man he was.

And at last, when he thought it would not answer, the power flowed up from the earth to bathe Aislinn in its magic.

When Aislinn roused, moving beneath the bedclothes like a fretful child, he released her fingers and rose. He put out his hand and caught the nearest bedpost to steady himself; he was dizzy, disoriented. The healing should not have been done alone. He had nearly lost himself within the overwhelming power of the magic, and he still trembled from the knowledge. But he felt the risk worth it;

after what he done *to* her, it was time he did something *for* her.

But Aislinn stared up at him in astonishment. "No," she whispered, clearly terrified. "Oh, gods . . . *no*—"

"It heals," he said hoarsely. "All it does is heal. I promise you that—"

"Promise *me?* You will slay me!" Her eyes were blackened by fear. "As you sought to slay me *before*—"

"No." He said it as clearly as he could, but his mouth did not work properly. He felt his knees buckle and clung desperately to the bedpost, sliding slowly to the floor. "I sought—sought only to know the truth. . . . I would *not* have slain you—I swear—"

Aislinn stared at him like a doe cornered by the huntsman. Red-gold hair tumbled over her shoulders; her mouth trembled. "I loved you," she said. "I loved you all my life. But—you already had *her*." Color crept into her waxen cheeks. "It was you I wanted, Donal—ever since I was a child. And—I wanted to bear children for you, as many as I could—but even *that* she had already given you!" One shaking hand was touched to her mouth as if she sought to halt her words, but she let them spill out with a ragged dignity. "There was no gift left I could give you that *she* had not already given—*no gift at all* . . . oh *aye*, I wanted her gone—I *wanted her gone from here!* But I *swear* I did not send her. Donal, I did *not!*"

"I know." He held himself up against the post. "I know it, Aislinn—"

"What have you done to me?" Tears spilled down her face. *"What have you done to me?"*

"Healing," he mumbled, "only healing. I want you strong again."

She recoiled utterly. "Why? So you may send me away as my father sent my mother?"

Donal felt his last reserve crumble. All the savage grief he had tried to suppress surged up into his chest until he nearly choked on it. He took handfuls of the silken counterpane, clenched it tightly in white-knuckled fists and wept. "I have no one." It hissed through a throat nearly sealed by grief. *"I have no one left at all*—" he closed his eyes "—except for you."

Aislinn said nothing at all.

"*Tahlmorra*," he said thickly. "All of it—" And he put his face down against the bed and knelt before her, a suppliant to the gods.

Aislinn's breath was audible. *"Do you expect forgiveness?"*

He heard the savagery in her tone. "No," he said, but the word was muffled against the bed.

"Then what *do* you want from me?"

He lifted his head and saw her face. The deathbed pallor was replaced by an angry flush high in her cheeks. Her emotion-darkened eyes glittered balefully.

"I want you to live," he told her plainly. "I ask for nothing from you save that."

"Why? So you may hurt me again?" Her hand shook as she touched her breast. "So you may hurt my heart again?"

Her broken, vulnerable tone broke the final barriers against emotion. "What promises can I make you?" he asked in desperation. "What words would you have me say? After all I have done to you, do you expect me to change with a wave of a hand?" He felt bitterness in his mouth. "Would you wish to have me beg? I will do it."

"Beg *me?*" She stared.

He shut his eyes. "Tell me what you want."

She swallowed heavily. "Once—I wanted your love. But that was too much to ask . . . you had given it to her." Tears ran down her face. One shaking hand tried to hide the quivering of her mouth. "I only—I only wanted a chance—a *chance* to know what it was—"

He could not answer her. He could only shut his eyes and put his head down on the bed again.

"You do not love me." The intonation was precise, as if she wished to make it clear.

He looked at her sharply, fearing she sickened again. But he saw high color in her face and a startled recognition in her eyes. "You do not love me," she repeated, with wonder in her voice, "but you *need* me. *You* need *me*."

The breath slipped out of his throat. "I need you," he admitted. "By all the gods, *I do*."

Aislinn stared at him a long moment, all manner of emotion in her face. He saw anger and pain and grief and regret, but he also saw something else. Something akin to *possessiveness*.

"Well," she said in an intense, peculiar triumph, "perhaps that will be enough."

Nine

Evan raised his goblet. "To Niall, the Prince of Homana. Four weeks old and thriving."

Donal smiled. He brought up his goblet to clash against Evan's, then drank down a swallow of wine.

They sat over their cups in Donal's private solar. Sunlight spilled through the casements. Evan sat slumped deeply in a chair; Donal stretched out on a snow bear pelt with Lorn collapsed against his side. Taj perched on a chairback.

Evan put up his feet on a three-legged stool. "What will you do about Strahan?"

Donal scowled into his cup of wine. "What *can* I do? He is Ihlini—he has what freedom he can steal."

"Could you not set a trap for him?"

"He has gone underground. There is no word of him. He could be in Valgaard by now, high in the Molon Mountains. He could be in Solinde, sheltered by those who still serve the Ihlini. He could be almost anywhere, Evan—there is nothing I can do. Except wait." *And the gods know I will do that, no matter how long it takes.*

Evan sighed and swirled his wine. "I know, I know—but it seems so futile to do nothing. You know he will do what he can to throw you down from the throne."

"He is a boy," Donal said. "I discount neither his power nor his heritage—but he *is* a boy. I think it likely he will wait until he grows older, old enough to inspire trust in other men. Oh, he will lead the Ihlini on the strength of his blood alone—but how many others will follow? I think he will play at patience."

"Donal?" It was Aislinn, standing in the open doorway. "A messenger has just come with word from Alaric of Atvia. It seems he is in Mujhara, intending to see you."

Donal pressed himself upright. "Alaric is *here?*"

Evan nodded. "I said he would come, did I not? He will offer fealty, does he have any sense at all."

Aislinn, hair braided and threaded with silver cord, pulled her pale green mantle more closely about her shoulders. "Shall we have his baggage moved into the palace?"

Donal, frowning, nodded. "Aye. It would transgress all decency did we leave him at an inn. Aye, send servants for his baggage. Gods!—I need a bath!"

Evan laughed. "Let him see you as you are."

Donal, draining the rest of his wine, cast Evan a sour glance. "I intend to—but I also intend to show him what courtesy I can muster . . . can I muster *any*." He turned to leave the room. "Aislinn—have Torvald set out fresh clothing."

"Aye," she said. "Cheysuli or Homanan?"

He stopped in the doorway. She faced him squarely, exhibiting no fear. What had passed between them after the healing had fashioned her into another woman.

One I do not know. "Which would you say is more fitting to receive a man who was once an enemy?"

Aislinn smiled. "The shapechanger, my lord. How can you consider anything else?"

Donal received Alaric in the Great Hall, ensconced in the Lion Throne. He had put on blue-dyed Cheysuli leathers and a torque of gold around his throat to match his heavy belt. To Alaric, he did not doubt, he would resemble nothing more than a crude barbarian. Which was precisely what he desired.

So I may lull him into carelessness? On the throne, Donal smiled.

Alaric was nothing like his brother. His height was average, no better; hair and eyes were dark brown. He dressed well but conservatively, in black breeches and velvet doublet, showing no ornamentation other than a silver ring set with black stone on one hand and a narrow chain of office—also silver—around his shoulders. He was accompanied by five Atvian nobles, all dressed more richly than himself, but none of them claimed the same intensity or the air of absolute command Alaric held even in silence.

Donal considered the formal greetings he had learned. He discarded them all at once. He disliked Alaric instantly; he disliked diplomacy even more.

He waited.

Alaric stood before the dais. He inclined his head a trifle. "My lord—I have come to offer fealty—and to tender an alliance."

"Why?" Donal asked.

A minute frown twitched the arched eyebrows. But Alaric's face retained its bland, cool expression. "Plainly, my lord, you have overcome my realm. My brother is slain and I am Lord of Atvia in his place . . . but I do recognize the virtue in admitting our defeat. You have—quite effectively proved your competence as a king."

Donal regarded him appraisingly. "Have I? Enough to keep you from our borders forever?—or only until you rally an army again?"

A muscle jumped in Alaric's shaven face. "A king does not offer fealty to another unless he intends to honor it, my lord."

"Usually." Donal relaxed in the Lion. "Not *always*, but—" He waved a hand. "Enough of this. You offer fealty, which you *owe* me, and an alliance, which undoubtedly *you* need more than I do."

Alaric's mouth was tight. "Aye, my lord—like you, I do not doubt it."

Donal studied him. He knew instinctively Alaric was more than a competent warrior. He was also a strategist. A diplomat. He would give up much to gain more. *But what does he want? And what will he give up in order to get it?* He gestured idly. "Once before you came here. To Carillon, after he slew Thorne, your *jehan.* Then, you said Atvia would offer fealty to no foreign king."

Alaric inclined his head. "I was a boy then. I am a man now—and king in my brother's place—and I must do what is best for my realm."

"Your fealty I will have—you can hardly refuse me now—but the alliance I must consider. What do you offer me?"

Alaric gestured eloquently. "My brother died without heirs. He had two sons, but both are dead of fever. I myself am unmarried, without legitimate heirs. What I offer Homana is quite simple: myself. And a binding peace between our realms when children are born of this match."

Donal frowned. "You wish to wed a Homanan woman?"

"No. I wish to wed your sister."

Donal's hands spasmed against the clawed armrests of the throne. "You wish to wed with *Bronwyn?*"

"Aye, my lord. If that is her name." Alaric did not smile.

Gods . . . he cannot mean *it!* But he knew Alaric did. When he could, he asked a single question. "Why?"

Alaric's smile was very slight. "My lord, I have said—to settle a peace between our lands."

"What *else?* We can make a peace without wedding my *rujholla* to you."

"Perhaps." Alaric's tone was negligent. "Perhaps not. But consider it in this light, if you will: a princess of Homana—though she be Cheysuli—is wed to the Lord of Atvia. From that union, provided the gods see fit to bless it, will come children. Sons, of course. And the eldest to rule in my place when I am dead." Alaric gestured idly. "He would be your nephew, my lord Mujhar—and never an enemy. How better to insure peace between our realms?"

"How better for you to make yourself a claimant for the Lion!" Donal's fist smacked down on the throne. "Do not play me for a fool, Atvian—I am no courtier with silken tongue and oiled palms, but—*by the gods!*—neither am I blind. You desire peace between our realms? Then keep your armies from my borders!"

Alaric's dark brown eyes glittered, but only a little. He kept himself under control. "But of course, my lord—I had intended to. And yet—it seemed such a perfect way to link our realms. As for *me* desiring to claim the Lion Throne, I say no. Of course not. Do you not have a legitimate heir?"

Donal smiled thinly. "Aye, my lord, I do."

"Then the continuance of your House is certainly insured." Alaric smiled. "I offer this alliance because I desire to insure the continuation of *my* House. And nothing more."

"Nothing more?"

"Perhaps support against Shea of Erinn."

Donal sat back again, conforming his back to the crimson cushion. "What quarrel have you with Shea?"

"He has usurped my brother's title: Lord of the Idrian Isles. It was my father's. It was *his* father's. Shea claimed it when Osric died." Alaric shrugged. "I want it back."

Donal frowned. "With Homanan help? Why should I offer that? Homana has no quarrel with Erinn."

"No. Nor do I wish to begin one." Alaric spread his hands. "Mere word of this marriage would send Shea back behind the walls of Kilore and keep him from my shores until I can regroup my demoralized army—demoralized because of my brother's death. I would not ask men of you; my lord, merely the *appearance* of support. It would be more than enough."

Donal frowned at the toes of his soft leather boots. "I cannot see a single sound reason for agreeing to this. It gets Homana nothing. You say it gets us peace, but that we should have anyway. We have defeated you."

Alaric shrugged. "And eventually the Atvian throne. Your nephew will be my heir. There will be Cheysuli princes in Atvia."

Donal shrugged. "I am not so certain that would serve anything—" Abruptly, he stopped speaking. His belly turned in upon itself. *By the gods—it is the prophecy . . . even from the mouth of the enemy!* He stared at Alaric in shock. *Four warring realms—*

He pushed himself back in the throne before he could display his shock to the Atvian. The pattern lay before him as clearly as if Evan had thrown it himself. *If I wed Bronwyn to him, her son will have the throne. Cheysuli in Atvia. Adding one more realm to the prophecy. By the gods, it will come true!*

Bronwyn in Ativa. No, he could not see it. She would never agree. The Cheysuli did not barter women or use them for sealing alliances.

And yet, things changed. So many things *had* to change. His own mother had told him how Finn had stolen her from the Homanans because for years the Cheysuli had needed to steal Homanan women, to strengthen the clan again. It was alien to him, but no less alien than the thought of wedding his sister to Alaric.

If I do it—if I do it—Bronwyn would never forgive me— Alaric still watched silently, all politeness, waiting for an answer. He was like a cat ready to spring, elegant in his readiness; Donal did not like him. He did not like him at all.

Give my **rujholla** *to this* **ku'reshtin** *of Atvia?*

And yet, if he did not and it was part of the prophecy— *I will not decide this* now. *There is no need to decide this* now— He steadied his breathing with effort. And then, as he prepared to give Alaric a diplomatic reason to delay the expected answer, he realized with blinding clarity the marriage could never take place. Even if the prophecy demanded it.

Slowly, Donal sat back. "You are guests of Homana," he said evenly. *"Cheysuli i'halla shansu."* But he knew he did not mean it.

Alaric frowned as Donal moved to rise. "My lord—your answer? May I know when you will give it?"

Donal stood. "I give it now," he said. "My *rujholla* may never marry."

Bronwyn, whom he tracked down in Aislinn's solar, looked on in silence as he banished everyone from the chamber save herself. She stood before an open casement with light falling on her shoulders. She wore a simple indigo gown embroidered with interlocking leaves in silver thread. He looked at her silently, wondering when she had grown up. She had done it without his knowledge; he clearly recalled her girlish laughter at his wedding; her tomboyish way at the Keep. Now she was a woman. Only sixteen and still young, but there was a new maturity in her eyes and grace to her movements.

He gestured her to sit down upon a stool even as he himself did. "A man is here," he said. "He has come to Homana-Mujhar because he wishes to wed the Mujhar's *rujholla*."

Color blossomed in her cheeks. "Wed *me?*"

"Aye. He offers you the chance to be a queen."

"Queen!" Bronwyn was clearly shocked. "Who would wish *me* to be his queen?"

"Alaric of Atvia."

Bronwyn shot to her feet. *"Alaric of Atvia!"*

Donal rose slowly. He heard the horror in her tone. *At least I may save her that.* "Bronwyn—Bronwyn, you do not have to wed him. I promise you that. Do not think I will send you away."

She shut her eyes. A breath of relief hissed out of her mouth. "Thank the gods—*thank the gods*—I thought it might be a political thing—" She shuddered. "There are dangers in being *rujholla* to the Mujhar."

"It *would* be a political thing," Donal pointed out. "Alaric offers alliance to Homana. It would also be a dynastic thing, binding the realms together."

She understood him perfectly. "It—seems to be sound reasoning—to bind the realms together." Her tone was very flat.

"Bronwyn, you need fear nothing. There can be no royal marriage. There can be no marriage at all."

"Not with Alaric." Relief put life back into her tone. "But someday—"

"No." He said it plainly, wishing to have it done with. "Bronwyn, you will never be able to marry."

She stared. "Have you gone mad? Of *course* I will marry! What would keep me from it?"

"I would." He said it flatly. "I have no other choice."

She laughed. The tone was incredulous and perplexed. "You *have* gone mad. Donal . . . *what are you saying?*"

He reached out and caught her shoulders. "That because of the blood in you, I can never let you wed. You can never bear any children."

She went stiff in his hands. He felt the convulsive shiver that shook her limbs. She tore herself from his grasp. "You are mad—you are *mad*—how can you say such things? How can you tell me this?" Slowly she shook her head. "Do you think my children would threaten the throne? By the gods, Donal—I am your *rujholla!* Our *jehana* bore us both! Our *jehan*—"

"—sired only me." He saw the spasm in her face. "Gods, Bronwyn, I wish I could spare you this. I wish it were not true. But—when you say I fear your children may threaten the throne—you may have the right of it. I cannot shut my eyes to the possibility."

Her eyes were fixed on his face. "You said—you said we do not share a *jehan*—"

"No. Another man sired you."

"*Who?*" she demanded. "Gods, *rujho*, I beg you who I am—"

He felt the tightness his throat. "You are *Tynstar's daughter.*"

Silence. Bronwyn stared. He could not look away.

"Oh—" she said. "Oh—oh—*no*—"

"Aye," he told her gently, and reached out to steady her.

Slowly he guided her to the stool and made her sit down again. "Bronwyn, you are still my *rujholla*, still our *jehana*'s daughter. Almost half Cheysuli, and bloodkin to the clan. It changes nothing. It changes nothing."

"It changes *everything*." The words were dead in her mouth.

"No, Bronwyn, it does not. Do you think I will send you away? There is too much blood between us—"

"—too much *spilled* blood between us." She looked up blankly to meet his gaze. "Why was I never told?"

"There was no reason for for it. You were raised Cheysuli—it was hoped you would never show Tynstar's power. And unless you have purposely hidden it—you never have."

Trembling, she touched the vicinity of her heart. "I have ever felt Cheysuli . . . Cheysuli and Homanan."

"You are both. You are. But—there is also Ihlini in you."
"How—?"

Donal sat down again. "You have heard how Tynstar had our *jehana* taken to Valgaard. I was just a boy. I wanted me as well, but I managed to escape." He looked down at her shaking hands as she clutched them in her lap. "He kept our *jehana* captive. And while she was there—"

"—he raped her?" Bronwyn shuddered. "Gods, oh gods—it makes me feel so *dirty*—"

"No!" He reached out and caught her hands. "It has nothing to do with you."

"But I do not *feel* Ihlini!" she cried. "How do you know it is true?"

He put out his arms as she slid off the stool to kneel on the floor. He soothed her head against his shoulder, as if she were Isolde requiring special comfort. One arm slid around her shoulders. He held her close, knowing he could never share her grief.

A woman told she cannot bear a child— He shut his eyes. He whispered inanities.

Bronwyn clutched at his leather jerkin. "I begin to see— all the times I sensed a barrier between us . . . something keeping us apart. That was it, was it not? The knowledge I was Tynstar's daughter?"

"Oh *rujholla*, I would do anything to lift this grief from you."

"*Jehana* never said. *Never* did she say—"

"She told it to no one. Only a few of us knew, and none of us ever spoke of it to others."

"Why did you let me live?" The question was hardly a sound.

"Bronwyn! Oh, *gods*, Bronwyn—do you think we would *ever* desire to have you slain? What do you think we are?"

"You are Cheysuli. And—I am the enemy."

"No enemy. *No enemy!*" And yet he recalled all the times he had watched her, wondering, and felt the guilt in his soul. *Not an* intentional *enemy.*

"But you will never let me wed." The tears welled up again. "Do you distrust me so much? Do you think I will work against you? Do you think I would ever aid the boy who slew our *su'fali?*" Bronwyn shook her head. "Gods, Donal—I would *never* do such a thing! You know I would not. We are kin. There is blood between us."

"There is blood between you and Strahan." He shook his head. "It is not *you* I do not trust—it is how your power might be used. By another, if not by you."

"Power!" she shook her head. "I *have* no power, Donal. I would know it. I swear—I would know it. There is nothing in me. Do you think I would not know?"

"Bronwyn—"

"Then test me." She rose and stood before him. "*Test* me, Donal! See if there is power."

He shook his head. "Bronwyn, I could not—"

"You did it to Aislinn!" she snapped.

"*And* I nearly slew her! Gods, Bronwyn, *have sense!* Do you think I wish to harm you?"

"You harm me now," she said. "You tell me I cannot wed, cannot bear children—you name me Tynstar's daughter. How can I live with that? You have given me a life of emptiness!"

He could not answer. He had no answer for her.

"Donal," she said, "I beg you."

He threaded his fingers into hers and pulled her down to kneel against the tapestry rug. He looked into her eyes. "Do I do this—do I test you, and learn you are Ihlini . . . you must promise never to wed. Never to bear a child."

Bronwyn shut her eyes. "*Ja'hai-na,*" she said. "Accepted."

*   *   *

Tentatively, he parted the curtain of her awareness. He slid through, hardly disturbing the threads of his sister's consciousness. What she felt he could not say; what he felt was a sudden unexpected communion that nearly threw him out of the link. It had been different with Aislinn, who had received him unwillingly. What he had done to her was little different from rape. But Bronwyn understood. Bronwyn desired his presence. She welcomed him willingly, but he sensed a trace of fear. She was not certain what he would find.

Gently. Gently. He left no residue of his passing.

The barriers went down.

In the web of her consciousness he saw the junctions of inner knowledge that buried itself so deeply. He allowed his own awareness to expand, touching the junctions carefully. He feared no trap-link in his sister, but it was possible that Ihlini were born with warding powers. That somehow, unconsciously, she would move to throw him back.

But she did not. He sensed only complete acceptance; a trust that nearly unmanned him. She had seen what he did to Aislinn, yet she did not fear the same for herself.

Gently, he expanded his awareness. And her own surged up to meet him.

Patterns linked. Meshed. Knotted. Everything fell into place.

He knew, without a doubt, Duncan had sired them both.

Bronwyn sagged. He caught her against his chest and stood up, holding her on her feet. Gently, he said her name, until she opened her eyes. She was dazed, clearly disoriented. But sense moved into her eyes.

"Rujho?"

He hugged her as hard as he dared. *"Rujho,* aye—there is no Ihlini in you." He felt the tears in his eyes. *All those years, all those years . . . oh* rujholla, *how we all have wronged you—*

Bronwyn's laughter was little more than a breath of sound. "It was worth it, *rujho . . .* oh, it was! To know I am not that demon's daughter!" She hugged him, laughing against his chest. But then she went stiff in his arms.

"Gods—*oh gods*—there was the boy! *He* told me the truth—"

Donal drew back. "Bronwyn—"

Her hand was at her mouth. "He said—oh, I recall it so well! We sat outside *su'fali*'s pavilion while he tested Aislinn. He showed me those runes—he asked me to try my own—" Her breath was harsh in her throat. "None of this was necessary! Sef gave me the answer *then*."

"Sef! What answer could *he* give—" And then he recalled it also. How he had seen them kneeling in the dust, drawing foreign runes.

Bronwyn nodded. "Something he said made no sense. I thought nothing of it. But—he said I was not who you thought I was." She frowned, shaking her head. "It made no sense: *You are not the woman your brother thinks you are*." She clutched at his shoulders. "Oh gods, Donal—he knew—he *knew* I was not Ihlini!"

"He tested you." The words were bitter in his mouth. "Even as Finn tested Aislinn, Strahan tested you."

Bronwyn shuddered. "How could I have been such a fool—?"

"No more so than any of us." Donal loosened his arms and turned her toward the door. "I am no less glad than you are to have it settled at last. But we have no more time for it now, either of us. Bathe and dress yourself as fits a princess, Bronwyn—we feast the Atvian tonight."

Bronwyn made a face. "Could I not plead sickness? I would rather not see this man who thought I would wed him."

"Let him see *you*—to know what he has lost."

She laughed. But then she frowned. "But I have nothing to wear!"

Donal merely sighed.

Ten

Donal saw Alaric's amazement when first he set eyes on Bronwyn. Undoubtedly he had prepared himself to charm a barbaric Cheysuli woman who hardly understood the niceties of courtship. Instead, he saw a lovely young woman in copper-colored silk with her heavy hair bound up in a mass of looped, shining braids pinned against her head with gold. Garnets glittered at ears and throat; a matching girdle of tiny bells dripped down her heavy skirts.

Donal realized, as he watched her, she knew precisely what she was about. He smiled inwardly. *Does my young* rujholla *play at being a woman? Well—perhaps she should. No longer is she a girl.*

Bronwyn, during the feast in the Great Hall, was seated next to Alaric. Donal, watching them both, noticed how quickly Alaric saw through his partner's subterfuge. He did not set out to charm her, as he had undoubtedly first intended; instead, he spoke courteously and sparingly. But Bronwyn was not won over.

Throughout the feast Alaric and his countrymen were unceasingly polite to the Homanan nobles. Nowhere was there a sign of hostility or resentment. Nor were there any signs the Atvians considered themselves the vanquished. They moved quickly, smoothly, speaking of unification. More and more Donal saw how members of the Homanan Council looked first at Alaric and then at Bronwyn. More and more he saw consideration in their eyes.

They will *ask,* he knew. *Oh, aye, they* will *ask . . . and I will have to answer them.*

And after the food was taken away, with Donal in an adjoining antechamber, the council members asked.

Donal listened. He heard the arguments for and against the match. Some members said Atvia was too distant, too unknown; the Mujhar could never keep constant watch on political happenings. Others said the match would unify the two realms, much as Carillon's marriage to Electra had, while it lasted, unified Homana and Solinde—save for a few insurgents who fought against the alliance.

But it was an elderly man, Vallis, former counselor to Shaine himself, who spoke most clearly to them all. "Many of us, my lord Mujhar, understand we are here to serve the gods. Cheysuli, Homanan . . . it does not really matter by what names we call our gods. It merely matters that we serve them." He was in his eighties, and frail, with a thin, soft voice and thinner hair. The dome of his skull was mottled pink. Only the merest fringe of fine white hair curled around his ears. "While it is true as Homanans we do not dedicate ourselves to this prophecy of the Firstborn, we do acknowledge its existence. We do not discount it—or *should* not." He looked at each of the men with rheumy, pale blue eyes. "Before the purge, Cheysuli and Homanans intermarried. You yourself, my lord, claim blood from both those races. And does not this prophecy say there must be more?"

Donal agreed warily.

Vallis nodded. "What I tell you now is by wedding your sister to Alaric of Atvia, you move one step closer to fulfilling that prophecy."

"I am aware of that." Donal kept his tone very even, giving nothing away of his private thoughts. "Say on, Vallis."

The old man braced himself against a chair. Ropes of veins stood up beneath his flesh. "Prince Niall bears the blood of Homana and Solinde, as well as the Cheysuli. Do you wed your sister to Alaric, and she bears him a daughter, in time that daughter could be wed to the Prince of Homana."

Donal raised his brows. "And does she bear him a son instead?"

Vallis shrugged narrow shoulders. "Doubtless by *then*, you and the Queen will have daughters enough to wed into every royal House."

He felt their eyes upon him. Slowly he walked to a casement and stared out, though he could see little in the darkness. Then he turned to face them. "Bronwyn does not desire it.

Some of the others smiled. Some faces expressed outright surprise. He knew his statement made no sense to them; Homanans wed their daughters to men most able to advance their rank or wealth.

Like bartering horses. He shook his head. "Bronwyn does not desire it."

They knew it was his answer. They had learned that much of him since he had become Mujhar. And so they filed from the antechamber and back into the hall, while Vallis stayed behind.

"My lord," he said, "I know you value your sister. Do not lump me in with the others. I am an old, old man . . . I have seen the Cheysuli elevated by Shaine and then destroyed by him—I know your customs well. She is not a broodmare. She is not a ewe. She is not a favorite bitch. She is a woman, a Cheysuli woman . . . but she is also a part of the prophecy." Slowly, the old man put out a palsied hand. Palm uppermost, with the fingers spreading. *"Tahlmorra lujhala mei wiccan, cheysu."*

Donal turned and left the chamber, returning to the hall.

Evan came up to him, holding two cups of wine. One he held out. "So solemn, Donal . . . did they put you into a corner and make you listen to their babble?"

Donal, smiling grimly, accepted the wine. "You know court habits very well."

Evan laughed. "Ellas is no different! Only the language." But his laughter died away. "I must go, Donal. It is time I went back to Ellas."

The taste of the wine turned flat. "Evan! So soon?"

"Soon?" Evan stared. "I have been here nearly a year."

"Stay another."

He shook his head. "I cannot. It is time I went home. There are things in Ellas for me."

Donal drank down the rest of his wine, gave the empty cup to a passing servant and got another to replace it. He saw his sister across the hall, laughing with Aislinn and Meghan. "Have you told Meghan you intend to leave?"

Evan's mouth turned down wryly. "No. I dislike tears cried into my velvet doublets."

"Tears from *Meghan?*" Donal shook his head. "She is stronger than you think."

"Oh, aye—strong . . . if you count willfulness as strength." Evan scowled into his wine. "No, no tears from Meghan. But I could wish for more complaisance."

"I warned you," Donal told him. "She is not meant for just any man. Not even for Evan of Ellas—does he desire no more than an evening in her bed."

"Ah, but he does desire more." Evan ran the rim of the cup across his bottom lip. "Lodhi protect me—but I invited her home with me."

"To *Ellas?*" Donal stared at Evan in surprise. "Did you really think she would go?"

"I—hoped." Evan shrugged. "It was useless. She refused me."

Donal saw the genuine unhappiness in the Ellasian's sleepy eyes. It was not like Evan to exhibit anything other than mild distress when a woman refused him; it did not happen very often, and generally he found another who suited him as well. But Meghan was different. And Donal realized Evan knew it.

He smiled. "I am sorry. She may be Cheysuli, but there is Homanan in her also. Living so close to Aislinn lately may have given her Homanan sensibilities when it comes to such things as men."

"Because she would not become my light woman?" Evan shook his head. "But I asked her to wed me."

"*You?*"

"Aye," Evan said gloomily. "And a waste of time it was."

Donal sighed. "I am sorry. I did not know it had gone so far."

"Oh, it had not. But I thought it was the only way I might get her to lie with me." Evan grinned. "Unlike all of the others, she did not believe I meant it."

Donal laughed and nearly spilled his wine. "You fool! Do you forget she is Finn's daughter? She will take a man on *her* terms, if she takes a man at all."

Evan raised his goblet. "To Meghan," he said. "And to the warrior who sired her."

Donal lifted his cup. And then, abruptly, he told Evan not to go. "What will I do without you?"

"Learn to govern Homana without me to offer bad advice." Evan shook his head. "My time here is done. I am sorry—but I must go."

"When?"

"Probably in the morning. Or, depending on my head after this celebration, perhaps in the afternoon. But I do have to go."

Donal reached out and clasped his arm. "In advance, I will wish you safe journey and good fortune in your games. And—I wish I did not have to lose you."

"No more than Carillon wished to lose Lachlan." Evan grinned. "But I am not so bound by responsibility as my brother, and I think I will come back. At least to bother Meghan once or twice more."

Donal released Evan's arm and glanced back across the hall. Alaric still lingered near Bronwyn. *Hoping, no doubt, she will have him. But why does he want her? What does he expect her to bring? Peace with Homana? Support for the island wars? Gods—I wish I could read that man.*

But he could not. Grimly, he drank more Falian wine. "You have heard, of course, that Alaric wishes to wed with Bronwyn."

Evan's tone was wry. "Who has not, by now? But—with her Ihlini blood, you dare not allow the match."

"She has no Ihlini blood. I tested her today."

"None!" Evan turned sharply to him. "None at all?"

"She is my full *rujholla*, Evan. She is Duncan's daughter."

The Ellasian shook his head, frowning perplexedly. "Then—if you could have tested her all along, why did you wait so long?"

"Because it could not have been done without her knowledge, without her willingness." Donal sighed. "It was our *jehana*. She wished to leave Bronwyn in peace. She did not wish to awaken potential powers *or* bring grief to Bronwyn. And so—she was kept in innocence."

Evan's blue eyes were fixed on the girl as she laughed with her two kinswomen. "Then—there is nothing preventing this marriage."

"No," Donal said. "There is nothing preventing this marriage."

Evan looked at him sharply. "Lodhi!—you *do* intend to honor Alaric's request!"

Donal shut his fingers on the heavy cup. "All my life I have been told there would be choices placed before me. Choices I would hate. I knew it, of course—but it is so easy to push the knowledge away." He heard the unevenness in his voice and worked to steady it. "I remember all the times I wanted to call Carillon a fool because of the choices he made . . . particularly the ones he made regarding *me*. And now—now it will be *Bronwyn's* turn to ask me what I do, and how—in the name of all the gods—can I possibly even *consider* it."

"I understand what you do." Evan said. "Being a prince, I can hardly *mis*understand why you do it. But—I do not envy you."

"No," Donal agreed. "But too many other people do."

Donal stepped forward. He waited until his stillness silenced them all. And then he beckoned Alaric forward. "Tonight, in this hall, we feast you, my lord of Atvia. Tonight we give you good welcome and blessings for your health. But you came to us with a purpose, that being to pledge us your fealty." Donal met Alaric's wary eyes. He did not smile. "Then pledge it, my lord. Here in this hall before us all."

Alaric's lips parted. Briefly, Donal saw the tic of a muscle in his jaw. But he knelt. In elegance, he knelt, making it not an act of submission but of calm willingness to sacrifice anything for his realm.

Donal unsheathed the Cheysuli sword. The ruby blazed in the pommel as he raised the blade toward Alaric's face. "Swear," he said, "by all the gods you have."

Alaric bent forward. He placed his lips upon the rune-chased blade and gave it the kiss of fealty. "I swear by all the gods of Atvia, by my rank and by my birth, that I am vassal to Donal of Homana. My sword, my life, is his. I pledge this in all good faith. I break this oath only upon my death. My liege—will you accept me?"

Unless he were a false man, willingly surrendering birthright and royal holdings, Alaric *would* die before renouncing so binding an oath. Donal did not believe the Atvian would risk his place so casually.

"I accept your oath and do hold you by it," he agreed. "Rise, my lord of Atvia."

Alaric rose. His intense gaze did not move from Donal's face. He waited.

Donal slid home the sword in his sheath. "By my right as Mujhar of Homana, I enter into willing alliance with this man. Let all know there is peace between our realms." He inhaled a steadying breath. "By my right as Mujhar of Homana, I enter into willing agreement with this man: that this oath of fealty be sealed with a wedding. He has asked for my sister in marriage."

He heard Bronwyn's gasp clearly. "Donal! Donal—*no!* You said I would not have to!" She thrust herself out of the crowd to face him in the center of the hall. She did not look at Alaric. "You *said*—"

"I said." His tone was harsher than he meant it to be: "I said, aye. But now it must be done."

"My lord." It was Alaric, urbane and calmly pleased. "My lord, you honor me."

"I do not honor you. I honor the prophecy." He would not hide the truth, blatant though it was; he would not hide his open dislike of the man. "Because of *that*, my lord of Atvia, I will give Bronwyn into marriage. But there are agreements you must make."

Alaric inclined his head and spread his hands. "Name them, my lord."

"That should Bronwyn bear you a son and heir, any daughter the Queen of Homana bears *me* shall be wed to him, thus fixing the succession." He did not smile. "That should Bronwyn bear you a *daughter*, that daughter will come to Homana and wed Niall, the Prince of Homana."

Alaric's smile was one of subtle triumph. "Aye, my lord, I agree."

"*Ku'reshtin!*" Bronwyn cried. "You are no *rujholli* of mine!"

"Fetch a priest," Donal told a servant.

"How can you do this to me?"

He looked into her angry face. "For the prophecy, I will do anything."

It was quickly done; too quickly. The priest was brought. The ceremony performed in front of everyone present over loud protestations from Bronwyn; so loud Donal doubted anyone else could hear the vows. It did not seem to matter to Alaric. He smiled a cool, satisfied smile. But the priest was clearly offended by her words. And a Homanan priest at that.

At last Donal stepped in and caught her elbow. "*Ruj-holla*," he said quietly, "you lend credence to the belief we are little more than beasts with such noise."

"Noise!" She stared at him through tear-filled amber eyes. "I will make more *noise* than this, given the chance. I want no part of this!"

"It is done," he told her. "You are wife to Alaric of Atvia."

"And I promise a fine celebration when we have reached Rondule," Alaric said calmly.

"I want nothing to do with *celebrations!* I want nothing to do with *you*. I want *none* of it, do you hear? And I want none of my *rujholli*, who turns his back on Cheysuli customs!"

"Bronwyn—"

"You *do!*" she cried. "You sell me off to a stranger, just to make an *alliance*—"

"Bronwyn, you cheapen your *jehana*'s name with such behavior."

"*You* cheapen it as well, Donal." Bronwyn shut her eyes a moment, teeth clenched so hard the muscles stood up along her jaw. "I swear, *I swear*, when I am given the chance I will show you all what gifts I claim. I will *show* you what the Old Blood means—"

"Old Blood," Alaric frowned. "I have heard rumors . . . the girl has it, you say?"

"*The girl* is now your *cheysula*, my lord of Atvia, and your queen. You might give her proper rank," Donal said tightly. "And aye, she does. Why? Does it make you wish to end the marriage almost as soon as it is made?"

"Not at all," Alaric said smoothly. "I welcome the Cheysuli with all their arts. I must. It may be that my children will reflect their mother's gifts—"

"There will *be* no children," Bronwyn said bitterly. "I will see to *that*—"

"Enough," Donal said gently. "You will send all our guests from here muttering of your intended witchcraft."

"Let them. *Let them.* Do you think I care?" And then, before he could move, Bronwyn brought the flat of her hand across his face. "I renounce you. *I renounce you.* You are no *rujholli* of mine!"

For a moment, Donal shut his eyes against the pain and humiliation. Then he swung around to face them all. "Get you *gone!*" he shouted. "Can you not see the celebration is done?"

Blindly, he watched them go. Bronwyn. Alaric. Even Aislinn, Meghan, Evan. And then the hall was empty save for a single man.

His hair was disheveled. A smear of dirt marred his face. His clothes were soiled. Mud clotted his boots. He wore no leathers, no gold; there were no *lir* at his side. But as he faced his Mujhar, Donal knew he was a Cheysuli.

"So, the travesty is concluded."

"Rowan—" He broke it off; the time for defense was past. "It is done."

Rowan smiled a little. "I came to bring news of a final victory in Solinde. Instead, as I make my way through the hordes of departing guests, I am given news of my own: the Mujhar of Homana has wed his *rujholla* to Alaric of Atvia."

"For the prophecy." The words came out listlessly.

"Of course. *Everything* is done for the prophecy." Rowan laughed, and then the laughter died away. "But I wonder—what would *Alix* say to see her daughter bartered away—"

Donal flinched. "We do not speak of my *jehana! I* have done this thing!"

"Oh, aye, you have. And now you must live with it."

Donal wanted to turn away. But he did not. The time for that was also passed. He was Mujhar; he must behave as a Mujhar. "I will live with it."

"Am I to assume the Homanan Council also desired this match?"

"Aye. And campaigned most eloquently, for it." Donal stared down at the cup in his hand. He had forgotten to drink. The tang of the wine filled his nose and head.

"So quickly you succumb to the desires of Homanans. Do you think Clan Council would have agreed?"

Sluggishly, anger rose in his defense. "This was done for Homana—Homana *and* the prophecy! A son of Bronwyn's will one day sit on the Atvian throne."

Rowan's eyes narrowed. Tiny creases fanned out across his cheeks. "Do you care *so much* for kingship?"

"*Aye,*" Donal answered harshly. "Would you tell me I should *not?* Is it not what Hale left to me when he fashioned a sword and took a Mujhar's daughter as his *meijha?*"

Rowan slowly closed his eyes. "Ah gods, ah gods . . . you have accepted it at last . . . after so many years." He opened his eyes and smiled a bittersweet smile. "Carillon used to despair that you would ever know the cost. The legacy of the thing. And a man, never knowing the *cost* of kingship, is never really a king."

"Carillon despaired . . ." The pain was worse than he had expected. "And you as well?"

"From time to time." Rowan's smile was a little broader, but his tone was still ironic. "*Now*—do you see what it does to others? Do you see what it does to *you?*"

"You do not approve." Somehow, he wanted Rowan to approve. He needed *someone's* approval.

"It is not my place to approve or disapprove."

At last Donal succumbed and turned his back on the man. He faced the Lion instead. "Do I see what it does to others?" he cried. "*Aye,* I see what it does! No doubt it was much the same for Carillon. And now—only *now*—I understand why a man curses his birth if only to escape the demands of his entrance into the world." He drew in a ragged breath. "Bronwyn's children will bring us another bloodline. *I do what I must do.*"

He expected Rowan to answer. When he did not, Donal turned. And found himself alone.

He wanted his *meijha.* He wanted his mother. He wanted his father, his uncle, his *lir.* He wanted his *rujholla.* And he could have none of them, because this he must face alone.

Donal turned back to look at the hall. He saw the casements, glowing dimly; the banners, the tapestries, the weapons. The Lion upon the dais.

Slowly, he walked the length of the hall. He stood before the throne. He felt all the pain and grief and fear well up into chest and throat. He could not bear it. He thought he might burst with all the anger and frustration.

Before he could consider the blasphemy of his actions, he hurled the cup of wine against the ancient wood. "*All* of them, gone!" he shouted. "*All* of them you have taken. You have robbed me of even my pride, even the pride in my *heritage*, because I must be a ruler before I am a Cheysuli. A man before a warrior. And a lion before a man: *The Lion of Homana*."

Wine spilled down to stain the crimson cushion. The Lion bled. Or cried. He could not tell the difference.

Donal put his hand upon the hilt of his sword and drew it from the scabbard Rowan had made. He heard the steel-song as it slid; the hiss when it rattled free.

By the blade, beneath the crossguard, he held it. He looked at the hilt from gritty, burning eyes, and saw how the weapon shook in his trembling hand.

Gold. Solid gold, with the mark of men's hands upon it. The curving prongs that caged the ruby, brilliant Mujhar's Eye; the avatar of his soul.

And the lion. The royal rampant lion.

Donal laughed. It was a sound of discovery, lacking all humor; the futile sound of a man who knows himself trapped by what he has done and what things he still must do.

He laughed, and the sorrow filled up the hall.

"I am Donal," he said when the echoes had died. "Just— Donal. Son of man and woman. Born of the Cheysuli and a dutiful child of the prophecy. But—just once—*just once*— I wish I could turn my back upon it all and be nothing but a *man!*" His challenging stare shifted from sword hilt to crouching Lion, looming on the dais. And then, abruptly, he shut his eyes.

I wish Carillon were here.

After a moment he turned, intending to leave. He stopped. Aislinn stood in the doorway with their child in her arms.

Waiting.

Donal sheathed the sword and went to his wife and son.

TRACK OF THE
WHITE WOLF

Prologue

I knelt in silence, in patience, right knee cushioned by layers of rain-soaked leaves. Boot heel pressed against buttock; the foot within the boot, perversely, threatened suddenly to cramp.

Not now, I told it, as if the thing might listen.

My left leg jutted up, offering a thigh on which I could rest the arm supporting the compact bow. Support I needed badly; I had knelt a very long time in the misted forest, keeping my silence and my patience only because the discipline my father and brother had taught me, for once, held true. Perhaps I was finally learning.

How many times did Carillon kneel as I kneel, lying in wait for the enemy?

My grandsire's name slipped easily into mouth or mind. Perhaps for another man, perhaps for another grandson, it would not. But for me, it was a legacy I did not always desire.

—Carillon *would keep still for* hours—Carillon *would never speak*—Carillon *would know best how to do the job*—

Distracted by my thoughts, I did not hear the sound behind me. I sensed only the shadow, the *weight* of the stalking beast—

Even as I tried to turn on cramping foot, the bow was knocked flying from my hands. Half-sheathed claws shredded leather hunting doublet and, beneath that, linen shirt. Weight descended and crushed me to the ground, grinding my face into damp leaves and soggy turf.

In the cold, breath rushed out of my nose and mouth like smoke from a dragon's gullet. *Mountain cat.*

I knew it at once, even as the cat's weight shifted and allowed me room to move. There is a smell, not unpleasant, about the cats. A sense of *presence.* An ambience, created the moment one of their kind appears.

I rolled, coming up onto my knees, jerking the knife free of the sheath at my belt—

—and froze.

A female. Full-fleshed and in prime condition. Her red coat was a dappled chestnut at shoulders and haunches. The tail lashed in short, vicious arcs as she crouched. Dark-tipped ears flattened against wedge-shaped head as she snarled, displaying an awesome assemblage of curving teeth.

She hissed, as a housecat will do when taken by surprise. And then she purred.

I swore. Slammed the knife home into its sheath. Spat mud and stripped decaying leaf from face and hair. And swore again as I saw the laughter in her amber, slanted eyes.

And suddenly I *knew*—

I glanced back instantly. In the clearing, very near the place I had waited so patiently, the red stag lay dead, the *king* stag, with the finest rack of antlers I had ever seen. And a red-fletched arrow stood up like a standard from ribs.

"Ian!" I shouted. "Ian—*come out!* It was not fair!"

The cat sat down in the clearing, commenced licking one big paw, and continued to purr noisily.

"Ian?" I looked suspiciously at the cat a moment. "No—Tasha." Still there was no answer. It was all I could do not to fill the trees with my shout. "Ian, the stag was *mine*—do you hear?" I waited. Wiggled my foot inside my boot; the cramp, thank the gods, was fading. *"Ian,"* I said menacingly; giving up, I bellowed it. "The stag was *mine*, not *yours!"*

"But you were much too slow." The answering voice human, not feline. "Much too slow; did you think the king would wait on a prince forever?"

I spun around. As usual, with him, I had misjudged his position. There were times I would have sworn he could make his voice issue from rock or tree, and me left searching fruitlessly for a man.

My brother sifted out of trees, brush, slanted foggy shadows into the clearing beside the dead stag. Now that I saw him clearly, I wondered that I had not seen him before. He had been directly across from me. Watching. Waiting. And laughing, no doubt, at his foolish younger brother.

But in silence, so he would not give himself away.

I swore. Aloud, unfortunately, which only gave him more cause to laugh. But *he* did not, aloud; he merely grinned his white-toothed grin and waited in amused tolerance for me to finish my royal tirade.

And so I did not, having no wish to hand him further reason to laugh at me, or—worse—to dispense yet another of his ready homilies concerning a prince's proper behavior.

I glared at him a moment, unable to keep myself from *that* much. I saw the bow in his hands and the red-fletched arrows poking up from the quiver behind his shoulder. And looked again at the matching arrow in the ribs of the red king stag.

Conversationally, I pointed out, "Using your *lir* to knock me half-silly was not within the rules of the competition."

"There were no rules," he countered immediately. "And what Tasha did was her own doing, no suggestion of mine— though, admittedly, she *was* looking after my interests." I saw the maddening grin again; winged black brows rose up to disappear into equally raven hair. "And her own, naturally, as she shares in the kill."

"Of course," I agreed wryly. "You would never set her on me *purposely*—"

"Not for a liege man to do," he agreed blandly, with an equally bland smile. Infuriating, is my older brother.

"You ought to teach her some manners." I looked at the mountain cat, not at my brother. "But then, she has arrogance enough to match yours just as she is, so I am sure you prefer her this way."

Ian, laughing—aloud this time—did not answer. Instead he knelt down by the stag to inspect his kill. In fawn-colored leathers he blended easily into the foliage and fallen leaves. Another man, lacking the skills I have learned, would not have seen Ian at all, until he moved. Even then, I thought only the glint of gold on his bare arms would give him away.

I should have known. I should have expected it. All a man has to do is look at him to know he is the better hunter. Because a man, looking at my brother, will see a Cheysuli warrior.

But a man, looking at me, will see only a fellow Homanan. *Or Carillon, until he looks again.*

For all we share a Cheysuli father, Ian and I share not a whit of anything more. Certainly not in appearance. Ian is *all* Cheysuli: black-haired, dark-skinned, yellow-eyed. And I am all Homanan: tawny-haired, fair-skinned, *blue*-eyed.

It may be that in a certain gesture, a specific movement, Ian and I resemble one another. Perhaps in a turn of phrase. But even that seems unlikely. Ian was Keep-raised, brought up by the clan. I was born in the royal palace of Homana-Mujhar, reared by the aristocracy. Even our accents differ a little: he speaks Homanan with the underlying lilt of the Cheysuli Old Tongue, frequently slipping into the language altogether when forgetful of his surroundings; my speech is always Homanan, laced with the nuances of Mujhara, and almost never do I fall into the Old Tongue of my ancestors.

Not that I have no wish to. I am Cheysuli as much as Ian—well, nearly; he is half, I claim a quarter—and yet no man would name me so. No man would ever look into my face and name me, in anger or awe, a shapechanger, because I lack the yellow eyes. I lack the color entirely; the gold, and even the language.

No. No shapechanger, the Cheysuli Prince of Homana.

Because in addition to lacking Cheysuli looks, I also lack a *lir*.

PART I

One

I think no one can fully understand what pain and futility and emptiness are. Not as *I* understand them: a man without a *lir*. And what of them I do understand comes not of the body but of the spirit. Of the soul. Because to know oneself a *lir*less Cheysuli is an exquisite sort of torture I would wish on no man, not even to save myself.

My father was young, *too* young, when he received his *lir*, and then he bonded with two: Taj and Lorn, falcon and wolf. Ian was fifteen when he formed his bond with Tasha. At ten, *I* hoped I would be as my father and receive my *lir* early. At thirteen and fourteen I hoped I would at *least* be younger than Ian, if I could not mimic my father. At fifteen and sixteen I prayed to all the gods I could to send me my *lir* as soon as possible, *period*, so I could know myself a man and a warrior of the clan. At seventeen, I began to dread it would never happen, never at all; that I would live out my life a *lir*less Cheysuli, only half a man, denied all the magic of my race.

And now, at eighteen, I knew those fears for truth.

Ian still knelt by the king stag. Tasha—lean, lovely, lissome Tasha—flowed across the clearing to her *lir* and rubbed her head against one bare arm. Automatically Ian slipped that arm around her, caressing sleek feline head and tugging affectionately at tufted ears. Tasha purred more loudly than ever, and I·saw the distracted smile on Ian's face as he responded to the mountain cat's affection. A warrior in communion with his *lir* is much like a man in perfect union with a woman; another man, shut out of either relationship, is doubly cursed . . . and doubly lonely.

I turned away abruptly, knowing again the familiar uprush of pain, and bent to recover my bow. The arrow was broken; Tasha's mock attack had caused me to fall on it. A sore hip told me I had also rolled across the bow. But at least the soreness allowed me to think of things other than my brother and his *lir*.

I have never been a sullen man, or even one much given to melancholy. Growing up a prince and heir to the throne of Homana was more than enough for most; would have been more than enough for me, were I not Cheysuli-born. But *lir*lessness—and the knowledge I would remain so— had altered my life. Nothing would change it, not now; no warrior in all the clans had ever reached his eighteenth birthday without receiving his *lir*. Nor, for that matter, his seventeenth. And so, I tried to content myself with my rank and title—no small things, to the *Homanan* way of thinking—and the knowledge that for all I lacked a *lir*, I was still Cheysuli. No one could deny the Old Blood ran in my veins. No one. Not even the *shar tahl*, who spoke of rituals and traditions very carefully indeed when he spoke of them to me, because—for all I lacked a *lir*—I still claimed the proper line of descent. And that line would put me on the Lion Throne of Homana the day my father died.

That, at least, was something my brother could not lay claim to—not that he would wish to. Being bastard-born of my father's Cheysuli *meijha*—light woman, in Homanan— attached no stigma to him in the clans. Cheysuli do not place such importance on legitimacy; in the clans, the birth of another Cheysuli is all that counts, but as far as the Homanans were concerned, Donal's eldest son was toler- ated among the Homanan aristocracy only because he was the son of the Mujhar.

And so Ian, as much as myself, knew what it was to lack absolute acceptance. It was, I suppose, his own part of the discordant harmony in an otherwise pleasing melody. It only manifested itself for a different reason.

"Niall—?" Ian rose with the habitual grace I tried to emulate and could not; I am too tall, too heavy. I lack the total ease of movement born in so many Cheysuli. "What is it?"

I thought I had learned to mask my face, even to Ian. It served no purpose to tell him what torture it was to see my brother with his *lir*, or my father with his. Most of the time it remained a dull ache, and bearable, as a sore tooth is bearable so long as it does not turn rotten in the jaw. But occasionally the tooth throbs, sending pain of unbearable intensity through my mind; my mask had slipped, and Ian had seen the face I wore behind it.

"*Rujho*—" so quickly he slipped into the Old Tongue— "are you ill?"

"No." Abrupt answer, too abrupt; I inspected the bow again, for want of another action to cover my brief slip. "No, only—" I sought a lie to cover up the pain "—only disappointed. But I should know better than to match myself against you in something so—" I paused—"so *Cheysuli* as hunting a stag. You have only to take *lir*-shape, and the contest is finished."

Ian indicated the arrow. "No *lir*-shape, *rujho*. Only human form." He smiled, as if he knew we joked, but something told me he knew well enough what had prompted my discomfiture. "If it pleases you, Niall, I will concede. Without Tasha's interference, you might well have taken the stag."

I laughed at him outright. "Oh, aye, *might* have. Such a concession, *rujho!* You will almost have me believing I know what I am doing."

"You know what I taught you, my lord." Ian grinned. "And now, if you like, I will go fetch the horses as a proper liege man so we may escort the dead king home in honor."

"To Homana-Mujhar?" The palace was at least two hours away; rain threatened again.

"No, I thought Clankeep. We can prepare the stag there for a proper presentation. Old Newlyn knows all the tricks." Ian bent down and with a quick twist removed the unbroken arrow from between the ribs of the stag. "Clankeep is closer, for all that."

I shut my mouth on an answer and did not say what I longed to: that I much preferred the palace. Clankeep is Cheysuli; *lir*less, I am extremely uncomfortable there. I avoid it when I can.

Ian glanced up. "Niall, it is your home as much as Mujhara." So easily he read me, even by my silence.

I shook my head. "Homana-Mujhar is my place. Clankeep is *yours*." Before he could speak I turned away. "I will get the horses. My legs are younger than yours."

It is an old joke between us, the five years that separate

us, but for once he would not let it go. He stepped across the dead king stag and caught my arm.

"Niall." The levity was banished from his face. "*Rujho,* I cannot pretend to know what it is to lack a *lir*. But neither can I pretend *your* lack does not affect me."

"Does it?" Resentment flared up instantly, surprising even me with its intensity. But this was intrusion into an area of my life he could not *possibly* understand. "Does it affect you, Ian? Does it disturb you that the warriors of the clan refer to me as a Homanan instead of a Cheysuli? Does it affect you that if they could, they would petition the *shar tahl* to have my birth-rune scratched off the permanent birth-lines?" His dark face went gray as death, and I realized he had not known I was aware of what a few of the more outspoken warriors said. "Oh, *rujho,* I know I am not alone in this. I know it must disturb *you*—a full-fledged Cheysuli warrior and a member of Clan Council—in particular: that the man intended to rule after Donal lacks the gifts of the Cheysuli. How could it not? You serve the prophecy as well as any warrior, and yet you look at me and see a man who *does not fit.* The link that was not forged." It hurt me to see the pain in his yellow eyes; eyes some men still called bestial. "It affects you, it affects our sister, it affects our father. It even affects my mother."

Ian's hand fell away from my arm. "Aislinn? *How?*"

His tone was unguarded; I heard the note of astonishment in his voice. No, he would not expect my lack of a *lir* to affect my mother. How could it, when the Queen of Homana was fully Homanan herself, without a drop of Cheysuli blood?

How could he, when there was so little of affection between them? Not hatred; never that. Not even a true disliking of one another. Merely—toleration. A mutual apathy.

Because my mother, the Queen, recalled too clearly that what love my father had to offer had been given freely to his Cheysuli *meijha*, Ian's mother, and not to the Homanan princess he had wed.

At least, not *then.*

I smiled, albeit wryly, and more than a little resigned. "How does it affect my mother? Because to her, my lacking a *lir* emphasizes a certain other bloodline in me. It reminds her that in addition to looking almost exactly like her father, I reflect all his Homanan traits. No Cheysuli in me, oh no; I am Homanan to the bone. I am Carillon come again."

The last was said a trifle bitterly; for all I am used to the fact I look so much like my grandsire, it is not an easy knowledge. I would sooner do without it.

Ian sighed. "Aye. I should have seen it. The gods know she goes on and on about Carillon enough, linking her son with her father. There are times I think she confuses the two of you."

I shied away from that idea almost at once. It whispered of sickness; it promised obsession. No son wishes to know his mother obsessed, even if she is.

And she was not. She was not.

"Clankeep," I said abruptly. "Well enough, then let us go. We owe this monarch more than a bed of leaves and bloodied turf."

A muscle ticked in Ian's jaw. "Aye," he said tersely; no more.

I went off to fetch the horses.

Once, individual keeps had been scattered throughout Homana, springing up like toadstools across the land. Once, they had even reached a finger here and there into neighboring Ellas, when Shaine's *qu'mahlin* had been in effect. The purge had resulted in the destruction of Cheysuli holdings as well as much of the race itself; later the Solindish king, Bellam, had usurped the Lion Throne and laid waste to Homana in the name of Tynstar, Ihlini sorcerer, and devotee of the god of the netherworld. With Carillon in exile and the Cheysuli hunted by Solindish, Ihlini, and Homanan alike, what remained of the Cheysuli was nearly destroyed completely. The keeps had been sundered into heaps of shattered stone and shreds of painted cloth.

My legendary grandsire had, thank the gods, come home again to take back his stolen throne; his return ended Solindish and Ihlini domination and Shaine's purge. Freed of the threat of extirpation, the Cheysuli had also come home from secret keeps and built Homanan ones again. Clankeep itself, spreading across the border between woodlands and meadowlands, had gone up after Donal succeeded to the Lion on Carillon's death. And though the Cheysuli were granted freedom to live where they chose after decades of outlawry, they still preferred the closeness of the forests. Clankeep, ringed by unmortared walls of undressed, gray-green stone, was the closest thing to a city the Cheysuli claimed.

As always, I felt the familiar admixture of emotions as we entered the sprawling keep: sorrow—a trace of trepidation—a fleeting sense of anger—an undertone of pride. A skein of raw emotions knotted itself inside my soul . . . but mostly, more than anything, I knew a tremendous yearning to belong as *Ian* belonged.

Clankeep is the heart of the Cheysuli, regardless that my father rules from Homana-Mujhar. It is Clankeep that feeds the spirit of each Cheysuli; Clankeep where the *shar tahls* keep the histories, traditions, and rituals clear of taint. It is here they guard the remains of the prophecy of the First-born, warding the fragmented hide with all the power they can summon.

And it was here at Clankeep that Niall of Homana longed to spend his days, for all he was prince of the land.

Because then he would be Cheysuli.

The rain began again, though falling with less force than before. This was more of a mist, kiting on the wind. Sheets of it drifted before my horse, shredded by the gusts. It muffled the sounds of the Keep and drove the Cheysuli inside their painted pavilions.

Except for Isolde. I should have known; 'Solde adores the rain, preferring thunder and lightning in abundance. But this misting shower, I knew, would do; it was better than boring sunlight.

"Ian! Niall! Both my *rujholli* at once?" She wore crimson, which was like her; it stood out against the damp grayness of the day as much as her bright ebullience did. I saw her come dashing through the drifting wet curtains as if she hardly felt them, damp wool skirts gathered up to show off furred boots of sleek dark otter pelt. Silver bells rimmed the cuffs of the boots, chiming as she ran. Matching bells were braided into thick black hair; like Ian, she was all Cheysuli. Even to the Old Blood in her veins.

"What is this?" She stopped as we did, putting out a hand to push a questing wet muzzle from her face; Ian's gray stallion was a curious sort, and oddly affectionate toward our sister. But then, perhaps it was the magic in her showing. "The *king* stag!" Yellow eyes widened as she looked up at Ian and me. "How did you come by this?"

'Solde seemed untroubled by the rain, falling harder now, that pasted hair against scalp and dulled the shine of all her bells. One hand still on the stallion's muzzle, she waited expectantly for an explanation.

I blew a drop of water off the end of my nose. " 'Solde, you have eyes. The king stag, aye, and brought down by Ian's hand—" I paused "—in a manner of speaking."

Ian glared. "What nonsense is this? *'In a manner of speaking.'* I took him down with a single arrow! You were there."

"How kind of you to recall it." I smiled down at 'Solde. "He set Tasha on me the moment I prepared to loose my own arrow, and the cat spoiled my shot."

'Solde laughed, smothered it with a hand, then attempted, unsuccessfully, to give Ian a stern glance of remonstration. At three years younger than Ian and two years older than I, she did what she could to mother us both. Though I had my own mother in Homana-Mujhar, 'Solde and Ian did not; Sorcha was long dead.

Rain fell harder yet. My chestnut gelding snorted and shook himself, jostling all my bones. I was already a trifle stiff from Tasha's mock attack; I needed no further reminding of human fragility. " 'Solde, do you mind if we go into Ian's pavilion? You may like the rain, but we have been out in it longer than I prefer."

Her slim brown fingers caressed the crown bedecking the king stag's head. "So fine, so fine . . . a gift for our *jehan?*" She asked it of Ian, whose stallion bore the stag before the Cheysuli saddle.

"He will be pleased, I think," Ian agreed. " 'Solde, Niall has the right of it. I will shrink like an old wool tunic if I stay out in this downpour a moment longer."

'Solde stepped aside, shaking her head in disappointment, and all the bright bells rang. "Babies, both of you, to be so particular about the weather. *Warriors* must be prepared for anything. *Warriors* never complain about the weather. *Warriors*—"

" 'Solde, be still," Ian suggested, calmly reining his stallion toward the nearest pavilion. "What you know of warriors could be fit into an acorn."

"No," she said, "at least a walnut. Or so Ceinn tells me."

The stallion was stopped short, so short my own mount nearly walked into the dappled rump, which is not something I particularly care to see happen around Ian's prickly stallion. But for once the gray did nothing.

Ian, however, did. "Ceinn?" He twisted in the saddle and looked back at our smug-faced sister. "What has *Ceinn* to say about how much you know of warriors?"

"Quite a lot," she answered off-handedly. "He has asked me to be his *cheysula.*"

"Ceinn?" Ian, knowing the warriors better than I, could afford to sound astonished; all I could do was stare. "Are you sure he said *cheysula* and not *meijha?*"

"The words do have entirely different sounds," 'Solde told him pointedly, which would not please Ian any at all. But then, of course, she did not mean to. "And I do know the difference."

Ian scowled. "Isolde, he has said nothing to me about it."

"You have been in Mujhara," she reminded him. "For weeks. Months. And besides, he is not required to say anything to you. It is *me* for whom he wishes to offer."

Ian, still scowling, cast a glance at me. "Well? Are you going to say nothing to her?"

"Perhaps I might wish her luck," I answered gravely. "Whenever has anything we have said to her made the slightest amount of difference?"

"Oh, it has," Isolde said. "You just never noticed."

Ian shut his eyes. "Her mind, small as it is, astonishes me with its capacity for stubbornness, once a decision is made." Eyes open again, he twisted his mouth in a wry grimace of resignation. "Niall has the right of it: nothing we say will make any difference. But—why Ceinn?"

"Ceinn pleases me," she answered simply. "Should there be another reason?"

Ian glanced at me, and I knew our thoughts ran along similar paths: for a woman like our sister, a free Cheysuli woman with only bastard ties to royalty, there need be no other reason.

For the Prince of Homana, however, there were multitudinous other reasons. Which was why I had been cradle-betrothed to a cousin I had never seen.

Gisella was her name. Gisella of Atvia. Daughter of Alaric himself, and my father's sister, Bronwyn.

I smiled down at my Cheysuli half-sister. "No, 'Solde. No other reason. If he pleases you, that is enough for Ian and me."

"Aye," Ian agreed glumly. "And now that you have taken us by surprise, 'Solde, as you intended all along, may we get out of the rain?"

'Solde grinned the grin that Ian usually wore. "There is a fire in your pavilion, *rujho*, and hot honey brew, fresh bread, cheese, and a bit of venison."

Ian sighed. "You knew we were coming."

'Solde laughed. "Of course I did. Tasha told me."

And with those well-intentioned words, my sister once more reminded me even she claimed gifts that I could not.

Two

The rain began to fall a trifle harder. Isolde flapped a hand at us both. "Go in, go in, before the food and drink grow cold. I have my own fire to tend, and then I will come back."

She was gone, crimson skirts dyed dark by the weight of the rain. I heard the chime of bells as 'Solde ran toward her pavilion (did she share it now with Ceinn?) and reflected the sound suited my sister. There was nothing of dark silence about Isolde.

"Go on," Ian told me. "Old Newlyn will wish to see the stag now in order how best to judge the preparation. There is no need for you to get any wetter. Tasha will keep you company."

Ian did not bother to wait for my answer; much as I dislike to admit it, he is accustomed to having me do as he tells me to. Prince of Homana—liege man; one would think Ian did *my* bidding, but he does it only rarely. Only when it suits that which he believes appropriate to a liege man's conduct.

I watched him go much as 'Solde had gone, fading into the wind and rain like a creature born of both. And she had the right of it, my *rujholla*; warriors did not complain about the weather. Warriors were prepared for anything.

Or perhaps it was just that they knew how to make themselves look *prepared, thereby fooling us all.*

I grinned and swung off my gelding, looping the reins over a wooden picket-stake before the pavilion doorflap. As I pulled the flap back, Tasha moved by me into the interior, damp fur slicking back against muscle and bone as she pressed briefly against my leg. I wondered if she hated the rain as most housecats did; but then, she would hardly thank me for comparing her to a common creature such as knew the tame freedom of Mujhara's alleys and the corridors of Homana-Mujhar.

Ian's pavilion was dyed a pale saffron color. The exterior bore a stylized painting of a mountain cat in vermilion, honoring his *lir*. The interior was illuminated by the small fire 'Solde had lighted, but because of the gray of the day the shadows lay deep and thick. Trunks merged with walls and tapestries, the divider curtain with the faint haze of silver woodsmoke. Nothing seemed of substance except the fire in the cairn.

Tasha wasted no time. She stretched her damp, substantial length upon the silver-blue pelt of a snow bear and began to lick herself dry. Unfortunately, I could not do the same with my own soaked skin, not having the proper tongue.

Wet leathers smell. So do wet mountain cats. Between myself and Ian's *lir*, there was little left that did not offend my nose. And because Ian and I were not at all of a size, me being both a hand-span taller and at least thirty pounds heavier, I could not borrow dry leathers from one of his clothing chests. So I wrapped myself up in yet another bear pelt, this one chestnut-brown, and hunched down beside the fire with my back to the doorflap. I poured a cup of hot honey brew and inhaled the pungent steam.

"Ian." The voice outside startled me into nearly spilling my drink. "Ian, we must talk. About your *rujholli*'s future and the future of the Lion—" Without waiting for the word admitting entrance, the man who spoke jerked aside the doorflap and ducked inside. "Your decision can wait no long—"

He broke off at once as I turned on my knees to look at him. He was a stranger to me; clearly, I was not to him. And neither was his subject.

I rose, shedding bear pelt, and faced him directly. He was young, but several years older than I. Quite obviously all Cheysuli and just as obviously all warrior. He wore leathers, damp at the shoulders, dyed the color of beech leaves. His gold bore the incised shapes of a rock bear, a breed smaller than that most commonly found in Homana, but doubly deadly. I had not heard of a warrior bonding with a rock bear for years.

By the *lir* I judged the man. And by the look of him, he

was not one to allow another man time to speak when he had words of his own in his mouth. Even in all its youth, his face was hard, made of sharp angles, sharper than is common. His nose was a blade that sliced his face in half. There was the faint tracery of an old scar cutting the flesh at the corner of one eye. Though not so much older than I in years, I knew he was decades older in self-confidence.

But I have learned how tall men can occasionally intimidate shorter men. I reached out and took up the weapon. "Aye?" I asked. "You spoke of me?"

I waited. Dull color stained his dark face darker, but only for a moment. The yellow eyes veiled themselves at once; he was not a man I could intimidate with height *or* rank. But then I should have known better than to try; Cheysuli are intimidated by no one.

" 'Solde said her *rujholli* was here." He gave up nothing in manner or speech.

"He is," I agreed. "Did she not say—*both?*"

He judged me. I could see it. He *judged* me, as if he sought something in my face, my voice, my eyes. And then I saw the brief glance at my left ear, naked of gold, and knew the judgment reached.

Or perhaps merely *recalled*, as if it were no new thing. "No," he said smoothly. "She mentioned only Ian."

My fingers clenched briefly on the cup; carefully, I unlocked the stiffened joints. With effort, I kept my voice from reflecting the pain his casual words had caused. That much I had learned from my father; kingcraft often requires delicacy of speech as well as subterfuge. This meeting would afford me the chance to practice both. "My *rujholli* is with Newlyn. But if you would prefer it, you may wait here for his return." I paused. "Or leave your message with me."

I knew he would not. I could smell it on him: a great need for confidence, secrecy; his manner bespoke an arrested anticipation. Whatever news he had for Ian was important to them both. And would therefore be important to me as well, I thought, a trifle mystified; I wondered anew at the stranger's attitude.

"With you?" He nearly smiled. And then he did, clearly, and I saw he was not so much older than I after all. "My thanks, but no. I think not, my lord; it is better done in private."

He spoke politely, but I knew well enough what he did. Cheysuli warriors only rarely give rank to another, and then only to a Homanan such as my grandsire had been. To another *warrior*, never, because Cheysuli are born and remain equal until they die. And so he reminded me, as perhaps he meant to, that he viewed me as nothing more than a Homanan.

An unblessed man, as lirless Homanans are called. Well, perhaps he is not so wrong.

Politely, he bowed his head in subtle acknowledgment of my rank. It grated in my soul, that acknowledgment; I would trade every Homanan rank in the world for acceptance in all the clans.

"Tell your brother Ceinn has words for him," he said quietly, using the Homanan tongue as if I were deaf to the Cheysuli. "And forgive me for interrupting."

He was gone before I could stop him; before I could say a word about my sister's marriage. It was not my place to say nay or yea to the union; Cheysuli women are free to take what warrior they will, but there was little good in making no effort to like the man she would wed.

Well, the effort would have to wait.

The cup was cool in my hand. It would be easy enough to pour out the cold liquor and refill my cup with hot, but suddenly I wanted no liquor, no food, no pavilion filled with my brother's *lir*. Thanks to Ceinn and his careful words, I wanted nothing to do with anyone.

Tasha still lay on the pelt. She had interrupted the grooming ritual to look at me with the fixed, feral gaze of the mountain cat, as if she sought to read my mind. That she could read Ian's I knew, but mine was closed to her. As much as hers was to me, and always would be.

Abruptly, I set down the cup and went back out into the rain. At once I shivered, but did not allow it to turn me from my intention. I jerked the reins from the picketstake and swung up into the wet Homanan saddle.

Homanan this, Homanan that—it is no wonder the Cheysuli look at me with doubt!

"Niall!" Ian, coming through the rain, lacked both stallion and stag. *"Rujho—"*

I cut him off. "I am for Mujhara after all. I have no taste for Clankeep today." I reined my fractious chestnut around. "Ceinn came looking for you."

Black brows rose a trifle; what I looked for in his face was missing. There was no guilt in my brother, no embarrassment, that he discussed me with others behind my back.

But I wonder . . . what does he say?

Ian shrugged, dismissing Isolde's warrior. "Niall, stay the night, at least. Why go back in this rain?"

"The rain has stopped." It had, even as we spoke, but the air was heavy with the promise of more. "Ian, just—just let me be." It came out rather lamely, which irritated me even more. "*Rujho . . .* let me be."

He did. I saw the consternation in his face and the brief tightening of his mouth, but he said nothing more. One brown hand slapped my chestnut's rain-darkened rump, and I was away at last.

Away. Again. Away. Gods, how I hate running—
—and yet, as always, it seemed the only answer.

I stopped running at sunset because my horse went lame. Not far from Mujhara—I could see torchlights just ahead—I pushed myself out of the damp saddle with effort (wet leather against wet leather hinders movement considerably) and dropped down into sucking mud. I swore, jerked boots free, slipped and slid around to the right foreleg to inspect the injured hoof. The gelding nosed at me and snorted as I insisted he lift the leg. I tried to ignore damp questing nostrils at the back of my neck as I dug balled mud from his hoof.

A stone had wedged itself in the tender frog of the hoof. Cold, stiff fingers did not accomplish much; I unsheathed my knife and dug carefully at the stone until I pried it loose. The frog was bruised. It was nothing that would not heal in two or three days, but for now riding him would only worsen the lameness and delay recovery. And so I took up the reins and proceeded to lead my horse into the outskirts of Mujhara.

The city is centuries older than I. My father once told me the Cheysuli originally built Mujhara, before they turned from castles and houses to the freedom of the forests. But the Homanans claimed their ancestors had built it, though artifacts of Cheysuli origin had been found in old foundations. I could not say who had the right of it, as both races had lived in Homana for hundreds and hundreds of years, but I thought it likely the Cheysuli had built at least Homana-Mujhar, for the palace was full of *lir*-shapes carved in rose-colored stone and rich dark wood.

Mujhara itself, however, resembles little of the city that once held court upon the land. Originally curtain walls had ringed the city, offering protection against the enemy. But Mujhara was like a small boy growing to manhood all at once, without warning. It had burst free of childhood's bones and sinews with new adult growth and strength, as I myself had so dramatically two years before; now the city walls and barbican gates lay nearly half a league yet inside the outskirts, leaving hundreds outside the Mujhar's official protection.

But we had not been at war for nearly twenty years, and all the treaties held. Homana was at peace.

The gelding limped behind me as I led him through the narrow, mud-clogged streets. Inside the walls the streets were cobbled. Outside they were not, since no one could say what dwellings might go up overnight, thereby creating new streets. Ordinarily the ground was dry and hardpacked, or frozen solid in winter. But now it was only fall, too early for true winter. And so I slogged through the mud with my limping horse behind me.

I headed straight toward the nearest gate leading into the inner city, but nothing in Mujhara is straight. Streets and alleys and closes wind around and around like Erinnish knotwork, lacking beginning and end. So the Prince of Homana and his royal mount also wound around and around.

In fall, the light dies quickly. With the sun gone the streets lay shadow-clad in deepening darkness. I frowned against those few torches that threw inadequate illumination from dwellings into the street, for they played tricks on the eyes by hiding real obstacles even as they created others.

Your own fault, I reminded myself. *Ian offered a warm pavilion, dry pallet, good food, company, drink.*

Well, so would Homana-Mujhar, providing the horse allowed me to reach it before the night was through.

The rising yowl of an angry cat broke into my thoughts.

The sound came closer still, rising in volume as well as tone; I turned, searching, and saw the dark streak come running at me from out of the shadowed wynd. Behind the cat came a dog singularly dedicated to catching his prey. Neither animal paid mind to me or my horse, both intent upon the moment. The cat flew by me, closely followed by the dog, and as I turned to watch them go I came face to face with a cloaked and hooded man.

I stopped short. So did my horse; he nearly walked over me. As it was, I felt hoof against heel before I could step away.

The cloaked figure did not attempt to move out of my way, nor did he offer apology. He stood his ground. I thought perhaps he mistook me for another; when he put out a restraining hand as I made to go on around him I knew he did not, and I closed my free hand around the hilt of my knife.

"A moment of your time," said the cloaked figure quietly.

The gelding, so close behind me, snorted loudly into my left ear and showered me with mucus as I jumped and swore. The stranger pushed the hood from his head and let it settle on his shoulders. I could see his face dimly in the diffused light of the torches. He was smiling; my horse's response had amused him.

I let the merest hint of knife blade show and hoped my voice sounded steadier than I felt. Thieves and cutpurses abound in any city, even Mujhara, and I was not in an area I knew well. For that matter, only rarely do I go into the city alone at all. Ian is almost always with me, or others from the palace.

"I carry no wealth," I challenged, attempting to sound older and more confident than I was. "I have only this horse, which is far from a valuable beast at the moment. Else I would be riding."

The smile widened a little. "If I wanted your horse and your wealth, my young lord, I would take both. As it is, I desire only a moment of your time. But first, let us have better light. I would let you see to whom you speak."

I opened my mouth to repudiate his arrogance and his demands upon my time; I said nothing. I said nothing because I *could not*, being struck dumb by the illumination he conjured out of the air.

A hand. The merest flick of eloquent fingers, sketching, and a rune glowed in the air. Deepest, richest purple, swallowing the darkness and creating light as bright as day.

I thrust up an arm to block the sudden flame and fell back two steps. Briefly I felt the bulwark of my horse's chest behind me. But then he, too, took fright from the fire and shied badly, lunging away so quickly he jerked the reins free of my hand. I whirled, trying to catch him, but for the moment his lameness was forgotten. He wheeled and went back the way we had come, spraying thick clots of mud into the air and liberally daubing my clothing as well as my unshielded face.

But the horse was the least of my worries. Much as he had spun I also spun, but not away. Not yet. I faced the man instead, though admittedly only through utter astonishment and no particular measure of courage. But I could hardly see him through the brilliance of his rune.

The hand dropped back to his side, hidden in woolen folds of darkest blue. The rune remained: hissing, shedding tendrils of brilliant flame . . . and yet there was no heat. Only the bitter cold of harshest winter.

"There." He was content with what he had wrought. "Light, my lord. Illumination. Not in the manner to which you are accustomed, perhaps, but light nonetheless. Which would lead me to believe there is no Darkness in my sorcery if I can conjure Light."

Illumination filled out the details of his face. He was an immensely attractive man, as some men are; not precisely *pretty*, but more than merely handsome. As a child he would have been beautiful. But he was no longer a child, and had not been for years.

Suspicion flared much as the rune flared, blinding and all-consuming. At once I looked for the telltale eyes and found the stories true. One blue. One brown. The eyes of a demon, men said of people with mismatched eyes; appropriate, in this case, for his name was linked with such. With Asar-Suti himself, the god of the netherworld, who made and dwells in darkness.

Black hair, worn loose and very long, was held back from his face by a narrow silver circlet. He was clean-shaven, as

if he wished all to see his face and marvel at its clarity of
features. No modest Ihlini, Strahan; he wore pride and
power like a second cloak, and finer than any silk. I saw
the glint of silver at one ear. His left, as if he mocked the
lir-gold of the Cheysuli.

But then perhaps he mocked no one; he could not wear
an earring in his right because he lacked the ear.

I took a single backward step. Stopped. Again, not because I found a sudden spurt of courage, but because I
found I could not move. Facing him, seeing for myself what
manner of man he was, I could not go immediately out of
the sorcerer's presence.

Ensorcellment? Perhaps. But I choose to call it consuming fascination.

I licked my lips. Breath was harsh in my throat. It was
difficult to swallow. A weight was pressing on my ribs. The
contents of my belly threatened to become discontent with
their surroundings.

The odd eyes watched me. Strahan judged, as Ceinn had
judged. And, like Ceinn, the Ihlini saw I had no gold of
my own. But then, undoubtedly, Strahan already knew
quite well of my lack.

He smiled. I wondered how much of Tynstar was in him,
his father, whom men claimed a handsome man. And his
Solindish mother, Electra, who had been Carillon's wife
and queen before Carillon had slain her. Oh aye, I wondered how much of Electra was in him, because she was in
me as well.

"Kinsman." Coolly, he acknowledged the blood between
us. "You must tender my regards to your father when I am
done with you."

I did not care for the implications in the statement. And
yet I knew I stood little chance against him, whatever he
chose to do. *Lir*less, I lacked the magic of my race. Nothing
would turn the Ihlini's power if he chose to use it against me.

Strahan smiled again. Women, I knew, would be at once
swallowed whole by the magnitude of his allure. *And* men.
For a different reason, perhaps, but the results would be
the same. Where Strahan had need of loyal servants, he
would find them. He would *take* them. And use them up
before he ever let them go.

"I have heard stories of you, Niall." *That* did not serve

to settle me at all. "Tales of how the Prince of Homana, young as he is, bears a striking resemblance to Carillon. Of course it is in the blood, you being his grandson, but I wonder. . . ." The smile showed itself again. There was speculation in his ill-matched eyes. "When I knew him, he was an old man made older by my father's arts, and he was ill. Ill and dying, slowly, as the disease devoured him. But still a strong man, as strong as he could be." Black brows drew down a little beneath the silver circlet; he was judging me again, and using my grandsire as the point of comparison. Like my mother. Like so many *Homanans*. "He was the enemy, of course, a man I desired to slay—*especially* once he had slain my father," the cool voice hardened, "but in the end, Osric of Atvia did the slaying for me." Briefly, one corner of his beautiful mouth twisted in an expression of irritation. "And now, in some strange manner, I see I must face Carillon again."

"No." Inwardly, I drew in as deep a breath as I could. It did not dull the fear, but it filled the emptiness of my belly with something other than utter panic.

Strahan's arched brows rose. "No?"

I wanted to clear my throat before I tried my voice again. I did not, because I knew he would take it as a sign of my fear. And then, looking into the sorcerer's face, I no longer cared what he thought or what he knew.

This man is kin to me . . . Ihlini, perhaps, and powerful, but still a man like me.

"You face *me*, Strahan," I told him as evenly as I could. "Not my grandsire. Not my father. *I* am the one you face."

The Ihlini smiled a little. "You, then." Casually said, as if I hardly mattered. So easily was I discounted by Tynstar's son. "Again; you will tender my regards to your father, the Mujhar."

I smiled. I felt it stretch my lips a little, and heard the steadiness of my voice. As even as I could want it. "Be certain I will, Strahan. And know he will be pleased you have shown yourself in Mujhara. He has sought you many years."

"And will seek me many more." He was patently unruffled by my bravado. "What is between Donal and me will be settled one day, but not tonight. Tonight I came seeking you."

"And if I said I had neither the time nor the inclination to trade empty threats with you?"

Strahan laughed. The rune hissed and spat and pulsed against the darkness, as if it laughed as well. "The wolf's cub hackles, snapping; the falcon's hatchling spreads his wings and tries to fly." The laughter stopped as quickly as it had begun. Softly, he said, "A suggestion, my lord prince: waste no effort in displays of dominance when you have no *lir* to mimic."

From a Homanan, from a Cheysuli, the taunts were bad enough. But from an *Ihlini sorcerer*—

Rage roared up from inside my head. I heard a voice shouting at Strahan, calling him foul names in Homanan and Old Tongue alike. That much I knew of the language. I felt my body take two steps forward, saw my hands rise up as if to clutch at the Ihlini's throat. And then my hands struck through the flaming rune and the bones filled up with pain.

Cold. Not hot. *Cold.*

I cried out. I felt myself crushed to my knees in the mud of the street. The rune ate through leather and flesh to my bones and turned my blood to ice.

Through the haze of pain and the glare of living flame, I saw the Ihlini's inhumanly beautiful face. Dimly, I saw how he watched me; glinting eyes narrowed, black brows drawn down as if he studied a specimen. Waiting. Watching. Examining the results of the specimen's foolishness.

I watched him watching me and remembered who he was. As well as *what* he was.

At last, he spoke. "Not now. Not yet. *Later.*"

No more than that. A fluid gesture of one hand and the rune ran away from my body, spilling out of my flesh like blood from an opened vein. It ran down my thighs to splash against the mud, pooling like rancid water. Puddled. Ran in upon itself. And then hurled itself upward to renew its form in the shadows of the night.

Strahan looked down upon me as I knelt in the mud of the street. Once again he smiled. I saw genuine amusement and a trace of pleasure in his eyes; a look of contented reminiscence.

"Your father once knelt to me," he said in a perfect contentment. He did not gloat. I think he did not need to.

"Did he never tell you?" A nod of his head as I held my silence; it was the least I owed my father. "No, he would never say it; not to you, but it is true. And now his son as well." Strahan paused. "His *Homanan* son; the Cheysuli would never do it."

So easily he reached into my soul and touched that aspect of my character which I hated. Not my brother. Never Ian. No—*myself*, for resenting the gifts Ian—and others—claimed. Gifts I should claim myself.

I wrenched myself from my unintended posture of obeisance. A small thing, to face the sorcerer standing, but the beginnings of rebellion. It was the least I would offer him.

"State your business," I said flatly. I have learned something of royal impatience from my father, who hates the demands of diplomacy. Too often he is trapped by endless petitioners.

Strahan's eyes narrowed a trifle. "You are betrothed to your cousin, Gisella of Atvia: *do not wed the girl.*"

Stunned, I waited for something more. And when he offered nothing, I laughed. It was unintended. The situation hardly warranted levity, but he caught me so off-guard there was nothing else I could do.

I laughed at him. And Strahan did not like it.

"You *fool*," he snapped. "I could grind you into the mud before you could utter a word, and never bestir myself."

Suddenly, he was no longer so awe-inspiring. I had touched a nerve. "Do it," I challenged, emboldened by his unexpected vulnerability. "What *better* way of keeping me from wedding my Atvian cousin?"

Something hurled me flat against the ground, pinning me on my back. Half-swallowed in mud, I lay there, staring up at the angry sorcerer. "Drown," he said between clenched teeth. "*Drown* in all this mud!"

I could not move. I felt the ground shift beneath my flattened body. It heaved itself up from under me, lapped over my limbs and began to inch up my torso. I felt it in my ears; at the corners of my eyes.

But even as I drowned, I was aware of a nagging question. Why did it matter to *Strahan* if I wed Gisella or not?

The mud was at my mouth. My body was nearly swallowed whole. I felt the first finger reaching into my nostrils. I shouted, but my mouth filled with the mud.

Drowning—

Insanely, I did not think of dying for itself. I thought
instead of disappointing others by the helplessness of my
dying. *Ah gods, not like* this—*Carillon would* never *die like
this—in such futility.*

Abruptly, the rune winked out. Darkness filled my head.

I thought it was the mud. I thought it might be death.
And then I realized that though I lay flat on my back in
the street, I was free of the drowning mud.

I lay there. All was silence, except for my ragged breathing. The abrupt disappearance of the brilliant rune left my
eyes mostly blinded; I saw nothing, not even the light from
nearby dwellings. Only darkness.

I twisted. Thrust one shaking hand into the ooze and
slowly pushed myself up. Mud clung to me from head to
toe, but it no longer threatened to drown me. I was weary
unto death, as if all the strength had been sucked from me.
I was cold, wet, filthy, stinking of my fear . . . and angry
that I was so inconsequential a foe for the Ihlini.

"Why should *I* do it?" Strahan asked. "Why should I
trouble myself with *you?*"

I twitched. Spun again to face him. I had believed myself
alone; that Strahan had gone into the darkness. And then
I saw the ghostly luminescence of his face in the light of
the quarter moon, and I realized the clouds had broken
at last.

I spat out mud. My reprieve made me momentarily
brave. "I think I understand, Ihlini. If I wed Gisella and
get sons on her, I have added yet another link to the chain.
Another yarn to the tapestry of the Firstborn." A muscle
jumped once in his cheek. "Aye, that *is* it! Atvian blood
mixed with that of Homana, Solinde, and the Cheysuli
brings us decidedly closer to fulfilling the prophecy." Suddenly, I laughed; I understood it at last. "By keeping me
from wedding Gisella you break the link before it is truly
forged."

"*Wed* her," he said sharply, abruptly changing course.
"Wed the Atvian girl; I do not care. One day you will come
to me; *I invite you now to do it.*" His odd eyes narrowed
a little. "If you have sons, I will make them mine. I will
take them . . . but I think you will never get sons upon
Gisella because the others will see you dead."

"Others?" I could not help the blurted question. "Who but *you* would wish me dead?"

It was Strahan's turn to laugh. "Has your father taught you nothing? Do they keep you in ignorance, thinking to ward your pride? Not any easy thing to know, is it, that you are the center of the storm." Silver glinted at his single ear. "Better to ask: who would *not* wish you dead."

"Not—?" I whispered hollowly, as if I were a puppet and he the puppetmaster.

Strahan pursed his lips in consideration. Black brows rose below the circlet. "Or, if not *dead* . . . at least replaced by another."

Replaced. Me? But it was not possible. I was the Prince of Homana, legitimate son of Donal the Mujhar and Aislinn the Queen, Carillon's daughter. The proper blood was in my veins. There were no other legitimate children; the Queen was barren, the physicians said. There was and always would be only me. How could they think to replace me, and—by the gods!—with *whom?*

One hand parted the darkness and filled it with light again. "Shall I prophesy for you, my lord prince?" asked the compelling tone. "Shall I show you what will come to be, no matter how hard you try to rewrite what the gods themselves have written?"

He did not wait for my answer. He lifted the hand again and lent it the fluid, eloquent language of brush against living canvas. I saw the fingers move, forming shapes amidst the darkness.

Colors poured out from Strahan's fingertips: argent purple, deepest lavender, palest silver lilac. And the lurid red of fresh-spilled blood.

He painted a picture of living flame: a rampant Homanan lion and a compact Cheysuli warbow. All rich in detail, even to the curling tongue of the gape-mouthed lion and the ornamentation of the warbow. They hung against the air as if they waited. As if I had only to pluck the bow from the darkness and loose an arrow at the lion.

I stared. Swallowed hard. There were no words in my mouth. All I knew was a sense of awed, awful discovery: the picture he painted was a true one, regardless that the artist was enemy.

"The Homanans want no Cheysuli shapechanger on the

throne," Strahan said above the hissing of the flame. "The Cheysuli want no unblessed Homanan on the throne. But Donal's son is *both and neither*; what do *you* think will happen?" The parti-colored eyes were eerie in the light of the glowing shapes. "Look to your people, Niall," he said. So softly, he spoke; so *gentle* was his tone. "Look to your friends . . . your enemies . . . *your kin*—lest they form an alliance against you."

Smoothly, he bled together the shapes of bow and lion. And out of the flame I saw born the face of my brother—and the face I knew as my own.

"I think I need not trouble myself with you," Strahan said in quiet satisfaction. "I will let the others do it for me."

Three

"You should have come to me *first*." She had both temper and tongue to complement the red-gold brilliance of her hair. "Do you know how I have worried since that horse returned without you?"

That horse had indeed returned (without me, of course) and my absence had set the palace into an uproar. Rather, my lady mother had. Most of the Mujharan Guard had been stripped from better duty and sent out looking for me, as if I were a foolish, spoiled child gone wandering in the streets. And they had found me, some of them, just as I approached the gates of Homana-Mujhar. It had been a humiliating experience trying to explain how my horse and I had come to be separated. Especially since I could say nothing of Strahan's presence in the city. Not to them. Not at once. Not until I faced my father.

But now, looking at my mother's pale face, I knew it had been worse than humiliating for her. Always she worried. Always she fretted, saying Ian alone was not enough to guard me against misfortune. This would give her fuel for the fire.

Deep down, I was touched she cared so much, knowing it arose out of insecurity because she had borne only a single son, but mostly I was resentful. Oh, aye, she meant well by it, but there were times the weight she placed upon me was nearly too much to bear.

You may not be his son, she often said, *but you bear his blood, his bone, even his flesh. Have you not looked in the silver plate?*

Oh aye, I had, many times. And each time I saw the same thing: a crude vessel lacking luster, lacking polish. But no one saw the tarnish because it was overlaid with the shining patina of *Carillon*.

Even now she gave me no time to explain; to say a word to my father as he came into my chamber and shut the heavy door.

And so I let the resentment speak for me. "Would you have me remain in my befouled state, then? *Look* at me!" I had gotten as far as shedding muddy boots, soaked doublet; I faced her in filthy leather leggings and damp linen shirt. Thin rivulets of muddied water ran down to stain the carpeted floor.

"Niall." That from my father; that only. But it was more than enough.

I looked back at my mother's taut face. "I am sorry," I told her contritely, meaning it. "But I wanted to bathe and change first, before I came to you."

"It *could* have waited. I have seen men in worse conditions, and they were not my son." The strain showed at the corners of eyes and mouth. She was still beautiful in a way harpers and poets had tried to describe for years, but it was a fragile, brittle beauty, as if she might break with the weight of who and what she was. Aislinn of Homana, daughter of Carillon; once a princess, now a queen, and the mother of her beloved father's grandson.

I think she judged herself solely by the fact she had borne Carillon an heir. A *true* heir, that is; a man with much of his blood, not a Cheysuli warrior handpicked because Carillon had no choice. No, my mother did not view herself as woman, wife, mother or queen. Merely as a means to perpetuate her father's growing legend.

The resentment died as I looked at her. I could not name what rose to take its place, for there was no single emotion. Just a jumble of them, tangled up together like threads of a tapestry; the back side, not the front, with none of the pattern showing.

I released a breath all at once. "I am well. Only wet and dirty. And more than a little hungry." I looked at my father, longing to tell him at once of my confrontation with Strahan. But I would not so long as my mother was in the room. I saw no good in giving her yet another thing to fret about.

"Ian?" he asked.

I shrugged, turning away to strip out of my clammy shirt. "At Clankeep. I think he will stay the night." I heard the servants in the antechamber, filling up the cask-tub with hot, scented water. Oil of cloves, from the smell of it.

"Niall—" It was my mother again, moving toward me, but she did not finish. My father put his hands on her shoulders and turned her away from me. He did it gently enough, but I saw the subtle insistence in his grasp.

"Leave him to me, Aislinn. We have guests to entertain."

Womanlike, she instantly put a hand to the knot of red-gold hair coiled at her neck to tend her appearance. There was no need. She was immaculate, as always. The bright hair, as yet undulled by her thirty-six years, was contained in a pearl-studded net of golden wire. Her velvet gown was plain white, unadorned save for the beaded golden girdle and the gold torque at her throat. My father's bride-gift to her some twenty years before.

"So we do." Her voice was flat, almost colorless. "But I wonder that you choose to host them at all."

"Kings do what kings must do." I heard an edge in my father's voice as well. "We are at peace with Atvia, Aislinn; let us not break the alliance with discourtesy."

Her eyes flicked back to me. Great gray eyes, long-lidded and somnolent. Electra's eyes, they said, recalling the mother's beauty. But in conjuring Electra's name they also conjured Tynstar's.

"This concerns you as well, Niall," she said abruptly. "More so than *us*, when it comes to that. And if your father does not tell you the whole of it, come to me. I will."

The tension between them was palpable. I looked from mother to father, but his face was masked to me. Well, I could wait all night. One thing he had bequeathed to me was more than my share of stubbornness.

My mother went to the door and tugged it open before either my father or I could aid her. She lifted heavy skirts and swept out of the door at once, leaving me to shut it and face my father alone at last.

My father. The Mujhar of Homana he was, but more and less than that to me. He was a Cheysuli warrior.

A son looking upon his father rarely sees the man, he sees the parent. The man who sired him, not the individual. I was no different. Day in, day out I saw him, and yet I did not. I saw what I was accustomed to seeing; what the son saw in the father, the king, the warrior. Too often I did not see the *man.*

Nor did I really know him.

Now, I looked. I saw the face that had helped mold my own, and yet showed nothing of that molding. The bones were characteristically angular, hard, almost sharp; even in light-skinned Cheysuli, the heritage is obvious in the shape of the bones beneath the flesh. The responsibilities of a Mujhar and a warrior dedicated to his *tahlmorra* had incised lines between black brows, fanned creases from yellow eyes, deepened brackets beside the blade-straight nose. There was silver in his hair, pale as winter frost, but only a little; we age early only in that respect, and with infinite grace.

For the first time in a very long time I looked at the scars in his throat and recalled how Strahan had once tried to slay my father by setting a demon-hawk on him. Sakti, her name was, and she had set her talons true, even as she died. But my father had not, thanks to Finn, my kinsman, and the gods who gave us the earth magic.

Earth magic. Another thing I lacked.

He was tall, my father, but not so tall as I, with all of Carillon's bulk. He lacked my weight, though no one would name him a small man; Cheysuli males rarely measure less than six feet, and he was three fingers taller yet. He was certainly more graceful than I, being more subtle in his movements. I wondered if that total ease of movement came with the race or age. The gods knew I had yet to discover it.

Beneath lowered lids, as I began to undress, I watched my father, and wondered how he had felt as Carillon bequeathed him the Lion Throne. I wondered what he had thought, knowing so much of Cheysuli tradition would have to be altered to fit the prophecy. To fit *him:* the first Cheysuli Mujhar in four hundred years.

I would be the second.

He said nothing of my mother to me. A private man, my father, though open enough about some things. Just—not about what I wanted to hear.

"Well?" That said, he waited.

I stripped out of my leggings and walked naked into the antechamber. Steam rose from the cask. The scent of cloves

drifted into the air. And then I waved away the servants
so my father and I could discuss things privately.

I considered telling him the whole of it, from the beginning of the hunt to my arrival, on foot, at Homana-Mujhar.
But that would be unnecessarily perverse of me, and I
thought the circumstances warranted more seriousness. So
I took a shortcut straight to the matter of most importance
to us both.

"I met a man tonight," I began. "A stranger, at least to
me. But he had a message meant for the Prince of Homana.
I took up the soap and began to lather my muddy skin.
"He said I was not to wed my Atvian cousin."

My father's motion to hook a stool over with one foot
was arrested in mid-reach. He did not sit down at all but
faced me squarely, an expression of astonishment mingled
with genuine bafflement on his face.

After a moment of startled speculation, he frowned.
"How odd, that such a thing is said today."

I dipped under the water to soak my hair; came up with
water streaming down my face. "Why only odd *today?*" I
spat out soapy water and grimaced at the taste.

"Because the Atvians we host tonight are here upon
business concerning the betrothal." This time he finished
hooking the stool over and sat down. "It seems Alaric has
decided it is time the betrothal became a marriage."

I stared at him. The scent of cloves filled my nostrils.
Water still ran down my face. But I did not try to wipe it
away. "Now?"

"As soon as can be." He sighed, stretching out long legs.
"Alaric and I made an agreement nearly twenty years ago.
He has every right to expect that agreement to be honored."

His tone was a trifle dry. My father has no particular
liking for Atvians, having fought them in the war; he has
less affection for Alaric, the Lord of Atvia himself. For
one, Alaric's brother had slain Carillon, making my father
Mujhar. And Alaric himself, upon swearing fealty to Donal
of Homana, had demanded my father's sister in marriage
as a means to seal the alliance. Though my father had hated
the idea, he had agreed at last because, in service to the
prophecy of the Firstborn, he saw no other way of linking
the proper bloodlines.

And to link them further, he had declared his firstborn

son would wed the firstborn daughter of Bronwyn and
Alaric.

Oh, aye, Alaric got the match he wanted. He even got
the daughter, called Gisella. But no other. For Bronwyn
died while birthing my half-Cheysuli cousin.

I looked at my father's face. He is a solemn man, the
Mujhar, not much given to impulsiveness or high spirits.
Once he might have been different, but responsibilities, I
am told, can often change even the most ebullient of men.
The gods knew he had known more of them than most, my
father. He had had mother, father, uncle, and Mujhar all
stripped from him, in the name of the prophecy. In the
name of Ihlini treachery.

Lir-gold shone on his bare arms. He was Mujhar of Homana, but he did not forsake his Cheysuli customs, even in
apparel. Certain occasions warranted he put on Homanan
dress, but mostly he wore the leathers of his race.

Our race.

I slid down against the curved wood of the cask and
flipped the soap into the water. "Well, I expected the marriage to be made one day. You never hid it from me, my
tahlmorra." I grinned; it was an old joke between us.
"Just—not *yet*."

My father smiled. No man would call him *old*; he is not
so far past forty, but neither would a woman call him
young. Still, his smile banished the gravity of his title and
set him free again. "No, not *yet*. But soon." A glint of
amusement showed in his yellow eyes. "You have a little
time. Atvian custom demands a proxy wedding before the
true marriage is made."

I frowned in distraction at a purplish bruise on my right
knee. "How soon will this proxy wedding be performed?"

"Oh, I think in the morning. . . . I did say you had a
little time." The glint in his eyes was more pronounced.

"In the *morning!*" I stared at him in dismay. "Without
warning?"

He sighed. "Aye, I would have preferred it myself. And
that is what upsets your *jehana*. She swears it is a purposeful insult and that we should send them home at once until
proper homage is made, along with a respectful request,
since Alaric owes *me* fealty, and not the other way
around." His smile was wry; my mother, born to such things

as royal rights and expectations, was much more cognizant of details my father thought less important. "But Alaric's envoy says a message was sent some months ago, though it never arrived. Perhaps it was." He shrugged, patently dubious. "Regardless of that *and* the lack of proper homage, the betrothal was made in good faith. Alaric has the right to ask the wedding be performed. At seventeen, Gisella is old enough. Once the proxy ceremony is completed, you will go to Atvia to bring your *cheysula* home to a Homanan wedding."

Cheysula. He used the Old Tongue word for wife. But his mouth shaped it differently than mine; like Ian, he had been Keep-raised. They were very alike, my father and my brother. I was like neither of them.

As Strahan had taken infinite pains to point out.

Almost at once I forgot about *cheysulas* and proxy weddings. *"Jehan,"* the Cheysuli word slipped out more easily than usual. "The man who told me not to wed Gisella—" I broke off a moment, not knowing how to say it. "It was the Ihlini. *Jehan*—the man was Strahan."

He stood up at once, my father; so quickly, so abruptly he overset the stool. I heard the thump of wood against stone. The hiss of his indrawn breath.

But *"Strahan"* was all he said.

In the heat of the scented, steaming water, I was cold. To see that look in my father's eyes—

"Aye." Mostly it was a whisper. *"Jehan—"*

"You are certain." The tone was a whiplash of sound. No longer did I face my father. Nor did I face the Mujhar. What man I saw was a warrior filled up with a virulent hatred, dedicated to revenge.

"Certain," I echoed. "I saw his eyes: one blue, one brown. And he lacked an ear."

"Aye, he lacks an ear! Finn made certain of *that* much before he died!"

He broke off. I saw the spasm of grief contort his face. Almost as quickly, the mask was back in place. But he did not veil his eyes. Perhaps he could not. And what I saw sent an icy finger down my spine. *"Jehan—"*

"By the gods, I have prayed that *ku'reshtin* would come within my grasp." Both hands were extended. Fisted. I saw how the sinews stood up beneath the flesh; how the nails dug into the palms. "By the *gods*, I have prayed for this!"

I had not known such hatred could live in my father. He can show anger, aye, and irritation, and more than a little intolerance of things he considers foolish, but to see such bitter hatred in his eyes, to hear it in his voice, made me a child again. It stripped me of size and confidence and made me small again.

I sat in the cask with water lapping around my chest and stared at the warrior who had sired me. And wondered what manner of man *I* might be had the Ihlini served me such pain and grief upon *my* platter.

"He did not harm you?"

Slowly, I shook my head. "He—gave me a taste of his power. But he did me no lasting harm." I thought again on his parting words to me and the vividness of his painting. True? Or false? A trick to undermine my trust in Homanans and Cheysuli? More than likely. It was the Ihlini way.

And I knew it might succeed.

I looked away from my father. Replace me, Strahan had said. With another. Friends, enemies, kin. An alliance uniting them.

"Niall." He reached down and caught my left arm, gripping me by the wrist. "He *did not harm you?*"

"No." I said it as calmly as I could. "He said I was to tender you his regards."

After a moment, my father released my arm. He swore beneath his breath. "Aye, he would. Ever polite, is Strahan. Even when he kills."

"But why *did* he let me live? Surely it would suit his plans better if I were not in his way to the throne?"

"You are not *in* his way, not really." My father, looking infinitely older, shook his head and sighed. "The gods know why, but it is an Ihlini trait to play with an enemy before the kill. They twist the mind before they twist the body, as if it makes the final snap that much more satisfying. Tynstar did it with Carillon for years, though in the end, as you know, Carillon slew Tynstar." Of course I knew. It was all a part of the legend. "It may be a perverse manifestation of the power." He shrugged again. "Who can say? Strahan did not let you live out of kindness. No. More like—anticipation." His expression was very grim. "It means he has other plans for you. It means you are part of his *game*. And when he is done playing with you, he will end it. As he ended it for Finn."

When he is done playing with you, he will end it. I shivered. My father's tone was so matter-of-fact, so certain of Strahan's intentions. He did not shout or bluster or claim we would put an end to Strahan's plans. And it emphasized the Ihlini's power.

I recalled how Strahan had invited me to come to him one day. I recalled how he had said he intended to take my sons. And I wondered how he could be so certain there would be sons to take, as well as that he would take them.

But mostly, I looked at my father. *What does Strahan mean to him?*

His face was stark. The man was a stranger to me. *"Jehan."* I straightened in the cask. "If—if I had known how much you hated him . . . I would have tried to slay him."

He did nothing at all at once. He only stared down at me, as if he had not heard what I had said. In perfect stillness, perfect silence; a statue carved out of human flesh.

And then he said something in the Old Tongue, something that came out of his mouth on a rushing of breath, and I saw the tears forming in his eyes as he knelt down on one knee to grasp my hand in both of his.

"Never," he said hoarsely, "Never, *never*, Niall. He would slay you. He would slay you. He would take you from me as he has taken all the others, and I would be *alone.*"

I stared at him. His hands were cold, so cold, and I realized he was afraid. I had meant to comfort him, to offer what I could of loyalty. Instead, I had broken the fox from its den and set the hounds upon its trail.

By the gods, my father is afraid. . . .

"How?" I asked, when I could. "How could you be *alone* when you have so many others?"

"Name them," he said unevenly. "Say their names to me."

"My *mother!*" I was amazed he could not do it for himself. "Taj and Lorn. General Rowan. Ian and Isolde." I stared at him. *"Jehan,* how could you be alone?"

His breath was harsh. "I have them, aye, I have all of them: *cheysula, lir,* children, trusted general. But—it is not the same." He rose abruptly, turning his back on me. His spine was rigid beneath leather jerkin and human flesh. Then, just as abruptly, he swung around to face me. "Look what I have done to your *jehana*. I would offer her the sort of love she craves, if I could, but so much was burned out of me when Sorcha—died." Even now, he could not speak the truth: that his Cheysuli *meijha*, Ian's and Isolde's mother, had slain herself because she could not bear to share him with a Homanan. "There is much affection between Aislinn and me, of course, and honor, regard, respect—but that is not what she wants. Nor is it what she needs." His anguish was manifest. "But I cannot offer falsehood to her when she is deserving of so much better."

I listened in shocked silence, grateful I knew the truth at last, but unsettled at the hearing. He was an adult speaking to an adult, man to man, and yet I still felt so very young.

My father sighed and scraped a lock of black hair out of his eyes. "As for Taj and Lorn, aye—I share everything with my *lir* a warrior should. But they are *lir*, not men. Not kin. As for Rowan—" He grimaced. "Rowan and I work well together in the ordering of the realm, but we will never be easy together in personal things. I am not Carillon, whom he worshipped." He bent and righted the stool. "Ian and Isolde are everything a *jehan* could desire in his children. But I am the Mujhar of Homana, and the Homanans perceive them as bastards. It makes them different. It soils them in Homanan eyes, and that perception affects me. And so it leaves me only you, Niall." He smiled a little, but it had a bittersweet twist. "None of them are you. None of them are born of the prophecy." I saw the trace of anguish in his eyes. "None of them will know the things I have known. Not as *you* will know them."

For a long moment I said nothing at all, being unable to speak. But when I could speak again, I asked a thing all men might desire to ask of warriors and Mujhars. "Would you have it differently?"

My father laughed, but there was no humor in the sound—only pain. "What warrior, looking fully into the face of his *tahlmorra*, would not?" His smile was twisted; wry and regretful. "I would change everything; I would change nothing. A paradox, Niall, that only a few men have known. Only a few men *will* know." He sighed. "Carillon could tell you. So could Duncan and Finn. But all of them are gone, and I lack the proper words."

"*Jehan*—"

But even as I began, he turned and walked out of the room.

Four

In my dreams I was a raptor, circling in the sky. I felt the
buoyant uprush of warm air beneath my wings lifting me
heavenward, carrying me higher yet. But higher was not
where I wished to go. And so I angled outspread wings,
tilting toward the ground, and swept downward, downward,
in an ever-tightening spiral, until I drifted in idleness over
the walls of the castle garden, and saw the two girls plainly.

Young. Very young, yet much the same age. They knelt
upon the lush grass of a new spring, surrounded by a profu-
sion of brilliant blossoms, and shared a game of their own
devising. I heard sweet soprano voices rising on the sibilant
breeze. And yet the sweetness was tempered by an odd
possessiveness.

Closer. My shadow was a winged blotch upon the ground,
darkness itself sweeping across the grass until it swallowed
both girls whole. Enough, I thought, to make even a man
shiver from the omen. But the two small girls took no notice
of my shadow, or of me. Instead, they fixed one another
with feral, angry glares and tugged in opposition at something held between them.

My shadow swept onward, turned, then hastened back
again. More closely yet I drifted, raptor's eyes caught by the
glint of something on the thing they shared. Closer still; the
thing, I saw, was a cloth doll, nothing more, with a cheap
gilt brooch fastened to its forehead in a child's mimicry of
a crown. But only one doll and two girls; no good would
come of it. Sharing does not always serve.

A glint from the brooch. A sparkle, bright as glass. Raven-
like, I yearned to make that brightness mine. But I was raptor, not raven; if I stooped to claim a prize it would never
be a bit of tin or glass. No. Something worth far more.

Angry, accusative voices, filled with hate and scorn. I had

*heard the like in my childhood, had shared the tone with
Ian and Isolde once or twice. But those days had long passed
and the girls below me were strangers.*

*I saw no faces, only the color of their hair as they knelt
stiffly upon the grass with the doll clenched in their hands.
Each was the antithesis of the other: blue-black hair/thick
gold hair. Young skin the color of copper-bronze/young skin
the color of cream.*

Antithesis, aye. As Ian and I to one another.

"Mine, mine!" cried the black-haired girl.

"Mine, mine!" cried the gold-haired girl.

*Closer. Closer. I saw how the doll's arms and legs were
spread and pulled taut, tugged at until the seams threatened
to split. Beneath the gilt brooch-crown someone had stitched
on a face with colored thread. The red mouth smiled. The
blue eyes gazed vacantly into the heavens, blissfully blind to
the fate I so clearly foresaw. And even as I opened beak to
cry out a warning, the tortured toy split apart and spilled
out its dried-bean blood onto the grass. I heard the hiss and
rattle as the beans poured out and a shriek from each of
the girls.*

*My shadow slanted across them both. Now they saw me.
Now they took notice of my nearness. Now they threw down
the two empty halves of the ruined doll and turned their
faces toward the sky.*

*And I saw clearly, as I had not from the beginning, that
neither girl had a face. Only blankness, endless blankness
amidst the black/gold hair, devoid of a single feature.*

Weight descended upon me. In a panic, I tried to sit up
and could not; I was pinned to the bed too securely. Even
as I opened my mouth to cry out, the warm, pungent breath
of a mountain cat rushed in to replace the sound I sought
to make.

Tasha loomed over me. I heard the deep staccato rattle
of her rumbling purr. Her cool nose touched mine briefly,
then she set tongue to flesh and began to lick.

"Ian!" Most of my strangled shout was muffled beneath
Tasha's tongue. I did not dare move. Forepaws on shoulders pinned my upper body; hind ones were thrust between
my naked thighs. No; it *was not* worth the risk. "Tasha—
enough!"

I felt the rap of tail against kneecap. The licking halted

momentarily, but the tongue, resolute, remained attached to cheek and chin. My flesh, abraded, stung; shaving would be painful.

The licking renewed itself, but only for one more swipe. Undaunted by gauzy summer bed-hangings, Tasha sprang through them to the floor and left me free once more.

I sat up at once, yanking the bedclothes over my nakedness. "Ian! What—"

"You needed waking," he interposed smoothly. Through the creamy gauze I could see him standing alone at the foot of my bed, blurred by the texture of the hangings. "Torvald meant to come, of course; I told him I would see to the preparations for your wedding." Ian grinned. "I am no *proper* body-servant, of course, but I know where the arms and legs go. I should do well enough."

The sudden waking on the heels of an ugly dream left me with a headache. I glared at Ian and rubbed my forehead, trying to draw out the pain. "Better I go naked to my wedding than leave the dressing to *you*."

"Your choice." Ian, still smiling, shrugged. "No doubt the bride, proxy or no, might prefer it that way."

I grunted. "Only if Alaric sends me a well-used girl in Gisella's place. . . ." I frowned at him through the draperies. "What are you doing here? I thought you would stay at Clankeep."

Ian shook his head. In the thin pink light of dawn the cat-shaped earring glowed against the blackness of his hair. "*Jehan* sent word through Taj late last night; I left before dawn." Briefly, he frowned. "Did you think I would miss your wedding?"

"*Proxy* wedding." I fought my way through layers of gossamer gauze and stood up beside the bed. Spring or no, it was cold; Torvald's absence meant an absence of heat as well, since Ian had not tended braziers or fireplace. I squinted toward the nearest narrow casement. "Dawn, just. Time enough for food and clothing before this ceremony."

"You will eat *at* the wedding breakfast, not before." Ian laughed as I swore beneath my breath. "Fasting might improve your temper."

"As much as Tasha improved my face." I glared sourly at the mountain cat sitting silently near the door. Amber eyes were slitted; the tip of her tail twitched once. "Your idea, *rujho*?"

"Tasha is fond of you." Ian, considering that explanation enough, sat down on the nearest of my storage chests, leaning against the tapestried wall, and brushed at a smudge upon an otherwise spotless boot toe. Wedding finery: he wore supple doeskin jerkin and leggings dyed a soft honey yellow. The boots he tended matched, worked with copper-colored thread. Tassles trembled as he worked at the smudge. Bare-armed, the *lir*-gold shone.

Looking at him, I saw what I was not; what I could never be. *Ah gods, I wish you would give me the right to claim a* lir *and wear the gold on my arms and in my ear.* But I did not say it aloud. Instead, I answered Ian's comment.

"Fond of me," I echoed dryly. "If she loved me, would she use her teeth instead?"

"And plenty of claw, as well." Thoughtfully, Ian looked at an old scar on the underside of one wrist.

Even as I started to move toward my clothing chests, I stopped. Swung back. "Ask *her*," I said tersely. "Ask Tasha why I have no *lir*."

I had never asked it of him before. The bond he and Tasha shared was intensely private, and even another warrior knows better than to ask of private things better left between human *lir* and animal. And yet I could not put off the request a moment longer. Something drove me to it.

If Ian was surprised, he hid it well. At first, I saw only a new rigidity in the line of his shoulders. He sat upright on the trunk, no longer leaning against the tapestry. And as he spread fingers against the wood of the trunk in a silent and subtle plea for strength from someone other than me (the gods, perhaps?) I saw the tension in his hands.

"I have," he said tonelessly. "Repeatedly. Did you think I would not try?"

"And her answer?" Consumed, for the moment, with discovering Tasha's response, I ignored the faint undertone of pain in Ian's voice. I had wounded him somehow, but I thought his cut lacked the infection of my own.

Ian looked away. Plainly troubled, he stared at the floor. The uncarpeted stone beneath his boots was red, rose-red, as were the walls of Homana-Mujhar. A shaft of light working its way through a blue panel of stained glass in the casement painted the rose a deeper red, until the shade was nearly purple.

I stood barefooted on the Caledonese carpet by my bed and waited, naked, for my answer.

"I have asked," Ian said again. I saw how the muscles jumped once beneath the firm flesh of his beardless jaw. Sharp as a blade, the bone beneath the flesh. And aye, beardless. Because the Cheysuli cannot grow them.

But I had to shave each morning, or look more like Carillon than ever. "And the answer?"

When he could, he met my eyes and shook his head.

"I have no answer for you."

"Not from *you*," I said roughly, "from *her*." I jerked my head in Tasha's direction. "She is *lir*. The *lir* have all the answers. They know much more than any warrior can ever know. Ask her *again* for an answer!"

Ian drew in a deep breath. "No." Flatly said, with no room for urging or argument.

I opened my mouth to urge, to argue, to plead. And closed it again, because I saw there was no point. All the anger spilled away as I looked at my older brother. Aye, he had asked. More than once. But saying nothing to me, until now, because to tell me was to hurt me.

Liege man. *Rujholli.* And more. *Ah gods, I thank you for my brother.*

"Niall." He stood up and faced me. I was taller, heavier, fairer—two puppies sired on different mothers, but sharing kinship ties stronger than full-blooded brothers.

"*Rujho*, I swear I would take the pain from you if I had the arts to do it."

"I know." I could not look at him. His pain reflected my own, and that I could not bear. "I do not mean to berate *you*."

"Nor should you berate yourself." He did not smile. "Do you think I do not see it? I know the nights you cannot sleep, cannot eat. I know when you drink too much. I know when you look to a woman to ease the pain. I am your *rujholli*, aye, and liege man as well, but I am not always with you. And yet—I can tell. I can see the marks on your back though the whip be invisible." He reached out and caught my arms above the elbows, where the *lir*-bands ought to be. "It does not make you less a man to *me*."

The emphasis was eloquent, though he did not mean it to be. To him, I was a man. But to the warriors in the clan, I was merely a Homanan.

I looked at him directly. "What did Ceinn wish to say to you?"

He had not expected it. His fingers tightened in reflex before he could release my arms. "Ceinn?" I saw the brief loathing in his eyes. "Ceinn is a—fool." He wanted to say more; he did not.

"It had to do with me."

"More to do with me." He shook his head. "No good would come of it. *Rujho*, let it go."

"And if I do not?"

He tried to smile, but it came out less than amused. "When have you ever been able to make me speak when I have decided against it?"

True enough. Glumly, I gestured toward one of the brass-bound clothing chests that lined fully two of my chamber walls. "What do I wear for this, *rujho*? What finery do I put on?"

Ian's look was level. "It depends," he said calmly, "on what man you choose to be."

I stared. "What man?"

"Cheysuli," he said, "or Homanan."

Ian and I were directed to one of the smaller audience chambers. Somehow I had expected the ceremony to take place in the Great Hall, so full of ambience and history. But the Mujhar, we were told, had selected the smaller hall, to promote intimacy rather than intimidation.

"Possibly a mistake," Ian said in a low voice as we entered the audience chamber. "I know little enough of statecraft, but I think the Atvians may require what intimidation we can offer."

"They shall face Cheysuli," I said lightly. "That should be enough."

Ian laughed. "A good omen: my *rujho* jests on his wedding day."

"*Proxy*," I reminded him as the servant shut the door behind us. Though considerably smaller than the Great Hall with its Lion Throne, the chamber was impressive enough in its own intimate way. Here the rose-red walls had been whitewashed. Stained glass tableaus of Homanan history filled the deep, narrow casements and lent the white walls a subtle wash of countless colors. The stone floors were bare of rugs, but here the natural rose-colored surface was allowed to go unpainted. Sunlight and stained glass filled the chamber with a pastel nacreous glow.

"Proxy," my father agreed. "And as binding as a proper Homanan wedding." The Mujhar rose from the cushioned chair on the low dais at the far end of the chamber. Lorn sat slumped against one wooden leg as if his sole responsibility in life was to hold up the chair. On the back perched the golden falcon, Taj, and beside the chair stood another for the Queen of Homana; at present, however, it was empty.

I glanced around quickly, searching for Atvians, but saw none. Only my mother, by one of the narrow casements, staring out into the inner bailey.

She turned abruptly. Yellow skirts swirled around her feet. I saw the sheen of silk; heard the sibilance of fold caressing fold. "Binding!" she said bitterly. "What binds us now is *idiocy*. Niall would do better with another."

"Aislinn, we have been through this," my father said in weary exasperation. "As for doing better, *how* better? Gisella is his cousin, and *harana* to you by your marriage to me. Throw a stone at Gisella, Aislinn, and you splatter its mud upon yourself."

Gold glittered at my lady mother's neck. Her hands were clenched in the folds of her silken skirts. There was gold on her hands as well, threading from the heavy girdle through rigid fingers to clash against the fabric. Her rich red hair was bound up against her head, and resting against her brow was a circlet of twisted gold wire.

"It is not *Gisella*," she said tightly. "It is her father. *Him*. The Lord of Atvia himself. Do you forget it was Alaric's *brother* who slew my father?"

"I do not forget," he told her plainly. "You do not *let* me forget."

She wanted to go to him. I could see it in her face; in the great gray eyes that harpers sang of, making her beauty into legend. But she did not go to him. She stood instead by the casement and faced him, proud as the Mujhar himself, and equally inflexible.

I glanced briefly at Ian, still standing next to me. His face bore the polite mask it always wore before the Queen of Homana and Solinde. But I wondered what he thought. I wondered what my mother's terrible pride in heritage did to the man who was not her son.

I sighed. My headache threatened to return. "Does it go on, then, this ceremony? Or do I go back to my chambers and take off my finery?"

My mother still looked at my father, even as he looked at her. I wondered if they had heard me at all. I wondered if they even recalled Ian and I were in the chamber. They waged some private battle, and I could not begin to name the stakes.

"No." My mother, at last, still looking at my father, though the answer was for me. "No, you do not."

There was neither triumph nor relief in my father's face. Acknowledgment, I thought, of my mother's surrender. And perhaps a trace of compassion, because he knew why she fought so fiercely.

"You look well." My father turned to me. "I approve the selection of Cheysuli leathers."

I shrugged a little. "It—there was no choice. But—I could wish my arms were not so naked."

"And *do* wish it," my father said. "I know, Niall. Better than you think."

The pain renewed itself. I had chosen, but the choice did not feel right. It made my belly churn and stab at me with a familiar burning pain. But I had not earned the leathers.

"You are Homanan *also*," my mother began, as always; it was her litany. "Put not so much weight in ornamentation and think of the blood in your veins."

"Carillon's blood?" Through the pain I could not smile. "Aye, lady, always. As you would have me recall it."

Color stood high in her flawless face. The gray eyes flicked to Ian. "Was it your suggestion?"

"No, lady," he said gently. "I merely offered him the choice."

Briefly, she shut her eyes as if to shut out his words. But almost immediately they opened again and she looked at him unflinchingly. Her tone lacked the bitterness of moments before. "No, no, you would not thrust one or the

other upon him. I know you better than you think, Ian. It
is *myself*—"

But she did not finish, because the liveried servant who
had shown us into the chamber was opening the door yet
again. And this time there came Atvians into the room.

A man and a woman. The man was tall, elegant, garbed
in understated blue velvets and an attitude too well-trained
to betray anything other than respect and graciousness, and
yet I sensed a power in him, leashed, as if he were a hawk
waiting for the jesses to be cut. His hair was very dark,
nearly black, and his eyes were an odd pale brown. The
only ornamentation was a silver ring on his left hand and
matching earrings in his lobes.

His outstretched left hand offered escort to the woman.
Though her right hand met his palm, they hardly touched
one another. An odd dance by two magnificent animals. A
bizarre sort of courtship rite, I thought, when the woman
was meant for me.

Looking at her, I reminded myself at once the ceremony
was proxy only. What I knew of the custom was no less
than anyone else: I would wed the woman in Gisella's place
to make certain the alliance between Homana and Atvia
was sealed by the blood of our respective Houses, but I
would not bed the woman. That was left for Gisella.

And yet I found I regretted it.

She put me in mind of a harp string, capable of a poignant, subtle power. Plucked this way, plucked that, she
would still emit a tone that would bind each man to its
strength, resonating in his soul. I thought almost at once of
my mother's mother, Electra of Solinde, whom legend said
could ensorcell men with a single glance from lambent eyes.
And yet what I knew of that woman did not apply to this
one. The white-blond hair was black. The ice-gray eyes
were also. The velvet gown was brilliant crimson.

Smiling faintly, she allowed the man to lead her forward.
The hem of her skirts brushed the stone of the floor; I
heard its subtle song. A woman's song, that sound, and
incredibly powerful. But it was not at her skirts I looked.

Her head was bowed in a perfect humility, but there was
pride in her posture as well, and a comprehension of her
strength. Beautiful, aye, and claiming that power as a matter of course, but there was more to her than simple beauty.

There was confidence as well. An acknowledgment of her place in the world of kings and princes.

My mother moved smoothly to my father's side. They stood together on the dais before the padded chairs, united in titles and goals, and waited to receive the Atvian envoy and Gisella's proxy bride.

Silver glittered. The woman wore it at hip and brow. A chain of interlocking silver feathers formed a girdle. A plain silver circlet touched her brow, then flared out at each temple to form delicate downswept wings; curving back to encircle her head. Black hair, unbound except for the winged silver circlet, fell in a silken curtain to girdled, crimson hips.

"By the gods," I whispered to Ian, "is there a way I can wed the *proxy* bride instead of the genuine thing?"

His answering smile was wry. "It might discompose Gisella."

"As well as the alliance." I sighed dramatically. "Ah, well . . . *tahlmorras* must be obeyed."

"Such sacrifice," Ian mocked. "*I*, however, am not already bound to such a course."

I opened my mouth to return a suitable retort, but the envoy was speaking and I shut my mouth on my answer.

"I am Varien, ambassador from the Atvian court to yours," the Atvian said quietly. "My lord Mujhar; Aislinn, Queen of Homana and Solinde; Niall, Prince of Homana—may I present the Lady Lillith, sent from Alaric himself, Lord of the Idrian Isles."

Shea of Erinn would dispute that particular title. And did, I knew, even now. A petty thing, to fight over petty titles, but it was not Homana's problem.

Varien's voice was a smooth, cultured baritone. He spoke with a fluent, meticulous courtesy in accentless, flawless Homanan. Envoys are required to speak many languages, but for a moment, oddly, I wondered how he would do in the Cheysuli Old Tongue, which defies those not born to its cadence and lyricism.

Lillith. An odd name not unpleasing to the ear. I rolled it over on my tongue silently and found it more difficult to say than to hear.

Crimson skirts flared and settled as she dropped into a curtsy before the dais. I saw her nails were tipped in silver, and her mouth was painted red.

Beside me, Ian drew in his breath in a sudden hiss of shock. I looked at him sharply and found him staring rigidly at the woman as she rose from her eloquent obeisance. Yet it was not the stare of a man struck by a woman's beauty, but by realization instead.

And then I heard Tasha's growl.

Almost at once, the chamber was filled with tension. Tasha still growled, tail whipping at Ian's right leg. Lorn rose to stand before the chairs, hackled from neck to tail. And Taj, still perched upon the chair, bated in agitation.

My brother's hand was on his knife. My father was off the dais and standing before the woman. "You *dare* to come into my hall?" His anger and astonishment were manifest. "You *dare* to come into my city?"

"My lord Alaric sent me." Her voice was low and husky. The Homanan words had a foreign lilt.

"Does *he* know what you are?"

After a moment, Lillith smiled. But only a little smile. "My lord Alaric knows everything about me."

I could not be as calm as the woman so obviously was, but neither could I experience the same measure of shock as everyone save my mother. "Ian—what *is* she?"

"Ihlini," he hissed in an undertone. Then, more loudly, "By the gods, she is *Ihlini!*"

"What is the meaning of this?" my mother cried. "Alaric sends an *enemy* to show what he thinks of the betrothal?"

"Not at all," Varien said smoothly. "He sends a lady he holds very highly in his esteem."

"I am Ihlini," Lillith said quietly. "I do not deny it. But what is between your race and mine has nothing to do with the betrothal. Be assured, Alaric desires the marriage."

"Ihlini and Cheysuli do not treat with one another." My father's tone was deadly. "Is this some trick of Strahan's?"

Arched black brows rose below the silver circlet. "My lord Mujhar, I say again: Alaric desires the marriage. Strahan has no hand in this. Was it not you yourself who agreed to this alliance sealed by a marriage between your son and your sister's daughter?"

"It was agreed by Homana and Atvia," the Mujhar said. "There was no mention of Ihlini."

"He did not know me then."

She was deadly serious. But I wondered if she was as

calm as she appeared. An Ihlini in the halls of Homana-Mujhar? No more calm, I thought, than I would be within the halls of Ihlini Valgaard.

"Did he know, when he sent you, he gave us every opportunity to break off this betrothal?" my father demanded.

Lillith's eyes were unwavering. Her expression did not alter. "The enmity between Ihlini and Cheysuli is known to all men, my lord. But Alaric intended no insult. He sent me because he wished to, regardless of my blood." Briefly, black eyes narrowed. "Are the Cheysuli so hostile they cannot set aside their hatred for the sake of realms and children?"

"Ask us where our hostility comes from," my father commanded. "Ask us how we came so close to being annihilated by our own Homanan allies. Because of the Ihlini, *Lady Lillith of Atvia.* Because fear and hostility were fostered by the Ihlini, who reaped the benefits of a mad king's attempted extirpation of my race."

Lillith did not answer at once. I had seen my father this angry only once or twice, and I liked it no better this time. A man of iron control; it is painful to see him let it go.

Varien made a movement as if to speak, but Lillith put a hand upon his wrist and he said nothing after all. Instead, she took a single step forward toward my father. They were close. Very close. She had only to put out her hand to touch him. Uneasily, I thought of Strahan and his cold Ihlini fire.

I heard the metallic scrape of a knife pulled from its sheath. Ian's lips were moving in silent prayer or silent curse as he clenched his hand upon the hilt; I could not say which. But I saw how the swollen pupils turned his yellow eyes black. I saw how he watched the Ihlini woman, and knew she would live no longer than was humanly possible if she sought to slay our father.

"My lord Mujhar," she said quietly in her honeyed, husky voice. "I see no Ihlini within the halls of Homana-Mujhar. I would say we *lost* the battle for the Lion."

Donal of Homana merely laughed. "Oh, aye, you lost the battle for the Lion. But never, *never* do us the discourtesy of thinking we are foolish enough to discount the Ihlini so long as they serve the god of the netherworld."

Lillith met his steady gaze. She did not so much as blink.

"And do you think, my lord Mujhar, that *I* serve Asar-Suti?"

After a moment, my father smiled. "Lady, I would wager you lie down with the dark god himself."

It was Lillith's turn to laugh. The husky sound filled up the chamber. "Oh, *no*, my lord Mujhar . . . I only lie down with Alaric."

Five

My mother recoiled a single step, then caught herself, as if she preferred not to show the Ihlini woman she could be taken by surprise. "You are Alaric's whore?"

Lillith looked at her calmly. "Whore? In the Cheysuli Old Tongue women such as I are called *meijhas* and offered honor. In the Homanan language, the proper word is *light woman*. Yet the Queen herself resorts to the low speech of the streets?"

"If it is the *truth*," my mother answered. "You insult the Mujhar, *Lady Lillith*. Do you forget his sister was Alaric's wife?"

"Bronwyn has been dead nearly eighteen years," Lillith told her calmly. "Before she died, she gave my lord little welcome in her bed. And once she *had* conceived, she denied him utterly. Do you expect Alaric to keep himself faithful when he is wed to a woman like that?"

My father's hand was a blur as he reached out and caught one of Lillith's velveted wrists. "That is *enough* from you, Ihlini! You will keep your mouth from my *rujholla's* name!"

I was a little surprised by my father's vehemence. He and my aunt had parted on unhappy terms when Alaric came awooing from Atvia. My mother had told me Bronwyn wanted nothing to do with the marriage, but because of politics and the prophecy, my father had seen fit to wed her to Alaric even against her wishes. They had neither seen one another nor corresponded again, though I knew my father would have given the world to make peace with his sister.

Lillith's chin rose a little. Sunlight set the winged circlet aglow against raven hair. "Plain speech, I freely admit; I meant it so, just as the Queen meant her question. But I

ask you this, *my lord*: if the Cheysuli are so dedicated to
the tolerance of *all* races—as claimed in the prophecy of
the Firstborn—then why am I renounced for mine?"

"Alaric's whore," my mother repeated distinctly. "Oh,
aye, I use the low speech of the streets. Because you are
not worthy of better." She stepped down from the dais and
moved to stand next to her husband, confronting Lillith
directly. The first shock had passed; she faced the woman
possessed of a quiet dignity and an equally eloquent air of
command. "You may return home to Atvia, Lady Lillith,
and tell Alaric he will have to look elsewhere for a husband
for his daughter."

"Take your hand from me." Lillith did not acknowledge
my mother's words, looking steadily at my father. *"Take
your hand from me."*

After a moment, my father did so, as if he could not
bear to touch her.

"My lord." Varien, smiling, still couched his words in
unruffled courtesy. "My lord Mujhar, I well understand the
Queen's feelings in this matter. But I think she may wish
to reconsider what she has just said." He inclined his head
to my mother. "It is true the Lady Lillith is Ihlini. But it
is as I said; my lord Alaric esteems her highly."

"In his *bed*." It was Ian, shocking us all with his virulence;
I stared at him in surprise.

Lillith turned her head far enough to slant him an inquiring
glance out of eloquent eyes. A delicate silver wing glittered
against her hair. "In his bed *and* out of it. Why? Do you
wish to share it as well?"

Ian's laugh was a gust of air expelled with all the force
of disbelief. "I would sooner lie down with a leper!"

Lillith's eyelids lowered as if she consulted an inner
voice. It gave her a shuttered, secretive look of incredible
insularity. It made me wish to ask aloud what she thought;
what she intended to say. But I did not. What Ihlini would
tell a Cheysuli the truth?

Shut up within her thoughts, she presented an incongru-
ous picture of maidenly decorum. I knew better. She was
Ihlini; I had faced Strahan. And as for maidenly decorum,
she had already proclaimed herself Alaric's light woman. It
gave her a passkey to vulgarity, if she wished to use it.

But apparently she did not. When the kohl-smudged lids

lifted again, baring her eyes to all, I saw nothing but resolute innocence.

Her head lifted minutely. Her chin and jaw were distinctly molded, so that a tilt of a head this way or that divulged a multitude of things otherwise left unsaid. Someone had schooled her well in the use of her body.

Or perhaps witches such as Lillith and Electra are born to manipulate men with a smile, a look, a sigh.

Pale hands gathered heavy velvet. Smoothly she put her back to the Mujhar and the Queen of Homana and turned instead to face Ian and me, hair swinging, skirts swirling, silver nails flashing against the rich texture of the velvet.

She looked at me, but briefly; her attention was blatantly fixed on Ian. "Are you kin to the Prince of Homana?"

Somehow, it was not what either of us expected. I frowned; Ian answered because of innate courtesy, though the tone did not reflect it. "We share the same *jehan*."

It was clear she knew the word. The painted lips, still smiling, parted in silent comprehension. "Then you are the *bastard* son."

It took us all by surprise, her pointedly casual comment, but Ian more so than anyone else, I think. I saw the color drain out of his face until it was chalky-gray. He was not one generally much perturbed by insults—being so obviously Cheysuli, he was used to occasional Homanan curses—and bastardy bears no stigma in the clans. But this was from a woman, emphatically unprovoked, and an Ihlini woman at that. Somehow her precise explicitness honed the words more sharply. Without a doubt the knife cut more deeply than ever before.

Angrily, I swung back a rigid hand, fully intending to bring it across her lovely face. But Ian stopped me by reaching out to catch my wrist. "No."

"*Rujho*—"

"No," he said evenly. "Do not soil your hands."

"Lillith." My mother's voice, calm, cool, supremely in command of the situation. She was all queen now, standing tall in yellow silk and royal gold. What I witnessed was Carillon's legacy.

I saw the instinctive response in the Ihlini woman as she turned almost at once; saw also how that reaction surprised her by its alacrity. And how much it sat ill with her.

"Lillith." My mother smiled her lovely, deadly smile. "I will allow you to insult my husband's son no more than I will allow you to insult my own." Her face was smooth, untroubled; I saw a glint of satisfaction in her eyes. "Or, regardless of *whose* bed you sleep in, I will have you cast bodily out of this palace."

I nearly gaped in surprise. To hear her protecting Ian so definitively was shocking as well as welcome; they said little enough to one another, being uneasy companions at best, and certainly nothing in the past had warranted such loyalty on the part of my mother. And yet she sounded as fierce as if she defended *me*.

Smiling inwardly, I flicked a pleased glance at Ian. His color was back, though a little more flushed than normal; shock had been replaced by anger at the Ihlini. No doubt my mother's defense startled him as much as it had me, but he did not show it. He showed nothing but a mask.

Lillith inclined her head. "As you wish, lady. No more insults. I offer choices instead."

The mask slipped. "Choices?" Ian demanded roughly. "What choices could an *Ihlini* offer us?"

Lillith looked at the Mujhar. "*Your* choice, my lord: send Varien and me back to Atvia, and have the betrothal broken." She tilted her head a little to one side. "I have given you reason enough."

"Purposely," he said lightly. "Aye, I have seen that clearly. There is a purpose to all of this." He smiled. It was not the smile of a man he showed her, but of a predator whose attention is fixed upon the spoor of lively game. "Now, Lady Lillith, give me the other half so I may know the choice."

But it was not Lillith who answered. Varien spread his hands. "Simple, my lord: ignore the lady's heritage and allow the ceremony to go on."

My mother laughed aloud. "Do you expect us to overlook what she has said, let alone what she *is?*"

No. My instinctive response was immediate. *If for no other reason than the pain she brought to my brother, I would send her back to Alaric.*

"Choices," Varien said. "My lord?"

My father did not answer at once. I saw the fine-drawn tension in my mother as she waited; and felt it in myself.

Not because I particularly wanted to marry Gisella—cousin or no, I did not know the girl—but because some deep-seated instinct told me the choice facing my father carried more weight than usual.

He knew it as well as I, perhaps better, being who he is. I saw him smile again, mostly to himself, and then he turned it fully on the Atvian envoy. "Alaric and Shea have made a truce."

I frowned. It made no sense; none of it. What had a truce between Alaric of Atvia and Shea of Erinn to do with my marriage?

Varien's lips tightened. Briefly, oh so briefly, I saw anger in his eyes, and then he covered it. He was himself again, urbane, diplomatic, yet I knew my father's response was not what he expected.

I looked immediately at the woman, knowing instinctively she was a truer diviner of emotions. But if Lillith was angry, she hid it well. Instead, she smiled, and nodded once to herself. As if she had won a wager.

Or understood us better than anyone wished to believe.

"A truce," my father repeated. Still smiling, he sat down at last in the padded chair and gestured for my mother to do the same. After a moment's hesitation, she did so. But I knew she understood my father's manner no better than I, even as he laughed. "Let me speculate aloud, envoy, for a moment. Please correct me if I am wrong." He straightened a little and tapped one finger against the wooden arm. "Alaric and Shea, regardless of their respective reasons, have agreed to a truce. I think it unlikely Shea would ally himself with Alaric for any reason, judging by the turbulent history of the islands; nonetheless, a cessation of hostilities leaves Alaric in possession of a united warhost for the first time in decades." He paused, and I saw he no longer smiled. "Have I the right of it thus far?"

Varien's schooled face exhibited neither resentment nor regret; he merely acknowledged my father's summation with a brief inclination of his head.

"What is he doing?" I whispered to Ian. "What has a truce between Alaric and Shea have to do with anything?"

I saw the ironic curling of his mouth; Lillith's insult had not banished his sense of humor. "If you would close your mouth and open your ears, perhaps you would find out."

But my father went on before I could respond. "If I broke off the betrothal for reasons well known to all of us in this chamber, Alaric would have the right to consider the alliance shattered; the right to levy war." The Mujhar's face displayed no tension, only calmness. He had the right of it. Wars had been started over more trivial matters than this. "The past has proven Atvia incapable of defeating Homana in battle because her armies have been divided. Shea's *meddling* made it necessary for a portion of the war-host to be left at home to protect Atvia, and so it was that much easier for Homana to defeat her enemy. Now, of course, with Erinn and Atvia at peace, no matter how brief the duration, Alaric can levy half again as many men against Homana."

"My lord." Varien said nothing more; nothing more was needed. Even I began to see.

"And so if the betrothal is broken and Alaric comes against me, as would be his right, it is potentially possible that Homana could be defeated . . . and Alaric made Mujhar." My father shut his mouth on that; patently, he was finished discussing the thing.

Varien said nothing. He did not dare to in the face of his supposedly neutral commission.

But Lillith did. "Enough Erinnish knotwork, my lord Mujhar. Let us speak plainly." She did not so much as look at Varien as she stepped in front of him to face my father. "You may interpret the reason for my presence here in any way you choose. You may even be correct. But bear in mind that *if* war came of a broken betrothal, Atvia might well lose all. There is always that chance in war. I think you realize, my lord Mujhar, that Alaric has more to gain by seeing your son and his daughter wed than by breaking the betrothal."

"Then why this elaborate farce?" my mother asked. "By the gods, woman, Ihlini or no—have you an explanation?"

Lillith smiled. "Of course. But I leave that for you to divine."

"Insult," my brother murmured to me. "No more than that; a petty attempt by a petty man to irritate his overlord."

I frowned. "All of *this* just for *that?*"

"United army or not, Alaric would be a fool to believe

Atvia could defeat Homana. But he cannot accept continuing vassalage graciously; he is sly, he is resentful. His pride aches, so he offers this idiocy merely to slip the nettle into our bed." Ian shrugged. "I doubt Alaric is stupid enough to believe we would fall for this foolishness."

My father looked at me. "I will let the Prince of Homana make the choice. It is *he* who must wed Alaric's daughter, not I."

Varien had not expected that. Neither, I thought, had Lillith. They had discounted me early in the game as too young, too unimportant to consider. It was the Mujhar for whom they had set the trap.

Well, *I* had not expected it, either.

Nothing would please me more than to pack Alaric's light woman back to Atvia in disgrace. But I think it is not worth a war.

I inclined my head briefly to acknowledge my father's trust. And then I crossed the chamber to the woman dressed in crimson and reached out to take her hand.

Silver-tipped nails glowed. The painted lips smiled a little, waiting for my answer. Close up, she was lovelier than ever. But it was a hard-edged beauty with nothing of softness about it.

No, she would never be the prey. She would wear the hunter's colors; she would run the prey to ground . . . and follow him into his burrow.

"Lady Lillith," I said evenly, "nothing would please me more than to have this wedding go forth."

Kohl-smudged lids flickered minutely. I saw the brief, considering glance slanted at me out of eloquent eyes, black as the unbound hair. The smile widened. And then she laughed her husky laugh. "You know the game after all."

"No," I returned, smiling. "But I am a passable student."

My father looked to my brother. "Will you have the priest sent for?"

Silently, Ian did so, even as Lillith continued to laugh.

Laughed as if she had won.

Six

" 'Will you, the Prince of Homana, promise to provide all things necessary to the station and well-being of the Princess of Atvia,' " my brother quoted. "Will you, Niall, clanborn of the Cheysuli, promise to provide succor and honor, respect and regard, to Gisella of Atvia?' And so on, and so on." He laughed. "You notice he left out the word *love.* For a Homanan priest, he has surpassing sense."

"Proxy or no, it was hard to say the words." I swallowed sour red wine to wash away the taste of the vows I had made. "I kept telling myself it was for Gisella the promises were meant, but I had to look at *Lillith.*"

"And now you are bound to her forever," Ian mused. "Homanan law is an unforgiving thing, allowing no man— or woman—the chance to end a marriage that does neither any good." He shook his head. "Foolishness. Look at Carillon. Surely he more than any man should have had the right to end his marriage. Had he been able to set Electra aside permanently and wed another woman, he might have sired a son. And you would not be Prince of Homana, in line for the Lion Throne."

No, I would not . . . and undoubtedly I would not be bound forever to Gisella.

I turned from the stained glass casement and faced my brother. We were alone in the audience chamber. The ceremony had been completed an hour or more before. I had not left because a servant had brought wine to us all, intended for celebration. But none of my kin wished to share wine with Varien or Lillith past the customary nuptial cup; everyone, including Tasha, had departed, and now Ian and I kept company in the presence of emptiness.

He sat in my father's padded chair. I had not drunk so much wine as to weave fancies of my thoughts, but I could not help but mark the appropriateness of his position. He resembled our father more and more with each year, as if his flesh grew more comfortable with his bones. His mother, Sorcha, had taken her life before I had been born; I had no one to compare him with except the Mujhar. And now, looking at him, I saw Ian possessed the same mouth in repose. It was only rarely that I saw my father this relaxed.

I swallowed more wine. It went down so easily, too easily; I would have to stop soon, or I would suffer for it in the morning. "Have you ever wondered what life would be like for *you* if you were heir to the Lion?"

Like me, he held a cup of wine. Unlike me, he did not drink. He stared at me fixedly over the rim. "Why do you ask?"

I shrugged. "No reason, save curiosity. We are so different; I merely wondered how you would feel if you were in my place."

"Deceased," he said succinctly.

"Why?" I was horrified. "Why would you feel *dead?*"

"Because I would probably *be* dead." Ian straightened a little. "Do you think the Homanans would allow *me* to succeed to the throne?"

"Why not?"

"I am a bastard, for one. Cheysuli for another." He paused. "More *blatantly* Cheysuli."

I waved a hand. "Let us dispense with the first and say you are not a bastard. How would you feel *then?*"

He smiled a little. "You dispense with it so *easily* . . . well enough—I am legitimate. I am the Prince of Homana. I would still be dead, because the Homanans would see to it I was slain."

"Assassinated?"

He shrugged. "If it was not an *accident.*"

I felt a cold finger brush my spine. "Because you are Cheysuli."

"Aye."

"Our father is Cheysuli."

"Carillon chose our *jehan.* From him they would accept any man." He did not look away from me. "Niall, *you* are in no danger. You are Aislinn's son. You bear the blood of the man."

"As well as the man's *flesh*." I swore and stared into the blood-red wine. "So I survive on sufferance."

"Do not mistake me, I do not accuse all Homanans of wishing to see Cheysuli dead," he said pointedly. "More and more are reconciled to the reinstatement of our people, even to the succession. But there are *some* who would prefer it otherwise."

"Oh. *Those*." I grimaced. "The zealots."

"A'saii," my brother murmured into his cup. "Like Ceinn."

"What?"

He blinked and looked up at me. "The Old Tongue word, *a'saii*. It means *zealot* in Homanan, or something close to that."

"What has the word to do with Ceinn?"

"Nothing." The mouth was taut as wire. Ian began to drink his wine.

I set my own cup down in the casement sill and went to my brother. Before he could speak, I caught his wrist and kept the cup from his mouth. "I am not deaf, *rujho*. Neither am I stupid. At Clankeep, Ceinn came to your pavilion seeking word with you. He made a mistake: he began to speak before he saw I was there. You yourself said he was a fool. Now you call him *a'saii*. I want to know what it means."

"It means what I said: Ceinn is a fool." Ian twisted away from me and rose, leaving me with his cup of wine. "He is more devoted to the old ways—the old *days*—than others in the clan."

"The days of the Firstborn?"

"Directly after, when the prophecy was first discovered." Ian turned to face me. "In those days, the Cheysuli bred only with Cheysuli, to keep the blood clear of taint. In the end, that is what nearly destroyed us; we *need* the new blood promised in the prophecy."

I nodded. "I know this. Ian—"

"I am answering!" he said sharply. "Gods, Niall, must you have it carved for you in stone? Ceinn adheres to the beliefs of the early days, when our women only lay down with our men. To keep the blood pure."

"And mine, of course, is not." I smiled tightly, though

the revelation of Ceinn's beliefs did not particularly shock me. "He thinks I should not be in line to inherit."

"Aye." It was clipped; Ian was angry with himself for letting me learn the truth.

"Let me guess: Ceinn believes *he* should inherit the throne."

"No," Ian said. "He says the Lion should be mine."

I shut my mouth so as not to resemble a simpleton. "You," I said. "*You?* But—I thought surely *he* would want it. Is that not why he pursues Isolde? To make his claim stronger?"

"No." Ian drew in a breath and released it through taut lips. "The *a'saii*—" he stopped short. "Ceinn feels I have more right than you. That my blood is purer."

"He forgets Sorcha was half Homanan," I said bitterly. "You are no more pure than I!"

"We have a *jehan* who claims the Old Blood from Alix, our granddame. That ensures *my* right. But on your *jehana*'s side there is Solindish blood in you; Electra was *your* granddame, never mine." Ian's face was a mask. "There. I have carved it out for you. Can you set the stone into place?"

"Electra, my mother's mother, was also Tynstar's *meijha*," I said flatly. "Aye, I can set the stone into place. So, the blood that endears me to the Homanans—the Queen is Carillon's daughter, and for that they will overlook even *Solindish Electra*—devalues me to the Cheysuli." The pain rose up to swallow my belly whole. Grimacing, I spun and threw Ian's cup at the closest wall. Instead, it shattered the nearest casement.

Colored glass rained down against the floor. I stared aghast as the shards splattered down like blood, spilling across the stone. Sunlight gaped through the lead frame: naked light filled my eyes until the tears spilled over.

My clan will not accept me. My race reviles me.

"Niall." Ian's hands were on my arms. "Sit down—*sit down!*" He guided me to one of the chairs and pushed me into it. "*Shansu, rujho, shansu.* Such anger can harm the soul."

As well as gripe the belly. Hunched over, I leaned against one of the padded arms. "How many, Ian? How many of the *a'saii*?"

"Too few, I promise you. And the canker is very small."

"Cankers grow. Cankers can overtake the healthiest of men."

"And cankers can be cut out." He knelt down in front of me. "Do you think I would ever allow Ceinn or any other warrior to harm my *rujholli?* What manner of liege man am I? What sort of brother am I to you?"

Brother. The Homanan word was accented. Ian was more accustomed to the Cheysuli. *While I only rarely resort to the Old Tongue.*

"Would you want it?" I asked. "The Lion?"

Surprising me, Ian smiled. "If I ever laid claim to the Lion, the Homanans would have my head. Do I look like a martyr to you?"

My laugh resembled a gasp. "No, nor a particularly ambitious man." I leaned back in the chair as the pain in my belly began to subside. "I need you, Ian. Liege man, *rujholli,* companion . . . I need you with me, Ian. Here or in Atvia."

"Atvia," he said. "I thought it might come to that."

"Even now the Homanan Council hammers out trade agreements with Varien as part of the marriage settlement. In a week the ship sails. And I must go with Varien and Lillith to claim my Atvian bride." I forced a smile. "I have no intention of going there *alone* with that Ihlini witch."

He sighed. "I suppose I have no choice."

The smile came more easily. "You never have. Your *tahlmorra* lies with me."

Ian sat down in the other chair. "A long trip," he predicted. "Tasha hates the water."

The week before sailing was both the longest and the shortest of my life. The thought of the trip itself was exciting, regardless that my future wife lay at the end of it. I had never been out of Homana before, and the idea of a sea voyage was almost intoxicating. At first there had been some disagreement over whether I should go. It would be easy enough for Alaric to send his daughter to Homana, but it was agreed at last that I would go to fetch her myself, as a mark of honor.

But now I had other things to think about; other things to gnaw at the back of my mind, even when I tried to keep my attention on matters of more importance.

A'saii, Ian had called them. Cheysuli warriors *too* dedicated to the refinement of the Old Blood.

And there was Lillith. Varien's overtures of friendship were easy enough to brush off: he was envoy, not prince; his rank did not match mine, and I found myself using an impatient condescension I had not known I possessed. But with Lillith, it was different. Being a beautiful woman, she knew how to manipulate men. Being Ihlini witch, she had recourse to more arts than most. And so I found myself agreeing to accompany her into Mujhara to show her the sights of the city.

"Alone?" I asked as we walked the length of the corridor. "You and I?"

She retied the wine-red ribbon threaded through her single braid. "We are wed. There is no law against it."

She was solemn-faced as we neared the main entrance, but I saw a glint of amusement in her eyes. It irritated me as much as she meant it to.

"*We* are not wed," I pointed out. "The union was never consummated."

Lillith smiled. "We could take pains to see that it *was*."

"No." I said it coldly, banishing any attempt at politeness or diplomacy.

Lillith's husky laugh rang out. "If you are *frightened* of me, my lord, why not have your warrior brother accompany us? His magic will prevent me from using mine."

Another man might have instantly refused the chance to gain an ally, being too proud and too full of himself; *I* was not a fool. Strahan had already impressed upon me how easy it was for an Ihlini to level sorcery against me, and I was not about to give Lillith the opportunity. I rousted Ian from conversation with one of my mother's ladies, ignored his muttered threat, and explained matters to him. He stopped complaining, summoned Tasha from his chambers, and went with Lillith and me into the city streets.

In the thirty-five years since Carillon had returned from exile and made the Cheysuli welcome in their homeland again, most of the Homanans had learned to coexist with warriors and *lir*. Tasha's presence no longer alarmed Mujhara's citizens to the point of taking action against her as they once would have against a mountain cat who happened into the city. While no one precisely *welcomed* her—

she is large, lethal, and incredibly powerful—neither did they hunt weapons with which to slay her.

Ian and I flanked Lillith out of good manners, nothing more. Tasha preceded us, clearing a path through the crowded streets as passers-by made way immediately. Though the streets were cobbled, a thin layer of dust rose to film Lillith's wine-red skirts and turn them a faded ocher-red. But she hardly appeared to notice. She observed everything around her with calm, discerning eyes, as if she fit the city into a private ordering. She did not appear aware of the stares she received from men, or the mutters from the women. They could not know she was Ihlini, but her vivid *apartness* made her a beacon in the streets.

Ian and I took her to Market Square, the hub of every city or country village. In Mujhara the Square is huge, hedged by buildings at every turning. It was here everyone brought wares to trade and sell, commodities meant for competitive distribution. Canvas stalls filled up the Square, narrowing the alleys and streets to winding walkways hardly wide enough for three to walk abreast. Even Tasha found the going more difficult.

"Is it always like this?" Lillith asked.

Ian was ahead, I behind. Jostled, I stumbled a step closer to her. "It is Market Day today. Another time it is not so bad, although the Square is always crowded." My foot squashed a sodden sweetmeat someone had dropped; grimacing, I shook the remains from the sole of my boot. "It is worse at Summerfair."

Lillith held up her skirts with both hands as Ian broke a path through the throngs of people. "Rondule is not so big as this. But then, neither is Atvia as big as Homana."

"Do you not come from Solinde?" I nearly had to shout over the babble of the crowds.

"Originally." She slanted a glance at me over a shoulder. "Atvia is now my home."

"Because of Alaric."

"Because I *choose* it as my home."

Ian was brought up short by a man on horseback, always questionable transportation in the Square. Lillith, still looking at me, bumped into him. Ian turned, intending to steady her; he stopped himself. For a moment they merely looked at one another, as if offering mutual challenges.

Then Lillith laughed. Ian looked away.

"Rujho," I said sharply, "look."

Ian turned. We had been stopped by the stall of a furrier, and the smell of freshly-dressed hides was pungent. There were pelts of every sort: coney, fox, beaver, bear, wolf, and mountain cat, countless other kinds. The largest pelts were tacked upon wood and hung from the back of the stall. Tails depended from nails. The plusher, finer pelts were piled upon benches and over the counter itself.

My hand had automatically gone down to brace myself against stumbling. It was buried in sleek softness; one look told me the hide had once clothed a living cat.

I recoiled. The color was Tasha's, lush red tipped with chestnut brown. Though there is no tenet in the clans against trapping or slaying animals who are not *lir*, the likeness to Tasha sent a shiver of distaste and superstition down my spine.

Ian's face was stark. Here we saw hundreds of pelts, and all the animals dead.

"Lovely," Lillith said, and her hands caressed the remains of the mountain cat.

A man stepped forward from behind his racks of pelts. He was small, quick, authoritative. "A discerning eye," he said, smiling warmly at Lillith, but not too familiarly. A shrewd glance at Ian and myself told him we could afford the price of any one of a hundred pelts; his smile became obsequious. "A fur-lined mantle, perhaps? A bit of coney for the collar?" He snatched up a night-black mountain cat pelt and swept it around Lillith's shoulders. "Black on black," he said. "Lady, you are lovely."

But Lillith looked past the man and lifted a slender hand. "No," she said, "the white."

The furrier glanced over his shoulder. His brown hair was tied back with a length of blue-dyed leather. His clothing also was of leather, with strips of fur at collar, cuffs and doublet hem. Red fox, I knew. I thought it fit his manner.

"Lady, that is not yet ready for sale." Still smiling, he took the black pelt from Lillith and offered a silver one instead. *"This* one suits you well."

"That one," Lillith said, and there was no mistaking her tone.

The furrier pressed palms against his leathers. "It has

only just come in. There are treatments. I must first render it suitable." He bobbed his head toward Ian and then myself. "Perhaps something else for the lady?"

"There is nothing here for her," Ian said flatly. "I hunt and skin animals when I must, for food and warmth and shelter, but I do not slay—or *sell*—so many as to make my living at it."

The furrier slanted a nervous glance in Tasha's direction. The cat's amber eyes were fixed on his face, as if she intended to leap on him momentarily.

"I wish to see it," Lillith said, and threw down the silver pelt.

The furrier complied. He settled the white pelt down in front of Lillith and folded his arms across his chest.

"Wolf," she said, and I thought I heard satisfaction in her tone.

"Aye," the furrier agreed. "Brought in this morning. The trapper gave it only a bit of a cleaning." Deft fingers peeled back an edge of the pelt to show the hide beneath. "It wants softening, brushing, dyeing; all the things I do to the pelts to make them lovely enough for a lady as lovely as you." No more merchant's chatter; he meant what he said, profoundly.

Lillith fingered the fur. "Will it be white again? True white?"

"Wants cleaning." He bobbed his head.

She smiled. "The wolf must have been a lovely animal, alive."

"Wanted killing," the furrier said. "Plague-ridden beast." Uneasily he glanced at me. "No more, of course. I'd never be selling a plague-ridden pelt."

"What plague?" I frowned. "There is no plague in Homana."

"North, across the Bluetooth River," he said. "Herders took sick after a white wolf got into their sheep."

"*This* wolf?" Ian asked.

The furrier shrugged. "Trappers are taking every white one they can find, for the coin. Herders are paying good silver."

"What are *you* paying?" I demanded.

He did not look away from me. "Copper," he said, and smiled. "There is no plague in Mujhara."

"And what will you sell it for?" Ian asked.

"Gold," the furrier answered. "White wolves are rare; there are people who crave the unusual."

"Lovely," Lillith murmured, burying fingers in the pelt.

"Enough," I said abruptly, "there is more for you to see." I put a hand on her arm and turned her away from the stall.

"Nothing for the lady?" asked the man. "Nothing for either of you?"

"We do not crave the unusual," Ian answered, "when purchased at the price of an animal's life."

"It carried *plague!*" the man insisted, then shut his mouth as if he realized he might lower his asking price.

"Plague," Ian said in disgust as we threaded our way through the throng. "More likely the *sheepdogs* carried the sickness."

"Or the herders themselves." Lillith smiled. "I have seen enough. I would like to go back to the palace."

"You have seen nothing," I said, surprised. "You have hardly tapped Mujhara—"

"I have seen enough," she repeated distinctly. A slim hand insinuated itself in the crook of my arm. "Will you escort me home, my lord?"

The emphasis as she singled me out was slight, but still apparent, and certainly so to Ian. I saw the slight twist at one corner of his mouth; amusement or irritation, perhaps both. He glanced at me, smiled, gave in graciously. But I thought he and Tasha fell back a few steps with an undue amount of alacrity.

Lillith said little enough as I escorted her back to Homana-Mujhar, keeping herself in companionable silence. Ian and Tasha followed, but she ignored them both. The hand still rested in my elbow; I could hardly strip it away, though I longed to do it. Common courtesy denied me the pleasure.

Ihlini or no, she is Alaric's representative—in bed or out of it, as she says. What little I have learned of statecraft from my father forbids outright rudeness unless I have no choice. And for now, there is *a choice.*

Still, I wondered if Lillith had truly seen enough. Or if, more likely, she had seen precisely *what* she had come to see.

Seven

We took ship from Hondarth, bound for Atvia. It was possible to go overland through Solinde to the western port of Andemir, then set sail for the island, but the fastest way was to go by sea entirely. Besides, we had no wish to enter Ihlini environs with Lillith in our company.

Aside from Varien, Lillith, Ian, Tasha, and myself, there was an escort of sixteen Homanan men handpicked from my father's personal Mujharan Guard. Ian, less inclined to approve of such things as royal escorts and decorum, was amused by it all. I felt a mixture of pride and resignation. I was content enough to accept my role as Homana's heir with all attendant traditions, but I realized, somewhat belatedly, that never again would I have the freedom to flee my princely concerns. The marriage, proxy or no, had locked the circlet around my head.

The weather, as we sailed out of Hondarth, was good. The rains had lifted entirely, leaving clear skies and a more temperate climate behind. Only a faint cool breeze snapped the blue sails of our ship and set the scarlet pennons flying.

Behind us lay the whitewashed city and lilac-heathered hills. Ahead of us floated the Crystal Isle, wreathed in silver mists. Ian, standing beside me at the taffrail, nodded toward the island. "All the history, *rujho*. Do you ever think of it?"

"I thought of it enough when the *shar tahls* made me memorize all the stories." Cautiously, I eyed the whitecaps slapping against the prow. I had not yet decided if I was born to sail or to keep myself to land.

Ian laughed. "I, as well. . . . but now those stories seem more alive. I think we should have come here *then*. Immediacy makes the lessons more comprehensible."

"I have no intention of reciting those lessons *now*," I

declared. "Still . . . you have the right of it. Perhaps we should have come."

"Why not recite those lessons to me?" inquired the husky voice from behind us. "Surely you know I learned a *different* history."

I turned to face Lillith. Ian did not. Beside him, wide paws spread, Tasha snarled and pressed against Ian's leg.

She wore an indigo mantle. The edges, stitched with gold thread, snapped in the rising wind. Her unbound hair blew freely about her shoulders. I was put in mind of a shroud. Black. Silken. And all-encompassing.

"Then shall I tell you what *I* know of the island?" She slipped between Ian and me, touching neither of us, yet I was as aware of her as if she were a wine too heady for my wits. As for Ian, I could not say how he responded, save to see how rigid was his posture. "It is the birthplace of the Cheysuli," Lillith told us. "The heart, if you will, of Homana."

Whatever I had expected of her, it was not that. Never the truth. Sidelong, I looked at her, and saw the distant smile. "The Ihlini rose out of Solinde," I said; it was common knowledge.

A thick strand of hair was whipped into her face. Slender fingers caught at it and pulled it away from the questing grasp of the wind; silver-tipped nails flashed. "The Ihlini rose out of *Homana*." The smile was gone, but there was no hostility in her tone, merely matter-of-factness. "I am certain Tynstar told Carillon, probably even your father. It is the truth, Niall; once the Ihlini and Cheysuli were as close—*closer*—than you and Ian."

She had never said my name before. Accented, the syllables had a different sound. The sound of intimacy, which did not please me at all.

"Lady," deliberately I denied familiarity, "I think you mouth lies we would rather not hear."

"Then tell me your truths," she invited. "Both of you: tell me what all Cheysuli children are told, when the *shar tahls* share the knowledge contained in the histories."

Ian turned abruptly. "What do you know of Tynstar?"

He took her by surprise. Arched brows rose slightly. Then she smiled, and the corners of her eyes creased. The wind put color into her cheeks. But before she could answer Ian, I asked her a question of my own.

"How old are you, Lillith?" In my intentness, I hardly noticed my use of her given name. "I have heard the stories of aborted aging."

Lillith laughed. "Along with other arts." She looked at each of us, one by one, and her smile grew wider still. "I shall answer both of you: I am more than a hundred years, and Tynstar was my father."

Ian physically recoiled. Behind him, Tasha growled.

"Tynstar!" I blurted. "How is it possible?"

"How is it *not* possible?" she countered. "Oh, I know, you are thinking of Electra, Tynstar's mistress. Your grand-dame, was she not?" Lillith nodded before I could answer. "Well, I can only say that when a man such as Tynstar lives for more than three hundred years, he will take more women than only one. Electra was the *last* one, perhaps, but hardly the first." She raised her head against the wind and let it caress her face. "My mother was Ihlini. We do not weigh the value of people by rank, only by power . . . but in your terms, she would have been a queen. As my father was the king." Lips parted in sensual pleasure. Eyes closed, she bared her flawless face to the rising wind.

"Strahan is your half-brother." I thought again of the man I had met in Mujhara, who had nearly drowned me in the mud.

"My younger brother," Lillith agreed. "*So* young . . . and so newly-come to his arts." She opened black eyes and looked at me. "There is much left for him to learn."

"But not so much for you," Ian said harshly. "Is that what you seek to say? To warn us of your power? Do not bother, lady. I have no intention of ignoring who or what you are."

"No," she said, "that is obvious. But why must you assume I bear you or your brother ill will?"

"You are Ihlini." It was explanation in itself.

"And kin to you, somewhere ages and ages ago." Lillith gathered in flying hair and contained it in a slender hand. "I am, albeit unspoken, Queen of Atvia. I am content with Alaric. What would I do with Homana? Why do you assume I *want* it?"

"You are Ihlini." This time from me, and equally inflexible.

"Ihlini," she said. "Second-born of the First, and therefore a threat to you." Lillith shook her head. "Not all of us seek to hinder the prophecy."

Ian's mouth opened, closed. I saw him visibly gather his thinning tolerance. "Lady," he said finally, with the infinite patience of a man who despises his opponent, "you have the right of it when you say Tynstar must have spoken to Carillon and my *jehan*. Aye, I know the truth that drove the demon: fulfillment of the prophecy means the end of the Ihlini. How can you *not* work against us?"

Lillith stood very still. Mostly she faced Ian now, but in her profile I saw a look of exalted triumph. "Aye," she said on a breath of accomplishment, "I think you begin to understand."

Ian shook his head. "Understand an Ihlini? I think not."

She backed away from us both; wind-whipped wraith, suddenly, indigo blue and black. And magnificent in her pride. "Why should we be any different?" she asked. "Why should we be hounded by your dogs of righteousness until no one in all the world can see the *sense* in what we do—why we fight for our survival! Do you see? Do you see it at all?" Her eyes searched my face and Ian's. "*Evil*, you claim us; *demons* you call us; seed of the dark god himself. And why? Because we do what we must to survive. *Survive!* Would *you* do any differently if promised demise by the fulfillment of a prophecy?" The mantle cracked in the wind. "Words," she said bitterly. "Words. And with them, you destroy an entire race. Even as you were nearly destroyed. Will you do the same to us? Unleash a Cheysuli *qu'mahlin*?"

"Enough," Ian said, white-faced. "You have said *enough*."

"Have I?" Lillith demanded. She glanced at me, then met Ian's baleful, yellow-eyed glare. "Looking at you, I say I have not. But then *you* are fanatic enough to be *a'saii*."

The last was bitterly said. But before I could ask her how she came to know so much of the Old Tongue, Lillith turned her back on us both and took herself out of our sight.

A'saii. Ian? I knew better. Until I looked at his face.

"*Rujho*—" I began.

Ian's face was the mask I knew so well. But his ashen color was not. "She has the tongue of a serpent."

"Can a serpent tell the truth?"

His head snapped around as he looked at me in shock. "You *believe* her?"

"No," I told him, troubled, "I think no Ihlini would ever bear us anything but ill will. But what if she tells the truth about their *reasons* for hating us so?"

"Truth, lies, what does it matter? Their knives are just as sharp." Ian shook his head. "Would it make you less dead if the man who slew you believed he was serving his race?"

The taste of salt was in my mouth. The tang was bittersweet. "No, *rujho*. No."

"See that you remember it," Ian told me flatly. "See that you never forget."

I watched him as he took Tasha with him to the other side of the deck. Alone, *incredibly* alone, I stood against the taffrail and wondered if there was, beyond the obvious, any real difference between Ihlini and Cheysuli.

We love and hate and fight with equal certitude. But then, so can brother and brother; so can sister and sister.

I shivered. The wind was decidedly cold.

The Idrian Ocean is a fractious beast, tame one day, wild the next. As we passed the crumbled headlands of southwestern Solinde, nearing the two islands known as Erinn and Atvia, the beast turned definitively disagreeable; I discovered I was a good sailor in good weather, a poor one in bad.

I stayed below much of the time, studiously ignoring what I could of the pitching ship, but when the swells deepened and the timbers began to groan alarmingly, I dragged myself up the slippery ladder to the sea-splashed deck above.

The sun was swallowed by clouds. I could not tell if it were evening or afternoon. Wind-wracked, sea-swept, I could not even tell if it rained, or if the water came from the ocean. All I knew was I was soaked through in an instant, and the deck was incredibly slick.

"Ian?" He was somewhere on deck, I knew; he spent as much time above as I did below. "Ian!" Slipping, sliding, swearing, I made it to the taffrail and clung with all my might. Spray nearly drowned me; the wind tried to batter me back.

I spat out the taste of salt. All around me the light was odd, an unearthly, ocherous green. My belly began to dance within the confines of my flesh.

"Gods," I muttered aloud, "if this is but a gentle blow, I would not care to see a gale."

The wind snapped the words back at me, along with the salty spittle of the sea. Eyes stung, mouth protested; I spat back, making certain I did it *with* the wind, and not against.

Ian came up behind me, looming out of the lowering sky. "The captain suggests we go below."

"No," I blurted instantly. "At least up here I can breathe."

Ian smiled as I turned to spit again. "Can you?" The humor faded as he squinted past me into the wind. "Niall— perhaps we should do as he says. The waves will surely swamp us."

I looked at the roiling ocean. The swells were watery mountains; the troughs a common grave.

I glanced back at Ian. Wet black hair was flattened against his head. Bare-armed, the water polished his gold. His leathers were soaked, but no more so than my woolen breeches and padded doublet.

"Where is Tasha?" I asked.

"I sent her below. She hates the water so, I could not bear to keep her with me." Ian squinted into the slanting rain. "Gods, Niall—look at *that!*"

I looked. Out of the pewter-green skies came a tracery of lilac. Delicate fingers touched here, touched there, insinuating themselves between the lobes of heavy clouds. It spread; spreading, it began to swallow the waves as well as the sky.

"I have seen nothing like *that* before," I declared.

"Nor have I," he agreed grimly, "but neither of us is a sailor."

No, we were neither of us a sailor. But it does not take a sailor to know when a storm is a bad one, or when the waves are more than *water*.

Gods—how they rise—how they prepare to swallow us all—

And then I forgot the waves and stared only at the heavens. "By the gods, the sky is *alive!*"

The ship dropped, prow-first, into a deep trough. It seemed almost to stand on end. I clutched the rail and braced myself against the slippery deck.

"Niall—the wave—*hold on*—"

Crushing weight descended upon me. It drove me to the deck, battering at flesh and bones, until I slid freely across flooded decking and came to rest, however briefly, against a pile of massive rope. I clutched at the nearest coil, locking rigid fingers as the huge wave rolled over the deck. Timbers groaned and shuddered. Like a surly stallion, the ship bucked beneath my body.

The water lived. It tried to swallow me down a sea-dragon's gullet, sucking, *sucking*, threatening to chew, until I lodged against a sore tooth and kicked, *kicked*, still clutching my coil of rope. Heaving, the sea-dragon spat me out; exhaled bleeding, screaming debris as well as silent bags of broken bone and shredded flesh.

My mouth was filled with blood and salt. My ears, deafened by pressure as well as by sound, throbbed painfully. Water and blood was streaming from my nose.

"Ian," I mumbled thickly. "Ian—*where are you, rujho?*"

The mast snapped. Spars broke and were flung through the air, skewering flesh and canvas. Sheets and shredded sail collapsed across the deck, tangling men within heavy folds and the deadly embroidery of knots and coils.

"Niall!" Distantly, I heard him. "Niall—*where are you—?*"

"Here!" But in the heart of the storm I could hardly hear myself.

Something pierced my leg. With the pitching of the ship I tried to pull myself onto hands and knees, but the slippery deck denied me proper purchase. Face down, I slid from my coil of rope toward the skeletal silhouette of the taffrail, fragile promise against the violence of the storm.

And heard the scream of a mountain cat.

Ian? No. More likely Tasha, searching for her *lir.*

Pitch, roll, heave . . . I slid nearer the side of the ship, knowing a negligent slap of the dragon's tail could sunder the wood and sweep me into the seas beyond.

Tasha. Screaming. Ian?

I lurched upward, lunging for solid wood. Found it; what

it was I could not say, knowing so little of ships. It creaked. Groaned. But it held.

Lurid lightning spilled like blood through the blackened clouds and lit up the drowning ship. In its glare I saw Tasha, huddled against a heavy sea chest. Wedged, the chest showed no signs of giving itself over to the storm. Timing the swells, I let go of my handhold and ran.

The ship rolled, wallowing like a drunken man in a pool of urine and vomit. I fell to both knees, skidded, slid into the terrified cat, apologized silently, and peeled myself up from the deck. The chest had brass handles; I grabbed one and held on.

Tasha's amber eyes were dyed yellow-green in the livid light. Tufted ears flattened against her head. Tightly, so tightly, she clamped her tail around quivering haunches. Diminished by the storm, she was little more than a terrified housecat.

It made me tremendously angry, that gods—or demons—would play with the mountain cat so.

"Tasha, Tasha—*shansu*. Be easy, my lovely girl . . . the storm will come to an end." A hand against soaked shoulder found rigid flesh and hardened sinew. She shook, even as I did; from the rain, from the cold, from the fear.

"Tasha, where is your *lir?*" I knew she could not tell me, but I could not hold back the question.

The cat snarled, baring lethal teeth in rage and pain. In the lightning I saw the gaping hole in her flank.

"Oh Tasha—*no!*"

It was deep. Jagged. It bled freely, but the rain washed it open again. And again; I watched her life spill onto the deck.

"No!" The shout tore out of my throat. "Gods, Tasha, *not you*—if you die, *Ian* dies—"

A heavy line slapped across my face, knocking me to the deck. Stunned, I felt the stinging spring up in my cheek and the pain growing in one eye. Groping fingers sought the welt and found it, as well as the cut over my eye. Already the lid swelled closed.

"Tasha—" I saw the cat's third eyelid rise. Sluggish, weakened, she panted, exposing slack pink tongue. From deep in her chest I heard the ongoing wail of pain and fatigue. Rising, dropping; a song of death and regret and futility.

If Ian was not already dead, Tasha's death would destroy him completely. Drive him into madness. Drive him into seeking the death-ritual.

Briefly, I thought of my grandsire, Duncan. Tynstar had slain his *lir*, Cai, the hawk. And so he had also slain Duncan.

Oh gods, if my brother must die, I beg you—let him die in another way. . . . Not a petition I was proud of, but I could not bear to lose him twice.

I crawled to Tasha. Peeled off my padded doublet, sodden and dripping with rain, and folded it, pressing it against the wound in Tasha's flank. My linen shirt plastered itself against my battered body. I shivered. My cheek and eye hurt; vision was restricted to my left eye only.

The ship rolled. Caught. Shuddered like a man expending himself in a woman. Stopped dead.

I was thrown to the deck, flung completely away from Tasha, and saw the taffrail tilt eerily. Beyond it lay the horizon, backlighted by saffron and silver. The moon, I realized, balanced itself on the blade of the horizon.

Free of trunk, of handle, of Tasha, I slid toward the maw of the dragon. Stiffened fingers and boot toes scrabbled against wet wood.

Shuddering again, the ship tilted farther yet and slid more deeply into the sea. Another wave drove it deeper, scraping the deck free of debris. At the broken rail I was caught by rigging; dragged up again as the ship wallowed, foundered, tried to pull free of the sea. As I grabbed for rope and spar, I saw Tasha swept by me into the dragon's mouth.

In shock, I could not grieve. I could only mouth the names of my brother and his *lir*.

The ship shuddered again, groaning as the hull splintered against jagged rocks. I felt the vibration through my body and realized what it meant.

"Land?" I croaked aloud. "But—how can there be land?"

I flailed in the rigging, trying to right myself. The ship, solidly aground, no longer pitched or wallowed. But it had tilted to an alarming degree; no more was there a deck on which I could stand. Knees grated against the rigging, lapped about with water, and slipped loose in the force of the waves.

"Niall."

I wrenched my head around and saw the woman clinging to a spar. It slashed a diagonal wound across the fabric of the sky. The storm had broken; behind her, the moon bled silver light.

"Lillith." The name was hardly a sound.

Sodden hair tangled at her hips. She had shed the indigo cloak. The gown she wore was deepest black, so that except for face and hands she was a part of the darkness itself.

I saw her reach out a hand. I saw the silver flash of her painted nails. But mostly I saw her beguiling smile, promising life, survival, continuance.

"Your choice," she said. "I will not make it for you."

I drew in a trembling breath. "And the price of Ihlini aid?"

"Whatever your life is worth."

I tried to swallow and found the task too painful. "My brother," I croaked, "and his *lir*."

Lillith smiled. And then she laughed. "I am sorry," she said at last. "His choice is already made."

I spat. And then I cursed her.

The pale hand rose. I saw a line of purple flame come hissing from out of the darkness to dance in the palm of her hand. In its lurid light her face was thrown into relief, hollowed: a fragile mask of death.

She carried the flame to her mouth, pursed her lips and blew. In the explosion of smoke and fire, Lillith disappeared.

Alone, alone, I cursed the woman. And then I threw back my head. "If you want me, *if you want me*—then, by the gods, you must *take* me!"

For a moment a hushed silence descended upon the ship. A quiver of fear and awe ran through my body.

The spar Lillith had clung to broke. Falling, it tangled me in its rigging. The weight of it crushed my chest.

I tumbled helplessly into the sea.

Eight

I roused to the taste of salt in my mouth, my teeth, in the crusted cuts on my lips. It burned. I sought to spit it out, but my mouth would not form the proper shape.

My flesh also burned and itched. The cloying touch of salt was in every crease of my skin, in every crease of the rags that remained of my clothing. One hand twitched. I pushed it weakly to and fro, relieving an itch by scraping the back of my hand against damp, rounded rock. Once done, my hand fell limply into water.

Water.

Realization awoke knowledge within my sluggish mind. Water. All around. It dampened my clothing and puddled beneath my cheek.

Asking nothing else of my battered body, I tried to open my eyes and found only one answered my bidding.

Sand and pebbles grated beneath my face. I tongued my lips and tasted salt, the ever-present salt, and felt the swollen dryness of split flesh and crusted sores.

Move, arm. The arm moved. It lifted and carried wet fingers to my face. The fingers awkwardly brushed away sand from my good eye and peeled back crusted salt.

Dimly, I saw tumbled rocks and rounded boulders. And the sea. Waves lapped gently at the stone nearest me, and I realized the tide was coming in.

I must move.

The pain was exquisite. Never had I felt such before, not even when the barber had jerked out a rotten tooth; the intensity astonished me. My hand, searching gently, felt damp cloth on my chest and shredded flesh beneath. My linen shirt was badly torn. The bones within bruised flesh ached with a fitful ferocity.

I twitched all over, once. The involuntary movement

awoke dull fire within every limb and brought full consciousness rushing in. I remembered it all.

Ian—

I sat up carefully, hugging my sore chest with one arm. The other I braced against the sand, holding myself upright. Dazedly I stared out to sea and saw the ship was gone.

Rujho—?

The crying of a seabird pierced the dullness in my ears and drew my burning eyes. Clusters of fellow gulls swooped and circled in the air, crying shrilly. I saw I was not on land at all, but a craggy fingerbone of stone. Sand clogged some pockets, water pooled in others. My salvation was but thirty paces from the shore; still, I felt too weak to make the attempt.

Ian.

Waves lapped at my feet. One boot was missing, sucked off by the sea-dragon's spite. I shuddered. The sea was my enemy, as it had been my brother's.

Oh gods, you have taken my brother from me—

But I was too dry for tears.

I felt at my waist and discovered my belt was whole, as was the silver-laced sheath; the knife itself was gone. But the ruby signet ring on my right hand glowed brilliantly in the sunlight, and I realized I had managed to keep my deliverance. For the worth of this ring, surely *someone* would give me aid.

I pressed myself to knees, then feet, and wavered alarmingly. My bones were brittle, hollow things; I feared they might shatter at any moment. My right eye ached and burned. The pain in my chest made me hunch, to relieve the strain on my ribs.

The tide is coming in. If you do not move, the sea will finish what the Ihlini witch began.

Slowly, with infinite care, I waded across the shallow inlet to the shore. By the time I reached it, the sea had swallowed my rocky perch. And so I stared inland, knowing my safety lay there, and wondered if I had come, however tragically, to Atvia at last.

Maps.

I thought back on the maps I had seen in my father's council chambers. I recalled the rugged coast of western Solinde; and even the channel separating Erinn and Atvia.

But no matter how hard I thought back, I could not recall if Rondule lay north or south, east or west. For that matter, I could not begin to say where I was in relation to the city.

Ian would say I deserve it, for shirking my geography. Oh, Ian, I would give anything to have you present. Your reprimand would be welcome.

I heard hoofbeats before I saw the riders. I turned immediately south toward the sound. Mounted men pounded toward me, garbed in plain, badgeless clothing that clearly was not household livery. The men wore caps on their heads. Baldrics dyed bright green slashed diagonally across their chests.

Perhaps some manner of household badge after all.

I waited, holding myself stiffly upright, and tried to think of what to say.

Twelve men. They surrounded me almost immediately at lancepoint. Somewhat startled by the reception—I was a single bedraggled man—I stared first at the gleaming points, then looked at the men who bore them.

Strong men all; I saw it at once. With all of Carillon's youthful height and bulk, I am hardly what one might regard as small. But, even horseback, I judged very few of the men would have to look up at me when they dismounted. They were bearded, toughened soldiers, fully experienced in what I believed had to be the Erinnish/Atvian war; I knew, looking at them, even clean, fed, and whole, I would offer them little threat.

I summoned what dignity I could. "Is this Atvia?" The croak I emitted was hardly human; a second try produced a hoarse but recognizable question.

Eleven men remained perfectly still atop wary horses; the twelfth rode slowly forward until the tip of his lance rested against my vulnerable, sunburned throat. He wore an age-polished leather cap fastened with a strap beneath his jaw, which was forested by heavy blond beard. His green eyes were shrewd. His expression was unrelenting.

"Atvia," he said softly. " 'Tis Atvia you're wanting?"

Swallowing was painful. What I needed was water; but would not ask for it from him. "My ship was bound for Atvia. It went down in the storm. I do not know where I am."

A humorless smile carved deep creases at the corners of

his eyes. "Not Atvia, lad. 'Tis Erinn, held by Shea himself, and Lord of the Idrian Isles. Erinn, lad, not Atvia. Atvia's *enemy*."

"You have a truce," I blurted, startled.

The green eyes narrowed consideringly. "What would *you* be knowing of a truce between your betters?"

"Betters," I muttered. I ached. I did not need this interrogation. "Take me to your lord, if you will. What I have to say will be for him."

The lance dug a hole in my neck, but did not cut me, quite. "What would *you* be saying to Lord Shea, ye bedraggled pup?"

I wanted to laugh, but could find neither strength nor voice. So I tried to strip the signet from my finger, to prove my right to a royal audience, but discovered my joints too swollen for the effort. Finally I extended my arm toward the man. "If you will look at the stone, you will see a rampant lion. I am Niall of Homana."

"Niall of Homana," the Erinnish man mocked. "What would Homana be wanting with Erinn?"

I wavered. "Nothing in particular, except aid for a bedraggled pup of a prince." I tried to smile disarmingly. "I did not intend to come here. It was the storm."

"Aye, the storm," the other interrupted. " 'Twas a fierce one, was it not?" He grinned, showing strong white teeth. "We are accustomed to a bit of weather, now and then, here in Erinn. How is it with you in Homana?"

I glared up at him, too weary to care about impressions. "In Homana I am treated better, being heir to the Mujhar."

The man exchanged grins with his fellow riders. "Heir, are ye, to the Mujhar? Is it Donal ye mean? And ye say you are his son?"

"Aye." The word was all I could manage.

"Legitimate, too, or is that too much to expect?"

"Ku'reshtin," I swore feebly, "I said I was his heir—" There was more I wanted to say and could not, being overtaken by a painful racking cough. I bent over at once; some of the sea I had swallowed came up to scour my teeth and throat.

I saw the sun glint off the lance tip as the man at last lowered the weapon. "Have ye had a hard time of it, puppy?" he inquired in mock solicitude. "Well, I'll be seeing to it you are treated befitting your rank—" as he paused I glanced up and saw his green eyes narrow "—once the rank is proven."

"Ku'reshtin," I muttered again. "Look at the ring, you fool."

The soldier frowned down at me. "What is that? That word? What name did you call me by?"

I summoned an ironic smile. *"Ku'reshtin?* It is Cheysuli, of course: The House of Homana is Cheysuli—or did you not realize that?"

I had expected further questions, or at least a mocking comment. Instead the soldier turned and gave a quiet order to one of his companions. In weary surprise, I watched as the man dismounted and brought his horse to me. The reins were held out in invitation.

"Take the horse," the leader said. "I'll be escorting you to Kilore."

"Kilore." I frowned. "Shea's castle?"

" 'Tis my father's home."

Reaching for the reins, I froze. I looked sharply up at the blond-bearded man.

"Aye," he said, when I did not bother to ask it. "Had ye not heard Shea has himself a son, even in Homana? 'Tis not *that* far away!" He grinned. "I am Liam. Prince of Erinn. Shea himself's own heir."

"No." I said it distinctly.

He laughed. "Oh, I admit I'm not looking much like a prince at the moment. Still, I am; underneath this soldier's garb is princely flesh, I swear. But 'tis enough to fool the Atvians, when they try to land their boats." He jerked his head toward the horse. "There is your mount, puppy; let us be going home."

Sluggish resentment rose. "Puppy," I muttered wearily. "When I am no longer so sore, I will knock that word from your mouth."

Liam of Erinn laughed and shoved the leather cap from his head. Blond curls fell around his face and I saw the years fall with it. Capped, bearded, with his weathered, wind-chafed cheeks, I would have said the man claimed at least forty years. But now he shed them easily: he was no more than ten years my senior.

I wavered, and Liam's laughter died. "The sea has

treated you poorly, lad, and I no better, have I? Mount your horse, Homana's heir, and I will see to it you're given the honor a prince deserves."

I turned to the horse in silence and clutched at pommel and cantle, hoisting myself from the ground. But if the Erinnish prince had not reached out and caught my arm, I would have fallen again.

Drooping in the saddle, I hunched forward over the pommel. "Ian," I mumbled, "where are you?"

"Here, lad," Liam told me, thinking I said his name.

"No—" I meant to explain, of course, but the light spilled out of the day.

Ropes fell away from wrists. Belatedly, I realized my face was buried in a horse's braided mane. I spat out the acrid taste of horsehair and pushed myself upright carefully, wishing I could neglect to breathe until my ribs had healed.

Liam stood by the horse, ropes dangling from his hands. "I tied you on because I thought you might fall off."

Undoubtedly I would have. I blinked, squinting, and peered around the cobbled bailey of a castle. The eleven soldiers—a prince's guard, I realized—arrayed themselves around me. "Kilore?" I croaked.

"Kilore. The Aerie of Erinn, my lord." Liam grinned and swung his cap by its leather strap. "Before you ask: I looked at that gaudy ring. I know the rampant lion, puppy, as well as I know my dogs." He rumpled brassy, tumbled curls. "Are you really Cheysuli, then? You lack the yellow eyes."

A chill washed over me. *Even here they know the difference.* "I *am* Cheysuli," I muttered, "but I look like Carillon."

Liam's heavy brows rushed upward to hide under hair that needed cutting. "Carillon, is it? I have heard of him. Was he not one of your heroes?"

"A man," I said crossly, having no desire to debate my grandsire's merits in Erinn any more than in Homana. "No more than that; a man."

Liam eyed me without expression. "A man who hacks away at legends builds little of his own.

"I have no *wish* to build a legend," I said in weary disgust. "All I want is a *lir*." I shut my mouth almost immediately; was Liam a sorcerer to bewitch such admissions from me?

"A *lir*?" he asked; no sorcerer, then, or surely he would know. "A charm, is it? A spell?"

"Animal," I answered. "A gift from the gods themselves. Without them we cannot shapechange."

Liam's escort muttered among themselves. Liam himself stared intently up at me. "And you are missing a *lir*."

"I am."

"So you lack all Cheysuli magic."

"I do." I said it between my teeth.

Grimly, he shook his head. "Not a wise admission, lad. Some men might be wishing to use you for their gain. 'Twould be better you made them think you have the magic."

" 'Twould be better you let him get off that horse," said a resonant, growling voice, "before he falls on his head."

I looked toward the castle and saw a tall, big-shouldered man in fine woolen dress descending the steps of the cavernous entrance. He was considerably older than Liam, but his manner and movements were those of a younger man. His blond hair and beard had silvered heavily, but still showed signs of the richness of youth. Green eyes were bright beneath an overgrown hedge of brows.

"Shea," I mumbled, "at last."

"Have him down," the old man said. "Unless he be Atvian, he is due some words to me."

"Homanan," Liam told him, moving forward to help me down. The dismounting was painful. I shut my mouth on a curse. "He says his ship went down in the storm."

"Accursed Ihlini storm," Shea growled. "Alaric's witch, again." He looked more intently at me. "Homanan, are ye? What word have you for me?"

"Nothing *prepared*, my lord. I was not originally coming here." I managed a weary smile. "Still, I have no doubts my father would wish you well."

Shea glared. "*Why* would your father wish me well, and who is he to wish it?"

"Donal," Liam told him. "Donal the Mujhar."

Shea's heavy brows jerked upward. Strip from him forty years, and he could be his son. "Truth?"

"Truth." Liam pointed at my ring. "The lion, my lord. The one in my grandmother's tapestry."

"Bring him in!" Shea bellowed. "See he is given food and drink!"

Fatuously, I smiled. Liam merely grinned. "The royal welcome, puppy. Shea himself has spoken!"

Food: rare beef, hot bread, sweet cheese. Drink: a powerful smoky liquor, as much as I could swallow. I ate as much as I could keep down on my brutalized belly, and drank too much of the liquor.

Shea sat in an iron-bound chair in the center of the hall. Liam paced silently, head bent as he turned the cap over and over in his callused hands. I watched him closely, wondering—uneasily—why the Prince of Erinn was not at home in his father's hall.

"Are you done?" Shea growled. "Have you slain the hunger and slaked your thirst?"

His speech, at times, was almost archaic. In my muddled mind, I had trouble deciphering the dialect. "For the moment," I answered at last. "My lord—"

"A shipwreck, you say. That I believe; what could survive that accursed witch's meddling?" He swore in a language I did not know. "If you were not coming here, where *were* you going, lad?"

"I was on my way to Atvia." I glanced sidelong at Liam.

Shea frowned, fingering the hilt of the massive knife at his belt. "What business have you with my enemy?"

Again, I said, "I thought there was a truce."

Briefly, Liam paused in his pacing. He looked intently at his father.

Shea buried bearded chin in the heel of his hand as he leaned upon one arm. He watched me silently; green eyes mostly hidden in lowered brows. I waited uneasily for his answer.

"Why were you Atvia-bound?" the Lord of Erinn inquired, and I realized that *was* my answer.

"I am to wed Alaric's daughter."

Shea's eyebrows shot up again. "The Cheysuli lass?"

Guardedly, I watched him. "She is my cousin, my lord. Her mother was my aunt."

Shea shifted in his chair. "I saw Bronwyn, once, before

she died. The lass, I am told, resembles her mother, not her father. Yet you resemble neither."

Liam was pacing again. "No," I agreed. "The heritage is mixed. If Gisella resembles her mother, she shows her Cheysuli blood. I—do not."

"Why do you wed the lass?"

The liquor was making me sleepy on top of all the food. "Alliance," I said succinctly, because it was all I could manage.

Liam strode between his father and me and faced me directly. "Alaric of Atvia calls my father usurper and outlaw. He claims the title Lord of the Isles for himself, when he has no right to it at all. Why is Homana desiring an alliance with the jackal of Atvia?"

After a moment, I nodded. "There *is* no truce, I see."

"Alaric believes there is." Shea displayed yellowed teeth. "Betimes a lie or two will help to win a war."

I stared at Shea a long moment. Then I looked at Liam. Neither man was a fool. Neither man was a friend.

My fingers and toes were numb: I rubbed distractedly at salt residue in my hair. Weariness made me dangerously frank. "Truce or no, it does not matter. It makes no difference to Homana *who* claims this island title. We have our own concerns."

Shea sat upright in his chair. "A petty feud between petty kingdoms. Is that what you are saying?"

"No." It was all I could do to mouth it.

"Then what *are* ye saying, pup?"

Liam gets it from his father. I licked my lips and tasted the smoky liquor. "My father defeated Alaric in battle nearly twenty years ago. Since then, Alaric has paid Homana tribute twice a year. Atvia is our *vassal.*" I struggled to speak sensibly. "My lord, outside of accepting tribute, we hardly know what Atvia does. Your battles are your own."

"I have seen the tribute ships," Shea mused. "Twice yearly, as you say." His eyes glittered shrewdly. "As vassal to Homana, Alaric has the right to request Homanan aid."

"He would never get it." I tried to sit upright in my chair. "My lord—my father loathes the man. It was Alaric's brother, Osric, who slew Carillon—my grandsire—and made my father Mujhar."

"He was not wanting the title?"

"Not at the cost of Carillon's life."

Shea nodded benignly. "Then why does he wed his son to Alaric's daughter?"

My good eye insisted on closing. My wits were failing too quickly. "My lord—?"

"Why does Donal wed Niall to Gisella of Atvia?"

The deceptively gentle tone woke me as nothing else had done. I looked at Shea more clearly. "For the alliance," I said. "We need no trouble with Atvia. We have enough with Solinde and Strahan."

"Ihlini," Liam said. "Kin to Alaric's witch."

Shea rubbed his beard. "Alaric desires this marriage?"

"I think he does, my lord. I am proxy-wed to—" I stopped. I could not bear to say her name: my brother's murderer.

"Alaric desires the marriage." Shea nodded. "Good."

I drew in an unsteady breath and tried to clear my head. "What will you do with me, my lord? Will you send me to Atvia?"

Erinn's gruff lord rose and walked to me. He stopped. Smiled down on me warmly, kindly; in infinite empathy. "You are weary, lad, and injured. You are requiring rest. I will ask my son to help you to your room."

Shea wavered before my eyes. "You have not answered my question." I waited. "My lord," I appended faintly.

Shea and Liam shared contented smiles. But it was the older man who spoke. "If Alaric's wanting this wedding so badly, then, he will pay for it, will he not?"

"Pay for it?" I asked dully.

"Aye," Shea said in satisfaction. "One way or the other, I'll be getting the concessions I want from him. In exchange for his daughter's betrothed."

The weariness washed out of me on a wave of comprehension. "And if he is unwilling to grant those concessions?"

Shea gestured eloquently. "You are heir to the throne of Homana, lad. We'll be treating you accordingly. You need not fear for your life." He smiled. "You will be honored as our guest . . . for as long as Alaric insists."

Nine

The Aerie of Erinn, Kilore is called. Apropos, I thought. *Surely Shea raises eagles in place of sons and daughters.*

Kilore perched atop a chalk-white, rocky headland at one nubby corner of Erinn. It afforded any long-sighted man a glimpse of Atvia, to the north across the channel the Erinnish call the Dragon's Tail. It was only a shadowed view, distorted by sea spray and distance; distorted also by tears of grief and the bitterness of frustration.

I stood on the windy battlements and glared out at the choppy channel, cursing the dragon whose capriciousness had stolen away my brother. An Erinnish wind blew in my ears, singing a lament I knew too well. Each night it kept me awake. Each night it made me dream; dream of my brother.

Grief dulls the pain of physical wounds and ailments. My ribs knitted, my eye opened, the scrapes and bruises healed. I was whole again because of Erinnish care, but I found I regretted it. It gave me time to think of Ian again.

"Longing for your Atvian bride?"

I turned. The wind dried the remains of my tears. I saw Liam had exchanged plain soldier's garb for finer garments of blue-dyed wool, fastened with hammered gold platelets. His shining curls were brushed smooth, but the wind already whipped them into brassy disarray.

"No," I said flatly. "It is difficult to long for a woman when you have never seen her."

Like me, Liam pressed his belly against the wall and hooked elbows over the top of the crenel, boundaried on either side by taller merlons. "A striking girl, she is. I saw her once, when she sailed the Dragon's Tail to get a better look at Shea's unruly children." He grinned. "Atvia is so close, she might as well have shouted."

I did not wish to talk with him, no more than I ever did. But Liam was blind to my sullen silences . . . or else he did what he did to ease them. "You want her for yourself." It was something to say; I said it.

Liam laughed long and loud. "Easy explanation, is it? Another thing to resent me for? *Hah!* I am already married, lad; I am wanting nothing of that girl. You may have her." He looked at me closely out of speculative green eyes. "But you should not be placing such trust in alliances made in the wedding bed, my lad. They do not always hold."

"What would *you* know of that?"

Liam nodded a little, staring out at the distant island. "More than you might be thinking. My mother was Atvian."

That snapped my head around. "Your *mother?*"

Liam picked at mortar with a blunt finger. The nail was already blackened; this would peel it back. "Aye, Atvian she was. Shea married her to settle this accursed feud between the realms. For a while, it did. Then I was born, and Shea desired a title for his son. So he took back his claim as Lord of the Idrian Isles." He glanced at me levelly. "Alaric is my uncle."

In disgust, I looked away. "My marriage will make us kinsmen, you and I."

"*If* you wed the girl."

"And what would keep me from it?" I turned to face him squarely. "Do you intend to do it?"

Liam smiled. Then he laughed. "The puppy growls. Then be growling as loudly as you wish; I know better than to judge a dog by the sound of his voice."

Inwardly, I swore. Outwardly, I showed him an expressionless face. "I am proxy-wed to Gisella. The marriage will be made."

"Proxy-wed to that *witch*." Liam swore, spat over the wall and made the ward-sign against Ihlini evil. "But at least you did not bed with her, or surely your loins would be cursed."

I grunted. "If I had bedded her, *that* marriage would be real."

Liam went back to picking at the mortar. "Lad, you *must* see it. Alaric is unlikely to succumb to Shea's latest raft of demands. He never has before; they are two old hounds baring rotten teeth over a bitch who does not care." Sunlight gilded beard and curls. "No insult to ye, lad, but he can get a man for his daughter anywhere. Homana is hardly the only kingdom in the world, nor you the only prince."

I reached impotently for the knife that did not rest in my sheath. Not to harm Liam, whom I judged the better fighter, but out of an almost insane wish to cut at *someone*, just to ease the bitter frustration. "Alaric sends no word?"

"None yet, save for that first one of calculated outrage." Liam's grin was crooked. "Methinks the value of his daughter's prince declines."

My teeth clicked closed. I forced the sentence through them. "Then let me send word to my father, and you will *see* what value I have."

Liam, laughing, lolled against the wall. "I am having no doubts Donal values his heir. But 'twould bring the entire Homanan army down upon our heads, when 'tis only a dogfight between Erinn and Atvia."

With great effort, I kept myself from kicking the wall with my boot toe. "How do you know *Alaric* has not sent word to my father? He would like nothing better than to have Donal of Homana needing something from him."

"Because I know Alaric's pride," Liam answered. "I have a measure of my own, lad; are you forgetting?" He rubbed distractedly at a sea-filmed clasp. "Alaric will wait. Alaric will play out the game. For now, Homana is not involved. There is no need for it."

"How is there no need?" I cried. "My father does not even know his other son is dead!"

Liam released the clasp at once and looked at me in shock. "You had a *brother* on that ship?"

"Had," I echoed numbly. *Gods, why did it have to be Ian?* "Aye. He went down, like all the others, swallowed by the dragon."

The levity was scrubbed clean from Liam's face. "You are certain he died?"

I shrugged listlessly and turned away; turned to stare out at the white-capped Dragon's Tail. "How could he survive?"

"*You* survived, lad. 'Tis possible he washed ashore as you did."

"Dead," I said. "Without Tasha. . . ."

Liam pushed hair from his eyes. " 'Tis hard on a man to lose a woman, but it does not always kill him, Niall. There is still a chance—" He broke off as I stared at him incredulously. "Why are ye gaping at me, lad? 'Tis not foolishness I spout, but truth!"

Slowly I shook my head. "Tasha was not his wife, Liam, nor even his light woman. Tasha was his *lir*. Without her, he is a dead man."

"How can you be so certain of that? Was he a sickling, then? A weakling?" The wind tugged at beard and hair. "Looking at *you*, Niall, I think he must be a tougher man than you think."

"It has nothing to do with toughness." *And* everything *to do with it.* I reached out and caught his wrist, baring the sinewy underside to the sky. "If I took a knife and cut deeply enough to spill all your blood onto the stone, would you die?"

"Are ye daft, lad? Of *course* the bleeding would kill me!"

"Because you require the blood to live." I let go of his wrist. "Think of a *lir* as that blood. Without Tasha, Ian dies."

Liam stared down at his wrist. Heavy blond brows knotted; he resembled his father more than usual. But when he looked at me, I saw compassion in his eyes. " 'Tis that, then? The price? The cost of being Cheysuli?"

I met his gaze squarely. "For every warrior—except, of course, myself."

Green eyes narrowed as he studied me. "Would ye be wanting it, then? This cost? If ye knew the animal, taken from ye, would result in your death though you be *healthy*—would ye still be wanting it?"

"Aye," I said. "If a god came to me and offered a *lir* in exchange for an eye, I would give him both of them."

"I am sorry," he said abruptly. "Prince or no, you are an honorable man—and due better treatment than this."

Hope rose. "Then you will let me send word to my father?"

"No."

I reached for his throat; closed my fists on air and shook them in his face. "*Gods*, Erinnish, do you do this to torture me? You are worse than the Ihlini!"

" 'Twould not serve my father," Liam declared, but I saw the glint of anger in his eyes.

"Your father!" I spat. "That old fool? You yourself call him an old hound with rotten teeth."

Liam caught my left arm in an iron grasp and shut off all the bloodflow. "In my place, would you be allowing me to send to mine? Would you risk bringing an army of shapechangers into your land? I think not, puppy—I think not at all!" Liam shook me. It was a measure of his strength. It was a measure of his anger. "Shea cannot be sending to Donal, or he leaves us open to the arts you shapechangers claim!"

"Gods, I wish I *had* them!" I shouted back. "I would break you like a rotten piece of bone!"

A quiet voice intruded. But it was not Shea's familiar growl. "Sometimes I'm wishing someone *would* break my brother. His arrogance knows no bounds."

Liam thrust me against the wall as he released my arm. I winced as spine met stone, but stood upright almost immediately. I tried to ignore the numbness in my arm.

Liam laughed aloud as he turned back to me and slumped against the wall, all his anger banished. "She is back, lad. We'll be knowing no peace at all." The laughter died away. "She is Deirdre of Erinn, Niall. My sister."

She was a feminine version of Liam, but lacking all the rough edges. Like him she was tall, but in her his bulk was slenderness. The hair was the same brilliant, brassy gold; unbound, the wind blew it away from her face. She wore green to match her eyes and no jewelry at all. She did not require it.

"Deirdre comes and goes as she pleases," Liam said casually. "Shea gives her inordinate freedom."

"For a woman?" she demanded. "He gives as much to you; *more*, being a man." Her features were more masculine than feminine, bearing the father's prominent stamp, but it did not lessen her striking looks. It merely gave them a different quality. "Why should I remain in this drafty pile of bricks and mortar when there is a world to see?"

"The world being Erinn," Liam retorted. "Give it up, lass; while the war lasts, you'll not be leaving the island."

"This war will last forever." She pulled hair away from her eyes and clasped it, forming a single thick plume. Her nose bore two golden freckles. Her cheekbones were sharply angled—as much as Liam's, I thought, but his were mostly hidden in his beard—and the wind whipped color into her cream-fair Erinnish skin. She smiled a warm, conspiratorial smile, as if we were boon companions embarked on a reckless childhood scheme. "Can you really break Liam for me?" she asked. "Like a piece of rotten bone?"

"Given the opportunity." And yet I knew I could not.

Defined brows rose consideringly. "Then I shall be seeing you get it." She glanced at Liam. "This is the hostage prince?"

Liam winced. "*Guest*, Deirdre . . . Niall is our *guest*."

She shrugged. "Hostage, guest, captive. . . ." Deirdre looked at me. "You are Niall of Homana. My father told me you were here."

"Against my wishes, aye."

She folded her arms beneath her breasts, tucking hair out of the wind's insistent fingers. "He did not tell me why. Will you?"

Liam reached out a booted foot and gently tapped the toe of her slipper. "If he was not telling you, lass, there is a reason for it."

"I am a *woman*. Shea forgets I am his daughter with as many wits as you." Her teasing smile was fleet and fading; she reserved most of it for me. "Why are you here, Niall of Homana?"

I wanted to answer sharply, bitterly; to strike out at another of Shea's proud eagles. But I did not. This one was not deserving of it.

"I was shipwrecked. Shea keeps me because of my value to his enemy."

Her brows quirked. "To Alaric? What value would *you* be having?"

In her the lilting cadence was softer, more attractive, though I did not doubt women longed to hear Liam's as well. "I am to wed his daughter."

"Ah," she said softly, as if in discovery. And then she laughed aloud, turning into the wall to stare out at Atvia. "So, my kinswoman will precede me into the marriage bed after all."

"Were you expecting otherwise?" Liam asked in affected irritation. "You send all the suitors away."

"Are you formally betrothed?" Deirdre asked me, plainly ignoring her brother.

"I am proxy-wed."

She nodded thoughtfully. "I was betrothed, once. When I was very young."

Liam growled deep in his throat. "You should have let me kill him, lass, for breaking the betrothal."

"I *wanted* him to break it. His heart was lost to another." She shrugged. "He went home to Ellas perfectly happy to leave me far behind."

"*Ellas!*" I looked at her sharply. "He was Ellasian?"

"Evan," she said. "Brother to High King Lachlan. He came here because his brother sent him, hoping to make an alliance. But there was another woman for Evan. He wanted none of me."

"Evan wed a kinswoman of mine!" I told her. "Meghan. Daughter to Finn, my father's uncle."

Deirdre watched me over an angled shoulder. She frowned a little, then shrugged. "I'm not knowing the names. Someday you will have to tell me a little of Homanan history."

I laughed. "Lady, there will *be* no 'someday' if I have any say. I intend to go to Atvia."

Deirdre smiled sympathetically. "A futile intention, I'm thinking. Shea will never allow it."

"There is an alternative." Liam turned to face me squarely with the wall at his back. "Make a *new* alliance, lad. One with Erinn instead."

I sighed. "I am proxy-wed, Liam. In Homanan law, it is the same as being truly married . . . and we do not end proper marriages. If I did not wed Gisella now, having already been proxy-wed to her representative, it would be justification for Alaric to cry war and sail to Homana with every soldier he can muster." I shook my head. "I am not a fool, Erinnish."

Besides, there is the prophecy . . . if I were not *to wed Gisella, what world become of my* tahlmorra? *Would I forego the afterworld?*

Liam squinted in consideration and scratched at his brassy beard. "Neither is Alaric. He would be thinking more than once about sailing to Homana while Erinn sits on his flank." Nodding a little, he smiled. "If he goes to

Homana, lad, it will be with no more than half his army.
The rest he would leave behind. Because if he were foolish
enough to take *everyone*, Atvia would be mine."

I shook my head. "Half a warhost or not, there is no
reason to plunge Homana back into war. Even with victory guaranteed."

Liam shrugged. "An idea, lad, and worth the trouble to
think it. I only meant there are other princesses in the
world besides Gisella of Atvia."

As he meant me to, I looked immediately at Deirdre.
Her back was to me. But she spun around to face us both.
"I am not a piece in one of your foolish games!" she cried.
"D'ye think I never wed because I waited for *him?*"

"Deirdre, I'm wanting less noise from you." He smiled
winningly. " 'Twas only an idea."

"Put it back in the acorn you call your head," she told
him crossly. "Leave my marriage to me."

"Then you'll never be wed at all."

"Perhaps 'tis what I prefer." She smiled, curtsied, gathered up her skirts. "I'll be leaving you now, *my lord*, if
you'll be having no objection."

He sighed. "Go, Deirdre. Take your babble to our father." She went, green skirts swinging, and Liam shook his
head. "Wild, too wild, my father's lass. But our mother
died ten years ago, when Deirdre was only eight. Shea took
a second wife—and a good woman, she is, but too timid in
the ways of raising children. Even I can make no headway,
no matter how hard I try."

I thought of Isolde, wild in her own way. Ian knew—*had
known*—her better than I, being full-born brother instead
of half, yet even he had muttered about her recklessness.
But 'Solde, I knew, was harmless. I thought Deirdre was
as well.

"She is not beautiful," Liam said bluntly, "but she has a
way about her. Your visit will be more comfortable now
that Deirdre is home."

"Why?" My tone was equally blunt. "Will she be sharing
my bed?"

Fast, so fast, he caught me by both arms and lifted me
off my feet, pressing me up and over the crenel. Parting the
veil of beard and mustache were taut lips and gritted teeth.

"Say it again," he invited softly, "and I promise you the *rocks below* will be your bed."

I did not have to look. I did not have to speak. I merely nodded to him.

Liam let me go. I slumped back against the crenel, clutching one of the merlons next to it. "You chafe," he said, "I know. It would drive me mad as well. But do not make my sister the target of your anger."

Slowly, I rearranged my clothing. I could think of nothing to say.

Liam shook his head. "Do as you wish. If you choose to make an enemy of my sister, you make one of my father. As for myself, I care little for what becomes of Donal's yapping puppy."

He left me alone on Kilore's windy battlements. As he went, I was aware of genuine regret.

On his part as well as my own.

Ten

Liam's anger did not last. He was too fair a man, too content with life to allow darkness to possess his soul for long. His empathy for my plight surprised me with its depth; he seemed to understand what I felt better than I did myself. And so we made our peace without passing a word between us, and life became infinitely easier.

As the days passed, the shackles were loosened a bit. I was given a horse out of the royal Erinnish stables, a pale gray gelding, and told I might ride whenever I chose. I chose to often, galloping across the endless heights and headlands. Liam assigned a six-man contingent to ride with me when he himself could not, and so I learned what it was to be a hostage to hospitality; on my honor as a prince—with no complaints to voice concerning my treatment—I could not attempt escape.

Often I sought refuge in solitude on the windy headlands overlooking the Dragon's Tail. This morning I watched what I always watched: fisherfolk, Atvian and Erinnish alike, sailing out with the tide into the Idrian to work the waters until the tide brought them back again.

The morning mist had lifted, but the brassy sun could not quite dispel the chill of approaching fall. I pulled my fur-lined cloak more tightly about my shoulders and halted my horse, staring bleakly at the beaches below.

Nearly fall. It has been months since I sailed from Hondarth. Three, they say, from Homana to Atvia. I swear it has been twice that, and my father in ignorance.

The distant jangle of trappings gave away an approaching rider. In irritation I looked up, prepared to order my human watchdogs farther away; they knew better than to bother me with close surveillance. But the words died in my mouth when I saw Deirdre, crimson cloak whipping as she came riding across the headland. A single braid slapped her back as she rode, all bent over in the saddle to let the dark gray gelding gallop on unhindered.

She rode straight at me, straight at the end of the headland, at the edge of Erinn itself. She was laughing. I saw crimson-dyed doeskin boots shoved into iron stirrups and the cloak went flapping, flapping as she galloped. laughing in joyous exultation. I had known the feeling myself, but not since my imprisonment.

Not since Ian's death.

She bobbed upright in the saddle and set the reins, calling something to the gelding. I watched him tuck dark haunches and slide, plowing through damp turf so that it flew up behind him like muddy rain. But he stopped. At the edge of the world, he stopped.

Deirdre was laughing breathlessly. The wind and the ride had pulled tendrils free of the single braid; they curled around her flushed face in gilded disarray. Her green eyes were alight as she turned the gelding to fall in next to my own. The horses nosed one another, grays dark and light, blowing, then picked with greedy teeth at succulent turf in perfect companionship. Bits and bridles clattered a counterpoint to the shrieking of the gulls.

"So," she said, "you have discovered the peace in turbulence."

I looked from her to the wind-whipped Dragon's Tail. "Are they not enemies to one another?"

Doeskin gloves matched the crimson boots. She made a sweeping gesture. "You see below us the turbulence of the wild sea, and feel the cold breath of the dragon whistling through his teeth. Wind and water have a peace of their own, and balm for a troubled soul." Her gaze was very green, very clear as she looked at me. "And are you not seeking that peace?"

"Why should *you* seek it?" I countered. "*You* are not a prisoner."

Beneath the crimson cloak she wore a fine white tunicked gown, belted with gold-plated leather. The colors became her as well as the wild wind that stripped hair from her braid and whipped it into her face. "Is a woman not prisoner first to her father, and later to her husband?"

I smiled. "If *you* are a prisoner to your father, it is the most unbalanced captivity I have ever witnessed. As for a *husband*—you have only to tame your tongue, and doubtless you would be wed within a six-month."

Deirdre laughed aloud, unoffended. "But what would my father do without me?" Abruptly, her laughter died. "He has wed two daughters into foreign lands and lost a third to childbed fever. I am his youngest, his favorite . . . of all his girls. He would rather keep me by him if I choose to stay."

"And do you choose to stay?"

She lifted one shoulder in a half-hearted shrug. "I would like to see the world. But not at the price of taking a husband I do not want."

"Shea would never force you into a political marriage."

"No," she agreed. "He is a loving man, my father, for all his gruff words and ways. He is not a harsh lord, no matter what *you* believe."

"He keeps me against my will."

She did not smile. "You could escape. Down there." She did not so much as glance down. "You could."

I could. Here the chalky cliff face was broken, crumbling downward toward the sea like a spill of riverbank. It was not impossible.

And yet it was. "I have given your father my parole. To break it is to break the honor of my House. That I would never do." A gull screamed overhead. "I do have *some* pride, Deirdre."

"Near as much as Liam," she said softly. "And as deadly, too, I think." She stared down at scarlet leather as she replaited her gelding's mane. "He said your brother went down with the ship."

"He did."

She looked straight at me, hiding none of her empathy. " 'Tis sorry I am, Niall. I lost a brother when I was very little. To fever, but death is one and the same, whatever face he shows." She looked at me a moment longer, then twisted her neck to peer fixedly out to sea. Gazing westward. "Were you in Homana now, what would you be doing?"

I almost told her it was possible I might be bedding my Atvian wife, but I did not say it. Somehow, before Shea's gilded, green-eyed daughter, I could not speak of Gisella.

"I would be in Homana-Mujhar—my father's palace—learning statecraft from my father's councillors. The gods know I have need of such training." Like Deirdre, I stared westward toward Homana. "Or I would be in Clankeep . . . wishing myself whole."

She looked back at me quickly. "Whole? Are you missing a part of you, then?"

I smiled, but it faded soon enough. "No. Not in flesh and bone. I speak of spirit, of soul . . . of the thing that makes a man worthy of the world. It is a Cheysuli thing." I waited for the familiar gnawing pain to rise in my belly; when it came, it lacked its normal intensity. Regret, as always, was present—the longing of a man in need of security, but the lack was not as painful. "A warrior without a *lir* is not accounted whole," I told her. "Such men do not stay with the clan, but seek death among the forests as soulless men, until the death is given to them."

I fully expected her to recoil in horror, remarking on the barbaric beliefs of the savage Cheysuli, but she did not. She studied me silently, as if she considered the implications of my words.

"You are here before me, alive," she said at last. "Why are you still alive?"

I looked away from her. "Because, never having had a *lir*, I did not lose one. I am not expected to perform the ritual. But—also because I am two men." Bitterly I defined them. "Prince and warrior. Homanan and Cheysuli. I am not wholly one or the other."

"And neither accepts you fully."

"No." The breath of the dragon whistled. I felt the touch of his icy teeth.

"What are you, Niall?" she asked. "Tell me who you are."

"What I am. . . ." I looked up into the skies. "I am a vessel the gods would make use of to shape a prophecy."

" 'Tis the fate of all men, that. To be part of their *own* prophecy, regardless of origin."

After a moment I reached out and touched her gloved hand. "I see why your father has no desire to lose you. Were I Shea, I would never let you go."

The wind whipped hair into her eyes and made them tear. Smiling sadly, she withdrew her hand from mine and turned her horse from me.

I watched her go at a gallop. Then I turned back to seek the peace in turbulence.

And to curse my *tahlmorra* in silence.

I dreamed. In my dream I was a raptor, circling in the sky. Below me, in a castle garden, two girls played with a doll wearing a gilt brooch-crown. Each was the antithesis of the other: blue-black hair/thick gold hair. Young skin the color of copper-bronze/young skin the color of cream.

And as the seams split and spilled dried-bean blood onto the ground, I saw Deirdre's tear-streaked face framed by bright gold hair.

But the other girl's face I did not know.

A sound awakened me. I could not put a name to it, knowing only it had intruded upon my dreams rudely, leaving me sitting upright in bed in a somewhat befuddled state. A glance at the candle with the hours marked in it told me I had only barely slept at all; perhaps half an hour, a little more. Enough only to lose myself so completely that it was difficult to recover all my senses.

There. Again. A voice. Muffled by the wood of my heavy door, but clear enough for me to identify.

Deirdre's.

The tone was urgent, both pleading and exasperated all at once. I heard her call out her brother's name, and then I could make no more sense of the words at all.

I considered trying to go back to sleep. It was none of it my business. But my curiosity was roused; I slid out of bed, pulled on trews, shirt, boots, and went to open my door.

The hinges creaked. I put my head into the corridor and saw the guard standing at one end, as he always did, by the spiral stairway, set there to keep an eye on me. At the other end, as I turned, stood Deirdre, half in a nightrail, half in woolen trews. She had stuffed the ends of the nightrail into the waist of the trews, but some of the linen still trailed over her rump to the backs of her knees. And over the linen trailed her brass-bright hair, unbound, unkempt, infinitely provocative.

"Ye *skilfin*," she told the closed door directly in front of

her face. "Why, when I'm needing you, d'ye drink yourself insensible?"

The door was opened. I saw only a portion of the face
in the crack between door and jamb, but it was definitely
not Liam's bearded features.

Ierne's. Liam's wife.

"Aye, he's drunk," Ierne told Deirdre. "Have mercy on
his poor head, Deirdre, and hush your shouting."

"But I *need* him!"

"Are we under attack?" Ierne asked calmly. "Has Alaric
come raiding again across the Dragon's Tail?"

"No, but—"

"Then be letting the poor man sleep, Deirdre. He doesn't
do it often, now, does he?"

"No, but—"

Firmly, Ierne said: " 'Tis a wife's prerogative to keep her
husband in bed, Deirdre. One day, you'll be exercising your
own." And, as firmly, Ierne closed the door in Deirdre's
face.

"*Skilfin,*" Deirdre muttered, threatening the door with a
fist. Then, sighing, she turned away and saw me. Her head
came up. Her face brightened. "Well, come on, then.
You'll do."

"*I'll* do? I'll do what?"

She tossed heavy hair back, strode down the corridor in
muddy boots and shut her hand upon my wrist. "You'll do
because I have no better, Liam so lost in drink. 'Tis Brenna,
you see. Come along."

She did not wait to let me close my door. "Brenna?" I
asked as I went with her, wrist still trapped in her hand.

"Brenna," she said firmly. "She's needing a man's help."

"A—man's?"

"Aye. I always get Liam to help, but he's lost for the
night. Brenna doesn't know you, but once I introduce you
she'll be fine. She doesn't like the others."

Deirdre led me past the guard and released my wrist as
she started down the twisting stair. Behind her, I saw hair
turned to molten gold in the torchlight; a slender hand sliding against rough stone as she went down and down and
down, never hesitating. Gone was the prince's sister I had
seen on the battlements of Kilore, green-clad against the
gray of the skies and the gray of the Aerie walls. Gone was

the elegant princess of Erinn in white wool, crimson, and hammered gold, atop the chalk cliffs on a storm-gray horse. It was a different woman I saw now: rumpled, half-dressed, all intent upon a thing. And as she turned her head to look over a shoulder at me as she reached the bottom of the stair, I found I wanted—suddenly, irrationally—to kiss her.

"Do ye know horses?" Deirdre asked.

With great care I removed myself from her immediate presence, taking two steps back up the stairs. "Horses?" Horses were the last thing on my mind.

"Aye. Why—were ye thinking Brenna was a woman?" *Her* mind, clearly, was only half on me; she frowned, then laughed. "No, no, a *mare*. And one about to foal. Come on, then, or she'll be done before we get there."

"Would that be so bad?" I thought surely a mare knew best how to bring her young into the world.

"D'ye know nothing of horses, then?" she asked impatiently. "Agh, go back to bed. I'll do it myself."

Obviously, Brenna was a favorite. Well, I'd had them myself. And at the moment, I had no desire to leave. "I'll come."

Deirdre took me out of the castle proper to the stable inside the curtain wall. There was almost no moon, so that I stumbled over the uneven cobbles like a child just learning to walk. Deirdre, knowing the bailey, cast me an impatient glance and hastened onward with only a single torch in her hand. It smoked and flared in her wake.

A man met us at the stable. He looked at me in mild surprise, then turned his full attention to Deirdre. He seemed unconcerned by his lord's daughter arriving at the stable in the dead of night in nightrail, boots, and man's trews. He simply took the torch from Deirdre's hand and told us to go on.

"She'll be having naught of me," he said quietly. "At least until the foal is born. 'Tis always Brenna's way."

"Aye." Distracted, Deirdre went by him into the stable and I followed.

"Oh, *breagha, breagha*," Deirdre said softly as she slipped into a stall. "Oh, my Brenna *breagha*, 'tis a fine foal you'll be showing us."

The stables were thickly shadowed, illuminated only by

a few lanterns. Looking into the stall Deirdre entered I could only see blackness, and then the blackness moved.

I saw the glint of eyes. Heard the flaring snort from velvet nostrils. Smelled the faint acrid tang of a horse in extremity.

The mare lay on her side. She heaved her head up, touched Deirdre's hands softly with muzzle, stiffened with exertion. I saw the contractions roll through the mound of glossy belly.

Deirdre moved away at once, stepping closer to me as she gave the mare room. Black Brenna grunted, strained, lay back again.

"There," Deirdre breathed. "See the hooves just under Brenna's tail? There's the sac. The foal will follow soon enough."

She spoke softly, so softly to the mare, soothing her with infinite care and affection. Brenna seemed calmer with Deirdre talking her through the labor; she gave a great heave and the foal slid out into the clean straw of the stable floor.

"Now," Deirdre breathed, and knelt down to tear the wet sac from the newborn foal. Brenna aided her, catching what she could with her teeth, then began to lick.

And stopped, almost as abruptly.

"Brenna *breagha*," Deirdre soothed. "A bit of a stud-colt for us, is it?"

She was soaked in birthing fluids, the ends of her bright hair stiffening into sticky curls. I saw the damp shine on her forearms as she shoved the sleeves of her nightrail above elbows, reaching down to free the colt's nose of residue.

"Ah, no," she said abruptly. "Ah, *no*." Hair whipped as she jerked her head around. "Seamus? Seamus—are you there? Quickly, man. The colt's not breathing!"

He was with us in an instant, hanging the lantern onto a nail. Now I could see clearly how still the colt was, how limp he was in Deirdre's arms and in the soiled straw.

He bent even as the mare lurched to her feet. Brenna turned her back on the colt. Her exhaustion was plain to see; so was her rejection of the stillborn colt.

"Hold her," Seamus told me plainly. I did as was told,

taking hold of Brenna's halter and keeping her in a corner of the stall as they ministered to the colt.

The mare was too weary to resent my presence. She shut her eyes as I stroked her face, marveling at the purity of her coloring. Black, all black, with not a single spot of white anywhere. Priceless.

"*Breagha*," Seamus said, and I knew he did not speak to the mare, "*breagha*, 'tis nothing left to do. He's gone from us."

"Ye *skilfin*, you've not tried hard enough."

"I have," he said solemnly. " 'Tis nothing left but to give him to the *cileann*."

"Nothing." Deirdre echoed. "Eleven months spent a-waiting for this birth, and now there is *nothing*—"

"You've got the mare, *breagha*."

"Aye," she said finally, and rose. She came to me, to Brenna, and clasped the mare's neck in her arms. "Oh Brenna, Brenna, such a fine little colt he was, so *fine* . . . fitting, I think, for the *cileann*. They'll give him honor and all the freedom of his days."

"I'll be bringing him, then," Seamus said.

"No." Deirdre swung around, but not before I saw the sudden kindling in her eyes. "No, 'tis for Niall to do, if he'll do it."

There was no need to ask me. And I think she knew it as well as I, though we dared not look at one another.

Seamus's face closed up. "Homanan," he said only. And then he added: "shapechanger."

"Surely the *cileann* won't begrudge him *his* fair share of magic," Deirdre chided. "They are honorable folk, and generous. They'll be giving him welcome, Seamus, as much as Shea himself."

Subtle reprimand, I thought, reminding the loyal servant that the woman he served was the daughter of a king. Reminding him also that what respect I was given by that king was owed by Seamus as well.

"Then I'll be tending the mare. She'll have me by her, now."

Deirdre looked at me. "Can you lift him?"

Silently, I did so, gathering the wet, still body into my arms. He weighed substantially less than one of Liam's wolfhounds.

She nodded. "Bring him, then. We've a thing to do."

Deirdre took me out of Kilore and into the hills of Erinn. With no moon to speak of it was difficult to see, and yet Deirdre seemed to know the way. I followed the pale luminescence of her linen nightrail and the faint gleam of burnished hair. She did not stop, did not speak, did not even turn as if to see how I fared with the weight of the colt. She simply walked on, intent upon her thoughts, and I left her to her silence.

At last, upon a crumbled hilltop, she stopped. Over the colt I saw the stone cairn and low altar beside it, also of stone, all carved with alien runes. I knew, without Deirdre's instruction, what I was to do, and so I lay the colt down upon the altar. Then Deirdre motioned me back, and I saw there was a thin circle carved into the turf. Chalk white, it glowed faintly in the darkness.

"The tor," she said, "belongs to the *cileann*, the oldfolk. They were in Erinn long before we were. Many have forgotten them, but not all. And none of the House of Eagles." Her eyes were black in the darkness, though I knew by day they were green. "We will wait the night through until dawn, so we know he is safely taken."

"Taken—?" I looked at the cairn and altar. "I mean no disrespect, but what would the oldfolk do with Brenna's stillborn colt?"

"What they do with anything born without breath in its body—give it welcome, give it life, give it the freedom of the *cileann*." She sighed a little. "I have seen women leave stillborn babies here, and children murdered kittens, all with equal grief. But also equal certainty that the death is only of the earth, and not real in the land of the oldfolk."

She sounded so certain, so absolute in her conviction. "And have *you* waited before?" I asked.

"Twice," she answered calmly. "There was Callum, my brother. And Orna, the sister who died in childbed."

"And did the oldfolk take them away?"

"That is a question best answered at dawn," she told me quietly. "And by the *cileann* themselves."

It was cold upon the tor, and windy, and heavy with ancient magic. *Lir*less I was, but neither blind nor deaf to power when it is so strong. I tried to sleep and could not; Deirdre did not ever bother to close her eyes. We lay on our backs on the cool turf with the cairn and altar behind us and stared up at the stars, talking of dreams and aspirations, sharing portions of ourselves we had never thought to share, holding them too precious, and waited for dawn to come.

And when it came, just as I put out a hand to touch her, Deirdre scrambled up and spun to look at the altar.

I was forgotten. She was lost in the rite of welcome given to a new day.

Sunlight gilded the cairn. The world was born again. And the altar was perfectly empty.

I moved, slowly, toward the cairn. Now I could see her face, where the sun touched it even as I longed to touch it; as the light set her hair afire. I saw a smile of blissful satisfaction. She murmured something in a tongue I did not know, and then she looked at me.

She wore a soiled, dirty nightrail and a pair of men's nubby wool trews. She had spent the night upon the sacred tor with a man she hardly knew, and yet knew better now than he himself. We had thrown open the corners of our hearts that men and women kept secret from one another, too afraid to set light into those corners for fear the other would laugh or, worse, find the secrets not worth the hiding.

And I had waited for her to grieve, speaking of the colt. But she had not. Like a Cheysuli, she locked it away. But I thought she waited for something.

I looked at her. At her smudged, proud face with the look of an eaglet in it, waiting to leave the aerie. Knowing the day will come when she will ride the air and lay claim to all the world.

Deirdre looked at the empty altar. She sighed a little, and turned her face back to me. "Now," she said. "*Now* I can cry."

And as the tears ran down her face, I shut my arms around her.

My captivity continued. I was well-treated, honored for my rank, assigned warm, comfortable chambers. I was allowed to hunt and hawk with Liam and his hounds. Shea taught me of ships and war.

But it was Deirdre who taught me what it was to love a woman.

Evenings were spent with the family: Shea, his wife; his son and daughter; Liam's wife and their two-year-old son. Sean was Liam's only child as yet, but Ierne had conceived again and was due in seven months' time. The boy was brown-eyed like his mother, but his hair, like Liam's, was brassy gold. Shea's stamp was on all of them; Kilore, the Aerie of Erinn, was home to magnificent eaglets.

And Deirdre. Present always, serving me even as her stepmother served Shea; as Ierne served Liam. Making no promises she could not keep, saying nothing of the future. But wanting as much as I did.

I sat before the cavernous fireplace after dinner and stared silently into the flames. Servants moved softly, removing platters and empty wine jugs. Shea and his clutch gathered some distance away; I was treated as part of the family until politics intervened. Then I was a hostage who must be kept in ignorance of his future.

Sean, defying his elders, came running across the floor to fall against my legs. He hugged one knee and grinned at me, saying something in what I believed was the ancient Erinnish language, until I realized it was only his childish mumblings. Obligingly I lifted him into my lap and settled him there. He squirmed around until he sat against my chest, head slumped on my collarbone and one fist thrust into my woolen jerkin. Like me, he stared into the flames in deep, thoughtful silence.

I realized I had never held a child before. I felt distinctly discomfited; did I have the arms and legs settled comfortably? Sean did not seem to notice my concern, so I assumed he fared well enough. But I was not certain I liked the responsibility. Children, I had always believed, were crying, petulant things when they were not shouting and shrieking in play, and yet Sean was quiet enough. Slowly my unease abated and left me feeling tentatively contented.

I felt her presence before she spoke, as always. "You are good with him." Deirdre stood behind me. "He does not always please himself so easily."

Having no wish to disturb the boy, I did not try to turn. "I am a stranger. He will lose interest soon enough."

"Sean is not one for losing interest in a thing. 'Tis independent he is, like his father."

"Like you."

Laughing softly, she moved around the chair and sat down on a stool at my feet. Pale yellow skirts of softest wool settled around her like a cloud. " 'Tis a good father you'll be making one day." Intently, she watched me, waiting; absently, one slender hand touched the fabric of my breeches.

Deliberately, I said: "If I am ever given leave to wed my betrothed."

Her eyes flickered in response to the wry challenge in my tone. She took her hand away. "Then 'tis still *Gisella* you desire."

"I do not desire *her*, Deirdre . . . only my freedom so I may wed her. There is a difference."

The firelight behind her set her bright hair aglow. Her face was in shadow, but I saw her clearly. I knew her too well by now. "What of me?" she asked evenly.

I looked away. I had to. "What *of* you?"

Her tone hardened. " 'Tis so easy for you, then, this thing between us? This thing that has the binding on us both?"

I drew in a careful breath. *Ah gods, forgive me for hurting her—* "There is a prophecy, Deirdre, to which I am bound more firmly than any woman."

"Even Gisella?" The barb was sharp. "Is she not a *part* of that prophecy?"

"She is a part of my *tahlmorra*, my fate, as you would call it. She is half Atvian. It is her blood we need, for the prophecy of the Firstborn."

"Are you forgetting, then? *I* am half Atvian, too."

She and Gisella are cousins even as Gisella and I are. Gods, what a tangled tapestry—

Sean squirmed, sensing the tension between Deirdre and me. I set him down and watched him make his way to his father, still talking with Shea near the door.

"But you have no Cheysuli blood," I said finally. "Deirdre, I have told you what I lack. No *lir*, no gifts, no strength as the warriors know it. I lack even the *color*—" I stopped. It would do no good to expose my insecurities and resentments. *"One day a man of all blood shall unite, in peace, four warring realms and two magic races,"* I quoted. *"All blood*, Deirdre. If I cannot hand on the proper gifts to my children, the prophecy will not be properly served." I drew in a breath through a painfully constricted throat. "Gisella is half Cheysuli. What *I* do not have, she does. I need her, Deirdre, for that."

She sat before me, rigidly upright; rigidly proud. "And I need *you*."

I reached out and touched her glowing hair. Beneath my hand she trembled with the strength of her conviction; with the strength of her desire. Even as I myself did.

Dry-mouthed, I said: "There is nothing I can do."

And hated the man who said it.

The old lord called me into his personal chamber weeks later. I went with foreboding in my soul, for hope had been banished months before. I found Liam present as well.

Shea waved me to a chair. "Sit, sit, lad . . . what I have to say is better heard in private."

I watched Liam's face for some hint of what was to come. He gave nothing away, nothing at all, save the gravity of the matter.

Shea sat down also. " 'Tis word from Donal, your father." His mouth, behind the beard, twisted in a grimace. "Alaric at last sent word of your presence with me, saying other messengers must have gone astray." He grunted. "I think Donal is no fool, lad. He'll not be believing *that*."

I felt light-headed with relief. "What does my father say?"

"He inquires after your health. I told the Homanan messenger it was excellent. He'll be taking that back to the Mujhar already."

All the relief fell away. *"You have sent him away?"*

"The messenger? Aye. I saw no reason to have you trade words with him, lad. I was not wanting you disturbed."

"Disturbed!" I overturned the chair as I jumped up unsteadily. "By the gods, you pen me up for five months and then send away a man who bears word from my father?"

Shea's thicket of eyebrows jerked up into his hair. "Has it been that long? I'd be saying three months, I think, not five." Frowning, he turned to Liam. "Five months, he says. Truth?"

"Truth," Liam answered.

Shea glanced back at me. *"Sit down!"* he roared. I righted the chair and sat down. Appeased, he rubbed thoughtfully at his beard. "I let him see ye, lad, to know how you fared." His faded green eyes were oddly watchful.

"You were with my daughter, lad. . . . Liam says you looked well content."

I felt heat and color spill into my face. I shut my mouth on a curse, but sent Liam an angry glance. He smiled crookedly and shrugged.

"He's wishing to send a personal envoy to Kilore," Shea said. "To negotiate for your release."

My hands closed over the arms of the chair. "Well?"

"I have agreed."

"To my *release?*"

"To his coming. No more than that, lad—'tis all I can give you, for now."

I pushed myself out of the chair and faced the old man. "My lord—"

"You'll be staying here till I see fit to let you go."

I drew in a careful breath. "And if the Mujhar sends forces with that envoy?"

"I'm thinking he will not," Shea remarked. "He is well occupied with Solinde at the moment."

"Solinde," I echoed blankly.

"The Ihlini have risen, lad."

Oh gods—it is Strahan— "My lord," I begged, "let me go home to my father."

"Until Alaric gives in, you go nowhere." Shea glared at me and shifted in his chair. "There's a thing I must ask you, lad. Will you give me honest answer?"

"Ask me." I was too overcome to dissemble.

"Would you be in mind of breaking your pledge to Gisella?"

I stared at him in shock. "I could not."

"And if I offered you your freedom?"

I looked at Liam. I saw compassion in his eyes; he knew what the answer cost me. "No," I said again. "I—cannot." But I would not cite the reasons. I thought Shea would not understand. And I thought *I* might not, if I ever spoke them aloud.

The old man nodded slowly, as if the answer was precisely what he expected. "Well," he said. "Deirdre told me what you would say. But 'tis sorry I am you cannot be my son."

I could not speak. Obscurely touched, I could only stare at the man.

Liam shrugged broad shoulders. "You'll be doing what you must. 'Tis what makes you the man you are."

I turned my back on them both, intending to walk from the room. And then I turned back again to face them. "Wait. *Wait*—perhaps there is something." I drew in a breath. "I cannot be a son or brother, but I *can* be a kinsman."

Shea glared. He tapped the arm of his chair. "Set it out here, lad, where grown men can see it plain."

"I will wed Gisella," I declared, "and when we have a daughter, I will offer that daughter to Sean. He will be lord of this island one day—and Lord of the Isles, no doubt—but my daughter will be a princess of Homana. Would that be enough for you?"

Shea grunted. "For myself, aye, 'twould. But I'll not be here to see it. 'Tis for Liam to say whom his son will be taking for a wife."

Expectantly I looked at the Prince of Erinn. His smile was crooked, half-hidden in his gilded beard. "I'm thinking Sean is a bit young, yet, to have his marriage settled for him, but I'll be considering it." He nodded. "*If* you get a daughter on the lass."

"Gisella and I were cradle-betrothed," I pointed out. "At least Sean is *walking*."

Liam laughed. "But Gisella is not even *bedded*."

"She will be. Once I am free of here."

Shea grunted. I saw affection and amusement in his eyes. "Take yourself away, lad, and leave me to my son."

I took myself away feeling oddly liberated.

Eleven

Liam sent word for me to meet him in one of Kilore's audience chambers, but when I went I found myself alone. No doubt *important* business kept him: one of his wolf-hounds was due to whelp, or a mare to foal, or perhaps even Sean demanded his attention. Wryly, I reflected that the Prince of Erinn's priorities were different from those of most men.

The chamber was cold. The fire had been allowed to die, or else a servant had neglected to light it. The sunlight coming in one of the deep, crudely-cut casements hardly reached the center of the room. Kilore was not a luxurious aerie for the Erinnish eagles, being more fortress than palace, but it served well enough. It did not matter to me that the rush-strewn floors were uneven, the tapestries faded and threadbare, the furniture but crudely made of knotty greenish wood. It was here Deirdre had been reared; that was all that counted.

I slumped against the edge of the casement sill and stared out. From here I could see neither the Dragon's Tail nor Atvia. All I could see was the green Erinnish turf stretching forever and ever to the edge of the world, where the wheel of life continued turning for everyone save myself.

The door creaked open (none of Kilore's heavy leather-hinged doors were silent) and I heard Liam's bootstep. "Niall."

Not Liam— I turned, then thrust myself off the wall. A stranger faced me, except he was no stranger at all. He had been a part of my life since birth. "Rowan!"

My father's closest companion—and Cheysuli general of all the Homanan armies—stared at me as if he distrusted his eyes. I did not doubt he *did*, after nearly a year. And then he smiled a smile I feared would break his face, so broad and transparent he was in his relief, and I met him halfway across the chamber in a bearhug that required neither apology nor explanation.

The rampant black lion on Rowan's crimson tunic clawed silk impotently as I stepped back from the embrace. In the months of my absence the general had aged. Cheysuli do not show the years as easily as Homanans, but Rowan was no longer young. I could not number his years precisely, but he claimed several more than fifty, I knew. And it had begun to show.

"The gods have been kinder than we expected," Rowan said on a sigh of relief. "I thought to find you weak and wan as an albino calf."

"No." Emotion welled into my chest with such intensity I feared I might shame myself. It is rare for a Cheysuli to show precisely what he feels. Oddly, I saw the same struggle in Rowan's careworn face.

Why not? He and I share the same capricious gods.

*Lir*less, both of us. Cheysuli born and bred, and yet we neither of us claimed a *lir*. Rowan's explanation was straightforward enough: orphaned in Shaine's purge of shapechangers some forty-five years before, he had been taken in as a foster son by immigrant Ellasian crofters who did not know he was Cheysuli. In those dangerous days no shapechanger was safe; he did not dare divulge his heritage, or he would give himself over into certain death. And so he had been reared Homanan, growing into Homanan habits and traditions; when the time come for him to go out and make a bond with the *lir* intended for him, he did not. *Lir*less he was and would remain so, until the day he died.

And I? Perhaps it is time I learned to live with it, even as Rowan has.

I motioned with my head. "What you see has been my prison. Kilore is not an unpleasant one."

Though the black hair was graying to a decided silver, his yellow eyes were sharp and steady as Ian's or my father's. The netting of sunlines and silvering scars in his face only underscored the years he had spent at the side of Homana's Mujhars, insuring domestic and personal security.

He frowned, just a little; enough to crinkle eyelids and pull at the weatherburned flesh over angular cheekbones. I thought he listened to my tone more than he did to my words.

"Have they suborned you with this?" In *his* tone I heard tremendous restraint, and yet I also heard a multitude of emotions. Traces only, but enough to emphasize what my disappearance had meant to my father and mother. And, perhaps, to Rowan.

I wanted to laugh at him and clasp a shoulder and lead him to a chair, to pour the smoky Erinnish liquor and laugh *with* him, that he could ask such a thing of me. But I did none of those things. I looked at him, steadily as I had looked at no man before and told him the truth.

"No. But I will not lie and tell you Shea has been a harsh lord or inhumane when he has offered me honor and affection."

"Eight months of it?—assuming, of course, the voyage took *you* the three months it took me." Rowan's posture was the rigid stance of a longtime soldier and officer at rest, which is to say he was not precisely resting. And his elaborately casual tone was as inflexible as his spine. "I think perhaps we misjudged your reaction to my coming; Aislinn said Carillon's grandson would devise an immediate means of departure. Donal said it was more likely you would leave the devising to me." The general did not smile. "Yet you say *nothing at all* of departure."

Carillon's grandson. Even now she does not refer to me as her son, only heir of her legendary father, one generation removed.

"There is no need to *say* anything," I told him curtly. "Shea will not let me go. Not until Alaric grants the concessions he demands."

"And what are those concessions?"

I shrugged. "He does not tell me such things."

Rowan looked away from me briefly, toward the casement. Then he turned and went to it, staring out even as I had before his entrance. "It is unlikely Alaric will grant Shea anything. He is too concerned with mustering men to aid Strahan against Homana."

I started. "But—the alliance—?"

"Contingent upon you making his daughter Princess of Homana." Rowan's tone was distant. "Oh, aye, the proxy ceremony makes you husband and wife in Homanan law, but until she is properly wed and acclaimed Princess of Homana, the alliance does not exist. And now it seems impossible that it ever *will* exist, does it not? At least, while Shea keeps you here." He turned to face me and the lion rippled, clawing at his right shoulder. "Eleven months ago you left Homana to fetch Gisella home to a Homanan wedding. Circumstances aside, Alaric has every right in the world to declare the proxy wedding invalid and the cradle-betrothal broken." His face was a mask; his tone was not so well-schooled. "A broken betrothal and an invalid proxy wedding taints a woman as well as a man, Niall. A father would be justified in levying war in his despoiled daughter's name. And as for you, who would you find to wed? Who would have you?"

Deirdre would—

"Who would bring the proper blood to the prophecy?"

Deirdre would not— Angrily, I glared at him. "I did not *put* myself here!"

"No." Frowning, Rowan stared down at his boot toes. "No, you did not. Alaric is aware of that; no doubt more aware than *we* are, being so close to Erinn, but . . . regardless—" He looked at me again, and I saw a weariness of spirit so totally alien that it brought me striding across the room to him.

"Rowan—"

His raised hand stopped me short. More intensely aware of the man and his feelings than I ever had been before, I marked the callused palms and battered knuckles, ruined nails and crooked fingers, all badges of his profession. His life. And I saw the bleakness in his eyes.

"Niall, there is trouble at home. Serious trouble."

Fear flared. "My father? *Mother?* Rowan—"

"Both well," he said at once. "No, it has nothing to do with their welfare. It is—"

"Strahan," I finished, "is it not?"

"Not—entirely." He straightened and thrust himself away from the wall, pacing away from me toward the cold fireplace. I noticed for the first time he limped, though only a little, as if his aging bones and muscles reminded him he had fought in too many battles. Most of them with Carillon, whom he had served for nearly twenty-five years. The last twenty had been with my father, but I knew the bond was not the same.

And now he must fight another.

He turned. I saw him muster the dry factuality necessary to a competent, effective general. Necessary to a ruler, for that matter. One day, I would have to find the same within myself. "It concerns you," he said flatly. "And—Carillon."

"Carillon!" I stared at him blankly. "How can this concern a man who has been dead for twenty years?"

"Because while he lived he sired children," Rowan answered in the same even tone.

Baffled, I nodded agreement with the obvious. "How else would I be his grandson?"

"I did not say *child*, Niall."

No. He had not. He had said *children*.

Suddenly, I was very cold. The chamber darkened around me. "A son," I said distantly. "A *son*."

"A bastard." Rowan's voice was very quiet. "We know very little. His age: thirty-five. His mother: a Homanan woman who followed Carillon's rebel army as he made his way from Ellas to Mujhara." He shrugged. "I remember her myself. Carillon was not the sort of man who wanted or needed a woman with every meal, and when he took one, he kept her. Sarne was—worth keeping."

"But he did *not* keep her, did he?" I was detached from the man who asked the questions. "No. Once she carried a *bastard*—"

"No." The word cut through my rising bitterness. "Once Electra came."

Of course. *Electra.* The witch who had bound even Carillon the Great into a web of deceit and ensorcellment until he nearly fallen victim to Tynstar himself. Electra the witch.

Electra: my mother's mother.

I looked for a chair. Found one; collapsed into it. Rubbed absently at my scalp; it itched from the sudden prickling of trepidation. "Well," I said at last, "he must have sent her away."

"She asked to leave. She came to me and said she had conceived. She no longer wished to remain with the army; she would go home."

"With Carillon's bastard in her belly."

"I gave her money. A horse. A soldier went with her."

Rowan's smile was very faint. "A crofter-turned-soldier, who discovered he was much better at wielding scythe than sword. He married her."

I looked at him sharply, frowning. "Then how do you *know* it is Carillon's son? If she married the crofter—"

"He is the image of an older you, Niall. Or a younger Carillon, before the disease aged him. As testified by a Homanan priest and a Cheysuli *shar tahl*."

Like Shea, he stamps his get— "They have *seen* him? Is he so bold as to press his claim based on bastardy when I am legitimate?"

Rowan did not avoid my eyes. "There are Homanans in the world who would prefer a descendant of Carillon on the throne who is *not* Cheysuli."

My laugh was a bark of sound. "How can they call me Cheysuli? I have no *lir*, no magic, no shapechange. . . . I am more Homanan than anything else."

"It is said you hide your magic, so as to *trick* the Homanans into believing you are wholly Homanan, and less of a threat than a man who assumes the shape of beast or bird." A muscle jumped in his jaw. "I repeat what is said by the zealots."

Under my breath, I swore. "I wish I had magic to *hide*."

"I know it, Niall." The tone altered; I heard a trace of empathy for the first time. "They claim you will unveil your true self only after you hold the throne."

"So, they want to replace me with Carillon's bastard, who *is* wholly Homanan."

"Aye."

"I am tainted by the Solindish witch's blood."

"Aye."

I sat forward and rubbed my eyes with rigid fingers. "What would they say if they knew there are some Cheysuli who feel the same?" I asked wearily. "Gods, I think I was never meant to inherit the Lion."

"You were. You will."

"Have *you* seen him?" I raised my head. "Have you seen this misbegotten image of myself?"

"No. He is too well-guarded by Homanans dedicated to his cause. They say if his location were divulged, Donal would have him slain. They wait to gather men to his cause." He spread his hands in a futile gesture. "They allowed the priest and the *shar tahl* to see him, to prove he exists. That is all. Neither spoke with him."

I slumped back in the chair again. "A pretty coil, Rowan. How do we get free of it?"

"By having you leave Erinn for Atvia, where you will settle things with Alaric and bring Gisella home to Homana," Rowan said flatly. "Your absence has strengthened the bastard's cause. When we feared you *dead*—" He shrugged. "We need you home. As soon as possible. With Gisella and Ian . . . I think only Ian can settle this thing with the *a'saii*, since he is the one *they* wish to put upon the throne."

"You knew," I mused, thinking of the *a'saii*. Then I was on my feet. "You do *not* know! Gods, Rowan, there *is* no Ian! He died in the storm."

All the color ran out of his face; leaving it a stark, empty mask of shock that only slowly was refilled by a comprehension and grief so intense it made me want to run from the man, the room, the castle.

To find my brother in the belly of the dragon.

"*Rujho*," I said; no more. The pain was new again.

After a moment, Rowan cleared his throat. "I must send word to Donal."

"*Take* it to him," I said at last. "I think—it would be better if you told him."

"And what do I tell him of *you*?"

"That I live." I drew in a breath that cleared my head. "That I will be home with Gisella as soon as possible."

"And if Shea does not let you go?"

"Then I will have to break my parole."

Looking at me steadily, Rowan shook his head. Just a little. "Whatever else this captivity has done, it has also tempered the sword."

"What is left to hone the edge?" I asked. "War?"

"Assuredly," he answered softly, and then came forward to hug me again. "The gods be with you, Niall."

"With them, without them—what does it matter?" I asked. "They are the ones who fashioned this *tahlmorra*."

I could not sleep. In the darkness of my room, my bed, my spirit, I stared sightlessly up at the woven curtains forming my Erinnish womb and tried to think of things other

than war, *a'saii*, bastards. I tried to think of everything, and
nothing at all made sense.

Until Deirdre came to me.

In the darkness, all unknowing, I thought of enemies. I
rolled and reached through the slit in the curtain for my
knife and remembered I did not have one.

"You'd be needing no weapon against *me*, Niall."

"Deirdre—"

"I heard you speak to your father's man. Is that what a
true Cheysuli looks like? So fierce, so solemn . . . so *dangerous.* I'm thinking I like you better as a Homanan."

"Deirdre—you *heard?*"

"There are secrets in Kilore even Shea does not know,
or has forgotten already. Do not worry. No one else was
there when you spoke of breaking your parole."

"Deirdre—"

"Have we driven you from us, Niall? Have we kenneled
you too closely, like one of Liam's hounds?"

The blackness of the room was not so all-encompassing
as my eyes adjusted to it. I could just see Deirdre in my
bed, and put out a hand to draw her to me. As she came,
she shed linen shift and I realized she was naked.

"Gods, you drive me only to madness . . ." I groaned
against her throat. "Deirdre—"

Her hand covered my mouth as I moved to cover hers.
"Do not speak. I have not come here for speech. There is
something more than that, I'm thinking, between us, you
and me."

I locked my fingers in her hair. Its color was muted in
the darkness, but I gloried in its texture. "I am not one for
gainsaying you in this, the gods know—" fervently "—but
do you know what you are about?"

She pressed herself against me, winding heavy locks of
hair around my neck as if she sought to set iron there.
"Only rarely am I *not* knowing what I am about, my lord."
Her breath was warm against my ear. Low-voiced, she said,
"Don't be worrying about what I heard today. I have no
intention of telling my father or brother. We'll be keeping
it between us."

I bore her down with me, shivering with pleasure at the
sensual touch of her hair and skin. "*Meijha*—" Then purposely, I used the Erinnish inflection "—you will have me

thinking you are not jealous of Gisella . . . and I am knowing better."

Laughing softly, she stroked my naked shoulder, tracing shapes of her own devising in a languid, sensuous fashion, then set lips and tongue against it. " 'Tis a jealous woman I am, but I know when I have lost. What was that word you called me?"

"*Meijha*," I breathed, "Cheysuli. . . ."

"That much I was thinking myself." A trembling forefinger traced the line of my mouth. "What does it mean?"

I kissed the fingertip, then reached for the hand, the arm, the breast. "Do not judge too hastily a people you cannot know," I whispered. "In the clans, warriors may have both wife and light woman—*cheysula* and *meijha*. There is no dishonor, none at all, for the woman who is not a wife. I swear by all the gods of Erinn and Homana—"

"Don't be swearing by gods you're knowing nothing about." Her breath came faster still. " 'Tis disastrous when they take note of it."

"Gisella is Cheysuli. I think she would understand the custom, once I have explained it."

She drew back a little. "Are you telling me 'tis what *I* would be? Your—*meijha*?"

Her accent twisted the word. I did not correct her. "If you wish it, Deirdre." *I wish it, I wish it.*

In the shadows I could not see her expression. "I might prefer to be a wife."

I set my forehead against her shoulder in defeat. "Deirdre—"

"But if I cannot be taking you *that* way, I'll be taking you the other. Now enough of this babble, Niall, and let us be making our *own* alliance between Erinn and Homana."

Laughing exultantly into her untamed hair, I covered her body with my own.

Twelve

It was three days before I could pursue my intention to escape, and even then it was coincidence that gave me the opportunity. Liam, riding out to hawk with me along the cliffs, was called back by a servant from the castle. And because Liam himself had come with me, the six human hounds had been dismissed.

I did not hesitate. I spurred the gray gelding toward the broken clifftop and rode off the edge of the world.

The gray plunged down the chalky slope, jarring my spine until I felt at least a handspan shorter. I cursed raggedly, not daring to shout my discomfort aloud, and hooked stirrups forward to brace against the jolting downward momentum.

Below me, fishing boats were scattered like pebbles along the shoreline, most of them untended as the fishermen dragged bulging nets onto the sandy beach. I must steal one quickly and, using the knowledge Shea had divulged, somehow sail it across the Dragon's Tail to the rocky coast of Atvia.

Almost down—

The horse stumbled beneath me, lurching forward onto his knees. I could not wait to see if he had injured himself or had the heart to go on. I threw the reins free and scrambled out of the saddle—

—sliding, sliding, scrabbling at the chalky escarpment of the tumbled base of the ciiffs—

Gods, get me down from here with both legs and arms left whole—

—sliding, churning up clouds of white chalk dust to coat my face, my clothing; to settle on my tongue and make me mouth my distaste. I wanted to spit; it would have to wait until I was down.

On my buttocks I went down, down, *down*, one hand thrust back to brace myself against the broken cliff. The chalk crumbled away, spilling me over like a round rock in a storm-fed stream. I fell; falling, I rolled—

—came up into a crouch at the bottom of the cliff; spitting, I thrust myself upward and ran.

I heard an outcry from the top of the cliff and knew the voice was Liam's. What he shouted I could not decipher, hearing only anger and epithets. I did not look around, intent only on reaching the boats before Liam could form a proper pursuit. I did not blame him for his rage, no more than I blamed myself for causing it.

And yet I *did* blame myself; a broken oath is no simple thing. I thought of how I had proclaimed myself incapable of ending the betrothal to Gisella because I could not break an oath. Now I broke an oath equally important.

For the sake of Homana— And I knew it was. As much as wedding Gisella was for the sake of the prophecy.

Chalk dust filled my lungs. I coughed, spat, wheezed, still running for the boats. Almost. *Almost.*

Netting tripped me up, throwing me sprawling to the wet sand. I scrambled up, trying to run again, but the net was tangled around my spurs. Cursing aloud I ripped frenziedly at the strands, then stopped yanking, still cursing, and carefully picked them free. I ran again.

The first boat was too far, bobbing in the waves at the end of its tether. I went on to the next one, reaching for the line that anchored it to the shore. Waves slapped at my boots as I bent to jerk it free.

I heard the pounding of hooves echoing against the cliffs. Closer, coming *closer.*

Oh gods, it is Liam!

I saw his furious face as he urged his horse on faster, riding directly at me. *At* me, as if he would ride me down.

Forgoing the boat, I dropped the line and ran.

The horse's chest caught me high on the left hip. A hoof ripped the heel off my boot entirely, clipped my heel, drove me headlong to the ground. I curled, sucking air as another hoof came down on the side of my thigh. The horse squealed, flailing thick legs desperately, trying to avoid me even as I tried to roll away. I tasted sand and salt and seawater. And blood from a bitten lip.

The hooves were gone. I tried to rise, to run again, but Liam leaned down from the saddle and buffeted me on the temple with a gloved, powerful fist. "False prince!" he cried. "False friend!"

I fell. I spat blood. Saw two of everything. Tried to clear my vision. By the time I did, Liam was off his horse and hauling me to my feet.

"I should slay you here, even unarmed as you are!"

I am tall, I am heavy, but Liam himself is not small. And in his rage he was larger than any man ever born. By my tunic, he lifted me almost completely clear of the sand. "Liam—"

"I should *slay* you! D'ye hear, ye faithless cur of a faithless bitch? By the gods, I swear I *will!*"

But he did not. He released me with a shove, as if he could no longer bear to touch me, and stood staring at me with chalk and spittle fouling his gilded beard. His chest heaved; like me, he panted.

"Liam—" Breathless, I could hardly manage a word. "Liam—I had to—I *had* to . . . for the war, for the realm." I tried to catch my breath. "Alaric—*Alaric* intends to join Strahan—there is domestic dissension at home!"

"I care *nothing at all* for your incestuous domestic wars!" Liam roared. "Not when you're in *Erinn* seducing my sister!"

Prepared to defend our incestuous domestic wars, I discovered we were at odds over something else. Something I could not defend at all. And so I shut my mouth.

"False prince," Liam said hoarsely, "you have betrayed my father's trust, and mine. When we have honored you with our favor!"

"Liam—"

"Were you armed—"

"Then give me a knife!" I shouted. "I am not shirking the fight!"

Liam spat blood and chalk. His green eyes were hard as glass. "I'll not be giving *you* the honor of a fight! I'll be letting you taste the hospitality you should have known *before.*"

No protest. I could not. Because before I could summon a word, Liam loosed a blow that felled me to the ground as easily as if I were a stalk of wheat.

*   *   *

The dungeons of Kilore are damp and smelly. Sore and more than a little sullen, I sat against a clammy wall because I had no other choice. Someone—Liam, no doubt—had ordered me chained in place, though there was no place I could go.

The stone beneath my buttocks was cold and damp. What straw existed was musty, stale, undoubtedly filled with vermin. Seawater dripped from the ceiling. I was cold and lonely and afraid, and also filled with guilt.

Deirdre came to me willingly, but how can I say that to her father and brother? What sense is there in besmirching her reputation?

None. What honor remained to me (little enough, after breaking my parole) kept me from being able to make the admission, regardless of the truth.

My ears rang. My head ached. Liam's blow had caught me solidly along the jaw, loosening teeth. I tongued them gently, afraid to push too hard for shoving them out entirely. Even my cheekbone hurt.

Footsteps. I turned my face toward the door and listened, trying to determine if the footsteps brought a man to me or to another prisoner, if there was one. I had no candle by which to see. There was no light in the cell save for what came in under the wooden door. And the gods knew *that* was little enough.

The footsteps stopped. Iron rattled: keys. Finally one was fitted into the lock. I waited, and at last the door was shoved open. It scraped along the slimy floor.

Shea himself. Not Liam, come to gloat. The old lord instead, holding a fat candle in one hand. It guttered, danced, flared up again as it took life from the corridor air.

Skin was stretched too taut across age-defined cheekbones. His jaw worked impotently beneath the thinning beard. I saw the gutter of anger restrained in the cat-green, grieving eyes.

Gods, forgive me for what I have done to this man.

" 'Tis how Donal rears a son to be Mujhar, is it? To be breaking parole and pledge when he has been honorably treated?" Tears shone briefly in his eyes. "To be taking a lass's virtue beneath her father's roof?"

I looked away and stared blindly down at my manacled hands. "No."

"No? *No?* 'Tis all ye have to say?"

I swallowed thickly. "Do not judge the father by the son."

The candleflame guttered violently. I did not look at Shea.

"Well," he said hoarsely, "come up. I'll say what I say above." He glanced into the corridor and jerked his head in my direction. "Loose the iron and bring him up. I'll be seeing him in the hall."

The old lord stood in the doorway as the guardsman slipped by and knelt to unlock my shackles. Limping from a badly bruised thigh—the horse had struck me squarely—I followed Shea up winding stairs to the audience hall. I had half expected Liam to be present. He was not. Neither was Deirdre. It was for Shea alone to pass judgment.

He gestured to the guardsman to leave us alone. I heard the door thud closed. Then I turned and faced the old man.

His nostrils flared. "Ye stink," he said, plainly offended by my dungeon stench.

I felt inordinately ashamed.

"Have ye an explanation?"

"No."

"Were ye for it merely because 'twas *offered*, or did ye truly want it—much as a dying man cries for water?"

I had thought him diminished by what I had done to his daughter. Now I realized he was not, it was just that I saw a man instead of a king. A father instead of a man.

I drew in a breath and released it very slowly. "I needed it," I told him clearly. "I *was* that dying man."

Shea hooked thumbs in his wide belt and considered me. And then he spoke, and his tone held all the gruff affection I had come to expect from him. "She was not meaning to betray ye, lad. 'Twas her unhappy manner that gave ye away. 'Twas the lack of her wildness and gaiety."

"My lord?"

"Oh, she was happy enough for having despoiled herself with you. She *told* me that. No. 'Twas knowing you must leave. But by the time I was realizing what she meant, you had ridden out with Liam." He paused. "She said she was willing, lad."

I was silent. Even now, I would say nothing that might

reflect poorly on his daughter, who was a princess. That much of rank I knew too well.

"By Erinnish law I am in my rights to have you slain."

"By any man's law, my lord."

"Yet you are the Mujhar of Homana's son. His heir. As much as Liam is mine."

"Aye, my lord."

Shea sighed. "Lad, lad, 'tis all bound up I am. I'd be seeing the two of you wed, but for that pledge to Alaric's daughter. That you cannot be breaking, for all you broke the one to me." There was no bitterness in his tone. "Deirdre told me what the Cheysuli general said to you. About war, and bastards, and a throne in jeopardy. Those things I understand. And so I will not be blaming ye for breaking your parole. There are pledges taking precedence over other pledges given." Through the beard, I saw the hint of a weary smile. "I will not keep ye here when your father needs ye so. I'll be seeing you sent to Atvia before the day is out."

"My lord?" I stared.

"Homana is not my enemy. I'm not wishing to see your father broken by that Ihlini demon or even Alaric's spite. Go wed your Atvian cousin, and take yourself home to your father."

Hope sprang up. "And—Deirdre?"

"She stays," he told me flatly. "My daughter will be no man's mistress, no matter how much *honor* it claims before the Cheysuli." He sighed. "But I will be asking something of ye, lad. A pledge. And this one ye'll not be breaking; Liam will see to that."

I touched my aching face. "Aye, my lord. I give it willingly."

"Ierne is due to bear the child soon. Be that child a girl, let her wed your firstborn son. Or the next one for *your* next one, if this one is not a girl and that one not a boy. But I want it, lad. I want a granddaughter of Shea of Erinn to be queen in Homana one day."

I smiled. "A fair enough exchange, my lord. A daughter of mine for Sean, a granddaughter of yours for my heir. I think it will please the gods."

" 'Twill be pleasing *me*," Shea growled. "And 'twill be enough, I'm thinking."

I put out my filthy hand to the man. He did not seem to notice as he folded it in his. "Deirdre—" I began.

"No," he said. "I'll be giving her your farewell."

After a moment, I nodded. But I knew it would not be the same.

I had been bathed, shaved, garbed in fresh clothing. No longer did I stink. But it did not wash away the sorrow I felt at leaving Deirdre behind.

It was Liam himself who came to escort me to the ship. He was sternness itself with his hard, stark face; he said nothing at all as he preceded me down the twisting stairway to the entryway. We were met by the eleven men who had accompanied him the day I was rescued. Rescued and taken captive.

There was little enough sunlight. Liam's brassy curls were dulled by the gray of the day, as much as by his unusual solemnity. His mouth, in the beard, worked a little; the words at last issued forth.

"Where would you go, lad, before we send you to your bride?"

Where would I go? To Deirdre, of course . . . and yet I knew if I asked it, he would deny me the thing I most wanted.

I looked out into the muted sunlight. "To the tor," I said. "To the altar of the *cileann*."

Liam's green eyes flickered. Still, he did not smile. He nodded, once, and gave the order for us to mount. Eleven prince's men; one heir to Shea's wild aerie; one hostage foreigner. Together, we rode out to the tor.

In daylight, with the sun well up, the place was different. Much different. I tasted no magic; smelled no hint of ancient power. And all I saw was an altar full of memories.

Deirdre. Deirdre and her colt. And the *lir*less man who loved her.

Liam's eleven men remained on horseback some distance away. Liam came closer, but even he gave me what distance he could. Privacy enough, for the moment. And so I used it. I used it to stand on the tor outside the old chalk circle and give Deirdre my good-bye.

"Time to go," Liam said, when he saw me lift an arm to scrub briefly at my face.

Aye . . . time to go. I turned. The Prince of Erinn held the reins of my horse. I walked down from the tor, took them out of his gloved hand and mounted the pale gray gelding. And thought of Deirdre's wild laughter as she rode headlong at the edge of the chalky headlands overlooking the Dragon's Tail.

"Lad," Liam said; all I could do was nod.

The escort stopped short of the dock. I boarded slowly, so slowly, then swung back to grip the rail. Liam stood on the dock. The wind whipped his brassy curls and reddened his high, sharp cheekbones, tugging at his beard. His cat-green eyes were cool. "So, puppy, you leave Erinn a wealthy man."

"Wealthy?"

"You've gained my father's trust, won my sister's love, and have pledged children neither of us yet have, saving Sean. Ye leave with a *little* pinch more than ye came with."

The wind stripped freshly-washed hair out of my face. "Perhaps you should have thrown me back into the sea the day you found me. . . ." I squinted against the wind. "Perhaps you should have let the dragon have me."

"No," he said. "You were too sickly, too battered. Not worth the trouble to feed an Erinnish dragon. I'm thinking there would have been little pleasure in it."

"The pledge we made together, and the one I made with your father—" I shrugged. "You will be king after Shea. It is for you to break them, if it is truly what you desire."

Liam bent and spat off the dock into the Dragon's Tail. He folded his arms across a broad chest. "I'm thinking not. I'm thinking I'm not much of a man for breaking pledges. Unlike *you.*"

I clutched the rail. "I can sail to Atvia later. We can settle this matter now. With knives or swords or fists." I grinned. "I leave it to you, *my lord.*"

Reluctantly, Liam grinned. The green cloak fastened to his wide shoulders curled and cracked in the wind.

"We are of a like size, I'm thinking, lad. I have spent nearly fifteen of my twenty-nine years fighting Atvians, and *you* are Cheysuli—even without the *lir.* I'm thinking 'twould not be so wise to strip Donal and Shea of their sons in a silly, boyish battle that could get either—*or both*—

of us slain." He shrugged. "Besides, my sister loves you. Where's the sense in beating a man for that?"

I laughed. "But it would have been something to see."

Liam, sighing, nodded. "Aye, 'twould. Well—perhaps another day, puppy. Now get you to Atvia."

I leaned over the rail as he gave the signal for the boat to be cast off. "Liam—a message for Deirdre?"

He squinted into the wind. "What would you be saying to her *now?*"

"That if she wants me—if she *needs* me—do not hesitate to send word. Even to Homana! I promise I will come."

"I'll be caring for her here."

"*Liam*—"

"No, lad. She needs no more of you." He stared hard at me. Then his bearded face softened. "But I'll be telling her what you said."

I clung to the rail as the ship moved out into the channel. Wind-whipped swells crashed against the prow. But I hardly noticed. I watched the dark bulwark of the Aerie silhouetted against the sky and then I watched the Erinnish shore. Until all I could see was the green speck of Liam's cloak. And then I turned my face to Atvia.

And to my Cheysuli bride.

PART II

One

Rondule, like Shea's city of Kilore, was a fishing port. Except for minor differences in architecture, I saw no real distinction between Rondule and Kilore, or between Rondule and Homana's own Hondarth, for that matter. I had sailed hundreds of leagues westward, and yet I saw little that made this part of the world any different from my own.

Until I heard the language. In eight months with Shea and his folk, I had grown accustomed to the lyrical lilt of the Erinnish tongue, which was little different from Homanan except for nuances and a few words held over from the old days of Erinn. I did not doubt that I had acquired a trace of the accent myself, after so many months. But I knew I would never acquire the sound of Atvia, no matter *how* long I stayed on the island.

I thought it an ugly language, choked with consonants rather than vowels, and those spoken harshly. It was a sibilant tongue that put me in mind of a serpent hissing in the darkness. I did not much like the imagery. More than ever wished I could avoid Atvia altogether.

The boat docked. In Erinnish finery borrowed from Liam (though we were both big men, the clothing did not fit well; the gods had put us together differently) I disembarked into a maelstrom of activity. The tide was turning; time for the fisherfolk to return home with the day's catch. And I in the middle of it.

I heard the hissing chatter of the men as they hauled in the nets; the women as they hastened down to help their men. I smelled fish everywhere. It clogged my nose and insinuated itself in my mouth, my clothing, my hair. A fleeting thought told me it had been no different in Kilore, but I chose to see Rondule in a harsher light.

"My lord." A boy's voice, speaking accented Homanan.

The familiar words were almost throttled in his throat, but I could decipher them. Just.

He was half my height, clothed in a bright blue tunic. An intricate border in white yarn drew my eyes; it was very nearly Erinnish knotwork. But there was a difference. Just as there was in the boy's attitude toward me. He was not rude, not precisely, but neither was he as warm as the Erinnish.

"Aye," I said shortly. "Has Alaric sent you to fetch me?"

He did not smile. I judged him ten, twelve; his brown eyes were older. "If you are Niall of Homana."

"Oh, I think so. And you, boy?"

"Belen," he answered. He pointed at two horses tied nearby, waiting patiently. "Come."

I came. Belen led me through the twisting cobbled streets toward the center of the city. And when we had reached it, I found myself having to close my mouth because I did not wish the boy to see my awe.

Like Kilore, Alaric's fortress perched atop a rocky cliff. But his did not have the headlands and heaths stretching in all directions. Instead, the castle capped a palisade that jutted up from the center of the city. The promontory was cone-shaped but lacked a smooth, uniform roundness, displaying craggy flanks full of crevices and treacherous faults in the stone itself. I saw no road or path at all winding its way up to the castle on top of the world. And I began to understand why Shea had told me, again and again, that a frontal assault on Alaric's castle was the strategy of a madman—or a fool.

Being neither, he never tried. They fight their wars on the seas and beaches.

"Come." Belen set heels to his spotted horse.

There was a path after all. It followed the natural grain of the stone, rising, twisting, zigzagging through faults and square-cut protrusions. Here and there pockets of turf carpeted the terraced face, but most of it was rock. Hard, cold rock.

The wind beat at my face, threading tiny fingers through the weave of my borrowed garb. I shivered. Belen, ahead, did not seem to notice the chilly breath of the dragon. He rode steadily onward, always ascending, never looking back. I heard the familiar wailing song of the dragon as its exhalations curled around the rocks and buffeted me front and back. I thought of Deirdre. I thought of the chalky, wind-whipped heights of Erinn, so close I could nearly touch them. I had only to put out my hand and reach across the Dragon's Tail, and Deirdre would be mine.

"Dragon's Teeth." The boy had turned in his saddle. He jerked his head a little, indicating the rocky ramparts of the cliffs. "The castle is beyond."

Higher still, and then atop the promontory. The wind spat into my face.

"Castle," Belen said.

A boy of few words. But I paid no mind to him. I looked instead at Alaric's fortress.

Unassailable, aye; no man foolish enough to risk himself against certain death would ever try to take the castle. Perhaps Rondule, or other cities. But never the actual fortress. Like Homana-Mujhar, it was invulnerable.

But once, Homana-Mujhar had fallen.

Belen led me through a barbican gate warded by six massive portcullises and into the outer bailey beyond. Guards hedged the sentry-walks and battlements. Colored pennons snapped in the wind. I heard the echoes of iron on cobbles as we entered the inner bailey.

Boys came running for the horses. I dismounted, hissed a bit as the landing jarred my bruised thigh, nodded irritably as Belen motioned me to follow. One might think I was the prisoner here, instead of Gisella's betrothed.

The boy took me through candlelit corridors and into a private chamber. Here the stone floor was carpeted with rugs I recognized as Caledonese; we had similar in Homana-Mujhar, including my bedchamber. Lighted braziers warmed the room. There were no casements; I could not stare out and search for Erinn from the top of the dragon's head.

"Someone will come," the boy announced, and then he shut the door.

Alone, I looked around the room. Chairs, a table, a chest, a jug of wine, and silver goblets. Having nothing better to do, I poured myself a cup.

Not wine. It was a clear, pungent liquor. I lifted the goblet, recognized the powerful contents and set it down again. *"Usca,"* I said in surprise.

"Trade routes," a voice commented equably. "All the way from the Steppes to Atvia." As I turned the man smiled and shut the door. "*I* am not Ihlini, Niall; did you think I conjured it?"

Alaric. I knew him at once, though I had never seen him. Once, my mother had described him to me, telling me how he had come to Homana seeking the Mujhar's sister as a wife. Then, she said, he had been tall, slender, brown-haired, brown-eyed. Handsome, she had added, if you liked men with silken manners and silver tongues. Bronwyn had not, but she had wed him anyway. My father had given her no choice.

Nineteen years had passed since then. I thought he was a year or two older than my father. He looked younger than his years, though time and wars had roughened the too-smooth edges. He had not thickened, maintaining a tensile slenderness, and he moved with an awareness of a subtle but acknowledged strength. In body as well as spirit.

In understated black, he put me in mind of Strahan. He reminded me of Lillith.

He smiled. His Homanan was quite good. His accent was very slight. "You are well come to Atvia. Although—for a moment—I thought it was a dead man standing before me."

"Carillon." I forced a smile, as always. "No."

Alaric moved to the table and poured *usca* for us both. Out of courtesy I accepted the goblet; I have no taste for *usca*. "I met Carillon once," he said reminiscently. "I was but a boy, no older than Belen, but I knew enough to be impressed. It was not long after Tynstar had stolen twenty years of his life. Already the disease ate away at his bones." Still smiling, he drank. I did not.

"My lord—" I began.

"I never saw him again." Clearly, Alaric was not finished. Until he was, he had no intention of allowing me to speak. "When my brother slew him, I was here. Beating back Erinnish wolfhounds from my shores." Alaric continued to smile.

I set down my goblet with a thud. *Usca* slopped over the rim. "It was for *you* to end my captivity."

If my curtness surprised him, Alaric did not show it. Politely he set down his own cup—he would not drink if I did not—and motioned calmly for me to be seated. I considered refusing. But my stiffening thigh ached and my head still rang from Liam's blow. I sat down.

"It was for me to end your captivity." Alaric sat down and crossed his legs. His boots, I saw, bore massive spurs of rune-worked gold. "And did you curse me for not doing it while you bedded Deirdre of Erinn?"

The breath ran out of my chest. There were no words in my mouth; no aborted explanation. Not before *this* man; he was Gisella's father.

Alaric rubbed idly at his clean-shaven chin. His manner was calm, too calm; he put me in mind of a cat waiting for the mouse to jump. "Well?"

"You ally yourself with Strahan and the Ihlini. Against my father."

A corner of his mouth twitched in amusement. He knew very well why I altered the subject. "What I do is my own concern." He shifted minutely in the chair. The golden spurs glinted. Oddly, they reminded me of *lir*-bands. "I have no intention of filling your head with Atvian history, Niall. Suffice it to say it was never my wish to give my fealty to Donal." He shrugged a little, dismissing it. "We are uneasy bedmates at best. He takes—I give. And I am weary of it."

I stood up "My lord, if you have no intention of honoring the alliance, I have no intention of listening to you."

"Sit down," he told me coolly. "If I have ruffled your feathers, accept my apology. But I am being frank with you, Niall. You are not a boy any longer."

No, I was not. The quick anger and affrontedness spilled away almost at once; I sat down. It would harm nothing to listen to the man.

"Think of what I would gain if the alliance were ended," he suggested.

"War," I answered promptly. "And my father has beaten you once."

Brown eyes narrowed a little. He studied me a moment. And then he smiled. "War. But even Homana grows weaker when the wars drag on for decades." Politeness forgone, he reached out and took up his goblet, swallowing *usca* again. "You *are* here," he said. "A trifle tardy, perhaps, but that is no fault of yours. I see no reason for invalidating the proxy wedding. Gisella would be—disturbed.''

He spoke so calmly of his daughter and the wedding when he knew about Deirdre and me. I wondered uneasily how he had gotten his information. If he had a loyal Atvian servant somewhere in Kilore—or, for that matter, a *dis*loyal Erinnish one—Shea and everyone else could be in danger.

"My lord, if you truly wish to let this marriage go forth, why did you not give in to Shea's demands?"

"Because I give in to no one."

It was my turn to smile. "But you gave in to my father. I know all about it. You knelt on the floor and kissed his sword and swore fealty to him."

"And in return I got his sister for my wife. Gisella for a daughter." He raised dark brows. "Who gained, who lost? Surely *I* benefited more than Donal did."

Surely he had. And he knew I knew it. "Is a title so important? Worth so many wars?"

"This one is." A signet ring glinted on Alaric's hand: silver set with jet. "It has belonged to the Atvian lord since before I was born. My grandsire, Keough, won it from Ryan of Erinn. Shea did not contest it until his heir was born."

"Your sister was wed to Shea. Does it mean nothing to you?"

He uncrossed his legs and leaned forward, elbows on his knees. "Boy, you must learn the practicalities of alliances and wars. When one is broken, the other invariably follows." A warning, perhaps? He rose. "For more than two hundred years Erinn and Atvia have been at war. Intermittently, of course—we cannot *always* fight. But it is as much a part of the Atvian and Erinnish way of life as shapechanging is of yours." He movement was arrested. "Ah, but of course—you cannot. I had heard you lack a *lir*."

I thrust myself out of the chair. Impotent rage welled up as Alaric continued smiling.

Gods, if only I could close that mouth forever—

"Niall," he said gently. "Did you expect us to be friends?"

With effort, I said, "I expected us to be civil."

He put his emptied goblet on the table. "This *is* civil, boy. I am not Shea of Erinn."

"Shea of Erinn possesses more integrity, honor, and manners than you could ever *hope* for!"

"No doubt," he said easily. "Nonetheless, he is a fool." He looked past my shoulder and smiled, gesturing a welcome. "Niall, there is someone who wishes to see you."

Gisella. I turned, trying to arrange my face into a mask of civility—Gisella was due it even if her father was not—and saw Lillith instead of Gisella.

Again, she wore crimson. She was cloaked in the weight of her hair. "I offered you a choice," she said calmly. "You refused to accept my help. But I see you had other alternatives."

No more would I look away from the woman. I stared intently back at her. "The gods look after their own."

After an arrested moment, Lillith began to smile. "The months have done you good," she said obscurely. And then she laughed.

I watched as she went to Alaric and kissed him intimately, ignoring my presence entirely. He locked one hand in the curtain of her hair. The other pressed her against his loins. Because they wanted to make me uncomfortable, I did not look away.

Lillith broke from Alaric and turned to me. Her black eyes seemed blacker yet. "I have come to escort you to proper chambers. Tonight we honor you with a feast; you will need to rest until then."

Her hand was on my arm. She waited. But before I went, I looked over my shoulder at Alaric.

The Lord of Atvia was smiling.

My assigned chambers, as I shut the door in Lillith's lovely face, were deeply shadowed. Again, there were no casements to let in the sunlight. Only candles, and most were not lighted. Though it was only afternoon, the room was gloomy. I wanted nothing to do with it.

Lillith had remarked on my lack of clothing, saying those lost in the shipwreck would be replaced with others. Now, made aware I had nothing of my own save the ruby signet ring and my silver-plated belt, I found myself longing for Cheysuli leathers.

"Niall." A shape moved out of the shadows of the room.

I spun, reaching for the knife I still did not have, and then I stopped moving altogether.

The face was thin, too thin, so *gaunt*, fined down to flesh stretched nearly to splitting over the prominent bones of the skull. I saw hollowed pockets beneath high, angular cheekbones; circles like bruises beneath eyes, the yellow eyes, filled with a dozen haunted memories of what it was like to lose a brother. What it was like to lose a soul. He was a stranger to me, my brother, and yet I knew him so very well.

"Ian!" And almost instantly: *Oh, gods, what have they done to my brother?*

He was thin. His clothes were of Atvian cut; no Cheysuli leathers here. When Ian had worn nothing else. His thick hair was dull, though clean, and had been cut much shorter than normal. It did not quite cover his ears; I saw the nakedness of his left lobe and realized what he had done. Or what they had made him do.

What have they made of my brother?

"*Rujho?*" he asked tentatively, and I saw the apprehension in his eyes.

I took a single step toward him. "Gods! Ian, I thought you were dead! I thought you had drowned in the storm!" I stopped. I wanted to go to him, to embrace him even as Rowan and I had embraced; to give him welcome as I could give no other man. But I did not. Something in his manner held me back.

"Niall," he said. "Oh—gods—I thought she lied—I thought she told me *lies*—" He shut his eyes so I would not see the tears. "But you are *here*—"

"Here," I echoed numbly. *Oh,* rujho, *what have they done to you? "*Ian. . . ." At last I stretched out a hand to touch his shoulder. But as I touched him he moved rigidly away. Like a hound afraid of his master.

"She said you were coming," he told me. "She *said* so, but I did not believe her. She tells me so many things." His heavy swallow was visible, even in the shadows. "When there is one truth in twenty lies, I cannot always choose which one to believe in."

"Ian, what is *wrong?* What is wrong with you?"

He flinched. Visibly. As if the master had struck the hound. "I know, now. I know what it is, now. The pain.

The emptiness. The void within a heart." He drew in an unsteady breath. "I have seen how it is, how it has been with *you* all these years—"

"Ian."

"—and now I know myself—"

"Ian."

"—what a *lir*less man goes through—"

"Ian!"

"—when his *lir* is taken from him." The sinews knotted even as his jaw muscles did. "I *know* what I must do. *But she will not let me do it!"*

I did not hold back. I crossed to him in a single stride and took him into my arms. And I thought how odd it was that I, the younger, the *lir*less Prince of Homana, now comforted a *lir*less warrior of the clan who had always comforted me.

With words and without.

Beneath the woolen Atvian doublet and linen shirt, I felt the nakedness of his arms. In shock I drew back. "Where is your *lir*-gold?"

"Gone. I put it off." He pulled away, turning away; turning his back on me.

As if he cannot face me. "Ian—"

"A *lir*less warrior has no right to wear the gold." and then he turned. *"You* should know that, Niall."

Niall. No more *rujho.* Had Tasha's loss also made him forget other bonds?

Or is it what they have done to him?

I wanted to shout at him. I did not. I drew in a steadying breath and told him, very quietly, "You have more right to wear the *lir*-gold than any warrior I know."

Ian laughed. There was no humor in it. Only the vast emptiness of a man who has lost himself. "It is what a warrior does," he told me bitterly, "this putting off of the gold. A true warrior. One who conducts himself according the Cheysuli tradition—"

"—and seeks the death-ritual?" I finished. "In Homana I would never question it. But we are in Atvia, and—"

Interrupting rudely, another sign he was not himself, Ian spat out an oath in the Old Tongue. "Do you think *that* matters?—what kingdom I am in? Oh, Niall, our customs are not determined by *where* we are but by *who*. I am Cheysuli. My *lir* is lost. There is only one thing left to do."

"Then why are you here?" I wanted to shout it, knowing the question was the only way to trick an explanation from a man who so patently did not want to give me one. "If you are willing to stand before me and prate about Cheysuli tradition and *lir*lessness, then why not complete the ritual? Live up to your heritage, shapechanger. Go out and seek your death."

He twitched. Suddenly he was not Ian before me, not my brother; not the boy to whom I had looked for guidance nor the man to whom I had looked for companionship and protection in the court of the Lion Throne. Somehow, he was—*diminished*.

"Oh *rujho*," I said in despair, "what have they done to you?"

"Not they," said a female voice distinctly. "What *she* has done to him."

This time it *was* Gisella. I had only to look at her as she shouldered shut the door. "You do not deny it, then?"

She did not answer. She came forward into the wash of candlelight and I saw her eyes: yellow as my brother's. No, Alaric had not stamped Gisella as Shea had stamped Liam and Deirdre. Nor as Carillon, through his daughter, had come back to live in me. In flesh and bone and spirit, Gisella was more Cheysuli than I.

Ian said nothing. Nor did I; I could think of nothing succinct that would express what I was feeling.

She wore a gown the color of blood. Not the bright crimson red of Lillith's velvet skirts, but the color of day-old blood. Dull, a man might say; ugly, a woman would, but on Gisella the color was right.

She smiled. Ignoring Ian, Gisella smiled at me. "I was not to let you see me before tonight's feast. But I could not wait." Her black hair was worn Cheysuli-fashion: braided, looped, twisted, fastened in place with golden combs that glittered with ice-white diamonds. She had a widow's peak. It gave her a look of elegance, of maturity, and yet I knew she lacked both. She was oddly childish. Or was it child*like?* "My father wanted you to be pleased with me. *Are* you pleased with me?"

It is as if Ian is not even in the room. "I think I might

be more pleased if I knew what Lillith has done to my brother."

Gisella shrugged. The gown was cut wide of her shoulders, displaying smooth dark skin, elegant neck, a rope of gold and diamonds. "Only what she has done before. Though they were not Cheysuli." She looked at Ian and smiled. Her eyes lit up and she laughed. "Because she *wanted* to do it. Because he hated her. Because he lacked a *lir*."

"I lack a *lir*."

Her lips parted in surprise. "Lillith would never ensorcell *you!*"

I turned to Ian. "We will discover what she has done, *rujho*, I promise. And then we will—"

"—do *what?*" Gisella came closer, skirts swinging. "He is *lir*less, Niall. Without a *lir* he will go mad. But Lillith will keep him from it. She said so . . . she said she *wants* him."

I stared. Her tone was utterly unconcerned, as if it mattered not one whit to her that the witch had ensorcelled my brother. "Gisella—"

She spun and spun in place, holding out blood-colored skirts. "Did Lillith not make me pretty?"

"Gisella!" I cried. "By the gods, girl, are you blind? The woman is Ihlini!"

She stopped spinning. The skirts settled. The diamonds stopped blinding me with their brilliant glitter. "The woman is my mother."

"Your *mother!*" Aghast, I gaped openly. "Has she driven the sense from your head? Lillith is not your mother. Your mother was Bronwyn, sister to Donal of Homana. My aunt—*su'fala* in the Old Tongue. You are my kinswoman, Gisella . . . my cousin. No matter what she has told you, Lillith is *not* your mother."

Gisella frowned. Lifted a hand. Her nails, like Lillith's, were silver-tipped. And they ripped a hole in the air to replace it with living flame.

Cold, *cold* flame . . . and a lurid Ihlini purple.

Two

Gods!

She ripped the air apart but a handspan from my face. I lurched back awkwardly, trying to escape the flame. Off-balance, I fetched up against a chair, overset it, went over myself, rolling, trying to get up before she could loose another blast of icy, encompassing flame.

"Gisella—*no!*" I heard my brother shout.

"But I *want* to," she said simply, and I wrenched sideways, thrusting up an arm to shield my blinded eyes.

Flame licked out, caressed shrinking flesh, charred wool and linen . . . singed the reddish hairs upon my forearm. Backward I scrabbled, gulping air; came up against the stone wall and was stopped. "Gisella," I gasped, *"no!"*

Sparks hissed form silvered fingertips, winking out even as they fell. A crackling aureole of livid lavender gloved her slender fingers. *"Godfire,"* she said, "do you see?"

Ian took a step toward her. Stopped. I did not blame him. No man, facing a girl as irrational as Gisella, would want to go closer to her.

What has Lillith done to her? What has that witch done to both of them?

"Ian," I began, "wait—"

He thrust out a silencing hand.

Gisella's eyes were fixed on me in an opaque, unwavering stare. Diamonds glittered. "Lillith said you would be *mine*."

Gods . . . do they expect me to wed this girl? Do they really expect me to bed her?

Ian's hand motioned for me to stay precisely where I was. Decisively; he was Ian again. And for the first time since Gisella's attack, I looked at my brother instead of my cousin.

He stood rigidly before her, in three-quarter profile to

me. He was intent only on Gisella, marking her posture, her position in relation to me, to the rest of the room, to him. Like me, he was unarmed, but I knew, looking at him, even lacking knife or bow he was as lethal as he was with them.

An odd juxtaposition. They were very like one another, Ian and Gisella, reflecting kinship as well as racial heritage. Again, it was *I* who was so different. *Lir*less I was even as Ian was, but still so very different.

Slowly, Ian stretched out a hand to Gisella. Their fingertips nearly touched. Gisella gazed at him fixedly, as if she sought to judge his intentions. Still the *godfire* clung to her hand.

And then his, as he touched his fingers to hers.

Ian?

"No," he told her gently. "Loose no magic at him, or you will surely anger the gods."

"Gods?" she whispered. *"Gods?"* Like a striking viper, her other hand shot out and clawed at his face. In its wake I saw the afterglow of flame slicing the air apart as easily as steel.

Ian caught her striking hand. The other he claimed as well. By the wrists he held her, nearly suspending her. She cried out angry curses I did not know, fearing them Atvian or, worse, Ihlini invective. Such curses could summon demons.

From rigid fingertips ran blood, raisin black. Or fire; I could not say. It ran down fingers to wrists and spilled onto Ian's hands. Gisella laughed even as he cursed.

I scrambled up, thrusting myself from the floor. Against both of us, surely, she could not persevere; I moved toward them both, intending to aid Ian however I could.

Gisella saw me. Her eyes, swollen black in the muted candlelight, shrank suddenly down to pinpricks. Yellow, so *yellow*, filled with the ferocity of a beast.

And so she was. Even as Ian cried out against it, I saw the precursor to the shapechange. A ripple. A blurring. The sense of a shattered equilibrium. And then the void, so all-encompassing, as it swallowed the woman whole and spat out the mountain cat.

She struck out, clawing, ripping the air where Ian had been only a moment before. She was black, black as pitch, with tufted ears pinned against wedge-shaped head. Yellow eyes glared at us with a feral intensity.

I have seen housecats, enraged, huddle back as if in fear. And I have seen the subtle sideways twisting of their heads; heard the eerie wailing of their song; sensed the awesome magnificence of their rage. In Gisella, that rage was manifested as clearly as was her madness.

She struck out twice more, slashing with curving claws. Had Ian not been quicker, she would have shredded wool and flesh. She did not try for me. Ian was her target.

He moved as only a Cheysuli can move, with a grace and fluency of motion echoing that of the cat herself. I wondered if it was born in the blood or came with the *lir*-bond. I thought the latter. I had none of my brother's grace. But then, *he* had none of my size.

She screamed. It lifted the hairs on the back of my neck. It was the cry of a hunting mountain cat who has decided on her prey.

I can slay her, I thought dazedly, leaping behind the overturned chair even as Ian lunged back against the wall. *I can slay her and* end *this madness.*

But to do that would end the prophecy before its final fulfillment.

One man of all blood shall unite, in peace, four warring realms and two magic races.

But how does a man get children on a woman such as Gisella?

"*Gisella!*" shouted Alaric from the doorway.

Almost instantly, she was back in human form. She twisted hands in heavy skirts, backing away even as her father advanced. "No," she said, "no. Please? No." The yellow eyes, once so filled with a virulent anger, now reflected the fear of a disobedient child discovered. "It is so hard *not* to—"

Alaric caught slender shoulders in slender hands. Gisella's hands splayed across her cheeks as she tried to look away from his angry face. "Again," he said curtly, "again. Will you never learn, Gisella? There are *reasons* for what I forbid."

"I will learn," she promised, "I will. But—sometimes I *have* to do it!"

"Even against your father's wishes?"

She threw back her head and laughed. *Laughed.* And then she wrenched out of his hands and faced him as defiantly as she had faced us. "You are only angry because *you* cannot shapechange! Oh, no. Not *you!* Not even *Lillith* can." Throwing out her arms, Gisella let her head fall back against her spine. She spun in place. How she spun, my poor, mad cousin. "I can," she sang, "I can . . . and nobody else can do it!" Spinning, spinning, she crossed the floor. Gold and diamonds spun with her, all aglow in the candlelight. And then she stopped short, so short; so close to Ian her skirts tangled on his boot tops. "Not even *you* can," she told him cruelly. "Not since Lillith took your *lir*."

I looked at the Lord of Atvia. "She is mad," I told him. "Quite mad."

He smiled calmly. "But you will wed her anyway."

"Wed me!" his daughter cried. "Niall is to *wed* me!" She left Ian behind and came at once to me, locking hands into the fabric of my doublet. "They have told me I must wed you and be Queen of Homana. Will you make me Queen of Homana?"

Gods. One day I *would*.

"Gisella." Gently, I tried to unlock her fingers. "Gisella, I think there is something I must discuss with your father."

"Why?" she cried. "He will only say *you* should not shapechange, either. He is always telling me that." She jerked her hands from my grasp, locked arms around my neck. "Niall," she said, "when will we be wed?"

"As soon as he takes you to Homana," Alaric told her smoothly. "Once all the celebrations here are finished."

I peeled Gisella away and set her aside, confronting Alaric squarely. "There will be none," I said briefly. "By the gods, you fool, why were we never told? Why was this travesty allowed to continue? Do you think I wish to wed *that?*"

"Does it matter?" he asked. "You will. Because your prophecy demands it." Even as I started to speak he silenced me with a gesture. "Turn your back on my daughter, *child of the prophecy*, and you twist that prophecy. Perhaps even end it precipitately." He smiled. "In addition, your father will discover me on his doorstep. Armed. With at least five thousand men-at-arms. Is that what you wish to see?"

"Twenty-five hundred," I countered bitterly. "Liam has promised me *that* much."

Alaric's brows rose. "The truce already broken? Ah well, I have other plans. I doubt Liam would be so willing to levy war against Atvia when all of his kin are slain . . . including his wanton sister." He smiled. "I thought that might get your attention."

"You *do* have an informant in Kilore—"

"Informants," he corrected. "Assassins, more like. A word from me—or a beacon fire on the cliff—and the royal Erinnish eagles are dashed to the rocks below." Alaric smiled. "I might even have it done tonight."

Gods— I bared my teeth. "Why not?" I asked. "What good do they do you alive?"

"I have been advised it might be best to play this game carefully." Alaric shrugged. "I am not so proud that I cannot accept assistance from someone more—patient—than myself."

"Lillith?" I demanded. "Aye, patient! And what *else* is she, my lord?"

"My mother," Gisella said promptly. Almost instantly a hand flew to cover her mouth; she looked at her father fearfully. "But that is not *really* true . . . is it? *You* told me—"

"I told you the truth," Alaric answered evenly. "Bronwyn bore you, Lillith raised you." He smiled. "How else could you combine Ihlini illusion with the Cheysuli shapechange?"

"Illusion," I said, startled. "None of it was real?"

Gisella thrust out a hand. Fingers snapped open. Even Alaric squinted in the glare of the blinding flame. "Real," she said flatly. *"Real!"*

"Real," he agreed patiently. "Of course it is, Gisella." He looked at my brother and smiled. "Lillith wants you, Ian. Had you not better go?"

Before my eyes I saw my brother diminished. He said nothing; indicated nothing by posture or movement, but he could not hide the revulsion in his eyes.

For himself. Not for Lillith.

"Rujho—" I began.

Ian did not even look at me. He walked past me and out of the room.

Alaric laughed. "Interesting, is it not? To see a Cheysuli humbled?"

"Not Ian." But even in my ears the declaration sounded hollow. "Do you intend to humble me?"

Alaric glanced at his daughter. "Gisella. The game."

She smiled delightedly. Eyes alight, she put out fisted hands. To me. "Choose."

"Not *too* quickly," Alaric cautioned. "Wait a moment." He moved behind her, resting hands on the bared flesh of her shoulders. Then he smiled at me, and I saw the game was on. "Should we humble you, Niall, as Lillith has humbled Ian? *Could* we? You are very different. Half-brothers, perhaps, but very different. Like two pearls from the same oyster: one black—" Gisella opened her right hand and displayed a pearl, a perfect pearl, blue-black in copper-toned flesh "—the other white. Do you see?" I saw. In the other palm was displayed the other pearl. White. Aglow against her hand.

"Very pretty." I granted it because I knew they would demand it.

Alaric moved around his daughter and took the pearls from her hands. Inspected them. "Aye," he agreed, "very pretty. But at their best only when given into a *woman's* keeping." His brown eyes were very steady as he looked at me. "Do you understand?"

"What does she want with him?" I ignored the implications in Alaric's game of pearls and men. "What does she *do* to him?"

Alaric, shrugging, smiled. "Some men keep hounds, some women cats. Lillith keeps men."

"You?" I thought it an odd arrangement: light woman to a king, yet collector of other men.

Alaric's eyes glinted. "She came to Atvia twenty years ago from Solinde. She had grown bored, she said, with her young half-brother's machinations; she wished to try her own. I saw her. I wanted her. And when I learned precisely what she was, I gave in gracefully." His smile grew. "She said she always wanted a tame Cheysuli."

"He will die," I said hoarsely, "or give himself ever to death."

"Because he lacks his *lir?*" Alaric laughed. "I do not

think so." He dropped the pearls to the floor. As they struck, they splashed. And I saw they were only tears.

"I must go," Alaric said brusquely. "There is a feast to oversee—in *your* honor, my lord Prince of Homana. Will we see you there?"

"Have I a choice?"

"Of course," he said politely. "You may come or not, as you wish." He looked at his daughter as he put his hand upon the door. "Gisella . . . you know what to do."

"I know what to do," she said brightly. "*I* know what to do!"

Alaric shut the door.

I stood very still in the center of the room. And then slowly, so slowly, hardly realizing what I did, I righted the overturned chair and sat down awkwardly, like a man with too little sleep. My eyes burned as I stared at Gisella.

Arms outstretched, she began to spin in place. "Did Lillith not make me *pretty?*"

I shut my eyes. *Oh gods—*

"Niall!"

Oh gods—

"*Ni*-allll!"

"Pretty," I mumbled. "Aye."

"But you are not *looking* at me!" Hands were suddenly on my face, peeling my eyelids back. "How can you see me when your eyes are closed?"

I caught her wrists and threw her hands away from me. I rose even as she protested. "Bronwyn's daughter, are you? By all the gods of Homana, girl, how could you turn out like this? Because of Lillith? Because of Alaric? Because you know no better?"

She tried to twist free of my grasp, but I held her too tightly. Still, I could not help thinking of how she had reacted to Ian's touch; how she had assumed the shape of a mountain cat as if to mock his loss of Tasha.

"Bronwyn's daughter," I said again. "You claim the Old Blood, do you? And take on any form at will?"

"When he *lets* me," she said, pouting. "He does not let me very often."

"Why not? Does Lillith then lose control?"

"Because of what happened to my mother. My *real* mother." She tried to twist free again. This time I let her go.

"What happened to your mother?" I was assailed by sudden suspicion as well as apprehension. "What happened to Bronwyn, Gisella?"

"She died." Bronwyn's daughter rubbed sore wrists and glared at me from beneath lowered brows. "She shapechanged, and she died."

"Shapechanged! Why? And *how* did she die?" Suspicion flared more brightly. "Was it Lillith?"

"No. My father." Gisella shrugged. "He did not mean it. He told me he did not mean it. Because he had no wish to slay *me.*"

"Gisella!" I caught her upper arms. *"Tell me how she died!"*

"He *shot* her!" she cried. "With an arrow! He thought she was a raven!"

"A *raven?*"

"In Atvia they mean death," she told me. "Ravens are death-omens." She shrugged. *"Everybody* shoots them."

So Bronwyn tried to flee her Atvian husband. "Gisella!" I tightened my hands. "What did he tell you happened?"

She twisted to and fro, protesting ineffectively even as she answered. "He said—he said he only meant to slay a raven. But it was *her* . . . it was her. . . ." She stopped moving. Her eyes were very clear. "He slew my mother, Niall. While she was carrying me."

"And she fell. . . ."

"I was born that day," Gisella told me, "before my mother died."

I looked into her eyes and saw no pain, no grief. Only a calm matter-of-factness; only the innocence of a child repeating what she has been told. What Alaric meant his daughter *never* to tell.

"Gisella," I said gently, "I am sorry."

Her smooth brow creased. "Do you think it hurt?" she asked. "The fall? I cannot remember any pain."

"No pain," I said, "not now." I let go of her arms. But Gisella moved in against me, like a child seeking comfort, so I enfolded her in my arms and gave the child the comfort she craved. "No pain ever again."

Her face was against my neck. "Sometimes I am afraid."

"I will take away the fear."

She murmured something against my throat. And then

she pulled away, laughing, and reached up to clasp my jaw in both her hands.

"Gisella—"

"She said you would be *mine*—"

—and I was falling, *falling*, even as I stood there; even as I tried to speak and could not; tried to reach out; tried to wrench away; tried to break free of the woman who held me trapped within her hands.

Something is in me, something in *me—something—*

—something indefinable—something reaching into my mind, my soul, my *self*—

—until there was nothing left—

—*nothing left*—

—of Niall at all.

"Niall," she whispered, "we have to go to *bed*."

Three

A torch was put into my hand. "Light the beacon-fire, Niall. We must warn ships of the dragon's presence."

The dragon. Aye, the dragon, with his cold breath and endless appetite, swallowing helpless ships.

"Light the fire, Niall."

The wind gusted. The torch flared, roared; streamers of flame were snatched from the pitch-soaked rag and shredded in the air, the *cold* air; the breath of Alaric's dragon.

Or was it Lillith's dragon?

"Light the fire, Niall."

I stretched out my arm toward the cone-shaped stand of faggots. Flame snapped, whipped; *yellow* flame, pure, clean *yellow*, with not the faintest trace of purple.

The flames drew my eyes. Transfixed, I stared. I could not look away.

"—*or a beacon fire on the cliff*—" Alaric had said. But I could not remember why.

We stood on the dome of the dragon's skull, wrapped in the dragon's breath. Visible yet intangible, it rose to cloak us like a mantle, all five of us: Ian, Gisella, Lillith, Alaric, and myself. At sundown, as daylight spilled out of the sky to be replaced by moonlight. Even now the platinum plate was visible scudding above the ragged chalky headlands of the island across the Tail.

Erinn. So close. So *far*.

Aerie of the Eagles.

"Light the fire, Niall," Alaric told me gently.

I twitched. Blinked. My eyes were filled with fire. I could see nothing but the fire.

Hands were on my right arm, tugging me toward the pyre. Slender, feminine hands, but almost masculine in their demand. "*Do* it," she said plaintively. "I want to see the fire."

And for her I would do anything.

I plunged the torch deep into the heart of the stack. Kindling snapped, caught, blazed up. I fell back, shielding my face against the flame.

"Fire," she whispered. "So pretty—"

Alaric removed the torch from my hand. He was smiling, but it was an odd, thoughtful smile, full of secret knowledge. He stepped to the edge of the promontory and was silhouetted against the rising moon; laughing, he threw the torch as far as he could into the darkness beyond.

I watched it fall, spinning, *spinning*, shedding light and smoke and flame.

"*That* for Shea of Erinn." His words were thick with a joyous satisfaction.

"And *Deirdre*," Gisella said sharply. "Deirdre, *too*."

Alaric turned. For a frozen moment he looked only at his daughter, seeing the fixed, feral stare of her yellow eyes, and then he stepped away from the edge to wrap her in his arms. He embraced her tightly, cradling her head against his shoulder. In the light of the blazing beacon-fire I saw the glint of tears in his eyes. "No more," he told her softly, rocking her in his arms. "No more Deirdre, my lovely girl; my beautiful, fragile sparrow. No more threat to your happiness. That I promise you."

"When will the baby come?" she asked. "When will my baby come?"

"Six months," he told her gently. "In six months you will hold your baby."

Her hands slipped down to touch her belly, splaying across heavy skirts. And then she broke away from her father and threw out her arms. Spinning, *spinning*, she tipped back her head and let the black hair spill out into the wind, whipping, *whipping*, as she whirled atop the dome of the dragon's skull.

"A baby!" she cried. "A baby of my own. . . ."

"Niall," Above the howl of the wind, I heard the other woman. "It is time for you to go home."

In the bright light of the roaring flames, I saw Lillith with my brother. She did not touch him; she did not have to. She had only to be near him, and he was lost.

Lost.

But in his grieving eyes I saw a reflection of myself.

The man came to me as I stood on the dock, prepared to board the ship. He looked familiar, but I did not know him at once. "My lord," he said, in a smooth, cultured baritone, "I am to sail with you. As envoy to your father's court, and as companion to the princess." When I said nothing, he smiled. "My name is Varien. Do you not remember me?"

And then, of course, I did. "I thought you drowned," I told him. "I thought you swallowed by the dragon."

"No, my lord." So polite, so sincere, so much in control of his emotions; I envied him. "The Lady Lillith saw to it I survived."

"She is generous," I said simply. "She kept my brother from drowning, as well."

"And you?"

"No." I shook my head. "No. I washed ashore . . . I think it was near Rondule. That is where they found me."

"Of course, my lord. I recall." He gestured gracefully toward the ramp. "Shall you board? Everything is prepared. Even your brother waits."

"Ian?" I looked at Varien sharply. "I thought Lillith was keeping him."

"No, my lord. She has what she wants from your brother. Ian goes home with you."

Alaric stood on the dock and hugged his grieving daughter. "Do not cry," he told her. "Do not fret, Gisella. You go to become a queen."

"But I want to stay here with you!"

"I know. But now your place is with your husband, not your father."

"But I will miss you so!"

"No more than I will miss you."

She clung to him a moment longer as if she would never let him go, then abruptly pulled back to look up at him expectantly. "Will he give me other babies?"

Alaric smiled and stroked her windblown raven hair. "He will give you all you want."

She reached up to kiss him. And then she boarded the ship.

* * *

"A gift," Lillith told me, *"to see you safely home."* And she put something in my hands.

I looked. A tooth. A smooth white tooth, thick at one end, narrow and curved at the other. A dog's tooth, or a wolf's. It was set into a cap and hook of gold, which depended from a thong.

"Wear it," she said, smiling. *"Wear it and think of me."*

I put the thong around my neck.

The sea is an endless place, a place in the world where time nearly stops and all a man knows is patience. I had found what little I had of it, rationed it well, and managed to keep myself whole. But for Ian, I could not say the same.

He stood at the rail near the prow of the ship, staring eastward, ever eastward, toward Homana. In two months I had watched him dwindle to a shadow, hardly a man at all. Physically he was present, but elsewhere he was not.

Homana, for me, is home. For Ian it is his death.

Waves slapped the sides of the ship. Timbers creaked. Canvas billowed, cracked taut. I heard the song of a ship under sail.

Midsummer, nearly. But it would be another month before we were home. I thought we would miss the Summer-fair in Mujhara. It would be the first time since I could remember. The first time for either of us.

Us.

Slowly I crossed the deck. Though I knew he heard me, he did not turn. He stood at the rail and clutched it, dark hands locked around the wood. Two months since we had set sail. His hair had grown to cover his ears; to cover the mark of his shame. To hide the naked ear. Even now, free of Lillith, he left off Cheysuli leathers and wore Atvian garb instead, much as I did: low boots, snug trews and a full-sleeved linen shirt, billowing in the salt-breeze.

I settled a hand on his shoulder. "Ian—"

"No."

"Rujho—"

"No."

"At *least* do me the courtesy of allowing me to share your company while you yet live," I snapped. "Gods, *rujho,* you will be gone from me soon enough. Why do you already leave?"

He turned so sharply I fell back a step. "*I* did not leave—it was *you!*" He clamped a hand around my arm. His eyes were filled with despair. "Gods, Niall—do you even *know* what you have done? What they have done to you? Or should I say: what *she* has done to you, since it takes a Cheysuli to do what the girl has done."

"It was to *you.*" I was precise in my amazement. "It was Lillith—"

"*Aye,*" he said harshly. "Lillith. And who was it for you?"

"I," she said. "It was I."

I turned. "Gisella!"

"It was," she said. "Lillith told me I could do it. She said I *should.* Otherwise you would never lie down with me." Hands cupped belly protectively. "And then there would be no baby."

Already the child showed. Gisella was slender, *too* slender; she did not carry the baby well. Though only five months along, she was huge. Ungainly. Wearied of the weight. The summer warmth was crueler to her than to others; though she wore a thin linen gown with sleeves cut off, I saw the dampness of perspiration soiling the fabric. A fine sheen filmed face and arms, already burned darker by the sun. She had tied her heavy hair back, but strands of it crept loose to straggle down the sides of her face.

She looked at Ian. "I am Cheysuli. I know a few Cheysuli customs—those they have let me learn." Much of her intensity had vanished, replaced with a weary vacancy. She seemed to have tired of what they had told her she must say and do. "Without a *lir*, you die."

"There is a ritual involved," he said; roundabout agreement.

"But you *die.*" Yellow eyes met yellow eyes. "I think Niall would not like that. I think I will give you your *lir.*"

Ian laughed. I could not.

Quick tears filled Gisella's eyes. "Do you think I *lie?* Do you think I would lie to you?"

He opened his mouth to answer at once. I knew what he would tell her. *Aye, Gisella, you lie. I think you would lie to me.* But he shut his mouth and said nothing, because we both knew she could not help it. She was incapable of knowing the difference.

The tears spilled over. A low moan issued from a trembling mouth, and then she spun and ran away. Thinking of the baby, I started to follow; Ian jerked me back.

"Let her go. Like a child, she means to cry. And then she will fall asleep, and the world will be right when she wakes."

I wrenched free of his hand. "How can you be so cold? There was a time you might have been the one to offer comfort."

"To Gisella?" he asked. "No. She has a *taint* about her. The smell of an Ihlini."

"Tricks," I said. "Lillith only taught her tricks. She has no Ihlini powers."

"Tricks," Ian mocked. "Aye. The sort of tricks Tynstar taught Electra." He looked at me intently and shook his head. "But what does it matter if she knows a few Ihlini tricks? She has done enough damage to you with the gifts the gods gave *us*."

And then Gisella was back, still crying. In her hands was the glint of gold. "Do I lie?" she asked. *"Do I lie?"*

She threw down the gold. It rang and thudded against the decking: a cat-shaped earring and two massive spurs. Alaric's rune-worked spurs.

Ian did not move. *I* did; I knelt. Picked up the earring and then the heavy spurs with their leather straps dyed black. Looked up at Gisella in amazement.

She rubbed the back of her hand across a sweat-sheened brow. "He melted them," she explained. "The bracelets. He wanted them for himself."

"Not bracelets," I said numbly. "*Lir*-bands. The mark of a boy become man." *Gods, what I would give for gold of my own—* I rose, turning to Ian. In shaking hands I held them out. *"Rujho—?"*

He did not move. "That is gold. That is not my *lir*."

"I could not carry *her*," Gisella said tearfully. "Not while I carry the child."

Ian's head snapped up. *"Her?"*

She scrubbed tears from sunburned cheeks. "Below," she said. "Below."

I hooked the straps over my wrist and grabbed her arm before Ian could. "Where?" I asked. *"Show us where."*

Gisella showed us. She took us below to the hold where the cargo was carried, where we had no cause to go. To the back, near the bilges.

"Wait," she said sharply, pushing through the chests and other gear. At last she bent over a canvas-shrouded crate. She plucked something from the crate and turned, hiding it behind her back. "You may come now."

Spurs clinking, I caught Gisella and dragged her hand into the open. "Gisella, let me see."

She resisted. Gave in. Opened her hand as I told her to. In the palm was the withered foot of a predator bird, curved talons spread as if to strike.

Gisella shrugged, twisting shoulders defensively. "She told me it was from a *lir*. A hawk, she said. She said she needed it for the spell." She glanced sidelong at Ian. "So you would not know the cat was in Rondule."

"Rondule!" I cried. "All this time Tasha has been in Rondule?"

"Lillith wanted to keep her. So she could keep *him*." Again, she looked at Ian. "But then—she said she did not care to keep him any more; that he had given her what she wanted. She said now it would be sweeter to know he gave himself over to death while his *lir* was so close at hand."

I looked at the thing in her hand. But even as she spoke, the withered foot and curving talons fell away into grayish dust.

Gisella sucked in her breath. "No more spell!" she cried in despair. And then, singing softly, "All gone away. . . ." She turned her hand palm down and poured out the grayish dust. "All—gone—away. . . ."

Ian tore open the crate as I stared at the girl who was my wife. My poor, fragile-witted wife.

Whispering, *"All—gone—away. . . ."*

"Gisella—"

"Gods, it is *Tasha*. It *is!*" Ian was almost incoherent. *"Rujho,* help me—"

He had not asked it for so long. I turned from Gisella to Ian and helped him lift the slack body from the bottom of the crate. We dragged Tasha free of the crate entirely and settled her on the flooring. She was alive, but only just.

Still, her eyes knew us both. One paw reached out weakly and patted Ian's foot.

He sat down awkwardly, as if he could no longer stand, and pulled what he could of the cat into his lap. I could tell by the look in his eyes that he spoke with her in the link. Once more, I was shut out. But this time I did not care.

"Whole," he whispered. *"No more a lirless man—"*

This time—this time only—it did not seem to matter to me that I still was.

When he had assured himself, or been assured by Tasha, that the mountain cat would survive, Ian looked up at Gisella. In his eyes I saw the tears. *"Leijhana tu'sai,"* he said unevenly. *"Leijhana tu'sai,* Gisella."

I rose. I caught her shoulders in my hands. "Those words are Cheysuli thanks," I told her, when I could. "You have made him whole again."

"But not *you*," she said obscurely.

And then she sat down and drew pictures in the dust of a murdered *lir*.

Four

She sang a song I did not know and hardly heard. It was not meant for me, but intended only for herself. And perhaps for the child.

"Gisella," I said gently, "there is nothing to harm you here. This is Homana-Mujhar."

She stood in a corner of the antechamber, hugging herself. Hugging herself, rocking herself, singing to herself. Softly, so very softly; she meant to disturb no one. She meant only to lock herself away from the fear of what must come.

I stroked the hair from her eyes. She had gone away from me to that very private place she had sought more and more the closer we came to Mujhara. I had lost her somewhere on the road from Hondarth. Physically she was with me, but otherwise she was not.

She sang. She hugged. She rocked.

I shut her up in my airs and tried to still the rocking. Her swollen belly pressed against me, intrusive and unyielding. She was bigger still than before, having two months less to wait for the birth of the child. Only two, now, before I would be a father.

"Niall? Are you here? I was told you would be here!" It was my mother hastening into the adjoining room; I felt Gisella stiffen in my arms.

"Wait," I called, perhaps a trifle curtly. No doubt it was the last word she had expected to hear form me. "Gisella," I said gently, "Gisella, I promise you. No one here will harm you."

She sang on, rocking herself within the circle of my arms. And so I left her to herself and went into the chamber to greet my mother.

I said nothing. What she felt was manifest in her face. I

crossed to her and let her put her arms around me, acutely conscious of how large I was in comparison to her. "Mother—"

"Say nothing." Her words were muffled; most of her face was pressed against my chest. "Just—let me *hold* you."

And so I let her hold me, even as I held her. It was odd to think of her as the woman who had borne me nineteen years ago, even as Gisella would bear *my* child. Somehow it was impossible to think of the Queen of Homana as ever being little more than a woman in travail, trying to give Homana an heir for the Lion Throne.

"Fourteen months," she whispered. "Oh Niall. I feared I would never see you again! Even after Alaric sent word that Shea of Erinn held you. Even after *Rowan* came home and said you fared quite well in Erinnish captivity." She pulled away and stared up into my face. "How much was the truth?"

"All of it," I told her. "Never once was I treated with anything less than my rank was due."

She sighed in relief. "Thank the gods!" She hugged me again, then stepped away. "There. Enough. I have no wish to embarrass you with tears or clinging ways." Laughing a little, she pressed one hand against her mouth. "You see? Already I cry again."

I smiled. "Embarrass *me?* No more than I might embarrass you. Gods, it is good to be home again!" And I pulled her back into my arms and hugged her one more time.

"Then the messenger had the right of it concerning your arrival," said my father as he came into the chamber. "His words were worth the gold I spent."

I released my mother and went at once to him, to clasp his arms Cheysuli-fashion and then pull him into an embrace. In all the years of my life I had wanted to do it, and yet somehow I never had. He had seemed closed to me, somehow; closed to demonstrations of affection.

"Leijhana tu'sai," he murmured fervently. "All those months I had to be strong for your *jehana* . . . yet there was no one to be strong for the *jehan.*"

I could not imagine my father needing anyone but himself. And yet, once I might have said the same about my brother. "You know about Ian?" I stepped back out of the embrace: "The messenger *did* tell you he is alive?"

"Aye," my mother said dryly. "Your father made him repeat it four times, just to be certain."

I searched for resentment and found none; she was genuinely relieved. But I was not certain how much was for my father's sake rather than my brother's.

"Where is he?" my father asked. "I expected him to be with you."

"Ian is—at Clankeep." I saw the minute twitch of surprise in his face. "He said he required—*cleansing* . . . and that you would understand."

"*I'toshaa-ni.*" My father turned away from me as if to hide his thoughts and feelings. But when he turned again I saw a residue of a fear I could not comprehend. "Is he all right?"

"Well enough," I answered. "Tasha is mostly recovered and so Ian is more himself, but—" I could not avoid the truth any longer, and so I would not "—he is not the warrior I knew before we left for Atvia."

"No. Not if he is in need of *i'toshaa-ni.*" Troubled, my father looked more grim than I could expect of a man who knew both of his sons were alive when he had believed them lost.

"What *is* it?" my mother asked. "I know so little of Cheysuli customs . . . but what could keep Ian away from his father when he has only just returned?"

"A ritual of cleansing," my father said, patently reluctant to speak of it at all. "It—is a private thing . . . when a warrior feels his spirit soiled by something he has done— or by what others have done *to* him—he seeks to cleanse himself through *i'toshaa-ni.*" He made a gesture of subtle finality and I knew the subject was closed.

It was obvious my mother knew it as well. She wanted to speak but did not, having learned his moods so well. I wondered if Gisella would ever know mine.

Or if any *man can know hers.*

"Niall," my mother said. "Niall, is this *Gisella*?"

I turned abruptly. It was. She stood in the doorway to the antechamber. The curtain was caught over one shoulder so that half of her was hidden. But not enough. It was obvious she was weary, too weary; overburdened by the child. I had thought to give her time to rest, bathe, change . . . but now that time was taken from us both.

I went to her at once. She was quiet, very quiet; no more singing, hugging, rocking. Under my hands she trembled. "Gisella, I promise you, there is no need to be afraid." I pushed the curtain off her shoulder and brought her into the room.

"By the *gods!*" My mother's tone was couched, all unintended, in the brutal honesty of shock. "The girl has already conceived!"

My father was less forceful than my mother, but his surprise was no less obvious. "Niall—"

"She is very weary," I told them quietly. "The sea voyage was hard on her, the journey from Hondarth harder. Once she has rested, you will see another Gisella."

"Niall," my mother said helplessly, "what am I to *say?*"

"Say she is well come," I told her. "Or—is she not?"

"Niall." There was no hesitation on my father's part, no careful search for diplomacy. "She is as well come as your *cheysula* ever could be . . . but what your *jehana* means to say is that the Homanans will claim the child is not your own."

"Does it matter what they claim?" Beneath my hands, Gisella trembled. "When have *you* ever cared?"

He did not smile, my father, being less than pleased with me. "On the day when I at last understood what my *tahlmorra* truly entailed, I was *made* to care. But you may not have that chance." He did not so much as look at Gisella, being too intent on me. "Even now there are growing numbers of Homanans who rally around a faceless, nameless bastard, known only as Carillon's son. Not his grandson, Niall—his *son*. And as those numbers grow, so does the threat to you. So does the threat to the Lion. And, by the gods!—*so does the threat to the prophecy of the Firstborn!*"

"Donal." My mother, as ever, seeking to turn his anger from her beloved son.

"No, Aislinn. He will have to know the truth." He moved closer to me, confronting me squarely, still ignoring Gisella. "On the day our kinsman has you slain in the name of *Homanan* rule, will you ask then if it matters what the Homanans claim?" His face, like his voice, was taut with suppressed emotion. And now he did look at Gisella. "Will you ask it when they have slain *her* as well, because she bears a child who might become a threat to them? Think of *that*, Niall, if not of yourself." He smiled, but there was no humor in it. "And now—ask me again."

"No." Chastened I was, but I did not look away. "No, there is no need. I spoke too hastily." I took a deep breath and started over again. "This is Gisella. And aye, she bears my child." I glanced briefly at my mother, still silent in her shock, then looked back at my father. "I do not doubt but that the wedding should be very soon. Not just because of the child, but because of Carillon's bastard." I shrugged. "How better to secure the Lion for *our* line instead of his?"

My mother turned away. The line of her spine was rigid; no doubt it troubled her deeply to know her father had sired a bastard. No doubt it troubled her more to know that bastard offered a very real threat to me.

"Niall." She turned, skirts swinging. "Niall—will you forgive him?"

Gods, how she needed me to say it; to say *aye, of course I forgive him.* As if it might absolve her of her guilt for believing in him so. So she could believe in him again.

"Carillon was not a god," I said clearly. "He was a man. A *man.* And so is his bastard son. *So is his daughter's son.*"

"Niall?" Gisella, breaking her silence. "Niall, is he the Mujhar?"

I laughed aloud, relieved to hear her voice after she had been so long silent. "More than that," I said. "He is your mother's brother. Your *su'fali,* in the Old Tongue."

Color came into her waxen face. Some of the weariness dropped away. "Donal of Homana! My father speaks of you."

My father's smile was wry. "Aye, no doubt he does. And does he speak of me with kindness?"

He did not expect her to answer honestly. He expected embarrassed prevarication. But then, he did not know Gisella.

"No," she said, with all the guilelessness of a child. "He says you are a leech upon the treasury of Atvia, and that one day he will squash you."

Before my mother could express her shock, my father laughed out loud. "Aye, well, I imagine he might well say so. In his position, I might say much the same. But then, it is a position *Alaric himself* brought about." No tact from him, not when she gave *him* none. "When you see him again, Gisella, you may tell him that for me."

"But I will never see him again," she told him seriously. "I must stay with Niall. Niall will be Mujhar. Niall will need me *here*."

"Surely he will allow you to visit your father." My mother hid much of her growing dislike, but I heard it plainly in her tone. "He will not keep you chained to Homana."

"But he will *need* me," Gisella insisted. "They said he would always need me."

I saw my mother begin to frown.

"Gisella," I said hastily, "this is my lady mother, Aislinn, the Queen of Homana."

But Gisella was uninterested in my mother. Her attention was on my father. "I forgot," she told him. "There is a thing I am to do." Giggling, she tried to curtsy deeply, offering him what awkward homage she could manage.

Immediately he stepped forward. "Gisella, there is no need for *that*—"

—and she was up, clawing *godfire* from the air with her left hand while her right hand clawed for his face.

No. Not *clawed*. Her hand was filled with a knife.

"Gisella—*no!*" I caught her from behind even as she lunged for my father. I clamped her arms against her body, hugging her with all my force, while she struggled impotently to twist free of me to strike at him again.

"Dead—dead—dead—" she chanted. *"Dead—dead—dead—"*

"Gisella—*no*—"

The air was choked with lilac smoke. The *godfire* was gone, but its aftereffects were not. My mother coughed, pressing an arm against nose and mouth. My father, having fallen back from Gisella's attack, now reached for the knife still clutched in her hand.

"Dead—dead—dead—"

"No," I told him, "let her be."

"Niall—"

"Let her be!" I shouted. "She is weary, so weary of the child. She is *not* herself—*not* Gisella—not Gisella at all." Still I held her, clamping her arms against her sides. "You do not understand her."

"I understand she has just tried to murder me," my father said angrily. "Am I not to question it?"

"*I* question it!" my mother cried. "By the gods, *I* will!"

"No," I told her flatly. "Let Gisella be. She will be better when she has rested.'

"Better!' My mother stood by my father now, buttressing his side as if she were a soldier. "You speak as if this were only a momentary aberration, Niall."

"She is *weary.*"

"She is *mad!*" my mother interrupted coldly. "Do you think you will marry *that?*"

"I have every intention of it."

"Mad?" my father asked. "Or is it something Lillith has done?"

Gisella stopped struggling. "Lillith," she said. "Lillith is my mother."

"No, no. . . ." Already I could see the shock forming in their faces. "No, *Lillith* is not your mother, Gisella. Bronwyn was your mother."

"She died," Gisella told them earnestly. "He shot her out of the sky."

My father recoiled as if she had struck out at him again, but this time the blade went home.

"Out of the sky," Gisella repeated. "And she fell . . . and she *fell* . . . and she crashed against the ground. . . ." She sighed. "After I was born, she died. She died of her broken body—"

"No more," I told her softly. "Gisella, say no more." Because I could not bear to see the look in my father's eyes.

"My father slew my mother," she said brightly, and sucked on a piece of hair.

"Gods," my father choked. "That *ku'reshtin* murdered Bronwyn, but it was *I* who sent her there."

"Donal, *no*, do not blame yourself!" My mother's hands were on his arm. "I beg you; do not do this to yourself—"

"*I* gave her in marriage to that man . . . *I* made her wed him when she wanted nothing of it!"

"Donal, you had no choice," she told him firmly. "You told me yourself—there was the prophecy to think of.

"*Prophecy.*" He said it like a curse. "Gods, Aislinn— when I think of the things I have done in the name of that thing . . . all the lives I have altered—"

"Donal."

"Even *yours*," he said. "Even yours."

There was the tone of bittersweet acknowledgment in her voice. "Aye," she said, "even mine. But do you hear me curse you for it?"

"No," he said at last, "though the gods know I deserve it."

"She died," Gisella said. "He shot her out of the sky."

"Hush." I pulled the hair out of her mouth. "Hush, Gisella . . . *please*."

My mother looked at Gisella. "You cannot marry *that*."

"He has to," my father said wearily. "The prophecy requires it."

"She just tried to *slay* you!"

"And once, *you* tried to do the same."

It was clear she had made herself forget that once she had been no less a tool for murder than Gisella. That once Tynstar, through Electra, had set a compulsion within her mind: to slay the man she was meant to wed. I knew the story. My father had told me once.

"Oh *gods*," she said brokenly, and tried to turn away.

But my father did not let her. *"Shansu,"* he said, "it is over. A long time over."

She turned back. She did not bother to wipe the tears away. They—and her anguish—remained. "And if Gisella tries again?"

"You did not," he told her.

"Because you had Finn go in and find the trap-link," she said impatiently. "Donal, have sense! Gisella has spent her life with an Ihlini witch as well as with a father who despises you. Do you think she will not try again?"

"Not if I defuse the trap-link . . . *if* there is a trap-link." He looked at me. "Niall, you know what I must do."

I shook my head. "You see how weary she is."

"All the better. There will be less resistance." He looked at Gisella, who still held the glittering knife. "I will risk neither my son nor myself to the chance she may be ruled by an Ihlini."

"My lord—"

"Prepare her, Niall. I have already summoned my *lir*."

* * *

I did my best to prepare Gisella, telling her what to expect though I hardly knew myself. All my life I had known Cheysuli magic existed, gifts from the gods themselves, but never had I seen my father use it past taking on the shape of wolf or falcon. Even Ian, who had as much power as any warrior, had shown me nothing other than the shape-change. Though father and brother also claimed the ability to heal, my childhood hurts had been allowed to heal naturally, without recourse to magic. Nothing had been serious enough to require it.

Now, I knew, there was. But I wanted no part of it.

I put Gisella to bed, covering the mound of her belly with a silken coverlet as she leaned back against the bolsters. She needed food, rest, sleep. She needed to be rid of the weight of the child.

"Two more months," I said aloud, splaying my hand across her belly. "Two more, Gisella, and you will be free of this burden."

Her own hand covered mine. "A baby, Niall. Something that will not drown as my puppies drowned, or break as my kitten broke."

Someone touched a cold fingertip against the base of my spine. But there was no one in the room. "Gisella—a baby is nothing like an animal. Nothing like a *pet*." I stroked black hair away from her weary face. "A baby is more important than anything in the world."

"More important than the Lion?"

Her tone was earnest. So was her expression. But there was opacity in her eyes, as if she hid from me the other side of her question.

I drew in a careful breath. "Gisella, if this baby is a boy, he will *become* the Lion."

She giggled. "How can a man become a lion? There *are* no lions, Niall. They have all gone out of the world. Not even *I* can become a lion!"

"He will be the Lion of Homana," I told her. "Mujhar." I put out my hand and let her see the ruby ring. "See the stone, Gisella? See the rampant lion?"

One finger touched the stone. I saw her pensive face as she traced the tiny etching in the flat ruby signet. "The Lion," she murmured. "The Lion of Homana. . . ." Abruptly she looked up at my face. "Are *you* the lion, Niall?"

I shook my head. "Not yet. Not for a long time to come."

She sighed. "But I want to be a queen."

A step sounded in the room. "Aislinn has no intention of relinquishing her title for a long time to come," my father told her bluntly. "Your pride will have to be satisfied by a lesser title."

"Father," I reproved, "she hardly knows what she says."

"Do you?"

"Do *I*? Of course!"

"*Do* you?" he asked again. "Is that why you almost never refer to me as *jehan?*" He was unsmiling. "Is the Cheysuli word so hard for you to say?"

It hurt. I felt the twist in the pit of my belly. "You have *Ian* to use the Old Tongue."

"And you for something else?" He shook his head as he moved to Gisella's bedside. Taj perched himself upon the casement sill as Lorn, lay down on the floor at the foot of the bed. "No, now is not the time; my *lir* remind me of it plainly. You are just home after more than a year away, and reprimands can wait. I apologize."

An apology from my father. I stared as he sat down across from me on the edge of Gisella's bed. I could not recall if he had ever offered me an apology before.

Or if I had ever deserved one.

Or if I deserved one *now*.

"I will not harm you," he told her gently. "I promise you that, Gisella. You are Cheysuli yourself; you know of all the gifts."

"*I* know." She was a petulant, impatient child, suddenly, claiming superior knowledge. "I know many things."

My father did not smile. "Aye. I imagine you do. How *much*, I will find out."

He did not touch her. He merely looked at her, even as I did. And then I looked at him.

His eyes matched hers in expression as well as color: pinpointed pupils, opacity, a look of total detachment. Though my father sat on the bed at Gisella's side, I knew he had gone *elsewhere*, seeking her. And I sensed Gisella's retreat.

Still I held her hand. I could feel the tension in it; the rigidity of flesh and tendons. She did not try to hold mine. I think she was unable. I think she was enmeshed in a battle of wills with my father, and had no time for me.

Suddenly, I was alone in the chamber. Gisella was in the

bed, my father on its edge, his *lir* present as well. And yet, I was alone. So *alone* . . . because I was a shadow-man, a shell of nothingness. *Lir*less, I lacked even the slightest hint of the power that was manifest in my father. Manifest in Gisella.

Is this irony? I asked the gods. *That certain* Homanans *desire to replace me because they believe I hide my magic, while certain* Cheysuli *desire the same because I have no magic at all?*

Irony, aye. Or my downfall.

Gisella's hand clenched itself within the palm of mine. I felt the fragile, rounded knucklebones rise up to test the flesh, as if they might break through. And I heard her moan of pain.

There was an expression of grim determination on my father's face, though the eyes retained the blank, detached stare. It was as if he were the hungry hunter running down terrified prey: unflagging flight and an unremitting pursuit.

Gisella writhed in the bed, though no one touched her but me. She cried out.

"Wait—" I blurted. "Father." No. *Jehan.* But I could not say the word. "Wait you—"

But his fingers locked around the wrist of her other hand—she screamed—

—Gods, how she screamed—

"*Jehan*—no!" Now the word came easily as I tried to break the grip. I tried to break it—but the sudden burst of fire within my skull hurled me back, *back*, away from the bed, until I crashed into the tapestried wall.

The world was upside down. Or was it me? I could not tell. I crawled on hands and knees to the bed, leaving a trail of blood behind. My nose was numb; I could not feel the blood, only taste it. My ears buzzed, rang, hummed. My vision was obscured by broken images.

—my father—Gisella—Taj and Lorn—

Bleeding, I sprawled face down across the bed and tried to touch my father, to tell him no, *no*—to somehow gainsay the power he leveled against her. Images blurred, twisted, revolved. The movement made me retch.

"Niall? *Niall!*"

My father's voice? *My* name? I could be certain of neither; my ears made too much noise.

"Niall—oh *gods*, let the boy be all right!" Hands caught me, pulled me up from the bed and then settled me on the floor with the side of the bed serving as backrest. "Niall?"

His face was split into sixths; I could make no order of the pieces.

"Niall, can you hear me?"

Blood ran down my chin. "Why? Why—harm—*her*—?"

One of his hands slipped behind my neck and cradled my wobbly head. "Never, *never*, touch a Cheysuli in mind-link, Niall. Have you not been warned against it?"

His face was in thirds, now. An improvement. And I could hear him better. "What did you do to Gisella?"

"Nothing," he said firmly. "Better to ask: what did she do to *me?*"

"You?" My eyes shut of their own accord. I put the back of my hand to my face and tried to stanch the blood.

"What you felt did not come from me, Niall. It was all Gisella's doing." His tone was grim. "Later, we will discuss it. Not now. Not in front of her."

"She will be my wife," I protested weakly. "It should all be in front of her."

"Look at me." I did as told. "Aye, you are better. Can you rise?"

Only with his help, and even then I nearly fell down again. I grasped the closest tester with one shaking hand; the other I locked under my nose. But the river was slowing to a stream. "What happened?"

"You broke the link," he said; now, looking at him with normal vision again, I saw the traces of blood in his own nostrils. "But it is just as well. Gisella was preparing to throw me out, which would have been more painful yet." He smiled a little and rubbed at bloodshot eyes. "For all she was raised far from any clan—and by an Ihlini, at *that*— she knows many of our tricks. And has many of our strengths." The smile fell away. "But none of our sense, I fear. When Alaric slew Bronwyn, he slew the girl's wits as well." He shook his head. "What happened to her cannot be healed, even by a Cheysuli—even by *several* Cheysuli. The damage was too severe."

I raised a silencing hand and turned to see if Gisella had heard. But she slept. She slept deeply; she slept smiling, as if pleased by what she had wrought.

I shivered. And then I looked at my father. "There was no trap-link, then?"

"No. There was no hint of Ihlini meddling—at least, not *within* her mind." His tone was level, unyielding; he would play no games with me. "Perhaps only *to* it, from things the others told her."

Others. Lillith, no doubt. And Alaric.

I nodded. "How soon can we have the wedding?"

I thought he meant to protest; to make some comment regarding *my* witlessness. But he did not. Bleakly, he said, "As soon as arrangements are made."

Again, I nodded. "Things will be better, then."

My father looked at Gisella. But he said nothing at all.

Five

Arrangements were made in an almost obscene haste. I knew it was Homanan custom, particularly *royal* custom, to invite neighboring aristocracy as well as royalty, as a means of sealing the ceremony. In this way no one could claim the throne was unsecured, and make plans to invade Homana. I had no doubts the Homanan Council, as well as my mother—and possibly even my father—would have preferred the custom adhered to, for the sake of displaying the Lion's successor and his Cheysuli bride to as many people as possible. But because of Gisella's advanced state and the domestic threat promised by Carillon's bastard, as well as Strahan himself, we could not afford to wait.

I put on the finest clothes I had for the wedding, since we could not even delay in order to have new ones made. And so Torvald made certain I was fit to appear before the guests, laying out the silks and velvets Homanans preferred, while also selecting Cheysuli ornamentation from my jewel chest. I wore garments of amber, sienna, and russet, set off with gold and garnets; a braided torque, hammered flat, with matching plated wristlets, and a belt studded with unfaceted garnets, glowing in the sunset.

As Torvald finished, my mother came into the chamber. At her nod he bowed and took his leave. And then she came to me. "You look well. Very well." But she did not smile. "Niall, there is still a little time."

I nodded absently, bending to adjust the droop of my amber-dyed boots.

"Niall, do you understand what I am saying? You do not have to go through with this."

Sighing, I straightened. In yellow, she was lovely. It made her gold-netted hair more vivid than ever. "I have said it before: I have every intention of marrying Gisella."

"Why?" she demanded. "That erratic, addled girl is a poor choice for Donal's heir!"

"And for Carillon's grandson?" I turned from her and paced to my jewel chest, studying the remaining contents idly. I approved Torvald's choices, but it gave me something to do. "We were cradle-betrothed, mother. Such a thing is not broken lightly, even if I *wished* to have it broken. And I do not." I picked through the brooches, wristlets, rings, then turned to face her. "She is mad. Aye. I will not deny it. But it does not mean she cannot be my wife."

"She will be *queen.*"

"One day," I agreed. "By then, perhaps she will be better."

She stared at me in obvious perplexity. Slowly she shook her head. "I do not understand. You are not—the same. Not since you went away."

"In fourteen months, I was bound to become a different man." I shrugged. "Perhaps I have grown up."

Again she shook her head. "There is something—" But she broke it off. "Niall, do you truly love her?"

"I think, as much as I am able." I shrugged. "I say that because you ask. My father would know better, being Cheysuli. So perhaps it is that the Homanan portion of me loves her, while what little Cheysuli is in me will not admit the feeling."

"Then you *do* have reservations." She came close, resting a hand upon my arm. "Niall, if you are not completely reconciled to this match, I will have it broken."

"And give Alaric cause to march against Homana?" I shook my head. "You are Queen, and undoubtedly you have the power to sway most if not all of the Homanan Council . . . but I doubt you would sway my father. I doubt you would sway the Cheysuli."

Her hand tightened. "I *know* there is the prophecy! How could I *not*, being wife and mother to men fully caught in its demands? But it does not name Gisella! It does not *say* she is the one you must wed, merely that you must wed to gain another bloodline. What of Erinn, Niall? Shaine himself wed an Erinnish princess before he wed Lorsilla. Save the Atvian line until later . . . the Erinnish might serve as well. We could speak with Shea."

"No." Quite suddenly, I felt ill. A hasty swallow steadied my belly again, but I could feel it threatening, waiting.

A beacon-fire on the cliff.

And I had lighted the fire.

"Niall?" A hand, tugging gently at my arm. "Niall?"

All I could see was the fire in my eyes, and the blackness of the night as I stood upon the top of the dragon's skull.

"Niall!"

The vision faded, but it left me with the bitter taste of guilt. An immense, abiding guilt, made worse because I could not say *why* I should feel guilty.

"No," I said. "I wish to wed Gisella."

"And so you shall." Ian's voice; he stood in the doorway, ablaze with Cheysuli gold: his *lir*-bands were whole again, unblemished by Alaric's hand. His leathers were pure, un-sullied white edged with scarlet silk. "Everyone waits below."

"Then we shall go." I put out my arm to my mother. Reluctantly, she took it.

To match the preparations, the ceremony itself was brief in the extreme. The Homanan priest said the same words he had said more than a year before when he had per-formed the proxy wedding. The *shar tahl*, summoned from Clankeep, echoed the other's sentiments, but in the Old Tongue. I understood all of it well enough, having learned the language in childhood, but Gisella, listening closely, merely looked left out. It made the bond between us stronger, I thought; I was left out of all the magic, while she lacked the language.

When it was done and Gisella and I were truly wed, my father announced the celebration would begin in an adjoin-ing audience hall. But those who had cause to give the Prince and Princess formal greeting were to stay behind and do so. And so I was able to watch and name to myself those Homanans who had no wish to greet me ·formally, and I realized that was precisely why my father had ar-ranged it that way.

Gisella was seated in a chair upon the dais, near the Lion itself. I stood beside her, noting with concern the weariness in her face. There was no hiding her pregnancy and no one had bothered to try; she wore loose, full robes that swathed most of her body, billowing over the mound that was my child.

My father and mother themselves went into the adjoining chamber, to give us this time alone. I knew why. There are men in the world who do things only when their lord's eye is on them, to curry favor, no matter what they think. And so by leaving, the Mujhar made certain those who stayed to greet me were doing so for reasons other than those. No doubt he would expect me to mark who said what, and report it to him later.

Enough Homanans came by with a word or two of congratulations that soon enough I could not name them all. I did not bother to keep track of each one, no more than I did with the Cheysuli. But when Isolde and Ceinn came through at the end of the line, I forgot my detachment entirely.

"So handsome!" But 'Solde's bright eyes mocked me as they had even in childhood. "I would have welcomed you to *my* wedding, *rujho*, had you not been gone so long."

"You have already wed?" I looked sharply at Ceinn, whose expression was once again blandly cordial and utterly closed to me.

"Aye," she answered. "About a sixth-month after you and Ian sailed for Atvia." One hand went out to briefly touch Ceinn's hand; for a Cheysuli, a broad display of emotion. But I saw nothing in his eyes that indicated he wished she had not done it.

Does he truly care for her? Or is she so valuable to his cause he will let her do as she wishes?

'Solde slanted a sidelong glance at Gisella, who was staring blankly into the emptied hall. "Is she—all right?"

I turned. "Gisella," I said. Then, more forcefully, "Gisella!"

Her black hair had been braided Cheysuli fashion and looped against her head, pinned with silver combs hung about with tiny silver bells. As I called her name, she started, and all the bells rang out.

'Solde, never one for hanging back, reached out and caught Gisella's hand. "I am Niall's *rujholla*," she said, "so now I am yours as well."

"*Rujholla?*" Gisella echoed.

'Solde frowned only briefly. And then she laughed. "I

forget. You have been reared in Atvia, so why should you know our language? It is only that you look more Cheysuli than anything else, and so I expect you to know the customs as well as the language." She glanced at me and laughed. "Niall will teach you *everything*, I am sure."

"Isolde is my sister," I told Gisella. "*Rujholla*, in the Old Tongue."

"Niall's sister?" Gisella stared at her. "Oh, of course, my father told me. You are the Mujhar's bastard daughter."

All the gaiety died out of 'Solde. White-faced, she stared blindly at Gisella. Then, abruptly, she let go of Gisella's hand at once and turned to leave the nearly empty hall.

" 'Solde—*Solde . . . wait!*" I caught up to her, leaving the dais and my blunt-speaking wife behind. " 'Solde, she does not understand our ways. And she is weary, *so* weary of the child. I beg you, try to understand."

'Solde's arm was rigid beneath my delaying fingers. "I understand," she said clearly. "I understand very well, Niall. I should have expected it." I had anticipated anger from her, and harsh words—'Solde is not a silent sort—but not the magnitude of her pain. She shrugged. "She was reared by the enemy."

"Gods, 'Solde, do not judge her so harshly. You do not understand."

Suddenly, Ceinn was at my side. "She understands as well as I do, *my lord*." His pupils had shrunk so that I saw mostly yellow, an intense, *intent* yellow. "Forgive my plain speech, my lord, but you have worsened your position with the clans by taking Gisella as your *cheysula*."

"She is half Cheysuli," I pointed out evenly, trying not to lose my temper. "She is the Mujhar's niece."

"She may be his *harana*—" the Cheysuli word was emphasized, as if to point out my use of Homanan in its place "—but she is also Atvian. Daughter to Alaric, who is no friend of ours."

"Atvian, *aye*." I was through with diplomacy. "And *necessary to the prophecy*." I caught his arm as he reached out to turn Isolde away, as if he intended to leave my presence and take my sister with him. "No," I told him plainly, "I am not finished with you."

His bare arm slid out of my grasping fingers as he jerked it sharply away. My nails scraped across the bear-shape worked into the gold of his *lir*-band. "Finished with *me?*" he echoed, though he knew precisely what I had said. "Oh, *no*, my lord. I think we are finished with *you.*"

"Ceinn!" 'Solde was clearly shocked by the virulence in his tone.

"I think the time *has* come for plain speech." Somehow I managed to summon an even tone, though I wanted to shout at him. "Well enough, hear what I have to say." I moved a step closer to him and was pleased to see that *this* time, he fell back a single step. "I am fully aware of the existence of the *a'saii*, and the preferences for my replacement in the line of succession. But I challenge you to tell me how *that* would serve the prophecy you claim to know better than other warriors." I made a beckoning gesture. "Well? I wait."

"Niall." Isolde, again, trying to turn my rising anger before it could burst its banks. "How can you say that to Ceinn? Of *course* he serves the prophecy."

"By seeing to it I am slain?" Though I watched Ceinn, I saw her twitch of shock. "What did you think he wanted from me, 'Solde—a peaceful retirement into the country?"

"Niall—"

" 'Solde—*enough*." That from Ceinn, as if he had no more time for verbal maneuverings even from his wife. "Plain speech, aye; and *aye*, I serve the prophecy! So do the rest of us." He turned a bit closer to me, edging Isolde out entirely. We confronted one another squarely. "You have some of the blood, it is true, but you also bear *other* blood—"

"So does Ian," I said clearly. "If it is true the *a'saii* desire a return to the days of purebred clans, how does it serve the prophecy? The prophecy *demands* a mixture—it *points* us to other realms."

"Other realms, aye," he agreed. "I do not contest the need for the blood of other realms; it can only strengthen us. But I do contest your absolute *lir*lessness, your lack of Cheysuli gifts, your lack of Cheysuli *customs*." He drew in a breath made uneven by the intensity of his anger; by the depth of fanaticism. "There are so few of us left now, those with untainted blood, and if it were possible I would prefer one of the *a'saii* to take the Lion on Donal's death. But we are not so blind as to turn our backs on a warrior who has more right than most—"

"—that warrior being Ian," I finished. I thrust out a hand and pointed at Gisella, still huddled in her chair. "In her body lies the *seed* of that prophecy, Ceinn—a child born of Homana, Solinde, Atvia, and the Cheysuli. How can you tell me *that child* should be replaced?"

"Because it should be. And *will* be." He reached out and caught Isolde's elbow. "Come, 'Solde. My business with him is finished. Let us go to the other hall."

"Ceinn—*wait.*" She pulled free of him even as he had pulled free of me. "Is it the truth? You want Ian to take Niall's place?" She thrust up a silencing hand even as he began to answer her question. "You know Ian would never do it. He is Niall's liege man as well as his *rujholli.* Do you think he would break that service merely to accept *yours?*"

Ceinn's mouth was grimly set, lips pressed tight against one another. "If he will not, we will simply find another with similar heritage."

"*Similar heritage*—" Isolde fell back a step. Then she stood very still. "Would *identical* be better?" she inquired bitterly. "Augmented by *yours*, no doubt . . . do you think a child from us would do?" Isolde smiled, but it was the smile of a predator. "My *jehan* is likely to live for at least another twenty years, perhaps more. By *then*, no doubt a son of ours would be old enough to accept the Lion. Is that it? Is that it, Ceinn?"

" 'Solde—"

"Just answer!" she cried. "Just *answer*. I do not want an explanation. Tell me aye or nay!"

Whatever else he was, Ceinn was not a liar. "Aye," he told her evenly. "I want our son to rule."

Isolde shook visibly, she was so angry; so shocked, so bound up in what she had learned. I saw tears welling into her eyes but they were not solely the tears of sorrow, though that was present also. They were the tears of rage and discovery; of a discovery so devastating it breaks the world into pieces.

'Solde's world, at least. I have shown her the man she has married.

"Well," she said, and I was amazed at her self-possession, "I think there will be no son."

" *'Solde!*"

"No." She did not shout it, scream it, cry it. She merely *said* it; I saw my father in my sister. "No." She pulled the bear-torque from her throat and dropped it to the stone at Ceinn's feet. "No."

Crimson skirts swirled as she turned. Ceinn reached out to catch an arm, but I caught his and jerked him back. "You heard what my sister said."

"*Ku'reshtin!*" he swore. "Do you think I only wanted her for the child? I wanted her—still *want* her—for herself!"

I laughed aloud. "Then tell me you love her, Cheysuli. Say the *Homanan* words to me, since there are none of the Old Tongue."

As I released his arm, Ceinn bent and scooped up the gleaming *lir*-torque, the mark of Cheysuli marriage. When he faced me again, I saw how tightly he clutched the torque; how tightly he clenched his jaw. But in clear, fluent Homanan, lacking Cheysuli accent or hesitation, he told me he loved my sister.

I had no answer for him. And he had none for me.

I watched the proud, angry warrior stride away from me, going after Isolde. And I began to think he was more of an enemy than at first I had believed. Because a man, so dedicated to a certain thing that there is no room for anything other than zealotry in his life, does not consider how or why he slays. But a man who loves, a man able to express that love, will think of what he does even as he does it, because he has something—some*one*—he believes is *worth* the thing he does. Even if it is assassination.

"Niall?" It was Gisella, at my side. "Niall . . . can we go see the dancing?"

I did not want to go. "You look weary," I told her truthfully. "It might be better if you went to bed instead."

"I want to see the *dancing*."

And so I took her to see the dancing.

Six

I saw to it Gisella was settled comfortably in a cushioned chair on the dais with three other chairs. Two were for the Mujhar and his queen, the other for me. But all three remained empty.

As I stood solicitously by Gisella, she reached out and caught my hand. The motion reminded me of 'Solde and how she had reached for Ceinn. It reminded me of the conflict in her face as she had removed the *lir*-torque from her throat and told Ceinn there would be no child.

Holding Gisella's hand, I looked down upon my wife and the child who swelled her body. Fruit of a man's labors, and a sign of fertility so necessary to the House of Homana. And yet—it seemed I could hardly recall the first time we had lain together. Only the faintest flicker of a fleeting memory that told me once I had known someone other than Gisella.

Inwardly, I grimaced. I had hardly kept myself celibate before sailing to Atvia. No doubt what I recalled so dimly were the women who did not matter, being more interested in *who* I was rather than in what I could do to pleasure them.

I thought suddenly of the children born of such unions, the fruit of a man's labors in fields that had already been well-tilled. I thought it likely I had no bastards because surely a woman who conceived of a prince would tell him in hopes of winning coin or jewel or favor. But I knew also it was entirely possible I *had* sired a child or two before the one in Gisella's belly. And it made me think of Carillon, who had gotten a woman with child, and how that child now threatened my very existence, let alone my right to inherit the Lion.

The Lion of Homana. Gisella had asked if I were the Lion myself. And now I looked at the man who *was*.

He wore Cheysuli leathers dyed a rich, deep crimson, hem and collar set with narrow gold plates stitched into the leather. On his brow he wore a simple circlet of hammered gold and uncut rubies. And at his left side, scabbarded in rune-worked leather, hung the sword others claimed was ensorcelled.

My father did not move about the room; he let the room come to him. Quietly he stood near one of the groined archways and received those who wished to have word with him. He might have done it from the chair upon the dais, next to me. But it was a mark of his nature that he did not, preferring to stay away from such trappings as thrones and trumpeted announcements of his arrival. That he wore the sword surprised me; only rarely did he clasp the belt around his hips. Only rarely did he ever put hand to hilt, as if reluctant to display his absolute mastery of it.

Of course, he would never admit to being the master; rather, the servant. He had told me how once the brilliant ruby, the Mujhar's Eye, had been perverted by Ihlini magic into a thing of ugliness. A dead black stone, dull and luster-less, had sat within the golden pommel prongs. For nearly all of the years of Carillon's rule the stone had remained dull black.

Until the day Donal put his hand upon it, and it came blazing back to life.

There is a legend within the clans that a sword made of Cheysuli craftsmanship bears Cheysuli magic, and knows the hand of its master even when the master is unknowing, he had told me. *The gods know I was aware my grandsire had made that sword, but it was for Shaine, I thought; for the Mujhar who began the* qu'mahlin *that nearly destroyed our race. Shaine gave it to Carillon, who bore the blade for all the years of his exile and all the years of his rule. Only when he was dead did it come into my keeping.*

And only at the cost of a warrior's life: Finn, my father's uncle. Strahan had sheathed the sword in Finn's body, and in so doing had unintentionally bequeathed the magic unto my father.

The magic that slew Osric of Atvia, Gisella's uncle, and put Alaric on the throne. I glanced down at her pensively.

So many people dead . . . and all in the name of the prophecy.

I saw my mother moving among the guests, speaking quietly with countless members of the aristocracy, Homanan and otherwise. The gold netting enveloping rich red hair shone in the light of the setting sun as it slanted through stained glass casements. The rose-red floor was awash with brilliant color.

And then I saw Isolde.

I turned to Gisella. "Forgive me if I leave you, but I must speak with my sister."

Her fingers tightened on my own. "Niall?"

"You will be well, I promise." Carefully I detached myself from her and stepped off the dais, moving through the throngs of people surrounding the dancers in the center of the hall. I answered greetings absently, too intent upon reaching 'Solde; when at last I did, I saw the desolation in her posture. She stood by one of the casements, back to the hall, as if by ignoring the people she could also ignore her loss.

She turned as I placed a hand on her shoulder, and then she tried to turn again; to turn her back on me.

" 'Solde—"

"Leave me be."

" 'Solde, *please.*"

"Niall—" She broke off the beginnings of her plea and swung back to face me squarely. I saw bitter grief in her ravaged face. "I would be the last person in the world to wish you in peril, Niall . . . but surely you will not blame me if, for the moment, I wish also to have nothing to do with you."

A flicker of grief; a larger one of defensiveness. "I did not *ask* you to renounce him."

"What *else* could I do?" Impatiently she brushed tears away, as if their presence was anathema. And in a way, they were; Cheysuli do not grieve in public. "Am I to renounce *you?*"

Sighing deeply, I took her into my arms and crushed her against my chest. She was rigid, denying herself comfort, until I rested my cheek on her hair and told her I would forgive her if she went back to Ceinn.

"Go *back!*" She pulled away to stare up at me. "How can you say that after what *he* has said?"

"Because I know what *else* he has said." And I told her.

I thought it would help. I thought it would make her happy to know her *cheysul* genuinely cared, not intending to use her merely because of who she was. But I misjudged her. I misjudged her badly.

"Do you value your life so little?" she asked angrily. "Do you value *me* so little? How can you expect me to go back to a man who wishes to see you stripped of your rank, your title—your *life?*"

"I think it will not come to that," I told her. "The *a'saii* are no longer secret, and I have no intention of allowing them to succeed. They are only a tiny portion of the Cheysuli, 'Solde, I doubt they have *that* much power."

She shook her head. "I will not take the chance."

" 'Solde—"

"No." She nearly choked on the word. "How *can* I, *rujho?* I already bear his child!"

Pain rose up in my belly, the old familiar pain I associated with *lir*lessness. Yet now it came as I thought of what 'Solde must face, bearing alone the child of the man she loved.

"Gods," I said, "does he know?"

"No. I planned to tell him after your wedding. But now," she shook her head. "Now I will say nothing."

" 'Solde, he is the child's *father.*" I thought of Gisella. I thought of myself in Ceinn's place, not knowing my wife carried my child in her body. For all I hated the man for his zealotry, I could not hate him for desiring a child.

Even one he would use against me.

'Solde drew in a deep breath. "Aye. And right now, not knowing, he plots to put Ian on the throne. You are safe so long as he and the others work toward that goal, *rujho,* because Ian will never agree. But once he knows I have conceived, they will have a new candidate. A candidate they can control." Through her tears, she smiled. "I am a child of the prophecy as much as you; do you think I will allow my *cheysul* to destroy it?"

I was touched by her resolve, deeply touched, but could not ignore the brutal truth of the undeniable transience of that resolve. " 'Solde, in a month—two, three—the child will begin to show. What will you say to him then?"

She stood very straight before me. "In a month or two or three, perhaps you will have cut out this canker in our midst."

I wanted to speak, to say something that might dilute her pain, if only a little. But 'Solde's pride and resolve took all the words from my mouth; took even the pride from *me,* because she was far stronger than I could ever be.

She gives her husband over to death.

And knew *exactly* what she did even as she did it.

I tried to swallow down the painful lump in my throat. *"Cheysuli i'halla shansu,"* I said thickly. I could think of nothing more fitting than wishing upon my Cheysuli sister the peace of the race she served so faithfully.

'Solde smiled a little. And then she put out her hand—palm-up, fingers spread—and made the eloquent gesture that had the ordering of an entire race. *"Tahlmorra,"* she said quietly, and then she walked out of the hall.

I watched her go, then swung around abruptly to return to Gisella. And I stopped just as abruptly, because Varien stood in my path.

The Atvian envoy smiled and inclined his head. "My lord, please accept my congratulations on your marriage to the Princess of Atvia." The smile, so smooth, widened only a fraction, not enough to offer offense. "And now the Princess of Homana."

"My thanks." I was brusque, but it was difficult to be polite after witnessing 'Solde's grief.

"My lord." He detained me easily with merely an intonation. "Here, my lord. I have brought you wine."

Each hand held a silver cup. I took the cup he offered because indeed I *did* desire wine . . . *anything* to ease the ache in my spirit. I felt bruised from 'Solde's decision. I could not argue that it was the right one, but neither was I the sort of man who would be pleased to see his sister in such pain.

Varien, unctuous as always, lifted his cup in a brief salute. "Your fortune, my lord."

I drank deeply. So deeply I drained the cup too quickly; Varien instantly motioned a servant to refill it. And then, as I drank again, the Atvian stepped closer. So close, a velvet-clad shoulder brushed my own.

"May I speak freely, my lord?"

My mind was not on Varien at all. "Of course." I looked past him toward the dais, and saw Gisella picking half-heartedly at her silken robes.

"My lord, I will be frank with you: your wife is not entirely like other women."

Looking at her, I recalled how changeable were her moods; how violent the swings. "No," I agreed.

"This is a delicate subject, my lord, but I am certain you would prefer it discussed. It has bearing on your future."

I frowned a little, looking at him more attentively. "If it concerns my wife, of course it has bearing on my future."

Teeth showed briefly, so briefly, as he laughed silently. And then the laughter was gone, leaving in its wake a cool, quiet amusement. "My lord, let us agree the lady is—of divergent humors. Because of these humors, it is entirely possible she will not always be a willing partner." He paused delicately and lifted the cup to his lips. But he did not drink. "*Bed* partner, my lord."

I looked at my wife. "That is something between Gisella and me, envoy."

"My lord, of course." He bowed just enough to emphasize his subservience. "But with you I feel I must be completely frank." Smiling, he said, "If Gisella ceases to please you, I can show you another way."

In distaste, I frowned at him. "Do I hear you aright? On the day of my wedding you offer other women to me?"

"Not—entirely." The smile did not fade. "My lord, let us say I have admired you greatly since first we met. Admired, respected—*desired*, my lord."

My fingers slipped on the cup; I nearly dropped it. But I recovered my grasp and clenched it tightly, so tightly my hand shook, and wine slopped over the rim to splatter against the floor. *"What did you say?"*

"I said I desired you, my lord." He made no indication of shame, regret, embarrassment. His tone was perfectly controlled, as if every day he said such to a man.

As perhaps he does. Incredulously, I stared at him. I was too shocked to be angry.

Varien sipped wine and smiled, infinitely patient.

I became aware that a hand had reached out and caught Varien's wrist in a crushing grasp. The hand dragged the silver wine cup away from Varien's smiling mouth. Sharply. So sharply it caused the cup to fall; falling, it rang, silver on stone; spilled blood-red wine across rose-red floor.

And I realized the hand was mine.

Around us, there was silence. A falling wine cup, even spilling its contents, is not so uncommon as to silence so many people. But the sight of the Prince of Homana confronting an Atvian envoy *is;* eyes watched avidly.

Sweat beaded on Varien's upper lip. His face was pale from the pain. But still, he managed to smile.

I wanted to shout at him that what he offered was worthy of execution, but I did not. Not before so many people; before Gisella, my father, my mother. I wanted to tell him that what he offered was worth his ostracism; at the very least I could send him home. But something held me back. Something shut up my mouth and chased the words back down my throat to my belly, where they twisted and tangled and bound up my guts with bile.

And *still* Varien smiled.

I let go of his wrist. "You are here at Alaric's behest."

"Alaric's—and Lillith's."

I frowned a little. My toe touched the cup; it rolled. "Lillith's?"

"Of course, my lord." Varien fingered the collar of his indigo doublet. I saw a hint of silver: a chain. He drew it forth, and from the links dangled a single curving tooth, capped with shining silver. "Lillith."

Lillith's gift. My hand went at once to my own collar. Beneath the wedding finery was a matching tooth, hanging from its thong. I had nearly forgotten.

Varien bowed. "Forgive me, my lord; I intended no offense."

I stared after him, bewildered by the sudden upsurge of emotions. Sorrow, anguish, emptiness . . . a horrible emptiness, as if someone had stolen from me a thing I had always desired, demanded, *needed*—before I could say what it was.

I was lost. Amid the throng of guests who had witnessed my marriage to Gisella, I was lost: an eye of emptiness in the middle of the maelstrom.

A shadow of a man.

And when the servant filled my cup, I drank.

I drank.

I drank—

—and when I could stand the confinement no more, I went out of the hall and out of the palace proper, climbing narrow stairs to the sentry-walks along the curtain wall. Night had fallen with the sunset, but Homana-Mujhar is never in total darkness. There are torches along the walls and tripod braziers in the baileys. There is always a pall of yellow light, flickering in fickle winds. Preying on the shadows.

Now I *sought* the shadows, seeking escape from the light, the noise, the *emptiness*. Except even here, atop the narrow sentry-walk along the parapet, I found solace in nothing; no answer to emptiness. Only redoubled sorrow, and an anguish born of nothing I could name.

In my hand was a cup of wine. A deep cup, and filled to brimming; tipping it slightly, albeit unintentionally, I heard the wine spill out to splatter against the stone. Even as I righted the cup I did not care; I had drunk so much already that stopping now would serve nothing at all.

I caught hold of the wall and leaned between the merlons of the parapet to hang over a crenel, pressing my belly against it. Lights from the city flared and danced and melted together, until I blinked away the dazzle from my eyes. My fingers dug into the stone. Digging, *digging;* I felt the protest of abraded flesh. But still I dug, as if the pain might give me surcease from the demon in my soul.

"An easy target, for an enemy."

I pushed myself up raggedly, still hanging onto the merlon. The torchlight from below set his gold to gleaming. All his gold; suddenly, I found I hated him for it. "I came out here to be alone."

"I know." Ian's tone was even, unperturbed even by the belligerence in my own. "That is why I followed."

"Why? Did you think I would throw myself from the wall?"

"You look as though the thought has crossed your mind." Like me, he bore a cup of wine. But he did not drink from his. "Niall, what did Varien say to you?"

I tasted something in my mouth that made me want to spit. Instead, I gulped more wine. "He said he desired me,"

I said flatly, when all the wine was gone. "Perhaps he thinks I will share his bed when I cannot share Gisella's."

The torchlight polished Ian's angular face. He was so much like Isolde. So much like our father. "There was a time I could have told you the truth of Varien. I grew to know him well in Atvia because I had no choice." He paused. "Not in the way he wishes to share with you, but because we spent time together. But as for telling you, I was not certain you would listen. I was not certain you could." He looked straight at me. "Can you, *rujho?* Can you hear the truth?"

"What truth?" I demanded. "I think I have heard it all."

He took the empty cup from my hand. "No. You have heard nothing." Smoothly, he threw the cup over the crenel. I saw a flash of silver in the torchlight; it was gone. "Do you hear it?" he asked, and I heard the dull clang of the cup striking stones below.

"Ian—"

"Gisella has addled *your* mind as much as her own is addled," he said plainly. "I know you cannot see it, but I can; I can see precisely what she has done to you, and I do not like it. It is time something was done to destroy the taint."

"*I'toshaa-ni?*" I asked rudely. "Or does that lie solely within *your* province?"

"It lies within the province of every Cheysuli warrior," he answered quietly. "Even within that of a *lir*less Cheysuli. "

He might as well have taken a knife and thrust it into my belly. I felt the invisible blade go home, twisting, *twisting*, until I nearly cried out with the pain. As it was, I clutched at the merlon. Sweat broke out on my face.

"*Ku'reshtin—*" I cursed him raggedly. "Look to *yourself* when you speak of taint. It was *you* Lillith kept."

"Aye. *You* she gave away." The silver cup glittered against the darkness of his hands. "You she gave to Gisella."

I swore again, very softly; I was nearly doubled over from the pain. "Gisella is my *wife.*"

"Gisella is your bane . . . and *will* be, until we do something to prevent it."

"We?" I asked bitterly, leaning against the merlon. "Do

you speak of the *a'saii?*" I laughed in the face of his sudden shock. "Perhaps you *do* desire the Lion; perhaps Ceinn and the others *have* found a willing substitute for me."

"The gods forgive you for that," he whispered. "How can you think it of me? I am your *liege man*—"

"You leave out *brother*," I said harshly. "Is it because we only share a father that you discount the kinship? Is it because I am Homanan and Solindish that you brush aside the other blood between us?" I laughed. "Why not? *Ceinn* is willing to let that be reason enough to drag me out of a throne I cannot yet claim as my own. Do you abet him? Do you abet the *a'saii?*"

"No," he said softly, when he could speak again. "I abet only the gods."

"In what? Your march to the throne?" I thrust out a rigid arm and pointed toward the massive palace proper. "It waits, Ian. In the Great Hall. All crouched down upon its wooden haunches with its wooden eyes gleaming even as the mouth spills out its wooden tongue. The Lion *waits*, Ian—why not claim it for yourself?"

His posture was so rigid I thought he might break. "Because I do—not—*want*—it." He thrust the words out between clenched teeth. "And one day, you will understand why. One day, I think you will beg me to take the Lion from you." He put his cup into my hand. "But even when you *beg*, I will not take it. Because I am the Lion's shadow . . . not the Lion himself. I leave that title to you."

"Ian—" But he had turned, going back into the shadows until I could not see him, only the glinting of his gold. All his Cheysuli gold.

Gods, why can I not have my own— "Ian! Ian, *wait!*" Unsteadily I ran along the narrow sentry-walk, still clutching the cup in my hand. Wine slopped over the ring and splashed against thigh, boot, stone. "Ian—come back! I need you, *rujho*. I *need* you . . . I need you to take away the *pain*—"

But he was gone. He did not hear, or else he did not care to answer.

I stopped running. I fell against the parapet and gasped for breath, trying to still the roiling in my belly. I wanted to spew all the wine over the crenel onto the stones below. I wanted to start over again, to tear up the spoiled parchment and begin again with a fresh one. I wanted to shout and scream and cry, because I was so empty, so gods-cursed *empty*.

And a man cannot live when he is made up of emptiness.

The cup in my hand was also empty. And so I threw it over the crenel to join its fellow far below, wishing I could be rid of *myself* as easily.

How can a man be rid of himself when he has no wish to die?

He leaves. He *leaves*.

Seven

I fled Homana-Mujhar on fleet horse and fleeter need to escape the blackness in my soul. That I had a demon in me I did not doubt; I could feel it within me, clawing, gnawing, shredding the interior of my belly. I shouted orders to the guard and clattered out of the cobbled outer bailey and through the wide front gates even as they were shoved open. Free of the outer curtain wall, I spurred through winding alleys and streets, ignoring the shouts of passers-by. Never an indifferent horseman, I took negligent care to avoid trampling anyone, and therefore no one went down beneath my stallion's iron-shod hooves.

Sparks flew; I bent low in the saddle and urged the horse on faster, past the watch and through the massive barbican gate, portcullis raised: the East Gate of Mujhara. Onward through the clustered spillage of outer dwellings; I recalled the night I had met Strahan. So long ago—had he really warned me not to wed Gisella?

Aye, he had. As well as promising to take my sons. Now the promise was more dangerous than ever; Gisella could bear me my first son soon, and set Strahan's plans into motion.

Through the winding footpaths of the outskirts; out of dirt onto heath, digging divots of tight-packed turf and clods of soil. I shut my eyes and trusted my horsemanship to keep me in the saddle as I battled the emptiness.

It is difficult to describe how overwhelming emptiness can be, how utterly encompassing, until even the thought of death becomes less important than the driving need to be *filled*. It is worse than melancholy; worse than the depths of despair. It is a complete cessation of functioning. A man simply ceases to *be*, and yet he knows that physically he still exists. It is only his spirit that has been torn asunder.

The need burned away the liquor in my blood. I was not drunk, though a part of me longed to be. Nor was I made ill by the poison I had poured so liberally into my body. I was simply *empty*.

Under the quarter moon the horse and I went on, galloping across the open plains until we could gallop no more, and then we slowed. I heard the whistle in the stallion's wind and knew I had come close to slaying him outright; I might even have ruined him permanently. He carried his head very low, dangling on the end of his shaven neck. His ears lolled back loosely, flopping as he walked. He staggered, stumbling repeatedly; at last I dismounted and led him. But I did not turn back. I led him ever eastward, into the deepwood that swallowed the eastern plains.

Spittle from the stallion had soiled my velvet doublet. It was past midsummer, moving into fall, but the night was not cold, only cool.

Ahead of me, hidden by leagues of deepwood, lay Clankeep. But I did not intend to go there; *could* not, in my need. I knew Ceinn and the other *a'saii* would mock me, denigrating me before the clan, using my emptiness and *lir*lessness to turn other warriors against me. And then there would be more than just a few; more, even, than twenty or thirty. There would be enough to pull me out of the Lion's presence and put Ian in my place.

At last, weary as the stallion, I stopped stumbling eastward and searched for shelter. In a copse of close-grown beeches I unsaddled the stallion, unpacked the few things I had brought with me—bow, full quiver, waterskin, a pouch of dried meat, one of grain, cloak—and made a bed of leaves. I threw myself upon it and rolled up in my cloak once I had tethered and grained the horse. I knew he would not try to break the rein and wander. Like me, he wanted nothing more than the forgetfulness of sleep.

I burrowed into the leaves, reflecting the Homanans would not believe it of their prince, and let the darkness overwhelm me. I heard the night sounds; smelled the sap, the soil, the fragrance of the forest. I stared up at the arching fretwork of limbs against stars and thought of the gods who had decreed there be a people put onto the land, and so they had put the Firstborn upon the Crystal Isle. I thought of the Firstborn who had watched their children become so blood-bred their very existence was threatened; until even the Firstborn knew they themselves could not recover. And I thought of the prophecy that bound the Cheysuli so tightly; that bound *me* so tightly, like the pillory that imprisons thief and liar.

The stallion grunted. I turned to look and saw him go down, shifting sideways, until he lay on his side; until, on his back, he twisted and hunched, flailing long legs as he rolled against deadfall and dirt. He shed dried sweat and discomfort in the age-old equine rite; I wished I could do the same.

He lay still a moment, blinking; the quarter moon set his eye afire with light. And then he was up, awkward in the attempt as horses always are; he stood, shook violently— shedding hair and debris—then locked his knees and shut his eyes. He would sleep standing, perfectly comfortable, while I tried to sleep lying down in leaves against a ground that would be damp by morning.

The night was colder than I had expected. When dawn chased away the morning mists I awoke shivering with a bone-deep chill. I tried to wrap the cloak more tightly, but it was only a summer cloak of fine-combed wool, not a heavier winter cloak lined with fur. And so I gave up on sleep altogether and rose, aware of a sourness in my throat that bespoke a belly gone bad on too much wine. I had thought the effects purged by the flight from Mujhara; they were not. The condition of my head told me that.

I drank water sparingly, ate dried meat, sat hunched on a cold log wishing myself a man who did not imbibe; knowing one day, and probably too soon, I would do the same again.

Finally I rose and went to the horse. With both hands I brushed his back free of the debris remaining from the night before, placed blankets across his spine and prepared to hoist the saddle up and settle it on top of the blankets. I had every intention of going back to Homana-Mujhar. *Every* intention: no doubt my brother and father worried— I *knew* my mother worried—and I had left Gisella as well. Poor, sad Gisella, deprived of the ordering in her wits that would have made her worthy of any man.

And yet, I thought she was worthy of me.

Grimly I reached for the Homanan saddle. But even as I caught hold and hoisted it, I realized the emptiness was not gone. Only a bit laggard in renewing itself in my soul.

Gods, what am I to do? Tell me what I am to do!

But the only answer was the snort of my chestnut stallion and the chatter of a jay in the tree.

Do I go back? Has anything changed from last night, except the condition of head and belly? No. I am still empty, still naked, still bound up in the need for the thing I need so badly.

And so I did not go back. I tended the stallion more carefully than the night before, pulling the blankets from his back, once again, and found him mostly recovered from my irresponsibility. I grained him, watered him as best I could by tucking the skin beneath an arm and pressing water into cupped palms. He drank, but I did not doubt he would prefer a stream or river.

"Later. First, we—*I*—need fresh meat. This pouch will not last long." I patted him, left him rein enough to graze around the tree, took bow and quiver and set out to hunt on foot.

After half a day spent tracking, I slew a roebuck and carried it back to the campsite slung over my shoulders. There I hung it up and butchered it, enjoying the messy task not because I enjoyed butchering, but because I took satisfaction in doing the thing myself. So often there were others to do it for me. Even Ian. And I thought of the red king stag.

I built a fire and roasted the meat, knowing most of it would spoil before I could eat it all. The stallion cropped contentedly at forest grasses and the grain I gave him, untroubled by his sojourn away from luxury into the depths of the shadowed forest. And even though I was empty still, I began to know a little peace.

We moved on, the horse and I, after another day. He had stripped the copse bare of grazing and I wanted to find a proper stream. So I saddled him, packed him, mounted him, intending to head back.

But instead, we went deeper into the woods. And, as the days passed, more deeply still, until I left behind all thoughts of Homana-Mujhar and contented myself with doing for myself, as I had never done before.

I let my beard grow, since I had only a knife with which to shave it, and no polished plate at all. I slew a deer and fashioned a set of boots, since my others—intended only for ceremonial wear—were nearly destroyed. The fur was lush against my legs. The remaining pelt I made into a rough jerkin—hair-in, hide-out, no sleeves—and belted it with a strip of leather. Beneath it all I still wore the soiled silks and velvets of my wedding finery, as well as the garnets and gold.

The horse began to grow his winter coat, losing the sheen of summertime and gaining the blurry outline of colder months. His mane, no longer shaved, grew straight up to a height the width of my hand before it began to fall. At Homana-Mujhar, he was stabled, closely tended, knowing shelter against the seasons. Here he knew only the honesty of the forest.

We moved on twice more, because the emptiness increased. Each day I awoke prepared to go back, to go *home,* and yet each day I felt myself emptier than ever. The only surcease I knew was to busy myself with living as I had never lived, learning the forest as I had never really known it. I thought of Gisella, growing larger with my child. I thought of Ian, whom I had sent from me with cruel temper and crueler tongue. I thought also of my father, deprived yet again of his legitimate son and heir so soon after he had finally gotten him back; needing him more than ever. And, of course, my mother, who no doubt worried every hour of every day and night. But this was my time, *my* freedom . . . my final chance to learn precisely who I was before I must become the man they *desired* me to be, and not the man I might have become on my own.

I did not go back. Because I *could* not, yet.

And then early one morning, just before dawn, a bear came into camp. I knew it at once by the smell, even as the stallion awakened me with the noise of his fear; his attempts to break free of the rein tying him to the sapling.

He broke it, but as he spun to run the bear was on him, and in the bright light of a full moon I saw the hunter clearly: a cinnamon-colored rock bear.

There was nothing to do for the horse. By the time I caught up my bow, the bear had slain him. And so I took what I could reach of my belongings, silently, and left at once, not wishing to contest anything so deadly as a rock bear for campsite *or* gear.

I went away as far as I could and slept the rest of the night beneath the spreading limbs of a huge old oak, rolled in my summer cloak. And when at dawn I awakened, I found the rock bear sitting beside me.

I was up before I could speak, running before I could walk, caught before I could pray. I felt the spread paw slap at my ankle, catch, jerk, and then I was down, rolling, trying to yank my knife free of its sheath even as the bear slapped my hand. The knife went flying. With unexpected precision, the bear used only one claw against the back of my hand. The stripe turned white, pink, red; opening, it spilled blood down through my fingers.

I sprawled on my buttocks, braced against one rigid elbow even as my booted feet scraped rotting leaves, searching for purchase in drifting debris. The bear sat back on his haunches. I saw the yellow eyes; the eyes of a Cheysuli.

And then, of course, I *knew*.

"*Ku'reshtin!*" I shouted hoarsely. "Is *this* how you mean to do it?"

The bear blurred before me. I squinted as the void swallowed the bear and spat out a man, a Cheysuli: Ceinn. Still he squatted before me, close enough to touch; I did not move. I knew better than to move.

"My lord," he said calmly, "there is a thing we must discuss."

"The two of us have *nothing* to discuss!"

"Oh, aye—we all of us *do*, my lord."

As he spoke the others came out of the thinning darkness, gliding from trees and shadowed pockets, all in human form, except for the *lir*. That hurt most of all, more than anything I had expected; that there were *lir* in the world who would join the *a'saii* in attempting to replace me.

I could not count them all, warriors or *lir*. I knew only there were more than I had expected. More than I had dreamed possible.

Ceinn smiled. It made the scar by his eye crease. It made him look like a man who would be a good friend. A man whose companionship would be valued.

As no doubt the *a'saii* valued him.

"My good fortune amazes me," he said. "We have been so patient, expecting to wait a very long time. *Prepared* to wait a very long time. Yet now you are here, and *we* are here, and this thing can be settled at last."

I still sprawled on my back, one knee thrust up. The claw mark continued to bleed. "How many?" I asked.

"Of the *a'saii*?" Ceinn shrugged. "Enough. I have not counted lately. At least two or three from every clan."

"*Every* clan?"

"Even those from the Northern Wastes, across the Bluetooth River."

I tried not to show my dismay openly. But I was stunned at the magnitude of the Cheysuli rebellion. There were, at last count, at least thirty clans in Homana, some large, some small, some smaller, but all invaluable to the completion of the prophecy. And now, in their misguided zealotry, they desired to destroy it.

I did not bother to look at the others, though I addressed them as well. I looked only at Ceinn. "How much of this is personal?"

"None of it," he answered instantly, so sincerely that I believed him even as I desired not to. "There were *a'saii* in Homana before Isolde and I ever lay down together."

It was a shock as well as an unpleasant realization. "And now?"

"Now?" He nodded thoughtfully. "I admit I enjoy the idea more."

Apprehension knotted my belly. I could not help it; I winced against the familiar pain. "Would it do any good if I told you there are *Homanans* who feel much as you do? That they also desire to replace me with another?"

"The bastard." Ceinn nodded. "We know."

I had hoped to buy my way free. I should have known better. "Ian will never agree," I told him. "And 'Solde has renounced you . . . who will you choose to hold the Lion now? You?" I thought perhaps to breed dissension among the others; Ceinn's personal ambitions might disturb them enough to delay their immediate plans.

"Ian may not agree while you are alive," Ceinn told me, "but what happens when you are dead? The Queen is barren. Donal has no other sons. Who else will succeed him?"

"Carillon's bastard."

Something flickered in his eyes.

I smiled, albeit was unamused. "If I am dead, it gives the Homanan *a'saii* more chance than ever to put the bastard on the throne. They are every bit as loyal and fanatical as you are; do you think they will suffer *Ian* to hold the Lion? You are a fool, Ceinn—you and the others. You will bring domestic rebellion to Homana again, and destroy all hope of fulfilling the prophecy."

"Eloquent," he said, "but our decision has been made."

Slowly I sat up all the way, forgoing my unintentional posture of submissiveness. In the muted light of early dawn, I looked at as many faces as I could. "How will it be? Will it be the *lir*? Or all of you in *lir*-shape, leaving only scraps of clothing and broken bone—with perhaps the ring remaining on my hand to make certain my identity is known?"

"That may well be your fate," he agreed, "but it will not be our doing. It will be your own."

"*Mine*—" I laughed. "I hardly think—"

"*I* do." He interrupted smoothly. "You are a *lir*less man, Niall. Cheysuli, for all you sublimate it beneath Homanan looks and customs." He glanced in distaste at my thickening beard. "And a *lir*less Cheysuli gives himself over to the death-ritual."

"I never *had* a *lir*." It took all my determination not to show my fear. "I am not constrained to the ritual."

"No," he agreed, "but when we are done with you, you will *believe* you had a *lir*—and you will believe you lost one."

Gods, they can do it. I tried to scramble up, to lunge away from Ceinn, but it did not matter. The others closed in even as he rose and brushed off his leathers.

"*Rujho*," —how he mocked me, in his inexpressibly gentle tone— "for Isolde's sake, I promise we will not hurt you."

Gods—

I tried to scream it. But by the time I opened my mouth,
I had lost the means to speak.

Or even the desire.

Eight

Oh gods—my lir—
   —*my* lir *is dead—*
   —*my* lir—
I knelt on the ground, hunched upon my knees so that my heels cut into my buttocks. My forehead was pressed against the layer of brittle fallen leaves; I shut my eyes so tightly all I could see were the pallid colors of my death: smutty blue, muddy black, an edge of maggot white in the ashen darkness of my grief.
   —*my* lir—*my* lir *is dead—*
Fists dug holes in the crumbling leaves; digging, *digging,* until they touched the cool dampness of soil beneath; the humid, sweaty soil; of the consistency of clay; the clay that is used to seal the eyes of a dead man closed.
   —*my* lir—
I have known grief in my life, much grief; I recalled how it was when I had believed my brother dead, but I have never known, have never *imagined* what it would be like to lose a *lir.* It was as if a man had thrust a hand through flesh and gristle and bone to grasp my heart; grasping it, he wrenches it from my chest and throws it aside, leaving me both alive and dead. Alive because I do not die; dead because everything within the fragile shell of human flesh is dead, so infinitely *dead.* How does a man *live* like this?
How can a man survive?
He does not.
And then I knew what I must do.
I wrenched myself up from the ground and ran, *ran;* running, I felt the grief rise up from my belly to clog my chest, my throat, my mouth, until I could hear it rising from my lips to kite upon the wind made of my own passing; a keening deathsong, a wailing griefsong; a song composed of all

the pain in my heart and soul and mind: *my* lir *is dead, my*
lir *is dead; why can* I *not be dead as well?*

I ran. *I ran.*

So hard. *So hard.*

—gods—*how is it you can gift a man with such a miracle
as a* lir, *and then take him away from that man—?*

I ran.

Vines slashed down across my face. A tree limb scraped
across my cheek, lifting skin and beard. A thorny creeper
looped my throat; tugged, tore.

I ran.

Bracken fouled my legs, slapping at my thighs. Deadfall
limbs cracked and rolled beneath my feet; I stumbled,
caught myself; ran on.

Gods—how I ran—

There is pain in my belly, in my chest, in my throat. I
can hear my breathing wheezing, hissing, whistling, like that
of a wind-broken horse. There is dryness in my throat, such
gods-awful dryness; it burns, it *burns* . . . I think it will
burn me alive—

Gods—why did you take my lir?

I trip. I fall. I rise.

—*run*—

Something is running behind me. I can hear it. I can hear
it coming; hear it slipping through the path I break as I
run; running more quickly than *I* can run as I try to leave
it behind.

I can hear it. I can hear it tearing through the vines and
creepers and bracken, unhindered by the thorns, the roots,
the traps that plants will lay for a man, seeking to bring
him down.

I can hear it. I can hear it breathing, *breathing*; I can
hear its heavy panting.

I can *hear* it—

—and then I realize it is *myself* I hear; there is nothing
behind me, nothing at all, except grief and pain and the
awful weight of knowledge: *my* lir *is dead, my* lir—*my* lir
is gone from me—

Oh gods. Will you not lift this weight from my soul?

Aye, they tell me. *Aye. You have only to trust in us; trust
yourself to us; give yourself over to us.*

Aye. It is best. For the best. It cannot be so hard.

—I give myself over to you—

No! A new voice I do not recognize. Not myself. The gods?

—I give myself—

No!

—I give—

And more urgently yet: *No!*

No? Who—or what—is that which tells me *no?*

I slow. I stop. I turn. But all I can see is the grayness of finality; the grayness turning black, so *black,* it promises relief. It promises an end to all the pain and grief and wretched *emptiness—*

No, the new voice tells me. Firmly, as if I am a child.

And I think: *perhaps I* am *one.*

Not a child. No. But a man. A man. A warrior. A Cheysuli.

And I laugh. Aloud, I shout: "How can I be a Cheysuli when I have no *lir?*"

And then I realize what they have done to me, Ceinn and the others; what they have tried to do.

And failed.

I fell. I fell down, painfully, and felt thorns clawing at my face, catching the corner of my eye; tearing. A stone was beneath my temple, pressing inexorably. I moved a little, seeking relief; found it.

Gods—I would have given myself over to death.

I lay face down in dirt and leaves and fern, nearly blind from overexertion. I had tried so hard to run both *from* my end and *to* it; to give myself over to the beast that would take my life, to relieve the pain of my loss.

Except there had been no loss. None at all: I had no *lir.*

You do now.

My breath stirred the crackling skeletons of leaves that were no longer leaves. Motes rose, danced, insinuated themselves beneath my lids. I felt sweat run down my nose, my brow, my jaw; the tears run down my cheeks.

Lir, you would do better to get up.

I felt stones beneath my hip. But I had no strength to move.

Lir.

Something cool, something damp, something impossible to ignore; it reached beneath my neck and nudged, nudged again; *pushed*—

I cannot lift you, lir . . . I am a wolf, not a man; not a warrior.

Am I?

It pushed. It *shoved*.

I rolled. Opened my eyes. Saw black nose, silver muzzle, green-gold eyes.

And *teeth*.

I lunged upward, away, *away;* then, kneeling, hunching, bent to spew the contents of my belly onto the ground.

You ran too hard. Lir, you should not have run so hard.

My belly was empty, but still it cramped. How it cramped, knotting itself like yarn from a woman's fallen spindle.

I will wait.

I clawed for my knife and found the sheath empty. I faced the wolf bare-handed.

Slay me and you slay yourself. The tone, unaccountably, gentled. *Lir—be not so witless. Have they made you deaf as well as blind?*

A wolf. Male. Silver-gray, with green-gold eyes, and a mask of deepest charcoal.

He sat down. He *sat*. And his tongue lolled out of his mouth.

"You are a—*lir?*" I croaked aloud.

I am Serri. I am yours. I have been empty so long, so long— Suddenly he rose, approached, butted his head into my shoulder before I could scramble away. *I am filled—I am* filled—*my spirit and soul are complete*—

I nearly fell over. My arms were full of wolf; my *lap* was full of wolf. So—much—*wolf*—

I am Serri, he said. *I am yours. And I am no longer empty*—

And I realized, neither was I.

"Serri?" I whispered. *"Serri?"*

There is no need to speak aloud, unless you wish it. We share the lir-bond, lir.

I laughed. Once only; I was too shocked, too utterly overcome, to blurt out anything more.

Serri?

You see? You may speak, or you may not—it no longer matters, lir.

"Serri?" This time, aloud; it was a croak, not a word, but the sound brought tears to my eyes.

Tears of joy, of disbelief; of relief and exultation. But also tears of an absolute *completion* I had known before only in a woman.

Sul'harai, Serri said. *That is what the Cheysuli call it. But do not judge it too soon.*

Apprehension lifted the hairs on the back of my neck. "Too soon?"

Too soon. You will see. It is often better than this.

"Better than *this?*"

Better. When you trade your shape for mine.

I laughed. And then I cried. And then I pulled the wolf into my arms and hugged him, *hugged* him, as I had hugged no one before.

Serri! I cried. *Oh gods—why did it take so long?*

Because it was your tahlmorra.

I hugged him harder. I hugged him until he sneezed; I laughed until he grunted.

"I am *nineteen,* Serri—am I not a bit too old?"

Your jehan *was too young, they say. You are too old, you say. But age has nothing to do with it,* lir; *it has to do with being ready.*

"And I am ready?"

For me, and for your tahlmorra.

I fell back against the ground, still hugging the wolf against my chest. I felt paws and nails digging into flesh as Serri tried to right himself; tried to regain some semblance of dignity. But I did not let him. I wrapped him more tightly yet in my arms and buried my face against the thick ruff warding throat and neck against attackers.

"Serri—"

Ihlini! The word rang a tocsin in my head. *Lir—on you—Ihlini—*

On—*me?* "Serri—"

Ihlini—Ihlini! And then he was grasping at my throat, lips peeling back from his teeth.

I thrust myself away at once, trying to ward my throat with a shaking hand. "Did Ceinn send you?" I asked. "Is this another trick?"

Ihlini—lir—Ihlini— Even as I tried to scramble away, the wolf was leaping for my throat.

My fingers caught the leather thong, and suddenly I knew.

Lillith's gift—Lillith's tooth—

I pulled the dangling tooth from beneath my clothing. "This?"

Be rid of it—be rid of it—lir, be rid of it at once!

I scraped the thong over my head. In my palm lay the curving tooth: thick at one end, capped by gold; pointed at the other. A dog's tooth, or a wolf's.

A wolf's.

"Such an insignificant thing. . . ." I said aloud.

Be rid of it, lir—at once—

I stared at the tooth. "Lillith," I said aloud. "Lillith, Alaric—*Gisella—*" And I knew what they had done.

What they had made *me* do.

My hand spasmed. Fingers shut over the tooth. Tightly, so tightly; the tooth bit into my flesh. "Oh gods— Deirdre . . . they have made me slay them all!"

Lir, be rid of the charm!

I thrust an arm against the ground and pushed, rising unsteadily. And then I hurled Lillith's gift as far as I could into the forest depths.

They have made me slay them all. Deirdre, Liam, Shea— even Ierne and the unborn child—

Oh *gods.*

I began to run again.

Lir! Serri came running behind me; running, *running,* even as I went running. *Lir—wait—*

Dead. All of them *dead.*

All the proud eagles of Erinn, proud, fierce Erinn, with its aerie upon the white chalk cliffs overlooking the Dragon's Tail.

Deirdre.

Oh—gods—*Deirdre—*

I stopped running. I stood in the sun-gilded clearing and felt the warmth upon my face as I turned it toward the sun. *Gods,* I said, *how is it that in the moment you give me the greatest gift of all, you take away another? You give me the knowledge of what I can do . . . and the knowledge of what I have done.*

Serri, beside me, lifted his head and licked my hand. *Lir, be not so bitter. What is done is done; look not to lay blame upon your platter when it was another who had the fashioning of that platter.*

The fashioning of that platter. . . . "Gisella?" I asked aloud. "No. It was Alaric who put the torch into my hand; Lillith who stood by him even as he did it."

I recalled it so well, that night upon the dome of the dragon's skull. And all the light in my eyes as I set torch to beacon-fire.

Gods. All dead.

Gisella: who had spun a web within my mind and bound me to her will.

At her own instigation? Perhaps not. Perhaps she as much as I was a puppet caught in the tangle of strings pulled by Lillith and Alaric. I thought she lacked the wits and concentration to make or carry out such plans.

And yet it had been Gisella who had ensorcelled a *lir*-less man.

A man who was *lir*less no longer.

"Serri," I said aloud, "there are things that I must learn, and I must learn them well. Things such as taking *lir*-shape. Things such as healing." I paused. "And the gift of compelling a person to do as I wish him to do."

Lir—

"And then we will go to Clankeep. And then to Homana-Mujhar."

Lir—

I looked down at the wolf, my *lir*, and knew myself complete even while I felt the emptiness of grief; the hollowness of despair. "Serri," I begged, "teach me what I must know."

Serri seemed to sigh. *It begins,* he said, *with the shapechange. . . .*

Nine

Gods—but I cannot begin to say what it is to trade human form for animal. There are no words to describe the melding of heart and mind and spirit, the perfect bonding of man and animal. I knew only that I could not comprehend how I had lived before, so empty, so insubstantial, so *unwhole;* so vague a shadow of what a man can be when he is a Cheysuli warrior.

It is a trade, the ability to put off one form and wear another. A transience unlimited by beginning and end, simply a time of *being;* when I was a wolf I was a wolf, not a man, not Niall; not even the Prince of Homana. Not even a Cheysuli. Just—a wolf, and bound by such freedom as an unblessed man cannot possibly comprehend. Not even a Cheysuli. Because even a warrior, in human form, lacks the perfection of the animal he becomes when he trades one shape for the other. Even a *Cheysuli* is less than he can be.

I began to understand. And I began to see why my race is so arrogant, so insular, so certain of their place within the tapestry of the gods. Our colors are brighter. We are the warp and weft of Homana, and all the patterns besides. Pick us from that pattern and the shape of the dream collapses. The shape of *life* collapses.

As Homana herself would collapse.

Gods, but what responsibility. And I began to understand what my father faced, trying to merge Homana and the Cheysuli. Trying to blend recalcitrant yarns into a harmonious tapestry.

I learned to think as a wolf, feel as a wolf, act as a wolf. I learned how vulnerable is a man's naked flesh; how much stronger are hide and fur. I learned sounds I had never heard, scents I had never smelled, flavors I had never tasted. I learned what it meant to be alive, *alive,* as no man can ever be until he claims a *lir.*

I learned that to be *lirless* and trapped forever in the shape of a man is a torture of the kind no Cheysuli should ever experience.

I thought of myself as I had been: *lir*less, unblessed, a shadow of a man, lacking a soul altogether.

And I thought of Rowan. And began to respect him as I had never fully respected him, knowing only I had resented him as I had resented myself, because we neither of us claimed a *lir.*

O gods, I thank you for this lir.

Serri taught me the shapechange and the responsibilities inherent in the ability. There was, he said, a matter of balance, a matter of retaining the comprehension of *self.* Without it, a man in *lir*-shape who grows too angry can also grow too careless, and he can tip the delicate balance. Tipping it, he loses himself, and slides over the edge into the madness of permanent *lir*-shape.

Because a man, he said, is a man; locked in *lir*-shape forever, he loses the thing that makes him human and becomes a beast instead.

I wondered aloud: would it be so bad to be an animal forever?

And Serri had answered that a man, born a man, was *intended* to be a man; the gods, seeing how unbalanced the scale had become, and why, would take their retribution.

And I had said: Our gods are not retributive; that is a thing of Asar-Suti, the Seker, the god of the netherworld.

And he had answered: *It is a thing of all gods, high and low, when their children go astray.*

Aye, a trade. The putting off of human form and the replacement with animal flesh and blood and bone. But where does the man-shape go when the man desires the guise of an animal? Into the earth. We vouchsafe our human forms to the power of the earth, whose magic gives us the ability to borrow the animal shape for as long as need be. We are so rooted in the earth, we Cheysuli; so intricately *rooted.*

And I wondered what it was like to be a Firstborn; to know myself foremost of all the children to come. To have power in abundance, more so than Ihlini or Cheysuli, and yet also to carry the seeds of self-destruction.

I thought of Ceinn and his fellow *a'saii*, harking back to the days of the Firstborn and desiring the power again. Their desire was not *wrong*, precisely—the prophecy, fulfilled, would give us that power again, with added stability gained from the bloodlines merged—but their method of attaining the power was. Could they not see they valued the Old Blood too much?

But zealots are too often blinded by the magnificence of their vision; while dedication can be an admirable, awesome thing, it can also be incredibly deadly. As it might have been for me.

Enough. The time for contemplation is done. "You have taught me," I told Serri, "and I have learned. Now it is time to go."

I have taught you a little, lir, and you have learned a little less. Be not so drunk upon the wine of accomplishment.

I laughed. "Drunk, am I? No, I think not. I think I am afraid . . . and I think I am angry, too. But not so angry as to forget what *little* I have learned; I have no intention of challenging all the *a'saii*. Only to ask for what is owed."

Nothing is owed *a man, lir. Unless it is the service the man himself owes to the gods and the prophecy.*

"Serri, you are sounding pompous. As for things owed— aye, a man owes service to the gods. But a man also owes respect to another man when that man has earned it."

As you have earned it?

"I have. I have gained my *lir*."

Serri sighed. *Not so much, I think, most of the time. But, then again, sometimes I think perhaps it is.*

"And *sometimes* we are in accord." I bent, tugged a charcoal-tipped ear, suggested silently we go on. It was time to go to Clankeep.

A long walk.

"Who speaks of walking when I can run?" I asked, and blurred into my *lir*-shape.

What joy it is to slip the bonds of human flesh and wear the shape of a wolf instead.

Gods, now we ran!

*   *   *

The guardsmen burst through the underbrush in a blaze of black and crimson. Horses beat the deadfall and brush aside, trampling it down even as the riders urged them forward. I saw the glitter of bared steel as the Mujharan Guard hacked their way through the forest.

Serri?

Taken by surprise—responding with the instincts of a wolf—I leaped over a fallen tree to hide behind a screen of limbs even as Serri leaped beside me.

Serri—

I am here. I am always here.

"*There!*" one of the guardsmen cried. "Did you see him? There—the white wolf—"

"And a second wolf as well," claimed another.

"But not white," said a third. "Gray or silver—I could not tell."

And then Ian, with Tasha leaping beside him, rode out of the trees to join the others. "We are not tracking *wolves,* captain. We are tracking the Prince of Homana."

Screened behind a veil of leaves and heavy fern, I saw my brother rein in by the man who had spoken first; an older man, brown-haired, with a coif of mail shrouding most of his head.

"Aye," the soldier agreed grimly, "but are we to ignore a white wolf when we see one? The plague—"

"We are not certain the plague is caused by wolves," my brother said mildly. "After all, how many white wolves can there be?"

White wolves? I *myself* was white when in *lir*-shape; it had concerned me greatly at first, for albino coloring is undesirable, signifying weakness. Albino stock is always slain; I had seen it done to an entire litter of puppies born to one of the captains' hunting bitches when I was just a child. But Serri had assured me I was *white,* not albino. My eyes were blue, not red; my hearing was unaffected. There was nothing in me of weakness.

But—plague?

I heard one of the men mutter: "There is a bounty on white wolves."

"And would you risk the plague to bring one in for a copper penny?" the nearest rider asked.

"Silver," the first retorted. "For silver, I might do it."

"Ride on," my brother said. "We are hunting a man, not a wolf; I think the Mujhar would pay more than a silver penny to the man who finds his heir."

I heard someone mutter something about a body, and realized they thought me dead. I am not a man much taken with jokes of death, real or not; at once I took back my human form and stepped out in front of them all. "But what coin for the heir if he finds himself?"

Hands went to swords and knives, then fell away. I heard startled exclamations, curses, murmurings of relief.

"*Rujho!* Gods, *rujho*, you are alive!" Ian swung a leg across his horse's neck and leaped out of the saddle, beating his way through the ferns and dangling creepers.

I met him half way and clasped his bare arms, grinning as I felt the gold beneath my fingers. "Alive," I agreed. "Ian—truly I did not mean to worry everyone. But—"

"It is enough that you are alive," he interrupted. "I am not our *jehan*—let *him* give you the reprimands."

I grimaced. Aye. No doubt he had more than one for me. "Ian—"

"Gods, we thought you were dead! We found the remains of your horse—the gear—" He shook his head. *"Rujho."*

"There was reason," I told him. "In a moment, I promise you will understand. . . ." I went from him to the captain, still mounted, and caught his horse's rein. "Captain, take word at once to the Mujhar and the Queen that I am well—*quite* well—and tell them I will be home in a few more days. There is something else I must do first."

"My lord." He stared. As if I were a spirit risen from the dead; perhaps, in a way, I was. But I had no time for such speculation when my father and mother believed I was dead.

I frowned. "Go at once, Captain. Do not tarry any longer."

He tightened his reins to turn, signaling to the others. But even as *they* turned, he hung back and drew in a deep breath. "My lord—forgive me, but . . . for a moment, I thought you were Carillon."

He was deadly serious. And he was old enough to be.

"You served him, did you not?" I pushed the horse's nose away from my face. "You knew him, then."

"I did not *know* him—not as General Rowan or others of higher rank; I was not a captain then. But aye, I served him." He smiled. He was older than I had thought, but career soldiers are often an ageless lot, become old before their youth is spent. "My lord, it has always been said of you; that you resemble the late Mujhar. But now it is doubly striking. Now that you wear a beard."

I had forgotten the beard entirely. I would have to shave it off. But—not yet. For the moment, I found I did not mind the comparison.

Carillon never had a lir. I smiled. "Go back, captain, and carry word the heir is alive. And I will be home soon."

"My lord." He spun his horse and was gone, leaving broken vines and bracken in his wake.

I turned to Ian. "I swear, I intended no one to worry."

"They did. We *all* did. Gods, *rujho*, what do you *expect?* I saw what your temper was before you disappeared; for all I knew, you had sought the death-ritual."

I shrugged. "I did."

Ian's face was taut. "Once we found the horse, I thought a beast had taken you."

"One did," I said grimly. "A Cheysuli beast called Ceinn."

"Ceinn!" Ian stared. "What has Ceinn to do with this?"

"What has Ceinn to do with *anything?*" I asked bitterly. "He very nearly had his heart's desire, *rujho*—Niall dead, and only Ian left to accept the Lion Throne."

"Rujho—"

"It is the truth," I told him gently. "And when we see him, you may ask him."

The first shock of my appearance had worn off. Now Ian looked more closely than he had before. I saw him begin to frown.

"The beard," I told him.

"No—well, aye, but not *only* the beard. There is more. You are—harder."

"Grown up," I told him. "Aye, a little." I bent down on one knee to greet Tasha as she glided through the trampled fern. She purred, butting her head beneath my jaw in her customary greeting. "Still the lovely girl," I told her warmly. "If Ian ever grows weary of you, you may come to me."

Ian grunted eloquent dissent.

"Oh, aye, I know. You would not weary of her anymore than I would weary of Serri." I grinned. "Would you care to meet my *lir?*"

Before he could answer, I summoned Serri through the link. And when the wolf came, eyes slitted against the sunlight, I turned to watch my brother's reaction.

He stood incredibly still for a long moment. And then, slowly, he knelt down amidst the tangle of deadfall, brush and bracken. "Oh wolf," he whispered, "*leijhana tu'sai—leijhana tu'sai* for making my *rujholli* whole. . . ." And put a shaking hand against Serri's lovely head.

A moment later, almost awkwardly, he rose and turned to face me squarely. "How could I not have seen it? How could I not have known?"

"How *could* you have known, Ian? I did not know myself."

He shook his head. "I myself have been *lir*-sick. I know what the craving is, the emptiness that drives a boy out into the forest to find his *lir*. I have seen it before; I have *felt* it before . . . *rujho*, I should have known."

"Well enough, I curse you for it." I spoke the weakest one I could think of. "Now, shall we go on to Clankeep? I have business there with Ceinn and the other *a'saii*."

He looked troubled. "Perhaps the *a'saii* might wait."

"Perhaps not," I suggested. "I would prefer to settle the question of my worthiness once and for all. I think now the clans might accept me willingly."

"*They* might," Ian agreed grimly, "but what of the Homanan zealots? Your blood at last asserts itself; your magic is no longer 'hidden.' It will give them further cause for alarm and outcry."

"But it will not give them the Lion."

He caught my arm as I turned to go. "It *might*," he said flatly. "Niall, have you forgotten how to count? You were in Erinn and Atvia for more than a year. And then, barely home again, you disappear for another month. You have given the Homanan rebels every opportunity to gain a foothold in this battle for the Lion."

"Carillon's bastard," I said grimly.

"*Aye,* Carillon's bastard." He glared. "Niall, he has begun to gather an army."

"The *bastard?*" It was my turn to stare in disbelief. "How can he do that?"

Ian shrugged. "How not? He wants to take the throne."

"But—our father is Mujhar."

My brother sighed a little. "The cost of growing up in a realm at peace is complacency, I see—or, perhaps, ignorance. Have you no comprehension of politics?"

"Do you?"

"Some," he said shortly. "Cheysuli or no, I understand what this means. As *you* should. . . ." He shook his head. "Even now he gathers an army as well as public opinion in his favor—"

"—and when he has enough of both, he can petition the Homanan Council for a change in the succession." I nodded, pleased to see the surprise in Ian's eyes; he had expected me to understand nothing at all. "And, of course, the Council, led by our father, will decline the petition—"

"—which will open the road to civil war," Ian finished. "It is no idle threat, Niall; no unlikely happenstance. And you forget something else: the Council is made up of Homanans. All of them served under Carillon; our *jehan* has appointed no one, except for Rowan, and even *he* might prefer Carillon's son as opposed to Carillon's grandson."

"Rowan?"

Ian shrugged. "Perhaps. Who can say for certain? When you look at the petition closely, you will see there are possibilities for its approval. He *is* Carillon's son, and therefore a part of the prophecy."

"But he is not Cheysuli."

Ian did not smile. "Let us say the Homanans are less impressed with the need to fulfill the prophecy than the Cheysuli are, Niall. But let us say also there are those on the Council who *do* desire to see the prophecy fulfilled . . . how better to lay proper claim to the Lion than to wed the claimant to a woman with the necessary bloodlines?"

"Cheysuli," I blurted. "But who would agree to such a thing? *I* am the rightful heir!"

"Gisella might," he said evenly. "With you dead, why should she decline the chance to be Queen of Homana? The title was promised her at birth the moment her gender was known."

It shook me, as he intended it to. Aye, Gisella might.

And the gods knew she had the proper blood; it was why *I* had had to wed her.

"Gisella!" I said bitterly. "Gods, but I wish she had *died* in her mother's fall!"

"Niall!" Again, Ian caught my arm. "Niall—by the gods, you *know*—"

"That she ensorcelled me? Aye, I know—I knew the moment I gained my *lir*. Whatever spell she wove must have had Ihlini origins, not Cheysuli. I remembered it all once I had linked with Serri." And then all the pain and grief welled up again. "Oh gods—Ian . . . *what they made me do*—"

"I know." He caught me in a compassionate embrace. "Oh *rujho*, I know . . . they made me watch as you lit the fire."

"*All* of them," I cried. "All the eagles in the aerie—" I hugged him as I never had before, never having required it so badly before. "Gods, they made me give the order to slay Liam—Shea—*Deirdre*—"

He heard the change in my tone as I said her name; the pain, the anguish, the grief. "Deirdre," he echoed, mostly to himself, and it intensified the pain to hear him say her name.

Oh—gods—Deirdre—

I sank down to kneel in the trampled grass and ferns. "They made me murder *Deirdre*."

Silently he knelt down on one knee and caught the back of my neck with a single hand, forcing me to look into his face. "*Rujho*," he said, "if you loved her that much, I am truly sorry."

It shocked me, even in my grief. "*You* speak of love?"

"Why not? It exists, no matter what the customs say. Do you think there is no love between our *jehan* and his *cheysula*?"

"*Is* there?"

"Of course. I see them differently, *rujho*, because they allow me to. Or—" smiling a little, he shrugged "—perhaps they do *not* allow it, and yet I see it. But be certain it exists."

"There was Sorcha first. *Your* mother."

"Aye. But she died many years ago, and there is no law that says a warrior may not love another woman."

I saw Deirdre in the distance. "Not I," I said remotely. "By the *gods*, not I . . . I will never love Gisella."

After a moment, he sighed. "No," he agreed. "No, I think not. I think no man will ever love Gisella . . . except, perhaps, her *jehan*."

"Alaric?"

"Aye. You were too bedazzled by what the girl had done to you—but aye, Alaric loves her. And I think he does not forgive himself for being the man who made her the way she is."

"Compassion for the enemy?"

"Compassion for the *jehan*." He clasped my neck briefly and pulled my head against one shoulder in a brotherly gesture of affection, then tousled my hair as he rose. "Perhaps you have the right of it *rujho*. I think we should go to Clankeep."

I stood up. "After telling me we should not?"

"There is something left for you to do." He grinned, and then he laughed aloud. "After all these years, have you forgotten the *lir*-gold? It is your right to wear it, now."

My right. I looked down at Serri, waiting beside my left leg. Lir-*gold, Serri!*

It is *your right to wear it.*

I laughed. "Aye! It is!" I caught Ian's neck and hugged him awkwardly, nearly jerking him off his feet. "Aye, *rujho*, let us go and get my gold!"

Frowning a little, he felt at the lobe that bore the cat-shaped earring. "We have only one mount, and you are too heavy for my horse to carry both of us. There are times he wants nothing to do with *me*."

"Who speaks of riding, *rujho*?" And as he watched be-musedly, I blurred into my *lir*-shape.

As I ran, I heard him curse, because he had a horse. Because, like me, he wanted to go in *lir*-shape.

And I laughed, because there is not a Cheysuli alive who prefers a horse when he has another form to serve him.

Gods—what freedom there is in lir-*shape—*

Ten

I took back my human form at the gates of Clankeep and turned to watch Ian come up on his stallion. Beside him ran Tasha, sleek and sinuous in the sunlight, chestnut coat burnished bronze. Serri warded my left leg, pressing a shoulder against my knee; through the *lir*-link, I sensed his insecurity.

A lir? I asked in surprise.

In my place, how would you feel? he returned. *Clankeep is a place of many people, many* lir . . . *and I have known none of them.*

It was amazing insight into how a *lir* felt about things. All too often it was easier simply to believe them above us all, closer to the gods, and yet Serri's defensive tone reminded me of myself when faced with a thing I could not fully understand.

Was it the same for Tasha?

Serri peered around my knee as the mountain cat came to join us. *The same for us all, when the link is first made. We are not so different from men.*

I would have disagreed, verbally or otherwise, but Ian jumped off his horse and called out in the Old Tongue for the warriors guarding the entrance to open the gates for us.

I waved away drifting dust, then stepped back as the wooden gates swung open. Once, I had been told, there was no need for gates to shut the Cheysuli in. But the time had come to shut the enemy *out*, and the gates had become traditional. More and more, Clankeep reminded me of Mujhara.

Ian, leading his fractious stallion, fell into step, beside me. "We will go to the *shar tahl*. It is for him to make the arrangements for the Ceremony of Honors."

I felt a shiver of pride and excitement lift the flesh on

my bones. *Ceremony of Honors* . . . and at last I would wear the gold.

But even as we walked away from the gates, one of the warriors called us back. "The *shar tahl* is not at his pavilion, Ian. He is with Rylan, and the Mujhar is with them both."

"Jehan?" Frowning, Ian glanced at me sharply. "Something serious, I think . . . what else would bring him out of Mujhara *now?"*

I thought the emphasis strange, and said so. But Ian, walking fast enough to pull the stallion into a trot, merely shook his head. "I will let him explain . . . no doubt he has much to say to you. *Rujho*—hurry."

And so I stretched out my longer legs and moved ahead of him entirely, which afforded me the chance to tell *him* to hurry. But Ian was too preoccupied to be amused.

Serri?

I cannot say, lir. *I am new to the politics of Homana.*

Then what does Tasha tell you?

Only that her lir *is very worried. It has to do with Ihlini, the plague, the bastard . . . there is much he concerns himself with. Much.*

Grimly, I agreed. *Ian is better suited to politics than I. He understands them better.*

We wound our way through clustered pavilions, dodging the black-haired children who played some game in the trees and knee-high bracken, spilling out into the beaten earth of the walkways. Woodsmoke smudged the skyline; I smelled oak, ash, a hint of fresh-cut cedar. But mostly I smelled the meat. Bear, I thought; someone roasted a bear. And it made me think of Ceinn.

"Ian." I intended to address the problem of the *a'saii,* but he was calling out to one of the running children; a boy, who swerved away from the game and trotted over.

"Blaine, will you do me the favor of taking my horse to my pavilion? I have business with the clan-leader."

"Aye." Blaine reached out for the reins. "Did you know the Mujhar is here?"

"Aye. *Leijhana tu'sai.*" Relieved of his horse, Ian nearly ran.

Worried, Serri told me.

That I can see for myself.

"Here," Ian stopped before a green pavilion bearing a

silver-painted fox half hidden in its folds, hardly noticing as Tasha threw herself down on a rug beside the doorflap. Lorn was there as well, blinking sleepily in the sunlight. Golden Taj perched upon the ridgepole. And the brown fox curling next to Lorn moved over to offer Tasha room. I did not know his name, only that he was Rylan's *lir*.

So little time have I spent here that I know too little of my clan, I reflected guiltily. *It is no wonder there are warriors who prefer to see Ian in my place. I think Ian knows everyone.*

My brother scratched at the doorflap and identified himself. A moment later the clan-leader himself pulled the folds aside; when he saw me he opened his mouth to speak, then shut it sharply. I saw the flicker of surprise in his eyes; I was the last man he had expected to see, and in such a guise as this.

And then he smiled. "You had best go straight to the Mujhar, Niall. He is with Isolde, walking the wall path."

"Go," Ian told me. "It is important he knows you are alive. I will stay here with Rylan and the *shar tahl* to speak of the arrangements."

"Wait!" I swung down the pouch from my shoulder and pulled wide the thong-snugged mouth. Reaching inside, I caught the heavy belt I had worn at the wedding and pulled most of it free of the pouch. "Gold," I told the clan-leader. "Cheysuli gold, made by a master's hands. I would wear it again, but in the proper shapes."

Rylan looked at the wolf who stood so close to my side. I saw him begin to smile.

Ian took the pouch and stuffed the belt inside it once again. "*Rujho*, go. I will see to the gold." But even as I turned, he caught my upper arm. "There is also *i'toshaa-ni*," he said seriously. "All will be explained, but you must prepare yourself."

"Will *you* be the one to explain it?"

He grinned, suddenly young again in the time before he had learned so much of responsibility, and the concern in his face was banished. "If that is what you wish."

"I wish." And then I was gone, running after my father, with Serri running at my side.

The wall path . . . Rylan meant the footpath that edged the green-gray wall surrounding Clankeep. It reminded me a little of the sentry-walks atop the battlements of a castle, ringing the parapets, but there was nothing of castles about a Cheysuli Keep. Only a wall, curving through the trees like a granite serpent, lacking merlons and crenels, showing only an undulating line of piled stone, unmortared, but sealed with moss and ivy. The vines threaded their way up lichened flanks and clung tenaciously, setting roots and questing fingers into cracks and crevices. Trees from the other side sent reconnaissance patrols across over the wall and down, breaching Cheysuli security. Mistletoe clustered in crotches. Columbine twined the boughs and mantled the top of the wall.

I saw them ahead of me. Isolde sat on a shattered tree stump with head bowed and all her thick hair hanging around her face. I could not see her expression. Then she cried, I knew; one hand was pressed to her face and I could see how her shoulders trembled.

My father stood over her, one hand placed upon the crown of her head. And then the other; he squatted down so he could look into her face, and I saw how gently he smoothed the hair back behind her ears.

I could not hear what he said. But I saw 'Solde lean forward, hug him awkwardly, then rise and hasten away. My father remained squatting by the stump a moment, head bowed, as if he felt a measure of his daughter's pain. And then, as I slowed from a run to a walk, he rose and turned toward me.

And *recoiled.* "Carillon—" he blurted.

I stopped walking. I stood in the middle of the footpath quite alone; Serri had paused along the way to make the acquaintance of a coney too far from his burrow. My first instinct was to resent the mistaken identity; once, I would have, but now I could not. I was too shocked. Though others often did, never had my father even remarked upon the resemblance. Never had he so much as likened me to my grandsire. *Certainly* he had never looked at me and called me by Carillon's name. Not even by mistake.

And it was not a mistake now. Because, for that instant, he believed I *was.*

It passed. It passed quickly. I saw the shock turn to startled recognition, and then the color was back in his face. But he did not move at once. We faced each other, my

father and I, across an acre of ground that was only the
length of a man.

"No," I said finally. "Niall."

"I know." His tone was odd. "I—know. Forgive me."

I shrugged. "It is nothing."

"It is *something*. Do you think I do not know?"

I started to answer, to dismiss the common mistake, but
his raised hand silenced me. "There are many things to be
said, not the least of which is to note you are alive when
everyone else believes you are *dead*, but even that will wait.
There is something else. Something I should have told you
long ago."

He sighed. And then he sat down on the stump Isolde
had vacated and sighed again, as if searching for the proper
words. "He was an incredibly courageous man. An incredibly *strong* man, and I do not speak of the physical, though
there was that as well. No. I speak of spirit, of dedication,
of the willingness to shoulder burdens far beyond the ken
of most men." He reached down, plucked a jointed blade of
grass from the ground, began to tear it apart. "After Tynstar stole his youth and gave him the disease, he lost much
of his remarkable strength. But none of the dedication.
None of the willingness to take on so many burdens. Because it was his duty. Because it was his *tahlmorra*."

He looked up at me; I nodded and he went on. "Every
day I looked at him, seeing how he drove himself to make
Homana whole—seeing how he drove himself to serve a
prophecy not even of his people, and I wondered. I wondered: *how will I ever be able to take the Lion from this
man? How will I ever be able to carry on the things he
has begun?*"

I stared at his hands. I watched him shred the stalk of
grass, and then I saw him spill the pieces through his fingers
as easily as now he spilled the self-doubts of his youth.

"He told me: *be Donal*. He told me: *you should not judge
yourself by others*. But, of course, I did. Even as you do now."

"I hate him," I said hollowly. "I hate a dead man, *jehan*."

"But mostly you hate yourself."

I sat down awkwardly in the middle of the footpath because I could no longer stand in the face of the realization.
"Aye," I said on rushing breath. "Oh, *jehan* . . . I have."

"Be Niall," he said gently. "Do not judge yourself by others."

I laughed. I heard the sound cut through arching boughs like a scythe through summer grass. "And when Carillon told you that, *jehan,* did it mean anything to you?"

My father did not smile. "It meant something that he said it."

Abashed, I looked at the dirt between my deerhide boots. "Aye. Aye, *jehan*, it does."

"He left me a legacy. He left me the knowledge I had nothing to be ashamed of; that I would do the best I could do, no matter what the odds. And I have." He smiled a little. "Oh, aye. There are people who will disagree; people who claim I serve only my own self-interests, but I try to serve Homana. Homana and the Cheysuli." I saw the smile begin to widen. "I think only as I watch my own children wrestle with the power of adulthood do I come to understand that I am not a failure. That I am not a bad Mujhar. And the day will dawn when *you* come to know the same about the Mujhar who follows Donal."

"The Lion of Homana." I shook my head. "I think what disturbs me most, now that I begin to see it more clearly, is that they have been so unfair to you. Always it is Carillon. Even from my *jehana.* It is so easy for everyone to see *him* when they look at me. And yet—they overlook that it was *you* who sired me. It is thoughts and memories of *you* I should invoke."

He laughed a little, showing the face I knew better as Ian's, albeit older than my brother's. "Aye. It brightens a man's pride to hear the son compared to him—when the comparison is *favorable.*" He nodded. "But I think the dye has been set, Niall. It is Ian who reminds them of me, and you who reminds them of Carillon."

I grimaced wryly. "Well, I think it no longer matters. I think—"

"—*I* think it is time we spoke of business and set aside self-examinations." He rose, stepped to me and caught my arm as I raised it. "I will not belabor it, Niall. You should never have left as you did."

I was up, brushing at my breeches. "No, but—"

"I want no excuses; what is done is done. But I expect you to accept more responsibility in the future."

"*Jehan*—"

"We are at war, Niall," he said plainly, as if I could not understand. "Strahan raises an army in Solinde. And so does the bastard, here." He sighed and scraped the hair back from his face, leaving it bare and bleak. "Everyone thought you dead. And so I had to contend with a Homanan Council who bestirred themselves to consider the possibility of naming the bastard to your place—they would sooner have *Carillon's* bastard in place of mine—and a *Cheysuli* Clan Council who spoke of Ian as your successor, citing the prophecy." He shut his eyes a moment. "Gods, I feel like I have been juggling unbalanced knives . . . Aislinn sick to death with worry—this plague that begins to spread—trying to placate hostile councils—and, of course, there is Strahan. Gods, there is always Strahan."

Abruptly he turned away, showing only his back to me. His hands were on his hips, head bowed; he looked more disgusted than anything else, but I thought perhaps he was only weary. Weary of all the burdens Carillon had bequeathed to him.

And that he will bequeath to me.

"Niall." He turned back. "There is yet another thing. Perhaps the *most* important—the gods know it turned the councils upside down." He smiled. "Suddenly they could no longer speak of which bastard would inherit, but who to name as regent for the Prince of Homana's heir."

"The Prince of Homana's—*heir?*" I stared. "Gisella bore the *child?* A *son?*"

"Two," he said succinctly.

"*Two?*"

"Both boys." He grinned. "And so I am made a grandsire."

"Both boys," I echoed in a whisper. "By the gods, I have an *heir.*" And then I looked at him more sharply. "Gisella?"

His grin faded. "She is well . . . but no different from before."

"No," I agreed grimly, "it is a permanent affliction." And then, unable to dwell on Gisella in the face of such news, I began to smile again. "Two boys! How will I ever tell them apart?"

"It is possible even now. But I will let you see for your-

self." He reached out and clasped my arm. "No more de-
lays, Niall. We must go back to Homana-Mujhar."

"No—*jehan.* . . ." I thought of the two boys at Homana-
Mujhar, and the choice suddenly became much harder.
Gods, what do I do?

"No?" my father asked in amazement. *"No?"*

Torn, I tried to pull away. "I—cannot. Not yet."

"Cannot." He swung me around to face him. "Niall, my
patience is wearing thin."

"So was mine!" I cried. "Why do you think I left Mujhara? Because I *could not wait* any longer!"

"Niall, I cannot express to you how precarious is our
position at the moment . . . nor my surprise that you can
so easily dismiss two newborn sons."

"I do not *dismiss*," I said curtly. "Gods, *jehan*, I could not.
But—I need to stay. I must. There is a thing I have to do—"

"What *thing* is more important than the security of your
claim to the Lion Throne?" He was angry, very angry; I
wanted to look away and could not. "Do you understand
what I have told you, Niall? As Strahan assembles another
army in Solinde, the bastard assembles one *here*. There is
plague all through the north, creeping down even now from
the Wastes into the rest of Homana. And you have the
audacity to tell me you *cannot come to Homana-Mujhar?"*

My answer was to summon Serri to me. I heard his response within the link, and even as I turned the wolf came
running, *running* to meet me. His ears lay back along his
skull and his mouth gaped open, allowing the tongue to
loll. The black-smudged tail stood out behind him like a
pennon in the wind. How he ran, my magnificent *lir*; how
he ran to answer my call.

I dropped to one knee and caught him in my arms. He
snugged his muzzle against my neck and muttered into my
flesh and beard, forgoing the link to express his feelings
aloud. And then I twisted my head to look up at my astonished father. "I left because I had to. I had to find my *lir*.
And now I stay because I have to, so I can be fully acknowledged a warrior—a *Cheysuli*—before my clan."

He said nothing. He did not have to. All the world was
in his eyes.

"Jehan—"

"Three days," he said quietly. *"I'toshaa-ni*, for the

cleansing, and then the Ceremony of Honors." He swallowed heavily. "For this, I can give you three days. I wish I could give you three years."

And then he walked away.

But not before I saw the tears of pride and thankfulness in his eyes.

Eleven

I'toshaa-ni.

It is a mystery to most men because the Cheysuli keep it that way, desiring no profanation. It has always been a mystery to me, not because I am not Cheysuli, but because it is a highly personal thing, an expression of the intense need for the cleansing of flesh, spirit, mind, heart, and soul.

For Ian, the need had come upon him twice: once, during the rituals associated with the Ceremony of Honors; again, when he had been so soiled by Lillith's Ihlini sorcery. He did not speak of his experiences to me, saying only that I would be born out of smoke and sweat and pain to be a man again, new-made, as no other man can be. Certainly not a Homanan.

At dawn, I went out of Clankeep into the forest. There I painstakingly built a shelter out of saplings, binding them with vines and sealing the cracks with leaves until the shelter was a hummock against the ground, closed to the world save for the tiny entrance.

I took stones from the ground and built a fire cairn in the center of the shelter. And when it was made I lighted a fire and fed it with herbs the *shar tahl* had given me. The smoke made me cough. The stench made my eyes water.

I shaved. Bare-faced, I stripped. My clothing I left in a pile outside the door; naked, *lir*less, alone, I sat down beside the fire and let the smoke form a shroud around my body.

I waited.

When at last the sweat ran down my flesh and the tears ran out of my eyes, I began to see a reason for the ritual of cleansing. For three days I would fast, until there was nothing left in my body; until the sweat cleansed the impu-

rities from my flesh; until I was a new-made man, lacking
the soil of the former life.

*I dreamed of Carillon. Though I remained in the shelter
I had built, a part of me broke free. It left behind the shelter
and the fasting and the smoke and went elsewhere, to
Homana-Mujhar; to the Great Hall, where I sat in the Lion
Throne. I stared down the length of the empty hall and saw
it was not empty at all; that a man approached, and I
knew him.*

Carillon.

*I knew it was him, though I had never seen him. Because
he looked like me.*

*He was—old. Though he stood rigidly straight, I saw how
his shoulders hunched a little; how his spine seemed to pain
him. And I saw the hands, so twisted, so wracked, so ruined.
But mostly I saw the spirit of the man, because its intensity
was such that it set the hall ablaze.*

*"Grandsire," I said. "You are dead. How can you come
to me?"*

*"I come to you because I am a part of you, as I am a
part of your mother, your sons, the children yet to come. I
am in them as much as I am in you, and so it will ever be.
You can rid yourself of me no more than you can shed your
flesh and become another man."*

*"Not another man," I agreed, "but an animal. I am Chey-
suli, grandsire."*

*"And in animal form, do you become someone who is
not Niall?"*

*I frowned at him. "No, grandsire—of course not. I am
still myself."*

*He smiled. And then the shadows swallowed him, and I
was back in my smoky shelter.*

On the second day, naked, *lir*less, alone, with only a
snare and a knife to my name, I caught and slew a young
ruddy-colored wolf. He fought his death. He fought me. He
left weals upon my flesh and anguish in my heart, thinking
of Serri, but I slew him. And then I bathed in the blood
and ate the still-warm heart, to vanquish that portion of
myself that might be suborned by the freedom of the *lir*-
shape.

*　　*　　*

*I dreamed of Ceinn. He stood before me as I sat upon
the Lion Throne of Homana and told me to get out of it;
that I was unworthy because I lacked the lir-gifts; because I
was not a proper Cheysuli. He told me I was forgotten by
the gods and therefore no part of the prophecy; my abdication would be a blessing to all the folk of Homana, Cheysuli
and Homanan alike.*

*I listened. I waited. And when he was done reciting the
things the* shar tahls *had told him since birth, even as they
had told me, I rose and stepped away from the Lion, relinquishing the throne. I gave it over to Ceinn willingly. And
as he stepped forward, intent on claiming it himself, I saw
the wooden lion's head move.*

*The jaws widened, waiting. I tried to cry out, to tell him
no; to say the Lion would swallow him—but he did not
hear; he did not choose to hear. And so as Ceinn sat down
upon the Lion Throne of Homana, the gaping jaws closed
over his skull and crushed it.*

On the third day I bathed in an isolated pool and washed
the blood from my flesh. With handfuls of sand I scoured
the grime and smoke-stench from my body, raising blood
into the wolf-wounds, and then I washed it off with clean,
cool water. And at last, clean within and without, I put on
the fresh leathers someone had left outside the shelter and
went back to Clankeep a newmade man, born again of
i'toshaa-ni.

In the center of the clan pavilion, I knelt on the hide of
a spotted mountain cat. Around me sat ranks of warriors
and their women—not all of them, because the pavilion
was no longer large enough—but those members of Clan
Council, the ruling body of the Cheysuli.

Once, it was believed there was only a single clan remaining in all of Homana, because of Shaine's *qu'mahlin.*
My royal Homanan ancestor had done his best to rid the
realm of every Cheysuli by ordering all of them slain. The
qu'mahlin had failed, thank the gods, but only after thirty
years of methodical elimination. And mostly because Carillon had stopped it once he had reclaimed the Lion Throne
from Bellam of Solinde. In those days an entire clan would

have filled only half of the pavilion; now most of the people had to remain outside.

It was evening. Only the fire in the cairn before me lighted the pavilion, throwing odd illumination over the faces of the warriors and the women. Looking at them, I thought of the days of the Firstborn, when all men and women of the clans claimed the ability to assume *lir*-shape. But because we had become so blood-bred, so isolated in our insularity and arrogance, the gifts had begun to weaken. Only through the fulfillment of the prophecy would we reclaim the power that we once took for granted.

So many faces. Nearly all of them characteristically dark, angular, polished bronze by the sun of Homana. Black hair, yellow eyes, so much gold in ears, at throats, on arms and hips and wrists. So much *strength*; why was it the people of other realms desired to break that strength?

Why did the *Homanans* desire it?

Not all, Serri said. *Many, still, because it is natural for the earth magic to frighten those who do not claim it, do not know it . . . but not all. Carillon began the change in common- opinion. Donal furthers it. And you will further it even more.*

He lay beside me on the edges of the pelt. I moved hand from lap and buried it in Serri's lush pelt. In so short a time he had become my world, my other *self;* I wondered how I had managed to live before we had found one another. How I had functioned without my *lir.*

Much of the ceremony had already been concluded. But there remained the most important part: the bestowing of the *lir*-gold to signify I was a warrior of the clan, a man grown, a Cheysuli in place of a *lir*less, soulless boy.

Rylan himself sat before me on the other side of the cairn. The firelight made his face a mask of black and bronze, stark in the harsh shadows, but smiling. And as he smiled, he spoke.

"Before all the old gods of the Cheysuli, I as clan-leader bear witness that you have sought and found a lir *according to the customs of our people. That you and the* lir *have linked as a* lir *and warrior must* link, *to make the magic whole. And I bear witness that through this link the* lir *has accepted you in heart and soul and mind as well as spirit, as you have accepted him."*

He waited. I inclined my head in affirmation.

"The lir-*bond is for life. While you live, the* lir *lives. But should your life be taken from you within the natural life-span of the* lir, *regardless of the manner, the* lir *shall be released from the bond to return to the freedom of the forests, no longer bound to the body that once was a Cheysuli warrior."*

Again, I nodded.

"Should the lir *die in battle or in sickness or by other unknown causes, you will be made soulless, empty, unwhole, and you will give up your name as a Cheysuli warrior to seek an ending however you may find it, in the death-ritual of the clan, unarmed and alone among the beasts of the forests."*

I had tasted *lir*lessness once already. I did not hesitate to accept the consequences.

Rylan's eyes held mine steadily. "For you, I must be very clear: the *lir*-bond requires payment, even from those who rule. You will be two men, warrior and Mujhar, but the bond will constrain you still. Should Serri die, my lord, you will be required to renounce the Lion and go alone among the beasts."

I thought suddenly of Duncan, my other grandsire, who had not ruled because he had helped to win Carillon the Lion. He had been clan-leader even as Rylan was, required to perform the rituals of the Ceremony of Honors as Rylan did now for me. Aye, I thought of Duncan, my long-dead grandsire, who had lost a *lir* and lost his life, giving it over willingly even though he also gave up the leadership of the Cheysuli.

And I thought of my father, who, too young, had accepted the responsibilities of the *lir*-bond before he had known he would be Mujhar.

And I thought: *It is not a thing done lightly.*

No, Serri agreed, *and no man will force you to it.*

I drew in a deep breath and nodded to Rylan. *"y'Ja'hai,* clan-leader. *Ja'hai-na."* I nodded again. "I accept. The price is willingly accepted."

"Ru'shalla-tu," he said quietly. *May it be so.* Quietly he moved aside and made way for the *shar tahl*, who carried a roll of bleached-white deerskin in his arms. He was Arlen; not young, not old, but the most high of all the clan mem-

bers, being a man totally dedicated to serving the prophecy and the histories of the Cheysuli.

Arlen knelt before the cairn and carefully unrolled the deerskin, making certain it did not wrinkle or tangle itself. Hands smoothed it efficiently; he must have done this so many times, too many times, and yet he made no indication he was weary of the task. He merely did it. And by doing it, he made me a place in my clan.

"One day a man of all blood shall unite, in peace, four warring realms and two magic races." A finger touched the rune-signs painted on the supple hide. "Already we begin to approach completion, the fulfillment of the prophecy of the Firstborn, *so:*" He touched a faded green rune. "Here is *Hale*, liege man to Shaine the Mujhar, and *jehan* to a daughter got on Shaine's Homanan daughter."

Arlen glanced briefly at me, as if to be certain I followed him; I did. I could not take my eyes from the finger that so carefully showed me my heritage.

He touched another rune, this one red, of a different shape. "Here is *Duncan*, born of the line of the Old Mujhars, in the days before we gave the Lion to the Homanans. Here is *Carillon*, born of Shaine's brother, *harani* to the Mujhar, and who took back the Lion from the enemy." The finger moved yet again. "And here is *Alix*, daughter of Hale and Lindir, who bore a son to Duncan: *Donal*, who accepted the Lion from Carillon, and who sired a son on Carillon's half-Solindish daughter."

The finger stopped on a bright blue rune. There were none under it, only a blank space waiting for the name of my newborn sons.

But Arlen looked at me. "And here is *Niall*, son of Aislinn and Donal, who shall inherit the Lion from his *jehan* and name a son to inherit it from him."

I smiled. "Brennan," I told the *shar tahl*. "There is a son already born; I shall call him Brennan. And beside him, Hart. Liege man if he chooses; *rujholli*, companion, *kinspirit*—they were born in a single labor of Gisella of Atvia, daughter to Alaric and Donal's *rujholla*, Bronwyn."

Arlen inclined his head briefly to acknowledge the furthering of the succession, then re-rolled the deerskin and moved back to his place in the front ranking of warriors and women.

It was Rylan's turn once more. "There is now the bestowing of the *lir*-gold upon the newborn warrior. It is customary for the warrior to choose a *shu'maii*, a sponsor, from among his fellow warriors. It is the task of the *shu'maii* to pierce the lobe and place the earring in it, as well as placing the bands upon the arms. It is a mark of respect from warrior to *shu'maii* to ask; it is acknowledgment from *shu'maii* to warrior before Clan Council and others of the clan that he accepts the responsibilities of a bond almost as binding as that of the *lir* or a liege man. That he honors the newborn warrior with all the honor of his heritage as a Cheysuli born of the clan and all its traditions."

He said nothing more, having explained the final task that faced me. Like the others, he waited for my decision.

I looked at the empty place in the ranks ringing me. Empty because my father had returned to Homana-Mujhar, unable to remain even for my Ceremony of Honors. I would have named him as my *shu'maii*, naming his name with great pride, but he had gone, and I could not say the name of a man who did not exist in the moment of my birth.

I looked at my brother, sitting beside the empty place, and saw how he waited with eyes downcast. He was the natural choice, I knew, and certainly the most appropriate. But Ian was already pledged to me.

And so I looked at Rylan. "I name the name of Ceinn."

I heard a woman gasp: Isolde. And I heard the low-voiced murmurings of the men.

It was to my brother I looked first, to see if I had hurt him. Perhaps I had, but he did not show it to me. He merely smiled a tiny smile, as if I had done a thing that surprised him with its shrewdness but also met with belated understanding. He smiled, did my brother, and I knew I had chosen well.

"Ceinn," Rylan said. "Do you accept the honor offered?"

His face was a mask to me, but his eyes were not. From out of the mask they stared, hard and cold and yellow, and in their depths blazed the flame of fanaticism. Oh, aye, he would accept. In the face of his dedication to clan and custom, he could not do otherwise.

"Ja'hai-na," he said only, and rose to make his way through the others to the cairn. He sat down on my right side; Serri was at my left.

Rylan accepted the leather pouch offered him by another warrior. From it he took a silver awl and handed it to Ceinn. Firelight glinted off the silver. The point was ground quite fine, but I knew it would hurt regardless.

I pushed the hair behind my ear and faced Ceinn, kneeling. Saying nothing, he pinched and pulled down my left earlobe, stretching it thin, then pressed the awl against the flesh. I set my teeth; the point slid in, beyond . . . I felt Ceinn twist it into my flesh, until I heard the pop of completion. He withdrew the awl and put out his hand; into his palm Rylan set the golden earring.

Wolf-shaped, of course; a small wolf born of incredible skill, showing face and paws and tail. From its back rose the curving prong. Ceinn shut his fingers on the wolf and pushed the prong through the hole he had made; hooked the tip into the loop with a deft twist. I heard the tiny snap and knew the thing was done.

My earlobe stung. The weight of the gold set up an ache I found bearable regardless of its irritation: I was very nearly a warrior.

Rylan set the heavy armbands into Ceinn's waiting hands. The mask was shown me again; such a hard, cold mask, expressing bleak acknowledgment that what he did made a pledge that could not be broken; his time with the *a'saii* was done, even if he preferred otherwise. He would not, *could* not break the bond, ·or forswear the traditions that bound him of all men so very tightly.

The armbands clinked together as Ceinn brought them closer to me. Such massive, magnificent things, full of runes braided one into the other, tangling cheek-by-jowl all the way around at top and bottom edge. And in the center of each, flowing around the curves, was the shape of a running wolf, fluid in the metal, as if he would leap out of the gold and into the midst of us all.

Gods—how beautiful is my lir—

Ceinn slipped one over my left wrist and slid it up until it went over my elbow and was snugged against muscles. Then the other on my right, holding my wrist as he settled the band into place. Again, he snugged it, and I saw the rich flash of his own gold in the firelight as he made me a man before the others.

"Leijhana tu'sai," I said quietly. And I meant it.

His lips thinned. *"Cheysuli i'halla shansu."* But I knew the *last* thing he intended me was Cheysuli peace.

And yet he could do nothing about it.

I swallowed heavily. I had no wish to show what I felt to the others. And yet I could not help but show it to Ceinn; he was too close, too intent. He could not help but see how moved I was. And I saw him begin to frown.

Rylan's voice broke the moment, and then made it more poignant yet. *"Ja'hai-na,"* he said simply. "By the clan, by the gods, by the *lir*, the warrior is accepted."

It was for Ceinn, the *shu'maii*, to begin the welcomings. I waited, and when he rose he also pulled me up, clasping my arms above the *lir*-bands to give me Cheysuli welcome.

At my right he stood, keeping himself in silence as the others filed by. Rylan. Arlen. Others I could not name. And Isolde, reaching up to kiss my cheek even as I bent down to hug her in a blatant display of affection. A side-long look at Ceinn showed a rigid, unyielding face as my sister went by him without a word, and then I saw the blaze of grief in his eyes.

Lastly, Ian, who forgot proprieties as quickly as our sister; who embraced me twice and said very little because he could not manage it. *"Rujho,"* he said only, "you make a man proud to be Cheysuli."

And then he and the others were gone, save for Serri, Ceinn and a handful of the *a'saii*.

They did not come to me. I knew I had taken their weapon from them because my *lir*lessness was banished, and yet they did not come to me. As one they looked at Ceinn, and as one they turned their backs on him and exited through the back flap. In their silence was eloquence.

He took a single step forward, as if he meant to go after them, to say a word or two; to ask them what they meant. But he knew very well what they meant. He of all people.

He stopped. He did not go after them. He did not ask. He stared blindly into the emptiness of the pavilion.

"Shu'maii," I said quietly, "when a man cannot make a friend of an enemy, he takes the enemy from his friends."

After a moment, he shrugged. "Why not?" he asked dully. "You have already taken his *cheysula*."

"'Solde does as 'Solde chooses; surely *you* understand that better than most. But I would not have it said she cannot change her mind."

He looked at me sharply. "Would she?"

I shrugged. "I cannot speak for her—not now; not anymore than I did when she publicly renounced you. But she renounced you because you were *a'saii* . . . and now you are *shu'maii*."

He expelled a ragged breath of realization. "Gods—do you think—?" But he did not finish. He stared at me in rigid silence, unable to voice his hope for the intensity of his emotion; the magnitude of his fear that, once spoken, the hope would be taken away.

"I think I took an enemy from his friends, and gave a friend back to his *cheysula*."

As well as saving him from the Lion.

A muscle leaped in his cheek. "Do you think it is so easy to fashion friends out of enemies? I *believed* in what I did. And if you were *still* a *lir*less man, I would do it all again!"

"I know that," I said gently. "A man can also be measured by the dedication of his spirit. Aye, you believed. Too much, perhaps, in the old traditions, but it was a true belief. I cannot condone it. You tried to slay me, but I can comprehend it. Can you not see it, Ceinn? It takes men like you to restore a blighted race. Men like you . . . Carillon . . . my *jehan*. And I will need every one I can find."

"For what?" he asked sharply. "What do you intend to do?"

"Rule Homana," I told him. "Hold the Lion, once my *jehan* is dead."

He looked at Serri. He looked at the gold he himself had given me in my Ceremony of Honors. And then he turned sharply as if to go; to leave me alone in the tent with my *lir* and my memories.

But he swung back. "*Ru'shalla-tu*," he said flatly, and then he was gone from the pavilion.

I smiled. And then I laughed aloud.

May it be so? Serri's tone told me he did not understand my amusement.

"Aye," I agreed, still laughing. "But—from *Ceinn*."

Twelve

My sons, I said to Serri in amazement. Slowly I shook my head. *Of this imperfect vessel are magnificent children made.*

Given time, Serri agreed as he leaned against my knee; the posture was becoming habitual whenever I stood still. *At this age, there is not much magnificent about them except a magnificent odor.* His lips peeled back from his teeth; Serri sneezed. And then he went away from me to flop down upon a rug near the fireplace.

Laughing softly, I hooked hands over the side of the big oak-and-ivory cradle and leaned down to look more closely at the contents. Two babies, swaddled in costly linens and mostly hidden beneath a white silken coverlet stitched with crimson rampant lions. That I had fathered *one* was a miracle in itself; two was utterly incomprehensible to me.

Carefully I smoothed the coverlet and felt the lumpy bodies beneath. "You will be warriors of the clan," I told them quietly, "as well as princes of Homana. And one of you will be Mujhar."

That one, Serri told me, even from the rug. *I can feel it in him as you touch him . . . he is firstborn—he will be Mujhar.*

"And the other?"

Prince of Solinde?

I grunted. "Solinde prepares for war yet *again* . . . I begin to think no Mujhar of Homana will ever hold that realm in peace. At least not a long-lasting peace."

Prince of Atvia?

I nodded thoughtfully. "Possibly. With no male heirs, Alaric has only Gisella's son to look for a man to succeed him as Lord of Atvia."

Then again, there is Erinn.

I felt the old pain flare up in my belly. The grief renewed

itself. "No, *lir* . . . not Erinn. I think the Erinn I knew is gone forever."

Again I smoothed the silken coverlet, trying not to recall how *I* had lighted the beacon-fire that signaled Alaric's assassins to begin. Two small heads I touched, very close together. Both soft with fine black fuzz; black-haired were my sons, my half-Cheysuli sons.

One of them stirred beneath my hand. And almost instantly, the other one did as well. Some form of communication? They were children of the same birth . . . who could say what the strength of their link would be?

"Mujhar," I whispered to the one Serri had named the firstborn. "Such a heavy title for such a little boy."

Face down, he turned his head even as his brother did. They opened their eyes and peered at one another uncertainly, as if to make sure the other one was present. And I saw, looking at their eyes, why my father had said one could tell them apart already. The older, Brennan, had the brass-brown eyes that would turn Cheysuli yellow. Hart, the younger, had eyes the color of the sky on a summer day. Very like my own.

I smiled and cupped a palm over each of the black-fuzzed heads. *"Cheysuli i'halla shansu,* little warriors. And may your lives be long and full."

Lir— Serri said sharply, and I swung around with a hand to my borrowed knife.

But it was only Gisella—no, not *only*. Never would I attach that word to her name again.

She stood in the open doorway and stared at me sorrowfully. "You went away from me," she accused. "On our wedding night."

I felt a vague sense of guilt; aye, I had left her on our wedding night, when a man and woman should spend the time together. Even heavy with the babies, she was due common courtesy from her husband.

And then the guilt evaporated; what I felt was anger. Anger and *helplessness*, because she was no more responsible for her actions than were our two small sons, soiling nightwrappings in their sleep.

"I went away," I told her, "because I had to go."

She trailed a wine-red bedrobe across the floor as she wandered into the chamber. Beneath the robe, which hung mostly off her shoulders, was a linen nightshift. Her feet were bare upon the cold stone floor.

"You went away from me." She was a heartbroken child, repeating the thing that had hurt her. "You left me all *alone*."

"Gisella—"

But her face brightened abruptly. "Have you seen my babies? Have you seen my sons?"

"*Our* sons, Gisella," I said gently, even as she hastened across the floor to bend over the cradle. "They are mine as well as yours."

"*Babies,*" she whispered, and reached down to tuck the coverlet more closely around their bodies.

"Gisella." I caught a shoulder and pulled her around to face me. "Gisella—do you recall the night upon the cliffs, when your father told me to light the beacon-fire?"

She stared at me blankly. Her hair was bound back from her face in a single loosely woven braid. It hung over a shoulder and dangled against her hips. Gone was the bulk and weight of pregnancy. Her face was reminiscent of Isolde's, I thought, but that was not unusual as many Cheysuli resemble one another. She had regained her grace and allure. In sheer cream linen and wine-colored velvet she was a woman who would make another man think of bed, but *I* could not think of bedding her without also thinking of Deirdre.

"Gisella, do you remember?"

"You mean—in Atvia."

"Aye. In Atvia."

Abruptly she twisted away from me, pulling out from under my hand. Her back was to me, but I saw her drag the bedrobe up to cover her shoulders. She pulled the velvet very tight around her body, nails scraping rigidly at the nap, and I saw the silver tips. They reminded me of Lillith.

"Gisella—"

"You think of *her* instead of me." I saw how the nails dug into the velvet, as if she meant to hurt herself. "You think of her instead of *me*."

I shut my eyes a moment; when I opened them, Gisella was facing me. I saw the tears in her eyes. I saw how the slender fingers worked their way into the weave of her braid, tugging, *tugging*, as if she intended to jerk the hair out of her scalp.

"Did you know?" I asked her. "Did you know what lighting the fire would begin?"

"I wanted you for *me!*"

"By the gods, Gisella, *did you know what it would begin?*"

She pressed the braid against her mouth and I saw the white teeth bite in. Gods, how she trembled. "It was so pretty," she whispered over the shining hair. "The fire was so bright . . . it lit up the dragon's smile and I could see all his teeth."

"Do you know what you have done?"

"But it was *pretty*, Niall!" Suddenly she was angry. She jerked the braid from her mouth. "I like to see pretty things. I *want* to see pretty things."

I caught her arms before she could finish. *"Do you know what you have done?"*

"Aye!" she shouted back. "I have borne you *boys*—the Lion is secure!"

I heard the rising wail issuing from the cradle. In a moment another joined it; we had disturbed their sleep.

I have borne you boys—the Lion is secure.

That much of things she understood well enough. She had secured her *own* place as well as the future of Homana. What manner of man would I be if I set aside the woman who had borne me two healthy sons at a single lying-in?

In that moment, looking at her, I knew a futile anger of the sort that might drive me to murder. What would it take to place my hands around her throat and squeeze, shutting off her breath forever? She was responsible for altering my consciousness, for making me a man with no wits or will . . . a man capable of giving the woman he loves over to the hands of an assassin. And yet I knew Gisella could not be held accountable. Not—entirely.

All the anger spilled out of my body. Deep despair was left in its place. "Oh—gods—*Gisella* . . . will you never understand?" I turned from her and locked my hands onto the side of the cradle, staring blindly at my sons. "You will never understand."

"The babies are *crying*, Niall. We have made the babies

cry—" And she was instantly at my side, bending over the side of the cradle to make certain of their welfare.

She sang. Some little atonal melody I had never heard, and which I found utterly unbearable. How carefully she tended the babies. How solicitous she was. How concerned she was for their welfare, even as she ignored—or forgot—how she had made it possible for Deirdre to be slain.

She sang. And as she sang I backed away. And when I reached the door I turned and lurched out of the chamber even as Serri lunged up from the rug.

I did not get far. Even as I shut the door with a solid bang, I fell against the wall, pressing my brow against it. Gods, if I could only shut away the memories and guilt as easily as I shut away the sound of crying babies; the sight of their half-witted mother. *If only. . . .*

If only I could go back to Erinn and repeat my captivity there, because then all the eagles would be alive.

"Niall."

I spun, feeling Serri's warmth pressed against my leg. And saw my mother approaching from a turn in the corridor.

"Oh, Niall," she said in sudden concern, "what has put you in such pain?"

"Need you ask? The woman I have married." I shook my head. "I wish I might have listened to you when you gave me the chance to gainsay the wedding."

"Well, you did not, but it was not within your power." Her eyes were on the wolf. "Donal told me of your *lir . . .* and how it was Gisella's sorcery that blinded you to the truth."

"Jehana," I saw the minute twitch of surprise as I addressed her in the Old Tongue. *"Jehana,* I think there is a thing we must discuss, you and I . . . will you give me the time?"

"Gladly," she said. "We have had so little of it to share this past year." She placed a cool hand upon my wrist. "You know I would give you anything that you desire."

Inwardly I grimaced; *but will you* give *me my freedom when I ask you for it now?*

I escorted her to her favorite private solar, a round room in one of the corner towers of the palace, with wide, glassy casements and whitewashed walls. She had six women to attend her whenever she desired it; three were in the solar now, but before I could request privacy my mother asked them to leave. And so we were left alone, save for Serri, and I found myself suddenly reticent to speak of the thing at all.

My mother smiled. She turned from me and went to one of the casements, staring out as if to give me time to assemble the words I wished to say. I looked at her back and saw the firm arch of her spine beneath the tight-fitting glove of the green-dyed linen gown. The sleeves also were very fitted, snugged against her arms from shoulders to midway down her hands. All the glorious red-gold hair was bound up in a green-wrapped loop of braid at the back of her slender neck.

Still so slim, my mother; still so youthful looking.

I drew in a deep breath, held it a moment, let it out carefully. "I am not Carillon."

The spine went rigid. She spun, bracing herself with hands thrust against the casement sill. *"What?"*

"I am not Carillon."

I saw a mixture of emotions in her face: astonishment, perplexity, a trace of apprehension. As if she began to understand precisely what I meant to say. "Niall—"

"And if you mean to tell me so emphatically that of *course* I am not, I wish you would gainsay it. Mother—" I stopped. "*Jehana*, too many times in the past you have made me to feel inferior. You did not *mean* it, I know. If anything, you meant to bolster what manhood I claim by comparing me to *him*, but it has always made me feel the reverse. Incapable. Incompetent. A shadow of the man your father was." I spread my hands. "I have his height, his weight, his color—certainly a legacy I might respect . . . were I allowed to respect myself."

Still she braced herself against the sill, head held rigidly upon a slender neck. Garnets glittered in her ears; I saw a flash of the gold chain around her throat. The links dipped down beneath the bodice of her gown, caught between flesh and fabric. I thought she might speak; she did not. She did not even move.

"He was not perfect," I told her. "He was flawed, as any man is flawed. It does not make him less than the legend he has become. It merely makes him a *man* . . . as his grandson is a man." I felt the weight of the gold upon my arms. The ache in my left earlobe. *At last, I am Cheysuli.* "I need to be myself. I need to know my own name. I need to walk unhindered by the weight of my grandsire's legend." I paused. "I need to be allowed to respect the memory of the man, instead of resenting it."

I saw the pain in her eyes. "Have I done that to you?"

"You did not *intend* it."

"Have I done that to you?"

I swallowed tightly, loath to hurt her any more. "I think—perhaps. . . ." I stopped short; why avoid the truth in the name of tact when I had already made the wound? "Aye."

She flinched. Only a little, but there was no doubting the blade had gone cleanly home.

"Oh—gods—" she said, and covered her face with her hands.

I went to her at once, wrapping her up in my arms. She did not sob aloud, merely cried silently into my leathers. Such dignity, has my mother . . . such rigid awareness of self.

When she was done with tears she lifted her head and looked up into my face. "I loved him so much. He was everything to me. I had no mother for most of my life . . . he had already banished her. And when at last I *did* come to know my mother, it was to know also that she intended to use me against him." The anguish laid bare her soul; she had carried her own weight of guilt. "He was my world for so many years of my life . . . and then he was taken from it."

"Men die, *jehana.*"

"Not Carillon of Homana." Her tone was very grim. "Men such as he are kept alive in lays and sagas; we have the harpers to thank for that."

"Then *let* him live," I agreed. "Let the truth of his deeds live on in the magic of the music."

"But not in the life of his grandson?" She nodded a little, though mostly to herself. "I know . . . he became what he was because he *had* to, to make Homana whole. I cannot—and *should* not—expect you to mimic him. The times are different now . . . the requirements different also. It is not fair to ask you to be someone other than yourself." She sighed. Fingers traced the shapes in the gold on my arm. "For so long you have been Homana's *Homanan* prince, when you are also Cheysuli. But it was so much easier to follow the mold already made, than to trouble myself with fashioning another."

I shrugged. "I am whatever I am: Cheysuli, Homanan, Solindish. The rest is up to me."

"The rest is up to the gods." She smiled even as I bent to kiss her brow, before I took my arms away. "It is difficult for a woman with only one child *not* to try to shape the clay precisely as she wishes. And more difficult yet to realize the clay may prefer to shape itself."

"Well, I think the clay is unfired." I smiled, shrugging. "Who can say what I will become?"

"All of *them*," she said seriously. "*All* of them will say. The councils, the races—the loyalists and the rebels. And certainly the enemy." Pensively, she smoothed the silk of her shining hair. "Be wary, Niall . . . be wary of everyone. Friend and foe alike."

And into the room on the tail of her words came the echo of Strahan's voice: *"Look to your friends . . . your enemies . . . your kin—lest they form an alliance against you."*

Thirteen

I lost my freedom almost as soon as I had won it. It was nothing my mother, my father, the Cheysuli, or even the Homanans had done. It was a combination of factors: imminent war, the plague, civil turmoil. Although the *a'saii* were, for the moment, disarmed, I knew it was possible the Cheysuli fanatics might seek other avenues to replace me. No one could say I lacked the gifts of my race, not with Serri and our link so blatantly obvious, but they *could* say they preferred someone with a different strain of the required blood. And perhaps they would.

The plague began to prey upon Homana in earnest. What had initially begun as a vague illness defined mostly as fever in Homanan herders and crofters spread down from the north to invade central Homana, and Mujhara lay in its path. Reports of deaths were brought to the Mujhar, and, too soon, the vague illness was diagnosed as something far graver. From Homanan crofters and herders, isolated in the Northern Wastes and the greater distances between towns and villages, the sickness reached out to touch even the Keeps, and word came of Cheysuli deaths.

The bounty on white wolves rose. A trip to the furrier in the Market Square showed me a man whose purse was fattened almost daily by trappers coming in with pelts. Some were ruddy, others silver, some a charcoal gray, as if the trappers took no chances and slew all the wolves they could catch. But there were white pelts as well . . . pelts as white as my own, when I wore my *lir*-shape.

And so, when I went into the city, I made the greatest sacrifice of all: I left Serri in Homana-Mujhar. I would not risk losing my *lir* to an overzealous citizen intent on ridding Homana of the plague, or—more likely—intent on putting a silver piece in the palm of his bloodied hand.

I did not like leaving Serri behind. Not at all. But certainly no more or less than my father liked leaving Lorn behind when *he* went into the city.

Or even to Clankeep.

My sons thrived, though I learned all too quickly demands upon my time by governmental matters stole away the hours I had meant to spend with them. I saw them infrequently at best; mostly I toiled with my father in sessions of strategy and hypothetical situations, learning how men plotted the course of war. Lessons in my youth had taught me Homana's history of wars and civil turmoil; I began to see why they had been required of me. All too often one of the councillors tossed the name of this battle or that into the discussions to cite an example of proper procedure, thoughtful initiative, even dismal failure. All too often I heard the name of Carillon invoked . . . and then one day, in listening to yet another discourse on what the late Mujhar had done as well as why, I began to see the reasons for the invocations. My grandsire, flawed man that he was, as I had taken care to point out to my mother, had known instinctively what might win the battle, and so the war as well.

Or *was* it instinct? Perhaps it was simply *experience*, won from out of the midst of carnage and put to use in later confrontations.

If it was instinct, perhaps I had inherited a portion of it. And if it was experience, I had little doubt I would soon know that as well.

Relations with Gisella continued much as before. She was quixotic, unreliable, unpredictable. Servants disliked serving her and argued among themselves as to who would take her trays, for she only rarely came down to meals in the dining hall, preferring, she said, to eat with the babies. Quietly I made certain there were always two or more women with her and the children; I did not wish to risk my sons to the whims and odd fancies of a woman such as Gisella.

We spent little time together because of the demands of the planning sessions. More and more my father asked me for my opinions in an attempt, I thought, to familiarize me with the idea of conducting a war as much as familiarizing the others with the idea of my contribution. Ian, also present, said less than I and was asked less, even by my father; his place was at my side, not in the line of succession for the Lion or even in orchestrating wars. But I did not doubt that when the time came, his responsibilities would be as great as mine. Simply drawn from a different background.

Gisella did not appear to miss my company, although she was always glad to see me. I thought surely she would stifle, ever keeping herself within the confines of Homana-Mujhar, but she said no. She did not wish to go to Clankeep or into Mujhara or even outside the walls of Homana-Mujhar. She wished only to stay with the babies.

I could not forbid it, any more than I could force her to leave the palace. And I was not certain I *wanted* her to leave Homana-Mujhar; there was no telling what she might do or say in the city or at Clankeep. The gods knew I could never predict it.

Any more than I could have predicted her desire.

I had not sought her bed since the birth of Brennan and Hart, even though enough time had passed to make it physically possible for her. It was repugnant to me. *She* was not—it was just that I could recall so little of the time before Serri had freed me from Gisella's ensorcellment. The idea that I had been little more than a toy to her, performing at her whim, disturbed me deeply. I had no desire to learn how malleable I had been in her bed.

And yet it seemed I would.

She came into my bedchamber as I prepared to blow out the candle. Naked, I glanced up as the latch lifted (I did not sleep with it locked) and stared in surprise as Gisella slipped through and shut it with scarcely a sound. She wore only a nightshift and the black cloak of her shining hair. As she turned toward the bed, seeking me, I heard the whisper of the linen; saw the cloak swing against breasts and thighs.

She saw me through the filmy screen of the gauzy hangings. She stopped. Stood very still. Then, slowly, a spread hand caressed her breasts, sliding diagonally from the left shoulder to stop eventually at the dimple of her navel. The hand trapped a portion of the linen and pulled the fabric tight against her loins.

Even against my will, I felt myself respond.

She said nothing. She crossed the room, came to me, placed her hands upon my shoulders. Her palms were warm as she kneaded my warming flesh.

She smiled. There was no doubt I wanted her, even when I thought I could say I did not. Her nails scraped down and caught in the gold on my arms; I heard a metallic scratching as she dragged tips across the flowing shapes.

"Wolf," she whispered, "I, *too*, can be a wolf. . . ."

She pressed herself against me. I caught handfuls of her hair. I thought suddenly of Serri, curled at the foot of the bed. Serri, who shared my life through the link.

And then I did not care.

"Wolves," she whispered. "Let it be as *wolves*."

"Niall? *Rujho*, the council has called an emergency meeting." Ian unlatched and pushed open the door, speaking even as he did it. And then he stopped short, silenced abruptly; he had not expected to find Gisella in my bed.

Well, no more than I had—at least, initially.

Light spilled through the casements. Early morning, *too* early; I rubbed a hand across my face and tried to wipe the dullness from my mind. "Emergency?"

Ian hovered between divulging an answer and leaving at once. Beside me, Gisella pulled the coverlet over her nakedness.

"Ian—" I began, frowning.

"Just—get dressed. I will wait outside." As he backed out he pulled the door shut with a thump.

I got up and dragged on leggings, jerkin, hooked a belt around my waist. Boots were last; I tugged them on, then turned and bent down to kiss Gisella briefly, but the brevity was replaced by elaboration. She smiled, stretched languorously, promised me the world with her half-lidded, sleepy eyes.

Gods—who can say what is ensorcellment or lust? I wondered vaguely, and went out the door with Serri at my heels.

Ian's face was conspicuously blank as I joined him in the corridor. Tasha sat beside him, cleaning a spotless paw. Wryly, I smiled; my brother would say it was not his place to comment, but it would not be necessary to say anything at all. By his very blankness I knew what he was thinking.

He gestured down the corridor and we matched our strides as we walked even as our *lir* trailed us. "I know little more than you," he told me. "Some word of the bastard."

I swore. "With this war becoming more and more imminent, the *last* thing we need is trouble with the bastard."

"Until he is dead, he will make it." Ian shook his head as I looked at him sharply. "No, I do not speak of assassination, but no doubt others do."

Assassination. It was a political reality, a tool kings and others used to remove potential rivals as well as very real ones. Alaric himself had used it against the House of Erinn.

And for that very reason, I could not imagine myself condoning its use against the bastard. Even to lessen the threat to me. Surely somewhere there would be someone who grieved. His mother. His foster-father. Perhaps even a wife.

We descended spiraling staircases one behind the other; the steps were too narrow to support more than one man at a time. Down and down, around and around, with only a rope for a guide on the inner column. The twisting staircase with its narrow confines was designed for ease of defense: it was easier to defend the palace against the enemy one man at a time, instead of one against many.

On the bottom floor we passed by guards in the corridor and nodded greeting to those just outside the wooden door. One reached in, unlatched, pushed the door open for us; we entered, had the door pulled closed almost at once—

—and walked into the eye of a storm.

No one took note of us. Where ordinarily men stopped speaking to acknowledge me with bows and murmured greetings, now none even knew I was present. The ranks of benches along the walls and just before us were filled; more men, standing, lined the walls and filled the aisles. Sitting, standing, they were shoulder to shoulder, blocking our view of the dais and its table where our father customarily sat. Over the low-voiced mumble of constant comments, I could hear someone haranguing the Mujhar.

Ian and I exchanged startled glances. Then he shrugged and began pushing a way through the standing men, murmuring apologies even as the others swore, shifted, glared. Many of them, as I followed, were unknown to me; no doubt they were annoyed by the audacity of two much younger men.

I stepped upon a boot toe, apologized, nearly tripped over another. The irritation was mutual as the owner of the toes and I exchanged scowls. Behind me, Serri grumbled aloud; within the link I felt his disgust with mannerless Homanans. But I also heard the murmuring arise in our wake; Ian and I were named by those who knew us, and by the time we reached the center of the hall, where room was left for speakers and petitioners, the men moved aside willingly. But by then we no longer needed the courtesy; our father, rising, was summoning us to the dais.

We went at once, crossing the open space in the center of the hall. A man stood before the dais in a posture that bordered on defiance. He turned as Ian and I approached; I saw his expression of outrage, as if he intensely resented the interruption. But as he saw me, following in Ian's wake, the expression changed. He stared. And I saw him murmur something silently to himself. A prayer. Or a curse.

The men on the benches rose. The sudden silence was loud and very brief; I heard the murmuring begin again almost at once. There was a note of anticipation in most of the low-voiced comments. Apprehension in others.

And even hostility.

Ian hesitated only a moment before he stepped up behind the table. Tasha was a shadow behind him, tail whipping as she paced silently onto the dais. Like Serri, she sensed the tension in the hall.

There were three chairs on the dais. The middle was obviously my father's: Taj perched upon the back. Lorn lay beside it, eyes slitted. Ian went by him to the left and waited behind it even as I took my place at the right. Into the hush my father spoke quietly, presenting both of us to those assembled. I saw faces I knew and faces I did not. The council members ringed the floor in the curving front row. I knew none of them well, save Rowan; I looked to his face for some indication of the gravity of the session, but it was a mask to me.

We sat down as my father did. Still there was silence. The man in the middle of the floor continued to stare at me.

"Be seated," my father announced, and the silence was

replaced by the sound of benches scraping, the ring of spurs, the clatter of sheaths and scabbards striking wood.

The stranger in the center waited in tense silence.

"This is Elek," my father said. "From the north, across the Bluetooth. He represents that faction of Homanans who support the right of Carillon's son to inherit the throne when I am dead."

Every man in the hall looked at me, to judge my reaction. No doubt they expected shock, anger . . . perhaps even hostility. And a few, probably, fear. But I gave them none of those things. Instead, I looked at Elek.

He did not look like a rebel, a fanatic, a madman. He looked like a *man*, and not so much older than myself. He was brown-haired, brown-eyed, clean-shaven with an open, earnest face. His clothes were plain homespun: tunic and breeches, without embellishment. His kneeboots were muddied, but otherwise the leather was good. Not a nobleman, Elek, but neither was he a poor man. No doubt his wealth lay in his convictions.

I rose, scraping my chair against the dais. Silently I bade Serri stay by the chair; slowly I stepped off the dais and crossed the open center of the floor. In silence I stopped before Elek, marking how he wet his lips; how he had to look up to meet my eyes. And marking also the faintest tang of perspiration. Elek was nervous, now that I stood before him. And so I knew he had been exceedingly eloquent, championing the bastard's right to usurp my place in the line of succession.

"Why?" I asked. That only.

He swallowed. His gaze flicked between me and the Mujhar. Clearly, he did not know how to answer.

I waited. So did all the others.

After a moment, Elek cleared his throat. "He is Carillon's son."

"He is Carillon's *bastard*."

His chin rose minutely. "It is customary for the *son* to inherit from the father."

"Rather than the grandson?" I nodded. "Aye, I grant you that. But the circumstances were different."

"We maintain that had he known, Carillon would have named his son as his successor, rather than Donal of the Cheysuli."

"I am his daughter's son," I said quietly. "If, in Homana, women could rule in their own right, Aislinn, my mother, would have inherited the Lion Throne. As it was, her husband did. Do you really think Carillon would have disinherited his daughter to make way for a bastard son?"

"Had he known—"

"How do you know he did not?" I looked past Elek to Rowan. "My lord general, you are the best man to answer my question. Did Carillon know the woman had conceived?"

Elek wrenched his head around to stare in disbelief at Rowan; had he thought to make his case uncontested?

Rowan's smile was very faint. As always, he wore the crimson silk tunic with the black rampant lion sprawled across its folds. With his Cheysuli looks, the colors were good on him. "Aye, my lord. He knew she had conceived."

Elek turned sharply to refute Rowan's statement, but my raised hand stopped him. "Before you ask it, Elek, let me answer your question: that is General Rowan himself, who served Carillon for nearly twenty-five years. Do you intend to question his veracity?"

"I question his prejudice," Elek answered curtly. "He is Cheysuli. Do you think he would prefer to have a Homanan replace a fellow Cheysuli in the succession?"

"There speaks ignorance," I retorted. "Were you never taught the histories? In your zeal to champion Carillon's son, did you never learn the names of those who served the father so faithfully?" I shook my head. "No, you did not. Else you would know that General Rowan is a *lir*less Cheysuli. He was raised Homanan, Elek . . . he has no *lir*-gifts, owes no loyalty to his race, does not claim a clan. What benefit would he gain from lying to you?"

Elek did not respond.

I looked again at Rowan. "He knew she had conceived, and yet he let her go."

"She requested it my lord." Rowan was so calm, and yet I sensed a trace of amusement beneath the surface of his tone. Did he have so much faith in me?

"She requested his leave to go."

"Aye, my lord. She wished to have the baby elsewhere, away from the brutalities of war. The Mujhar made no attempt to dissuade her."

He did not notice his slip. *The Mujhar.* To him, no doubt, Carillon would always be the Mujhar. But I thought in this instance the mistake was a good one; Elek, turning again to look at Rowan, frowned a little, as if disturbed by the reference. A man who was so dedicated to Carillon that he still referred to him as Mujhar unconsciously emphasized where the depth of his loyalty lay.

"Were you present when he gave her that leave to go?"

"Aye, my lord. He gave her coin and his best wishes for the birth of a healthy child."

"And did he say nothing about bringing the child to him? That if it was a son, he would want the child given into his keeping?"

"He said nothing of it, my lord."

"Why do you think he would not? A son is a son."

"A bastard is a bastard." Rowan did not smile. "He intended to wed Electra of Solinde."

"And expected a son of *her*."

"It—was hoped. Certainly." Rowan's faint smile was gone. No doubt the questioning aroused old memories. Painful memories of earlier days, when Carillon's youth precluded the thought of illness and accelerated age.

"Aye!" Elek shouted triumphantly. "But he *got* no son of her—only a daughter." He swung to face me again. "Only a daughter, my lord . . . who could not inherit the throne."

Still I looked at Rowan. "You knew him better than most, general. Do you recall at any time that Carillon considered—or *wished* to consider—sending for his bastard?"

"No, my lord. He said nothing of it."

"To *him!*" Elek cried. "But does a man—a *Mujhar*—confide everything to another, even his general? I say no, he does not. I say he divulges what he wishes, and keeps some things private, as every man does. Even a Mujhar."

I laughed. "And do you seek now to tell me my grandsire's private thoughts?"

"No. There is no need for me to do it. I will let the woman do it instead." It was Elek's turn to laugh even as I stared at him. "Aye, my lord—the woman. The *bastard's* mother. Why not ask *her* these questions? She is just outside the door."

I did not dare show him my concern. It had become quite

obvious many of the strangers in the hall were companions
of Elek's, fellow supporters of the bastard. And I could not
be certain how many of the men supposedly loyal to my
father intended to remain so. It was possible Elek and those
present with him hoped to gather more supporters even
within the walls of Homana-Mujhar.

"By all means," I said quietly. "Have the woman
brought in."

There was no sense in confronting her as I confronted
Elek. And so as a man was sent to fetch the woman, I
returned to my seat upon the dais.

My father's face was grim. "He did not say the woman
was here."

I glanced at him sharply. "Do you think *that* will
change anything?"

"He is making a formal petition of the Homanan Council," my father answered. "It is possible a majority of the
members might agree with his claim in the name of Carillon's bastard."

"But you could *overrule* it."

"And I would immediately do so. But it would have serious repercussions. It could split the council entirely, which
would more or less split Homana. And the gods know I do
not need a hostile, divided council, going into war."

"What of the Cheysuli? Have *they* no stake in this?"

He did not appreciate my tone. "And will *you* speak of
the *a'saii*? Or will Elek?"

I did not answer because the woman had arrived. I
watched pensively as the men made way for her as they
had not for Ian and me.

At first I was surprised. She was short, too heavy, at least
ten years older than my father. Her graying brown hair was
pulled back from a sallow, puffy face into a knot at the
back of her head. She wore, like Elek, simple homespun,
but the quality was not as good.

A gray woman, I thought. Gray of dress, gray of hair,
gray of spirit. Nothing in manner or appearance spoke of
the young woman who had captured a Mujhar's interest.

She stopped beside Elek. She curtsied awkwardly, as if
she had forgotten how. Her eyes were downcast, yet as she
raised her lids and looked at my father, I saw they were
also gray. But a large, lovely gray, clear as glass and bril-

liant. No matter what else she was, she was not a stupid woman.

Carillon bedded this woman and got a son upon her.

Rowan rose. "My lord?"

My father nodded.

The woman turned toward him as he approached. I saw the look they exchanged; an agreement to disagree. He knew her, she him, and yet their loyalties were spent on different men.

He nodded. Silently he returned to his bench. "My lord." Again, Rowan looked to my father. "It is the woman, my lord. Her name is Sarne."

"Sarne." My father leaned forward in his chair. "You bore Carillon a son."

"Nearly thirty-six years ago, my lord. When I was twenty." Her voice was as cool as her eyes; whore she might be, but she was also bound to the man they called the bastard.

"And now you come to us claiming he should be Prince of Homana in place of *my* son."

"My lord—he is *Carillon's* son."

"*Illegitimate* son." I knew how much the emphasis cost my father, with Ian seated beside him. It is not a Cheysuli custom to curse a bastard for his birth, and yet for my sake he had to.

"Bastard-born, aye," she answered forthrightly. "But acknowledged by his father."

The Mujhar nodded. "By his father. Which one? Carillon—or the crofter you married?"

Her sallow face was suffused with angry color. Her eyes glittered. I was put in mind, oddly, of my own mother, when I had seen her angry. The eyes were similar.

And I wondered, suddenly, if that had been the attraction. My mother's eyes were *her* mother's, and Electra was notorious for the power of her gaze. If Carillon were susceptible to the color, it became more understandable how Sarne had appealed to him.

"He was acknowledged by his *father*, my lord, when I brought him to Homana-Mujhar."

I heard the gasp go up from the assemblage. No one had expected that; no, perhaps some of them *had*. Not everyone looked surprised.

A sidelong glance at my father's face showed the faintest trace of consternation in his expression. Beyond him, Ian frowned blackly at the tabletop. Almost idly, he picked at a blemish with his thumbnail. But I knew my brother too well; he was also deeply concerned.

"And when did you come to Homana-Mujhar?" my father inquired calmly.

Sarne nodded a little, as if she had anticipated the question. "You weren't here, my lord. You'd gone to the Crystal Isle to fetch home the Princess of Homana." She nodded again. "It was before you wed her. When the only son you claimed was also a bastard, like mine."

I was on my feet at once. "You go too far," I told her plainly, over the murmurs of the throng. "Give my brother no insult *here*."

Her dignity manifested itself subtly, and yet I was aware of its presence. "Then give *my* son no insult here, my lord." She took two steps forward; a short, heavy woman, yet powerful in her pride. "Do you think I don't know Cheysuli custom? Do you think we put forward my son out of some perverse desire to *steal* the throne from you? *No*, my lord— we only want what's right for him—what's *his* right, because he is Carillon's son! Bastard, is he? *Aye*, he is! And so is that man there!" She thrust a hand toward Ian. "So is that man who sits at the Mujhar's *side* bastard-born, and suffering none because of it. Cheysuli he is, and therefore not pushed aside because his father never married his mother. And I say to you—what right have you to push aside *my* son? What right have you to refuse him his proper place? *Carillon* never did!"

"What place did Carillon *give* him?" my father demanded. "By the gods, woman, nothing was ever said! Not to me, not to Rowan . . . if Carillon promised you a place for your son—a title or otherwise—no one ever knew it!"

"Why would he say so to *you*?" she countered. "He had already promised you the throne. Everyone in Homana knows how the shapechangers serve their prophecy. Perhaps he thought you or the other Cheysuli would try to harm my son."

My father nearly gaped. "You are mad," he told her, shaking his head slowly from side to side. "You are *mad*."

"Am I?" she retorted. "As mad as the Princess Gisella?"

"Enough!" I shouted. "Woman, you go *too far!"*

"Everyone knows it!" she cried. "You are wed to a mad-woman, my lord. Who can say what manner of children you will get?"

Even my father was on his feet. "No more," he said. "By the gods, woman, *no more!"*

"Why? Because I speak the truth? Because I *dare* speak the truth before all the others?" She whirled, facing the gathered men. "It's true! *All* of it! My son was acknowl-edged by Carillon, who intended to give him a place. And now when we *ask* for that place, the Mujhar denies it to us." Her body vibrated with the intensity of her emotions. "He fears my son. He *fears* what it means for the prophecy. But I say we are *Homanan*—we need no prophecy. Why not make Homana *Homanan* again?"

Men were on their feet, trying to shout her down. Others shouted over them declaring their support of the woman's son. And all the while I watched in astonishment.

Ian pushed back his chair. "I will fetch the guard."

"No." My father caught his arm as he moved to rise. "Remain here. I do not want you going near that crowd."

"Jehan—"

"I said *no."*

"She is mad," I said dazedly. "Madder than Gisella."

"What sort of man do you want on the Lion Throne?" the woman was shouting. "A Cheysuli? A Homanan? The child of Carillon's son? Or the child of mad Gisella?"

I looked at Elek. He was smiling. He watched the woman and smiled, as if he waited for something.

Beyond him, Rowan had turned to the men. I saw his mouth move, but his shout was lost in the tumult. Like Ian, I wanted to fetch the guard. But I did not move to try it.

"It was a *Cheysuli* who slew Carillon!" I heard the woman shout. "A *shapechanger* slew the Mujhar. He gave him shapechanger poison!"

"Oh *gods,"* I heard my father exclaim. "How can she know about the *tetsu* root that he wanted for his pain?"

"Carillon's son should be Mujhar—Carillon's Homanan *son—let the Lion remain Homanan."*

I saw men draw steel in the midst of the shouting throng. I heard shouts, curses, threats; I heard the woman's voice rising over it all like the shrill cry of a hunting hawk.

"Let the Lion remain Homanan!"

And then, abruptly, a man broke free of the throng. He darted forward even as I leaped over the table and onto the floor, trying to turn him aside. But I was late, hobbled by a poor landing; he thrust, left his knife in the woman's body, and looked directly at my father. "My lord—that was for *you*—to prove my loyalty."

And almost at once he was dead. Elek, rising up from Sarne's crumpled body, thrust with his own knife and drove the man down to the floor.

I heard the ring and hiss of steel from more than a hundred swords and knives. I caught a glimpse of Rowan battering back an attacker. *Gods—they will not slay* Rowan—

And yet I knew they might.

They advanced: a wall of human flesh. Elek was a target; so, I thought, was I.

"Niall, *get back!*" My father's voice, shouting over the others.

Elek twisted, mouthing obscenities at me. Others held him, knocking the bloodied knife from his hand. I did not think he wished to slay me, only to curse me for Sarne's murder. And yet clearly the others thought he did. En masse, at least twelve bore him to the ground.

"Do not slay him!" I shouted. "By the gods, *do not slay him!*"

"*Rujho*—get back!"

And then I felt Serri go by me into the mass of men, snapping at a throat. "'*Serri! Serri no—*" *Gods—they will say he has gone mad—they will say he must be slain—and then I will be slain as well—* "Serri—*no!*"

I dove after the wolf, trying to catch him in my arms. All I caught was the tip of his bristled tail, and then I was down, sprawled on the floor, with stomping boots too close to my face.

Serri—

"My lord, get you *up*." Someone caught the back of my jerkin and yanked me to my feet, steadying me even as I staggered. I felt a knife pressed into my hand. "My lord, *arm* yourself!"

Serri—

There was no answer in the link.

Hands were on me. I felt something sharp slice through my jerkin. My belly stung.

Someone is trying to gut me like a fish—

"My lord!" I was turned, shoved, the knife in my hand sank deeply into flesh.

"No!" I cried in horror.

Elek's face, mouth gaping in shock and horror. Blood flowed over my hand. And then he sank down slowly to his knees until he was lost in the crowd.

Gods—say I did not do it—

And yet I knew I had.

"Serri!" I shouted. *"Serri!"*

"The prince has slain him!" someone shouted. *"The prince has murdered Elek!"*

Hands were on me, dragging me back from the throng. I twisted frenziedly, trying to free myself, until I heard my brother's voice. "Stop fighting me, *rujho*, and let me save your life."

"Serri," I said dazedly. "Oh gods—*where is Serri?*"

Here, came the familiar tone. *Lir, I am well. You need have no fear for me.*

Ian jerked me down behind the table, thumping my head into the chair. "Stay down," he said. "Let the guard do their job."

"The guard—?" I sat up even as Ian tried to shove me back down. And then Serri was in my face. "Oh gods—*lir—*"

I am well. I am well. Lir, do not fear for me.

His nose was pressed into my throat. I latched an arm around his neck and hugged as hard as I could. *Lir, where did you go?*

There was a man who was trying to slay you. I had to stop him, lir.

I heard the ring and clash of steel on steel, the shouts of the Mujharan Guard. Benches overturned, men cried out, cursed, petitioned the gods for deliverance even as I had myself.

I tried to thrust myself up to peer over the table, but Ian jerked me down again. "You fool," he said, glaring. "You did precisely what they wanted, so they could claim you murdered Elek. Do not give them more satisfaction. *Stay down!"*

"Where is our *jehan?*"

"Here," he said from behind me. "I was fetching Rowan out of that mess." He knelt even as I twisted my head to look. "Are you harmed?"

I looked down at myself. Blood stained my leathers, but none of it was mine. "No. This is all Elek's, I fear."

Behind the Mujhar stood the general. His fine silk tunic had been torn. But the ringmail beneath was whole. "Almost clear," he reported. "I think the madness is over."

"But for how long?" I asked in disgust. "Gods, what an ugly thing."

"As it was meant to be," Rowan agreed. "It was elaborately planned."

"Planned?" I stared up at him as I reached out to touch Serri for reassurance. "Some of it, aye, I can see it easily enough. But—Sarne's murder? Elek's?"

"How better to divide loyalties as yet unsecured than by inflaming them with murder?" Rowan shook his head grimly. "My lord, she was murdered by a man claiming his loyalty to the Mujhar . . . it was made to look as though Donal desired it. But Elek was not quite careful enough. I saw him speaking to the man in the corridor just before the audience began."

I recalled how he had looked, as if he waited for something. "So she was sacrificed."

"Aye," my father said grimly. "And so was Elek, though he did not expect it. It makes these people doubly dangerous. They will slay their own to lay the blame on us."

"Gods! Will it work?"

"It might," Rowan answered. "Word of it will get out: that *Niall* slew Elek, and it will draw more people to the bastard. The rebels will use it against us all."

"How do we stop it?"

"We do not," my father said. "Not physically. We do not dare, on the heels of what has happened today. All we can do is deny it."

I shook my head. "Not a powerful weapon."

"But the only one we have. We cannot afford another. All we can do is let this rivalry sort itself out—with what subtle aid we can give the sorting—until the Homanans will listen to reason." He offered his arm and pulled me up.

I blew out my breath in shock even as Serri pressed against my knee. Men littered the floor. Some were dead. Some were near it. Others were merely wounded. Much of the Mujharan Guard still filled the hall, though others remained in the corridor enforcing the Mujhar's peace.

"Gods," I said in despair, "what madness infects this realm?"

"Not madness," Rowan said. "Rather, call it ambition. The desire for a throne."

"And Carillon's bastard is behind it."

Rowan's expression was horribly bleak. "How the father would hate the son. . . ."

"Would he? Could he really?"

"For this?" Rowan nodded. "If he could rise up from out of his tomb, he would put an end to this. He would put an end to his son. But he cannot . . . and so we must do it for him."

"*You* would do it?" I asked. "Could you slay Carillon's son?"

Rowan smiled a little. "I am pledged to the Mujhar of Homana, and after that to his son. Carillon's time is done; Donal is Mujhar. And the son I will serve is you."

I grinned. "You will be an old, old man."

My father grimaced. "And I will be a *dead* one. Let us speak of something else." He turned as if to step out from behind the table and off the dais, but one of his guard approached.

"My lord, a message has arrived." He held out the sealed parchment. "It was to be given to you at once."

"My thanks." He broke the wax and unfolded the creased parchment. And then he looked at Rowan. "Ships," he said. "Solindish ships, sighted off the Crystal Isle. Hondarth is in danger."

"And so it begins again." Rowan wiped and sheathed his bloodied sword. "My lord, how shall you deploy us?"

"I will do it as Carillon once did, when he was endangered on two fronts. You and I will go to Hondarth. My sons I will send to Solinde."

Rowan smiled a little. "And I will say of *them* what once I said of *you*: they are unschooled in warfare and the leading of men."

"Aye, but they will learn. I send the Cheysuli with them—"

Gods, I thought, *Solinde*.

My father looked at his sons. "I cannot put it more plainly: in the morning you go to war."

Gods, I thought, *Solinde*.

PART III

One

"*Rujho—get* down*!*"

Even as I lunged out of the saddle I felt the nip of arrow at shoulder, plucking at the leather of my jerkin. My foot was half-caught in the stirrup; the horse, shying a single step from the wail and whistle of arrows, dragged me off-balance. I fell, twisting awkwardly as I tried to free my foot before my knee was wrenched out of its proper alignment. Heard hum and hiss of additional feathered shafts; jerked my head aside as fletching dragged at a lock of tawny hair.

"Get *down*," Ian repeated.

"I *am* down." Irritably, I jerked my boot from the stirrup and rolled, flattening on my belly, scowling at my brother. Like me, he lay belly-down in the thin dry grass of the Solindish plain, barren in the first gray days of winter. "Where are they? How many?"

Ian, peering westward through the screen of grass, shook his head. He pulled his warbow out from under a hip, rolled sideways to take an arrow from his quiver, nocked it. Slowly he rose, hunching behind the thigh-high grass. He blended perfectly with the stalks and scrubby vegetation: amber, ivory, sienna; no greens, no browns, no richness, only the dull saffron of banished fall. The land was made bland in brassy sunlight as it burned through the flat light of a winter's day.

Just beyond Ian, at his left, crouched Tasha, chestnut indistinctness dissected by slanting stalks. Nothing moved to indicate she lived, not even the tip of her tail. She was stillness itself; I was reminded, oddly, of the wooden lion in Homana-Mujhar, crouching on the dais.

Serri?

He came, even as I thought of him, dropped low in the slouching walk of a wolf who skulks, avoiding contact with the enemy. His tail was clamped at hocks, curving inward to brush tip against loins, protecting genitals. Tipped ears lay back against his skull. He was hackled from ruff to rump.

Beside me, he crouched, much as Tasha crouched. He stared at the distances. *Ihlini*, lir. *Ahead.*

I looked at once at Ian, intending to tell him; saw the grim set of his mouth and realized there was no need for me to speak. Tasha had already relayed the information.

Ihlini. At last. After two months in Solinde, entangled in skirmishes that did little but waste our time—as well as wasting lives—we were to meet the true enemy in this war. Not the Solindish, though they fought with fierce determination. No. *Ihlini.* Strahan's minions, who served Asar-Suti.

Ihlini. And it meant Ian and I were summarily stripped of our Cheysuli gifts.

Even now I could feel the interference in the link with Serri. A numbing, tingling sensation, faint but decidedly present, lifting the hair on my arms, my neck, my legs. Irritability: something insinuated itself within the link I shared with Serri, shunting the power aside. It was as if someone had split a candleflame in two, snuffing one half entirely . . . spilling the other half into a darkness so deep even the *light* was swallowed up. I could feel the power draining away into the earth, leaving me, going back into its mother. And I was not certain it would return.

I shivered. *How eerie that the gods give us the gifts of the earth magic, then take them away when we are faced by the Ihlini. . . .*

How *disconcerting* that we are stripped of our greatest weapon when confronting our greatest enemy.

"More than Ihlini," Ian muttered. "They do not use the bow. They leave that to others."

"Atvians?"

"Atvian bowmen are perhaps the most dangerous in existence."

"Except for the Cheysuli."

Ian cast me a glance. "Do you forget? There are only two of us. I am the last to decry our warrior skills, *rujho*, but I am also the first to face realities. Judging by the number of arrows loosed, we are badly outnumbered."

"Only for the moment. The camp is not far from here— I will send Serri for reinforcements."

Ian nodded grimly. The link no longer functioned normally, but I trusted Serri's instincts better than my own. As I put my hand on his shoulder, the wolf rose, turned, loped away, heading eastward. Toward the Homanan encampment.

For two incredibly long months we had been in Solinde, breaching the borders and advancing steadily until we were easily three weeks from the Homanan border. From Mujhara, farther yet. And from Hondarth, where our father remained, we were at least a two-months' ride.

We had come in with mostly Cheysuli, but Homanan troops had followed on our heels. It was not war such as I had expected, being comprised primarily of border skirmishes and raids by quick-striking Solindish rebels, but I soon learned that death was death, regardless of its manifestation.

Carillon's methods, one of the captains had told me. *It was what defeated Bellam when Carillon came home from exile. If nothing else, the Solindish have learned in the intervening years.*

Oh, aye, they had learned. They knew that if you cannot raise a warhost of thousands, you raise what you can of hundreds. And use them carefully.

How many times? I wondered. *How many more times will Solinde levy war against Homana?*

"They come," Ian whispered.

Aye, they came. As I crouched in the thin Solindish grass, I watched the Solindish come. So carefully. So *very* carefully; like locusts methodically consuming the life of every stalk, they trampled down the grass even as they used it for a shield. I could see no men, no shapes; hear no words or weapons. Only the soft and subtle sibilance of an approach through winter grass.

There was no question the enemy knew where we were. Though we were screened by the grass even as they were, our horses marked our presence. Grimly I looked at them: Ian's gray stallion and my own red roan, browsing idly in the grass. Bits clinked, trappings clattered; Ian's stallion snorted.

And then, abruptly, the horses no longer grazed. They stared. Westward. Toward the enemy.

Serri, I said, *hurry*. Though I knew he could not hear me.

Ian darted upward, loosed an arrow, crouched down almost at once. I heard a shout from the enemy—it was of discovery, not of pain—and realized what Ian had meant to do. They marked our position very well now . . . and it was time we left it.

Ian caught my eye, pointed toward the horses. It was unlikely we could mount and escape without detection, but we could use the stallions for a distraction. Also a living screen. Much as I disliked the thought of sacrificing my horse, I disliked more the thought of sacrificing myself.

I nodded. Flattened. Tried to belly-crawl toward the horses without disturbing so much of the grass as to give our purpose away.

But we reached neither of the horses. Without warning, the grass in front of us burst into smoke and flame.

It was an acrid, oily smoke that filmed our faces, our eyes; tried to breach our mouths and make its way down our throats. I coughed, gagged, spat. My eyes burned. Teared. I could see nothing but smoke and flame.

The horses snorted, squealed, ran. Westward, away from the enemy.

Gods, but how I wished Ian and I could do the same. But we could not see to do it. We could not even *breathe*.

Out of the smoke there came a man, and then another. Solindish, with swords in their hands and determination in their eyes.

Another. Another. But I could not see to count the others.

Beside me, Ian lurched to his feet. I wanted to jerk him down again, to catch an arm and *jerk,* but I did not. I could only cough, wheeze, spit—and watch as he loosed arrows from a bow that trembled from the trembling of his hand upon it. He could not see, and yet he fought.

Two of the Solindish went down at once; Ian's skill was such that even half-blinded, even choked by acrid smoke, he could find the target. In this case, two. And in silence he nocked yet another arrow.

More men stepped out of the billowing smoke. And behind them came the Ihlini.

I knew him at once. Somehow, I *knew* him, though I had never seen him.

Blood calling to blood? No. That was Strahan's weapon, to make me think we were linked through blood and heritage.

And yet, it made me wonder.

Much as my brother had, I lurched upward to my feet. I jerked my sword from the sheath at my hip. The first man came in with his rusted blade—*rusted blade*—and swung at my head. It surprised me; not that he would strike, but that he left himself so open. No swordsman, this. Just a man. A man with an old, old sword. And a man about to die.

A single step forward, even as I ducked beneath the blow. A single thrust with my own blade. I felt the tip cut through the leather of his belt, scrape momentarily against a soft brass buckle, continue onward into belly, parting flesh, muscle, the vessels thick with blood. And how it spilled, the blood. How it ran out of the man to stain the fabric of his tunic, the silver of my steel; to splash, drop by rubescent drop, against the thirsty stalks of saffron Solindish grass and dye it lurid crimson.

I unsheathed the blade yet again, pulling it from the human scabbard, and turned to face the enemy once more.

This time it was the Ihlini.

Smoke peeled back from his shoulders as he crossed the ground to me. He wore gray, a pale lilac gray, twin to the smoke billowing at his bidding. His hair was black, his eyes blue; I thought at once of Hart, my second son.

"My lord," he said, "a message from Strahan." The Ihlini was calm, quiet-spoken. And he smiled. I judged him only a year or two older than myself. Young, strong, powerful. Filled with the confidence of his mission. Consumed by his dedication. "He says: *'Tell Donal's cub he should never have wed Gisella. Tell Donal's cub one day he will come to me.'*"

The sword hung from my hand. I had only to lift it—

But I did not. He had taken the intention from me. "No doubt," I answered. "No doubt I should not have, because it will be Strahan's undoing. I have children of the woman, Ihlini—sons. *Sons.* And so the new links are forged."

The smoke was a nimbus around him, clinging to his shoulders, hands, boots, like seasalt to a spar. It rose, billowed, built a wall, swallowing those around us until we were two men alone, confronting one another across generations of hatred, distrust . . . *fear?*

Could it be the Ihlini feared *us?*

Honesty undermines the falsehoods of arrogance: I knew I feared the Ihlini. And I was not afraid to admit it.

Silence lay around us. Within the walls of smoke there was no sound. The world had surely stopped. And without? Perhaps the wheel had warped; I thought he had made the time to stand quite still.

I faced him. "Strahan has said Ihlini and Cheysuli are kin. Children of the Firstborn."

He smiled a little. "It is said we are."

"Do you believe it?"

"I know better than to *dis*believe a thing that may be true." He shrugged; ash spilled down his shoulders.

"Is it repugnant to you?"

His black brows rose a little. "That the races may be linked? No. Not repugnant. Perhaps—*unappreciated.*" Again, he smiled. "Why do you ask, my lord?"

He gave me my rank, even as Strahan had. And without irony; a simple statement of address. Moment by moment, he peeled away the preconceptions I had built out of ugly stories.

Prejudice? No doubt. But I was not certain the Ihlini did not deserve it.

"I ask because if it is true the races are linked, you and I are kin."

He laughed. "The beginnings of a plea for leniency? You require mercy of me, my lord? Well, do not waste your breath. I intend to do to you what you desire to do to me." He tilted his head a little, as if he listened to a thing I could not hear. "Even were we *brothers,* it would not alter the melody." He began to smile even as I began to frown. "Can you not hear it? It is played, my lord, for us; because we will dance the dance of death."

He lifted a hand in a gracefully eloquent motion. In his fingers I saw the glint of silver, polished bright. Brilliant, blinding silver. But it was not, I saw, a knife.

He inclined his head in a gesture of subtle deference. Or was it in farewell? "My lord."

The hand was thrust skyward. I saw how the smoke

parted, making way for the thing in his hand. It glimmered, flashed, streaked upward into the sky.

I watched it. I tipped my head back, watching the silver fly; I saw it arc upward, slicing through lilac smoke, and then I knew what he intended.

I snapped my head down. "Oh, no," I told him, "you do not divert me with childish tricks of misdirection."

He did not even attempt to avoid my blade. I spitted him cleanly, front to back, and heard the scrape of bone against blade. And as he lay in a spreading pool of brackish, blackened blood, he laughed.

He *laughed.*

"My lord," he said, still smiling, "say to me *which* diversion was misdirec—"

—and he was dead. I stared down at the face gone suddenly slack in death, the abrupt cessation of *life*, leaving him empty, *spent* . . . so devoid of that which had made him a man. Ihlini, Solindish, even Homanan or Cheysuli. He was a man. And he was dead.

And then the silver lanced out of the sky and buried itself in the top of my left shoulder, and I understood his words at last.

Misdirection, aye. And now it might prove lethal.

The pain drove me to one knee. Of its own accord my right hand loosed the hilt of the sword and flew to clasp my shoulder. I felt steel, sharp, deadly steel, wafer-thin, deeply imbedded; a flat, curving spike was all that protruded above the surface of my flesh, my jerkin; the rest was firmly sheathed in muscle and bone. My left arm dangled helplessly at my side.

I caught the elbow, dragged the forearm around so I could cradle the limb against my abdomen.

—oh—gods—the *pain*—

"Serri—" I gasped. "Ian—?"

The smoke was gone. I saw the last wisps of it sucked back into the Ihlini's body as if it were a part of his soul; now that he was dead, so was the power dead. Crushed grass was his shroud; bloodied soil became his bier.

My fingers twitched. Again. All the muscles in my arm tautened, from shoulder to fingertips. My fingers curled up, tucked beneath my folded thumb. The rigidity was absolute.

"Ian—"

I vomited. Shuddered. Retched. Sweat ran down my flesh beneath the clothing. I twitched. I smelled the tang of fear. The stink of helplessness.

Oh—gods—Ian—

I put out my hand and touched the face of death.

Two

I heard someone cry out. The sound hurt my ears. It set my head to throbbing. Inwardly, I cursed the man who made the noise . . . and then I realized he was myself.

"Gods!" I blurted aloud. "What are you *doing* to me?"

Lir, *be still.* That from Serri, seated next to the cot.

"Pulling a tooth." Ian's voice, and very near.

"Tooth?" Dazed from pain I might be, but I knew well enough that what resided in my shoulder was not anything like a *tooth.*

"Sorcerer's Tooth," Ian answered. "An Ihlini weapon . . . the name suits, I think."

I lurched nearly upright as the pain renewed itself. Hands pressed me back down upon the cot. Ian's. Another's. And yet a third dug at the tooth in my shoulder. "Gods, Ian— can you not do this yourself? Save me some pain—use the earth magic on this wound!"

Lir, *be still. Do not bestir yourself.*

"I cannot. The Tooth is an Ihlini thing. It will have to heal of its own."

"Give him wine," someone suggested. "Let him drink himself into a stupor."

"No." A third voice, also unknown to me. "I know little enough of the Ihlini, but I *do* know they resort to poison much of the time. I think the Tooth was not tampered with—but I will not take the chance. Give him no wine, or we may kindle the poison."

I gritted my teeth so hard I thought they might fall into dust in my mouth. "Just pull it out. *Cut* it out . . . will you rid me of this thing?"

"My lord, we are trying."

"Try harder." Sweat ran down my face and dampened

the pillow beneath my head. Poisoned or not, the Tooth was setting my body afire.

"*Rujho*—" Ian again "—one more moment—"

Hands tightened on me. I felt the sharp pain slice into my flesh, and then abruptly the thing was wrenched free.

"There," someone said; fatuous satisfaction.

"Let it bleed," the other suggested. "If there is a poison, the blood will carry it out."

"And if there is not, the blood will carry out his *life*." Ian had never been impressed with the sometimes questionable skill of Homanan physicians; being Cheysuli, he had alternatives. But at the moment, I did not. "Pack it, bind up the wound," he said calmly, but I heard the note of command in his tone. "Then let him sleep."

They did as he told them, and so did I. I slept.

Something landed on my chest. A small weight only, but it awakened me. I opened my eyes, saw Ian standing by me, shut them again.

"The Tooth," he said. "You are lucky; it carried no poison. You will survive, *rujho*."

I did not feel like it. I felt wretched. My mouth was filmed with sourness; I licked my lips, wanted to spit. Wanted to swallow wine or water, hoping to wash away the bitter tang.

I opened my eyes and looked up at Ian. The light in the field pavilion was thin, hardly enough to illuminate the interior, but the fabric was unbleached ivory and lent meager strength to the dim winter light. Still, Ian was mostly clothed in shadow; his eyes, lids lowered, were black instead of yellow.

"Tooth," I muttered. I scraped my good hand across the rough army blanket and found the thing my brother had dropped. Picked it up; felt the cool kiss of the shining steel. Ice in my hand, I thought. And yet the wound in my shoulder burned.

It was a thin, circular wafer of steel, perfectly flat, edged with curving spikes honed to invisible points. Starshaped, in a way, except the shape was too refined, too fluid; the spikes flowed out of the steel to form a subtle vanguard at the wafer's edge. There were runes etched in the metal.

I grimaced. This thing, thrown from the sorcerer's hand,

had lanced out of the sky to imbed itself in flesh and bone. As if it had a life of its own. As if it knew its target.

Abruptly, I held it out to my brother. "Take it. The Tooth is out of the jaw; now you may dispose of it."

Ian, accepting Ihlini steel, smiled a little. He tucked it into his belt-pouch.

Serri?

Here, lir. I felt a nose, cool and damp, pressed against my hand. I opened my fingers and stroked the place between his eyes, in the center of his charcoal mask. His eyes watched me avidly. *You will recover,* lir.

I did not really doubt it. I looked at Ian again. "How many slain?"

"Ten Solindish; there were only twelve of them. The reinforcements arrived directly after you went down."

I nodded. "How many of us were slain?"

"Two Homanans. Two wounded."

I frowned. "What is it they mean to do? Here we are in Solinde, where we have been for two months, and yet we hardly fight. Occasionally, aye—I do not discount the men we have already lost . . . but I am perplexed by the enemy's intentions. We have Cheysuli with us as well as Homanans, and yet we hardly see more than twenty Solindish at a time."

"Gnats nipping at horses." Ian nodded. "As Sayre says, it was Carillon's way. But I think there may be an explanation." He shrugged a little. "A thought, only—but what if the enemy's numbers have been vastly overestimated? What if the rebellion itself is far smaller than we have been told?"

"But the intelligence comes out of Lestra, from the regent." I frowned. "You cannot mean Wycliff is a traitor. . . ."

"No. He is a loyal Homanan, serving our *jehan* as best he can. No. I think the intelligence is manipulated before it reaches Wycliff. I think he is given reports of numbers that do not exist; where there are ten men, forty are reported. By the time the news reaches Lestra—and later Mujhara—the number is ten times greater than the truth."

"Then the Ihlini are *using* us . . . drawing us away from their true objective." I frowned. "Hondarth? *Jehan* is there, and Rowan. There were Solindish ships. . . ." Ian shook his head. "News travels slowly in war—slower yet in winter . . . who can say how things stand now in Hondarth? And each day the weather worsens. Sayre says there will be snowfall before the day is out."

A winter war. I shivered from the suggestion. "Is it possible the Ihlini manipulate the Solindish? That there really is little more than *mutters* of rebellion, no rebellion of itself?"

"I am quite certain the Ihlini manipulate the Solindish. What I *cannot* say for certain is if this realm truly does wish to attack Homana." His expression was grim. "I have no doubt there are many here who desire independence from Homana—before Carillon defeated Bellam, Solinde never had a foreign overlord—but are they as dangerous as we fear? Oh, aye, there are rebels, raiders . . . zealots—" he did not smile "—but there are always those who seek to throw down the power and take it for themselves. *Regardless* of the competence of the king."

"*Jehan* should be told."

"I am sure he knows. He has fought Solinde before."

"But that was with Carillon."

He did not answer at once. And when he did, his tone was full of infinite understanding. "A man learns, Niall. How to fight, how to lead, how to rule." His face was oddly serene; I saw compassion in his eyes. "You are learning now."

I shut my eyes under the cover of weakness from my wound. I knew what he implied: that soon I would lead the army in fact as well as name. For I did not lead it now. Wisely, my father had not expected me to know what a man must know in order to conduct a war. He expected me to *learn* it—and so he had dispatched veteran Homanan captains to lead us through this war.

"Niall."

I opened my eyes.

"The gods choose only worthy men."

I grimaced. "The gods can make mistakes."

He smiled a little; I had been very decisive. "Blasphemy?"

"The gods made the Ihlini."

The smile was banished. "Aye. They did. And often—I wonder why."

No more than I. No more than any Cheysuli, beginning to wonder if indeed the gods *had* sowed a second crop.

A winter crop, I thought; a deep-winter harvest. There was no warmth in the air. No spring. No summer. No light. Only Darkness.

Sayre tipped back his cup of warmed wine and drained it. He took it away, wiped the excess from his mouth with a forearm, nodded consideringly. "You may have the right of it, my lord."

It was a concession. Sayre and I got on as well or better than any of the captains, and I had taken to discussing strategies with the veteran. He had fought with my father and with Carillon. He was not old, but his youth had been spent on the battlefield. He lacked half his right ear; it put me in mind of Strahan, lacking the ear entirely.

He scratched idly at a reddish eyebrow. A thin pale scar bisected it. His ruddy hair was liberally sprinkled with white. "Complacency would be deadly, but I think the men are prepared. Fit. When the Solindish come, we will take them."

I shifted on the stool. "This encampment has stood safely for five weeks, captain. We have fought no one for that long. How can you be certain the Solindish will *ever* come?" I put a hand on Serri's head and buried fingers in the lushness of his pelt. "If they do not, we waste our time. But if the *Ihlini* come instead. . . ." I rubbed my left shoulder. The wound left by the Tooth had healed well enough, but the scar was tender still. It ached almost constantly in the bitter cold.

Sayre rose, thrusting his stool away from the table. He reached for the leather-bound tankard, poured, filled his cup and mine again, though I had drunk only half. He scowled blackly out of his wind-chafed, reddened face, gulping wine again. It set watery blue eyes ablaze.

"Let them come," he said flatly. "Let them come. My Homanans will be ready."

I said nothing. I knew the captain too well. And in a moment he did as I expected: he cursed and sat down again.

"Aye, aye—you may have the right of it. How better to suck the will to fight from men than by frightening it out of them?" He swore again, set the cup down so hard wine slopped over the rim. It splashed against the wooden table and filled nicks, scratches, divots hacked out by steel. Saying nothing, I retreated from the spillage by lifting my arms and leaning away from the table. "My Homanans are veterans, but they have fought only men," he said. "Who can say what they will do when faced with Ihlini sorcerers?"

"Captain—" But I stopped. His eyes had taken on the glazed expression of reminiscence; he was lost in battles long past.

"I recall the night Tynstar came upon us," he said in an almost eerie detachment.

I looked at him more attentively.

"Tynstar came upon us and took away the moon. He filled it up with blood." His mouth tightened in a faint grimace of distaste. "He sent a mist across the land, a *miasma*, intended to swallow us all. And all the army panicked, as he intended, save for Rowan, Carillon, Donal . . . and even the Ellasian prince, Evan, your father's boon companion." He frowned a little, lost in his recollections. "He meant to slay us then, to defeat us *before* the battle, and yet he was unable. Donal threw the magic sword at Tynstar, and the sorcery was broken."

I thought of the sorcery *I* had faced, in the circle of lilac smoke.

"The sorcery was broken," Sayre repeated. "But it was by a Cheysuli—the Homanans were too afraid."

"Then perhaps we should seek out the rebels," I suggested. "Perhaps we can finish this war for good."

"Perhaps we should let them come to us." Sayre was unsmiling. "They know this land; we do not."

I rose abruptly, went to the doorflap of the field pavilion and pulled it aside. Beyond me lay the horizon. The day was cold, windy, depressing. Clouds huddled on blue-frosted plains.

"There is little to recommend a winter war," I said quietly, rubbing again at my shoulder. "I think the Solindish will not come. And I think we should go to Lestra."

"By your leave, my lord—I think I must disagree."

I smiled. "You are welcome to disagreement. But I say equally freely: I do not think the Solindish will wage war against us *and* the weather."

"So you want us to winter in the city instead of here on the plains." Sayre's tone was eloquent in its careful intonation. "If we do so, my lord, we leave open the leagues between Lestra and the Homanan border. Open, to the *enemy*—" He paused. "Open to the enemy *and* those men who serve the bastard."

My teeth gritted. Aye, the bastard. His fame grew each day, and each day we lost one or two Homanans who decided to change allegiances in hopes of better food, warmer bedding, higher pay. I could not openly curse the bastard for leading his growing army in skirmishes against the Solindish borderers—intended ostensibly to *help* me—but privately I cursed him at least once every hour. Those skirmishes mostly helped *his* reputation; word of Elek's murder had tainted my own name and brightened that of Carillon's misbegotten son.

"What profit in taking the borders in deep winter?" I demanded curtly, swinging to face the man. "I think they *keep* us here for purposes of their own."

From outside there came a call. Ian's voice; I turned again. With him was a young man all wrapped in winter furs and leather.

"*Rujho*—messages from Mujhara." Ian ducked through the flap and into Sayre's pavilion, nodding a greeting to the man. He wore heavy furs against the cold and gloves upon his hands. No gold showed, not even in his ear. Against the wind he wore his hair longer than normal, even as I did myself.

The young man entered also. He was hooded, wrapped in woolen scarves. In his hand there was a sealed parchment. "My lord." He pulled wool away from his mouth. "My lord—for you."

I took the damp parchment, broke the brittle seal, opened it with difficulty—the parchment stuck, tore, nearly came apart in my hands—then looked at the messenger in dismay. "I can read none of this. The paper is mostly ruined, and the ink has run."

"My lord, I am sorry." Weariness made him almost curt. "It—was difficult reaching you. The Ihlini have fired the land."

"Fired?" I frowned. "Be plainer of speech."

"*Fired,*" he repeated. "Everything between here and the Homanan border has been put to the torch. People are dead, game dispersed, all winter supplies destroyed. My lord—do you see what they have done? They have cut you off from Homana. You must go farther inward in order to survive."

"*In*ward." I looked at Ian. "So now we know their plan."

Sayre swore violently. "An old trick," he said flatly. "Drive the enemy homeward and into starvation—or drive them inward to death in battle. I should have seen it. I should have *known* it!" He shook his ruddy head. "By the gods, I should have listened to you."

I looked at the messenger. His expression was limned in starkness against the bleakness of the day. "*You* made it through."

"Aye, my lord. But I was one man. I carried some winter rations with me, and grain. But—an *army*. . . ." Uncomfortable with the truth, he shook his head and shrugged. "What little game is left will die of starvation soon. There is no grass for the horses, no feed or grain stored away. All has been destroyed."

I turned abruptly and gestured for wine. Sayre acceded at once, handing over a freshly-poured cup of steaming wine. I put it into the messenger's hands. "You will be fed. You will be given time to rest. But first—were you given the message verbally as well as written out?"

He sipped. Nodded. Sighed. "Aye, my lord. General Rowan said parchments may go astray; he gave me the words as well."

"You have come from Hondarth?" I asked in surprise. "But this seal is the Queen's."

"The general is at Homana-Mujhar, *with* the Queen." He sipped again; color began to steal back into his pallid flesh. "Two messages, my lord: from the general, from the Queen."

"Rowan's first," I said at once. And then, thinking of my sons, I wished I had said the other.

The young man nodded. His brown eyes blanked a little as he sought to recall the words precisely as they had been said. "There is plague in Mujhara," he told me. "It spreads throughout Homana."

"*Plague!*"

"It slays one out of every family, sometimes more," he continued. "The Homanans fall ill of a fever, but most recover, unless they are very young or very old. But—it is the *Cheysuli*—"

He stopped. He looked at Ian, at the *lir*. Lastly he looked at me.

"Aye?" I asked with mounting dread.

He wet his lips. "For every five Cheysuli stricken, four will die. And—so with the *lir*, my lord."

"The *lir*—" Ian moved stiffly closer. "This touches the *lir* as well?"

"My lord." He stared into his wine. "Often the warrior recovers. But if the *lir* does not. . . ." White-faced, he looked at me. "If the *lir* does not, the warrior dies anyway."

"Two-fold," Ian whispered. "Slaying one, the plague slays *both*."

I put a hand on Ian's arm, more for me than for my brother. "This plague is in *Mujhara?*"

"Aye, my lord—and Clankeep. It spreads throughout Homana."

"My sons," I said blankly. "My sons are in Mujhara."

"And our *rujholla* is in Clankeep, along with other kin." Ian's face was bleak. "Gods, *rujho*, how can we stay here?"

"My lord." The messenger's tone was raised, as if he knew we meant to leave him before he had completed his task. "My lord, there is the other message. From the Queen of Homana."

I nodded, still too numb to do much more. *My sons are in Mujhara.*

"My lord, she sends to say the Princess has conceived."

I gaped. "Gisella—?"

"In five months, my lord—less than that, *now*—you will have another child." He paused. *"Ru'shalla-tu."*

I looked at him more sharply. *"You* are Cheysuli?"

"No, my lord. Homanan. But it seems a wise thing to learn the tongue of those who rule."

"Thank the gods for a little wisdom." I looked at Ian. "You know we have to go."

"*I* know. But you heard what he has said. No game, no people, no supplies. . . ." He shrugged. "It will not be easy, *rujho*."

"And if we do not try, we will never sleep again."

"No," he agreed bleakly. "Yet I think I will not regardless, until I know our kin are safe."

I nodded. *A child. Oh gods, another child. Now* three *will be at risk—*

I turned to look at Sayre. "In the morning we will leave. Only Ian and I; it would profit no one to take more. Captain—" I paused, "—do what you can to win this war. However you have to win it."

"Aye, my lord. Of course."

Oh gods, I thought, *my children.*

The heirs to the prophecy.

Three

The land lay in ruin. Although the Solindish plains lacked the heavy forests of Homana, it had boasted its share of scrubby trees, tangled hedges, thick turf, lush grasses. Now there was nothing, *nothing at all*—only charred turf, skeletal remains of blackened trees, ash and grit in place of grass. The land rolled on forever in its funerary finery, stretching eastward toward Homana.

Our horses sluffed through grit and ash, stirring a pall of pale gray dust that filmed our *lir*, our mounts, our clothing. Ice and frost rimed stones, frozen piles of hoof-churned earth, even the naked, twisted trees. Like jewels, ice crystals glittered. Beneath its wealth, the charring lent false glory to ruined wood. Like diamonds, like jet, it blazed and glittered in the thin blue light of an early winter morn, cloaking itself in transient ornamentation.

Though much of my face was hidden in woolen wrappings, my breath still escaped; plumed frost in the frigid air. I was weighed down in hood, furs, leathers, woolens, but still I was cold. Yet I could not say if the chill I experienced was born of temperature or sickened disbelief.

I squinted against the bite of bitter cold. We walked; we did not gallop, did not trot, shadowed by our *lir*, but still the movement stirred our eyes to protest. Tears gathered, spilled over; I scrubbed briefly at my cheeks with a gloved hand, not desiring to let the tears freeze in the winter-chafed creases of tender flesh. For warmth, I had grown back the beard that made me Carillon, but mostly I was *cold*.

"How could they do it?" I asked, though most of it was muffled behind the wool. "How could they destroy so much of their homeland?"

"Desperation?" Ian, also hooded, shook his head a little.

"Dedication, determination . . . perhaps those and more. I do not doubt it was a difficult decision."

"But to *slay* people? Their own people?"

His shrug was swallowed by the bulk of heavy leathers. "If you are engaged in a war to which you are fully committed, and a portion of your own people refuse to join or render aid, perhaps it becomes easier to sentence them to death."

"Indiscriminate *murder?*" I stared at him in amazement. *"How?"*

Ian pulled the wrap from his mouth. "I did not say I understood it, Niall—I only offer a possible explanation."

"Gods." I was sickened by the thought. "I could never make such a decision. Determine the fates of innocent people? Never. It is not a man's place."

"It will be yours, one day."

"No."

"Rujho—of course it will. What do you think kingship entails? You have attended council meetings, have heard our *jehan* render judgments. He makes choices, *rujho.* So will you."

"Our *jehan* would never order a thing as ghastly as this," I declared. "Murder, destruction . . . *rujho,* look around you! Crops ruined, dwellings burned down . . . even the livestock and wild game stripped of food and homes. How will the land recover?"

"It will. It will take time, but vegetation will grow back, crops will recover, crofts and hovels will be rebuilt, even the game will begin to return." He looked around grimly. "This is a waste, a terrible, senseless waste, but it is not complete destruction. The land will live again."

I shivered. "Idiocy," I muttered. "When we have won this war, the Solindish will see that this benefits none of their people."

"No, no benefit," Ian agreed. "But if you are going to lose a war, you take desperate measures. And if that war is lost regardless of those measures, at least you have left nothing to benefit the victor."

I looked at my brother. There was little of him I could see, just a shapeless mass atop a winter-furred tall gray stallion. But with the wrappings pulled down, I could see nearly all of his face. Beardless, I thought he looked younger than I. And yet he was so much wiser.

"You should be the heir," I said finally. "You should be, Ian. You are better suited. I think the *a'saii* have had the right of it all along."

He shook his head at once. "I am *not* better suited, Niall. You do not live in my skin; you cannot know how I think, how I feel about things. I am not right for the Lion. That task is meant for you."

"And if I died? If the plague took me, or a Solindish sword—or even a Sorcerer's Tooth. . . ." I looked at him with a calm expectation that was as surprising to me as to him. "If I died, *rujho*, could you accept the Lion?"

The shock made a mask of his face; he stared. And there was apprehension in his eyes. "Niall—"

"Could you?"

After a moment, he blew out a rushing breath that wreathed his face in fog. "You have two sons, *rujho*, and perhaps a third yet to come. The choice, thank the gods, will never be mine to make."

No. It never would be. Unless all of us were slain. And I thought that supremely unlikely.

I looked down at Serri, trotting by my roan. *Unless the plague took every one of us.*

"Why did you ask, Niall? Why is it important for you to know?"

I shrugged. "But for an accident of birth, it might be *you* who was meant for the Lion. In the clans, there would be no question of it. You were firstborn. And yet, because of Homanan law, only Aislinn's son can inherit. It seems unfair."

"It is not." Ian reined his stallion around a frozen hummock of charred turf, searching automatically for Tasha. Against the blackened, frost-rimed earth, her ruddy coat glowed like heated bronze. "It is what the gods intended, or they would have put us in one another's places." He smiled. "I am the fortunate one, *rujho*. My choices will be easier than yours."

"No." I disagreed in pointed affability. "Because I will make you help me with *mine*."

My brother laughed.

*   *   *

We watered our mounts, our *lir*, and ourselves at whatever streams and burns we could find, although many were frozen solid. Otherwise we drank sparingly of the contents of our waterskins and refilled them at the first opportunity. Food we rationed carefully, along with grain; we could not afford to waste a single pinch because it was unlikely our stores could be replenished. There was no game, no crops, no winter supplies. What we carried was our portion.

I wanted to avoid the charred wreckage of crofts and the remains of other dwellings, sickened by the first two we had visited in search of life and food. But Ian insisted we stop at each one because, he said, a man could not afford to ignore any opportunity. He had the right of it, my brother, but I did not enjoy the discoveries of bodies buried in the wreckage, burned, battered, broken, as if they were only toys. But the enemy had been thorough. There was no food, no water, no stored supplies that had not been methodically spoiled or destroyed.

And so we crossed the charnelhouse of Solinde praying we would reach Homana before our rations—or courage—gave out.

I thought often of the plague. So clearly I recalled how, more than a year earlier—nearly *two*—the furrier in Mujhara's Market Square had spoken of a plague in the north, believed to be carried by white wolves. And I recalled also, but a six-month ago, how the guardsmen seeking me had spoken of white wolves as well, desiring to slay *me* for the bounty. The thing had begun so long ago, and yet we had ignored it, believing it a fleeting thing, a piece of nonsense embroidered with falsehood, a story told at the sheepherders' fires to keep them awake while dogs warded the flocks against wolves of any color.

But now the tale was true. Now the beast was loose.

We crossed the border at last and saw how the Solindish had taken care not to raze any of Homana. With the naked eye a man could see the ragged line of demarcation, the sword's edge that divided Homana from Solinde. Here there was grass, though frosted; here there was life, though sluggish in the cold; here there was the promise of continuance. In Solinde, there was only the promise of ending.

And here there were also men, confronting us on horseback as we rode across the border.

Like us, they were bundled in furs, leathers, woolens. Caps and hoods hid their heads and much of their faces; I recognized none of them. They were Homanans, but that was all I could discern.

Ian and I, with our *lir*, crossed into Homana and the Homanans told us to halt almost at once. Muted light ran the length of their bared swords, but dully; the sun shone only fitfully through the mesh of scalloped snowclouds hanging low across the plains.

One man rode a little forward of the others (I counted fourteen in all) and halted. He looked at the *lir*, then at Ian, marking his yellow eyes. Lastly he looked at me, and he frowned. "Cheysuli," he said. "Both of you?"

"Aye," I told him, waiting.

He looked at me a trifle harder. But, as was his, most of my face was hidden; it is difficult to recognize a man well warded against the winter. "There is plague," he said abruptly. "Have you heard? All throughout Homana."

"And are you a patrol sent to turn us from our homeland?"

The other men murmured among themselves. This one did not answer at once. He squinted a little, peering past me toward the ravished plains of Solinde. "Are you from the Homanan army?"

"No," Ian answered wryly. "We are from the *Solindish* army."

The man's brown eyes flicked back to Ian. There was a glint of disapproval in his eyes. Not much of a sense of humor. "Shapechanger," he said levelly, "this is no time for levity. Least of all for you." A jerk of his head indicated the men waiting behind him. "We are men who serve the son of Carillon."

Inwardly, I swore. Outwardly, I did nothing.

Ian nodded slowly. "We have been long out of Homana. How does the petition proceed?"

The other shrugged. "The Mujhar is in Hondarth, the Homanan Council divided because of the war. The petition, for now, is set aside, but only for a while. When the war is done and spring is come, we will set *our* lord in Niall's place."

"Murderer," one of the other men said. "He slew Elek."

No, he did not—at least, not intentionally. But I did not dare to say it aloud.

Idly, Ian smoothed the pale mane of his dark gray horse. "This plague—how serious is it?"

"Serious for the Cheysuli. You would do better to stay in Solinde."

"No," we answered together.

He eyed us more attentively. "We will not turn you back. Cheysuli, Homanan, it does not matter. Our duty lies with our lord."

"Are you recruiting?" Ian asked.

The brown eyes narrowed. "And are you of the *a'saii?*"

So, even the Homanans knew of the zealots. "Why?" I asked aloud. "Have the *a'saii* joined with you?"

"We asked. They declined: our objectives are too different. And so the pact was never made." He shrugged, re-wraping his dark blue muffler. "But I think the *a'saii* are finished; too many of them are dead."

They were my enemy, the *a'saii.* But they were of my race, my clan, my kin; I grieved for their deaths. I grieved for the deaths of their *lir.*

"What of you?" Ian asked. "The plague is not *that* selective. Homanans are dying also."

I heard murmuring again. A glance at the others showed me furtive looks exchanged; expressions of bleakness and affirmation. No matter what was said, the bastard's adherents also suffered losses. *Many* losses; like the *a'saii,* their cause might be overcome by misfortune rather than anything I might do.

"We will win. We have the gods on our side."

"Tahlmorra lujhala mei wiccan, cheysu," Ian quoted. "The fate of a man rests always within the palm of the gods."

The Homanan turned his horse aside. And we were home at last.

We found little more welcome in Homana than we had in Solinde. Here the land was whole, the dwellings unburned, the crofters alive, the game and livestock healthy, but fear and suspicion also thrived. We were Cheysuli, and Cheysuli carried the plague.

Ian and I learned quickly that it was best if *I* went to

the doors and asked for food and water, offering coin in return; for once, my Homanan looks stood me in good stead. But even so, as we drew closer to Mujhara the wary welcomes turned to rude refusals.

And then, with a week's ride left to Mujhara, we stopped at a snowbound croft and were given warm welcome, both of us, and invited in for a meal. The old woman was alone, but did not appear to fear us or the plague. With our *lir* she took us in and served hot food and tart cider, spiced with a twist of cinnamon. And when at last we took our furs off in the heat of the tiny dwelling, our *lir*-gold was bared to a smiling—if toothless—reception.

"Aye," she said, "I knew you were Cheysuli. Even buried under fur and leather. *You* have the eyes—" she looked at Ian "—and the animals are more than pets. *Lir*, are they? Aye. Lovely beasts."

Her white hair was quite fine, thinning; it straggled out of a tight-wrapped knot of braid at the crown of her head. All the days of the world were in the tapestry of her face. Her faded blue eyes were rheumy, eaten away with the promise of milk-blindness, but even when she could no longer see with them, I knew she would see with her heart.

"Lady," I said, *"Leijhana tu'sai."*

She sat in her chair and rocked a little, grinning at my words. "Old Tongue." She nodded, knotting her hands in the ends of her faded brown shawl. "Been so long since I heard it. But even then, it was strange to me. My mouth did not want to shape the words."

I looked at her in startled supposition. "You are not Cheysuli?"

"No, no, not I. Not Cheysuli, no." She grinned. She rocked. She laughed.

"Lady," Ian said. "You know there is plague in the land, and yet you invite us in. You invite *Cheysuli* in."

"I am old. I have no one but myself, and my cat." The gray tabby, in the face of much larger kin in Tasha, had retreated to the mantel over the fireplace. "When my time comes, I will give it good welcome. But I think this Ihlini mischief will not send *me* to the gods." She nodded. She rocked. She smiled.

"Ihlini." I exchanged a glance with Ian. "You say the *plague* is Ihlini?"

"Born of Strahan, aye." Again she nodded. Her eyes were closed. She rocked. "It has been coming a long, long time. I remember the days of Tynstar, in Solinde, when he first told Bellam that Homana was his for the taking. And so together they took it, once Shaine was slain in the Great Hall of Homana-Mujhar. Tynstar chased Carillon out of his homeland and into exile in foreign realms. . . ." Her recital trailed off. Ian and I stared at her in silence, shocked to hear her repeat so much of our House's history. "But he came home again, he did, and took Homana back, and then Tynstar stole his youth. Tynstar was strong, but so was Carillon. And in the end, Carillon prevailed." She smiled briefly; it faded quickly enough. "But Tynstar sired a son on Carillon's queen, and now that son is loosed upon the land. Like the plague of Asar-Suti."

She said nothing more. In the silence of the tiny room Ian and I waited for her to finish. But she said nothing more.

"Lady," I said at last, "how is it you know so much of Tynstar? So much of Shaine?"

"Because I was alive when Shaine was Mujhar." Her rheumy eyes creased in good-natured humor. "And Tynstar was my lord."

"Your *lord?*" I was on my feet at once, hand closing on my knife hilt. "Lady—"

"Aye," she said, "he *was*. And aye, I am Ihlini. But I bid you not to slay me: I am not the enemy. Save your anger for Tynstar's son."

She stopped rocking. She sat very still in her chair, a small, old, fragile woman, who had suckled at a Solindish breast.

"Why are you in Homana?" Ian asked, genuinely curious as well as wary. So was I.

"Because I like it," she answered. "Because now it is my home." Suddenly she laughed. From some hidden place beneath her shawl, she withdrew a thing that glittered. She held it out in the candlelight, and we saw the stone. A multi-faced crystal; pale, perfect pink. "Take it," she said. "Take my lifestone. If you believe I mean you harm, you have only to crush it, or throw it in the fire. And the world will lack one more Ihlini witch."

After a moment, I put out my hand and took the stone

from her withered palm. I was ungloved; the crystal took on the color of my flesh, altering texture and hue until it was hidden in my hand. Perfect camouflage. It seemed weightless, though it was not. It seemed to have no temperature, though when I first had touched it the stone was undeniably cool.

"Lifestone," I echoed. "What does it do?"

"We have no *lir*," she told me. "We have a stone instead. It is a locus for our power." Her eyes were on the stone. "I have so little, now; I am too old. And I renounced Asar-Suti."

"Renounced him!" Ian stared at her. "And you were left alive?"

The old woman tilted her head a little. "Betimes I think I was not. But that is only because I am so old. I lost my youth when I broke faith with the Seker. It was the cost. And now, I wait for the day I will die."

I frowned a little. "How old, lady? How many years have you?"

Briefly, she counted on fragile fingers. And then she grinned her toothless grin. "Only two," she said. "Two hundred. Not so old, when you think of how old Tynstar was. Or how old Strahan will be, if no one seeks him out and slays him." She looked at us both. "You might," she said. "Go to him, seek him out, end the Seker's plague. It is the only way you will save your people. The only way the world will survive."

She put out her hand. I returned the stone. Before my eyes, it flamed, sent a single tendril of lilac smoke into the air, and then its momentary brilliance was snuffed out. "If you could take his lifestone, his power would be ended," she told me. "If you cannot, at least destroy the white wolf."

"Gods," I blurted, "you wish me to slay *myself*?"

Her hand spasmed, shutting away the pale pink stone. "You?" she said. "*You* are the Prince of Homana?"

"Aye, lady—I am."

"Then you *must* go. It is a task you must perform." Distractedly, she pushed at the wisps of pearlescent hair encroaching into her face. "Go home, my lord of Homana. And then go to Valgaard, Strahan's fortress, in the mountains of Solinde. It will be Homana's deliverance."

"And that is what you desire?" Ian asked gently. "Forgive me, but you are Ihlini. What reason can you give us to believe what you have told us?"

"Reason?" Clearly, she was shocked. "I have told you the truth. It should be enough."

Ihlini, my conscience whispered, as Ian and I exchanged dubious glances.

"Reason." She whispered it to herself. "I am *too* old; I have forgotten what hatred lies between the Firstborn's children—what prejudice there is—"

"Lady." Ian's tone was distinctly displeased; I recalled how he had reacted when Lillith had discussed our supposed kinship on the voyage to Atvia. "We are not bloodbound, lady. Not Ihlini and Cheysuli."

"No?" She smiled, shrugged, rewrapped her faded shawl. "No, then. As you wish."

I looked at Serri. *Lir?*

He remained conspicuously silent. Old the woman might be, and lacking most of her magic, but the link was affected by her nearness to us.

I caught Ian's eye and hooked my head toward the door in a silent suggestion. Equally silent, he nodded once and rose. We put on pounds of leather and fur again, wrapped our faces in wool and pulled up our hoods from our shoulders.

"Lady," I said, "our gratitude. *Leijhana tu'sai.*"

Unsmiling, she looked at us. "I will give you proof."

"Proof?"

"Reason to believe." She pressed herself out of the chair. She was tiny, fragile, bowed down with the weight of her age. "Proof," she murmured. "My gift to you—my gift to *Homana*—" And with amazing accuracy she threw the crystal into the fire.

"No!" I leaped for her, trying to catch her in my arms as the lifestone fell into the flames, but by the time I touched the woman she was only made of dust. Only *dust* in the shape of a woman, and then even that was banished.

Slowly I opened my hands. Tiny crystals glittered against the flesh of my callused palms. Slowly I tipped them; dust sifted, drifted, settled against the earthen floor.

I looked at my brother in silence.

"Gods—" But he stopped. There were no words for this. He turned and walked out of the croft.

Four

There were marks on the doors in Mujhara. At first Ian and I stared at them blankly in ignorance, and then the answer became quite clear. A red slash meant plague was in the dwelling. A black one signified death.

All around us was silence, except for the sounds of our horses. Grayish snowdrifts stretched from doorway to doorway, filmed with grime and ash. Down the center of each street was beaten a narrow path of dirty slush over frosted, muddy cobbles. Our horses slipped and slid, pressing slush into horseshoe-shaped crusts of ice. Behind us came Tasha and Serri.

Though it was midmorning, passers-by were infrequent. As they saw us, they huddled more deeply into their wrappings and hastened out of our way. I saw ward-signs made against our *lir*, our horses, ourselves, and realized yet another reason for distrusting Cheysuli had acquired significance. Now they feared us for the plague.

The pewter-colored sky spat snow at us, but fitfully. Flakes no larger than the end of my smallest finger drifted diagonally across my path of vision, sticking to leathers, wool, horsehair, waiting for others to follow. I squinted, burrowing bearded chin more deeply into wool; the path before my roan was quickly transformed from gray to white.

After so many weeks of riding, not knowing what I might find, I discovered I wanted to do it again so the answer would be delayed. I did not want to halt at the bronze-and-timber gates of Homana-Mujhar and see the crimson slash of a plague-house, or the black of a house of death. I did not want to look at all; even as Ian halted before me, I stared steadfastly at the ground.

"My lord!" someone cried.

"My lord prince!" cried another, and the wide gates were opened to us.

I looked up. I saw the leaves of the gate swinging slowly open before me. And I saw the red mark upon them.

"Rujho?" Ian waited. And I realized I had not moved to enter the outer bailey.

"My lord." Someone took my roan's damp rein. "My lord?"

I bestirred myself to look down at the man. I did not know his name, but I had seen him frequently around the exterior of the palace. One of the Mujharan Guard whose duty it was to tend the gates.

"No soot," I said. "No soot upon the gate."

"No, my lord—not yet."

"Niall." Ian again. "Here is where we part."

I looked at him in surprise. "You are not going to come in with me?"

"I will go to Clankeep. Isolde is there, and others." He reined back the gray who wanted to go home to a stable he knew. "I will be back as soon as possible, *depending*—" He broke off, looked eastward, yanked wool away from his face. "Gods, *rujho*, I am afraid of what I will find."

Snow gathered on his shoulders and on the rim of his hood. There was no sun, only the dim flat light of a winter day, so that most of his face was hidden in bluish shadow. There was tension in the set of his mouth and jaw; in the flesh around his eyes. Freed of the woolen wrappings, his breath smoked in the frigid air.

"No more than *I* am afraid." I looked past him toward the inner bailey. Patiently, the guardsmen waited to close the gate. "Go on," I said abruptly. "Go on. Come back when you can." And I rode past him with Serri trotting at the roan's right side.

I did not look back again. And as I passed through the outer bailey into the inner, I heard the gates thud closed.

Boys came running to take my horse, slipping and stumbling in the snow. I flung them the reins and jumped down from the roan, thanking him with a slap upon one furry shoulder. And then I rare up the steps of the palace with Serri loping next to me.

Gods, lir—*what if my sons have taken the plague?*

Do not beg misfortune, lir. *See if it is true, first.*

But even Serri's customary wryness did not make me feel better.

My sons—and who else? My mother?

I thought of everyone as I climbed more stairs inside the palace, but I went to see my sons.

There were women in the nursery, talking quietly as they sat and tended their stitchery. But all talk broke off as I entered; five women stood as one and then dropped into startled curtsies.

"My sons?" I asked. That only.

"Well," one of the women answered at once, as the others only stared. "My lord, see them for yourself."

I was already at the oak-and-ivory cradle, hanging on to the inlaid rim. They slept, did Hart and Brennan, swathed in soft-combed wool. There was no sign of illness about them.

"They thrive, my lord," the woman—Calla—told me. "You need have no fears for them."

"And Gisella? My mother?" I could not look away from my sleeping sons.

"Both well, my lord."

"I saw the mark on the gate. The *red* mark." Now I looked at her. "There is plague in Homana-Mujhar."

"Aye." She stared down at her hands. In them she clasped forgotten stitchery. "My lord, it is the general. The Queen is with him now."

"Rowan?" *Oh—gods—no—* "You do not mean General *Rowan?*"

"Aye, my lord, I do."

A knife blade teased at the interior of my belly. "Where?"

"In his chambers. The Queen said to leave him where he would be most comfortable, though others wished to lock him away." Calla's face was pale. "My lord." She followed on my heels as I turned abruptly to leave the nursery. "My lord—it would be best if you did not go."

"So I do not risk myself?" Grimly, I shook my head. "For Rowan, it would be worth it."

But as I turned, determined to go to him, I came face to face with Gisella.

Once again, swollen with the weight of an unborn child. Or, perhaps, two? This time I could not be certain.

Hands clutched a soft wool shawl over her distended abdomen. "You did not go *in*," she said. "Not into the nursery!"

"Gisella."

"You did not expose my sons to *plague*?" She was astonished, angry, genuinely frightened. "Niall?"

"I saw them," I told her gently. "Did you think I would stay away?"

"You exposed them!" She wrenched past me and ran to the cradle, even as I turned back from the door. "Oh, my boys, my little boys, has he visited you with the plague?" Her hands were on the soft wool wrappings, peeling them back to expose sleeping faces. And then, abruptly, she turned on the other women. "I *said* he was not to come in. I *said* he was not to be allowed. I *said* I wanted him kept away from my little boys."

"Gisella." I cut into her diatribe before she could flay the white-faced women with her tongue. "Gisella, *no one* in this palace has the right to refuse me the opportunity to see my children."

"*I* do!" she cried. "*I* do—their mother! I do not want you to touch them. I *told* these women you were not to touch the babies."

She stood between me and the cradle, warding it with her body. How rigidly she stood; how fierce was her defiance. And I could not really blame her.

"I have no plague," I told her. "I promise you, Gisella— there is no plague in me. Do you think I would wish to risk them any more than you?"

"White wolf," she said. "*White wolf.* How can you tell me *you* do not carry the plague. *You* are a white wolf when you take on the shape of your *lir!*"

"Gisella—"

"*No!*" She stared defiantly at Serri, then transferred it to me. "I—say—*no!*"

Lir, Serri told me, *you cannot battle fear so fierce as this. Give her time. Let her see you do not sicken. She will accept you then.*

They are my sons, Serri.

And she is their jehana. *Do you think her fear is misplaced? Do you think she is wrong to guard them with her life?*

Inwardly, I sighed. *No. No—perhaps I do not. But I might wish the target were other than myself.*

No doubt. But you have just come through a plague-ridden realm, and everyone knows what your lir-*shape is.*

"All right." I said it aloud. "All right, Gisella, I understand. But when you see that I am well, there will be no more of these demonstrations against me in the presence of my sons."

Her teeth showed a little. "There is *plague*," she said. "Plague all through Homana. Do you think I will risk my sons? Do you think I will risk the inheritor of the Lion?"

No, I thought she would not. I thought she would risk only herself in order to protect the inheritor and his brother. Even against their father.

Mad she might be, but I could not question her desire to save her sons. Nor would I disregard her loyalty to the Lion.

I sighed. "Well enough, Gisella. I surrender the battle to you." Through the link, I asked Serri to stay with my sons; I did not entirely trust Gisella's temper.

And as she sang a song to my sons, I left the nursery to find the sickroom.

Rowan's chamber was full of shadows. The weight of them lay thick upon the furniture and wavered in the corners. I smelled the scent of beeswax and the promise of coming death.

My mother's back was to me as I entered noiselessly. I saw only the chair and the top of her head above it, red-gold hair muted in the dim glow of candlelight. As I approached, I saw how she sat very quietly in the chair, hands folded in her lap. And when I reached her, I saw how rigidly her fingers were locked together.

I heard how she spoke to him.

"—so faithfully," she was saying. "He had no one as faithful as you. Oh, I know, you would argue there was *Finn*, as loyal a liege man as could be, but the loyalty did not last. Not as it should have lasted. Not as *your* loyalty lasted." Fingernails picked absently at the soft nap of the jade-green wool of her skirts. "I know the story, Rowan: how as a boy you swore to serve Carillon as no other man could serve him, even as he was driven from Homana by Bellam of Solinde. How you never failed your duty to the rightful Prince of Homana. And when he came home again, the rightful *Mujhar* of Homana, you gave him what aid you could. You helped him become a king."

I looked at the man in the bed. Much of him was hidden beneath layers of heavy blankets, and I could not see his face. I could not see him breathe.

"And when my father was slain by Osric, and Donal became Mujhar, you were there to help him also. To help him hold the Lion." I heard the minute wavering of her voice. "One day, my son will need you, as the others have needed you. How can you leave us now? How can you fail Niall?"

"Mother," I said, and she leaped up from the chair.

"Niall! Oh—*gods*—" She pressed a hand against her breast. And then she shook her head. "Oh *no*, do not come here. Not *you!*"

"*You* are here," I told her.

"But I will not be Mujhar. Niall, please go back."

"I owe this man my attendance. As much as you owe yours." I stopped beside the chair and looked at the man in the bed. "He has served the House of Homana longer than anyone I know. It is the *least* I can do for him." She said nothing. I moved past her to the edge of the bed. "Does *jehan* know?"

"I had a message sent. But I doubt Donal can come. Not in time. The plague waits for no one."

Indeed, it did not. Rowan's face was gray and very gaunt. Even his lips were gray, but they were also swollen and cracked. His breathing was distinctly labored.

I looked at my mother sharply. "Is there no one we can call?"

"Nothing is left," she told me gently. "What *can* be done has already been done twice over."

"Is there no kin to share his passing?"

"He is quite alone," my mother said. "His family was all of us."

Bleakly, I shook my head. "Gods," I said, "what *sterility*. No wife, no children, no clan . . . not even a *lir* to grieve."

Rowan began to cough. It was a harsh, hacking cough, coming from deep in the lungs. Spittle soiled his chin; his cracked lips split again and bled.

I bent over him instantly, smoothing his coverlet in a

futile bid to soothe his pain, though I knew there was nothing for it. The silvering hair was dull and lacking life. Pushed back from his face, it bared the fragility of his skull, showing the bones beneath the drying flesh. There was so little of Rowan left.

And then he opened his eyes; there was more left than I had expected. "My lord," he said, and smiled. "My lord—you have been away so long."

The voice had been ruined by his coughing. He sounded nothing like himself. "Aye," I said, "but home now. And will stay here, for a while."

The lids drifted closed, then opened once again. "My lord—" He drew a rattling breath. "*Carillon—*

I froze.

"Carillon, I beg you—take Finn back into your service—"

I shut my eyes. "Rowan."

"I know what constitutes an oath . . . I know you made one, broke one, according to Cheysuli tradition . . . but make a new tradition. You both need one another."

Looking at him, I saw how it hurt to speak the words. And yet he continued to try to speak them. "Rowan, do not trouble yourself—" But in the end I did not finish. It was not for me to tell this man what to do.

His hand was on my wrist. The fingers were so dry, so hot, so oddly insubstantial. Even the calluses were losing their customary toughness. "Oh, my lord," he whispered. "Oh, my lord, it has been an easy service. I could not have asked for a better lord—"

I shut his limp hand up in both of mine. "Nor could I have asked for a better *friend.*"

Rowan's smile was blinding. Tears were in his eyes. "Do you recall, my lord? Do you recall the day we met?"

I opened my mouth to urge him into silence; said nothing. I let him tell me how he and my grandsire had met.

"You were in chains," he said. "Thorne of Atvia had slain your father and taken you prisoner—and *me*, the same day, but I did not count. I was nothing—*you* were the Prince of Homana." He smiled a little; blood welled into the cracks in his lips. "And you spoke to me—to a boy made wretched by captivity—and you called us *kinspirits*." A tear rolled down one temple to stain the pillow beneath his head. "But Thorne took you away to his father, Keough, and I thought they would slay you. And then later, when *I* was taken, I thought they meant to slay *me*—"

He coughed. His hand tightened in mine. I felt my mother next to me. "Rowan," she began, but he went on when the spasm had passed, and she did not try to dissuade him.

"It was Keough—it was Keough who would have had me slain—when I spilled the wine . . . Thorne would have slain me, but you begged for my life. You *begged* for it, my lord—you offered to take my place. . . ." Again, he coughed. His hand clutched mine. "But—they did not listen. And I was flogged . . . for spilling wine. And when Alix rescued me, I swore then I would serve you all my life—even when you went into exile." The smile brought fresh blood to his swollen lips. "How I wished I could have been Finn . . . when I heard a Cheysuli had gone with you, I wished it could have been *me*—"

Breath rattled in his chest. I thought he could not go on. But he did. "All those years—all those years I envied him his position as liege man to Carillon . . . and yet by denying my race as a boy—by denying my *lir*—I also denied any chance *I* might have been the warrior you trusted so readily. And when he was gone—when you sent him from your service—I thought I would rejoice . . . but I did not. I was not Finn . . . and you needed him. You needed us *both*. . . ." He sighed. "Oh my lord, take him back into your service. Homana has need of all her children."

His voice stopped. I swallowed heavily. "Rowan—*Cheysuli i'halla shansu.*"

He laughed only a little; his voice was nearly gone. "Cheysuli peace, for me? But I am a *lir*less man. . . ."

"Cheysuli i'halla shansu."

He lifted his head from the pillow. "Carillon—" And then it fell back, and I knew he would not speak again.

I sat there for countless moments, trying to master myself. And when I could, I detached his hand from mine and set it carefully on the coverlet. It was hard to believe he was dead. Hard to believe the hand would never again lift a sword in the name of Homana's Mujhars.

Impossible to believe.

"I am sorry." My mother touched my shoulder. "But surely you understand."

"Why he mistook me? Oh, aye . . . and I do not care. If it gave him peace to believe I was Carillon, it is a gift I would gladly bestow." I rose. I saw the tears on her face. "I will see to it arrangements are made."

"Niall." Her hand closed on my wrist and held me back. "It is for others to do."

I snapped my wrist free of her hand. "If you think I will delegate the responsibility for this man's disposal to someone else merely because of *rank*—"

"No," she said clearly. "It has nothing to do with rank. If I thought it would bring me peace, I would dig the grave myself. But they would never allow me the honor."

"They?" I frowned. "*Who* would not?"

She looked past me to the dead man in the bed. "There is no choice. It is a time of plague . . . a time of new—and ugly—traditions. A time requiring measures ordinarily we could refuse. But not even those of the House of Homana may ask to be excused."

"*Jehana*—"

"They will take him away," she said plainly, "to a common grave outside the walls. And there he and the others will be put to the torch so the plague will be consumed."

"Not *Rowan*. He deserves so much more than that—"

"And if it were you," my mother told me, "they would do precisely the same. There are no titles in death."

No. No titles. Nothing but an obscene *absence* from the world.

I looked at Rowan a final time. And then I drew my mother into my arms even as she locked hers around me. Together we grieved in silence. Together we offered comfort even as it was asked.

Ja'hai, I said to the gods. *Accept this Cheysuli warrior.*

Five

I labored over the letter as I never had done before, trying to find precisely the proper words. It would be easy to simply say: *Jehan, Rowan is dead*, but the man was worth more than that. So, I thought, was my father.

I had thought of having a scribe do the work, saying aloud what had happened and letting the other write it down, but that lacked privacy. It gave me no chance to say what I really felt. So I sat at my father's table and wrote it out myself.

And as I signed my name, my brother came into the room.

"Ian." Quickly, I sanded the parchment, shook it, set it carefully aside. "How does 'Solde fare? How bad is the plague in Clankeep?"

"I had forgotten," he said. "I had forgotten she was to bear a child."

I sat back in my chair. "By the gods—so had *I!*"

"Well, it was a boy. Four months ago. 'Solde named him Tiernan."

I would have smiled, but there was a question I had to ask before I expressed my pleasure. "A healthy child? And 'Solde?"

"Healthy child? Aye." He nodded. He shrugged. "Ceinn said the birth was easy. But the plague has taken 'Solde."

I did not move. I *could* not. I sat in my chair and stared at the stranger who stood before me.

"Last night," he said listlessly. "Last night, as Tiernan cried for the breast she could not give him—the plague had dried her milk."

Shock was a buffer between comprehension and grief. "Not 'Solde—" I said; I begged. "Ian—not *Isolde.*"

I waited. I watched. I knew he would deny it. Ian *had*

to deny it. This was all part of the same obscene jest fostered by Strahan upon us. I waited. I waited for Ian to admit it; to say Isolde lived.

But he did not. He wandered aimlessly into my father's private chamber. Tasha, following, flopped down beside a storage trunk even as Ian sat down on the lid. "I watched it, *rujho*. I just *watched*. There was nothing I could do."

No—not Isolde—

"I thought perhaps the earth magic might help to turn the plague away. But nothing answered. Nothing came at my call." He sounded weary, confused, remote, as if the death had taken away more than just Isolde. "I *watched* and knew there was nothing I could do."

"No." I saw Rowan's face before me, his gaunt gray face clad in the somber flesh of death. "No, there is nothing."

"The baby cried. *Ceinn* cried. But Isolde slipped away." And then suddenly his listlessness was banished and I saw the ragged blossoming of his grief. "No—she did not *slip away!* She was *taken* from us! Like a lamb caught in a bear-trap."

I shoved my chair back an crossed the chamber to him. But even as I reached out, intending to grasp his shoulder, Ian rose and pushed my hand away. He brushed by me almost roughly; I watched him stalk to the fireplace and stare into the flames. The line of his shoulders was incredibly rigid.

It is not a Cheysuli custom to openly acknowledge grief.

But I had seen him acknowledge other things without a qualm, flouting Cheysuli custom.

He and Isolde had always been close. Closer than 'Solde and I; they had shared *jehan* and *jehana*. And I wondered: *Perhaps it is an indication of how* deeply *he feels this grief, that he cannot share it with me.*

"Ceinn is inconsolable."

I saw 'Solde before me, in the rain, clad in crimson wool and the brightness of her spirit. How she had loved the rain. How she had loved the children. How she had loved Ceinn.

Still his back was to me. But I knew better than to go to him. "And you?"

Slowly he turned, but not before I saw the telltale gesture

of hand pressing tears away from flesh. "Forgive me. I have no right to be selfish, *rujho* . . . she was your *rujholla*, too."

"Aye." I drew in a steadying breath. "Rowan is dead as well."

"*Oh*—" he said, when he could, "—oh, *gods*, but how keenly Strahan strikes!" Like me, he sucked in an uneven breath. "Niall—it is worse. Much worse than we imagined. The plague has slain half our numbers."

"*Half?*" All the flesh stood up on my bones. "*Half* of us are dead?"

"At least. They have not counted properly, but they tally what they can. Each day, there are no less than three new deaths. And that is not counting the *lir*."

It was my turn to sit down on the trunk lid. Half. Half of our clan only? Or of the Cheysuli as a whole?

I asked him. His eyes were bleak. "*Our* clan has lost half. But the others send word of additional deaths. I think we can say half of all clans are dead. Strahan begins his own *qu'mahlin*."

Half of all the Cheysuli.

I thought of Shaine, our ancestor, who had nearly destroyed a race. I thought of Carillon, who had come home from exile to end a tyrant's reign and end the *qu'mahlin* as well. I thought of how the clans had increased until they had divided, living in freedom again, building Keeps where they wished to build them, raising children in tranquility.

Half of all the Cheysuli.

Taken by Strahan's plague.

Gods, deliver us from the Ihlini. "The old woman," I said suddenly. "The old Ihlini woman. She had the right of it. This thing is born of evil. Born of Asar-Suti."

"There was another thing she said." His tone was hard as iron. "There was a thing she said we must *do*."

I looked at him. "We will go to Strahan's fortress."

In silence, Ian nodded.

"His lifestone," I said intently. "That, or slay the white wolf." I looked over at the table. The parchment lacked my seal. But I knew now I would not send it. I would have to send another. "Ian—it is late, I know . . . but will you ask for the council to be summoned?—those members who are here. If we are to go in the morning, I must name my heir."

"Without *jehan*?"

I shook my head. "We cannot wait for him. And even if he *did* come, he would say we could not go." I shrugged. "An informal council, perhaps, and a more informal acclamation, but one that must be made. The Lion must remain secure."

"Aye." He turned to go. And then he paused. "What will you say to the Queen?"

What *would* I say to my mother? I sighed. "I will think of something."

In the end, I simply said I was going. I told her when. I told her why. I told her what must be done. And I waited. For refusals, anger, tears. But she gave me none of those things.

"Go," she said. "Do what you must do."

I waited. But she said nothing more. In the end, it was up to me. "*Jehana?*" I shrugged a little beneath her calm gray gaze. "I—thought you would forbid it."

She sat in a cushioned chair, swathed in a bronze-colored robe. She had prepared herself for bed; the glorious hair, unbound, spilled about her shoulders and gathered in her lap.

"No," she said. "The realm is near to ruin. There will be nothing left for Donal—nothing left for you. Something must be done. Strahan must be stopped."

Still, I waited. Anticipating all manner of remonstrations, I had come prepared. My verbal quiver was full of arrows. But she had stolen my bow.

"Ian, too?" she asked.

"Of course."

"And the *lir*." She nodded. "I can think of no two warriors better equipped for this confrontation."

I smiled a little. "Such faith."

"You are both of you Donal's sons. I think it is not misplaced."

After a moment, I drew in a quiet breath. "Ian has called the council. Before I go, I must name Brennan as my heir. And Hart as *Brennan's* heir."

My mother nodded. Her face was oddly serene. "You are a wealthy man. *Two* sons to guard the Lion."

I knew she had always regretted her barrenness. One son. Not enough, not *nearly* enough, when war lives on your doorstep. But the House of Homana had nearly always been poor in sons; she should hardly blame herself.

Two sons. Aye, I was a wealthy man. Perhaps now the tradition changed. I claimed two heirs already, and Gisella was nearly due to deliver another child.

I went to my mother. I bent, cupped her head in my hands, kissed her smooth, fair brow. *"Tahlmorra,"* I told her gently.

She smiled. Squeezed my hands, then let them go. *"Cheysuli i'halla shansu."*

I smiled. I wanted to laugh out loud; to tell her how accented was her Old Tongue, but I did not. I think she knew. And so, in silence, I went to open the door. And at the door, briefly, I turned back, to wish her a final goodbye; to thank her for her strength.

But I said nothing at all, watching the tears run down her face. And then I went out of the room.

Gisella stared at me. "Strahan?" she said. "You are going to find the Ihlini?"

"Find him. *Slay* him, if I can. He must be destroyed."

Her yellow eyes were very wide and startled; she was a child, I thought, afraid of losing something. "You are leaving me."

I sighed. "No," I told her. "No. Not permanently. I will be back, if the gods are willing."

She sat in the center of her big tester bed, crumpling the coverlet into ruin with rigid, clawlike fingers. "You are leaving me. Because I am not like Deirdre of Erinn."

Gods, how she knew to provoke the pain. "I am going to stop this plague," I told her harshly. "It has nothing to do with you. Nothing to do with Deirdre. How *can* it, Gisella? Deirdre of Erinn is dead!"

"And if you go, *you* will be dead." Awkwardly, she scrambled forward to grab my hand. She pressed it against the mound of her swollen belly. "Stay here. Stay here. Stay here."

"Gisella—I cannot. It is a thing I have sworn to do."

"Stay here. Stay here. Stay here."

I tried to detach my hand, but she hung on with all her strength.

"—stay here—stay here—stay here—"

"No," I told her. *"No."*

But I knew she could not hear me. The chanting had grown too loud.

Beneath my hand, the child moved.

"—stay here—stay here—stay here—"

Gods, my child moves—

"—stay here—stay here—"

Child or no, I broke her grip. Because I had to.

I stood up. Moved away from the bed.

The chanting abruptly broke off.

Gisella began to rock. Gisella began to sing.

I closed the door on her song.

I faced what remained of the council in one of my father's audience chambers. It was not the same chamber that had borne witness to the murders of Sarne and Elek, but it was enough like it to instantly set the memories before our eyes. I saw glances exchanged among the Homanans as I took my place in a chair upon the dais, and knew precisely what they recalled. Precisely what they thought.

Ian stood beside my chair. He did not sit, though he had the right; though a second chair stood empty. He stood. As if to illustrate the reality of my rank, and my right to call the assembly in the absence of the Mujhar.

Old men, most of them, or hampered by illness and ancient injuries. Those who were young enough, strong enough, competent enough had assumed their places with the armies. But *these* men were enough, I knew, to bear witness to my announcement.

I leaned forward a little. I felt Serri's warmth and weight against my foot; he lay beside the chair. "This plague is not happenstance," I told them. "Not a cruel test devised by the gods and visited upon us. It is Ihlini treachery, meant to strip Homana of the Cheysuli."

Once again, sidelong glances were exchanged. And I knew what some of them meant: *strip Homana of the Cheysuli, and the land is Homanan again.*

"In the morning," I told them, "I will leave Mujhara. Ian and I are bound for Solinde across the Bluetooth River, across the Northern Wastes. We seek Valgaard, Strahan's fortress. We seek the root of this demon-plague."

"My lord." One of the councillors rose. "What does the Mujhar say to this?"

"There is no time to inform him before we go. He will be told, of course—but Ian and I will be gone."

I heard murmuring. I heard low-voiced comments made. I knew what many of them were thinking. And I knew I would have to gainsay it.

"You have served the Mujhar well," I told them. "And, gods willing, you will serve me equally well when the time is come. But for this moment we must look farther down the road and see another man who is meant for the Lion Throne."

They were silent now, staring at me attentively.

"Carillon," I said. "Carillon betrothed his Homanan-Solindish daughter to a Cheysuli warrior. He did it because he had to. He did it because he was *meant* to, to make certain the throne was secured. And, in time, a son was born to the Prince and Princess of Homana, and the Lion *was* secured." I drew in a steadying breath. "A son has been born to the son; a boy intended for the Lion. And I will not leave this place until your loyalty is sworn."

Another of the councillors rose. "My lord, this is unnecessary!"

"Is it?" I shook my head. "If I am slain, there must be an heir for my father. In my place, I put my son. He will assume the title if Strahan takes it from me."

"My lord—"

"I require it," I said quietly. "I am not blind to the knowledge I may be slain, or the threat offered by Carillon's bastard. My first responsibility is owed to my father, my second one to the throne. My third to the prophecy." I knew they were one and the same, and equally important, but I thought it would please the Homanans if I made each one separate. "It is not so much," I told them. "Surely it is a loyalty you would offer one day anyway. Why not do it now?"

When no one offered argument, I took it for acquiescence. And so I signaled to the guard at the door, who stepped outside a moment, and then the door was opened. Two women came in with my sons.

They brought them to the dais, where I bade the women to face the assembly. Two swaddled bundles, hardly enough to carry the titles I would give them. But I knew it could be done. I had done it myself.

I rose, rounded the end of the table, took my place between the women. One hand I placed on Brennan's head. The other I placed on Hart's. "Before the gods of Homana and the Cheysuli, I pledge the lives of my sons into the service of the Lion; into the service of Homana. My firstborn, Brennan, I acknowledge as my heir; he will be Prince of Homana. My second son, Hart, I acknowledge as Brennan's heir until such a time as Brennan weds and sires his own. He will be Prince of Solinde."

I saw the startled expressions; heard the startled exclamations. But what better way of stating my confidence in the army than by making Hart prince of a realm we fought?

Beneath my hands the smooth soft brows were cool. "I request these acknowledgements be formally accepted by the Homanan Council. I request that fealty be sworn."

They could refuse me, each and every man. I had no power over them; I was not Mujhar. Such a request is more ordinarily made by the king, but my father was not present. If nothing else, my request was a test of their loyalty to *me*. And I think each one of them knew it.

It was Ian who took the oath first. He left his place beside my empty chair and came around the table with Tasha at his side. He stopped in front of the dais where I stood between the women who held my sons. He drew his Cheysuli knife from its rune-worked sheath, kissed the hilt and blade, then bent to kiss each of my sons. He was my liege man, but he offered them his service also. He offered them his life.

He stepped aside. And one by one, slowly, what was left of the Council came forward. My sons were acknowledged my heirs; the Lion was secured.

If the gods see fit to take me, my death will not be in vain.

Six

Twelve days out of Mujhara, Ian's stallion broke a foreleg. Crashing through crusted snow to treacherous deadfall beneath, the gray snapped his leg and threw my brother as he fell. Ian dug himself out of the snow quickly enough, but the stallion was not so lucky.

I said nothing. I watched, hunched in my saddle, as Ian knelt down and cut the stallion's jugular. And then, as the bright life spilled into the snow, Ian stroked the speckled jaw and spoke quietly to the gray until the life was spent.

He rose. His boots were sodden with blood. He unlaced the saddlepacks and tugged them free of the fallen horse, then pushed through the snow to me.

I reached down to catch the packs as he handed them up. "I am sorry."

"Better the horse than me." But beneath the brutal candor I heard the trace of genuine grief.

I draped the packs across the pommel in front of my thighs and kicked free of my left stirrup. Ian stepped up, swung a leg across the roan's wide rump, settled himself behind me. "We will buy another," I told him.

"We will have to," he agreed. "Or risk slaying this one with too great a burden in heavy going."

I watched as Tasha and Serri ran ahead to break a trail. "There will be another," I told him confidently.

There was not. It crossed my mind we should turn back, to go home for another horse. But we were two weeks out of Mujhara; the choice had been taken from me. It was unlikely my own horse would survive even the journey home again.

Eighteen days out of Mujhara, the roan died even as we dismounted. Although during the shapechange we could

store in the earth such things as clothing, weapons, packs—
perishables would spoil. And so we did not bother to carry
the packs. In *lir*-shape, we went on.

Five days later, Ian began to cough. And as we neared
the Bluetooth he fell markedly behind. I stopped, turned
back, looked for two cats and saw only one; saw my brother
on hands and knees.

In wolf-shape I ran back to him, but as a human I knelt
beside him. *"Ian!"*

He clawed wool from his face and coughed, spitting into
the snow. His breathing was loud, labored, rattling in his
chest. I heard a sound I had heard before. I saw a face I
had seen before.

Rowan's before he died. "Oh gods—" I said, "—oh, *no*—"

He knelt in the snow, coughing; obscene obeisance to the
plague. His face was deathly gray, filmed with sweat; his
lips had begun to swell. His eyes were mostly black.

"No—*no*—" I cried. "—*not Ian*—"

He coughed. His eyes glittered with fever. Sweat dampened his hair and dripped into the snow.

I thought of Rowan. I thought of Isolde. Pain enough, in
those deaths. More than enough grief. But I could not *begin*
to consider what life would be like without Ian.

*Not again—gods, not again—I have already done it once.
I could not bear it again—* "Serri!" The wolf was at my
side. "Serri—find shelter! Any sort; it does not matter. But
let it be warm and out of the wind."

Even as the wolf sped through the snow Ian tried to call
him back. "No," he croaked. "Niall—do not bother."

"No bother," I told him. "You would do the same for me."

He coughed. It rose from the deepest portion of his chest
and brought up foulness with it. Fingers clawed at his
throat; freed at last of the woolen wrappings, the swollen
buboes were plain to see.

Frenziedly I dragged him up from the ground. Even as
he protested, I half carried him to the nearest tree. There
I settled him, putting his back against the trunk, and
wrapped his throat again.

He coughed. Gods, how he coughed, and it ripped his
chest apart. Lips split, bled, crusted, split and bled again.
His face was a mask of pain.

Do not take him, I begged the gods. *Do not take my brother. Once already I feared he was dead—do not make me go through it again—*

His eyes were closed, but he did not sleep. He simply breathed, as Rowan had breathed. And each time the rattle stopped, I prayed it would start again.

Oh gods—not Ian—better me instead—

I thought he might be cold, even with Tasha pressing herself against one side. And so I took on the shape of wolf and warded his other side. I waited for Serri to come.

It was later, much later. *A place,* lir. *A dwelling near the river.*

It took us hours. I stumbled, weaved, staggered beneath the weight of my brother. Ian did what he could to help, but he was so ill and so weak he only made things worse. Tasha and Serri ran ahead yet again, breaking a track as best they could, and at last I saw the glimmer of lantern light through the close-grown trees.

"There," I told Ian. "You see? I have brought you to safety."

"Who would succor a man with plague?" he asked in his ruined voice.

"Someone will. I promise." *O gods, I beg you—deliver my brother from this—*

We staggered onward. And at last we were free of the trees. The dwelling was very small, a stone hut with thatched roof huddling against the snow-cloaked shoulder of a mountain. Beyond it lay the Bluetooth.

"The ferry-master's," I gasped.

Ian sagged. I fell as he fell, pulled off balance, and felt myself swallowed by the snow. I was so weary, *too* weary. I struggled up with effort.

My brother was unconscious. Serri and Tasha instantly wrapped themselves around his body as they had throughout the journey to the dwelling, whenever we had stopped. I got up unsteadily and staggered to the door.

"Ferry-master!" I called. "Master—I need your help!" I fell against the door, banged my gloved fist on the wood. "Ferry-master—"

The door was pulled open even as I thrust myself aside. I saw a blur of graying mouse-brown hair, brown eyes, a face creased by winter chafing. "Nae, nae, ye'll nae be need-in' me," the man told me in a thick northern dialect. "Yon beast be frozen. A man may walk across, wi' nae need o' my ferry."

"No." I said. "No, I need no ferry. I need your *help*—"

"*My* help?" He frowned.

"My brother—" Leaning against the cold stone wall of the hut, I gestured toward the *lir*-shrouded shape of my brother. "He is ill."

"Cheysuli," the ferryman said sharply. "It be plague, then, aye?"

"I need your help," I begged. "Warmth, shelter, food, drink—is it so much to ask? I can even pay you—"

"He'll likely die of't," the ferry-master told me flatly.

I could barely stand up myself. "Then let him die in a bed beneath a roof!" I cried. "Let him die as a man!"

Brown eyes studied me fiercely a moment. Then he stared past me to Ian. At last he hawked, spat out the door, wiped his mouth and nodded. "Aye. Aye. Ye hae the right of't—isna my place to turn away a sick man. Coom then, lad, we'll bring him under yon roof."

We brought him under 'yon roof' and settled him in the ferry-master's cot. I shook with a fatigue so deep it nearly made me helpless. As it was, the ferry-master tended Ian more than I myself did. He stripped my brother of his furs and settled hot cloth-wrapped stones against his flesh and covered him up again.

As I bent to look at Ian, the ferryman jerked his head toward me. "Sit ye doon, boy, afore ye *fall* doon and crack yon head. I'll get ye food and *usca*."

Lir, do as he says, Serri told me, pressing against my leg. He guided me to a chair near the cot.

Nodding weakly, I fell into the chair. It was roughly made, uncomfortable, but it supported my weary body. "*Usca*," I said. "You have *usca* here?"

The ferry-master moved to a shelf pegged into the wall. He caught down an earthenware jug and two dented pewter mugs. "Aye. Yon ferry be the on'y one on the river road out of the Mujhar's city. There be a road from Ellas as well, and a trade route into Solinde. Most days I see men, I see their goods as well." He poured, held one mug out to me. "I hae other drink, but this one warms a man's soul faster. I keep *usca* for the cold."

Indeed, it warmed my soul, and everything else besides. I slumped in the chair and sipped, taking strength from the bite of the liquor. It burned all the way down to my belly, but it gave me life again.

I pulled myself up in the chair and leaned to look more closely at Ian. Tasha lay just beside the cot, eyes locked on Ian's face. He did not move except to breathe; I heard the rattle in his chest.

Oh gods—I beg you—

"Be bad," the ferryman said. "I've seen men die of't afore."

"So have I." I thrust one hand into Serri's pelt and tried to take hope from him. "Master—"

"My name be Padgett," the ferryman told me. "Nae *master*, me. Jus' Padgett."

"Padgett." I smiled a little and slumped back again in the chair. "I must trust you with his life. I cannot stay here to nurse him."

The dark brown eyes narrowed shrewdly. "I've been on yon beast near thirty years. I've seen a thing or two, but ne'er a man journeying in such weather. What do ye do it for?"

The *usca* threatened to put me to sleep. "The plague," I said thickly. "Strahan. I must stop him before he slays more of my race—before he destroys Homana."

Padgett's surprise was manifest. "This plague be 'lini-made, then? Not a thing o' the gods?"

"Strahan's," I said succinctly. "A thing of Asar-Suti."

Padgett's brows rose, then knitted as he frowned. He sat down on a stool and picked at a blackened thumbnail in consternation. "They've ne'er done a thing to me," he said quietly. "Oh, aye—a man could say they hae need o' yon ferry, but they be sorcerers. They canna fly, but there are other ways." He sighed and looked at Ian. "Folk say the 'lini are evil, and most'y I gie a nod o' the head and go on—because they ne'er done *me* any harm. But—*plague*—" He shook his head. "Plague be unco' bad. If Strahan turns his hand to harmin' the folk o' Homana—Cheysuli, Homanan, whate'er—I want nae truck with them." He sighed pensively. "Go where ye will, lad. I'll do what I can for yon boy."

Boy. Ian was nearly twenty-five. It made me smile, but then the smile died. I did not want my brother to be this age forever, become only a memory.

"Our coin is gone," I said, stripping the signet from my finger, "but there is this in place of gold." I tossed him the ring. "If you save him, ferry-master, be certain I will give you more than simple trinkets."

Padgett turned the ring in the firelight, squinting to study the incised rampant lion. And then he swore aloud. "Simple trinket? *This?* I know what this is, boy—how did ye coom by it?"

I smiled. "My father gave it to me."

"And does he steal from the Mujhar himself?"

"No." I shook my head.

Padgett stared at the ring. "I saw one like this on another man's hand. But then I dinna know it—I thought it on'y a ring. 'Twas another man, a soldier in royal liv'ry, who told me what it was." He turned it; the ruby glowed in the light. "A long time ago—" He broke off. He looked at Ian and frowned. He rose, went closer, frowned again, and then, in amazement, he swore. "Hae ye turned back years, then, lad? Hae ye kept the Mujhar young as the 'lini keep themselves?" He looked at me. "I saw the Mujhar once, near twenty year ago. This ring was on *his* hand—this face was on his face."

"Well," I said, "Ian is his son. The resemblance is not surprising."

Padgett frowned. "Ye called this boy your brother."

"Aye."

"And this ring is from your father."

"Aye."

Padgett opened his mouth, shut it. Then he shook his head. "I canna tak' it, lad. No' from the Prince o' Homana."

The ring lay in his hand. But I did not take it from him. "If you keep my brother alive, even *that* is not payment enough!"

"My lord—"

I thrust myself up from the chair and went to kneel by Ian. I did not look at Padgett. "If *you* will not keep it, give it to someone else. But that is my payment to you."

After a moment of silence, I glanced back. Padgett's

hand shook a little. The ring rolled once in his palm. Then he shut his fingers on it and turned away from me.

I caressed Tasha's sleek head and tried to comfort her. I knew she was in fear. I could see it in her eyes.

If the ferryman can keep my brother alive, I swear, if I could, I would offer him half of Homana.

Serri tucked his head under my elbow and pressed against my side. *You will need it,* lir. *As a legacy for your sons.*

And if Strahan destroys Homana? What legacy is that?

It is for you to determine, lir. *The question will be answered.*

I sighed. I rose. I turned away from Ian. "In the morning, I go on."

I heard Padgett's indrawn breath of shock. "So soon ye leave your brother?"

"I have no choice!" I said defensively; the guilt was a weight in my belly. "Ian himself would be the first to tell me that Homana is more important. That she is worth the sacrifice." Inwardly I disagreed; I thought nothing was worth the life of my brother. But he would say there was, and so I would respect his wishes.

"What do I tell them, then?" Padgett demanded. "What do *I* say to them if this man dies, and the Prince o' Homana doesna coom back?"

I looked at Tasha. She lay so still by the cot, maintaining a silent vigil. I thought of Ian, dead, and his *lir* sentenced also to death. I thought of my father, lacking both of Sorcha's children. And I thought of myself, brotherless—

I shut off the thought at once. "Tell them the truth," I said. "They know where we have gone. They know the risks involved."

"Do *you?*"

Oh, aye, I thought I did. And I was willing to take them. I knew I *had* to take them. For Ian as well as Homana.

Seven

"Would you know?" Serri and I stood on the southern bank of the Bluetooth. "Would you know if my brother died?"

My *lir* stared across the expanse of ice-choked river. His green-gold eyes were slitted; I thought he avoided an answer.

"Serri—"

Not if he died. But if he did, Tasha would also die—that I would know at once.

I turned back and stared at the trees that hid Padgett's tiny hut. All I could see was a smudge of bluish smoke drifting above the bare-branched limbs.

Oh gods—if I leave him—if I leave him and he dies—

Resolutely I turned away and stared blindly across the river. "Come," I said, "we must go." And I blurred into my wolf-shape.

We went north, fighting the winds and snows. Behind us lay the Bluetooth; we traversed the Northern Wastes. Around us rose bleak walls of slate and indigo, the backbone of the world. Here there were no trees but wind-wracked scrub and brush. No grass, no dirt, no turf, only layers of blue-white ice locked beneath wind-carved layers of crusted snow.

We climbed. Where men could not go *we* could, picking our way through narrow traceries cutting through turreted mountains and wind-honed rock. Our coats thickened, our pads toughened, our eyes remained perpetually slitted. But we knew we would not turn back.

Forests thinned, fell away far below us. The mountains became little more than upward thrustings of barren rock, blank and blue in the howling winds.

Higher. Higher still. And then we were through the

Molon Pass and into another realm, climbing down out of the Wastes of Homana into the canyons of Solinde.

Serri, I said, *my brother?*

We are too far for me to ask.

But you would know if Tasha died.

I would know if Tasha died.

Small enough comfort. But it was something; I did not overlook it.

The mountains began to shift their shapes. The slate-blue shadows of Homanan rock took on a darker, more menacing aspect. There were trees again, but twisted, deformed by cruel winds. Roots burst free of the soil. Bare, blackened roots, twisting across stone like a tangle of tapestry yarn. And I began to see shapes in the rocks. Avid faces, gaping mouths, the bulging of eyes in terror.

It made the hair on my neck rise. *Lir—*

Ihlini, Serri said. *They mock us with their stone menagerie.*

Beasts. Hideous, horrible beasts, all locked in blackened stone. I felt my hackles rise; my lips curled back to bare my teeth in a visceral, wolfish snarl.

Serri—

Ahead, lir. *Valgaard lies ahead.*

Through a narrow defile into the canyon beyond. And there, abruptly, was Valgaard, thrusting out of the earth in a gout of glass-black stone. Curtain walls, towers, parapets, all forming one wall of the canyon. It put me in mind of a massive bird, wings outspread to enfold the world.

How it broods. How it makes the canyon its mews.

Sheer walls jutted upward over our heads. We were small, so small, so insignificant in the ordering of the world. Valgaard crouched before us, cloaked in rising smoke.

My lips drew back. *Gods—how it stinks.*

The breath of the god, Serri told me. *The stench of Asar-Suti.*

It was a field of folded stone, spreading out in all directions. There were waves, curls, bubbles, but all was made of rock. An ocean of steaming stone.

"Serri—something is *wrong*—"

What is right about the Ihlini?

I shuddered. I was not cold; winter had been banished. Behind us lay the defile and beyond that the wind-wracked

walls of basalt. But here there was nothing but warmth. A
cloying, putrid warmth that made me want to vomit.

Serri— I said. *Serri, the link is fading*—

Too close, he told me. *Too close to the Ihlini.*

We were. I could feel the weakening of the link, the
dilution of the power that lent me the ability to shapechange. Even as I concentrated, trying to keep myself
whole, I felt the magic fading. I felt myself caught between.

Serri!

I felt the power drain away like so much spilling wine.
It splashed against the ground; was turned into hissing
steam. And then dispersed upon the air and blown out of
Valgaard's bailey.

Abruptly, too abruptly, I was wrenched out of my *lir*-
shape and thrown back into human form. But the transfer-
ence was *too* sudden, too overwhelming for me to
withstand.

I cried out. It started as a howl, ended as a scream.

Stone bit into my face. I tasted sulfur, salt, iron. I tasted
the spittle of the god. It made me spit out my own.

I pressed myself up from the ground. I was a man again,
booted, furred, armed with sword and bow and knife. But
I knew—gods, how I *knew*—I needed none of the weapons.
This was Strahan's domain, the Gate of the god himself.
Nothing but wits could ward me against their power.

The stone was warm beneath my bootsoles. The field
stretching before me was pocked with vents that vomited
steam into the air. Valgaard was wreathed in smoke.

"Gods," I breathed, "look at that. Look at the hounds
who guard the lair."

Hounds? I could not be certain. They were beasts, but
none that I could name. Merely shapes. Merely *things*. Ex-
tremities only hinted at; formlessness made whole.

Inert, they waited like black-glass gamepieces upon the
dark board of Asar-Suti.

I shut my eyes. *Gods—I am so frightened*—

But I knew what I had to do.

"Serri." I looked down at him, then knelt and swept him
into my arms. "*Lir*, I must ask you to stay here."

Here? Serri's tone was only a thread within my mind, the
merest shadow of the link. And fading even as we conversed. *My task is to go with you.*

"Not this time. *This* time, your task is to stay behind. I cannot take you with me."

Lir—

"I dare not risk us both. This is for *me* to do."

He pushed his nose against my neck. *Lir—*

"Serri, say you will stay. Say you will wait for me."

But if all goes wrong—

"If all goes wrong, at least *you* will retain your freedom. You are young yet, even by human standards; you will not be given to death."

This is not part of your tahlmorra.

"I *make* it a part of it." I hugged him firmly. "There is a chance, albeit a small one. But perhaps it will be enough. Perhaps he will be content." I unwound my arms from his neck. "Say you will stay, Serri. Say you will wait for me here."

Serri's tail drooped. He laid his ears flat back. The tone was only a whisper: *I will wait. What else is there to do?*

Serri— But the link was broken.

I left him. I stepped out from the defile into the field of steam and stone and did not look back at my *lir*. The link was utterly banished; there was nothing binding us now. Only the knowledge of what we were.

Of what there had been between us.

Strahan smiled. "Somewhat belatedly, you accept my invitation."

"I thought never to accept it at *all*."

He nodded. "People do change. Even princes." He sipped wine. "All men eventually grow up."

"Will you?"

We confronted one another in one of Valgaard's tower rooms. The black walls were curved, cylindrical, polished to glassy brilliance. Tapestries cut the chill; one quick glance had showed me I did not wish to see what pictures were in the yarns. Something that shrieked of demons and the god of the netherworld.

Strahan sat. I stood. It was a measure of the circumstances.

"Will I?" the Ihlini echoed. "Well, perhaps—it depends on how I feel." He sipped again at his wine. I had been offered a cup of my own, but had not accepted. "It is not closed to you, Niall: the ability to turn back the years. No more than to anyone else; mind you, I do not make the mistake of inviting you to join me." He grinned. "I know better. I know you would never do it. But there *is* an opportunity, for those who desire the power."

"And how many have accepted?"

"This year? Or last? Or all the years of the past?" He set the cup down on a table and rose, thrusting himself out of his chair. He wore hunting leathers, brown ones, and more than a trifle scuffed. His long black hair, spilling over his shoulders, was glossy and fine as a woman's, and held back by a circlet of beaten bronze. There were shapes in the metal, odd shapes, much as there were shapes in the ill-made stones in the field of the breath of the god. "So, Niall—you come to me in hopes I will put an end to my plague."

I watched him. He rummaged in a rune-carved trunk with curving lid. He did not look so much a sorcerer as he did a distracted student, having lost a favorite book.

This is Strahan, I reminded myself, *most powerful of all the Ihlini. Be not misled by the face he wears or the platitudes in his mouth.*

"And I ask you: why? Why should I wish to end my plague?"

My plague. Was he so pleased by it, then? Did he consider it a thing of which to be proud?

Aye. He probably did. "If ending it gave you something in return, it might be worth it for you."

"But only if the thing was a thing of value." Still he rummaged through the trunk, only absently paying attention to what I said.

It was disconcerting. He acted more man than sorcerer; more human than demon-born. "I think it might be," I told him. "You wanted it once, though—out of perversity?— you did not take it then."

He stopped rummaging. Straightened. Turned. Looked at me thoughtfully. "Willingly you came here."

"I was not forced—not *physically*. But it was you who brought me here. You did tell me I would come; now, of course, I have."

"Willingly you came here." Now he did not smile. "And—*willingly*—you offer yourself to me?"

I had forgotten how eerie were his eyes, how uncanny in their mismatched brown and blue. He stared, did Strahan; he waited. And I knew not what to say.

He turned back to the trunk. Reached in yet again, drew something forth. I could not see it. He shut it up in a hand.

"Strahan—"

"I have listened," he said. "I have heard. But I think you are mistaken." He closed the lid of the trunk. I heard the catch click shut.

I wanted Serri. I wanted Ian. I wanted free of this place.

I wet my paper-dry lips. "There was the night you came to Mujhara. For *me*, you said you came. And it was then you told me not to wed Gisella."

"Aye." He shrugged. "I said you should not, but you maintained you would." He crossed to a heavy book lying open on a stand. "You know, of course, I might have slain you then," he said casually. "It would have been simple enough. But I knew you would be coming. I *prefer* to make men do my bidding before I end their lives."

I looked at the book. *Grimoire?* I wondered. *The source of so much Ihlini magic?*

Frowning absently, he paged through the book. And as each page turned, I saw the faintest of flames flash out of the red-scripted pages.

"Strahan—"

"You wed her, Niall. You wed Alaric's addled daughter."

"Aye." My lips were dry again. "I will offer you a bargain."

He did not appear to hear. He stopped turning pages, read something with close attention; then nodded and closed the book. "I thought so. Not so hard, I think." He smiled at me, and the distractedness was gone. He was decidedly intent. "So, you came here to offer yourself in exchange for the ending of the plague. To offer me something of *value*."

"I *am*," I said with what dignity I could muster. "I am part of the prophecy."

He nodded. "Part of the prophecy. A tarnished link, perhaps? Or dross instead of gold?"

He meant to make me angry. And he very nearly succeeded. Inwardly I seethed, but I would not show it to him. "Dross, gold—does it matter? I am the Prince of Homana."

"Donal's son," he mused, "and Aislinn's as well, which makes you my kinsman as well as my enemy." Briefly he glanced down at the thing he held in his hand. "Well, once I might have accepted, when the bargain was a bargain, but now there is nothing in it. Nothing for you *or* me."

"I give you the prophecy!" I cried. "Its future is in your hands!"

"Well, no—not precisely." He shrugged a little, brows raised, and shook his head at me. "Indeed, it is some measure of sacrifice to offer yourself to me, but there is little value in it. *You* have little value; you married Alaric's daughter. And she has given you sons."

I opened my mouth. Shut it. And all at once I understood.

Not me. Not me at all. Once, aye, before my sons were born—but now the seed is planted. My link is no longer the last.

Strahan spread his hands. "You are too late, Niall. The wheel has turned without you."

I wanted to sit down. I wanted to *fall* down. I wanted to turn my back on the man. But I could do none of those things.

"Of course," he said, "were you to offer me your *sons*—"

"*No*—" I blurted. "Give over my sons to *you*?"

"But *then* the bargain would be worth the making." He shrugged. "You may give them, or I may take them. The choice is up to you."

So—this is what he has wanted all along; why he did not slay me once he determined my eventual worth—as a sire, if nothing else—like a horse valued for his bloodlines. He wanted the sons I would get on Gisella.

I smiled. "No," I told him plainly.

"All right," he said calmly, "all right. Then I shall simply *take* them . . . when Gisella brings them to me."

"*Gisella!*" I stared. "Gisella would never bring them!"

"But she will," he said gently, "when Varien tells her to."

Slowly I shook my head. "You are mad."

"No," he said, "*Gisella* is mad. . . ." He paused deliberately, smiling. "Unless, of course, she is *not*—and does this for other reasons."

He had silenced me at last. In the face of Gisella's treach-

ery and deceit I could do nothing but stare at the Ihlini.
Not mad? All of it contrived—an act?

Strahan watched the play of emotions in my face. And
he laughed. "Something to consider, is it not?" He was
truly amused. "Oh, aye, Lillith is a dutiful sister—she serves
me very well. And when Alaric wed a Cheysuli woman, it
was Lillith who suggested the children—or *child*—be made
to serve as well."

"Not Gisella. Gisella is *Cheysuli!*"

He made a dismissive gesture. "Cheysuli, Ihlini—do you
think it really matters? We were born of identical parents,
the gods who made Homana." He lifted a silencing hand.
"Cheysuli, aye, she is, and therefore immune to much of
our power, but there are tricks that can be taught. Beliefs
that can be instilled. *Loyalties* that are secured. I warned
you, Niall. That night in Mujhara when your horse had
gone lame . . . I warned you not to wed her." How he
watched me, gloating silently. "But you *did*—and so I devised another plan."

"You will *not* harm my sons!"

"No, Niall. Of *course* not—I have no wish to harm them;
I only wish to *use* them." He smiled. "And I shall. One
son upon the Lion, one son on the throne of Solinde. And
answerable to *me*."

Alaric. Lillith. Varien: Even, I knew now, Gisella. All
serving Strahan's interests? Gods, but how tightly was I
bound. How helpless had he made me.

"Gisella," I said aloud. "Gods, they are her *sons!*"

"But she has been *mine* since birth. My sister made her so."
For nothing—everything for nothing— "For *nothing!*"
Overcome, I shouted aloud.

Strahan smiled as I shouted. "No. Not for *nothing*. You
believed in what you did. Some men never have anything
to believe in." He gestured toward the door. "Now, come
with me. There is something I will show you."

He took me out of the tower into the bailey, and then
ordered the gates swung open. Before us lay the field of
stinking smoke. The breath of Asar-Suti.

"There," he said, "lies your freedom. I think I will give
it to you."

"I am not a fool," I began. "If you think I will believe
that—"

"Then believe *this*." He held out something that dangled on a chain. A tooth, capped with gold, and hanging from a thin golden chain. I had had one of my own, before I threw it away at Serri's behest.

"Take it," he said, and put it into my hand.

I did not want it. I wanted nothing to do with it. And as he took his hand away, I threw it into the smoke.

Strahan laughed. "I thought so. And now the beast is free."

Out of the smoke and stench was born an Ihlini wolf. His pelt was white, his eyes were blue; he looked a lot like me.

"Illusion," I said curtly.

"Was it illusion on the Crystal Isle when I slew Finn?" Strahan asked. "Aye, you know the story—how I slew Donal's uncle. Aye, I see you know it." He smiled. "And do you recall what happened to his wolf?"

"Storr—died. He was too old to live without his *lir*."

"He—*died*." How he mocked me. "Aye, as a *lir* dies—supposedly there is nothing left when an old *lir* dies. But there was a little left of Storr. Only a *little*—four teeth, and those I claimed for myself once your father and the Ellasian had gone. And with those four teeth I fashioned powerful magic with the aid of Asar-Suti—*powerful* magic, Niall . . . enough to hide Varien's identity; of course that is easily done . . . but also enough to raze Homana. Enough to purge the land of all Cheysuli." He looked at the white wolf wreathed in the breath of the god. "Illusion, you say. Is he? I think not. I think he is the deliverance of Homana." The Ihlini smiled as I looked at him sharply. "The plague is born of wolves, Niall. *White* wolves—animals of legend and superstition. All but one is dead now, slain for the bounty offered, but now it does not matter. They have done their work." He nodded at the wolf who waited, cloaked in hissing steam. "Slay him, Niall, and you will end the plague."

"Why?" I asked. "Why do you give me the answer? Why do you give me the chance?"

He shrugged. "Enough have died already. I prefer to rule *living* subjects, when I have made Homana mine."

"I do not believe you," I said.

Strahan looked at the wolf. "Go," he said. "Your task is

incomplete. There are Cheysuli in the world—rid Homana of them."

The wolf turned, ran, disappeared, even as I cried out. "Go," Strahan told me. "You have knife, bow, sword. It is up to you to stop him."

I thought, very briefly, of trying to slay Strahan instead. But by then I would lose the wolf.

Strahan's smile was one of subtle triumph, but I saw speculation in his eyes. "Your choice, Niall. Save your sons—or save the Cheysuli." The smile grew. "But which will you choose, I wonder? Gisella . . . or the wolf?"

The chasm opened beneath my feet.

"Your sons . . . or your race?"

I made my voice as steady and cold as I could. "I can make other sons."

Strahan laughed. "But how many on Gisella? How many who will claim the *proper* blood—the blood the prophecy requires?"

I stared after the running wolf. *Without the Cheysuli, without Homana . . . there is no need for my sons. . . .*

I ran.

First the wolf—then Gisella—

Gods, how I ran.

The stench filled my nostrils. Rising steam veiled my vision. I tasted the tang of sulfur and bile.

I ran, threading my way through hissing vents and puddles of steaming water, trying always to see the wolf. But he was gone, made invisible, swallowed by smoke and steam.

Serri! In the link I screamed for help, but the echoes remained unanswered. The task was mine alone.

The ground roared. Vibration stirred my feet. Tongues of flame licked lips of stone; darted out from gaping mouths.

I tripped, fell to one knee, thrust myself up again. Hot water splattered my face.

I ran.

A shape loomed out of the steam. I ignored it—until the shape reached out of itself and tried to swat me down, like a man swatting a fly. I ducked, dodged, nearly fell again as I gaped; the shape was made of stone. Moving, stalking stone.

I ran. And as I ran, I coughed.

—the breath of the god is foul—

Scraping followed; the grate of stone on stone. The gurgle and belch of sulfur; the hiss and roar of vomited steam. And through the smoke-smeared distances I heard the howl of a wolf who sings for the love of it. For the joy of being alive. But not the song of Serri; I know his voice too well. It was the white Ihlini wolf; the demon in the pelt: singing his song of death.

The deathsong of my race.

Gods, how I *ran*—

I was through the defile: out of heat I was thrust into cold. I shivered. Shivered again; snow still clogged the canyons. Vented steam was now the plume of breaths expelled. My sweat shapechanged to ice.

"Serri?"

Lir, *I am here.* And he was, suddenly, *here,* bounding toward me out of the snow.

Briefly, I stopped, gasping; preparing to go on. But I thought now I had a chance. I thought: *now it can be done.*

But I had reckoned without interference; without Ihlini irony.

Serri saw it first. Lir—*beware the hawk—*

Like a fool, I looked at the sky. And the hawk descended upon me.

Descended—

—and took an eye.

Eight

—hands—
—hands touching—
—touching me—
Oh gods—the *pain—*
Serri—Serri—Serri—
Hands touching me. Moving me. *Lifting* me.
NoNoNoNo—not with all this pain—
Serri—Serri—SERRI—
Oh gods, what has happened?
What have you done to me?

"What have you done to me?"
The question jerked me into awareness; I realized *I* had asked it. A trace of my voice still sounded in my ear.
"Be still. Be calm. Be tranquil. The worst is over now."
I twitched in shock. It sent a shaft of pain through bandaged eyes. I winced, gasped, hissed; the pain was all-consuming.
"Be *still*. Do not bestir yourself. Pain is a wolf at the door in winter: fob him off with a morsel or two and he may wait for spring before he comes again."
The voice painted pictures with intonations; with subtleties of emphasis. Such a *magnificent* voice. "Wolf—" My voice was more croak than anything else. "Oh gods—the *white wolf—*"
"Gone," the clear voice told me. "And for now, you must *let* him go. Aye, he must be caught, be slain, but there is nothing now you can do. Not yet. Wait a bit; I promise, you will fulfill your own *tahlmorra.*"
All was darkness. My eyes were sealed shut by bandages. I smelled the tang of herbs; felt the warm weight of a poultice against my right eye.

Oh gods—my eye is gone—

"Be still," the calm voice warned me. A hand was against my shoulder, pressing me down even as I tried to sit up.

—the pain—the pain—the pain—

"Serri? *Serri?*"

"He is here," the voice told me, and I felt the cold nose pressed against my neck.

Lir, *do as Taliesin tells you. His skills will heal you.*

"Taliesin?"

"Aye," the voice answered. "But you are too young to know me. And my name is no longer spoken."

"Where have you brought me?"

"To my cottage. You need not fear discovery; Strahan does not come here."

"*You* know Strahan? You know he did this to me?"

"I know Strahan, aye. And I know what he did to you." The voice hesitated a moment. "Not so very different from what he did to *me.*"

I shut my teeth in my bottom lip. My eye throbbed with increasing pain. I thought I might swoon from it.

Serri—Serri—

I am here. I am here. Do not fear I will go. I will not leave you, lir.

"Here." A hand was slipped beneath my head, tipping it up. Such a strong, wide hand, cradling my skull so gently. Another pressed a cup against my lips; I drank the bitter brew. "It will help the pain," Taliesin told me. "Sleep, my lord—let the herbs do their work."

My lord. . . ."You know me?"

"I do not *know* you—how could I? But aye, I know who you are. Be at ease, my lord. Solindish I may be, but I have no quarrel with Homana. Certainly none with *you.*"

"Your voice—" I was slipping into sleep. "I am sorry. I could not say if you are man or woman."

Taliesin laughed. "Well, a true bard may be either or both when he sings his lays and sagas. But when your eye is free again, you will see I am a man."

When your eye is free again. . . . How odd it was to know I had only one.

How it twisted the blade in my belly.

The hawk has stolen my eye—

Be still, Serri told me. *Rest. Cheat Strahan of his triumph. He meant to slay you*, lir.

The hawk? Serri—Serri—that hawk—

Dead. Did you think I would let him live?

I shut my hand in Serri's ruff. I wanted to hug him, to pull him into my arms and press him against my chest, to bury my face in his fur.

Mostly I wanted to cry.

But even as I tugged at his pelt, seeking strength and reassurance, I felt myself slipping away. *Serri, do not go—do not leave me—*

I will never leave you, lir.

I slept.

"You said I would fulfill my *tahlmorra*."

"Aye. You will."

"But you are Solindish. What do you know of *tahlmorras*?"

"Better to ask: what do I know of Cheysuli?"

I lay on the pallet beneath warm furs. As yet I was a blind man; Taliesin told me the hawk had torn the flesh near my left eye as well as destroying the right. Until the wounds were healed, I would be kept in darkness.

Serri was additional warmth stretched the length of my body. He slept, twitching in dreams; I wondered what he chased.

"*What* do you know of Cheysuli?" I asked obligingly. But my curiosity was genuine.

"I know of *tahlmorras* and *lir* and responsibilities. I know of the dedication that drives your race; the loyalty of the fanatic; the arrogance of a man who believes he is a child of the gods."

"*Believes!*" I did not like his attitude, regardless how quietly he expressed it. "We *are* children of the gods."

"Oh, aye, I know. The word *Cheysuli* means that precisely. But it means other things, as well: zealotry and intolerance, single-minded determination, the willingness to sacrifice many for the sake of a single man: the Firstborn. The child of the prophecy. The Lion of Homana."

"By the gods, you sound like an *Ihlini*."

"I should. I am." A hand pressed me down again. "Be

still, my lord. I am not one of Strahan's minions. That I
promise you."

"Do you set a trap for *me?*"

"Do I? Test it. Test *me*, my lord." The hand released
me. "Get up from your sickbed and walk out of my hut
forever. I will not keep you. I will not call you back. I will
tell no one you were here."

Sweat broke out on my flesh. "You know I cannot. You
know I can hardly raise myself without the pain throwing
me down again."

"Then ask your *lir*," he told me. "Ask Serri. *Think*,
Niall—has the link between you been broken?"

No. Serri and I conversed as we always conversed. There
was no weakness in the link, no interference that drained
the power away.

"If you are Ihlini, this is not possible."

"It is. I am not one of Strahan's Ihlini; nor am I one of
Tynstar's, though once he was my lord. No. I am Ihlini,
aye, but no more your enemy than your *lir*. There is a
difference, my lord, a divergence of opinion. Strahan does
not rule us all, only those who wish it. Only those who
serve Asar-Suti."

"And you do not." My dubiousness was plain, but Taliesin was patient.

"Asar-Suti is the god of the netherworld; the Seker, who
made and dwells in darkness. But I caution you, my lord:
be not so quick to lump us all together. Be not so ready
to give me over into darkness when I prefer the light."

I thought suddenly of the old woman in Homana, the
old *Ihlini* woman, who had sacrificed her life to make certain Ian and I believed she told the truth. She had not done
it for us. She had done it for Homana.

"How can it be?" I asked blankly. "How is it possible?"

"It is possible because the gods gave us the freedom to
choose. Even you. Aye, I will admit there seems to *be* no
choice when you know you deny the afterworld by denying
the prophecy, but there still exists the choice. You could
renounce your title, your birth, your blood. You could renounce your *tahlmorra*."

"I would die!"

"All men die eventually."

"I have no wish to hasten it!"

I heard him move. No longer did he kneel beside me. I heard footsteps, the scrape of a chair, the sound of him sitting down. But still his voice carried to me as if he knelt beside me.

"I have no wish to shake your faith; to question your dedication. Once, I shared it myself, though I gave it to my lord and Asar-Suti. I *believed*, because Tynstar made certain I did. And I served as well as I could, until I began to question the validity of Tynstar's intentions. Why, I wondered, was it so important for him to have Homana? Why was it so necessary to destroy our brother race in order to claim the land? And so, one day, I asked him."

My fingers were locked in Serri's pelt. "What did he say?" I asked tightly. "What was Tynstar's answer?"

"He said if the Ihlini did not destroy the Cheysuli, the end of the world would come."

"He *lied!*"

"Did he?" For a moment there was silence. "Be not so certain, Niall."

"Tynstar *lied!* How could the world end? Do you think the gods would let it?"

"I speak of perception, my lord, not of absolutes. You know what enmity lies between the races. You yourself are a victim of it; do you not distrust and hate Ihlini? Do you not slay one when you can?"

"Taliesin—"

"Perception, Niall: if the Cheysuli are allowed to live and the prophecy is fulfilled, the bloodlines will be merged. The Firstborn will emerge. And, in time—as it is with horses, dogs, sheep—the original bloodlines will be overtaken by the new." He paused. "Tynstar spoke the truth: if the Ihlini do not destroy the Cheysuli, the world will come to an end. The world as *Ihlini perceive it.*"

"But if that were *true*—"

"It is all we have, Niall—our only legacy. And the prophecy will destroy it."

Survival, Lillith had called it. Nothing more than a struggle to keep a race complete, undivided, *undiminished* by the thing that would destroy the Ihlini: the prophecy of the Firstborn.

How can I blame them for it? How can I hate them for

it? They do what I would do; what anyone *would do, trying to keep a race whole.*

"Oh gods," I said aloud, "you turn me inside out."

"I do not ask you to question your convictions, Niall. I do not say you are *wrong*, or that the Cheysuli are. I say only that when I realized the cost of Tynstar's intentions, I knew I could not afford it."

"But if we did *not* serve the prophecy—" I broke off. It was unthinkable. It was impossible to envision.

Take the prophecy away and what have we to live for?

I dug rigid fingers more deeply into Serri's pelt. "How better to overcome the enemy than by removing his reason for living?" I asked bitterly. "Is this what you try to do?"

"I ask you to make no judgments. I do not intend to shake your faith. I only explain how it was that one Ihlini chose to deny his god, his lord . . . and renounce the gifts the Firstborn gave us."

"Gave *you?*"

"Aye," he said gently. "Not all of us are evil. Not all of us serve Asar-Suti. And when we do not, when we have not drunk of the Seker's blood, we remain only men and women who have a little magic. A *little* magic, Niall . . . the sort *you* would claim if Serri left you."

Serri? Serri? But my *lir* did not answer. It frightened me. "I would *die* if Serri left me!"

"No. If Serri left you *of his own volition*, you would not die because of it. You would lack the shapechange, the healing—the things the *lir*-bond gives you. But you would not die."

"There is the death-ritual."

"Because suicide is taboo. It does not matter, Niall. The ritual is in force only if the *lir* is slain—not if the *lir* deserts you."

"Serri would never desert me! No *lir* would desert a warrior!"

I expected Serri's immediate agreement; he remained oddly silent.

Serri—you promised you would not leave me!

"Not in your lifetime," Taliesin said calmly. "Perhaps it will not happen even while your sons rule the realms you give them. But *some* day—*one* day—when the child of the prophecy is born . . . the *lir* will know a new master."

No.

" 'One day a man of all blood will unite, in peace, four warring realms and two magic races,' " Taliesin quoted. "What happens *then*, Niall? What becomes of the Ihlini? What becomes of the Cheysuli?"

No.

"The races, merged, form a new one. The one that lived before. The one with *all* the power."

Serri, say it is not true.

"It is what the gods intend. It is what the Ihlini must stop—those who serve Asar-Suti. Because when the First-born emerge again, the Seker will be defeated. The Gate will be sealed shut; the netherworld locked away. The First-born shall rule the world in the names of other gods."

"And you renounced Tynstar because of that?" I asked. "Because you *support* the merging of the races?"

"It means life, my lord, for all of us. I want the Cheysuli destroyed no more than the Ihlini. And the only means for settling our feud forever is to change the face of hatred."

In darkness, I could not see it. But I doubted anyone could.

Serri? Serri?

Nothing.

Gods, I thought, *I am* afraid—*afraid he tells me lies. But more afraid because he may be telling the truth.*

Nine

"There is someone *here!*" I said sharply. I levered myself up on one elbow next to Serri; the pain was mostly bearable now. "Taliesin."

"Your ears are keener," the Ihlini told me. "Aye, there is someone here, but Caro has always been here."

"Caro?"

"My guest. My friend. My hands."

"Hands?" I pressed fingers against the bandages and gently scratched the itching flesh beneath. "Gods, could you use your hands to rid me of these bindings? I am going mad."

"Aye, I think it is time. But Caro will unwrap you."

In a moment I felt hands on the knots of my bandages, loosening, untying, unwrapping. Light crept in, then blazed as my left eye was freed. The right one saw nothing at all.

I shut my left eye. "It hurts—the light hurts me—"

"Because it has known darkness for too long. Be patient. The eye is unharmed. You will see clearly again."

Tears ran out from under my shielding lid. I could not stop the watering. "And my right eye?"

"Gone," Taliesin told me gently. "You will need a patch; I will have Caro make you one. I could, but he will do it better."

Caro's big hands were gentle and familiar. All along it had been *he* who tended me, not Taliesin. Not *physically*. But with his voice, oh, aye—his beguiling, beautiful voice.

With a cloth Caro sponged the tears away, then rubbed tender flesh with an herbal salve. Now that I *knew* he was here, I wondered how I had not known it all along.

"Leijhana tu'sai," I told him. "My thanks, Caro."

"He cannot hear you," Taliesin said quietly. "Caro is deaf and dumb."

My eyelid jerked open. I squinted as tears welled up

again; my empty socket throbbed. But I ignored it. I looked at Caro. Wide-eyed, I *stared*, trying to see him clearly. And when I could, I began to laugh.

It hurt. But I laughed. I *cried*. I could not help myself. Because Caro *was* myself.

Gods, how I laughed.

"Did you know?" I asked Taliesin, when the laughter and tears had faded. "Did you *know*?"

He did not answer at once. For the first time I looked upon him as he sat in a lopsided chair. His hair was white, bound back by a thin silver circlet, but his face was smooth, unaged; the face of a man eternally young. His clear eyes were very blue.

I looked at his hands. Twisted, gnarled things, once whole, now not; someone had *purposely* destroyed them, for nothing else could do such tremendous damage.

Gods—who would do that to a man like Taliesin?

I looked again at Caro, who knelt in silence beside my pallet. "Did you know?" I repeated to Taliesin.

Did you know? I asked my lir.

You were ill, in pain—what profit in telling you before you needed to know?

"They told me his name," Taliesin said. "Carollan. They asked me to keep him safe."

Carollan/Carillon. Not quite the same, but close enough. Like father, like son—except the son was deaf and dumb.

"Safe," I echoed, looking at my kinsman; at Carillon's bastard son. "They believed my father would slay him?"

"They were convinced of it. There was nowhere in Homana he would be safe, they said, and so they brought him nearly two years ago to Solinde. To Taliesin the bard, who once sang in the halls of Solindish kings; in the halls of Ihlini strongholds. They knew. They knew I could never harm him. And they knew no one would look for him here. When they need him, they borrow him. But they always bring him back." He paused. "It was how I knew you, Niall. This close to the border even *I* hear news of how the Prince of Homana resembles his grandsire; how the bastard resembles his father."

I looked at Caro in fascination. He was me. But *not*, quite. He was thirty-six, nearly sixteen years older than I. His face was older, as was to be expected; windchafed, with traceries of sunlines at the outer corners of his eyes. His beard was more mature. But everything else was the same: tawny, sunstreaked hair, darker beard, blue eyes, almost identical shape of facial bones. Carillon had well and truly stamped his progeny.

I laughed once. But this time it was little more than an expulsion of ironic comprehension. "And so the Homanans who wish to replace Niall with Carillon's bastard want nothing more than a puppet. An empty vessel upon the Lion, so *they* can rule Homana."

"Aye, I believe they do."

I thought of Elek. I thought of Sarne, who had so eloquently campaigned for her disabled son. Gods, but how steadfastly she had insisted Carillon had promised his son a place in the succession. And I thought of the people who had rallied to Caro's standard. Gods, how ludicrous it all seemed now.

I shook my head. "Surely they understand once the truth is known, the petition will be denied."

"Surely they do," Taliesin agreed. "But I am sure they feel the truth will never be discovered, or—if it is—it will be too late; the Lion will already be theirs. Look at what they have already accomplished, even with him hidden." He shook his white-haired head. "Do not forget, Niall, many people never see their king. Many people know only his name, not what or who he is. They toil to pay his taxes, they die in his armies, they celebrate his name-day and the birth of sons and heirs . . . but only rarely do they set eyes upon the man. He is a *name*. And it is possible for a realm to be governed for years by only a name."

Frowning, I shook my head pensively, carefully. "But they were all so *willing* to follow him, to put him on the throne. So willing to slay Carillon's *grandson* to make way for the bastard son."

Taliesin nodded. "He is legend, now, as you should know so well. How better to recapture the man himself? By elevating his son. A son is a *son*, and closer than the grandson. And there are those who desire to keep the throne Homanan, to use it for themselves. But mostly I think there are those who desire only to serve the man they believe to be the rightful heir; it is not so impossible to believe Caro is that man. He *is* Carillon's son. Can you blame them? They know only that, nothing more; that he is a son, not a grandson—Homanan, not Cheysuli." His voice was very quiet. "They believe in what they are doing."

I stroked Serri's coat. *As so many of us believe . . . Cheysuli, Ihlini, Homanan.*

As so many of you must *believe.*

Aye—*must.* I thought of Strahan and Lillith, serving their noxious god while they also served themselves, desiring to save their race. I thought of Alaric of Atvia, opportunistic Alaric, who no doubt realized he alone could not defeat Homana but that he might come out the victor if he aided the Ihlini by giving his daughter to Lillith. And I thought of the *a'saii*, who sought the purest blood of all and were willing spill mine in order to get it.

Oh, aye, *all of us*, doing what we had to in order to make certain we survived; to secure the best possible of places in this world and the next.

Serri's tone was warm and wise. *Because, wrong or right, you* believe *in what you do.*

Aye. Every one of us.

Aloud, I said: "Nothing excuses bloodshed. Nothing excuses the *annihilation* of a race."

Taliesin's smile was incredibly sweet. This one was also compassionate. "And do you refer to the Ihlini? Or do you speak of the Cheysuli?"

Bitterly, I glared at him from out of my single eye. "Both. *Both.* What *else* can I believe?"

He sighed. His ruined hands twitched in his blue-robed lap, as if he longed to clasp them in victory; knowing he could not.

Caro leaned down to rub more salve into my flesh. But I stopped him. I caught his wrist, sat up slowly, confronted him face to face.

I looked for some indication, some *sign* he knew who he was; *what* he was, and what he might have become. But there was only patient curiosity as he waited for an explanation.

I let go of him. "They told him nothing."

"No. I think they believe him a lackwit, unable to comprehend. He is not, of course. But neither is he fit to be Mujhar."

Slowly I shook my head. "And so the great plan is undone. I have only to announce his disabilities, and the Homanan rebellion is over."

"So it is."

Said too sadly; I looked at the Ihlini in sudden consternation. "Would they slay him?—the Homanans? Would they destroy the useless puppet?"

"I think it more likely they would simply cut the strings. But I will pick them up." He lifted his ruined hands. "There is some movement left; I think I can work those strings. Better yet, I will cut them off entirely and let him go without."

I looked at Caro. I could not tell what he thought. But I knew he was not the enemy, intentionally or no.

I reached out, clasped his arm, nodded to him a little. "My thanks, Caro," I told him clearly. "In the Old Tongue—*leijhana tu'sai.*"

His eyes watched the movement of my mouth; the emotions in my face. I could not be certain he understood. But he smiled. He smiled my smile, returned my clasp, and went to sit upon a stool.

I looked at Taliesin. "Who did that to your hands?"

"Not Tynstar." The blue eyes were clouded with memories. "No, for many years I pleased him with my skill. Instead of remaining an itinerant Ihlini bard, I gained a permanent patron . . . until I asked him why he wanted to destroy the Cheysuli; why he wanted to steal Homana." The mouth tightened a little. "But he did not ruin my hands. No. His punishment was of a different sort entirely. He gave me the 'gift' of eternal life. He said that if I was truly a man who did not believe in what he and others sought to achieve, he would make absolutely *certain* I was alive to see it when he achieved it. So I could make songs about the fall of Homana and the rise of the Ihlini."

"Then who *did* destroy your hands?"

"Strahan did this. He felt I was deserving of graver punishment. Once his father was slain by Carillon, Strahan showed his grief by punishing those who would not serve him. And so he destroyed my hands; that I would live forever without the magic of the harp."

Strahan did this. Aye, Strahan did much to ruin the flesh of others. Retribution for the ear he had lost to Finn?

"I must go," I said finally. "I cannot remain here longer.

I fear for the safety of my sons, and there is a wolf I have to slay."

Taliesin rose. He went to a trunk, lifted the lid, drew out a piece of polished silver. He brought it to me and put it into my hands. "So you will know," he said.

When I found the courage, I looked. And saw the price of Strahan's humor.

I tried to remain dispassionate, to study my face without emotion. But I could not. All I saw was the lidless, empty socket and the livid purple weals.

All I saw was disfigurement; the ruination of a man. I let the silver fall out of my hand.

Taliesin picked it up with his gnarled claws. "Caro will make a patch."

"Patch," I echoed blankly. *Oh gods, lir, what will the others think? What will the others see?*

What they have always seen, those who know how to look.

Gently, I touched the puckered talon scars. They divided my right brow in half, stretched diagonally across the bridge of my nose to touch the lid of the other eye, reached downward out of the empty socket to cut into my cheekbone. There was no question the hawk had known precisely what he was meant to do. But for Serri, he might have done it.

"They will fade, soften . . . in time they will not be so bold." Taliesin told me. Gently, with compassion. With endless empathy.

Lir, they will heal.

The bard and my *lir* took such care to reassure me. But I *knew* the scars would heal. Of course. I knew that. One day I would grow used to the disfigurement; would hardly notice the scars.

But what they would look like in five or ten years had nothing to do with *now*.

"Maimed," I said hollowly.

"Niall, you have another eye. Once you are accustomed, you will find the loss of one hardly interferes," Taliesin said quietly. "Even as I—"

"Maimed," I repeated. "Do you know what it means to a Cheysuli?"

He frowned a little. "Is it—does it mean a thing apart from other races?" He shrugged a little. "Forgive me, but I fear I do not comprehend your fear."

"A maimed warrior is useless," I told him steadily, defying myself to break. "He cannot hunt food, protect his clan, his kin."

Taliesin's raised hand stopped me. "No more," he said. "*No more.* Forgive me for speaking openly, but I say that is foolishness. What is to stop you from lifting a sword? From loosing an arrow? From slaying deer and others for food? *What*, Niall? Do you mean to tell me you will give up because you have lost an *eye?*"

I tried to frown and discovered it hurt too much. "You do not understand. In the clans—"

"You do not live only in the clan," he told me quietly. "You will be Mujhar of Homana one day; do you give up the service of your realm and your race because you lack an eye?" He lifted his twisted hands. "I can no longer play my harp. But I can do other things. Not well, perhaps, but enough to keep me alive. With Caro, it is easier. But as for *you*—" he shook his head "—you are young, strong, dedicated . . . there is no reason in the world you cannot overcome a minor disability such as the loss of an eye."

"Minor disability?" I stared at him. "I lost an *eye!*"

"And have another." Taliesin looked at Caro. "He has no voice. He hears nothing. And yet he does not give up. Why should you?"

I lost an eye. But I did not say it aloud. I edged back down on the pallet and lay flat, staring one-eyed at the uneven roof of the little hut. But I saw nothing at all.

"It will be difficult," Taliesin told me. "You need time, Niall, more time than you have allowed yourself. The loss of an eye requires adjustment. Your perceptions will be different."

That I had already learned by simply moving about the hut. But I had no more time to spend on myself, not even for needed healing. I had to reach my sons. I had to slay the wolf.

We stood just outside the crooked door. Sunlight spilled through limbs and leaves to make fretwork shadows on the slushy snow. Caro and I were bookends to Taliesin in the middle. Serri stood a little apart, twisting to lick a shoulder into order.

"I have to go. I have—responsibilities." I smiled a little;

too well I recalled his gentle diatribe about Cheysuli intransigence and unshakable dedication.

"The gods go with you, Niall. *Cheysuli i'halla shansu.*"

"Ru'shalla-tu." I resettled the shoulder pouch the bard had given me, filled with rations for when I was not in *lir*-shape. I set a hand on Taliesin's shoulder. "*Leijhana tu'sai.* Not enough, I know . . . but for now the words will have to do." I looked at Caro. "You will protect him, Taliesin? Let no one use him falsely."

"That I promise you."

Briefly Caro and I clasped arms. He opened his mouth as if he meant to speak, closed it reluctantly. Regret bared his teeth a moment, an eloquent moment, until I pulled him into an embrace. "It does not matter," I told him clearly, when he could see my face again. "I know what you mean to say."

He smiled. *My* smile.

Serri?

Here, he answered. *Time to go,* lir. *The white wolf will not wait.*

Then let us go at once. And I blurred myself into *lir*-shape. Shoulder to shoulder we sped through Solindish forests toward the Molon Pass and the border of Homana.

Ten

I lost *lir*-shape as we approached the northern bank of the Bluetooth. Pain lived in my skull, centering in the empty socket, and I could not summon the concentration required for the shapechange. I felt it slipping, tried to rekindle the magic, stumbled even in wolf-shape, lost the shape entirely. On one knee I knelt in the snow, bracing myself against a stiff arm, and waited for the pain to die away.

Lir. Serri pressed against me, but gently, resting his jaw on the top of my shoulder. Lir, *we must go on. The wolf—*

"I know," I gasped aloud. "I know, Serri, but—" I sat down awkwardly, sliding over onto one hip, and pressed fingers against my skull. *Oh gods, take the pain away—*

Lir, *we must go. I feel* him—*he is near the ferryman's cottage.*

Caro's patch warded my empty socket against the bite of cold weather and the brilliance of the sun. I fingered it gently, resettling it; too new, it was uncomfortable. It cut diagonally across my forehead, above my right ear, tied at the back of my head. And though Caro had knotted it gently, at the moment it felt like an iron manacle pressing in against tender flesh.

Lir—Serri again.

"I know . . . a moment." I gathered my knee under me, waited, carefully thrust myself to my feet. It was all I could do not to vomit.

Lir, *the wolf has crossed the Bluetooth.*

"Then so will we . . . but I think I shall have to walk."

Lir, *it is your* rujholli *he seeks.*

"Ian!" I stared at my *lir.* "Finally you can reach Tasha? Ian is *alive?*"

Alive. But endangered. The wolf is seeking him.

Oh—gods— "Serri—let us *go!*"

The river was still frozen, but the first signs of thaw had begun. I heard mutters in the ice and the occasional snap of cracking floes. Serri ran back and forth along the bank, trying to find the safest way across; at last he plunged ahead. He slipped, slid, fell, got up and ran again. But he had four legs to my two and was unhampered by a missing eye. Carefully I followed his lead, but my progress was slowed by uncertainty of footing as well as the pain in my head.

Slick—so *slick* . . . no matter how careful and deliberate I was, my bootsoles slid on the ice. My arms flailed out as I tried to maintain my balance; I bit my lip and cursed.

Lir . . . *come*—

Slipping, sliding, jerking uncontrollably. Patches of crusted snow hastened my progress, but treacherous ice often lay beneath.

Lir . . . *the wolf*—

Halfway. *Halfway.* I set my teeth and refused to look at the southern bank for fear I would lose my fragile balance. One step at a time. . . .

And then I heard the howl of a stalking wolf.

My head jerked up. I saw the bank—the smudge of smoke along the treeline—Serri on the other side. And then my balance was lost.

I fell. Landed on shoulder and hip, cracked forehead against the ice. Slumped down and moaned as the pain erupted inside my skull.

Lir—*you must come!*

My cheek was pressed against the snow-crusted ice. My breath rasped and blew smoke into the air. It tickled my only eye.

Lir—

I moaned. Curled. Rocked a little, back and forth, hugging arms against my belly.

Lir—

I heard the sound again: the song of a wolf on the trail of prey.

Ian. Ice and sky exchanged places as I tried to regain my senses. *The wolf is after Ian.*

Up. I pushed myself up, up again, until I was on hands and knees. My empty socket throbbed; I thought my head might burst.

Lir— Back and forth along the bank: silver-gray wolf with green-gold eyes.

Ian. Up. Up again. Standing. Wavered. Stared blindly at my frenzied *lir.*

Ian.

I heard the howl of the wolf.

I shut my eye. I blocked out all the sounds, the sights, the cold and pain and weakness. All of it, gone, swallowed by concentration. I was aware of the great void waiting to take me away, to clasp me against its breast. Calmly I welcomed it, even as I was welcomed.

Lir-shape, I told it. *I need it.*

It examined me. Tasted me. Spat me out again.

I went on in the guise of a wolf.

Serri hardly waited. As I scrambled up the icy bank he went on ahead, streaking through the trees. I followed his lead, on the track of Strahan's wolf.

The hut. It was mostly a blur as I ran: a smudge of gray stone and the weave of careful thatching. And Ian, standing in front of the door.

He turned. Frowned; he had heard the wolf. From out of the trees the wolf exploded: a streak of purest white. Heading for my brother.

Serri—warn Tasha—

Already done— Ahead of me, Serri ran.

Ian saw all of us: two white wolves and one of silver-gray, each running directly at him. He fell back a step toward the hut. Stopped. Half-drew his knife, but did not finish. His confusion was obvious.

"Niall?" I heard him ask.

Gods, he cannot know which one of us is me!

One-eyed, even in wolf-shape, it was difficult to differentiate shadows, angles, splashes of sunlight across the brilliance of blinding snow. I had not yet learned to decipher all the signals. It would take time, *too much* time—and I had none of it now. So I ran.

I altered my route, moving to dissect the white wolf's path. Even as *he* prepared to leap, Serri hit Ian, knocked him down, turned to protect him. By then I was on the wolf.

Jaws closed on pelt and muscle, locking on his throat. We tumbled, rolled, were up—

Like me he went for the jugular, trying to tear out my throat. It was an obscene dance of death, a ritualistic courtship. We tore, shook, growled, tried to throw one another down. One-eyed, I was hampered; two-eyed, he was not.

Ian was up, gone, back. His bow was in his hands; an arrow was nocked and prepared.

But I saw his indecision. He could not tell which wolf was brother and which was not.

Hind claws scored my belly—teeth locked in my flesh— I smelled the stench of rotting meat—the stink of the charnel-house—the ordure of the netherworld.

Jaws closed, chewed, tried to tear. I lunged backward, then sideways, trying to throw him down. Paws scrabbled, claws ripping into the winter-hard turf . . . he growled and gasped and choked.

Backward again, again, *again*—then I lunged forward and took even more of his throat into my jaws.

I shook him, I shredded, I ripped. I felt the tearing in his flesh. I heard the rattle in his chest and tasted the salt-copper flavor of blood.

He tore loose. Stumbled backward. Staggered, bleeding profusely. His tongue lolled, dragged, dangled. He fell. Scrabbled briefly. Died.

My head hung low. Blood was a mask on my muzzle, painting me up to my eye. My tail drooped. I turned, saw Ian's arrow aimed at me, realized he could not know which wolf had won. And then I lost the *lir*-shape.

"Niall! Oh—gods—*rujho*—" He threw down the bow and leaped, catching my shoulders as I wavered on my feet. "Niall!"

He broke off so abruptly, staring at me in such horror, that at first I could not comprehend what had happened to him to cause it. And then I remembered my face.

I hung onto his arms. "Alive," I gasped. "Thank the gods—you are *alive*—"

"Niall—what *happened?* Gods, *rujho*, what has happened to you?"

I could not believe I could touch him and know he was alive. "I feared the plague was always deadly. Gods, but I thought you were dead! Serri could no longer reach Tasha in the link."

The cat was next to Ian, leaning against one knee. "I was not nearly as sick as the others. But—*Niall*—"

I put a trembling hand to my head. It hurt. It hurt so badly. "Strahan," I said briefly through gritted teeth. "Strahan sent a hawk."

"Niall, come in and sit down. At *once*."

"No. No—first there is something—" I pulled away from him and turned to the wolf. There was no doubting he was dead; his throat was completely gone. I could still taste the tang of blood in my mouth. "Burn it," I said hoarsely. "He is the last of the plague-wolves; Homana will be free."

"I will," he said after a moment. "I will. But come inside. You look near to collapse."

I was. My head pounded unmercifully; I thought if perhaps I carried it rigidly on my shoulders, I would not stir further pain. Ian took me into Padgett's dwelling and made me sit down in one of the crooked chairs. The hut was empty.

"Gone for supplies." Ian told me as he moved to pour refreshment. *Usca*, again; I took the cup he gave me, drank, shut my eye. "He should be back soon. I had planned to leave today."

"Leave?" I opened my eye as Serri sat down between my knees. "For Mujhara?"

"No." Ian frowned. "No, Niall, of course not. I meant to come after you."

I wanted no more of the Steppes liquor and gave it back to him. "I thought surely you were dead. And you might have been *yet*—Strahan sent that wolf to carry plague to those Cheysuli who were left."

Ian squatted before my chair. He looked a little older; the plague had scuffed the edges off his youth. "Niall—"

"We have to go home at once. The enemy is harbored in the halls of Homana-Mujhar." I rubbed at my right temple, trying to massage away the pain. "Gisella serves Strahan. And Varien is Ihlini. They mean to steal my sons."

"Your *sons?*"

"He means to use them. To *twist* them, then place them on the thrones of Homana and Solinde. And he could succeed, if Gisella takes them to him." I grimaced, then shut my teeth on the moan I longed to make. "We have to go *now*."

"No. In the morning, perhaps. You can go nowhere, now." He rose, put the cups and *usca* away, asked me if I was hungry.

"If I eat anything right now, it will only come up again." I leaned back a little and shut my eye. "Ian—do you recall what the old woman said to us? The old Ihlini woman?"

"Aye." He moved around the but behind me; I could not see what he did.

"Well, I begin to think what she said was true. About Ihlini and Cheysuli being brother races . . . both children of the Firstborn. Taliesin said it also."

"Taliesin?"

"Ihlini," I answered. "Once a bard for Tynstar himself. No more." I told him then how Taliesin had tended me. But I said nothing of Caro, not yet; another time, perhaps.

Ian listened, then came around to sit down on a stool in front of me. "It is heresy, Niall. You know that. It goes against all the teachings—what the *shar tahls* have told every child."

"Perhaps they had reason for censoring the teachings . . . for withholding all the truth."

"*Why* would they do it, Niall? There *is* no reason for it!"

"There is," I told him wearily. "How would *you* react if you were told you were kin to the Ihlini; that once you lay down with Ihlini women?"

He did not answer.

"If you were a *shar tahl* and your duty—your *honor*—lay in defending the prophecy, would you shake the foundations of that honor by tainting it with the entire truth if *part* of that truth had to do with the kinship between Ihlini and Cheysuli?" I sighed. "Consider it, *rujho*—do you think a Cheysuli warrior would keep himself from an Ihlini woman merely because of her race—if he wanted her badly enough?"

Silence filled the hut. And then Ian broke it. "I am the *last* one to answer that . . . after what Lillith made me do."

My eye opened. I straightened. Slowly I leaned forward.

His face was ravaged. There was shame, guilt, disgust; more than a little self-hatred.

"Do not blame yourself," I told him. "You believed yourself *lir*less—you *were*, since Lillith used a spell to cut off the link between you and Tasha. Do you think I cannot understand?"

His face was gray. "I thought *i'toshaa-ni* would help. I thought it would absolve me. But I am still soiled. I remain *unclean.*"

"Ian, stop." I touched his arm. "Lillith had a purpose. It becomes clearer even now. Do you see? Merge the blood and you merge the power . . . Cheysuli and Ihlini."

He looked at me in horror. "She wanted a *child* of me—"

And I thought it likely she had gotten one. Even Varien had said it: *she has what she wants from your brother.*

"But—it would not be a Firstborn, not a *true* one," I mused. "The other blood is needed. Yet if the Ihlini got a child of both our races, they would move perilously closer to fulfillment of the prophecy."

"But it means their *death!*" Ian cried. "Why would they do such a thing?"

I released a breath of comprehension. "If they bred their own—if *they* controlled the bloodlines, they could control the prophecy. They could make the Firstborn theirs. They could *twist* the prophecy." I stared at him in realization. "A Firstborn child in Ihlini hands would be the demise of the Cheysuli. Taliesin even said something about it." I frowned, trying to remember. "He said—he said when the child of the prophecy is born, the *lir* will know a new master."

"Gods—*no*—" He stared at me in horror. "The *lir* would never leave us!"

"But if they *did.* . . ." I looked at Tasha, so close to Ian's leg. And then I looked at Serri. *Lir,* I said, *would you?*

Serri did not answer. And neither, I thought, did Tasha, as Ian asked her the same.

My brother slid off his stool. He knelt. He locked his hands in the plush velvet pelt of Tasha's hide. I saw how rigid was his posture; how tightly he hung onto his *lir.* "They will go?" he asked. "The *lir* will go from us?"

"He wants my sons," I said blankly. "Strahan wants my sons. As Lillith wanted *your* child. . . ."

Ian looked at me. "Then I will have to kill it."

Eleven

"I think the plague is over," Ian said. "People are in the streets again."

"And they do not spit, do not run, do not make the ward-signs against us," I agreed. "Gods, I thought it would slay us *all*."

We walked through the streets of Mujhara in human form with *lir* on either side. We were warm in our heavy winter leathers; the first tentative tendrils had unfurled from the blossom known as spring, melting the snow and the mud and turning the streets into slushy quagmires. Even the cobbles did not help.

"If you wish to rest, *rujho*, say it."

I smiled a little. Already Ian knew when the headaches came upon me. Such painful, blinding headaches, sometimes so bad I had to stop, lie down, not even *move* until the pain had passed. Sometimes so bad I could not keep food or water in my belly.

I shook my head. "We are too close, now." And we were. Even though I was weary and had the beginnings of a headache, I was not about to stop. "One more corner, and we will be at the gates." *And Gisella will be unmasked.* "Do you know, there is a chance she is not mad at all. That she has presented herself so under orders from Strahan through Lillith."

"*Not* mad?" Ian stared at me in surprise. "If that is true—if she *has* fooled us all—she is the best mummer I have ever seen."

"Aye. And it means the choice is taken from me."

"Choice?"

"What to do with her," I told him grimly. "Do you think I will keep her by me? She means to give my children to

Strahan. I cannot allow her to remain near them. Who is to say she would not try it again?"

Ian nodded. He frowned thoughtfully. "What choice, *rujho?* What will you do with her?"

"Either put her on the Crystal Isle, as Carillon did with Electra . . . send her home to Atvia . . . or have her executed."

"The latter is—serious."

"But the crime is worthy of it. Giving my sons to the enemy?"

"The Council may disagree."

"The Council will have no choice. When I tell them about the bastard, they will have no choice at all. They will see that I am the one who is the rightful heir."

"Tell them *what* about the bastard?"

"What I am intending to tell you." So I told him, quietly, the truth. And when I was done, we stood before the bronze-and-timber gates of Homana-Mujhar. Both leaves bore the black slash identifying a house of death. It made me think of Rowan.

Ian shook his head as I signaled the gates open. "After all that—all their plotting and planning . . . it is futile. For *naught.*"

"Thank the gods. And when the Council learns of it, the petition will be dismissed."

We hastened through the baileys, outer and inner, briefly acknowledged welcoming shouts and good wishes of the men and boys, climbed the stairs into the archivolted entrance. Even as Ian was detained by one of the servants, I went on. I climbed the stairs to the nursery and went in to see my sons before I faced my wife.

But she was there as well.

Squinting a little against the worsening pain in my head, I drew my sword. "Stand away from my sons, Gisella. Stand away *now.*"

She swung, fell back a step, pressed herself against the oak-and-ivory cradle. She was cloaked, hooded, patently prepared to leave. In her arms she held a bundled baby.

"What happened to your *face?*" she asked in shock.

"*Put him down,*" I told her distinctly. "Put him down, Gisella, and stand away from the cradle."

She was transfixed by my face, until her attention was

switched to the tip of my sword as I advanced. Her mouth hung open inelegantly; had she thought I would be slain, and her plans never known?

"Put him down," I repeated.

She blinked. Shut her mouth. *"Her,"* she declared indignantly. "Do not call your daughter a *him."*

"Daughter!" My hand twitched on the grip; the sword tip wavered. I looked at Gisella more closely and saw that beneath the cloak she was slender again. "By the gods, you have borne the child!"

It should not have surprised me. I could not say how long I had been gone, but certainly long enough; she had only been two months away from the birth when I had come home from Solinde.

She clutched the child more closely against her breast. But she looked sideways at a second cradle. From it I heard the squall of a baby disturbed from sleep.

The tip wavered once more; I lowered the sword. I was diverted from my intent. *"Again?"* I asked weakly.

Gisella nodded slowly, still staring at my face; at the scars and the leather patch. "A girl. A boy. Three sons and a daughter, now."

"And all meant for Strahan?" I let the tip drift up again; teased the air before her face. *"All* of them, Gisella?"

Her eyes filled with sudden tears. "But—I *have* to—I *have* to—Lillith said I *had* to. Varien says I *have* to—I have to do it because all of them *told* me to."

"Stop." No more diplomacy. "Put the baby down, Gisella. Put her with her brother."

She turned abruptly and did as I told her to. Relief allowed me to breathe again.

"I *had* to," she said. "They *told* me I had to do it."

"Gisella—look at me."

The tears had spilled over. She thrust a hand against her cheeks and tried to wipe them away. She trembled. She clutched at the cloak and waited for me to sheathe the sword in her body.

By the names of all the gods, how do you ask someone if they are sane or mad? How can you know if they tell the truth?

Must you ask her at all? Serri inquired. *Look at her,* lir. *What manner of woman do you see?*

"Gisella," I said helplessly, "do you understand what they meant you to do? What the result would be?"

"They told me I *had* to do it."

"Why?"

"Because Strahan *wanted* it."

"Do you know why? Did they tell you what it meant?"

"They said I *had* to."

"Gisella!"

She trembled even harder. "I just—I just—did what they said to do. There was the spotted puppy—*two* of them— there was the gray kitten—they said I had to do it. Strahan *wanted* me to do it."

I stared at her in growing alarm. "Wanted you to do *what*, Gisella? The puppies—the kitten—?"

She tangled a hand in her hair, twined it through her fingers. "They said—they said I *had* to—so I did—I *did!*"

"Did *what*, Gisella?"

Her mouth opened, closed. Opened again. Her breathing came very fast. "I—put the puppies down a well—because they *told* me to!"

I drew in an uneven breath. "And—the kitten?"

She shrugged one shoulder a little. "The cliff—the top of the dragon's head." She shrugged again. "I let him *fall.*"

"Why?" I asked in horror. "Because they *told* you to?"

She was sobbing now. "They said I must get used to losing things—losing *live* things—because one day I would have to give up my children—"

"Oh—*gods*—" I sheathed the sword. Went to her. Pulled her into my arms. "Oh—Gisella—oh *gods* . . . what have they done to you?"

"It was what we *needed* to do." Varien's voice, so smooth and silken, as he came into the room. "Do you think it is a simple thing to ask a woman—even a *mad* one—to willingly give up her children? Gisella had to be *trained.*"

"You filth," I told him, when I could speak again. "You gods-cursed *filth!* How could you do this to her? How in the name of all the gods could you do this to a woman?"

"No," he said urbanely. "Not in the name of *all* the gods—in the name of only one. My lord is Asar-Suti."

"Gisella—stand away." I pushed her, gently but firmly. And as she went, I drew my sword.

Varien frowned a little. He studied my sword intently. Then his expression cleared. "A Homanan sword," he said.

"Still a sword," I told him. I lunged.

"A *Homanan* sword," he repeated, and put up an eloquent hand. Easily, so *easily*, he caught the blade in his hand.

Well enough—sever the hand, then sever the neck.

But he stopped the blade dead in his palm. I saw fire explode from his fingers, coat the blade, run down from tip to cross-piece. The steel turned black at once.

As he meant me to, I released the hilt. And *only* the hilt struck the ground; the blade no longer existed.

What is left to lose—he will take the children anyway—

I leaped. Empty-handed, I threw myself across the room and caught handfuls of Varien's doublet, bearing him to the ground. He went down easily enough, but was sinuous as a serpent; writhing, he nearly squirmed away.

We struggled for dominance on the floor on the nursery. I thought of my children, so close to violence. I thought of how I risked them. I even thought of Gisella.

"*Serri*," I shouted, "*the children!*"

There was no answer discernible in the link. There could not be, with Varien so close. But I knew my *lir* would protect the children. He would give his life for them.

And, of course, give mine.

Varien clawed at my face and caught a corner of my patch. He tore it away, snapping the leather strap; tried to scrape away tender flesh. The pain was manifest, but it only gave me another reason to fight.

We rolled. My head was slammed against the stone floor. I cried out—the pain of the headache was magnified at once, filling my skull with coruscating light. I felt my belly rise.

Fingers reached again for my empty socket. Childishly, I retaliated by grabbing the stones in his ears and ripping them through the lobes.

Varien screamed. I thought it odd. Torn lobes are painful, I imagine, but hardly enough to make a man *scream*.

Unless, of course, it is not the pain that makes him scream but the loss of the stones themselves.

I clutched both in my fist. I thought of the old Ihlini woman with the pale pink crystal called a lifestone.

Varien was shouting at me, denying me the stones. I was one-handed now as well as one-eyed, not daring to risk the loss of the stones clutched in my fist. Varien was on the bottom, pinned beneath my substantial weight, but now he bucked and twisted and nearly succeeded in flinging me off.

Again, we rolled. I felt an obstruction against my spine; the tripod legs of the nearest brazier. It rocked, tipped, fell, spilled oil across the floor. A sheet of flame followed and set the stone afire.

I laughed aloud. "Burn, Varien—*burn!*"

I slammed the stones into the fire.

He screamed. Gods, how he *screamed*—

And then the stones were consumed and I was covered with dust that had once been a man.

I scrambled up, ignoring the pain in my head. "Gisella, your cloak."

She stood and stared at me. So I ripped it from her myself and smothered the oil fire.

People were in the room. Women ran to tend crying children, men drew hungry swords. But there was no enemy to be slain.

"Niall?" Gisella asked. "Niall, Varien is *gone.*"

"Varien is gone," I looked at one of the guardsmen. "Escort the princess to her chambers. Be gentle, but firm. See that she remains there."

"My lord—" He broke off, nodded, did not question the oddness of the order. Perhaps everyone knew Gisella.

"My lord." Another man. "The Mujhar is in the Great Hall."

I gaped. "My *father?*" I looked for Serri. Lir—*at once.* We ran.

I jerked open one of the hammered doors, stepped through, swung it shut behind me. *"Jehan?"* I saw him at the end of the hall, on the dais near the Lion. *"Jehan!"*

Ian was present as well, and Tasha. And also my mother, caught in my father's arms. I grinned, strode the length of the hall, opened my mouth to give him greeting—

—and stopped.

My mother cried. She *cried*, but it was not from happiness. It was the sound of a woman consumed by wracking grief. "No," she told him, "*no*—say you will not do it—say you will *renounce* it!"

Ian's face was stark. His yellow eyes were empty. He stood rigidly by the throne.

"Say you will not," my mother pleaded. *"Say you will not go!"*

His arms were around her, but they did not comfort her. They kept her from harming herself. His eyes, when I looked, were angry, bewildered, lost. They were the eyes of a *lir*less man.

The pain of my head was abruptly swallowed up by comprehension. "How?" I asked. That only; it was the only word I could manage.

"Plague," my father answered. "Taj in Hondarth. Lorn here, two days ago. I should have gone then, but—" He stopped speaking. I saw the grief in his empty eyes. "Oh, Niall, what has he done to you?"

I had forgotten the missing patch. I put a hand to my face, then took it away. "He set a hawk on me."

"Gods," he said raggedly, "he does not alter his methods." He touched the old scars in his neck, and I recalled the story. Strahan had set a hawk on my father, some twenty years ago, and nearly slew him then.

But now, he had succeeded.

My mother stared in horror at my face. "Oh—gods—Niall—"

"I lack an eye, but not my life." I looked only at my father. *"Jehan*—" But I knew an appeal was useless.

"The war is over," he told us evenly. "Solinde has given in. The rebellion was never theirs. Now they weary of the deaths. The realm is ours again."

"How can you speak about the war?" Ian cried. "Gods, *jehan*, what of *you?"*

"You know what I must do." His arms still cradled my mother. "What every warrior must do."

"But you are the *Mujhar!"* my mother said. "Can you not overlook Cheysuli custom even *once?"*

"No." I answered for him. "No, *jehana*, he cannot. It is the price of accepting the *lir*-bond."

Her head twisted on its neck as she glared at me. "And am I to expect *you* to do the same thing if *you* lose your lir?"

"Aye," I told her gently. "I am a Cheysuli warrior."

"Oh—gods—*two* of them—" She turned her face away.

"I have—things," my father said. "Something for each of you. It was why I did not go at once, hoping you might return." He set my mother aside. "Aislinn, I beg you—"

She shut her eyes. But she did not touch him again.

He turned to the Lion. I saw bundles in the cushioned seat. He lifted one: a blue-suede bag the size of a shoulder-pouch. "Aislinn."

With effort, she kept her tears in check. I saw the tremendous strain in the tendons of her neck. She stood quietly before my father.

He lifted her hands, put the pouch into them, closed her fingers over it. "Duncan made Alix many things. Now I give them to you."

Her fingers clutched the leather. She stared at the hands that held the pouch: his were firm and bronzed, hers were smooth and fair.

"Do you know," she said. "I only realize this now. That even when you were in love with Sorcha, desiring her in place of me, it did not matter. I *thought* it did, then . . . but I know now I was mistaken." She smiled a little; a sad, bittersweet smile. "Sharing you was better than not having you at all."

His hands tightened on hers. "The things in the pouch are love-tokens from my father to my mother." He used Homanan deliberately. "I have always lacked the skill. I can only give you what another has made . . . and swear the feelings are the same."

He caught her in his arms, lifted her, kissed her as I had never seen him kiss my mother before. For Cheysuli, such emotions are private ones and kept from other eyes, but now there was no reason for it. They did not care who saw.

He set her down again. "I am sorry . . . *cheysula*, I am sorry—"

My mother nodded. She stepped away, hugging the pouch to her breasts, and in silence let the tears run down her face.

"Ian." My father bent and took another bundle from the Lion. He unwrapped it carefully, and from the folds he took the black-and-tiger-eye Cheysuli warbow he had used for as long as I had known him. "This was Duncan's warbow. He gave it to Carillon, who brought it home again; who gave it to me on your grandsire's death. Now I give it to you."

Ian stared at the floor. "Niall should have it."

"No." But my father silenced me with a look.

"Niall shall have something else," Ian was told. "This is for you. This is for my first-born son. The first-born of *all* my children."

I could not help but think of Isolde. And I knew my father grieved, even as he prepared to give himself over to death.

Ian accepted the bow and looked beseechingly at our father. He said nothing; he did not have to. All the words were in his eyes.

"Niall." My father took the last bundle from the Lion. He stripped the velvet away. I looked on the scabbarded sword. "This was—mine," he told me. "It served others as a sword is meant to serve, including Shaine and Carillon. It served *me* as my grandsire truly intended when it was forged out of star-magic and other Cheysuli rites. With me, the magic will die, but a sword is still a sword."

"Hale's sword," I said.

He put it into my hands. The scabbard was smooth, oiled leather, worked with Cheysuli runes. I knew Rowan had put them there.

I stared at the sword. I heard him strip the gold from his ear and from his arms. He gave them to his *cheysula.* "Do not watch me go."

"Donal!"

"Do not watch me go."

She shut her eyes and turned away, clutching my father's gold.

Resolutely, Ian stared at the floor. I looked at the shape in the hilt of the sword: the rampant Homanan lion. The ruby, called the Mujhar's Eye.

I smiled a little. *One-eyed, both of us.*

When I looked up, my father was gone.

I could not sleep. I lay awake in my bed and stared blind-eyed into the darkness, knowing it could not match the darkness of my grief. And when at last I could not stand it, I got out of bed entirely.

There was a thing I had to do.

I drew on leggings, house boots, a winter jerkin. I asked Serri to stay in my chambers; this was for me to do alone. I took up a candle and the sword my father had left me; went alone to the Great Hall with its silent, looming Lion.

I lighted a torch with the candle, but did not take it yet. At the end of the firepit I set the sword down, kicked ash and cold logs out of the way, bared the iron ring. Two-handed I grasped it, prepared myself, wrenched it up from the stone floor of the firepit. The lid, peeled back and clanged against the rim.

I hissed, held my breath; the effort had set my socket to aching. In time, the frequent bouts of pain would pass. For now, I had to bear them.

I waited a moment, then took up the torch and retrieved the sword from the floor. I went down into the narrow staircase cut beneath the floor.

The torch roared in the darkness, throwing odd patterns against the shadowed walls. I felt confined by the narrow space, but I descended anyway. All one hundred and two steps.

At the bottom there was a closet. I lifted the torch, sought the runes and the proper stone, pushed, waited as the wall fell open. Flame was snatched from the torch and sucked into the vault.

I took a breath and went in. It had been long since I had been in the vault, *too* long. I had nearly forgotten about it. My father had brought Ian and me here once, to show us the Womb of the Earth; even now, the memory made me shiver.

The walls were of gold-veined, creamy ivory, carved in the shapes of *lir*. I could not name them all. I did not wish to, now.

I thrust the torch in front of me, entered, then set it into a bracket by the door. Ahead of me, mostly hidden in the shadows, lay the oubliette. The Womb of the Earth itself.

I took four steps into the vault. I stood at the edge of the pit. I could not say if there was a bottom to it; no one—*alive*—knew. But legend said there was not.

I unsheathed the sword. In the torchlight the runes ran like water against the steel. I read them aloud into the silence: *"Ja'hai, bu'lasa. Homana tahlmorra ru'maii."*

I heard the echoes fall into the pit.

"Accept, grandson. In the name of Homana's tahlmorra."

I waited. I heard no sound. Only the song of silence.

I smiled. *"Ja'hai, O gods. Homana Mujhar ru'maii."*

The ruby blazed up in the light of the torch. Such a deep, warm crimson. The Mujhar's Eye was made of blood, as much as mine had been.

"Not my sword," I said softly. "Not mine at all—and he will need it where he goes." I held the sword over the oubliette. *"Accept, O gods. In the name of Homana's Mujhar."*

I let it go. It fell. Down, *down*, into the hollow darkness of the Womb—

—and was *welcomed*.

Epilogue

I stood alone on the sentry-walk along the parapet and let the wind beat at my face. Below me spread Mujhara in the bright garments of true spring: new flowers, new babies, new clothing for the people.

And then I was not alone; I heard the familiar step of my brother.

He came as far as the crenel next to mine, so that only a merlon stood between us. Like me, he leaned against the wall and stared down into the city. "Do you regret your decision?"

I shook my head. "No. She will do better in Atvia. There is no place for her here. Let Alaric tend his daughter—he made her the way she is."

"Some will argue you are too cruel, to separate a *jehana* from her children."

"I *am* cruel . . . but I would be crueler still if I let her give them over to Strahan." I looked at him pensively. "She would, you know, given the chance. Because they *told* her to."

Ian sighed. "Poor, addled Gisella. . . ." Then he straightened. "Here—I came to bring you this. I do not know the seal."

I took the parchment from him. I looked at the seal: a wolfhound in green wax. "Erinn!" I said in surprise. "*Liam* used this seal!" I broke it, tore the parchment open, read the scrawl avidly. And then I stared at Ian. "By the gods—they are *alive*—Liam and Deirdre *alive*—"

He snatched the parchment from me and read it for himself. And then he looked at me. "Only *Shea* was slain, and he took the assassin with him into the afterworld. Liam is Lord of Erinn."

I sighed. "For Shea, I am sorry. He was a good lord, a man I admired and respected." Grief tarnished the moment, then retreated in the bright light of better news. "But Deirdre is *alive!*"

"And on her way to Homana." Ian grinned. "And so I lose my *rujho*."

"You will not *lose* me! You gain a true *kinspirit*." I could not damp down my smile. "Deirdre is not like other women."

"No," he agreed with mock gravity. "Since she is in love with you, she could not possibly be."

The jest was well-meant, but my mind was on other things. I touched my leather patch in sudden consternation. "Gods, *rujho*—what will she say when she sees *this*? What if she cannot bear to look at me?"

"You have just said she is not like other women. I doubt she will turn away." Ian handed back the letter. "Will you accept the betrothals Liam offers?"

"Since I was the one who originally *suggested* them, aye, I think I will," I told him dryly. "My daughter for his son: Keely shall wed Sean. And *his* girl for my heir: Aileen will be Queen of Homana when Brennan inherits the Lion."

Ian sighed. "So—it is settled. But what does that leave for Hart and Corin?"

I scratched idly at my right cheek. "Well, Brennan shall have Homana, and Keely will go to Erinn. It leaves Solinde and, eventually, Atvia." I nodded. "Solinde is Homana's now; I will declare Hart its lord—formally name him prince of the realm, to take the throne when I judge him ready. As for *Corin*, I think Alaric of Atvia will leave his island to a grandson. Corin will not be overlooked."

Ian nodded. "A just distribution, *rujho*. But what about the Erinnish girl? What about the daughter Deirdre bore you?"

I stared at him. "Daughter? Deirdre bore me a *daughter?*" I tore the letter open once again. "By the gods—I did not *finish!*"

"I thought not," Ian agreed. "Well, *rujho*, I think we can safely say the Lion is secured—as well as the prophecy. Four realms in all. Shall I count them out for you?"

I looked up at him blankly. "What?"

"Homana, Solinde, Erinn, and Atvia." He smiled. "Four warring realms. If we can just get Erinn and Atvia to stop fighting over a petty island title, we will be that much closer."

"Oh, aye, but I imagine with Keely as the Lady of Erinn, and Corin in Atvia, the battles will end of themselves."

Ian's smile widened. "Or they will *create* the battles out of kinship perversity."

I reread the letter again. "Deirdre has borne me a *daughter.*"

My brother sighed. "Aye, *rujho*, she has. And five is an uneven number . . . I think the battles will be *frequent.*"

Blissfully, I smiled. *"Deirdre has borne me a daughter—"*

Ian laughed.

—*Deirdre is coming home.*

APPENDIX
CHEYSULI/OLD TONGUE GLOSSARY
(with pronunciation guide)

a'saii (uh-SIGH) — Cheysuli zealots dedicated to pure line
of descent.
bu'lasa (boo-LAH-suh) — grandson
bu'sala (boo-SAH-luh) — foster-son
cheysu (chay-SOO) — man/woman; neuter; used within
phrases.
cheysul (chay-SOOL) — husband
cheysula (chay-SOO-luh) — wife
Cheysuli (chay-SOO-lee) — (*literal translation*): children of
the gods.
Cheysuli i'halla shansu (chay-SOO-lee ih-HALLA shan-
SOO) — (*lit.*): May there be Cheysuli peace upon you.
godfire (god-fire) — common manifestation of Ihlini power;
cold, lurid flame; purple tones.
harana (huh-RAH-na) — niece
harani (huh-RAH-nee) — nephew
homana (ho-MAH-na) — (*literal translation*): of all blood.
i'halla (ih-HALL-uh) — upon you: used within phrases.
i'toshaa-ni (ih-tosha-NEE) — Cheysuli cleansing ceremony;
atonement ritual.
ja'hai ([French j] zshuh-HIGH) — accept
ja'hai-na (zshuh-HIGH-nuh) — accepted
jehan (zsheh-HAHN) — father
jehana (zsheh-HAH-na) — mother
ku'reshtin (koo-RESH-tin) — epithet; name-calling
leijhana tu'sai (lay-HAHN-uh too-SIGH) — (*lit.*): thank
you very much.
lir (leer) — magical animal(s) linked to individual Cheysuli;
title used indiscriminately between *lir* and warriors.
meijha (MEE-hah) — Cheysuli light woman; (*lit.*): mistress.
meijhana (mee-HAH-na) — slang: pretty one
Mujhar (moo-HAR) — king

qu'mahlin (koo-MAH-lin) — purge; extermination

Resh'ta-ni (resh-tah-NEE) — (*lit.*): As you would have it.

rujho (ROO-ho) — slang: brother (diminutive)

rujholla (roo-HALL-uh) — sister (formal)

rujholli (roo-HALL-ee) — brother (formal)

ru'maii (roo-MY-ee) — (*lit.*): in the name of

Ru'shalla-tu (roo-SHAWL-uh TOO) — (*lit.*): May it be so.

Seker (Sek-AIR) — formal title: god of the netherworld.

shansu (shan-SOO) — peace

shar tahl (shar TAHL) — priest-historian; keeper of the prophecy.

shu'maii (shoo-MY-ee) — sponsor

su'fala (soo-FALL-uh) — aunt

su'fali (soo-FALL-ee) — uncle

sul'harai (sool-hah-RYE) — moment of greatest satisfaction in union of man and woman; describes shapechange.

tahlmorra (tall-MORE-uh) — fate; destiny; kismet.

Tahlmorra lujhala mei wiccan, cheysu (tall-MORE-uh loo-HALLA may WICK-un, chay-SOO) — (*lit.*): The fate of a man rests always within the hands of the gods.

tetsu (tet-SOO) — poisonous root given to allay great pain; addictive, eventually fatal.

tu'halla dei (too-HALLA-day-EE) — (*lit.*): Lord to liege man.

usca (OOIS-kuh) — powerful liquor from the Steppes.

y'ja'hai (EE-zshuh-HIGH) — (*lit.*): I accept.

THE HOUSE OF HOMANA

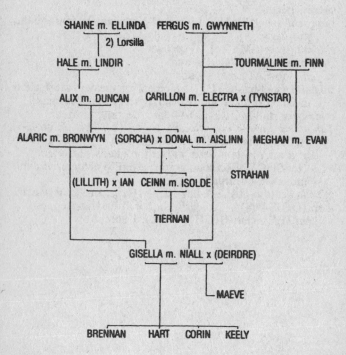

JENNIFER
ROBERSON

THE NOVELS OF TIGER AND DEL

Volume One   0-7564-0319-7
    Sword-Dancer & Sword-Singer
Volume Two   0-7564-0323-5
    Sword-Maker & Sword-Breaker
Volume Three   0-7564-0344-8
    Sword Born & Sword-Sworn

CHRONICLES OF THE CHEYSULI
Omnibus Editions

SHAPECHANGER'S SONG   0-88677-976-6
LEGACY OF THE WOLF   0-88677-997-9
CHILDREN OF THE LION   0-7564-0003-1
THE LION THRONE   0-7564-0010-4

To Order Call: 1-800-788-6262
www.dawbooks.com

DAW 49

The Golden Key

Melanie Rawn
Jennifer Roberson
Kate Elliott

In the duchy of Tira Verte fine art is prized above
all things. But not even the Grand Duke knows
just how powerful the art of the Grijalva family is.
For thanks to a genetic fluke certain males of their
bloodline are born with a frightening talent: the
ability to use their paintings to cast magical spells
which alter things in the real world. Their secret
magic formula, known as the Golden Key, per-
mits Gifted sons to vastly improve the fortunes of
their family. Still, the Grijalvas are fairly circum-
spect until two talents come into their powers:
Sario, a boy who will learn to use his Gift to make
himself virtually immortal; and Saavedra, a girl
who may be the first woman ever to have the Gift.
Sario's personal ambitions and thwarted love for
his cousin will lead to a generations-spanning
plot to seize control of the duchy.

0-88677-899-9

To Order Call: 1-800-788-6262

Melanie Rawn

"Rawn's talent for lush descriptions and complex characterizations provides a broad range of drama, intrigue, romance and adventure."
—*Library Journal*

EXILES
THE RUINS OF AMBRAI	0-88677-668-6
THE MAGEBORN TRAITOR	0-88677-731-3

DRAGON PRINCE
DRAGON PRINCE	0-88677-450-0
THE STAR SCROLL	0-88677-349-0
SUNRUNNER'S FIRE	0-88677-403-9

DRAGON STAR
STRONGHOLD	0-88677-482-9
THE DRAGON TOKEN	0-88677-542-6
SKYBOWL	0-88677-595-7

To Order Call: 1-800-788-6262

DAW 33